WESTERN APPROACHES

WESTERN APPROACHES

Graham Hurley

First published in Great Britain in 2012 by Orion Books,
an imprint of The Orion Publishing Group Ltd
Orion House, 5 Upper Saint Martin's Lane
London WC2H 9EA

An Hachette UK Company

1 3 5 7 9 10 8 6 4 2

A CIP catalogue record for this book
is available from the British Library.

ISBN (Hardback) 978 1 4091 3152 6
ISBN (Export Trade Paperback) 978 1 4091 3153 3
ISBN (ebook) 978 1 4091 3154 0

Typeset by Deltatype Ltd, Birkenhead, Merseyside

Printed in Great Britain by Clays Ltd, St Ives plc

The Orion Publishing Group's policy is to use papers
that are natural, renewable and recyclable products and made from
wood grown in sustainable forests. The logging and manufacturing
processes are expected to conform to the environmental
regulations of the country of origin.

www.orionbooks.co.uk

In memory of Deb Graham, 1972 – 2012

The sea has never been friendly to man. At most it has been the accomplice to human restlessness.

Joseph Conrad

Prelude

He awakes, as usual, at 03.55. For a second or two he lies in the clammy darkness, trying to work out what's gone wrong.

The last couple of days a thick tongue of high pressure has pushed up from the Azores, exciting weather forecasters all over northern Europe. He's listened to the headlines on the short-wave radio: 32°C in Amsterdam; hotter still in Paris; 35° expected this afternoon in London.

Christ, he thinks. London.

He searches for the T-shirt he carefully folded two hours earlier, checks with his fingers that it's not inside out. His mouth tastes of the tin of sardines they'd shared last night and he knows that his breath stinks. Sardines on Ryvita. Again.

He runs his tongue along his teeth and tries to pinch the darkness from his eyes. Something's definitely wrong. He knows it is. But, still groggy, he can't quite fathom what.

He pulls on the T-shirt. The last week or so, before the high pressure arrived, the weather and the ocean have been brutal. Sheer concentration has kept exhaustion at bay, but now, in the eerie calm, he feels totally wiped out. Yesterday he spent hour after hour checking their progress on the GPS, a habit – in Kate's phrase – that has become a nervous tic. But he can't help it. Without the suck and gurgle of a following sea, no matter how hard they pull, they seem to be going no-where. He's sure of nothing except the heat of the day, a thick blanket that presses down on them, bringing everything to a halt: conversation, energy, belief, even the small comfort of a

I

decent horizon. The ocean, poster blue, shimmers in the heat. Everything has become a blur. And now, as dawn breaks, this.

He struggles into his shorts, wincing with the effort. He has a couple of boils on his arse, incredibly painful. He checks them with a mirror when Kate's not watching. She's squeezed them dry as best she can and made him start on the antibiotics against the infection but he can feel, or he thinks he can feel, another one coming.

He's on his side now, up on one elbow, waiting for his arse to settle down. He can feel tangles of hair hanging round his shoulders and his head nudges against the roughness of the cabin roof. Ten days ago, riding out yet another storm, he'd popped a bottle of cooking oil in this khazi of a cave and everything still feels sticky to the touch. They lost a jar of coffee too, same storm, and the granules are everywhere. They melt in the sweat from his body and he's yet to emerge from the cabin without the telltale smears of brown all over his face. Kate, who seems immune from Nescafé Gold, has taken to calling him Coco the Clown. He thinks she means it as a joke but there are moments, especially recently, when he's not altogether sure.

The alarm on his wristwatch begins to ping. Four o'clock. He's learned to hate this sound with a fierce passion, the way some people react to the whine of a nearby mosquito. It means he has to move, gather himself together, face another day.

His fingers find the stainless-steel latches that keep the hatch in place. At last, thicko, he's realised what's wrong. The boat isn't moving. He can't hear the regular splash-splash of the oars, can't sense the faint tug as the boat inches forward. He feels nothing but the gentle sway of the ocean.

Anxious now, he fights to open the hatch. He knows how much Kate loves the slow drama of sunrise, that hour or so when the huge orange ball eases itself free of the ocean. Yesterday, she told him, was the best ever. Today, just maybe, might be better still.

Kate is keeping a record of everything. As the last latch comes free he can picture her squatting midships, her face to the rising sun, steadying her Nikon for yet another shot.

Daylight floods the chaos of the tiny cabin. He blinks at the familiar tableau of boat, of lashed-down gear, of sea, of the rich yellow spill of the new day. He wriggles his upper body through the hatch and rubs his eyes again, looking round, trying to find his wife.

But Kate has gone.

This, at least, was the way he explained it in the first of several interviews with Devon and Cornwall CID.

One

Nearly a year later, D/S Jimmy Suttle stumbled downstairs, knotting his tie, his mobile wedged against his ear. In theory, this was a precious weekend off. In theory, he should still be in bed.

'Where did you say?'

'Exmouth Quays. Sus death. Mr Nandy wants to blitz it. Asap, Jimmy. Do I hear a yes?'

The line went dead, leaving Suttle in the chaos of the tiny kitchen. In these situations, D/I Carole Houghton seldom bothered with anything but the barest of facts. That way she was already on to the next call.

Suttle gazed around. The tap he'd promised to fix this very morning was still dripping onto the pile of unwashed plates. Two empty bottles of cheap red and the remains of yet another Chinese takeaway were stuffed into the lidless waste bin. Even the cat, a tormented stray Lizzie had rescued from down the lane, wasn't interested in the curls of battered fish in gloopy sauce.

Suttle found it next door in the sitting room, crouched behind the sofa. Here, the carpet stank of animal piss and a fainter smell that signalled a more general neglect. In one of her blacker moods Lizzie had christened the cat Dexter in memory of a nightmare boyfriend at her long-ago Pompey comp. Now, his back to the wall, Dexter would do anything

4

to defend his patch against all-comers. Suttle, wondering why he hadn't swallowed more ibuprofen last night, knew exactly how he felt.

Upstairs, he could hear Grace talking to the mobile over her cot. This, he knew, was a prelude to the full lung-busting wail with which she greeted every new day. Normally it would be Lizzie who got up and answered the summons, leaving Suttle with a few snatched extra minutes in bed. Last night, switching off the light, he'd promised to sort out his daughter himself, giving Lizzie a lie-in. Now, looking for his leather jacket, he was trying to remember whether the car had enough fuel to get him to Exmouth.

Grace began to howl. Pulling on his jacket, Suttle headed for the door.

Exmouth, an old-fashioned low-rise seaside resort with a reputation for kite surfing, birdwatching and lively Friday nights, lies nine miles south of Exeter. Exmouth Quays is a marina development built around the basin of the old commercial docks, a quieter frieze of expensive waterside homes in various shades of New England pastel. Suttle, who'd been here before, had always regarded it as a film set, not quite real, a showcase destination for people who wanted to make a certain kind of statement about themselves.

He parked the Impreza beside Houghton's Vauxhall estate. Her dog, a mongrel terrier, lay curled on the back seat. A couple of uniforms had already taped off an area of walkway beneath the biggest of the apartment blocks, a towering confection with a faux clapboard finish and stainless steel trim.

Suttle crossed the bridge that spanned the dock entrance, flashed his ID at the uniforms and ducked under the tape. The apartment block was called Regatta Court. A banner draped across the fourth floor warned that only three apartments remained for sale while an accompanying poster asked WHY LIVE ANYWHERE ELSE? Why indeed, thought Suttle, eyeing the body at the feet of the grey-clad Crime Scene Investigator.

He'd worked with the CSI on a job in Torquay only last month. Difficult guy. Ex-marine. Mad about R & B. Lost his left leg after stepping on an IED in Afghan.

'Houghton about?'

The CSI was making notes on a clipboard. Suttle was trying to remember his name.

'It's Mark, if you were wondering.' The CSI didn't look up. 'And she's talking to Mr Nandy.'

Suttle was still studying the body sprawled among the puddles on the wet paving stones.

'So what happened?'

'He has to have fallen.' The CSI glanced up at last. 'We're thinking the top apartment. Big fuck-off place. Number 37.'

'The guy's got a name?'

'Kinsey. According to a neighbour.'

'Anything else you want to share?'

The CSI gave him a look. Wet weather made his stump ache.

'Some arsehole's been spewing round the corner if you want to take a look.' He nodded at the sea wall at the end of the walkway. 'Apart from that? No.'

Suttle was circling the body, examining it from every angle. The guy was on the small side. He was wearing a pair of Nike track pants and a red singlet. A crest on the singlet featured a pair of crossed oars. His feet were bare and there was something awkward in the way the body seemed to change angle around the neck. Blood from both ears had pooled on the paving stones and more blood had matted in his thinning hair. Guessing his age wasn't easy but Suttle thought around forty. His eyes were open, the lightest blue, and the last seconds of his life had left him with an expression of faint surprise.

Suttle knelt to examine the big Rotary on Kinsey's left wrist. The impact had smashed the face of the watch. Four minutes past three. Suttle's eyes strayed to the name beneath the crest on the singlet: *Jake K.*

'Has Mr Nandy asked for the pathologist?'

'Here, you mean?'

'Yeah.'

'No.'

'Why not?'

'He thinks there's no point. And he's probably right. A fall from that kind of height you're talking head first. If there's anything else, it'll show up at the PM.'

'You think he jumped?'

'I've no idea.'

Suttle nodded. His early years as a uniformed probationer in Pompey had taught him everything he ever wanted to know about the way the weight of the human head can turn a jumper upside down. Twice he'd had to deal with deranged adolescents who'd turned their backs on the world, or on a fucked-up relationship, and stepped off the top level of the city's Tricorn car park. Fall dynamics was a phrase he'd never grown to like.

He turned to the CSI again.

'CCTV?'

'There isn't any. The nearest cameras are in the town centre. We're talking nearly a mile away.'

'None at all?' Suttle was amazed.

'Zero. *Nada.*'

'Right.' He nodded. 'So how's Mr Nandy?'

'Manic. Argyle lost again yesterday and he thinks they're stuffed.'

Suttle turned to go. CID-wide, Det-Supt Malcolm Nandy was recognised as the king of lost causes. Trying to defend his empire against the marauding cost-cutters at force HQ was one of them. Plymouth Argyle was another. His beloved Pilgrims were on the edge of bankruptcy, and among the Major Crime Team Nandy was rumoured to be bunging them the odd fiver, doing his bit to help them stave off oblivion.

Fat chance on both counts, Suttle thought, ducking under the tape again.

7

Lizzie knelt beside the fireplace in a third attempt to coax a flame from the pile of damp kindling. Grace stood in her play-pen by the sofa, shaking the wooden bars in a bid to attract the cat's attention. Her morning bottle and a modest bowl of porridge had at last put a smile on her tiny face.

'Daddy?' she gurgled.

'He's at work, my love.'

'Daddy gone?'

'I'm afraid so.'

Lizzie abandoned the fire. Even the balls of newsprint beneath the kindling, the leftovers from last week's local paper, seemed reluctant to light. She pulled one out and flattened it against the cracked slates on the hearth, wondering if she'd missed anything. PENSIONER'S HANDBAG LEFT ON BUS went the headline. Breaking news in Colaton Raleigh, she thought. *What the fuck have I done?*

She was still taunted by dreams of her last day at work and the get-together in the pub afterwards. Starting her maternity leave in Portsmouth, she'd had every intention of one day resuming her job at the Pompey *News*. As the favoured feature writer, she'd cornered the market for the plum interviews and the occasional foray into serious investigative journalism, and she'd loved every minute of it. She'd scooped one of the big provincial awards for a feature on racial tensions among the city's Kosovan community and there'd been a couple of flattering calls from one of the national tabloids, inviting her to send a CV and a representative sample of her recent work. But then came Grace, and nine months later Jimmy had managed to score a promotion of his own. By this time she'd begun to know a different Pompey composed of fat mums at the health centre, ever-partying student drunks down the road and a manic neighbour – heavily tattooed – who claimed to have once met the Pope.

She remembered the morning the letter from Exeter had

arrived only too well. That night she and Jimmy had celebrated with champagne and blueberries with lashings of double cream. It had never been part of her career plan to move to Devon, and she'd never realised that her husband had fallen out of love with Portsmouth, but seeing the grin on his face as they emptied the second bottle she realised that she and Grace had no choice. Jimmy had grown up in the country, a straggly little village on the edge of the New Forest, and now he couldn't wait to introduce her to what he called the sanity of rural life.

Chantry Cottage had been his idea. His new employers – Devon and Cornwall Constabulary – had wanted him to start rather earlier than he'd expected, and he'd headed west without taking the extended leave he'd promised her. The Major Crime Investigation Team he was joining put him through a two-week force induction programme which gave him a little spare time at the end of each working afternoon. Within days, a trawl of the Exeter estate agencies had produced half a dozen potential buys. All of them, in Lizzie's view, were way too expensive. Property prices in Pompey were beginning to sink and mortgage companies were starting to demand ever bigger deposits country-wide. Jimmy was disappointed – she could hear it in his voice – but a week later she was looking at yet another set of estate agent's particulars. Chantry Cottage, according to Jimmy, nestled in a fold of the Otter Valley. It had half an acre of garden, mature fruit trees and space for a garage. The estate agent was the first to admit the property needed a little work. Hence the giveaway price of £179,000.

Needed a little work. Lizzie understood language, made a living from it, knew the multitude of blemishes a well turned phrase could hide. *Needed a little work?*

She lifted Grace from the playpen and wandered through to the kitchen to put the kettle on. She'd first seen the property back in high summer last year. It was a beautiful August day with real heat in the sun, and driving down the Otter Valley from the quaintly named Newton Poppleford even she had to

9

admit that this little corner of England was hard to resist. The way the greenness of the valley cupped the water meadows beside the river. The silhouette of a lone buzzard circling high over a waving field of corn. The lumbering herd of cattle that brought them to a halt a couple of minutes later. Grace had kicked her little feet with excitement. She'd never seen cows before.

The cottage lay about a mile outside the village. According to the estate agent, it had once been a chapel, but on first glance Lizzie thought this highly unlikely. Grey slate roof. Red brick construction. Ugly metal-framed windows. The broken gutters were brimming with moss and there were water stains down the exterior walls. The estate agent's photo had been taken from the back of the house, the view artfully framed by shrubs and a fruit tree. On this evidence, and her husband's obvious enthusiasm, Lizzie had been expecting something that would grace a calendar. Instead, she found herself looking at a run-down property that might have belonged on one of the more distressed Pompey estates.

Inside, it got worse. The moment you stepped inside, the sunshine vanished. The place smelled of damp and something slightly acrid that she couldn't place, and there was a chill thickness to the gloom that made her physically shiver. You went in through the kitchen. The units, obviously home-made, were chocked up on wooden blocks. One door had lost a hinge and a couple of drawers were missing. Ancient loops of electrical wiring hung from the walls and the walls themselves were wet to the touch.

Next door, in the tiny living room, the floorboards moved underfoot beneath the scuzzy carpet. One of the windows didn't close properly and there were gouge marks in the metal frame where someone had tried to get in. The open fireplace looked promising but on closer examination Lizzie found neat piles of mouse droppings on the cracked stone hearth. When Jimmy – still wrestling with the window – finally managed to get the thing open, the draught down the chimney carried a thin drizzle of oily soot.

Under-impressed, Lizzie had tried to get her thoughts in order, tried to puncture the bubble her husband had made for himself, but he was already leading her through the chaos of the garden towards the tiny stream at the bottom, his daughter in his arms, fantasising about the life that awaited them in this new home of theirs. Walks on the common up the road. A cat or two for company. And evenings around the barbecue he'd install on the refurbed patio, toasting their good fortune in cheap red from the village store.

In the end, that evening, she'd said yes, not really understanding his passion for this horrible house but knowing how much it mattered to him. He'd already negotiated a £15K discount on the asking price, which brought the place within their budget, but the work she insisted had to be done right now would be down to Jimmy. No problem, he said. His dad was handy. He'd get him across from Hampshire the moment they exchanged contracts. Between them, they'd sort the electrics, install a new kitchen, do something about the bathroom, give everything a lick of paint and generally clean the place up. He might even be able to tap his dad up for a loan to cover new windows. By the time Lizzie and Grace were ready to move out of Pompey, the place would be unrecognisable.

None of it had happened. Jimmy's dad fell off his moped and ended up in hospital the day contracts were exchanged. Jimmy himself had made a start on a couple of the jobs, but the pace of life on Major Crimes was unforgiving, and by the time Lizzie had sold their little terraced house it was nearly November. Stepping into Chantry Cottage, she recognised the smell and the damp only too well, realising why Jimmy had been so keen to keep her away. His apology had taken the form of a huge bunch of lilies, beautifully wrapped, which he'd propped up in the cracked sink in the kitchen. It was a sweet gesture, and she'd done her best to smile, but she'd hated lilies ever since.

Now, with Grace still in her arms, her mobile began to ring. She went back into the living room and deposited Grace in her playpen before stepping outside to take the call. Mobile reception in the valley was patchy at best. Another nightmare.

'Lou? It's me. How are you?'

Lizzie closed her eyes, glad – at least – that the rain had finally stopped. The only person who called her Lou was Gill Reynolds. The last thing she needed just now was an hour on the phone with an ex-newsroom colleague eager to tell her what she was missing.

'I'm fine. Busy. You know ...' Lizzie tailed off. As ever, Gill had no interest in listening.

'Great news, Lou. The buggers have given me a couple of days off. You remember that promise I made to pop down?'

Lizzie tried to fend her off, tried somehow to wedge herself into the conversation, tried to explain that this wasn't the best time to make a flying visit, but in her heart she knew it was hopeless. Gill would be down on Tuesday, around teatime. Directions weren't a problem because she'd just blagged a new TomTom off the paper. They had loads to catch up on and room in her bag for something nice to kick the evening off. Stolly or something else? Lizzie's call.

Lizzie opted for Stolly. Under the circumstances, she thought, vodka and oblivion might be an attractive option. Gill was still giggling at a joke she'd just made about some guy she was shagging when she rang off.

Lizzie watched the rain returning down the valley. Over the winter life seemed to have physically penned her into this godforsaken place. She'd become someone else. She knew she had. Through the open door she could hear Grace beginning to wail. For a moment she didn't move. A fine drizzle had curtained the view. She lifted her face to the greyness of the sky and closed her eyes again, knowing she should have thought harder about trusting her husband's judgement. Underfoot, she could feel the paving stones shifting with her weight. That was another thing he'd never done. The bloody patio.

Jimmy Suttle found Nandy and Houghton in the apartment that served as the Regatta Court sales office. Houghton stood by the window, staring out, her phone pressed to her ear. Nandy occupied a seat at the desk, eyeballing an attractive middle-aged woman who evidently looked after the development. Her name was Ellie. She'd just put a call through to a local firm she used for work around the apartment block. They'd have someone down in ten.

Nandy glanced up, seeing Suttle at the door. He did the introductions.

'Ellie's whistled up a locksmith,' he said. 'We're talking number 37. Fifth floor. You OK with a flash intel search? Mark needs to meet this locksmith guy before he sorts the door for us.'

Suttle nodded. As ever, Nandy was moving at the speed of light. Thirty years in the Major Crimes game had taught him the investigative importance of the first twenty-four hours of any enquiry. Pile all your pieces on the board, give the shaker a good rattle and pray for a double six.

'So what have we got, sir?' Suttle asked. 'What do we know about this guy?'

Nandy threw the question to Ellie. Suttle sensed she was enjoying the attention.

'You mean Jake Kinsey?' she said.

'Yes.'

'He's been with us ...' she frowned '... a couple of years now? Nice enough man. Lived alone. Kept himself to himself.'

'What did he do for a living?'

'I'm not quite sure. I think he may have been an engineer at some point. He was never one for conversation but we once had a fascinating little chat about alternative energy sources.

Some of the residents were wanting to install solar panels and he told me why they'd never work on our kind of scale. Then we got on to wind turbines. He knew a lot about them too.'

Nandy glanced at his watch. He was sharp as a tack but famously impatient.

'Is there anything special about number 37?' Suttle again.

'Yes. It's the biggest apartment in the block. It's huge. I like to think of it as the jewel in our little crown.'

'How much?' Nandy this time.

'Space?'

'Money. How much did he pay for it?'

Ellie paused. The bluntness of the question seemed to trouble her. She looked briefly at Suttle, one eyebrow raised, then returned to Nandy.

'One point four five million.' She smiled. 'As I recall.'

'A rich man, then?'

'Not hard up, obviously.'

'You checked him out at the time? When you agreed terms?'

'Of course we did. Not personally. But yes.'

'Did he raise a mortgage? Some kind of loan?'

'I can't remember.'

'Can you check? I'd be grateful.'

Ellie nodded and reached for a pad to scribble herself a note. Nandy had got to his feet and was feeling for his watch again. A lean man in his early fifties, he wore the same grey suit regardless of the season and in situations like these reminded Suttle of Samuel Beckett. Recently Lizzie had taken to reading *Krapp's Last Tape* in bed, and Suttle had clocked the author photo on the back. Nandy had the same hollowed-out face, the same shock of iron-grey hair, the same unforgiving eyes. This was a guy who brought an unyielding sense of mission to every enquiry, every exchange. Suttle rather liked him. There was madness in those eyes. Stuff had to happen quick-time and Nandy was there to make sure it bloody well did.

Houghton was off the phone. Nandy wanted to know whether she'd secured a slot for the post-mortem.

'Tomorrow morning,' she said. 'Half nine.'

'Best they can do?'

'Yes.'

'Pathetic.'

'I agree.'

Nandy headed for the door. He was off up to the local nick to commandeer a couple of offices where his team could camp out. The enquiry already had a name: Operation *Constantine*.

Houghton and Suttle paused a moment, then followed him out of the door. Nandy was halfway across the car park, heading for his Volvo. Houghton and Suttle exchanged glances. Houghton was a big woman with rimless glasses and a blaze of frizzy silver-blonde hair. She had huge hands, a live-in partner called Jules and spent a great deal of her spare time riding horses on the eastern edges of Dartmoor.

'I'll field the locksmith and liaise with Mark,' she said. 'I'll bell you when we're ready for the flash intel.'

'And me?'

'Talk to Ellie.' She nodded back towards the office. 'She likes you.'

Suttle did her bidding. He'd worked for D/I Carole Houghton for more than six months now and had developed a healthy respect. The steadiness of her gaze told you a great deal. This was someone you'd be foolish to underestimate.

Ellie offered him coffee. The kitchenette was next door. It wouldn't take a second.

Suttle shook his head. He wanted to know more about Jake Kinsey. And about what he might have been up to last night.

'That's easy.' Ellie was smiling. 'He was in the pub.'

'Which pub?'

'The Beach. It's just across the way.'

'How do you know?'

'Because we were there too. My partner and I.'

Kinsey, it turned out, had been in the middle of some kind of celebration. Saturday night the pub had been packed. Kinsey had turned up around eight with a smallish bunch of guys in tow. Ellie hadn't recognised any of them but there had to be some kind of tie-up with the local rowing club because they were all in badged training gear, and Kinsey had made a big play of the silver cup he was carrying. Ellie was vague on the details but thought they must have been taking part in some competition or other and had won.

'He bought champagne over the bar,' she said, 'and that doesn't happen often in the Beach.'

Kinsey and his mates had stayed for maybe an hour. They'd all had a fair bit to drink.

'What happened then?'

'They left. Like you do.'

'Where did they go? Do you know?'

'Not really, but my guess would be home, Kinsey's place. There was talk of phoning for a takeaway. I suppose Kinsey lived the closest so that's where they went.' She looked at the phone. 'There's a Mr Smart who lives in one of the flats below. Nothing gets past him. Do you want me to give him a ring?'

Suttle shook his head, making a note of the name. Organising the house-to-house calls would fall to D/I Houghton. He'd pass the intel on.

'This rowing of Kinsey's. How does that work?'

'You get in a boat. It has oars.' Ellie was flirting now. Suttle knew it. He was thinking of the badge on Kinsey's singlet, the crossed blades.

'Yeah ... sure ... so is there a club?'

'Of course there's a club. I just told you. ERC. Exmouth Rowing Club. Pride of the town. There's someone else you ought to talk to. She's the club secretary. Her name's Doyle, Molly Doyle.'

'You've got a number?'

'I'm afraid not. Look on the website.' The smile again. 'Nice woman. Fun. Everyone calls her the Viking.'

Houghton kept her laptop in the back of her estate car. Still waiting for the locksmith, Suttle borrowed the keys, woke the dog up and made himself comfortable in the front passenger seat. It was raining again, harder than ever, and the CSI had draped Kinsey's body with a square of blue plastic sheeting before taking cover in the Scenes of Crime van.

Suttle fired up the laptop and googled 'Exmouth Rowing Club'. The website was impressive. The home page had an eye-catching banner featuring a crew of young rowers powering a boat towards some imagined line. This giant collective effort made for a great picture. Their mouths open, their backs straight, their faces contorted, these kids were exploring the thin red line between pain and glory, and Suttle lingered on the image for a moment, wondering how an experience like that might have triggered the celebration in the pub.

From the front of Houghton's car, he had line of sight to the scene of crime across the entry to the dock. The warmth of his body had misted the windows but he wiped a clear panel with his fingertip, gazing across at the hummock of blue sheeting, trying to imagine the sequence of events that had linked several bottles of champagne to this inglorious death four or five hours later. Was the guy a depressive? Had he got so pissed he'd done something stupid and gravity-defying and just toppled off his own balcony? Or was the story more complex than that?

A keystroke took Suttle onto the contacts page. Molly Doyle's number was listed under 'Club Secretary'. He made a note and was fumbling for his mobile when Houghton appeared beside the passenger door.

Suttle wound down the window. The locksmith had arrived.

It was still barely nine o'clock by the time Lizzie got Grace washed and changed. Despite the weather, she knew she had to get out of the house. Jimmy had taken the car so the only option was yet another walk.

She watched Grace tottering towards her, then scooped her up, hugged her tight and strapped her into the buggy. During nearly two years of motherhood Lizzie had often wondered about this new role of hers, but there were moments when they seemed bonded, and this was one of them. She wouldn't wish a rural winter on anyone, least of all her own daughter, but apart from the odd tantrum and a recent talent for ignoring the word no, Grace seemed to have weathered the discomforts. Lizzie put this down to her husband's evenness of temper. She'd never met anyone so tolerant, so easy-going, and it had always been a surprise – back in Pompey – to talk to his mates in the Job and learn how relentless and proactive he could be. So why hadn't some of this can-do spirit spilled into their own little lives? How come she still had to wrestle the back door open because the wood had swollen with the incessant rain?

She pushed the buggy along the lane, keeping to the right, splashing through the puddles in her wellington boots. One of the early lessons she'd learned about the countryside was how difficult it was to find anywhere decent to walk. From a car, or an armchair in front of yet another episode of *Countryfile*, it was all too easy to imagine a world of endless outings, mother and child spoiled to death by this magnificent landscape: crossing fields, pausing beside rivers or streams, watching the first of the spring lambs, glorying in the freedom and the fresh air.

The reality, alas, was very different. Everywhere you looked turned out to be someone else's property. Everything was badged: PRIVATE, NO ENTRY, BEWARE OF THE DOG, TRESPASSERS WILL BE PROSECUTED. And if you finally managed to make it through the long straggle of village and down to the river, chances were that the footpath was ankle-deep in mud from the last downpour.

The rain came often, blowing in from the west on the big Atlantic depressions. Early on, before Christmas even, Lizzie had learned to read the sky, recognising the telltale wisps of cloud that promised the arrival of yet another frontal system as the light died, and it wasn't long before her battle with the weather became intensely personal. She hated the wet. She loathed having to dry everything in front of a one-bar electric fire. She spent hours every day trying to hoover mud from that horrible carpet in the sitting room. And night after night she lay awake, trying to distinguish between a multitude of drips. Water came in through the roof, spreading patches of damp across every ceiling in the house, and leaked from a crack in the back boiler behind the fireplace.

Worst of all was the dribbling tap in the kitchen. Jimmy, as ever, had been oblivious to her pleas to do something about it, and after months of listening to the slow drumbeat of water in the stainless-steel sink she'd caught the mobile library, found a book on DIY and tried to change the washer herself. She'd attacked the thing with an adjustable spanner she'd managed to borrow from the man who ran the village store but had given up in tears when water threatened to fountain everywhere. That evening Jimmy had found her tight-lipped, curled up in bed, Grace asleep beside her. He'd fetched ibuprofen from the bathroom cabinet, filled a hot water bottle, suggested a slug or two of Scotch, convinced she must be heading for a cold, but only later – once he'd reappeared with a plate of pasta – did she tell him the truth. I'm going mad, she said. This place is driving me fucking insane.

In more positive moods, increasingly rare, she'd tell herself that this husband of hers was doing his best. There was no money for a plumber, or a roofer, or a crew of fitters to turn up with a vanload of double glazing. There was also, it seemed, precious little time for Jimmy to have a go himself, or organise his dad to make good on the promised help that had never happened. And so, instead, they'd retreated to separate corners of their new lives, increasingly withdrawn, pretending that everything was OK, or nearly OK, or OK enough for the spring to finally arrive and take them somewhere sunnier. But even by mid-April that hadn't happened. On the contrary, the weather seemed fouler than ever, taunting her optimism, snuffing out the last flickers of hope that kept her going. No wonder they call frontal systems depressions, she thought. Even *Krapp's Last Tape* beat life in Chantry Cottage.

She trudged on, wondering whether to put a call in to Jimmy, asking about the wreckage of his day off, about how he was getting on, reaching out for a little company, a little comfort, but then she paused in the road, fumbling for a Kleenex to blow Grace's nose, knowing there was no point. For reasons she didn't begin to understand, she'd ended up in a prison cell of her own making. And whatever happened next, she knew with growing certainty, was absolutely down to her.

The locksmith turned out to have a duplicate set of keys for Kinsey's apartment. He pushed the door open and then stepped back. Mark was wearing a one-piece Scenes of Crime suit. The locksmith and Suttle had left their shoes at the foot of the stairs. Later, the CSI would do the full forensic number on the landing and the flat itself. If Nandy wanted the lift boshed too, no problem. But for now it was down to Suttle to do a quick trawl through the apartment, scouting for obvious indications – bloodstains, signs of some kind of struggle – that would turn an unexplained death into a likely murder.

Suttle stepped into the apartment, astonished and slightly awed by its sheer size. He'd no idea how much living space a million and a half quid could buy, but nothing had prepared him for this. The hall alone seemed to stretch for ever, and at the far end lay a huge living area. Lounge? Playground? Romper room? Viewing platform? The biggest kitchen-diner in the world? Suttle looked around. The flat occupied the entire width of the building. Everywhere else in the block, according to Ellie, this space would have accommodated two apartments, but Kinsey's money had bought him a view like none other.

Glass-walled on three sides, even in shit weather like this the flat's trophy room offered a panoramic view on the very edge of the estuary.

Suttle walked to the nearest of the huge windows. It was half tide, and the water was sluicing out through the harbour narrows. Beyond the narrows lay a long curl of sand fringed with grass. To the right, trawlers and yachts tugged at their moorings, and through the curtains of rain, on the other side of the river, Suttle could just make out the grey swell of the Haldon Hills, shrouded in mist. To the left lay the long curve of Exmouth seafront, the beach already exposed by the falling tide, while the whaleback of an offshore sandbank had appeared, a long ochre smudge in the murk.

'Are we doing this or what?'

Mark, the CSI, was Exmouth born and bred. He'd probably lived with this view most of his life but Suttle found it difficult to tear himself away. *If I had that kind of money*, he thought, *I might just live here myself.*

The CSI had disappeared again. Suttle could hear him padding around in one of the other rooms. He reappeared a minute or so later, shaking his head.

'Fuck all. Someone's had a party but we can't nick them for that.'

Suttle nodded. The hugeness of the lounge was underfurnished. A shallow crescent of sofa had been placed to suck in the best of the view and there was a free-standing plasma – not large – for after-dark entertainment. To the left, Kinsey had positioned a desk and executive chair beside another of the windows. Within reach of the chair was a big brass telescope on a wooden tripod with a scatter of charts on the floor beneath. One of the charts covered the south Devon coast, and Suttle paused a moment, gazing down at it, wondering precisely where this belonged in the story of Kinsey's final days. Beside the chart was a set of tide tables for Dartmouth, open at the month of April. Saturday the 9th had been ringed in pencil. High tide at 09.03. Was this where Kinsey had been yesterday? Some kind of race? Might this have accounted for the champagne in the pub?

Suttle looked round. A room this big and this bare could swallow a multitude of sins, but the evidence for a serious post-pub party was remarkably modest. An area at the back of the room housed a kitchen so spotless it might never have left the showroom. Suttle noted a couple more bottles of champagne, both empty. There were six glasses neatly lined up on the work surface beside the double sink, all washed, and a collection of crushed tinnies – mainly Guinness – in the swingbin. The bin also yielded the remains of a sizeable takeaway.

Mark limped across and took a sniff. 'Chicken jalfrezi.'

Suttle accompanied the CSI to the master bedroom. It was a decent size, nothing huge, with a view of the river beyond the rain-pebbled glass. The en suite bathroom had the usual goodies – recessed lighting, slate-tiled floors, big jacuzzi – but there was nothing to suggest violence.

In the bedroom the CSI had found a silver cup on the floor beneath the window. Suttle stooped to inspect it, remembering the chart beside the telescope. They were celebrating in the pub last night, he told himself. This has to be why.

The CSI was looking at the bed. The duvet had been thrown back, along with the top sheet, and the bed appeared to have been slept in. Given that this was the master bedroom, it was reasonable to suppose that the bed's occupant had been Kinsey.

So what had got him up and taken him to his death? Suttle returned to the lounge. There were twin balconies on the right and the left of the view, flanking the front of the apartment. Access to both lay through big sliding glass doors. Kinsey's body had been found by a local walking his dog. It was lying on the harbour side of the apartment block, directly under the left-hand balcony.

The CSI was inspecting the latch on the big sliding door.

'Here ...' He beckoned Suttle closer.

The latch was unsecured. Under his gloved hand the door moved sweetly open. Suttle stepped out. The rain was lighter now, no more than a thin drizzle, and he went across to the rail, peering over. The blue shape of Kinsey's shrouded body lay directly below, and Suttle stared at it for a long moment, trying to imagine how a fall like that could have happened. Kinsey was on the small side. Mounting the rail and throwing yourself off would have required a definite decision, not something that could have happened by accident.

Suttle looked up again, trying to work out whether anyone might have witnessed what had happened. The balcony overlooked the entrance to the dock. According to the CSI, this was where fishing boats and water taxis and the ferry that crossed the river tied up. There was a line of working units on the dockside, rented by fishermen, with a terrace of 1960s-looking flats beyond. To the left, looking out over the basin of the marina, another row of properties had line of sight on Kinsey's balcony. Suttle made a mental note, fixing the view in his head. He estimated at least thirty front doors. More priority calls for the house-to-house teams.

He took a last look round. Kinsey's watch had stopped at 03.04. At that time of the morning, of course, it would have been dark. He needed to check the harbourside illumination and whether the throw of light would reach up as far as Apartment 37. He sensed that a lot of these properties would belong to retired couples, wealthy enough to buy a share of a view like this. People that age often had trouble sleeping. Someone might have seen something, a flicker of movement, something unexplained. Worth a try.

He stepped back inside, wiping the rain from his face. They already knew that the front door had been closed on the latch but not bolted inside. Now he wanted to know about the interior lights.

The CSI shook his head. 'Everything off.'

'Including the bedroom?'

'Yes.'

'Right.' Suttle nodded. 'So the guy gets up in the dark, comes through here, opens the exterior sliding door, finds himself on the balcony. Yeah? Is that what the scene tells us?'

'Spot on.'

'Then what?'

'Fuck knows.'

Suttle took a look at the other rooms. There were two other bedrooms, both en suite, and one of them appeared to have been used as an office: desk, filing cabinet, whiteboard on the wall. There was nothing on the whiteboard, and apart from a PC and a phone there was nothing on the desk either. This bareness extended to the rest of the apartment, and as Suttle did another walk-through he got an overwhelming sense of emptiness, of a life somehow on hold. When it came to furnishings and decor, this was a guy who'd stripped his surroundings down to the bare essentials. The stuff was functional, well made, served a purpose, but there were no pictures to brighten the bareness of the walls, no framed faces of friends or family, no hats doffed to any kind of private life. Even the fridge yielded nothing but a one-litre carton of milk, half a pound of butter, a Tesco fillet steak and a stalk or two of broccoli.

Beside Kinsey's desk, the CSI was checking the answering machine. Suttle threw him a look but he shook his head.

'Nothing,' he said.

D/I Carole Houghton drew the *Constantine* team together at 10.07. Ellie had volunteered her office, plus a supply of coffees, and Houghton sat on the desk, letting her anorak drip onto the carpet.

So far she'd managed to rally eight D/Cs. Nandy was looking for a couple more but they lived out of the area and wouldn't arrive for at least an hour. In the meantime, she said, D/S Suttle had conducted a flash intel search of the apartment and drawn up a priority list of addresses for house-to-house. The duty Inspector at the local nick was preparing three rooms for *Constantine* and all of them would be operational by lunchtime. Depending on initial inquiries, the investigation might or might not transfer to the Major Incident Room at Middlemoor. At the moment, she stressed, the jury was out on Kinsey's death. Nothing in the flat suggested anything but a man who had fallen off his own balcony. If the truth proved otherwise, it was up to *Constantine* to find out.

There were very few questions. Houghton wanted the D/Cs working in pairs. She divided the house-to-house calls between them and sent the most experienced team to the Beach pub. She wanted a full account of Kinsey's visit last night, plus names and addresses of fellow drinkers for follow-up.

By the time Ellie returned, the detectives had gone. Houghton eyed the tray of coffees she was carrying and offered her apologies. Ellie put the coffees on her desk.

'That nice young man I was talking to ...?'

'He's gone to meet the club secretary.'

'Ah ...' Ellie failed to mask her disappointment. 'The Viking.'

Molly Doyle opened the door on Suttle's second knock. She was wearing a scarlet dressing gown, loosely belted at the waist, and her hair was wet from the shower. The blush of colour on her face, plus the muddy Nikes on the square of newsprint inside the porch, suggested recent exercise. He'd phoned ahead but she'd failed to pick up.

'I've been out on the seafront.' She was still looking at Suttle's warrant card. 'My Sunday treat.'

After a moment's hesitation, she invited him in. It was a neat house, warm colours, comfortable, lived-in. A line of family photos on the mantelpiece suggested a sizeable brood of kids and already, from somewhere upstairs, Suttle could hear a stir of movement.

'So what's going on? What's this all about?'

Suttle explained about Kinsey. The news that he was dead

froze the smile on her face. She looked visibly shocked.

'Dead?'

'I'm afraid so.'

'But how can that happen?'

'I've no idea. That's what we have to find out.'

Suttle wanted to know about yesterday's race. Kinsey, it seemed, had won himself a cup.

'He did. He texted me. The Dart Totnes Head. First proper race of the season. His guys did well. Better than well.' She frowned, knotting her hands in her lap. '*Dead?*' She stared at Suttle, wanting him to change the story, to apologise, to explain that it was all some kind of joke.

Suttle pressed for more details. 'You've got names? This crew of his?'

'Of course. Our events secretary is having a baby. I did the race entry form myself.'

'You've got contact details?'

'For the crew, you mean?'

'Yes.'

'Absolutely. That's my job.' She hesitated. 'You want me to get them?'

Suttle shook his head. He'd collect the names and addresses before he left but right now he was more interested in Kinsey. What kind of man was he?

'He was ...' she frowned, unhappy with the past tense '... different.'

'How?'

'Hard to say.' The frown deepened. She seemed affronted as well as upset. Who was this man to barge into her house, into her precious Sunday morning, and throw everything into chaos?

'The man's dead, Mrs Doyle. And at this point in time we don't know why.'

'Christ, what else are you telling me?'

'I'm telling you nothing. And that's because we know

nothing. Except that he probably fell from his own balcony in the middle of the night and ended up dead. There has to be a reason for that. Which is why I'm here.'

'But you're suggesting ...?'

'I'm suggesting nothing. You used the word "different" just now. What does that mean?'

'It means that he wasn't – you know – one of the usual crowd. We're a club. Quite a successful club as it happens. How much do you know about rowing?'

'Nothing,' Suttle said again. 'Tell me.'

'Well ...' She gathered her dressing gown more tightly around her. 'It's a sport, obviously. It's pretty physical, and it can be pretty challenging too, in our kind of water. People love that. It becomes a bond, a glue if you like. It sticks us together. When you're out there you have to rely on each other and that can build something pretty special. Not everyone races. A lot of our guys are social rowers. But I guess it boils down to the same thing. The sea's the sea. You don't mess with it.'

'And Kinsey?'

'He was never a social rower.'

'Meaning?'

'Kinsey was a competitor. In everything. Winning mattered.'

'And that's unusual?'

'To his degree, yes. This is me speaking, my opinion, but – hey – you did ask ...'

She offered him a bleak smile. She believed him now. Kinsey was dead and gone. No more cups. No more glory.

Suttle let the silence stretch and stretch. Footsteps hurrying overhead and then the splash of water in a shower.

'Did you like him?'

'*Like* him?'

'Yes.'

'Why do you ask?'

'Because these things can be important. I'm getting a picture here. People like Kinsey can be uncomfortable to have around.'

27

'That's true.'

'So was he liked? Was he popular?'

She looked at him for a long moment, then shook her head. It had been obvious from the start, she said, that Kinsey was rich. Not just that, but he was arrogant too. Wealth, like winning, mattered.

'He came to us from nowhere. Just walked into the clubhouse on a Sunday and signed himself up.'

'Had he rowed before?'

'Never. He said he'd watched us out of his window when we rowed up the river. That was important.'

'Seeing you row?'

'Telling us where he lived. That huge penthouse flat. It wasn't just pride. It was something else.'

'Like what?'

'He needed us to know the kind of guy he was. Rich. Successful. All that nonsense. Ours is a funny little club. We get all sorts. But money never comes into it. In a boat on the sea you are who you are. Kinsey never seemed to quite get that.'

Coaches at the club, she said, had taught Kinsey the basic drills. After a couple of outings, like every other novice, he'd sculled with an experienced crew, one oar in either hand, and hadn't let himself down.

'Was he good?'

'Not really. Some people are naturals. You can see it. Their body posture is right. They pick up the rhythm, the stroke rate, really quickly. They know know how to turn all that energy into real power. It's a bit like dancing. Either you have it or you don't.'

'And Kinsey didn't?'

'No. Don't get me wrong. He was OK, he was competent. But he got into bad habits from the start and never really listened to people who wanted to put him right.' The smile again, hesitant, almost apologetic. 'Am I making sense?'

Suttle nodded. He could hear a radio now from upstairs.

28

Heart FM. The last thing he wanted was one or other of the kids to stumble in through the door and bring this interview, this conversation, to an end.

'Tell me about the racing,' he said. 'How many other cups did he win?'

'None. Yesterday was their first outing. That was why he was so chuffed.'

About a year ago, she said, Kinsey had bought the club a brand new quad.

'Quad?'

'Four rowers and a cox. This was a sea boat. They don't come cheap.'

'How much?'

'Eighteen thousand, including the bits and pieces that go with it.'

The extras, she said, included oars, safety equipment plus a couple of trailers for the road and for the beach. The club had never had a windfall like that but Kinsey soured the gift with a major precondition. He and his crew always had first claim on the boat, regardless of who else might be in the queue.

'And that was unusual?'

'Absolutely. And it didn't stop there.'

Kinsey's crew, she said, was hand-picked. These weren't a bunch of mates he happened to get on with, like-minded souls with a taste for exercise and a laugh or two, but serious athletes he cherry-picked from the club's membership.

'It was like he was playing God. It put a lot of backs up. Here was a guy from nowhere, a virtual stranger, buying himself into the top boat. And no one could lift a finger because he was happy to pay for it.'

One of the crew, she said, wasn't even a club member. His name was Andy Poole. Kinsey had come across him on some business deal or other. It turned out Andy had been in the Cambridge blue boat two years running and had nearly made the national squad before a move west brought him to Exeter.

'Don't get me wrong. Andy's a nice guy. He's a bloody good rower too. We've been lucky to have him. Even on Kinsey's terms.'

Kinsey, she said, had enrolled Andy Poole in the club, paid his annual membership and designed a training programme around the guy's work schedule. The other guys in the crew had undoubtedly learned a huge amount from Andy's tuition, one reason why the crew had swept to line honours in yesterday's race, but the whole point was that access to this kind of coaching was strictly limited. Only Kinsey and his crew ever laid eyes on Andy Poole. To the rest of the club, he was Mr Invisible, the big man with the Mercedes who popped down from Exeter to do Kinsey's bidding. There were even rumours that Kinsey had paid him start money to make sure he turned up for yesterday's race. Not that Andy Poole was short of a bob or two.

'And that upset people?'

'Big time, if you let it get to you.'

'You're telling me he had enemies?'

'I'm telling you he was unpopular. And, to be frank, a bit of a joke.'

'Because he was so naff?'

'Because he was so crap in a boat. Some people called him The Passenger.'

'And he knew that?'

'I've no idea. But even if he did it wouldn't have made any difference. To be honest, he was the most thick-skinned person I've ever met. This is the kind of guy who takes what he wants and turns his back on the rest. He thought money could buy him anything.' The smile again, even bleaker. 'And – hey – it's turned out he was wrong.'

Footsteps clattered down the stairs. The door burst open to reveal a girl in her mid-teens. She was wearing a blue tracksuit and pink runners. Ignoring Suttle, she tapped her watch.

'Shit, Mum, I'd no idea. I'm supposed to be down there for ten. Tansy'll go mental.'

'They won't be launching today. It's a south-easterly, 4.3.'

'I'm talking Ergo, mum. You know what she's after for the 5K? After a night like last night? Twenty dead. I'm gonna be toast. See you.'

As suddenly as she'd appeared, she'd gone. Suttle heard the front door open and then slam shut again. Ergo? 4.3? Twenty dead? This had to be rowing talk. Had to.

Molly Doyle was on her feet. Like her daughter, she was tall and blonde. Hence, Suttle assumed, her nickname. Under the circumstances, the Viking thought coffee was a good idea. In the meantime, Suttle could help himself to the details on Kinsey's crew from the files she'd got upstairs.

'They went back to his place,' she said. 'After the pub last night.'

'All of them?'

'Yes.'

'How do you know?'

'He texted me an invite. Silly man.'

It had finally stopped raining by the time Lizzie got to the village church. It lay on the road that led down to the river, a sturdy plain-looking structure with a bulky tower that seemed out of proportion with the rest of the building. She opened the gate and pushed the buggy up the path towards the half-open door. Lizzie had never been a practising Christian and had avoided worship for most of her adult life, but this morning, for whatever reason, she felt the need to quieten herself, to find somewhere she might find a bit of privacy and a little peace.

Until she stepped into the gloom of the nave, it didn't occur to her that the church might be in use. *Shit*, she reminded herself. Sunday.

Heads turned, all of them old. There weren't many people, twenty tops. The nearest face looked familiar. She lived down the road, Mrs Peacock. They'd talked a couple of times in the village shop. She'd become the village's self-appointed chronicler and archivist, contributing badly punctuated articles to the parish magazine on various episodes in Colaton Raleigh's long history. It was May Peacock who'd confirmed the estate agent's belief that Chantry Cottage had once been a Nonconformist chapel, and – in the depths of winter – it was Mrs Peacock who'd battled through the snow and posted some additional information through Lizzie's letter box. There was some kind of tomb, she'd written, at the bottom of the cottage's garden. It had been constructed hundreds of years ago and was rumoured to contain the bodies of two children.

At the time Lizzie had dismissed the story as a figment of Mrs Peacock's imagination. This kind of legend was the currency of village life and Mrs P was obviously a big spender. Lately, though, as the damp walls of Chantry Cottage pressed closer and closer, Lizzie had begun to think more about the story. *Anything to revive the numbness that used to be my brain*, she'd thought. *Anything to stop me becoming a complete vegetable.*

Now, aware of Lizzie's hesitation, Mrs Peacock was beckoning her into the church. She had a long, slightly horsey face and wisps of white hair curling from her chin. *Come in*, she seemed to be saying. *We won't bite.*

Lizzie found a perch on the end of an empty pew. Grace, mercifully, seemed to have gone to sleep. At the altar a line of elderly worshippers waited to take communion. They were all women and most of them used walking sticks. Watching them as they shuffled painfully towards the altar rail, Lizzie found herself wondering what had happened to their menfolk. Were their husbands at home, sorting out the midday roast, or had the retirement years in Colaton Raleigh finally throttled the life out of them?

She had no way of knowing, of course, and as Mrs Peacock threw her another smile and struggled to her feet to join the communicants, Lizzie remembered the morning she'd taken up the carpet in the sitting room. Back then, in December, she'd still had the energy and the self-belief to pit herself against the challenges of Jimmy's little find. Chantry Cottage, she'd told herself, was simply bricks and mortar. She could make a difference; she could roll her sleeves up and have a proper sort-out.

The previous occupant, according to Jimmy, had been a lifelong hippy who'd read a couple of books about some Indian guru and become a yoga teacher. Living on virtually nothing, she'd tried to bypass the electricity meter with the aid of instructions from an anarchist site on the Internet but she'd screwed up badly and nearly burned the place down. This seemed to explain both the lingering sourness Lizzie caught from time to time, plus the sooty patches on the living room ceiling, but the latter, according to Jimmy, had come from the candles the woman had burned every night. This was someone who'd evidently lived by candlelight for most of her life and saw no reason to change. Quaint, he'd said. And very Devon.

It was at this point that Lizzie had decided to turn the year on its head and go for an early spring clean. The following morning, once Jimmy had gone to work, she moved Grace's playpen into the kitchen, shooed Dexter into the garden, cleared the tiny sitting room of furniture and began to roll up the carpet. For once the sun was shining. She'd strung a rope between two fruit trees and intended to give the carpet the beating of its life. With luck, she'd thought, the rest of the house would listen and take note. Pompey girl on the loose. Mend your ways.

In the event, though, the house – yet again – had won. The carpet had seen better days. Years of abuse had larded it with every conceivable spillage – grease, candle wax, coffee, wine – and when she took her gloves off to get a firmer grip it was sticky to the touch. That was bad enough, but as she began to roll the carpet back, she found herself looking at layer after layer of newsprint. These were papers from the early 60s. Headlines about the death of JFK. Feature articles asking why the Brits had to suffer yet another sterling crisis. She started to go through the papers story by story. This was a treasure trove of living history, she told herself, something to spark conversation when Jimmy came home. But then her interest flagged, and she stopped turning the pages, only too aware that Chantry Cottage had the feeling of a morgue, of time arrested under her very feet, a malevolent force dragging her unaccountably backwards, into a darkness that first alarmed and then depressed her.

That night, with the carpet in all its squalor back down on the sitting room floor, she'd tried to voice a little of this to her husband. She and Grace were still newcomers to the country-side. They'd been living here for barely a month. But already she could feel a sense of near-despair beginning to seep into her life. In some dimly remembered past she'd been the one pitching stories, conducting interviews, writing copy, dreaming up headlines, earning herself the beginnings of a serious repu-tation. Now, as the days implacably shortened and yet more rain blew in from the west, she felt totally helpless, a creature without either direction or worth.

Jimmy, as ever, had tried to understand. The winter was bound to be tough. They'd both known that. But the seasons would roll round, and spring would come, and then they'd all have a chance to take stock. At work, he said, they still think I'm great. He'd made sure that word of his last job in Portsmouth had reached the ears of his new colleagues, and there were still moments in the MCIT offices when he could feel the warmth of all that reflected glory. He'd been the key to the undercover operation that had potted Pompey's biggest criminal. If there'd been a medal struck for the death of drug baron Bazza Mackenzie, it would have had Suttle's name on it.

Lizzie loved her husband in moods like these. He'd always been a blaze of auburn curls in her life. With his freckles and his easy grin, he had an untiring optimism, an almost visible sunniness that was the very bedrock of their relationship. She'd always fancied him, and there were times even now when she still did, but she knew that her depression had begun to affect him as well, yet another reason to hate her new self. Evenings at home were beginning to be difficult. There was too much stuff that was better avoided – the state of the house, Lizzie's sheer isolation – and once Grace was tucked up, they both settled for silence or the telly rather than risk another row. But deep down, where it had always mattered, she suspected that Jimmy was right. Stuff comes and goes. You have to walk tall on life's road. But how on earth was she going to get back to the person she'd once been?

Thinking suddenly of Gill Reynolds, she watched the communicants returning to their pews. The last to take her seat was May Peacock. Lizzie gave her a little wave, hearing Grace beginning to stir, knowing that she had to get out of the church before the service came to an end. Her dread of conversation extended to pretty much anyone. She'd lost the knack of talking to people. She was no longer able to get the right words in the right order. Better therefore to keep the world at arm's length and pray that something, anything, turned up to make things better.

Suttle phoned D/I Houghton from his car. He had names and contact details for Kinsey's crew and knew that these would be priority interviews for the *Constantine* squad. When Houghton at last picked up, she told him to come to Exmouth nick for half eleven. Mr Nandy had sorted a couple of offices before departing for another enquiry in Torbay and he wouldn't return until mid-afternoon. By half eleven, she was expecting feedback from the house-to-house calls. After which she and Suttle could plot a sensible path forward.

Suttle checked his watch. Nearly eleven. Exmouth nick was round the corner, a two-minute drive. With time in hand, he fancied a little detour.

Molly Doyle had given him directions to the seafront

compound which served as the base for Exmouth Rowing Club. Suttle found it tucked up a wide alley behind a building that belonged to the RNLI. A wooden fence enclosed a patch of scrubland beneath the looming shadow of a half-completed leisure complex. A raised Portakabin served as a clubhouse and one of the sagging doors was an inch or two open. Suttle picked his way between a litter of abandoned rubber bootees, pausing on the steps to check out the ERC fleet.

In the compound he counted five big sea boats, all of them red and white, readied on launching trolleys beneath the spreading branches of a huge tree. Someone had attached a plastic owl to the roof of the Portakabin. Suttle was looking at the boats again. If the owl was a bid to keep the gulls off, it had failed completely. There was bird shit everywhere.

Suttle pushed at the door of the clubhouse and stepped inside. Neon tubes threw a cold hard light over the sparseness of the interior. Lighter boat shells hung from racks on the walls and a pile of ancient yellow life jackets occupied a corner at the back. There was an overpowering smell of sweat and effort, and among the handful of faces on the rowing machines he recognised the Viking's daughter. Even now he didn't know her name but he responded to her nod of recognition, wondering whether news of Kinsey's death had yet to reach this far.

A coach was squatting beside the nearest rowing machine, monitoring the performance readout on the tiny heads-up screen. The last thing Suttle wanted was a conversation, but the guy got to his feet and asked whether he could help.

Suttle shook his head. It was way too early to extend the investigation this far and in any case the circumstances were all wrong. He needed four walls, a desk, a couple of chairs and a door to ensure a little privacy. Not this place.

'You're interested?'

'I'm sorry?'

'In rowing. Only we do taster sessions for novices. Think of it as three free goes. If you like it, you become a member. If you don't ...' He shrugged. 'No harm done.'

Suttle looked around. It seemed like the place was falling apart: the sagging doors, the piles of abandoned kit, the bird shit. Yet at the same time there was no arguing with the buzz. These kids were really going for it.

'So anyone can turn up?'

'No problem.'

'When?'

'Sundays are best. As long as the weather's not too evil, you'll find us on the beach.'

The coach turned back to the rowing machine and checked the readout again. Suttle couldn't resist a look: 4,567 metres. In 19.03. The rower, a young lad of maybe seventeen, was cranking up for a final push. Sweat darkened his T-shirt. His face was contorted with effort, and every time he pushed back against the footstretchers the effort squeezed a grunt from his gasping lungs.

Suttle caught his eye. 'This is *good* for you?' he murmured.

The boy had the grace to muster a smile.

'Fuck off,' he mouthed back.

Exmouth police station occupied the middle of an otherwise picturesque square on rising ground beyond the main shopping centre. An undistinguished 1960s building, it had a slightly alien presence. An apron of parking contained a handful of cars and the clock on the church opposite had stopped at twenty to four. Suttle, already struck by the slightly retro feel of the seafront, regarded this as somehow symbolic. Exmouth, he thought. The town that time forgot.

Houghton was putting the finishing touches to the smaller of the two offices commandeered for *Constantine*. Three desks: one for Nandy, one for Houghton, the third for Suttle. A poster featuring a Thai beach occupied one wall. A second poster warned uniformed coppers that FIRST IMPRESSIONS COUNT.

'This used to be the sergeants' locker room,' Houghton grunted. 'You should feel at home, Jimmy.'

Suttle tallied the names of Kinsey's crew he'd picked up from Molly Doyle. Eamonn Lenahan, he said, served as cox. He lived up the river in Lympstone. Andy Poole, who turned out to work for a hedge fund partnership, had a flash apartment in Exeter. Tom Pendrick, who rowed in the seat behind Poole, was listed with an Exmouth address. While a guy called Milo Symons evidently dossed with his girlfriend in a caravan on farmland near Budleigh Salterton. She'd been at the party too. Her name was Natasha Donovan.

Houghton had scribbled down the names. Kinsey's body, she said, had been removed after the Scenes of Crime photographer had done his work. A Crime Scene Manager had joined the CSI and they'd made a start on boshing Kinsey's apartment. Documents from the desk that served as his office and from a filing cabinet in one of the spare bedrooms were waiting for Suttle's attention, and Kinsey's computer had been bagged for full analysis.

'The CSI also pinged me this.' She beckoned Suttle closer. 'He found it on the man's Blackberry.'

Suttle read the text on Houghton's iPhone. It read, 'V. We stuffed them. The whole lot. Decent time too. The Krug's on ice. Usual place. J. xx'.

Houghton wanted to know who V might be.

'The Viking. Her real name's Doyle. Molly Doyle. She's the one who gave me the crew names.'

'"Usual place"?'

'Yeah. Interesting.'

'You sound surprised.'

'I am, boss. The woman's no fan of Kinsey.'

'Are we sure?'

'Of course not.'

'But?'

Suttle shrugged. He honestly didn't know. Molly Doyle, in

his judgement, had her finger on the pulse of the club and her description of Kinsey had sounded all too plausible.

'The guy muscled his way in,' he said. 'No one liked him. He thought money could buy him anything.'

'Including her?'

'I doubt it.' Suttle made a mental note to check the lead out.

Houghton nodded, then updated Suttle on the house-to-house calls. Gerald Smart, who occupied the apartment below Kinsey, confirmed that his neighbour had entertained guests last night. He'd heard laughter and music and a bit of stamping around but not much else. Getting on for midnight, everything had gone quiet and after that he and his wife had retired to bed.

'Nothing afterwards?'

'No.'

'What about the other properties? Line of sight?'

'Zilch. The guys aren't through yet but we seem to be talking a particular demographic. These are retired people. They're older rather than younger. I get the feeling they party early, get pissed and go to bed.'

'How many of them knew Kinsey?'

'Very few. There's a residents' association which is pretty active but it seems he could never be arsed. Most of these good folk knew him by name because of the property he'd bought but that's pretty much as far as it went. You're going to ask me whether he was popular but I don't think it's that simple. When it came to socialising and all that, he just wasn't interested. Apparently he didn't even have a Facebook account.'

Suttle nodded. This is exactly what Molly Doyle had told him. *This is the kind of guy who takes what he wants and turns his back on the rest.*

'Mr Loner,' Suttle muttered.

'Exactly.'

'What about the pub?'

'The landlord was pretty helpful. Turned out to be an

ex-marine. His line on Kinsey was pretty much everyone else's. The guy very rarely made an appearance and when he did stuck to fizzy water. Last night seems to have been a one-off. Three bottles of Moët? The landlord couldn't believe it.'

'And the crack? The chat? Anything there?'

'Not so far. The landlord was too busy to listen in but he's given us the names of some regulars who were in last night in case they picked up a clue or two. I've scheduled the follow-ups for this afternoon.' Her eye strayed to the list she'd made of Kinsey's crew. 'These guys need sorting. Where do you want to start?'

Eamonn Lenahan lived in a rented cottage in Lympstone, a waterside village a couple of miles upstream from Exmouth. Suttle's first call had been Tom Pendrick, but his attempts to raise an answer on the phone or in person had come to nothing. Before leaving Exmouth nick, he'd run all six names – including Kinsey – through the Police National Computer but drawn a blank. No previous convictions. No one ever charged or even arrested. Model citizens, all of them.

Lenahan's cottage lay in a tiny cobbled street with a glimpse of the river at the far end. Clouds of gulls swooped over the rooftops and Suttle could hear the soft lap of water on the pebbles that fringed the tiny harbour. He knocked again, wondering if Kinsey's cox was still sleeping off last night's piss-up, and then stepped back from the door and offered his face to a sudden burst of sunshine. The weather had brightened from the west, and standing in the quiet of this little village, listening to the gulls, Suttle realised that he was beginning to enjoy *Constantine*.

Most of the jobs that came to Major Crime were, to be frank, tacky. In Portsmouth he'd lost touch of the number of pissed retards who'd ended up battering a friend or a stranger to death. There was no mystery, no challenge, to enquiries like these, and even the drug scene – a dependable source of more interesting work – was riddled with lowlife. Heading west, he'd somehow assumed that he'd be stepping into a different world, classier, more sophisticated, but crime hot spots like Torbay and Plymouth were as squalid and mindlessly violent as anywhere in Pompey. To date, he'd worked on two murders and an alleged stranger rape. In all three cases the real culprit had been cheap vodka and the girl reporting the rape had turned out to have been as pissed as the rest of them. These were lives in free fall, tiny domestic tragedies played out against a landscape of crappy bedsits, cheap drugs and increasingly elaborate benefit scams.

Constantine, on the other hand, already looked a great deal more promising. An alleged millionaire with no apparent reason to end his days plus five partygoing crew mates who may or may not have wished him well. Molly Doyle had painted a picture of each of these people. These very definitely weren't lowlife. Eamonn Lenahan was a medic. Andy Poole worked in hedge funds. Pendrick was an electrician. These people had jobs, education, prospects. Booze had undoubtedly played a part last night, but it was a relief not to be looking at SOC shots of fat battered women lying dead on yet another stretch of fag-cratered orange nylon-pile carpet.

Suttle was about to knock for the last time when the cottage door opened. A small figure in a pair of black boxers was rubbing the sleep from his eyes. He'd found a pair of pink slippers from somewhere and hadn't shaved for a while.

'Mr Lenahan?'

'The same. Who the fuck are you?' Irish accent. Inquisitive smile.

Suttle offered his warrant card. He'd appreciate a word or two.

'No problem, my friend. Always a pleasure.' He stooped to retrieve a pint of milk and stood aside to let Suttle in. The house smelled of burned toast. Lenahan blamed his fellow tenant.

'Sweet wee girl. Off out early, she and her lovely friend.

How can I help you?'

The sitting room was tiny and dark – a single tatty armchair, a battered sofa and a trestle table in the corner loaded with books and a copy of yesterday's *Guardian*.

Suttle took a seat. There was a row of framed photos on the opposite wall, randomly hung. Somewhere hot. A village setting. Some kind of open-air market in the background. A crowd of black faces mugging for the camera, many of them kids.

'Sudan.' Lenahan had found a T-shirt from somewhere and a pair of trackie bottoms. 'Know it at all?'

'No.'

'Shame. We all need a bit of Sudan. Keeps you fucking sane.' He perched on the sofa, his legs tucked beneath him. 'So what have you got for me?'

Suttle explained about Kinsey. The news that he'd been found dead sparked no reaction whatsoever. Lenahan just looked at him.

'You're not surprised?' Suttle asked.

'Nothing surprises me.'

'You're not ...' Suttle frowned, hunting for the right phrase '... upset?'

'Never. You go, you're gone. That's pretty fucking final. Dying would have upset yer man, for sure. Kinsey was one for the options, you know what I mean? That's how he operated. Always. Options. Possibilities. That sweet little opportunity no other fucker ever spotted. Dying's a terrible option. And you're talking to an expert.'

Suttle blinked. He'd been right. This definitely wasn't Torbay. Lenahan hadn't finished.

'Under that apartment of his, you say?'

'Yeah.'

'So you're going to want to know about yesterday, about last night. Am I getting warm?'

'You are.'

42

'OK, so here's the way it was. We need to start with the race. The race is everything. And why's that? Because the race, my friend, is where it begins and ends.'

Yesterday's outing, he explained, was a head race, nine and a bit miles down the River Dart from Totnes to Dartmouth, pretty as you like, acre after rolling acre of God's fucking England. The boats start every thirty seconds and the trick is to knock them off, one by one.

'Knock them off?'

'Pass them. That's the trick, that's what we're there for, that's what Kinsey wants us to do. Fastest boat wins. And if you pass every other bugger, you're home safe.'

Off the start line, he said, they were towards the back of the fleet. Lenahan is in the cox's seat face to face with Andy Poole. Andy is stroke. He sets the rate. Lenahan's known Andy for ever, rowed with him for years on the Thames, won oodles of fucking cups. Between them, they'll boss the race.

'So we're half a mile down the course, a long straight bit before the first bend, and already we've reeled in the boat ahead. The guys doing the work have no idea what's going on because they're all looking backwards, but I haven't said a thing so far because it's good to toss the guys the odd sweetie, and so I'm nudging towards the right bank for the overtake and you know what? It's Kinsey, the man himself, who's up there in the bow, he's the one who susses what's happening and steals a little glance over his shoulder, just a little look now, one of his trademark looks, and here's the point, here's what I'm trying to tell you. As we step on these guys, as Andy pumps up the rate and we go surging past, *racing* past, I get to see the expression on Kinsey's face. He's creamed them, he's fucking *buried* them, and the sweetness of that knowledge, that big fucking jolt of adrenalin, puts this nasty little smile on his face. He's top dog. He's up there with the angels. The heavenly fucking chorus is giving it full throttle and every last cell in his body tells him he can do this for ever. He doesn't feel a whisper of knackeredness. That man's got the world by the throat. All the nausea we've gone through in training, all the money he's spent, all that has paid off, big time, in spades, and all he needs now is more of the same. One bunch of muppets crushed. Eleven to go. And you know what? Yer man's right to think that. Because that's called winning.'

Lenahan shifted his weight on the sofa and offered an emphatic nod, driving the point home. There was a moment of silence and Suttle wondered whether to applaud or not. Was Kinsey's prize cox like this all the time? Or was the performance strictly for Suttle's benefit? Either way, he needed to find out more.

Lenahan was cranking up again. By the time they got to Dartmouth, he said, Milo and Kinsey had hit the wall and even the last couple of overtakes couldn't mask their pain. But they still crossed the line in 58 minutes 27 seconds, an easy win, and an hour or so later they're in the Dartmouth clubhouse on the right side of a couple of pints and they're scooping up the trophy and milking the applause and feeling thoroughly pleased with themselves when Kinsey starts again.

'Starts what?'

'Post-race analysis. That's his fucking phrase, not mine. My friend, you need to make an effort, you need to *imagine* it. We've won. We've done the business. We're all getting happily bladdered and Kinsey starts banging on about *post-race analysis*. Where we got things wrong. What we could do better next time. How we need to sharpen up on the catch or the extraction or changes of rate or any fucking thing. Can you believe that? We've pissed all over the opposition. We've come close to setting some kind of course record. And he's talking about *rate changes*? The man's an eejit. Was an eejit. And that's being kind.'

Suttle wanted to know what happened later, back in Exmouth.

'This is last night, right?'

44

'Right.'

'OK. So we tuck the boat away in the club compound and kiss it goodnight and then we go to the pub. This is a proper pub that's stayed scruffy and real and for once in his life Kinsey uses it the way you should. Maybe Andy's had a word. Maybe Andy's told him to lighten up, enjoy himself, tie a couple on. That's probably the way it was because Andy's the only one Kinsey ever listens to. The freemasonry of the minted, right? Both these guys have got money, real money, and so Andy deserves a hearing. The rest of us? We're just bad-arse drinkers, also-rans, trophy fodder for the man's fucking ego.'

At the pub, he said, they were joined by Milo Symons' partner.

'Now this girl is a piece. Her name is Natasha – Tasha if she knows you. She's late thirties, maybe older, good nick, works out, blonde, describes herself as a resting actress. Way back in the day she probably did it for real on some crap telly series, but we've been around her for the best part of a year now and I can't remember catching a single fucking gig, not one. But fair play to the woman, she's still got it, she's still good-looking, and she's funny and sexy in the way that those two words often go together, you know what I mean? She rows with us sometimes when one of the other guys can't make it, and while she'll never win any prizes for technique she makes us laugh. She's also taken Kinsey's fancy big time, which is funny in itself because the guy's a midget and she's way taller than he is. Not that little me can talk.'

'So how long were you in the pub?'

'An hour, tops. Kinsey's ordered champagne. In the end we do three bottles, no problem, and then Kinsey orders us all back to his apartment round the corner for a nightcap or two, and at that point it's Tasha's idea to sort out a curry because that woman eats for England. So she takes orders and gets in her little car and then the rest of us halloo round the corner to Kinsey's place.'

Suttle tried to imagine this little knot of revellers making its way through the windy darkness. Kinsey, it turns out, has more champagne in his fridge but no Guinness. Pendrick thinks that's a shame and so Milo gets on the mobile to Tash and tells her to pick up some resupplies.

'Tash has gone for the takeaway by herself?'

'Yep. Now I'm with Pendrick on the Guinness. Excellent fucking call. So we're all lying around Kinsey's pad, helping him with the Krug, and then Wonder Woman turns up with a whole load of takeaway plus an armful of tinnies. Me and Pendrick split the tinnies between us and we're drinking toasts to how fucking *invincible* we are and all the time the temperature's dropping because the sliding door to one of the balconies is open and then it occurs to us that Kinsey's out there chucking up over the rail. You can hear the *splat-splat* on the promenade below. Nice.'

Suttle made a note, remembering the CSI telling him about the puddle of vomit on the other side of the apartment block round the corner from the body. Then he looked up again, asking what had happened to Kinsey. It was Pendrick, it seemed, who'd sorted Kinsey out, taken him to his bedroom and tucked him in. Meantime the rest of the crew were getting stuck into the curry, which turned out to be a big disappointment.

'Splodge, you know?' Lenahan pulled a face. 'No theme. No story. Nothing to remember it by. It's one of those nights you pick at the best bits but our hearts aren't really in it. A lounge that big isn't the cosiest place in the world and the truth is we've all had enough. Nine hard miles? Our collective fucking bodyweight in Guinness and champagne? Definitely time for bye byes. So Tash dumps the curry in the waste bin and does the washing-up. She's got the little sports car for her and Symons but we need a cab so she makes the call. The guy's there within five minutes. He has to do a bit of a circuit to drop the three of us off. Andy lives in Exeter so he'll be the last man standing but you know what yer man does? He gets a price from the driver and then takes a whack from each of us before we even get in the bloody car. That's how you get rich, I guess. That's the kind of stroke Kinsey would pull.'

Suttle wanted to know more about Kinsey. Was he still in bed at this point? Or had he got up again?

'Still in bed. Yer man's spark out. This guy and alcohol are strangers. He doesn't know what's happening to him. But that's not the point. The place has got three en suite bathrooms and we're still all thinking why hasn't the eejit used one of those if he wants to be ill, but it's Pendrick who puts his finger on it. Guy's a dog, he says. The man has to leave his smell everywhere.'

It was a neat phrase. Suttle scribbled it down. Later Lenahan would have to volunteer a formal statement, but in the meantime – as precious background – this stuff was gold dust.

'So you left ...' Suttle suggested.

'Sure we did.'

'Time?'

'Gone midnight. Ask the cabbie.'

'And you pulled the door shut behind you?'

'Yeah. We do that grown-up stuff really well.'

'No one else around? No one you saw? Inside the building? Out by the marina?'

'Didn't see a soul.'

'And no calls when you were up in the apartment?'

'Nothing. Just us.'

'But a couple of hours later the guy's dead.'

'So it seems.'

'Don't you find that odd? Being a doctor?'

The word doctor brought the ghost of a frown to Lenahan's face.

'How do you know I'm a doctor?'

'Molly Doyle told me.'

'Ah, the Viking.' The smile was back. 'And did she tell you what kind of doctor?'

'She said you worked abroad a lot. Médicins Sans Frontières.' Suttle nodded at the photos on the wall. 'I take it she's right.'

'She is. Fine woman.' He studied his hands a moment, then his head came up again. 'You really want to know about death, my friend? Then let me tell you. It's getting towards sunset. It's hotter than you can believe. Even the lizards are getting fucking stressed. But yer family are desperate and so they bring little you into the clinic. They've probably walked ten miles to get you to where it matters, and a journey like that hasn't done you any good at all. So there you are on the knackered old trolley we use as a bed and after your last ten breaths your breathing stops and then you're gone.' He nodded, his voice soft, his eyes never leaving Suttle's face. 'You're a couple of years old, maybe younger. Your mother screams and leaves the room. All the relatives outside, dozens of the fuckers, start to wail. Your father squats on the cracked old plastic chair which is the only one we've got and puts his face in his hands. A nurse cleans you up, removes the IV, swabs all the fucking blood and mucus away and then drapes something half clean over your face. Then your dad ties your big toes to keep your little legs together and wraps your feet and puts your hands together and binds your thumbs like this.' He mimed the action, showing Suttle. 'Then your dad lifts you onto a piece of coloured cloth and wraps you for a final time and takes you away. Me? I'm watching all this. It's something I've got used to. It happens maybe five times a week. It's like a little piece of theatre. The gennie's fucked again and the lights are flickering on and off and you stand there in the dark and you listen to make sure they've all gone. You have absolutely nothing to say. You padlock the drugs cupboard and then step outside. With luck, you're alone. You have a cigarette, you look up at the stars, and you wonder if the rest of the guys back in the compound have left any beers in the fridge. But on no account do you allow yourself to think. No way. Never. Why not? Because that's the truth about death. It's ugly. It's unsparing. And it's fucking everywhere. So from where I sit, Kinsey probably had it easy.'

There was a long silence. Gulls again, more distant this time, and a stir of wind in the street outside. Suttle, for once in his life, was lost for words. He wasn't sure if any of this stuff served any evidential purpose but it was hard not to be touched.

'You're going back? To Sudan?'

'Sure. And to Uganda and to Somalia and to all the other fucked-over places.'

'So what does it do to you? Long term?'

'I dunno. I guess that's a treat to come.'

'Are you worried?'

'Sure.'

'Do you think it damages you?'

'I hope so.'

'*Hope so?*'

'Sure. Because it's real. Because this is what's waiting for us all, some place down the road.' He stirred again in the chair, his hand reaching for a packet of Gitanes on the floor. Suttle shook his head at the offered cigarette, watched Lenahan light up and suck the smoke deep into his lungs. 'Look at it this way,' he said finally. 'You go to some fancy dinner party. It happens a lot around here. You're heading for the cheese course and everyone's still talking about house prices or private schools or which four-by-four is best for towing jet skis or the horse fucking box, and then comes a bit of a lull, because there's always a bit of a lull, and you sense it's your turn. But what the fuck can you offer by way of conversation? Have any of these people got a clue about Sudan? About cholera, malnutrition, pneumonia, kidney infections, measles, meningitis, gunshot wounds, snakebite, sepsis after female fucking circumcision? Has any one of them ever heard an infant's heart stop? No fucking chance.'

'So who do you talk to? Who understands?'

'Is that a serious question?'

'Yeah.'

'Then it has to be Pendrick. This is a guy who lives in a dark part of the forest. He lives in the shadows. He lives in his head. But he's good, bloody good, and he's done a bit too, one way or another. Jesus, has he ...' He tailed off, took another drag, expelled a thin line of blue smoke up towards the ceiling. 'If you want the truth, we talk about it a lot. Once you've been out there, I tell him, once you've seen it, lived it, been part of it, been *swamped* by it, you're ruined. There's a gap between you and the rest of the world. Nothing's real. And nothing matters. You knock at my door and tell me Kinsey's dead and you know what? I couldn't care a fuck.'

'You think he killed himself?'

'I don't know.'

'You think he fell by accident?'

'Maybe.'

'What else might have happened then?'

Lenahan's eyes drifted to the copy of the *Guardian,* then he was looking at Suttle again. He was smiling.

'You tell me.'

Suttle was with Houghton by half past twelve. One of the other desks was occupied by a young D/C trying to raise someone in the marina. Suttle pulled a chair towards Houghton. Boiling down Lenahan's account to the kind of brisk summary the D/I favoured was beyond him so he stuck to the essentials.

'The guys all left in a taxi around midnight,' he said. 'We need to check out the booking and statement the driver, but I've talked to the girl Lenahan shares with and she confirms he got back around that time. There's no way he could have got up and gone out later because the girl's best mate was kipping on the sofa downstairs and the front door opens straight out into the street.'

'Not Lenahan, then.'

'Not if we're talking murder.'

'And what's your view on that?'

'I haven't got one. Not yet.'

'And this guy Lenahan?'

'He says he's agnostic.'

'Meaning?'

'He thinks the jury's out. He says Kinsey was too self-interested to end it all, and too sensible to put himself in harm's way.'

'Kinsey was pissed,' Houghton pointed out.

'Sure. But he'd thrown most of it up. I'm not saying he was sober. Just that he'd probably have stayed in bed.'

Houghton nodded, said nothing. Then she glanced over her shoulder at the adjacent desk. The young D/C's name was Golding. He'd just spent half an hour in Exeter with Andy Poole.

'So how was he?' Suttle adjusted his chair.

'Same story, Sarge. They won the race. They had a bevvy or two. Kinsey got rat-arsed. The girl sorted a taxi. End of.'

'But how did he take it?'

'Take what?'

'Kinsey dying.'

'He was gobsmacked. He couldn't believe it. Neither could his missus.'

'She's alibied him?'

'Yeah. She was still up when he got back, watching some DVD or other. They talked a bit about the race then they went to bed.'

'She knew Kinsey?'

'Not especially well but I think they'd all socialised a bit. Poole couldn't get his head around it. At one point he was wondering whether he ought to have stayed in the apartment last night, kept an eye on the guy, stopped him doing anything silly.'

'As if.'

'Exactly. That's what his missus said. Sanest man I ever met. Direct quote.'

'Because he was the go-to guy?'

'Because he was rich. Because he had it all. Because he'd just won his first race. Because he had everything to look forward to.'

'And Poole?'

'Agreed. In spades. Apparently he'd helped Kinsey map out a whole load of these regatta things, pretty much every weekend over the whole summer. Money was obviously no problem. They were going everywhere. The big deal was to get into the South Coast Championships. On yesterday's evidence, Poole thought that might be possible.'

'Even with The Passenger aboard?'

'The who?'

Suttle explained about Kinsey's nickname around the club. The D/C consulted his notes.

'Yeah. Poole had just found another old mate who'd really strengthen the crew but Kinsey was obviously there for the duration.'

'So who was going to get dumped?'

The D/C went back to his notes again. 'A guy called Symons. Apparently he's really good for a novice, but Poole knows this other bloke will row the arse off him.' He looked up. 'Milo Symons? Name ring any bells?'

Lizzie was back at Chantry Cottage in time to give Grace her lunch. The prospect of Gill's visit had begun to weigh heavily on her and she was wondering whether she might dream up an excuse and put her off. They'd been mates for years, fellow journos on the Pompey *News,* and they'd ended up forging a friendship that owed more to Gill's pushiness than anything else. This was a woman who always needed a best friend, a mother confessor, someone she could rely on to share a drink or two and an account of her latest conquest.

Last in a longish line of failed relationships had been with a Major Crimes D/I called Joe Faraday, much respected by Jimmy, who'd brought his life to an end with three packs of painkillers and a bottle of decent red. Gill had regarded Faraday's suicide as a personal tragedy, hers rather than anyone else's, although her claim to a special place in her new beau's life had never stood up to serious scrutiny. Jimmy had discovered that his boss had shagged her just twice before locking his door and taking the phone off the hook.

The real problem, in Lizzie's view, was simple. Gill Reynolds had never mastered the knack of letting a relationship develop at its own pace. She had a bad habit of crowding her man from the off and never understood why thigh-length boots and a dab or two of Chanel wouldn't guarantee the love affair of her dreams. In this respect Lizzie suspected that nothing would have changed and wasn't at all sure whether she could cope with a couple of days of heavy-duty angst. Gill never arrived at any meeting without an agenda. Taking an interest in anyone else's life was beyond her.

But what could she say? And wasn't company – of any description – a brighter prospect than yet another wet after-noon banged up in Chantry Cottage?

The endless rain had made the front door stick again. She turned the key and gave it a kick at the bottom before stamping the mud from her wellies and wrestling the buggy indoors. For some reason she'd left her mobile in the kitchen. Half-expecting a text from Jimmy, she took it out onto the back patio and fired it up. She wasn't wrong about a text, but oddly enough it came from Gill. She'd had to change her plans. Instead of descending on Tuesday she'd arrive tomorrow in time for lunch. 'Lucky us,' she'd texted at the end, 'Can't wait.'

It was mid-afternoon before Suttle got to Tusker Farm. *Constantine* had yet to be upgraded to a full HOLMES 2 enquiry and in the absence of a statement reader, Houghton wanted Suttle to sort out the scraps of feedback from the marina, which were beginning to fatten into something more substantial. The house-to-house teams, while failing to unearth the bankable evidence that would turn *Constantine* into a fully fledged murder enquiry, were reporting widespread resentment of Kinsey and his behaviour.

According to one resident, a mainstay of the Exmouth Quays development, this was a guy who'd never had any time for his neighbours. He openly flouted some of the by-laws by having midsummer barbecues on his balcony and riding his mountain bike around the marina basin. He never turned up at the community fund-raising events – Canapes on the Quay, Carols on the Quay – that had become such a feature of waterside life. He never put his hand in his pocket when appeals were launched for a commemorative bench or a fighting fund to battle a nearby development, and when she'd confronted him, knocking on his door and trying to shame him into writing a cheque, he'd told her to go away and get a life.

None of this, of course, suggested grounds for dumping the guy off his own balcony and leaving his body to cool in the rain, but it confirmed a wider irritation. The landlord of the Beach pub, re-interviewed at his own request after the Sunday lunchtime drinkers had drifted away, confirmed that Kinsey had also upset a fair number of locals in the town, firstly by writing to the local paper and complaining about early-morning noise from fishermen putting to sea from the dock beneath his apartment, and later by mounting a vigorous defence of a bunch of developers planning yet another multi-storey block of flats within shouting distance of the marina. To upset these two very different groups of locals – working trawler men and middle-class worthies – took some talent, and in the view of the landlord Kinsey definitely had some kind of death wish. The interviewing D/C had underlined the phrase, bringing it to the attention of Houghton when he got back to *Constantine*'s temporary home.

Suttle was thinking about it now, as he bumped the Impreza into the farmyard. Houghton wanted him to develop the intel picture on Kinsey – the kind of guy he'd been, the risks he'd run, the people he'd upset – and barely hours into the enquiry he was already tallying an ever-longer list of potential enemies. Paul Winter, a Pompey D/C who'd taught him everything he needed to know about the darker arts of CID work, had once told him that money, serious money, carried a smell of its own. At the time Suttle hadn't really understood what Winter had been getting at, but his years on the tastier Major Crime jobs had wised him up. Money puts you in the bubble, he thought. And that's when you're truly vulnerable.

The farmer's wife answered Suttle's knock. Molly Doyle had been wrong about a caravan. Half a field away, tucked beside the shelter of a hedge, he could see what looked like a mobile home.

Suttle introduced himself. He said he was looking for a Mr Milo Symons. The farmer's wife was still studying Suttle's warrant card.

'In trouble is he?' She didn't seem surprised.

'Not at all.'

Suttle asked whether she'd been at home last night.

'Of course I was. We both were.'

'And does Mr Symons come in this way? Through the farmyard?'

'No. They've got a separate entrance up beyond their place. It's a gate we use to get the tractor into the field.'

'So would you hear anything when they come and go?'

'Depends.'

'On what?'

'On the wind. And Bess.'

Bess, it turned out, was their sheepdog. Ears like a bat.

'So last night?'

'She heard nothing. Nothing that I can remember.'

'Around midnight? Maybe later?'

'Nothing. But the wind had died so she probably wouldn't.'

Suttle brought the conversation to an end. Symons and his

fancy woman had evidently been renting the mobile home for a couple of years. So far the farmer's wife had no complaints. The woman dressed like a tart, but these days that was so common you barely noticed.

Suttle thanked her and set off up the field. The grass was still damp underfoot but the sky was cloudless and there was a definite hint of the coming summer in the golden drifts of buttercups. Several fields away, Suttle could see lambs worrying their mums to death and he found himself thinking of Grace. There were lambs on a hobby farm up the lane from Chantry Cottage. Maybe Lizzie had wheeled their daughter up there for a look. Maybe.

The mobile home was bigger than he'd expected. A line of washing was flapping in the breeze and a sodden cardboard box beside the door was brimming with crushed tinnies. Behind the mobile home, invisible from the farmhouse, Suttle found a white Transit van. The van was pocked with rust around the sills. There was paperwork all over the passenger seat, and half a cup of something that looked like tea was balanced on the dashboard. In the well beneath the glovebox, a litter of empty crisp packets.

Suttle had phoned ahead, making sure Symons was available for interview. He'd wanted to talk to his partner too, but it seemed Tash was elsewhere.

Symons came to the door. He was tall and thin, dark complexion, single ear stud, a mane of jet-black hair tied at the back with a twist of yellow ribbon. He was wearing jeans and a black T-shirt under an embroidered waistcoat. With the gypsy look went the hands of an artist: long fine-boned fingers, delicate wrists.

'Come in. Yeah. Good.' Symons dismissed the proffered warrant card with a wave of his hand. Already, he seemed to be saying, Suttle was some kind of mate.

On the phone Suttle had been vague about the reason for his visit. Now he told Symons about Kinsey.

'*Dead?* Shit. How did that happen?' His amazement seemed genuine.

Suttle said he didn't know. In the circumstances it was his job to put together Kinsey's last movements and try and understand what might have led to his death.

'But the guy was cool with everything. Why ...?'

Suttle was looking around the space that obviously served as a living room. There was a built-in sofa that probably doubled as a spare bed and an Ikea rocking chair that had seen better days. The far end opened into a galley kitchen and Suttle could smell fresh coffee. But what took Suttle's eye was the PC on the desk in the corner. An image hung on the screen, two bodies on a bed. One of them was Symons. Straddling him was a woman. The long fall of hair down her naked back was a violent shade of mauve.

'That's Tash.' Symons laughed. 'You want to see the rest?'

Without waiting for an answer he stepped across to the desk. A single keystroke brought the sequence to life. Tash was moving very slowly, barely lifting her arse, her hands cupping her breasts. Symons' eyes were closed. These people have been at it a while, Suttle thought. Years and years. Perfect control. Lots of practice.

'Then this.'

Symons bent forward. Tash seemed to be almost immobile, waiting, poised. Then, seconds later, she arched her back and grunted and the shot cut to a stretch of sand, black with birds erupting from their roost. White flashes from a thousand wings filled the screen, a dizzying explosion of movement as the camera held them in frame, slowly panning across the gleaming expanse of the estuary. Suttle was transfixed. He'd seen exactly this landscape only this morning. From Kinsey's apartment.

'This is some sort of movie?'

'Yeah. It's a rough cut. You want to see more?'

Suttle shook his head. He had business to transact, questions to ask. Luke Golding, the young D/C who'd talked to Andy

57

Poole, thought that Kinsey had backed Symons on some kind of project by bunging him money. Maybe this was it.

'Tell me about yesterday.' Suttle took a seat on the sofa. 'Talk me through it.'

Symons, sprawled in the rocker, described the race. They'd been great. It was his first ever race. 58.27. Total result.

'And afterwards?'

'Afterwards was great too.' He described the pub. Toasting themselves in champagne was definitely a novelty. It was good, he said, to see Kinsey so relaxed. He deserved it. And so did everyone else.

Suttle wanted to know about the impromptu party afterwards. Had Kinsey shown any signs of stress? Had Symons noticed anything that might account for what happened later?

'The guy threw up. Then he went to bed.'

'And the rest of you?'

'We pushed off. Tash organised a cab.'

'For everyone?'

'No. She'd driven over. It's a sports car. It's only got room for two. The rest of the guys went off in the taxi.'

'Leaving Kinsey by himself?'

'Yes.'

'So what time did you get back here?'

Symons thought about the question.

'After midnight,' he said at last. 'Then we crashed.'

'Anyone else see you?'

'I doubt it.'

'And this morning?'

'I ran Tash up to Honiton and dropped her at the station. It's her mum's birthday. Normally you can get a train to Yeovil but on Sundays there's a coach service. She was well pissed off.' He grinned. 'Back tonight though. I'm driving over to pick her up. You know Yeovil at all? Evil place.'

Suttle shook his head and scribbled himself a couple of notes. There was something slightly childlike about this man. In ways he couldn't quite define he reminded Suttle slightly of J-J, Joe Faraday's deaf-mute son. The same hints of vulnerability. The same feeling that bits of the wiring didn't quite connect.

'So how did you come across Kinsey?'

'I didn't. It was Tash who met him first. Someone told her about the club after she'd seen the boats when she was out jogging and she went down to find out more. Kinsey was on the beach. He was still a bit of a novice himself in those days – he hadn't bought the new boat – and they sort of shared notes. He bigged himself up from the off, did Kinsey, told Tash all about his penthouse apartment in the marina, how he'd watched the club boats from his window going up the estuary, and how he'd fancied getting involved. They went out together that morning, same boat, half experienced guys, half novices, and it was funny because Tash came back and told me how crap he was, completely out of time, always ahead of the stroke. Stick insect she called him.'

'You were a rower then?'

'No. It was Tash who got me into it. That was a bit later. She said it was brilliant and she was right. She's like that, Tash. She's the one who sorts me out. Always has done. Ever since the off.'

They'd first met, he said, when he was in his early twenties. All his life he'd lived beside the river up in Topsham, but after leaving school with pretty much nothing to his name he'd bailed out of Devon and signed up for a film course in west London. Too much dope was doing his head in, and after a near-terminal bust-up with his dad he knew he had to get his shit together. The film course included a chance to work with professional actors and one of them had been Tash.

'We'd spent the afternoon shooting a whole load of stuff in some studios in Hammersmith. Afterwards we went to the pub, a place in Chiswick down by the Thames, and I was telling her about my own river, and what it meant to me, what it's always meant to me, and how hard that feeling was to express,

59

and she said film, you need to make a film about it, you need to dream up a story, or make something associative, an image-based thing, something that does justice to this feeling of yours. And you know what? That was the most wonderful thing I'd ever heard. It was like a door opening in my head, or maybe somewhere way down in here ...' He touched his chest, leaning forward in the rocker, trying to draw Suttle into this story of his. 'Tease it out, she said. Take it in your hands. Nurture it, understand it, shape it, *treasure* it. Why? Because something's calling you. Maybe it's the spirit of the river. Maybe it's something else. But either way you're lucky. Because that kind of thing doesn't happen very often. So be aware. Stay in tune. *Listen* to the river. And *do* it.' His eyes found the PC on the desk. 'She was right, too. And it's worked.'

Suttle smiled. He could imagine a conversation like this. It sounded more like therapy than idle pub chat. Symons was a good-looking guy, no question, and Suttle could picture this new woman in his life, probably older, undoubtedly wiser.

'And this film has a story?'

'Sure. It's about the river. Actually it's more than that. It's a story about the river and a story about a love affair, about two people who live *on* the river, who are *part* of the river, who maybe *are* the river, its mirror image, its other self, the river made flesh. They live on an old barge. The barge sits on a mooring up off Dawlish Warren. That's where the tide flows strongest, where the river talks loudest. These two people, the man, the woman, they have no names. They just *are*. They're part of the river, part of each other. The word Tash uses is flux.'

'Flux?' Suttle was lost.

'Yeah. Wonderful word. Perfect. *Flux*.' Symons grinned. 'Partly this is about geography. Here, let me show you. This is Tash again. Her idea. Her trope.'

Symons unfolded his long frame from the chair and rummaged around behind the desk. Seconds later Suttle found himself looking at a framed map of the Exe estuary. Symons knelt beside him, visibly excited at this sudden interest in his life.

'OK, so what I'm wanting is a narrative, a story that does justice to the river, that captures its essence, its soul. The framing device is the affair. But the affair, this relationship, has to be shaped by the river itself. And here's what Tash came up with.' One bony finger settled on the river upstream of Exmouth. Then the finger tracked slowly south until it paused at the mouth of the estuary.

'Look at that. Look at the river just there. What does it remind you of?'

There was a hint of impatience in his voice. This, he seemed to be saying, is obvious. Suttle was trying to make sense of the shape of the river. The way the harbour nosed into the tidal stream. The long curl of a feature on the bank opposite. The narrowness of the gap between them.

Suttle asked about the bank opposite. What was he looking at?

'It's called Dawlish Warren. It's a protected bird site. Magic place.'

Suttle nodded. He was still no closer to an answer.

'You can't see it?' Symons couldn't keep the disappointment out of his voice.

'No.'

'Truly?'

'Yes.'

'It's a fanny. A woman's vagina. That was her insight, Tash's, a stroke of total brilliance. Just here, where the river gets tight, is where the barge is moored. That's where the action takes place. Within touching distance of the Warren. Just here. Just across the water where the sweet spot is. And here's another thing. *Touching distance*. Tash again. The perfect title. Why? Because we're talking every kind of distance. Geographical distance. Historical distance. The distance between two people.

And the way that passion, or the tide, or the history, can *bridge* that distance, even *abolish* it.'

Way back in the eighteenth century, he said, a group of Dutch seamen got themselves shipwrecked on the Warren. There was a big south-easterly blow and their ship ended up on the beach. The locals came over from Exmouth and slaughtered every last man.

'That'll be in the movie too. My idea this time, not Tash's.'

His finger had found the sweet spot again. Suttle was looking hard at the map. This time he got it.

'That's Regatta Court. That's where Kinsey lived.'

'Exactly. He thought it was really funny. We needed a development budget and Tash thought he might like the idea. He knew nothing about flux but he understood the rest of it.'

'You're telling me he gave you money?'

'Not me. Tash. She did the negotiations, got him sold on the idea. First off he wanted to see the kind of stuff I'd done already. I've got some work from way back but Tash said we could go one better and shoot a couple of scenes from the script and show him those.'

Suttle's eyes had gone back to the PC. He was beginning to understand.

'So that's what you did?'

'Yeah. Kinsey bought us a decent camera and gave Tash a couple of grand to make it happen and we did the rest.'

'You're talking about the stuff I just watched?'

'Yeah.'

'So who chose the sequences?'

'Tash did. She chooses everything.'

'And Kinsey?'

'He only saw a rough cut. I gave him a DVD and he watched it on his laptop.'

'And?'

'He loved it. Totally knocked out.'

'He told you personally?'

'Yeah.'

'When?'

'Last night, in the pub. He'd told Tash already but last night he made a big thing of it. He said the rest of the budget wouldn't be a problem. Not after watching what we'd done.'

'How much are we talking?'

'Forty-five grand. Quite a lot of that is for the hire of the barge.'

'Right.' Suttle nodded. 'Right.'

There was a long silence. Would someone about to field a cheque for forty-five thousand pounds toss their benefactor into oblivion? Suttle thought not.

'How well did you know Kinsey?' he asked. 'Be honest.'

'Not well. Not really. If you want the truth I got into his crew because of Tash.'

'I'm not with you.'

'Kinsey fancied her. He'd do anything for her. And that turned out to be a bit of a blessing.'

'For you?'

'For both of us.'

'Because of the movie?'

'Of course. And the rowing too. Yesterday was magic. That guy Andy Poole's taught me loads.'

'He thinks you're good.'

'Does he?' The grin was unfeigned. 'Did he *say* that?'

'Yeah. Not to me. Not directly. But yeah. So tell me – what did you make of Kinsey?'

Symons thought about the question. Finally he sat down again, leaning forward, his voice lowered, almost conspiratorial. A kid. Definitely.

'This is just between us two, right?' Suttle didn't answer. Symons went on regardless. 'I think he was lonely.'

'Why?'

'I don't know. I just got the feeling. He didn't seem to have any friends, any mates. Mates matter.'

'No girlfriends? No one special?'

'I don't think so.'

'Was there a wife once?'

'Dunno. I suppose there may have been.'

'Right.' Suttle nodded. 'So you're telling me the guy was pretty much alone?'

'A loner, sure.'

'And Tash?'

'Tash?'

Suttle recognised the flicker of alarm in Symons' eyes.

'She got close to him?'

'He fancied her. I told you.'

'That's not what I'm asking.'

'Listen, man. The woman's my partner. She's beautiful. Everyone fancies her. So what are you suggesting?'

'I'm suggesting nothing.' Suttle had noted the sudden flash of anger. 'I'm asking you whether she might know more about Kinsey than you do.'

'And not tell me, you mean?'

'Yes.'

Symons considered the proposition before rejecting it with a vigorous shake of his head.

'No way,' he said. 'No fucking way.'

Suttle held his gaze. At length he asked how Symons made his living.

'I do stuff for my dad.'

'What sort of stuff?'

'You've seen the van out there? I collect and deliver bits and pieces of furniture. He's got a couple of antique shops. He bids in the auctions and I pick the stuff up.'

'And that gives you enough to live on?'

'Yeah.'

Suttle nodded and scribbled himself a note. The earlier warmth had gone out of this conversation. Symons was visibly upset now. Suttle asked him where Tash would be tomorrow morning.

'Here,' Symons shrugged, 'I guess.'

Suttle took her mobile number and then got to his feet.

'There's a guy called Pendrick,' he said. 'He rows in Kinsey's crew. You'll know him.'

'Of course.'

'Any idea where he might be?'

'No.'

'He didn't mention anything last night? Plans he might have had for today?'

'No.' The smile had returned. 'But then he wouldn't.'

'Why's that?'

'The guy's another loner. Just like Jake.'

Suttle was back at Exmouth police station in time for the first of the *Constantine* squad meets. Nandy had returned from a busy afternoon in Torbay, and the house-to-house teams filled the rest of the office. As a courtesy, Houghton had also asked the duty uniformed Inspector to attend.

She kicked off with a brisk summary of progress to date. House-to-house teams had knocked on every door in Regatta Court. They'd scored a response from maybe two thirds of the apartments but failed to gather anything of evidential use. Only one resident had laid eyes on Kinsey's partying crew. She'd seen them streaming out of Regatta House around midnight. Hand on heart she couldn't be sure but she thought four or five people, one of whom was definitely a woman.

Detectives had also covered every property with line of sight on Kinsey's balcony. Again, nothing.

'What's the lighting like?' This from Nandy. One of the D/Cs fielded the question.

'Crap, sir. We're talking lights at knee level on the walkway by the dock. No way would they reach the fifth floor.'

'So no witnesses?' Nandy was looking at Houghton.

'None, I'm afraid.'

'And definitely no CCTV?'

'No.'

Houghton went on to describe the kind of ripples Kinsey had been making. No one seemed to like him. His reputation for arrogance had spread beyond Exmouth Quays. There was even a question mark about the crew he'd put together.

'Who says?' Nandy again.

'Me, sir.' Suttle told him about Lenahan and Symons. In his view Kinsey had bought their loyalty. These were guys who got on among themselves, and after yesterday's win they might still carry on rowing with someone else in the bow seat, but neither Lenahan nor Symons seemed over-distressed by Kinsey's passing.

'So what are you telling me?'

'Nothing, sir. Except no one seems surprised that the guy's dead.'

'You think someone killed him?'

'I think he may have had it coming.'

'And we can prove that?'

'Of course not. Not yet.'

'But you think we might?'

'I think it's possible, sir, yes.'

Suttle was getting uncomfortable. The last thing he wanted was a public pissing match with Nandy.

Houghton stepped in. The post-mortem, she reminded everyone, was scheduled for tomorrow morning. After that, things might be a great deal clearer. In the meantime, D/S Suttle would be pulling together the background intel.

Suttle nodded, glad of the reprieve. There was a pile of Kinsey's files on his desk, material seized from the apartment, and he'd be spending most of tomorrow trying to build a picture of the man's life.

Houghton wanted to know what they'd missed. She was still looking at Suttle.

'Pendrick,' he said. 'We still haven't nailed the guy.'

Houghton nodded. Detectives had returned to his flat throughout the day but failed to raise him. Messages left on his mobile had gone unanswered. She'd tasked two D/Cs to sit on his address throughout the evening. If necessary, they'd be relieved by another shift at midnight. SOC had already retrieved some shots of last night's celebration from Kinsey's camera, and a process of elimination had ID'd Pendrick. If the guy hadn't turned up by first thing tomorrow morning, she'd be circulating the mugshot and other details force-wide.

Houghton had printed a couple of photos. Suttle, reaching for one of them, found himself looking at a big guy in his mid-thirties. A brutal grade one darkened his shaved skull and there was something about the cast of his face that seemed vaguely familiar. He had a deep scar that tracked diagonally down his right cheek and he was wearing jeans and a blue sweat top that had seen better days. Unlike the rest of the crew, he wasn't punching the air. On the contrary, he seemed preoccupied, almost detached. A loner, he thought, remembering Symons' parting shot.

The meeting broke up. Nandy told Suttle to stay put. Already Suttle sensed what was to come. It was this man's job to match ever-thinning resources against the incessant demands on the Major Crime machine. MCIT inquiries were horribly expensive, as the headbangers at HQ were only too eager to point out. In any enquiry the only currency that mattered was evidence.

'We've got Kinsey's crew alibied. Am I right?'

'Yes, sir. With the exception of Pendrick.'

'And Scenes of Crime have found nothing material in the apartment?'

'Not so far.'

'We've no witnesses to what happened?'

'No.'

'And not much prospect of finding any?'

This was a question Suttle wasn't prepared to answer. He didn't go as far back as Nandy, nowhere near, but his years on the Major Crime Team in Pompey had taught him never to discount a surprise. Solid effort, meticulous investigation and a helping of luck could sometimes transform a faltering enquiry and something told him that *Constantine* was far from over.

Nandy rarely left a suspicion unvoiced.

'You don't think this man had an accident, do you?'

'No, sir.'

'And you don't think he topped himself?'

'I think it's unlikely.'

'Why?'

'Because he doesn't seem that kind of guy.'

'Who says?'

'Pretty much everyone.'

'I see.' Nandy nodded and turned away.

There was a long silence. Suttle thought the conversation was over. He asked whether the Det-Supt would be down in Exmouth tomorrow. Nandy ignored the question. He hadn't finished with Kinsey.

'You think these people knew him, this man? Really knew him? You think anyone knows anyone? You really think there aren't parts of us we keep hidden? You? Me? Every other poor sod?'

Suttle blinked. This was suddenly personal. He seemed to have touched a nerve in Nandy, stirred feelings much deeper than irritation at defending his precious budget.

Nandy hadn't finished. He said he'd lost count of the sus deaths he'd tried to stand up as murder. As a younger copper he'd taken far too much notice of people telling him that so-and-so would have been incapable of suicide. They were probably sincere, they probably meant it at the time, but the truth was that deep down we were all in the dark, all strangers to each other.

'You don't believe that?' There was something almost

plaintive in his voice. 'You don't think that's the way we really are?'

Suttle left the nick shortly afterwards. He'd phoned ahead, checking in with Lizzie, but had raised no answer. The road back to Colaton Raleigh took him down into the town centre. On an impulse he headed for the seafront. The rowing club lay at the far end of the long curve of yellow sand. He found a parking space on the promenade and got out.

The days were lengthening now and the sun was still high in the west. The tide had turned a couple of hours ago and water was pouring back into the mouth of the river. After a morning of low cloud and drizzly rain Suttle could scarcely credit the transformation. A sturdy little trawler was wallowing in through the deep-water channel, a cloud of seagulls in pursuit. More gulls wheeled and dived over the distant smudge of Dawlish Warren while a pair of cormorants arrowed seawards, barely feet above the churning tide.

Watching the cormorants, Suttle thought suddenly of Joe Faraday. His ex-boss had been a manic birder. On a number of occasions down by the water in Old Portsmouth he'd abandon a review of this job or that to bring some passing blur to Suttle's attention. Suttle, who knew absolutely nothing about birds, had always been touched by this passion for the natural order of things. Faraday, to his certain knowledge, had despaired of the chaos that passed for daily life, and from the world of birds he appeared to derive both comfort and solace. Nature, he'd once confided, represented sanity. You could rely on a mother to feed her chicks. You could set your watch by the arrival of birds of passage. Spot a skein of Brent geese lifting off for the long flight north, you knew it had to be April.

Suttle paused on the front, enjoying the sun on his face. Nandy, somewhat to his surprise, seemed to share a little of Faraday's view of the world. In Faraday's case, deep pessimism had hardened into despair – and it was that despair, in the end, that had taken him to his death. Nandy, on the evidence of six busy months, appeared to be far more robust, but after their last exchange, just minutes ago, Suttle was beginning to wonder. Was there something that came with higher command, some subtle alteration to your DNA, that took you to a very bad place? Had Nandy been serious about the stranger at the heart of every friend?

In truth, he didn't know, and just for a moment, standing in this puddle of sunshine, the wind in his hair, he knew he didn't much care. He liked this new job of his. There wasn't much of a social life as far as work was concerned because most of the guys lived a fair distance away, scattered across the hugeness of Devon. Some lived up near the north coast, an area they referred to as the Tundra. A commute like that didn't leave much room for a pint or two after work, and in any case most of his new colleagues had young families to think about, a gravitational tug about which Suttle knew a great deal.

He grinned to himself. Despite the grief he was occasionally getting from Lizzie, he loved going back to Chantry Cottage. He wasn't the least bit daunted by the ever-lengthening list of jobs he had to sort and rather liked the way they'd managed to turn camping into a way of life. Nocturnal scufflings from the mice, he told himself, brought you closer to nature. That had to be good for Grace, and good for all of them in the end, and if Lizzie occasionally lost her sense of humour then so be it. Faraday, he thought, would have definitely approved.

On the point of returning to the car, his eye was caught by wheel marks tracking down to the water's edge. Then he spotted a boat trailer, tucked up beyond the tideline. The trailer was tiny, way too small for the big sea boats he'd seen earlier in the club compound, and he peered out at the water, shading his eyes against the glare of the sun, not quite sure what he might find.

For a long moment he could see nothing but the dance of

the incoming tide. Then he caught a movement, a black speck, away to the east.

The speck was moving fast, buoyed by the tide. Within seconds he could make out the shape of a single rower. He was big, powerful. He was wearing a red singlet. Each stroke seemed to flow effortlessly into the next one, his long arms reaching forward, his legs driving hard, his hands tucking the oars into his body until the cycle started all over again and he leaned forward over his knees, his hands feeling for the grain of the water, driving the tiny scull closer and closer.

Suttle grinned to himself, suddenly recognising what Lizzie needed in her life, what would chase the demons away, what would put the sunshine back. She should be down here. She should have her three free rows and get stuck in. She'd never been frightened by exercise. Back in Pompey she'd been running two or three times a week. She loved the water too, and they'd often fantasised about getting a little dinghy and sailing across to the Isle of Wight.

Suttle fumbled for his mobile, hoping Lizzie would pick up. Good news was for sharing. The sculler had stopped now and was drifting down with the tide, his body sagging, his head on his chest. Then came Lizzie's voice on the phone. She sounded exhausted. And there was something else there. Anger.

'Thank Christ it's you,' she said. 'I've had enough.'

He found her curled in a ball in the darkness of the living room. He'd never seen her sucking her thumb before. Even Grace, safe in her playpen, was looking anxious.

Suttle squatted beside her. She'd been crying. He knew it. Another first.

'What's happened?'

'I don't know.' She clung to him. 'I just don't know.'

'Shit.' He held her close. 'Tell me. Just tell me.'

'There's nothing to tell. I'm just ... Fuck ...' Her hand felt blindly for the tissues balled beside her. 'This is horrible ... I'm sorry ... I'm really sorry.'

'But what is it? Tell me. What's happened?'

She began to cry again, gulping for air, real pain, real misery. Suttle tried to get to his feet but she wouldn't let go. Grace couldn't take her eyes off her.

At last she released her grip. Her face was shiny with tears.

'I'm useless,' she whispered. 'Totally pathetic. Ignore me. Forget it. I'm sorry to get you back like this.'

'I was coming home anyway,' Suttle pointed out.

'I know but ...' She sniffed. 'This is the last bloody thing you need.'

Suttle struggled to his feet and she stared up at him then turned her head away. Grace was agitated now, shaking the wooden bars of her pen in bewilderment. Suttle lifted her up and gave her a cuddle. She struggled in his arms. She wanted to be with her mum.

Lizzie reached out, taking the baby.

'It's on the table,' she said.

Suttle found her mobile. It was still switched on. He read the message.

'Who's this from?'

'Gill.'

'Gill Reynolds?'

'Yes.'

'And she wants to come down?'

'She *is* coming down.'

'You said yes?'

'I did.'

'Shit.'

'Quite.'

Suttle absorbed the news. He'd never had any patience with Reynolds. Once you got past the obvious there was nothing there but self-obsession. As long as she'd just been a mate of Lizzie's, Suttle had bitten his tongue, but after what happened to Joe Faraday he'd consciously blanked the woman from his life.

'I'll cancel her,' he said. 'Leave it to me.'

'I've tried.'

'When?'

'This afternoon. I gave myself a talking-to. I knew you wouldn't want her down. It took me for ever to make the call but in the end I did it.'

'And?'

'It made no difference. You know what she's like. She never listens.' She took a deep breath and held Grace tight. 'Tomorrow morning. Around twelve.'

'I'll phone her again.'

'It's pointless. You could go one better though.'

'How?'

'By being here.'

Suttle thought about it, tallying the work he had to get through by lunchtime. Day two of *Constantine*. No chance.

'I can't, my love.'

'You could. If it was that important.'

'Of course it's important. You're important. You're both important. All this is important. But I can't just—' He broke off. 'Leave it to me. I'll phone her.'

Lizzie began to protest again, telling him she'd cope some-how, but Suttle wasn't listening. The weakness of the signal drove him onto the patio. It was a beautiful evening, the sun sinking in the west, the wind beginning to die. They'd discovered a troop of ducklings on the stream at the bottom of the garden only yesterday. Suttle could hear them pestering their mother.

'Gill?' Suttle could feel the patio slabs moving under his weight. 'Is that you?'

'Of course it is. Jimmy?' She sounded surprised.

'Yeah, me. Listen. Something's come up. Lizzie's not too good. Some kind of bug. She'd never tell you in a million years but I honestly think—'

73

Gill broke in. She had a habit of ignoring the end of other peoples' sentences.

'She sounded fine this afternoon. It won't be a problem. You know me. Iron constitution.'

'It's not you I'm worried about. It's Lizzie. She needs—'

'I know what she needs. I know that girl like a sister. I probably know her better than you do. I expect she needs a bit of TLC. I'm good with that. Just ask her.'

Suttle wasn't having it. It was flu. Definitely. Lizzie needed peace and quiet. She needed to be left alone. Please, Gill. Just this once.

There was a brief silence on the line. The mother duck had mounted the bank, an unsteady line of fluffy nothings behind her. Under any other circumstances this would have been a precious moment. He'd run for the camera. Grace. Lizzie. The ducklings. One for the family scrapbook. Then Gill was back. There was something new in her voice, a definite edge.

'I'll be there for lunch, Jimmy. You won't regret it.'

'I beg your pardon?'

'You heard what I said. You'll be around too?'

'No.'

'Then I'll stay for dinner. Don't worry. No pressure. I'll sort an Indian or something. Do they have takeaways in the country?' She laughed, then hung up.

Suttle was still staring at the phone. *You won't regret it?*

For a moment he thought about phoning back, upping the ante, going for broke, but then he heard a movement behind him and he turned to find Lizzie standing in the open doorway. She'd heard every word he'd said.

'See?' she said.

'Fucking woman.' Suttle risked a smile. 'We're doomed.'

They didn't talk until later. Suttle had bathed and changed Grace, leaving Lizzie to do her best with a packet of pasta and what was left in the vegetable basket. After he'd put his daughter down and blown on the mobile over her bed, he drove down to the village store and bought a bottle of Chianti. The wine turned out to be on special so he grabbed another before returning to Chantry Cottage.

Lizzie had made a definite effort with the pasta. She'd even found a candle to soften the overhead light in the gloom of the living room. Suttle uncorked the Chianti and poured two glasses, raising his own in a toast.

'To us.'

They touched glasses but then Lizzie put hers down.

'Something wrong?'

She smiled. For some reason she seemed to find the question genuinely funny.

'You want a list?' she said.

'Yeah. Since you ask.'

'No, you don't. And I'm sorry. I'm really, really sorry. I'm supposed to be better than this.'

'You're lovely. I love you.'

'Really?'

'Yeah, really. I know I'm not, you know ...'

'Here much?'

'Yeah.'

'It's not that. It's this. All of it.'

'What?'

'Everything.' She made a vague, circular motion with her hand. 'You, me, Grace, this horrible cottage, the country, the rain, the silence – it's driving me nuts, Jimmy. I just don't know who I am any more. Have you ever had that feeling? Not knowing what's happening to you? Not knowing if it's ever going to stop? I'm out of tune, my love. I'm not me any more. Do you know what I'm talking about? Has something like this ever happened to you?'

Suttle had to shake his head. Life had dealt him a number of evil hands. Twice he'd been hospitalised after making the wrong call in dodgy circumstances, once in the Job and once in his private life. That had hurt, sure, but he'd never suffered anything remotely like this.

'I'm sorry,' he said. 'I'm really, really sorry.'

'Sorry doesn't cut it. Not any longer. I've got to *do* something, Jimmy. I've got to take some decisions.'

'About?'

'Us.'

'Ah.' Suttle's head went back. He reached for his glass. For the first time he realised they were facing something really serious. Not once had he ever thought she might leave him.

'Is it me?' he said at last. 'Be honest.'

'Yes, in a way it is. Because this, all this, is you. You love it. I can see you love it. You love the country, the space, the fresh air. Even the fucking rain seems to turn you on. Me? I loathe it.'

'Then we'll move.'

'Where to?'

'Somewhere the roof doesn't leak. Somewhere with windows that fit. Somewhere mouse-proof.'

'In the country?'

Suttle didn't answer. Just looked at her. The silence stretched and stretched. She'd said her piece. The situation couldn't have been clearer.

'You want to live in a town,' he said. 'Or a city.'

'Yes, please.'

'Plymouth? Exeter?'

'I don't care. Pompey, if I have to.'

'That sounds like a threat.'

'You're right. That's where I am. Mrs Desperate. Dreaming of Copnor Bridge.' She smiled and reached for his hand across the table, throwing Suttle into confusion. He was lost now. Was she really packing her bags? Were they really headed for some shitty ground-floor flat in a gutty part of Guz?

He voiced the thought aloud. Cards on the table.

'Guz?' she said blankly.

76

'Plymouth. It's what the locals call the place. Tells you everything you need to know.'

'I see.' She was toying with her glass. 'How come the ground-
floor flat?'

'Because it's all we could afford. I've been round this course
before. Prices are astronomic down here.'

'Dearer than Pompey?'

'Big time.'

She nodded, then took a tiny sip of wine. Maybe she's not
aware of all the implications, thought Suttle. Maybe this isn't
quite as dire as I thought.

Wrong.

'I talked to Gill for quite a while this afternoon,' she said
softly. 'We had a proper conversation for once.'

'And?'

'She's just moved into a new flat. Three bedrooms? In
Southsea? Can you believe that? It turns out they gave her a
rise. She's mad about the place. It's even got a bit of garden.
She says it's lovely.'

Suttle's heart sank. The implications couldn't be clearer.

'You're telling me you'd move in with her?'

'Either that or my mum's, yes.'

'Both of you?'

'Obviously.'

Suttle stared at her, not quite believing his ears. Lizzie and
Grace? Camping out with Gill fucking *Reynolds*?

'Cheers,' he said, reaching for his glass.

Lizzie waited for him to swallow a mouthful or two. Then
she leaned forward across the table. She wanted him to be
reasonable. She wanted him to understand.

'Think about it. My job's still open if I want it. I could go
back to work, earn us a bit of money, give us some options.'

'And Grace?'

'My mum would look after her.'

'You've asked her?'

'No. But she would, I know she would.'

'So how long would this ...' Suttle shrugged '... go on for?'

'For as long as it takes. Until we had a decent stash.'

'That could be years.'

'Yeah. It could.'

'Living apart? Me down here? You back in Pompey?'

'Yeah. Unless you did what I'd do.'

'Go back to my old job?'

'Exactly.'

'I doubt they'd have me.'

'Of course they'd have you. You're the guy who put Mackenzie away. Local hero, you.'

'No.' Suttle shook his head. 'Going back never works, never.'

'How do you know? When you've never tried it?'

'Because I wouldn't. No way. You go on in life. You look forward.'

'So what does that make me?'

'Good question.'

Silence again. Upstairs, Suttle could hear Grace beginning to grumble. If you caught her early enough you could head off the tears and get her back to sleep. He was half out of his chair but Lizzie beat him to it.

'Leave it to me.'

Suttle listened to her footsteps on the stairs. All the earlier drama seemed to have gone. This was a different Lizzie. She must have been planning something like this for weeks, maybe months. He should have seen it coming. He should have headed it off.

He poured himself another glass of wine. By the time Lizzie was back at the table, his glass was empty again.

'Well?' she said.

Suttle began to talk. He told her about *Constantine,* about the lone dog walker from Exmouth Quays finding Kinsey's body sprawled on the promenade, about his involvement with the rowing club, and about the investigative pathways Suttle had to start exploring first thing tomorrow. Despite herself, Lizzie found herself engaged. At heart she was still a journalist. Stories like this had always fascinated her.

'So what do you think?' she asked.

'Honestly?'

'Honestly.'

'I think somebody killed him. I haven't a clue who and I might well be wrong, but that's not the point. Hunch isn't a word my bosses have much time for. They prefer evidence.'

'And?'

'There isn't any. Not yet.'

Lizzie reached for his hand again. In the early days he'd often let her into the world of the Job, sharing odd titbits from ongoing investigations, and she'd always loved him for it. It was an act of trust. It made her feel special. It made her feel loved. Lately all that had stopped. These days Jimmy very rarely talked about his work. Now this.

'So how do you –' she reached for her glass '– progress something like this?'

'By grafting. By looking. By building the intel picture. By establishing a timeline. By wondering about motive and opportunity. By getting inside this guy's head.'

'The killer's?'

'Kinsey's.'

'And then the killer?'

'Maybe ...' he nodded '... if it pans out that way.'

'But it will, won't it? You're good at this. Paul thought you were the best.'

Lizzie was the only person Suttle knew who always called Winter by his Christian name. Winter had a famously soft spot for Lizzie. He'd once told Suttle she was the only journalist in the city with real bollocks. At the time Suttle hadn't known quite what to make of the comment but in time he recognised it as a shrewd judgement. Winter was right. This lovely wife of his rarely lost her nerve.

Now she wanted to know more about Kinsey. Suttle shook his head. He'd said enough.

'Then why bring all this up?'

'Because of the rowing. I've spent most of the day talking to people who are crazy about it.'

'And?'

'I think you should have a go.'

'*Me?*'

'Yeah. Why not? You need to get out, my love. You need to put this place behind you once in a while. I'm sure running helps but maybe it's not enough.'

'Running round here is crap. Grace obviously comes too. I do my best with the buggy but on these roads you take your life in your hands.'

'Lives. Plural.'

'Exactly.'

'OK.' Suttle nodded. 'So maybe I'm right. So maybe rowing's the answer.'

Lizzie wasn't at all sure. Suttle could see it in her face. She'd started this conversation with her bags practically packed. Now this husband of hers was talking about some rowing club.

'How would it work?'

Suttle explained about the trial offer, three free rows. Suttle would drive her down to Exmouth next Sunday, and if her maiden voyage worked out OK then she could return for the club sessions on Tuesday and Thursday night.

'But what about Grace?'

'I'd look after her.'

'You'd get back in time?'

'Of course I would.'

She nodded, doing her best to fight her excitement. She'd always relished a challenge.

'Does anyone know about this?'

'About what?'

'About your missus maybe joining up? Only the way I read it most of your suspects belong to the club.'

Suttle had the grace to laugh. In truth, he hadn't thought this thing through at all. Not properly.

'So what would you prefer?' he said. 'How would you want to play it?'

'I'd need to be me,' she said. 'Lizzie Borden.'

'Not some copper's wife?'

'Exactly.'

'Fine.' He shrugged. 'In that case you'd drive yourself down on Sunday. Use the TomTom. There's no drama finding the place.'

'And you'd really stay behind? With Grace?'

'Of course.'

'Do the washing? Sort the cat out? Peel the spuds? Mend the fucking door? Not go mad?'

'No problem.'

'And you're telling me it's not a hard thing to do? Rowing?'

'I'm telling you you might like it. I'm telling you you might love it. And I'm telling you it's the least we can do.'

'To keep this thing afloat?'

'Exactly.'

Lizzie pondered the proposition, then emptied her glass and reached for the bottle. Her turn to propose a toast.

'Here's to Guz,' she said.

'Meaning?'

'We'll see.'

Two

Lizzie woke early on Monday morning, recognising a sound she dreaded. In the distance, coming down the lane outside the cottage, she could hear a squad of young marines from the nearby Commando Training Centre at Lympstone. They spent all night on Woodbury Common, doing God knows what, and then jogged down through the village to be picked up by trucks at first light. When she'd first got used to this early-morning wake-up call, she'd thought it mildly quaint. If Grace had woken early, they'd stand at the window and wave as the young lads sped by. But then she'd realised that the rhythm of all these boots could tell her what the weather was doing. And this morning, as the *splash-splash* of the approaching squad grew louder, she knew it was raining again.

She closed her eyes, willing herself back to sleep, telling herself that it was a passing shower, that she'd wake later to bright sunshine and maybe the prospect of a new chapter in this life of theirs. Sleep came more quickly than she expected, and she woke again an hour or so later, reaching for Jimmy's hand under the sheet, but he'd gone. Downstairs, the kettle and the teapot were still hot to her touch and she realised that the growl of the car that had woken her up was probably the Impreza. She checked the clock on the wall: 07.03. Even earlier than usual.

*

Suttle was at Exmouth nick by half seven. To his surprise, Carole Houghton was already at her desk, busy on the phone. Suttle sorted a couple of coffees from the adjoining kitchenette. By the time he got back, Houghton had finished her call.

'We found Pendrick,' she said. 'He turned up last night.'

'Where?'

'Back home at his place. He told us he never checks his phone. Not on Sundays.'

Pendrick, she said, had evidently gone to north Cornwall in search of some decent surf. He'd returned late afternoon and gone down to the rowing club to use one of their single sculls. You couldn't waste a sunset like last night's, he'd told the D/C.

'We get the feeling he likes exercise.' Houghton was reaching for a pad of jotted notes.

Suttle was back on the seafront at Exmouth, watching the lone sculler in the red singlet powering back on the flooding tide. This had to be Pendrick, he thought. Had to be.

'So what did he tell us?'

'Not a lot, to be frank. He confirmed all the other accounts. They won the race, came back, got pissed, went over to Kinsey's place. Kinsey, as we know, started throwing up off the balcony. Pendrick thought he'd gone out for a breath of air. He put the guy to bed and soon afterwards they all left in a taxi. Pendrick was the first to be dropped off.'

Pendrick, she said, lived alone in an upstairs flat in an area of Exmouth known as the Colonies. Saturday night the flat below was empty. One of his neighbours in the terrace had heard the taxi arriving but had gone to bed shortly afterwards. Pendrick had stayed up a while to check out the weather on his PC and watch the first half of a DVD. He'd been out of the house by eight the next morning to catch the tide at Widemouth Bay. The surf, he'd told the D/C, had been crap. He'd tried other beaches further north but had drawn a blank. Hence his visit to the rowing club.

Suttle wanted to know what the interviewing D/Cs had made of Pendrick.

'They thought he sounded pretty credible.'

'Was he surprised? About Kinsey?'

'Yes, apparently he was.'

'Upset?'

'The guys think not but we can't do him for that, can we?'

Suttle smiled. The coffee was horrible. He was trying to imagine this man, trying to get beyond the slumped figure in the red singlet. How did he present himself? What kind of place did he live in?

'Very tidy, very together. Andy says the guy reads a lot. Loads of music too, neat little sound system. Not too much furniture but loads of photos on the wall. Apparently the man's surfed everywhere: California, Oz, New Zealand, Hawaii, the lot. Been around a bit.'

Suttle nodded. Simon Maffett was one of the older D/Cs on the squad, an ex-marine who'd put in a couple of decent years on the force rugby fifteen until his knees gave out and his missus persuaded him to chuck it in. Andy could build a rapport as quickly as any detective Suttle had met. He also knew a thing or two about pushing the physical limits. Pendrick, Suttle suspected, would have recognised a fellow soul.

'What else did he say about Kinsey?'

'Not a lot. Like I say, Andy got the impression there was no love lost but he didn't press him.'

'And the rowing?'

'He loves it. Nearly as much as surfing.' Houghton paused, a rare smile on her face, and Suttle realised there was something she was holding back.

'Well?' he said. 'What else?'

'Pendrick? Doesn't the name mean anything to you?'

Suttle shook his head, remembering the prickle of recognition he'd felt when he'd seen the slightly scary face in the photo Houghton had circulated but failing to suss exactly why.

'Tell me.'

'It was last year. Summer. June 24 to be exact. I just looked it up on CIS. You remember the bloke who rowed the Atlantic and lost his wife en route? That was Pendrick.'

CIS was force-speak for the Crime Information System, a database that listed everyone who'd appeared on the Devon and Cornwall radar. Suttle had it now. The story had been all over the media. The couple had been rowing west to east. They'd made the Western Approaches after God knows how long at sea and Pendrick had woken up early one morning to find his wife missing. He'd alerted the Coastguard, and the rescue centre at Falmouth had coordinated an air search that had lasted a couple of days before being called off. At this point Pendrick could have made a landing in southern Ireland or been retrieved by any number of ships in the area, but he'd insisted on completing his voyage alone, ending up in Penzance Harbour, fighting for balance on the quayside as media crews battled for a word or two.

'He had hair then,' Suttle said. 'Lots of it. Hippy-looking guy. Never said much.'

'You're right. A couple of the uniforms at PZ took a statement, and there was a longer interview afterwards, CID this time.' Houghton scribbled a name and slipped it across the desk. Suttle stared at it. D/I Gina Hamilton. Another face from the past.

'You know her?'

'Yeah. Not well, but yeah.'

Hamilton, he said, had been part of a Devon and Cornwall intel operation a couple of years back. They had a bunch of local dealers plotted up and had successfully traced a supply source back to a Spanish fishing port called Cambados in Galicia. The cocaine, lots of it, was coming into the UK through Portsmouth, and Suttle, then a D/C, had been tasked to give her whatever assistance she needed when she drove east to coordinate the surveillance.

In the event Ms Hamilton been impressively well organised and the operation had ended with a meticulously planned hard arrest on Honiton bypass. The Drugs Squad had actioned a whole pile of warrants that same night, scooping up dealers across the entire force area. Hamilton herself had made a bit of an impact up in the social club at Fratton nick. Tall, blonde, nice leather jacket, bit of a looker. Even Faraday had been impressed.

'You know her?' Suttle asked.

'Of course.'

'Wouldn't have done her any harm, that job.'

'It didn't.'

'But?'

'But nothing.' Houghton nodded at the contact details. 'You might want a conversation. I gather she did the interview with Pendrick herself.'

Minutes later, Houghton was gone. She had a meet with Nandy at force HQ in Exeter, and then she was due at the Royal Devon and Exeter Hospital for the post-mortem on Kinsey. She'd be back, fingers crossed, in time for a bite of lunch. By which time, the future of *Constantine* might be a great deal clearer.

Suttle went through the morning's tasking for Houghton's squad of D/Cs. In truth, the guys were already beginning to run out of doors to knock on and Suttle knew that the preliminary findings from the PM would probably be decisive. Evidence of injury to Kinsey before the fall would bump up the enquiry to a full murder investigation. Anything else, especially with Nandy at the helm, might well be curtains.

Already Suttle had started the process of applying for the dead man's financial records, plus billing on his landline and mobile. It would be a day or two before the banks and the phone companies came through with anything solid and in the meantime Suttle needed to get a feel for exactly how this man had led his life. What did he do for a living? Where had his money come from? And who else might have shared his life in Regatta Court?

By late morning, with the help of a couple of phone calls, Suttle had the answers to most of these questions. Kinsey, it turned out, had been an engineer. For a while he'd worked for Boeing in Seattle. Afterwards, still living in the States, he'd run a one-man consultancy, Kittiwake, which specialised in wind-turbine technology. He'd come up with a new way of configuring the power train that converted blade movement to grid-ready electricity, and had sold the process to a major international corporation with operations across the globe. The proceeds of this deal appeared nowhere in the files at Suttle's disposal but a conversation with a contact in the Department for Business, Innovation and Skills put the figure at not less than $35 million. In three short years Kinsey had made himself a very rich man.

At this point, though, his success had been evidently soured by two developments. An industrial competitor, in the shape of a Swiss engineer called Henri Laffont, had threatened to sue Kinsey for patent infringement. Laffont claimed that Kinsey had ripped off key elements of his own wind-turbine design and owed him compensation that would have taken a huge bite out of the $35 million.

As far as Suttle could judge, this was an ongoing battle. Kinsey had refused Laffont's claims point blank and hired a firm of expensive commercial lawyers, Zurich-based, to put the Swiss engineer back in his box. The last email in the file was dated 8 February 2011, barely two months ago. Laffont, it seemed, was currently working on a contract in Shanghai. He was due to fly into London 'in early April' and was demanding a meet. He was tired of dealing through attorneys and suggested they could sort out a settlement, amicable or otherwise, face to face. Kinsey didn't seem to have replied to this suggestion but Suttle made a note to check on the seized PC. 'Amicable or otherwise' was an interesting phrase and he ringed it before putting the file aside.

Kinsey's other source of grief was his ex-wife. He'd met Sonya in Seattle. Her half-brother lived in Bristol. Suttle had found a phone number in one of Kinsey's files and given him a ring. Sonya, of course, needed to be made aware of Kinsey's death, but the brother-in-law, whose name was Bill, was more than happy to fill in a little of the background.

His half-sister, he said, had been making a decent living in the real estate business when she married Kinsey, but the crash of 2008–9 had wiped her out. At this point Kinsey had decided to return to the UK to look for new business opportunities. With some reluctance Sonya followed, but the marriage was a disaster. After less than a year, she'd maxed out her credit cards, emptied the joint bank account, left a pile of plastic on Kinsey's desk and flown back to Seattle. Since then she'd been fighting to extract every last cent from the divorce settlement. Even now, said Bill, she was still harassing Jay for money, and lately her demands had escalated. Only last week, to his certain knowledge, she'd been threatening to pay her ex-husband a personal visit.

Surprised by his candour, Suttle had asked Bill how things were between himself and his half-sister.

'You want the truth?' he'd said. 'Those two folks deserved each other. Anything for money. And I mean anything.'

'Do you see her at all, Sonya? Fly over for the occasional visit maybe?'

'Never.'

'And Kinsey?'

'I wouldn't spend a second with the guy. You've got an experience to share with him? A holiday, maybe? A trip to some nice Polynesian island? He's been there already, probably owns the place. You're proud of your new Prius? Want to show off about it a little? He tells you you've just made the dumbest purchase of your life. He knew everything about everything.

88

He just didn't need the other ten trillion people on the planet. This is a guy happiest in his own company. This stuff about the rowing is news to me. Those other guys must have had a lot of patience.'

The conversation had ended shortly afterwards. Reviewing his notes, Suttle knew he'd unearthed two fresh lines of enquiry, both of which needed serious attention. A multi-million-dollar settlement for patent infringement might offer ample motivation for a personal visit, while a vengeful ex-wife – under the right circumstances – could do worse than dump her ex-husband off his fifth-floor balcony.

He was still deciding how to develop each of these when Houghton returned. She eyed the spread of paperwork on Suttle's desk. He brought her up to speed. Two more potential suspects for the pot. Maybe.

'But what has he been doing since selling up?'

'Property development.'

'Where? How?'

'He's got a new company now, Kittiwake Oceanside. He seems to be catering to a particular demographic. These are couples in their sixties, made a bit of money – often in London – and they want to buy somewhere down here, nice view, private beach, total privacy, total peace of mind, full service, like-minded people, all that bollocks. Think retirement lite.'

Suttle had skimmed the Kittiwake files. Kinsey had been paying estate agents in Cornwall to scout for suitable sites. So far he'd identified three and was in ongoing contact with the relevant planning authorities. In every case his pitch was the same. As a successful businessman committed to developments of the highest standard, he was keen – in his phrase – to add value to outstanding locations. In this context, he defined value in terms of employment opportunities, net capital inflows and what he called 'the aesthetic and social gain from the provision of signature destinations'.

Kittiwake Oceanside, he said, would attract high net worth individuals to areas of Cornwall that were demonstrably struggling. These discreet, beautifully designed retirement communities would kick-start the local economy. From every point of view, he wrote, 'we're looking at the perfect win-win'.

Houghton was studying one of the brochures Suttle had extracted from the Kittiwake files. A sleek collection of apartment blocks towered above a line of sand dunes. There was lots of glass, lots of boasts about sustainability, and lots of hints that slouching in front of crap telly was strictly for losers. Couples playing tennis. A peleton of gym-honed retirees departing for a spin on their bikes. A woman in a bikini heading for the nearby surf. Kittiwake Oceanside, thought Suttle, was selling a kind of immortality. Settle here and your body will never let you down.

'I wonder what the locals think?' Houghton was equally unimpressed.

'Exactly. Maybe we should talk to the local journos and find out. People are getting pissed off with tosh like this. Views are for everyone. They shouldn't be something you have to reserve with a huge deposit.'

'Sweet. Where have you been these last few years?'

Suttle ignored the question. He sensed already that *Constantine* was dead in the water.

'So what happened at the PM?'

'Nothing. The guy died of impact injuries. Cranial contusions, severe spinal trauma and heart failure. Quick, if you're looking for a way out.'

'And you think he was?'

'There's no evidence to suggest otherwise.'

Suttle nodded. Post-mortems were never less than thorough. Scrapings from under the fingernails to indicate some kind of resistance. Special attention to the throat and larynx to determine possible strangulation. Try as he might to find evidence of prior assault, the pathologist had drawn a blank. Houghton was right: there was absolutely nothing to suggest that Kinsey hadn't been alone when he met his death.

'But why?' Suttle asked, 'Why would he have done it?'

Houghton shrugged. 'Not our call, Jimmy. People do what they do.'

'And Mr Nandy?'

'I haven't managed to talk to him yet. We've got a body in a field down near Bodmin. It hasn't got a head. I expect Mr Nandy thinks that's a bit of a clue.'

Gill Reynolds turned up just before lunch. Lizzie, deeply grateful that the sun had come out, met her on the patch of muddy gravel that served as parking for Chantry Cottage. She was driving a new-looking scarlet Megane convertible, a perfect match for her nails. Newsroom pay rates were clearly on the up.

She swung her long legs out of the car and leaned back to retrieve a bag of goodies. Lizzie had Grace beside her. When Gill knelt for a kiss Grace turned away and hid her face in Lizzie's jeans, plainly terrified by this sudden intrusion.

'Lunch?' Lizzie led Grace back towards the open kitchen door, determined to stay ahead of the game. Even when she was fit and well, doing a job she loved, Gill had always had a habit of swamping her.

The kitchen, for once, looked almost presentable. Lizzie had worked all morning to clean the place up. There was nothing she could do about the dripping tap and the state of the units, but she'd brightened the general shabbiness with the last of the daffodils from the garden and she had a pot of chilli con carne bubbling on the stove. Gill had a famous appetite, a tribute to her hours at the gym.

With the chilli went hunks of newly baked bread and a salad Lizzie had bought from the village store. Gill was in the garden, striding through the long grass, peering into a hedgerow, stooping to retrieve something from the reeds beside the stream. Frothy white blossom was beginning to appear on both fruit trees and she paused, gazing up, her face splashed with sunshine.

Seconds later, she was at the kitchen door.

'Fantastic,' she announced. 'So wild. So unspoiled. So fucking *authentic*. Lucky girl. Lucky old you. You have to keep it exactly this way. Promise me you will.'

Lizzie smiled but said nothing. She was tempted to suggest that Gill stay a while, get a real taste of life in the country, see whether she could cope with the isolation and the damp and the mobile signal that seemed to come and go like the wind. Instead she perched Grace in her high chair and dished out the chilli.

Gill had already started on office gossip. It seemed there'd been a big turnover of staff recently, and most of the new people Lizzie had never heard of, but Gill – as ever – had identified a target or two and was currently shagging a married man in his thirties who worked on the sports desk. Three times a week they'd been meeting at the leisure centre for a midday game of squash. Lately they'd given up on the squash and gone straight back to Gill's new place.

'The guy goes at it like a madman,' she said. 'The squash used to knacker me but this is ridiculous.'

She paused to try and tease a spoonful of chilli into Grace's mouth. Sex was the closest Gill had got to ever having babies and she'd always been clueless about the dos and don'ts of motherhood. Grace spat the chilli out and started to cry.

Gill seemed oblivious. A couple of months back she'd been offered the kind of feature pieces that had always gone Lizzie's way and she'd leapt at the chance. Her speciality just now was celebrity interviews, and she was speculating on the chances of bedding a soap star Lizzie had never heard of when she remembered a call she had to make.

Lizzie was still trying to settle Grace. Gill poked at her Blackberry, not understanding why it wouldn't respond.

'You have to take it outside,' Lizzie said. 'Point it at the sun and hope for the best.'

'You're not serious.'

'I am.'

'What about the laptop? Have you got broadband?'

'Dial-up.'

'*Dial-up?* Christ. You'll be sending pigeons next.'

Lizzie offered her landline but Gill was already out of the door. Minutes later she was back. Pointing it at the sun had evidently worked. She'd also remembered there was someone else in the room, another life, so different to hers.

'So tell me,' she said. 'How's it going?'

Lizzie had been anticipating this question all morning. In truth she'd have liked nothing better than to get the whole thing off her chest but she was determined to hang on to what was left of her dignity.

'It's fine,' she said. 'Just different.'

'You hate it.'

'That's not what I said.'

'You don't have to. I can see it on your face. So let's start again. What's it *really* like?'

Lizzie was nonplussed. This was the last thing she'd expected. Gill Reynolds, it turned out, was infinitely more tuned-in than she'd ever remembered. No wonder they'd given her promotion.

'You want the truth? It's a nightmare.'

She talked about what she'd found when they'd first moved down. She described the state of the cottage, and the garden, and the life she seemed incapable of putting together when her husband was at work. She told Gill about Christmas, two long days of unrelieved gloom while Jimmy tried to coax a little heat from the fire. And then she brought the story up to date. She'd decided she was a lousy wife and – even worse – a hopeless mother. By giving in to Jimmy, by agreeing to go along with his rural fantasy, she'd probably inflicted untold damage on her daughter. Kids were smart. They sensed when things were going wrong. For her sake and for Grace's, before it was too late, she needed to take a few decisions.

'You'll *leave* him?'

'Not him, Gill. This. I'll leave this. We both will, me and Grace. It's beaten us. I've tried. Believe me I've tried. I've *really* tried. But every time I think I'm getting somewhere something else kicks off and I'm back where I started. Central heating? Windows that fit? Maybe a little car to get out in? Is that too much to ask?'

Gill was trying to think this thing through. Another novelty.

'Maybe you haven't tried hard enough,' she said at last.

'That's an insult.'

'No, it's not. Of course this is different. You must have expected that. No way is this Fratton or Southsea or wherever. It's the country, Lou. Different mindset. Different everything. Like I say, try harder. *Adapt.*'

'Christ ...' Lizzie turned away. She had an overpowering urge to cry again. Then came an arm round her shoulders.

'I believe you, Lou. I really do. I'm just thinking about the alternative, that's all. Where will you go? What will you do?'

Lizzie was back in control of herself. She apologised for losing it and began to get to her feet.

'Don't.' Gill put out a restraining hand. 'Just answer my question. What will you *do*?'

Lizzie gazed at her for a long moment. The fact was she didn't know. On the phone yesterday she'd nearly asked Gill whether there was room for them at this new place of hers but in the end she'd drawn back. That wasn't something she'd shared with Jimmy last night but it hadn't seemed to matter because she'd assumed Gill's answer would be yes. Now she wasn't so sure.

'You're think of coming back?' Once again Gill was ahead of the game. 'Staying at my place?'

'It had crossed my mind, yes.'

'Forget it, Lou. It won't happen.'

'Why?'

'It just won't.'

'You don't want us?'

'Of course I want you. That's not the issue.'

'So what is? I don't understand.'

Gill studied her, then shook her head. No clues. No conferring.

'We'll go to my mum's then.' Lizzie was getting angry again. 'She'll definitely have us.'

'Not a great idea.'

'But why? Is it the job?'

'The job's fine. I'm sure the job's yours for the asking. It's just ...' She shrugged, picked at her chilli, then looked up again. 'Never go backwards, Lou. It never works.'

'That's what Jimmy said.'

'Then believe him. He's right. One way or another you have to make this work.' She paused. 'Is the seaside near here? Only I really fancy a walk on the beach.'

By mid-afternoon, Jimmy Suttle suspected it was all over. He'd tasked a handful of D/Cs to start exploring the new lines of enquiry – Henri Laffont and Kinsey's vengeful ex-wife – but Nandy was due any time and Suttle knew that Houghton would have told him about the post-mortem. These days, through no fault of his own, Nandy had become a juggler, forever trying to keep all the force's investigative balls in the air. As calls increased on precious Major Crime resources, there were balls he knew he'd have to put to one side, and while he'd never abandon an enquiry that showed genuine promise, he was bound by the iron demands of the Criminal Prosecution Service. No one had ever invented a form for a hunch, and if there was no evidence to suggest that Kinsey had died at someone else's hands, then Detective Superintendent Nandy would be moving swiftly on.

He arrived at the makeshift office within the hour. Suttle briefed him on the problems Kinsey had been facing in his business and personal life and tallied the actions he'd commissioned to find out more. Nandy nodded, unimpressed. No one, he said, got that rich without making enemies. That was one of the joys of capitalism, something you could rely on, but from where he was sitting there wasn't a particle of evidence that a pissed-off Swiss engineer or a homicidal ex-wife had chucked Kinsey into oblivion. The thing just didn't fly. While he was happy to have Suttle's D/Cs complete their preliminary enquiries in both instances, he was minded to redeploy the rest of the squad.

'Including me, sir?'

'No.' Nandy closed the door. 'Carole tells me you've been under some pressure lately.'

'Does she?' Suttle was astonished.

'Yeah. Not much gets by her, believe me. You should be grateful, son.' He paused. 'Everything OK at home?'

'Yeah ...' Suttle ducked his head. 'More or less.'

'Good to hear it. From tomorrow onwards I want you to take over the *Constantine* file and prepare it for the Coroner. We're looking at a couple of weeks, max. That's the good news. The bad news is you're on your own. Happy with that?'

'Perfectly.'

'If you really need help D/I Houghton might release D/C Golding on a temporary basis but that's absolutely last resort. We understand each other?'

'Of course.'

'Good. Any questions? Anything you're not clear about?'

Suttle gave the question some thought, then nodded.

'Yes, sir. What happens if ...?'

'If what?'

'If I end up believing there's grounds for further investigation?'

'Then you lift the phone –' he offered Suttle the ghost of a smile '– and we crank it all up again.'

It was gone six by the time Lizzie and Gill returned to the rowing club compound. They'd spent the afternoon on the beach at Exmouth, walking the couple of miles past the ochre jut of Orcombe Point and onwards to the distant wall of rock that marked the end of Sandy Bay. It was low tide and the sand was firm underfoot. Oystercatchers were feasting on the weed-strewn rocks at the water's edge and in the distance they could hear the *pock-pock* of live firing from the Royal Marines' range at Straight Point.

Gill's delight at what they'd stumbled on was unfeigned, and even Lizzie had to admit that this stretch of God's coastline was pretty special. Gill had insisted on carrying Grace, who was already getting too big for the chest sling, but she and Gill seemed to be friends at last, and Gill paused every now and again to show her something that had caught her eye. The beach was big and bare and flawless, gleaming as the sun began to sink, and when a couple of horses appeared, clattering awkwardly down the concrete slip from the caravan camp above, the picture was complete. They thundered past, splashing through the shallows, heading back towards Exmouth, and the noise and the movement drew shrieks of pleasure from Grace. Lizzie had remembered to pack a couple of spare bottles and some mashed-up swede in case she got hungry, but as they approached the rowing club she seemed content.

Gill's Megane was parked beyond the compound. Lizzie had told her all about Jimmy's suggestion that she join and Gill was adamant that she should, at the very least, give the thing a try. She was curious about this new departure in Lizzie's life and demanded a look at what lay in store. When they got to the compound, the doors to the clubhouse were open. Lizzie hung back, a little uncertain, but Gill wasn't having it.

'Come,' she said. 'We need to do this.'

Lizzie knew she was right. She negotiated the steps up to the clubhouse and pushed in through the door. The near-darkness took her by surprise. She could make out shapes on the rowing machines, three of them. Slowly, one by one, they came to a halt. They were all women.

Lizzie explained she'd come for a look, apologised for the interruption.

'Not at all. Are you interested?' The nearest woman had got off her machine and extended a hand. She said her name was Tessa. When Lizzie confirmed that she fancied having a go, Tessa grinned.

'No problem.'

'Now?'

'If you like. You don't need the anorak. Runners and jeans are fine. Nothing strenuous. Just the basics.'

Lizzie gave her jacket to Gill. This wasn't at all what she'd expected. She perched on the seat which slid up and down towards a tiny electronic screen. A handle was attached to a flywheel by a chain. The trick, said Tessa, was to use the muscles that really mattered to get the flywheel spinning.

She strapped Lizzie's feet into the footstretchers beneath the screen, asked her to take a pull or two and stepped back to watch. With a glance towards Gill, Lizzie did her bidding. She'd never been on a rowing machine in her life.

'You're bending your arms way too early.' This from Tessa. 'The real power comes from your legs. Push away and use your arms as levers. Only bend them at the end of the stroke. You'll be amazed at how much difference that makes.'

'Difference how?'

'Watch the readout. The figures never lie.'

The other two girls laughed. Too right, they seemed to be saying. Lizzie gave it another go, keeping her arms straight this time. Tessa was right. The numbers zipped forward.

'Much better. But you're holding the handle way too tight. It needs to be loose. Right. That's it. Now concentrate on getting the rhythm. It's a cycle. Your body leans forward, your hands go over your knees, you push back with the legs to take the stroke, you tuck the handle under your ribcage, then it's hands away quickly and you repeat the cycle all over again. Excellent. You're a natural. I didn't catch your name.'

'Lizzie.'

'I'm serious, Lizzie. This could be for you. Am I right, girls?'

There was a murmur of approval. Lizzie was still on the machine, still rowing, trying to get one of the numbers down. According to Tessa this calculated how long she'd take to cover 500 metres. Two minutes seventeen seconds, for a novice, appeared to be OK.

'More than OK. Now give it some welly. We're talking flat out. You've got a minute. After that we stop.'

Lizzie took it as a challenge. She increased her rate, driving hard against the footplate, trying to keep her back straight as she took the stroke, throwing her hands forward, keeping the movement going, chasing the numbers on the readout. By now she was fighting for breath, the lactic acid beginning to scald the muscles in her calves and thighs, the numbers dancing in front of her eyes. She could feel the sweat beneath her T-shirt, on her face. Two minutes ten. Two minutes seven. Two minutes six.

'Twenty seconds to go, Lizzie. Work for it. *Want* it.'

She shut her eyes, pushing ever harder. She was hurting now and the sheer effort lifted her bum from the seat at the start of every stroke. Then it was over and she slumped on the seat, sucking in the cold air, aware of the whine of the flywheel as it began to slow.

From somewhere above her came a noise she dimly recognised as applause. All the girls were clapping. Gill was clapping. Even Grace looked pleased. Lizzie grinned, trying to get to her feet. She hadn't felt so good, so complete, for months.

'Thank you, ladies,' she managed.

Tessa helped her up, said she'd done well, better than well, then her attention was caught by a movement in the doorway and Lizzie turned to see someone else silhouetted against the brightness of the sunshine outside. It was a man, tall, broad-shouldered, perfectly still. He was wearing shorts and a red singlet. He didn't have much hair.

'This is Tom.' Tessa laughed. 'Impress him, and you'll never look back.'

On the way home Suttle made a detour to Pendrick's flat. He was still in two minds about Nandy's real motivation in charging him with the preparation of a file for the Coroner. A task like this usually fell to a D/C, and something in Nandy's manner told him there was more to this decision that met the eye. Maybe Nandy wasn't convinced that *Constantine* had really hit the buffers. Maybe this was a clever move to keep the investigation at least semi-active. Either way, he didn't much care. Suttle had never had a problem working by himself. On the contrary, he rather enjoyed it.

Pendrick lived in the top half of a terraced house a couple of minutes' drive from the nick. A sign in the downstairs window read, *Dominic Widdows – Chiropractor. For appointments ring 01395 268078.* Suttle made a note of the name and number and rang Pendrick's bell. No reply. He rang again. Nothing. He stepped back into the road, gazing up at the top window. The curtains were pulled tight against the world outside.

Suttle drove home. Expecting to find evidence of Gill, he was surprised to find the parking area empty. He killed the engine and checked his watch. Nearly seven. He sat in the Impreza a moment, aware of the acids churning in his stomach. It's a beautiful evening, he told himself. They've gone for a walk.

The house was locked. He fumbled for his key, pushed at the door and stepped into the kitchen. Plates were piled in the sink and the remains of a chilli con carne had crusted in the saucepan. He wondered about a note but found nothing. There were still a couple of Stellas in the fridge. He fetched one out and snapped open the tinnie, trying to resist the obvious conclusion. Lizzie had spent the morning packing. Gill had arrived. Lunch would have been over in no time at all. Lizzie had strapped the baby in the back of Gill's car, stuffed her bags in the boot, and all three of them had fucked off back to Pompey. Job done. Game over. End of.

At this time in the evening a long low slant of sunshine added a rare warmth to the kitchen. Suttle inched his chair sideways, taking full advantage, reaching for the tinnie again. Was this what was left of his marriage? A sink full of washing-up and a spoonful or two of cold mince? He fought the hollowness inside, knowing that life banged up by himself would be a hard ask. He'd miss Lizzie like hell. He'd probably miss Grace even more. Family life, with all its imperfections, was what softened his working days. He was lucky enough to love what he did for a living, at least most of the time, but never for a second did he kid himself that it was enough.

Over the years he'd met countless cops who'd let the Job drive everything else out of their lives, and in every case they'd come to regret it. These were the guys suggesting a drink or two in the pub around the corner after work. These were the loners desperate for company and a listening ear. Suttle had always resisted these invitations, telling himself he'd never make the same mistake, but now – for the first time – he realised how easy it was to miss the obvious clues. He was a detective, for fuck's sake. So how come he'd let his marriage come to this?

He was contemplating the prospect of the other Stella when he heard a car slowing outside. Then came the crunch of wheels on gravel and a peal of laughter as a door opened. Moments later he was out in the sunshine. Lizzie hadn't laughed like that for weeks. Months. She was standing there with Grace in her arms. She had a huge grin on her face. Suttle put his arms round her, kissed them both. Relief had seldom tasted so sweet.

'And me?'

He kissed Gill too. She had a bottle of vodka in her hand. Bliss.

Gill had collected two bags of assorted Bangladeshi dishes from a takeaway in Exmouth. Suttle fired up the oven while Lizzie disappeared for a shower. The shower never got beyond lukewarm but on this occasion she didn't seem to care. By now Suttle was upstairs readying Grace for bed. Lizzie joined him, drying her hair with a towel.

'What happened?' he asked. 'Where did you go?'

Lizzie explained about the walk, and then the rowing club.

'They let you have a go?'

'They insisted. We're talking machines not the real thing but – hey – who cares?'

'It was good?'

'It was better than good.'

'Difficult?'

'Yeah. But good.'

She explained about the three girls in the Portakabin, the warmth of their welcome, her five-minute introduction to the mysteries of rowing and her dash for the line when Tessa cranked up the pace.

'The longest sixty seconds of my life,' she said.

Suttle was delighted. Was this Gill's doing?

'Yeah. I'd have wimped. She's been great, really supportive, really strong.'

Suttle was impressed. Maybe he'd got Gill Reynolds wrong. Maybe life had dealt her a wonderful hand these past few months and turned her into a human being. Either way, he wasn't complaining.

He found her downstairs, laying the table. He poured her a huge vodka and found some lemonade to go with it. The lemonade was flat but she never said a word. Another first.

By the time Lizzie came down, Suttle was dishing out the curry. Gill had brought a couple of bottles of wine too, and proposed a toast to life in the country before they started on the food. Barely hours ago, thought Suttle, his wife would have turned her head away, her glass untouched, but now Lizzie was the first to respond.

'*Salut*,' she said. 'And thanks.'

The evening slipped by in a warm fug of alcohol and laughter. They never left the kitchen. Suttle sorted the dodgy fuse in the plug that fed the one-bar electric fire, shut all the windows, left the oven door open and found a couple of candles for the rough wooden table. The soft throw of light danced on the walls, the perfect counterpoint to Lizzie's Muse CD, and Suttle allowed himself to get gently pissed. The girls at the rowing club, it seemed, were insisting that Lizzie return for a proper training session the following evening. Tuesday nights were club nights and boats would be on the beach from six onwards. When Gill suggested that Suttle drive her down there, he shook his head. This was Lizzie's gig, he insisted. He'd stay behind and play mum.

By half ten, with both bottles empty, Lizzie was knackered. She'd made up a bed for Gill in the spare room upstairs. She'd see them tomorrow. She gave Gill a hug and offered Suttle a lingering kiss. Then she was gone.

Suttle was suggesting a nightcap when he felt Gill's hand on his arm. She was very close. For a moment he thought she was coming on to him but then she ducked below the table, rummaged in her bag and emerged with a letter.

Suttle peered at it. Manila envelope. A single scribbled name. Suttle.

'What's this?' he mumbled.

Gill told him to open it. She had the impression it was important. Something in her voice told Suttle she wasn't as pissed as he was. Far from it.

'This is why you came down? To give me this?'

'Partly, yes.'

'So what is it?'

'I don't know. Like I say, open it.'

Suttle did what he was told. Moments later he was looking at a single sheet of paper. The message, poorly typed, was brisk: 'You'll know where to find Paul Winter,' it went. 'We need an address. leave a message on the number at the bottom and there won't be a problem.' Suttle reached for the candle, trying to read the handwritten number. Mobile. For sure.

Problem? He looked up.

Gill was shaking the envelope. A photo fell out. Then another. She took a quick look then slid them across to Suttle. He stared at them for a moment, side by side on the table. In one shot Lizzie was emerging from the village store with Grace in the buggy. In the other, presumably the same day, mother and child were walking away towards the road that led to Chantry Cottage. Same clothes. Same weather.

Suttle studied the photos a moment longer, his brain beginning to function at last. Paul Winter was the guy who'd taught Suttle everything he knew as a rookie detective on divisional CID. The guy who'd copped the lead role in a complex undercover operation to snare Mackenzie. The guy who'd resigned in earnest after Operation *Tumbril* had gone tits up and nearly got Winter killed. After that Winter had joined Pompey's top criminal. For real.

For years afterwards Mackenzie had laundered his drug millions and gone from strength to strength as a legit businessman. Paul Winter, as Bazza's key lieutenant, had been at the wheel for most of that ride, but a couple of episodes had opened his eyes and by last year he was ready to grass Mackenzie up. The result was Operation *Gehenna*, in which both Suttle and Gill Reynolds had played key roles.

This time Mackenzie had ended up the loser, shot dead by the ninjas from the Tactical Firearms Unit. Now Mackenzie's mates were obviously interested in settling a debt or two. And the guy they needed to find was Paul Winter.

'So where did this lot come from?'

'They came to the *News* in another envelope.'

'Addressed to you?'

'Yes.'

'Hand delivered?'

'By post. First class.'

'Postmark?'

'Pompey.'

'With my envelope inside?'

'Yeah.'

'Right.' Suttle was looking at the photos again. 'So why did it come to you in the first place?'

Gill wanted to read the note. Suttle passed it across.

'Because these people knew where to find me,' she said. 'My name's in the paper most days.' She looked up. 'So where's Winter?'

'I haven't a clue.'

'Really?'

'Really. And if I did I wouldn't be telling these numpties.'

'Even if they ...' Her eyes strayed to the photos again. Lizzie and Grace. These people knew where they lived. They knew where to find them. Scary.

'They wouldn't.' Suttle shook his head. 'They won't.'

'How do you know?'

'I don't. But I'll make sure it never happens.'

'That might be difficult.'

'You're right.'

Gill was watching him carefully.

'You really think Winter's more important than Lizzie and Grace?' she said at last.

'Of course he's not. But that's not the point.'

Winter, he explained, had done a deal with Hantspol in return for a significant cash settlement. With this, Suttle suspected he'd bought himself a new identity and moved abroad.

'Like where?'

'I haven't the faintest idea. If you were Winter, you wouldn't tell a soul.'

'You think he's alone?'

'Pass.'

Gill frowned, not quite believing him, then leaned forward. Suttle could smell cardamom on her breath.

'Mackenzie knew Winter had got it on with Misty Gallagher.'

'Is that right?'

'Yes. He told me himself when we were shagging. He said I was as good as her. I think he meant it as a compliment.'

'I'm sure he did.'

'So it stands to reason they might be still together, Winter and Misty.'

Suttle, far later than he should, realised she was fishing for details. Once a journalist always a fucking journalist. He told her again that he knew nothing. He liked Winter. He'd always liked Winter. He owed the man a lot. Winter's move to the Dark Side had disgusted him and he'd told Winter so, but their friendship had survived pretty much intact.

'And you're telling me you're not in touch?'

'I'm telling you the best favour I can do the guy is to stay well clear. What I don't know I can't pass on.'

Gill didn't want to believe him. He could see it in her face. Too bad.

'Have these guys been in contact with you?' Suttle was back with the photos. 'A name would be handy.'

'No. All I ever got was the envelope.'

'No phone calls? No pressure?'

'Nothing.'

Suttle didn't believe her. Mackenzie had always been able to call on muscle from the 6.57, a bunch of tooled-up football hooligans at the core of Pompey's away support. These guys were middle-aged now but no less handy. In any situation, no matter what kicked off, they always favoured direct action.

'They've been down here,' he said.

'Obviously.'

'So who told them where to find me? Who knew where we lived?'

There was a edge of accusation in his voice. Gill caught it at once.

'You think that was me? You think I'd sell my best mate down the river?'

'I'm asking, that's all.'

'Then the answer's no. Fuck knows how they found you. Maybe they looked in the phone book. Maybe they did a Google search. Maybe they've got sources in the Filth. There's nowhere to hide these days.'

'Really? You believe that?'

'Of course I do.'

'So how come they can't find Winter?'

It was the obvious question and she sat back, annoyed at falling into Suttle's little trap. *Filth*, thought Suttle, was an interesting word. This was fighting talk. This was what the 6.57 called the men in blue. Gill had definitely been mixing in bad company.

Suttle pushed his chair back and confected a yawn. He wanted to know whether Lizzie knew anything about the photographs.

'Of course not. They'd scare her to death.'

She stared at him. She was upset now. She'd started by bossing this conversation and somehow she seemed to have lost control.

'There's something you ought to know,' she said. 'Lizzie wants to move back to Pompey. And guess who told her she shouldn't?'

'You.'

'Yeah, me.'

'Because of these?' Suttle was looking at the photos again.

'Yeah, partly.'

'You knew they were in the envelope? You'd taken a look?'

'Fuck off. Mail turns up out of the blue. I find an envelope with your name on. You don't have to be super-bright to know it's not going to be good news.'

'So you're telling me you guessed the rest?'

'Pretty much. Don't look surprised. It's what I do for a living.'

Suttle offered her a nod. Touché. He was about to offer an apology but Gill hadn't finished.

'If you want the truth, I came down because of you guys, because of Grace, the family thing, the whole shtick. Fuck knows how but you've got a great thing going. That was the way I read it in Pompey. That woman loves you, believe it or not. I'm not sure living in the country was a brilliant decision but that's something you have to sort out. Me? I'm just the messenger.'

She checked her watch and bent down for her bag again. Time for bed.

Jimmy reached across as she began to get to her feet. He put his hand on her arm, gave it a little squeeze. She hesitated, looking down at him, a new expression on her face, surprise salted with something else.

'I just want to say thank you,' he muttered.

'For the note? For the photos?'

'For what you did this afternoon.'

For a moment Gill was lost. Then she remembered.

'The rowing, you mean?' She bent and kissed him on the lips. 'You need to be careful, Jimmy Suttle. You might lose that woman one day.'

Three

Suttle was at his desk at Exmouth nick by eight next day. Already the bulk of *Constantine*'s D/Cs had been redeployed on other inquiries and a text from Houghton instructed Suttle to vacate their temporary office and return to MCIT's permanent base in Exeter. The message was plain. In the absence of hard evidence, *Constantine* was effectively over.

An admin assistant from up the corridor supplied Suttle with a couple of cardboard boxes. He filled them with the seized files from Kinsey's apartment and headed out to the car park. That morning, for once, he hadn't been woken by Grace. Both Lizzie and Gill had still been asleep when he'd left. With last night's photos tucked safely in his jacket pocket, *Constantine*'s demise gave him a little time to frame up some kind of plan.

Houghton's Major Crime Investigation Team worked out of a converted police house on the sprawling force HQ site at Middlemoor, on the edges of Exeter. Suttle's desk occupied a corner of a ground-floor office with views of the car park. The other three desks in the room belonged to squad D/Cs, all of whom had been with the MCIT far longer than Suttle. As well as the usual maps and whiteboards on the wall, tracking progress on current investigations, he'd arrived to find a World War Two poster (KEEP CALM AND CARRY ON), a photocopy of the Obama electoral chant ('Yes, we can') and a medal for the Exeter half-marathon draped over a framed copy of a Robert Frost poem, 'The Road Not Taken'.

Suttle was looking at it now. The office was empty.

> Two roads diverged in a wood, and I –
> I took the one less traveled by,
> And that has made all the difference.

Really? He dumped the file boxes on the floor and sank into his chair. Twice in the last twenty-four hours he'd had to face the consequences of his move west. First, his wife threatens to leave him. Next, her best friend arrives with evidence that he and his family are under surveillance. On both counts, Pompey's shadow was far longer than he'd ever imagined.

He got out the note and the photos. His only real lead was the mobile number. He was tempted to add it to the list going to the phone companies but knew that the intel techies would be the first to review the data that came back and he didn't fancy trying to explain how a Pompey address might fit into the vanishing phantom that was *Constantine*. In any case, it was odds on that the phone was pay as you go, registered to a hookey name and address. These people weren't stupid.

His phone began to ring. It was Luke Golding, the young D/C tasked with chasing up Henri Laffont and Kinsey's ex-wife. More bad news.

'I've nailed Kinsey's missus, Sarge. I talked to that guy in Bristol again, Bill. He gave me a couple of numbers in Seattle.'

Sonya, it turned out, had spent the weekend with a bunch of religious fundamentalists on a retreat in the Cascade Mountains. If Suttle fancied taking this thing any further, Golding had a list of witnesses who'd willingly attest to her presence. It seemed she'd discovered Christ big time. The Cascade Mountains, he added as an afterthought, were on the west coast of America so it seemed unlikely she'd find the time or opportunity to dispatch her ex-husband to his death.

'And Laffont?'

'We're still working on that but my money's on Shanghai. I managed to make contact with the woman who organises his diary, Chinese lady, very helpful. I don't think he ever made it to London.'

'Great.'

'Sorry, Sarge. You want me to stick at it? Only time might be a problem now.'

'Of course.'

The phone went dead, leaving Suttle gazing at the whiteboard. To date, *Constantine* didn't even merit a mention because inquiries had been coordinated out of Exmouth. He got to his feet and found a marker pen. The fact that both Sonya and Laffont were probably out of the frame was, he tried to tell himself, a definite plus. It meant that he could concentrate on the ripples that Kinsey had been making locally. The guys in the boat. Maybe other rowers at the club. Possibly someone from Exmouth Quays, or the wider community, who'd nurtured some kind of grudge. This was a guy who was serially offensive. He thrived on pissing people off. That, at the very least, Suttle knew he could prove.

He blocked off a square of the whiteboard and scrawled *Constantine* across the top. Then he returned to his desk and fired up his PC. It took him seconds to find D/I Gina Hamilton's details. She was working out of the Plymouth HQ at Crownhill. She answered on the second ring.

Suttle introduced himself, mentioned their previous meeting back in Pompey. For a moment there was silence. Suttle could hear her talking to someone else. Then she was on the line again.

'You had a beard,' she said. 'And an office on the third floor.'

'That was my boss. D/I Faraday. I was the one who took you for a drink.'

'The younger guy? Reddish hair?' She was laughing.

'That's me.'

'Gotcha. What can I do for you, young man?'

Suttle explained about Tom Pendrick. He understood Hamilton had interviewed him down in Penzance after the Atlantic crossing.

'That's right. I did.'

'You mind if I come and see you? Talk about him?'

'Of course not.' She paused. 'What's he done?'

'I don't know.' Suttle was looking at the whiteboard. 'Yet.'

It took more than an hour to drive to Plymouth. An accident near Ivybridge had brought traffic to a standstill and Suttle spent the time reviewing his options on the surveillance photos. The thought of a bunch of Pompey heavies sniffing around Lizzie first angered then alarmed him. Last night, with Gill, he'd tried to be cool about it, telling her he'd get the thing sorted, but in the cold light of day he knew that wouldn't be simple. The temptation was to call in a favour or two from CID mates still working in the city. He could think of a couple, in particular, who'd relish the chance to have a quiet conversation and stir these guys up. But that, he knew, wouldn't hack it.

Neither was he prepared to make it official by lodging the evidence with Det-Supt Gail Parsons. His ex-boss on the Pompey-based Major Crime Team would doubtless view the photos as yet another opportunity to advance her ACPO prospects. She'd take the issue to the top. She'd knock on the Chief's door and tell him it was a direct threat to the force's standing in the city. The moment these people were allowed to get away with a threat this crude was the moment Hantspol should call it a day and look for something else to do. A threat against one of us, she'd say, was a threat against us all.

In this, thought Suttle, she was probably right, but leaving a bunch of Pompey heavies to the likes of Parsons wouldn't work either. They played by different rules. They didn't care a fuck about ambitious detective superintendents banged up in a bubble of their own making. The Filth, in their view, were like the weather. A minor inconvenience.

So what to do? As the traffic at last began to inch forward he was no closer to cracking it, but minutes later, as the dual carriageway crested the last hill before the distant sprawl of Plymouth, he thought – quite suddenly – of Paul Winter. A situation like this, back in the day, would have been meat and drink to Suttle's one-time mentor. He'd have studied it from every angle, looking for advantage, scenting a weakness here, identifying an opportunity there, finally lifting the phone to arrange a meet. Somewhere quiet. Somewhere companionable. Some pub where he could open negotiations, bait traps, orchestrate an outcome that the enemy, far too late, would recognise as a total stitch-up. Suttle could imagine him now. Steady on, son, he'd say. You always have more time than you think.

Suttle caught the first of the gantry signs indicating the turn-off for Crownhill. He indicated left, slipped into the nearside lane, hoping to God that Winter had it right.

It was mid-morning before Gill Reynolds left Chantry Cottage. Three ibuprofen and a plate of scrambled eggs had softened the worst of her hangover, and by the time she and Lizzie said their goodbyes she was feeling mildly euphoric. Their little stroll yesterday afternoon, Gill announced, had been fantastic. The rowing was going to do Lizzie a power of good. She wanted – demanded – regular progress reports including Lizzie's take on the available crumpet. East Devon, to her surprise, was only three hours away. With the right incentive, she could be back any time.

Lizzie waved as she accelerated away down the lane. To her relief, Gill's brief visit had turned out to be a real pleasure. Better than that, it seemed to have lifted the depression that had threatened to swamp her little boat. Gill was right about the rowing. She needed exercise. She wanted new people in her life. After her initial misgivings, she was now relishing the chance to conquer something difficult and worthwhile. She took Grace back inside, gazing at the wreckage from last night's meal. All this, she told herself, could wait. They needed supplies, something for Jimmy to cook this evening while she was down at the rowing club. With the sun out again, she and Grace should make the most of it.

It was a fifteen-minute push to the village store. Lizzie bought bread, milk, fresh vegetables, bananas for Grace, and – as an afterthought – a bottle of Jimmy's favourite Rioja. On the way back she paused outside the store to talk to an elderly woman she recognised from her recent visit to the church. The woman was collecting for an Aids charity in Africa and Lizzie dropped a pound coin in her box.

Shortly before noon, Lizzie and Grace were back at Chantry Cottage. She let herself in, settled Grace in her playpen and returned to the chaos of the kitchen. Minutes later, clearing the table, she caught sight of something tucked beneath the breadboard. It was a Pompey programme, the last home game, Portsmouth vs Preston North End. She gazed at it, trying to work out where it had come from. Gill, to her certain knowledge, loathed football. Jimmy, she knew, had been at home last weekend. So what on earth was this little bit of Pompey doing in her kitchen?

The phone rang. It was Jimmy. He'd just arrived in Plymouth and he wanted her to know if she was OK.

Lizzie was still looking at the programme.

'I'm fine,' she said. 'Don't be late tonight, eh? I'm going rowing.'

Crownhill was the biggest of the force outposts in Plymouth. D/I Gina Hamilton occupied a first-floor office close to the lift. Something had changed since they'd last met and it took Suttle a moment or two to work out what.

'The hair,' he said. 'Am I right?'

Hamilton had got to her feet, extending a hand.

'I had it done last week. I was going for the full butch but it hasn't worked, has it?'

She was right. Back in Pompey, five years ago, her blonde hair had been shoulder length, maybe longer. Now, still blonde, it was savagely cropped, giving her face a younger look. Delicate features. Flawless complexion. Full lips. And hints of fatigue shadowing her pale blue eyes.

'Anything interesting?' Suttle nodded at the paperwork on her desk.

'Performance reviews.'

'What did you do wrong?'

'That's not as funny as you think. Do you want a list?'

'Yeah, if you're offering.' Suttle had yet to take a seat.

She looked at him a moment, amused. Suttle was trying to guess her age. Forty? Maybe a year or two younger?

'Tell me about Mr Pendrick,' she said. 'I got hold of the file after you phoned, just to remind myself. Interesting guy.'

Suttle told her about Kinsey's death, about the resources Nandy had piled into *Constantine*, about their fruitless attempts to turn a sus death into something they might one day take to court. In the end, he said, they seemed to have drawn one fat blank with absolutely nothing to show for hundreds of man-hours of investigative effort.

'Except Pendrick?'

'Yeah. Maybe.' Suttle sat down at last. 'So what did you make of him?'

Hamilton pondered the question. Back last year, she said, she'd been relief D/I down at the far end of Cornwall. The Coastguard had been in touch with force HQ as soon as Pendrick had alerted them to the mystery disappearance of his wife, and Hamilton had been nominated to sit on top of the job. A couple of uniforms had taken a statement after Pendrick made landfall in Penzance and Hamilton had invited him up to the nick a couple of days later to expand on one or two elements in his account.

'HQ were getting twitchy by then.' She laughed. 'The papers were starting to speculate about what might have happened and we needed to be sure we had the thing covered.'

Suttle wanted to know about Pendrick's account. How much detail had he offered?

'Not a lot, to be honest. The way he told it, the crossing had been pretty boring. Most of the time they just rowed, which you can believe, and the week before it happened they'd had some pretty shit weather. I got the impression the thing had been a bit of a let-down, a bit of a disappointment. And then, of course, the wife disappeared.'

She talked Suttle through the sequence of events. They'd had a little cubby at the front of the boat. Pendrick used to sleep from two in the morning until four. Then he'd take over from his wife. They'd worked it this way for pretty much all of the crossing. On this occasion, like always, he'd been ready to take over and let her get some kip but when he emerged from the cabin she'd gone.

'Just disappeared?'

'Yeah.'

'No huge waves during the night?'

'No. According to Pendrick it was flat calm.'

'No note? No reason she might have gone overboard?'

'Nothing.'

'Did she ever take a dip? Just slip over the side and paddle around?'

'I asked him that and the answer was yes. But they only swam when the other one was there too. And only when they had knotted ropes trailing in the water.'

'So not at night?'

'Never. He said she was really responsible that way. They both were. House rules.'

Suttle nodded. He remembered an article in one of the tabloids. They'd never gone as far as directly accusing the hippy rower of getting rid of his wife, but they had run a series of articles profiling other guys who'd tried to fake the death of a spouse or a partner.

'Did you believe him?'

'I had no grounds not to.'

'That wasn't my question.'

'I know.'

Suttle held her gaze, aware that she was enjoying this exchange. Anything to liven up another Tuesday morning, he thought. Any escape from the pile of performance reviews.

'What about third parties?' Suttle asked. 'Did they have some kind of shore-based thing? Someone who kept an eye on them? Someone they checked in with?'

Hamilton nodded. Back in Woods Hole in Massachusetts, where they'd begun the voyage, were a couple of friends who fielded regular reports. Calling them a control centre was a bit of a stretch but they'd sent stuff on to the US media and generally done their best. After a while the reports from mid-Atlantic had become sporadic and – to be frank – a bit thin.

'They were their words, not mine.'

'You talked to these guys?'

'Of course.'

'And?'

'They didn't seem to have any cause for concern. Until the wife disappeared.'

'And then?'

'It became a bit of a news story. For a day or two.'

Suttle nodded. He was thinking about the crossing, what it must have taken to make the initial commitment.

'Did you *like* Pendrick?'

'What sort of question is that?'

'Well? Did you?'

'I liked what he'd done, what they'd both done. Rowing the Atlantic? You had to give the guy a bit of respect.'

'Sure but ... you know ...' Suttle smiled. 'Did you get *through* to him?'

'No, I don't think I did. From where I was sitting the man was on another planet.'

'Because of his wife?'

'You couldn't tell. Did he miss her? Yes, I think he did. Was that the end of the story? No way.'

'There was other stuff?'

'There had to be. He wasn't difficult or uncooperative, don't get me wrong. He just didn't say a lot.'

'Meaning he had something to hide?'

'Meaning there were limits, places you didn't go. I can't remember meeting anyone so private.'

'Fuck-off private? Or private private?'

'Private private. We're not talking aggression. Far from it. I had the impression he'd be a good guy to have a drink with.'

'Because?'

'Because, deep down, he probably had lots to say. And most of it would be worth listening to.'

Suttle smiled. Nicely phrased, he thought.

'What about other evidence? Did SOC bosh the boat?'

'Of course.'

'And?'

'Nothing material. They found traces of blood on a runner beneath one of the seats but it turned out to be mackerel. Our man was home safe.'

'What was the gap between his wife disappearing and Pendrick making it back?'

Hamilton frowned, doing the calculations.

'Over a week. He was single-handed. That boat must have weighed a ton.'

'So he had plenty of time to give the thing a proper seeing-to?'

'Of course.'

'When he could have been picked up? Gone for early doors?'

'Yeah.'

'Did you think that was dodgy at all? Carrying on the way he did?'

'Not really. I put it to him that it was a strange thing to do, rowing single-handed when most people would have been in bits about what had happened, but he just shook his head. The word he used was tribute.'

'Tribute?'

'To his dead wife. To Kate. Finishing was the least he owed her. It's in the transcript. I remember him saying exactly that.'

Suttle scribbled himself a note. *Finishing was the least I owed her.* It was an arresting phrase.

'What about passive evidence?'

'She had a camera which she apparently took with her when she went over the side.'

'Stills? Video?'

'Both.'

'And you're saying it disappeared?'

'Yeah.'

Suttle bent to his pad. Made another note. Then his head came up again.

'Did she keep a diary? Some kind of journal?'

'Yeah. Plus an audio account.'

'You seized them?'

'Of course.'

'And?'

'Evidentially it took us nowhere. I got the impression she was quite a literal-minded woman. From time to time the wild life would do it for her – the birds, dolphins, a couple of whales – and sunsets and sunrises always got a mention, but most of the stuff was pretty dull. Distance covered. Weather details. How much water they were making every day. Worries about the food stocks. Housekeeping really. One thing was interesting, though.'

'What?'

'I remember thinking the deeper they got into this thing, the less she wrote. It was the same with the audio. You could sense it in her voice. There was a weariness there. You could hear it.'

'She was probably knackered.'

'Sure. Of course she was. But there was something else. It was as if she couldn't be bothered any more.'

'Right.' Another note. 'And what about Pendrick? Was he keeping any kind of diary?'

'He said he wasn't.'

'Did you believe him?'

'No.'

'Why not?'

'Because he was so thoughtful, so *deep*. Pendrick was exactly the kind of guy to write stuff down. But no way would you ever get to read it.'

'Because he was hiding something?'

'Because he was so private.'

'What about the state of the relationship? What impression did you get about that?'

'They'd been married for a while. Five, six years, something like that.'

'Kids?'

'No.'

'But they were tight? Made it work?'

'I imagine so. You're going to be spending a lot of time together. Why do something like that with someone you don't much like?'

Suttle said he didn't know. Relationships were complicated enough on dry land. Just imagine what a couple of months alone at sea would do to most marriages.

Hamilton said nothing. Just shot him a look. Suttle asked her about the couple's life insurance.

'They'd both taken out policies. They were raising money for some charity and the people in charge insisted on proper cover. That was interesting.'

'How come?'

'The insurance thing was a bit of an issue for a couple of the media guys. One of the reporters did a bit of digging and discovered that Pendrick stood to gain half a million dollars from his wife's death. Of course it wasn't as simple as that. The insurance company wanted proof of death and it was months before they accepted the claim, but when I put it to Pendrick he just shrugged, said he wasn't interested, told me the money had never crossed his mind.'

'Did you check with the insurance people? Later?'

'Yeah. We had a wash-up at the back end of last year.'

'Performance review?'

'Very funny.' She had the grace to laugh. 'I put a call through and after the usual dramas they confirmed they'd paid out.'

'To Pendrick?'

'To the charity. It turned out that's what Pendrick and his wife had wanted all along. That was their decision. That's what they'd stipulated. And I'm guessing that's why Pendrick was never bothered about the money.'

'OK.' Suttle was impressed. 'So which charity are we talking about?'

'I knew you'd ask.' She opened a drawer and produced a file. Lovely hands, Suttle thought. No rings. Hamilton looked up, one finger anchored in the file. 'It's called Phra Mae Khongka. She's a Thai water goddess. I gather it's something to do with the tsunami.'

'How come?'

'You want the truth?'

'Please.'

'I haven't a clue.'

Lizzie got Gill on her mobile shortly after lunch. She was speeding through the New Forest with the top down and Muse full blast on the audio. She'd borrowed the CD from Lizzie and would bring it back next time round.

Lizzie wanted to know whether she'd had anything to do

with a football programme that had appeared on the kitchen table.

'A what?'

'A football programme. Portsmouth versus Preston. Last weekend.'

Lizzie heard the music level dip. Then Gill was back on the phone.

'Nothing to do with me,' she said. She wanted to know how come it had got there.

'Good question.' Lizzie was watching Dexter stalking something in the long grass.

She rang off as the signal began to fade and went back into the kitchen. The programme was still on the table. When she'd found it she'd done nothing but stare at the front cover. Blue shirts in front of a sea of faces. A white blur might have been a football. Now she went through the programme page by page. She found the phone number at the end, a line of carefully transcribed figures beneath an advert for a demolition company. The number was underlined and there was a question mark at the end. She studied the number a moment and wondered what would happen if she phoned it. Then something else claimed her attention.

The last time she'd checked the dodgy window in the living room, it had been loosely secured. There was no way it would ever keep anyone out but this way it at least minimised the draught. Now, though, it was completely unlatched. Someone had been at it. She knew they had. There was no other explanation. Someone had reached in, opened the window and climbed inside.

She peered hard at the windowsill, then at the carpet beneath. Sure enough, among all the ingrained crud, she could see tiny fragments of gravel and dirt. She turned away from the window, feeling a sudden chill despite the warmth of the sun. Grace was in her playpen, taking wet bites at her stuffed rabbit. Lizzie stared at her for a long moment then summoned the courage to venture upstairs. Both bedrooms were empty. She came down again, her pulse back under control, wondering what to do. Should she phone Jimmy? Or should she wait until this evening?

She glanced at her watch and decided not to bother him. Mercifully, the bolts on both the front and back doors still worked. With a bit of ingenuity, she might be able to re-fasten the window. Whoever had left the calling card was probably miles away by now. Her eyes strayed to the programme again and despite everything she found herself wondering what on earth lay behind its sudden appearance in this tomb of a house. Pompey, she thought. Never lets you down.

Suttle had decided to nail the photos as soon as he got back to Middlemoor. Apart from the Admin Manager and a lone D/C, the MCIT offices were empty. Suttle closed his door and extracted the mystery number from his wallet. Using his own mobile, he keyed in the digits.

The number rang and rang. Finally, a voice. Gruff Pompey accent. No surprise there.

'My name's Suttle. You want to talk to me.'

'That's right. We do.'

'When? Where?'

'How about this afternoon?'

'You have to be joking. I'm in fucking Exeter.'

'So are we, mush.' The voice was laughing. 'Bet your life we are.'

Suttle was thinking fast. They've been back to the village, he told himself. He'd talked to Lizzie a couple of hours ago. She'd seemed perfectly OK.

'Listen.' He bent to the phone again. 'If anyone lays a finger on my family, they'll regret it. Are we cool with that? Are you listening?'

'I'm listening.'

'So leave it out, yeah?'

The guy was still there. Suttle could hear him. Heavy breather. Probably fat. Probably enormous. Finally he came back on the phone.

'Pub called the Angel. Opposite Central Station. You know it?'

'Yeah.'

'Three o'clock. If you're not there by quarter past, all bets are off.'

'What's that supposed to mean?'

'You don't want to know, mush.'

The line went dead. Suttle slipped the phone back in his pocket and checked his watch. 14.27. Getting into the city centre and finding somewhere to park would take at least twenty minutes, probably longer. And no way was he going into this without back-up.

In the next office D/C Luke Golding was on the phone. He'd been with Major Crimes less than a month. Suttle barely knew the lad.

He stood over him, tapping his watch. Get off the phone. Like now.

'Sarge?' Golding looked startled.

'There's a meet we have to get to.' Suttle was already heading for the door. 'That's me and you, son.'

In the car Suttle left the details vague. When Golding asked which bit of *Constantine* this linked to, Suttle said it was impossible to say. Call it a fishing expedition. Call it any fucking thing. Just do what I say, right?

Golding nodded. He was small and slight but Suttle had listened to a couple of the other guys on the squad and knew the boy could handle himself. In uniform, still a probationer, he'd evidently faced down a bunch of pissed marine recruits in an Exmouth pub. That very definitely took bottle. Good sign.

The traffic, mercifully, was light. Suttle was in the city centre by five to three. There was even a parking space outside the

Central Station. He killed the engine and sat in silence for a moment. The Angel was directly across the road. He'd never been in the pub in his life but a big plate-glass window offered a view inside. It was dark, impossible to see further than the tables beside the window.

'So what now, Sarge?' Golding had to be back for a meet by four fifteen.

'You watch my back, OK? I'll be sitting at one of those tables you can see across the road there in the pub. There'll be someone with me. If anything kicks off I want you to call for the cavalry. You happy with that?'

'No sweat.' He could see the lad warming to the task. Maybe he enjoyed physical violence. Maybe he was a stranger to the strokes the 6.57 could pull.

Suttle got out of the Impreza and crossed the road. The pub was near-empty, a couple of derelicts at the bar, a younger man with a copy of the *Independent* curled on the sofa beside the brick fireplace. None of them looked remotely Pompey. Suttle asked for a small shandy and took it to the table beside the window. He could see Golding across the road. He was studying his mobile.

Moments later the door opened. Two guys, one fat, one black. Suttle recognised neither of them. The fat guy muttered something Suttle didn't catch to his mate and dispatched him to the bar before wedging himself into the chair across the table from Suttle. His tiny shaved skull seemed to wobble on the folds of fat at the back of his neck. Baggy jeans and a black leather jacket over a black woollen polo neck.

'So who's the kid in the Impreza?'

'A mate of mine.'

'He knows about this?'

'He knows I'm meeting someone heavy.'

'Too fucking right. Does he know why?'

'No.'

'Straight up?'

'Yeah. There'd be no point telling him. Pompey's a mystery to these people.'

'You're right, mush. Wrong fucking league, eh? Wrong fucking end of the country. What's it like then? Life in the sticks?'

Suttle didn't answer. He hadn't any interest in conversation. He was simply here to deliver a message.

The black guy was back with the drinks. Two pints of Stella and a packet of cheese and onion. Suttle was looking at the fat guy.

'You've got a name?' he asked.

'Of course I've got a fucking name.'

'What is it?'

'None of your business. If it helps you can call me Jonno.'

'OK, Jonno, so why don't you say your piece? What exactly do you want from me?'

'You know what we want.'

'All I know is you've been sniffing around my missus. Nice pix, by the way.'

Jonno had caught sight of the crisps. He was staring at the black guy.

'I said salt and vinegar, didn't I? Can't you fucking read?'

'They've run out.'

'*Run out?*' His eyes revolved. 'Fucking carrot crunchers.' He opened the packet and emptied the crisps across the table. 'Help yourself, mush. Lunch on us, eh?' He gave the crisps a poke. The back of his right hand carried an eagle tat. On his left, a name framed in an elaborate scroll. Even upside down Suttle had no difficulty deciphering it.

'He lives down this way.' Suttle nodded at the tat. 'Not many people know that.'

'Who?'

'David James.'

'Know him, do you?'

'I've met him a couple of times, yeah. He's big on the charity front. Nice bloke.'

David James had been a legend at Fratton Park, a commanding goalie with a huge Afro and a string of England caps.

Jonno was impressed.

'You talk to him at all?'

'Of course.'

'Fuck me,' he said. 'You're starting to sound half human.'

He pushed the crisps towards Suttle. He wanted be out of
this khazi of a city and back on the road east as soon as possible. So why didn't Suttle do himself a favour and help him
out?

'How?'

'You know how. That cunt Winter was totally out of order.
You think we can let something like that go? In case you don't
remember, Mr Filth, your guys shot the Man dead. That's life,
mush. That's what happens. Some tosser pulls the trigger and
Bazza Mac's history. You'll be glad to know we don't have a
problem with that. The arsehole with the shooter's doing a job.
But what we don't put up with is a fucking two-timing lowlife
grass like Winter. Without him, the arsehole with the shooter
would never have been anywhere near Bazza Mac. And so our
Mr Winter's on a slapping. Happy to oblige.'

'I don't doubt it.'

'You shouldn't, mush. We're quality when it comes to slap-
pings.'

'Great. So what do you want from me?'

'An address. Nothing more, nothing less. Give us an address
and we're out of your face. Never trouble you again.'

'I haven't got an address. I haven't got a clue where he is.'

'Think again, mush. It happens we know how you cunts
operate. Witness protection? New ID? Plastic surgery? Set the
fat cunt up in some fucking bungalow on the other side of the
globe? Make sure he blends in with the wildlife? Dunsnitching?
Dungrassing? We know all that. And so do you.' He picked at
a crisp. 'So where is he?'

'I just told you. I don't know.'

'OK.' Jonno nodded. 'And if you did know?'

'I still wouldn't tell you.'

'Really?' The expression on his face could have been a smile. 'So how do we know you're not lying?'

'You don't. You have to believe me.'

'But what's the point, mush?'

'There isn't one. Our gang's bigger than yours. Which is why you're best off forgetting all about Winter.'

'That ain't going to happen, mush. And you know it. You know something else? Young Karl here, the genius who doesn't know a salt and vinegar crisp from the hole in his arse, thinks you're probably wearing a wire. You mind if he checks?'

'Go ahead. Help yourself.'

The black guy took his cue. He swallowed a mouthful of Stella and then gestured Suttle to his feet. Suttle stood up. A single nudge with his knee was enough to upset all three glasses, sending a tidal wave of cold lager across the table.

'Fuck me.' Jonno, outraged, was looking at a lapful of soggy crisps. He tried to push away from the edge of the table. More lager.

Suttle was aware of Golding racing across the road, body-checking through a line of cyclists. Then he was in through the door. Suttle told him to cool it.

'Little accident, son.' He shot Golding a grin. 'I think my new friends are leaving.'

As promised, Suttle was back at Chantry Cottage by half five. It was a thirty-minute drive to Exmouth, absolute max, and he knew Lizzie wanted to be on the beach by six. He reversed the Impreza and left the driver's door open.

Lizzie emerged from the back door. She was wearing shorts and a T-shirt with a trackie top draped over her shoulders. She'd just fed Grace, she said, and there was plenty of food in case Suttle fancied getting some supper together. She'd no idea when she'd be back but imagined it wouldn't be late.

Suttle was still standing by the Impreza. There was an edge in Lizzie's voice he didn't much like.

'Everything all right?'

'No.'

'What's happened?'

'There's a message on the answering machine. I don't know what's going on but maybe you ought to check it out.'

Suttle watched her drive away without a backward glance. He ducked into the kitchen. The phone had been readied in the living room. Grace gave him a little wave and rattled the bars of her playpen.

Suttle recognised the voice at once. The message couldn't have been simpler. 'Top mistake, mush. Next time, eh? Looking forward to it.' Suttle hit the replay button. He and Golding had left the two guys in the pub. Mercifully, Golding hadn't had time to call for help, deciding that his D/S could do with a bit of physical support. For this Suttle had been genuinely grateful but he'd spent most of the journey back to Middlemoor fending off the lad off. Yes, these guys were very definitely the enemy. No, he couldn't reveal more at this stage. And, by the way, would he mind keeping radio silence for the time being?

'Radio silence' hadn't cut much ice with Golding. He was both curious and alarmed. Curious because he had a nose for serious trouble, and alarmed because he didn't begin to understand why Suttle wasn't pushing all the panic buttons. The young D/C had seen enough to suss that the two heavies in the Angel had fuck all to do with *Constantine*. Bosses existed to take care of situations like these and D/I Houghton, in Golding's eyes, was one of the best. Getting out of the Impreza back at Middlemoor, he nodded up towards Houghton's office window.

'Just tell her, Sarge. Whatever it is, she'll understand.'

'Sure.'

'I'm serious.'

'Yeah, thanks ...'

Golding had shrugged, leaving him to it, but now – hours later – Suttle suspected he was right. In the pub he'd definitely overstepped the mark. The sudden gust of Pompey, like the stale breath of a party you'd prefer to forget, had irritated him. The cartoon threats hadn't helped. And when those numpties had played him like he was an extra in some Al Pacino movie, wanting to pat him down, he'd truly had enough. You didn't put up with stuff like that, not if you had an ounce of self-respect. Hence the spilled lager and the soggy crisps and the fat guy shouting to the barman to bring him a fucking cloth.

Suttle replayed the message again, sitting in the armchair, Grace in his lap. If he took Golding's advice and went to Houghton she'd have no choice but to refer the whole matter back to Hantspol. Hantspol meant Gail Parsons and the new Head of CID who'd replaced Willard. He trusted neither of these people not to cook up some clever plan to flush Winter out. Someone at the top of the force would probably have a lead on his whereabouts and one way or another this info would find its way to the 6.57. They'd jump on the next plane, give Winter a thorough battering, maybe even kill him. At Hantspol HQ there'd be a quiet flurry of nods and winks – Winter nailed, justice finally done – and up in his new office in the West Mids force ACC Willard would doubtless raise a glass when Parsons phoned with the news. Did Suttle really want that? Did he want to spend the rest of his life knowing that he'd sent a man he liked and still admired to his death? He thought not.

He nuzzled Grace and gave her a cuddle. Then, for the first time, he saw the football programme, propped against the bars of the playpen. He picked it up, clocked the date, and leafed through until he found the number at the back. Now he understood why Lizzie had been so iffy. They must have slipped it through the letter box, leaving her to puzzle out the implications. First a Pompey stranger at the door. Then the voice on the answering machine.

He got to his feet and carried Grace to the window. These people, he knew, were serious. They had reach. They had limitless patience. Winter, in their view, had killed Mackenzie. And, one way or another, they were going to settle the debt.

He thought of Parsons again. Maybe – after all – he should lift the phone, tell her exactly what had happened, then leave it for his old employers to sort out. That way he might get these animals off his back. But deep down he knew a call like that would solve nothing. There has to be a better way, he told himself. Has to be.

Lizzie saw the boats the moment she hit the seafront. There were two of them, still on their trailers, down by the water's edge. Among the gaggle of rowers rigging the oars were the women she'd met in the Portakabin. Spotting a parking place, she pulled in.

It was Tessa who saw her first. Lizzie waved back. A concrete slip offered access to the beach. She was unaware that anyone was behind her.

'Come back for more?'

She spun round, recognising the big guy she'd briefly met yesterday. Shaved head. Three-day stubble. And an intriguing scar down the side of his face.

'Tom?' she said, uncertain.

'Yeah. Tom Pendrick.'

He fell into step beside her. He was wearing shorts and a scruffy top he must have used for painting. He was tall, way over six feet, and his sheer bulk made her feel almost comically small. Stepping onto the beach, she might have been back at school.

Tessa was organising crews. Lizzie's arrival was a godsend. With one seat unfilled in the second boat, she'd slot in perfectly.

'But I've never done this,' Lizzie pointed out.

'No problem.' Tessa was already rigging the second boat. 'Tom?'

The big man did the honours. With the help of Tessa and a couple of others, he slipped the quad off the trailer and into the water. The tide had just turned and was beginning to push back into the estuary. Another rower held the nose of the quad into the current while Pendrick helped Lizzie into the bow seat. Adjusting the footstretchers to the length of her legs, Pendrick told her to push back in the seat. Lizzie watched him tightening the pegs that secured the footstretchers.

'Try now,' he said.

'Try what?'

'Try moving the seat. Here ...'.

The oars had been stowed across Lizzie's midriff. Pendrick pushed them out through the gates until Lizzie was in the rowing position.

'OK. Now come forward. Keep the blades out of the water. Just get a feel for the weight and the movement. That's good. That's fine. Thumbs on the ends of the handles. No pressure, eh? Just treat them like a friend.'

Lizzie took a couple of practice strokes. Pendrick would be rowing in front of her. The rest of the crew, all women, were still on the beach, watching.

'How does it feel?' Pendrick again.

'Fine.'

It was true. The seat moved sweetly beneath her bum. The oars, to her surprise, were nicely balanced. She couldn't wait to get going.

Pendrick was still squatting beside her, briefing her on this detail and that. She couldn't take her eyes off his hands. Worker's hands. Big. Calloused. Dirt under the nicely shaped fingernails. He tested the tension on her foot straps, then made an adjustment to a bungee that secured the life jackets on the bulkhead behind her.

'Anyone ask you whether you can swim?'

'No.'

'Well?'

'I can swim fine.'

'Good. If anything happens, stay with the boat. The guy to listen to is the cox. She's in charge. OK?'

He got to his feet and threw a look at Tessa. He didn't seem to smile much.

Tessa, it turned out, would be cox. She told Pendrick to get in the boat. For such a big man he moved with surprising grace. Tessa steadied the quad as he stepped in and settled his weight on the number two seat. The rest of the crew joined them.

'Just do what I do, OK?' Pendrick again.

Lizzie nodded. The woman holding the boat gave the bow a push. Lizzie could feel a shiver of current beneath them as the quad slipped free from the beach. It was an extraordinary sensation and she wanted to cherish it, this first taste of the real thing, but she was concentrating too hard on Pendrick.

'Take a stroke,' he said. 'Just the right-hand oar. Help me pull us round.'

She did her best. Her blade skidded across the surface of the water. She felt hopelessly awkward. She panicked and tried again. This time her blade clashed with Pendrick's. Horrible sound. Deeply embarrassing.

'No problem. We've all done it. Just take it really easy, yeah?'

He reached forward, took another long slow stroke. Lizzie did the same. This time it worked. They were out now in the current, clear water between the boat and the beach, landmarks up on the promenade slipping by. She couldn't believe it.

'Even pressure.' Pendrick's head was half turned.

'What's that?'

'Both oars.'

Lizzie did what she was told. Another stroke. Another little triumph.

'Easy up. Sort yourselves out.' Tessa this time.

Everyone stopped rowing. The boat drifted on. Tessa wanted to know whether Lizzie was OK, whether Tom was taking care of her. One of the other girls laughed. Lizzie said she was fine. The crew numbered off from the bow, Lizzie first.

'I'm fine,' she repeated.

'Two.'

'Three.'

'Stroke.'

'Come forward to row.' Tessa again. 'Ready to row. Row.'

At the other end of the boat Lizzie had no idea what was happening. All she could do was follow the big man in front of her, do her best to mirror his every move and try not to screw things up. Most of the time it worked, stroke after stroke, fierce concentration, trying to store Pendrick's muttered asides in her teeming brain, reaching forward to take the catch, keeping her arms straight as she pushed back against the footplate, remembering not to bury the whole blade in the water as she pulled hard before the extraction. By the time they'd made it down to the dock, she was wiped out. Not physically but mentally.

Tessa had called for another stop. Pendrick turned in his seat. Lizzie was staring up at the biggest of the apartment blocks on the waterfront. It had to be at least six storeys.

'What's that place?' she asked.

'Regatta Court.'

'It's gross.'

'You think so?'

'I do. And the colour. Who ever let that happen?'

'Fuck knows.'

The big man was shaking his head. And when he turned to her again, he at last had a smile on his face.

An hour or so later, back on dry land, he walked her to the Impreza.

'You were good,' he said. 'I mean it.'

Lizzie was touched. She wanted to thank him. She wanted to thank them all. She'd arrived with zero expectations, pre-occupied with not making a fool of herself. She sensed it might be tricky and she hadn't been wrong, but there was something about these people that gave her immense confidence. They'd made room for her. They'd expected her to measure up. And that's exactly what she'd done. No drama. No girly hysterics. Just the calm sweep of water at the end of each new stroke and the comforting tug as the boat surged forward.

Pendrick wanted to know whether she'd enjoyed it.

'It was brilliant,' she said.

'You mean that?'

'Yeah, I do.'

'You'll come again?'

'Definitely.'

'Thursday?'

'For sure.'

They were at the car by now and she was looking for her keys. Pendrick was gazing out at the water. Another crew was pushing hard against the tide.

'Got far to go?'

'Colaton Raleigh.'

'Country girl?' He seemed surprised.

'Far from it.'

She'd found the keys at last. She thanked him again, then paused.

'You mind me asking a question?' she said.

'Of course not.'

'This guy who was found dead the other day. The one on the TV news. The guy the girls were talking about in the boat.'

'Kinsey?'

'Yeah.' Lizzie bent to re-tie her shoe lace. 'You knew him?'

'Sort of.'

'So ...' Lizzie glanced up. 'What do you think happened?'

Suttle was at the stove when Lizzie got back. There was a pile of sliced potatoes ready for the frying pan and he'd opened a tin of baked beans to go with the sausages. Grace had been bathed and might fancy a story. So far, Lizzie hadn't said a word.

'So how was it?' he asked at last.

'Great,' she said. 'Fantastic. They're all talking about Kinsey. Fascinating.'

'Really?'

'Yeah. Don't worry. No one knows I'm married to a cop.'

'Thank fuck for that.'

'So how's it going? This Kinsey thing?'

Suttle studied her a moment, then turned back to the stove.

'Later,' he said. 'Why don't you sort Grace out first?'

She was back downstairs within minutes. Grace was already asleep. She'd showered and changed and now she had something else on her mind.

'That message on the answering machine,' she said. 'What was that about?'

Suttle explained. Lizzie had always had a soft spot for Winter. 'You're telling me they want his address?'

'I'm telling you they want to hurt the man. Maybe worse than that.'

'You mean *kill* him?'

'These things can get out of control. It's best if they never catch up with him.'

'Shit.' Lizzie told him about finding the Pompey programme on the kitchen table.

Suttle stared at her.

'On the where?'

'There.' Lizzie pointed at the table. 'I was out for maybe an hour. Maybe less. When I came back, there it was. They must have got in through the window next door.'

Suttle gave up on the potatoes. His briefcase was still in the car. When he returned he had the photographs. Lizzie was horrified.

'Where did you get these?'

'Gill brought them down.' He explained about the envelope

that had landed on her desk at work. It would have come from mates of Mackenzie, he said. And Gill had been chosen to play postman.

'Why?'

'Because they know you two are mates.'

'How?'

'Because Gill had been shagging Mackenzie and probably told him.'

'Christ.'

Lizzie sat down. She understood now why Gill was less than keen to have her and Grace around the new flat. The last thing she needed in her life was a bunch of middle-aged heavies from the 6.57.

'So what do we do?' She was looking at the photos again. 'These people frighten me. They shouldn't but they do.'

Suttle had already decided to spare her the details of this afternoon's meet in the Angel. Now he told her that he had the thing under control.

'I don't believe you.' She looked up. 'Have you told someone? Reported it?'

'Yeah.'

'Who? Who have you told?'

'Someone in Pompey.'

'Police? Someone in the Job?'

'No.'

'Why not?'

'Because I don't trust them.'

'Don't *trust* them? Christ, Jimmy, this is our daughter we're talking about, our house, everything we have. The police are supposed to look after us, protect us. Isn't that the way it works or have I got this thing wrong?'

Suttle did his best to explain. It was about Winter, he said, not them.

'You think he's more important? More important than us? Than Grace?'

'That's not the point.'

'It's not? Jesus, you're supposed to be my husband. My daughter's father. What is this?'

Suttle held his ground. He'd thought the thing through. Tomorrow he'd be going to Pompey. By Thursday he'd have everything sorted.

'How can I know that? How can I be sure?'

'You have to trust me.'

'Sure, but ... fuck, Jimmy, these people are creepy. Worse than that they want to hurt us.'

'No.' Suttle was emphatic. 'That won't happen.'

'You say.'

'I say.'

She looked at him for a long moment.

'I could phone the police myself,' she said at last.

'You could. Of course you could. Then it would be your fault.'

'My fault what?'

'Your fault when they get to Winter.'

'You really think that would happen?'

'I think it might. And that's enough.'

Lizzie had slumped in the chair. The fight had gone out of her. She felt physically smaller. Suttle went back to the stove, started cooking again.

After a while Lizzie stirred. 'What would the police do?'

'I've no idea. We're thin on the ground just now. Plotting up the house would be a no-no. What with the cuts and every-thing, there just aren't the bodies any more. If we're lucky we might get some kind of alarm.'

'Like old people? Wear it round our necks?'

'Yeah.'

'Call for help after they've burned the house down?'

'Yeah.'

'OK.' She shrugged. 'You win. Just make sure Grace stays in one piece, yeah?'

Suttle served the meal. The sauté potatoes were fried to a crisp and the sausages in the oven had dried out. So much for the meal of his dreams.

Lizzie mentioned Kinsey again. She'd been chatting to a guy at the club. He'd sorted her out in the boat, been really helpful.

Suttle speared a sausage, dipped it in a puddle of mustard.

'He's got a name, this guy?'

'Tom. Tom Pendrick.'

Suttle nodded. The mustard had done nothing for the sausage.

'So what did you make of him?' he said after a while. 'This Pendrick?'

'I liked him. He was solid. He was kind too. Rowing isn't as easy as it looks.'

'I'm sure.' Suttle's face was a mask. 'So what did this guy have to say about Kinsey?'

'You're fishing.'

'I am.'

'He said he was rich. He said he wanted to be a winner. And he said something else too.'

'What?'

'He said guys like that are driven. They never lift their heads up, never look around, never see the obvious in front of their noses. In Kinsey's case that might have been fatal.'

'He *said* that last bit?'

'No.' She pushed her plate away. 'I just did.'

Four

Suttle drove to Portsmouth the following afternoon, telling Houghton on the phone that he had a couple of domestic difficulties to resolve. Houghton, as far as he could gauge, was unsurprised.

'Take care,' she said. 'If you want a couple of days, book it as leave.'

The road east was clotted with late-spring traffic and it was early evening on the M27 before Suttle was stealing a glance at the familiar sprawl of Pompey in the thickening light. He took the exit at the foot of the motorway and drove through the suburbs of Cosham before taking the road up to the top of Portsdown Hill. There was a car park here with a view over the entire city. He'd used it a thousand times, often with Winter when they were working together on divisional CID, and it was ideal if you wanted to steal a little time for a coffee or a think.

Suttle killed the engine and settled back. Marie was Mackenzie's widow, a classy High School girl whom Bazza had kidnapped and made rich. Opinions differed on exactly how keen Marie had been to join the world of the young Bazza Mac, but Winter, who was in a position to know, had always insisted that she'd made the running. She was wild as well as beautiful, and she'd seen something deeply promising in her new beau. Life with Bazza, as it turned out, had been everything he'd promised – unpredictable, never risk-free, always fun – and when he'd died at the hands of the Tactical Firearms Unit, she'd been beyond consolation.

Suttle had seen photos of Marie following her husband's coffin into the cathedral. She'd maintained a dignified silence in the face of ceaseless media attention, and at the funeral, a step or two behind the pall-bearers from the 6.57, she'd graced the occasion with poise and elegance. In a brief tribute to her dead husband she'd talked about his loyalty and warmth. He'd been the rock at the very centre of countless lives, she said, and his absence left a void that would never be filled. She'd spoken without notes, her eyes moving from face to face in the packed congregation, and she'd ended by calling for one of her grandsons to read a poem he'd penned only the previous night. The poem was moving in its simplicity and stirred a low rumble of applause that had ended by engulfing the entire cathedral. If anyone would understand the importance of family life, Suttle thought, then it had to be Marie.

She answered his call within seconds. They'd already been in touch on the phone the previous day and she was prepared to meet. Now she named a restaurant in Southsea. She'd be there in half an hour.

Suttle knew Sopranos well. He and Lizzie had used it regularly before they'd left the city and the food was never less than excellent. He arrived a couple of minutes early and found himself a table in the corner. He'd bought a copy of the *News* from the Co-op down the street and he flicked through to the back to check on the football news. The Preston game had ended in a 1–1 draw. Pompey, it seemed, had been lucky to steal a point.

'Hi.'

He looked up to find Marie standing beside the table. She was wearing a white knee-length dress that definitely hadn't come from a chain store and the tan suggested a recent holiday.

Suttle got to his feet. A handshake would have been too

formal, a kiss way too familiar. He pulled out the other chair and gestured for her to sit down.

She told him she hadn't come to eat. When he suggested a drink she asked for a spritzer. Suttle went to the bar and ordered himself a San Miguel. The owner, whom he knew, raised an eyebrow at the sight of Marie.

'Known her long?' She was smiling.

'Not that long.'

'Business or pleasure?'

'Both.'

'So how's life in Devon?'

'Fraught.'

He returned to the table with the drinks. Marie looked up at him. The last thing Suttle wanted was silence.

'Been somewhere nice?' he enquired.

'Madeira. Big mistake.'

'No good?'

'The weather was lovely. But you need to be over seventy to have a conversation.'

'You went by yourself?'

'No.' Marie glanced at her watch. 'So what's this about?'

Suttle saw no point in glossing over what had happened. A bunch of Pompey guys were giving him a hard time. They wanted to lay hands on Paul Winter and thought Suttle had the key to his door. All this he could cope with but he drew the line at pressure on his wife and daughter. They'd staked out his house. They'd photographed Lizzie and Grace. The threat was explicit. We know where you live. We know who you love. He needed this kind of stuff to stop.

'What's any of this got to do with me?'

'These people were mates of your husband. They think Winter needs a seeing-to.'

'Maybe they're right.'

'Maybe they are, but that's not the point. Number one I

haven't a clue where Winter is. Number two I wouldn't tell them if I did.'

'Do they know that?'

'Yes.'

'You told them?'

'I did.'

'And?'

'They weren't pleased.'

For the first time Suttle detected a flicker of approval. Was she applauding the heavies who'd driven down to Devon? Or was there something in Suttle's defiance that had won her respect? In truth he didn't know but sensed there was no point in taking his foot off the throttle.

'I could take this to the police,' he said.

'You are the police.'

'I know. But I could make it official, make life hard for these guys. That's not something I want to do.'

'Why not? I thought that's what you people were for?'

'It's not as simple as that.'

'It never is.' She leaned forward, toying with her drink. 'You know what I liked about Winter? Apart from the fact that he made me laugh? I liked his mind. I liked his deviousness. He did us a lot of favours, that man. I'd be the first to admit it. Which makes what he did all the more unforgivable. We took him in. We treated him as one of the family. And then he betrayed us.'

Suttle nodded. He wasn't here for a moral debate. If you were looking for devious, serious devious, Paul Winter was world class. All Suttle wanted to do was to get these monkeys off his back.

Marie hadn't finished. Winter, she said, had often talked about Suttle. This was the young kid he'd turned into a detective of real quality. More to the point, Jimmy Suttle had remained one of the few ex-colleagues prepared to give Winter the time of day.

'Is that true?' she asked.

'Yeah. More or less. I'd no time for what he'd done and I told him so, but yeah, we stayed friends.'

'He told me you once saved his life.'

'I did what I could. He was a sick man.'

'He appreciated that.'

'I'm sure he did.'

'And he appreciated the way you stuck with him.'

'That was different. I had a job to do. There was always a reason we got together.'

'On his part?'

'On mine.'

'I see.' She was watching him carefully. 'So does that make my husband's death your fault?'

'Yes. We never set out to kill him ... but yes. It's my job to put people like your husband away and that's exactly what we did.'

'We?'

'The team.'

'Including Winter?'

'Obviously. It wouldn't have happened without him. I've no idea how much you know about all this, Mrs Mackenzie, but your husband exposed Winter to situations that seriously upset him.'

'Are you telling me that came as some kind of surprise? That's what he signed up for.'

'Really? Murder? In cold blood? Not just the target but the target's girlfriend? Someone this guy had known for a couple of days? Someone who never deserved to be killed?'

Marie blinked. *She knows nothing of this*, Suttle thought. Absolutely fuck all.

'This is nonsense,' she said. She didn't sound convinced.

Suttle shook his head. The day before he'd ghosted himself into another life, Winter had shared a story or two that explained his decision to grass Mackenzie up. One of them had to do with a contract killing in the shell of a hotel near Malaga.

Winter had been the sole witness when the gunman stepped into a half-built bar and blew two people away. Minutes later he was still picking tiny gobbets of brain off his best suit. The memory had haunted him ever since and the nightmare had worsened as the prospect of a European Arrest Warrant drew steadily closer. The last thing Winter wanted was the rest of his life in a Spanish prison cell.

'Are you going to tell me more?' Marie was reaching for her drink.

'No.'

'Why not?'

'I promised him I wouldn't.'

'Do you always keep your word?'

'I try.'

'That's admirable.' She offered Suttle a cold smile. 'Tell me something else then.'

'What?'

'This friendship with Winter. Do you think he deserved you?'

'That's a silly fucking question.'

'Is it? Is it really? I trusted that man. I trusted him with our lives. And you know what? He screwed us.'

Suttle fought the waves of scalding anger that threatened to engulf him. For reasons he'd never understood, he also regarded Winter as family.

'I'm sorry.' He ducked his head. 'I'm not here to lose my rag.'

'Whatever. I just want you to know how I might feel about it.'

'It?'

'Winter. He killed my husband.'

'Got him killed.'

'Sure. And from where I'm sitting that's hard to forgive.'

A silence settled on the conversation. Then Marie pushed her glass away and stood up.

'It's been a revelation,' she said. 'And I mean that.'

Suttle didn't know what to do with himself afterwards. It was still early, barely half past seven. He'd set up this conversation in the hope that he might be able to sweet-talk Marie into calling off Bazza's attack dogs, but blood and battle ties were thick in this city and he was beginning to suspect that the guys he'd met down in Exeter were way beyond listening to the likes of Bazza's widow. Even if she put the word out, tried to call them to heel, Suttle doubted they'd listen. Winter was a grass. Winter had fucked Bazza over. Winter deserved everything that was coming to him.

Suttle left the restaurant and walked the half-mile to the Royal Trafalgar Hotel. Barely a year ago this had been the jewel in Bazza's crown. A fourth AA rosette was living proof that he could cut it as a legitimate businessman, and he'd relished the evenings when he hosted discreet dinners for the city's movers and shakers, paving the way for his bid to become one of the city's two MPs. It was Winter who'd sussed that the general election would trigger Mackenzie's downfall, and so it had proved. With his commercial empire in free fall, Bazza had staked everything on a final throw of the dice. His campaign for Portsmouth North had burned money he didn't have, and by the time he died, taken out by the Tactical Firearms Unit in a shop called Pompey Reptiles, he was effectively bankrupt.

The Royal Trafalgar had gone to a rival businessman, a heavyset Pole from nearby Southampton, which made him a Scummer. Suttle paused at the door and then stepped inside. The bar lay beyond reception. This was where the 6.57 would gather for a drink on football nights, reliving old campaigns over a couple of Stellas, and Suttle half-hoped that a face or two would still be around. Maybe he should talk to these people in person, get them to recognise that Winter was history. Maybe Marie had been the wrong place to start.

The bar was empty. Suttle ordered a Guinness, sensing at once that the hotel was on the skids. One look at the clientele in the adjacent restaurant told him that Dobreslaw, the Pole, had taken the whole operation downmarket. Coach-loads of pensioners from up north were tucking into mountains of chicken nuggets. There wasn't a soul under sixty-five, and when a guy in a shiny tux arrived to announce a bingo session afterwards, Suttle knew that this was the last place that any 6.57 would show up. The Pole had bought the hotel for a song and carefully destroyed Bazza's hard-won reputation as a hotelier of serious quality. Revenge, in the ongoing war between the two cities, couldn't have been sweeter.

Depressed, Suttle swallowed the Guinness and crossed the road to the seafront. No closer to fending off his new friends, he knew there was no way he was going to tackle the long drive home until he'd settled down. Maybe a walk by the sea. Maybe another pint or two. Anything to shake himself free of the troubling suspicion that life was beginning to gang up on him.

Lizzie spent the evening alone with Grace. After putting her daughter to bed, she drifted around the kitchen wondering what to make for supper. She'd no idea when Jimmy might be back and had half-expected a call by now. In the end she settled for making a salad with boiled eggs and new potatoes. By gone nine, when he still hadn't appeared, she loaded a plate on a tray and ate a glum supper in front of a repeat of *Shameless*. At ten came the news. By now she was seriously worried. What if he'd had some kind of accident on the way home? Far more likely, what if his attempts to head off the threat to their little family had gone horribly wrong? She was on the point of putting a call through to A & E in Pompey when the phone rang. It was Jimmy. She knew at once he'd been drinking.

'Where are you?'

'Southsea.'

'*Still?*'

'Yeah.'

'Why?'

'It's complicated. I just wanted …' He tailed off.

'Wanted what? What did you want?'

'It's hard, my love. It's just hard.'

'What's just hard? For fuck's sake, Jimmy. I'm sitting here waiting for you. We both are. So when are you back?'

'Tomorrow.'

'*Tomorrow?*'

Lizzie was staring at the dodgy window. It was open again. Her clever wedge must have dropped out. *Great.*

Suttle was trying to apologise. He'd talked to someone he thought might help. Afterwards he'd had a bit of a think, trying to work out exactly what to do. This thing's really tricky, he kept saying. It's not as simple as you might expect.

Lizzie had ceased to be interested. A cold hard anger had iced what was left of her patience. She was alone in the middle of nowhere with an infant daughter and a bunch of lunatics trying to barge into her life. The very least she wanted was her husband back home to take care of them both. Yet here he was, 130 miles away, pissed as a rat.

'So what's going to happen?' she asked.

There was a long silence. In the background Lizzie thought she caught the parp of a ship's siren. Then Suttle was back on the line.

'Fuck knows,' he said. And rang off.

Suttle walked and walked, wondering whether he should drive home. The third pub had been a mistake, and he'd known it, but after the fourth pint he hadn't much cared, a feeling of release that had taken him by surprise. The temptation now was to get back on the phone, bell a couple of his ex-colleagues, seek a little advice. That way, he told himself, he'd at least have something to show for his evening in Pompey, but the moment he tried to imagine these conversations the more he realised the idea was a non-starter. These guys would suss at once that he was shit-faced. He'd left this city with a decent reputation. Why put all that at risk?

The cheapest Southsea B & Bs were in Granada Road. By now it was raining. The first three doors he knocked on didn't answer. The fourth was opened by an Asian guy in a grease-stained Pompey shirt. Yes, he had a room upstairs. Forty-five quid cash. In advance.

Suttle peeled off the notes, too knackered to barter. The room was horrible: pink bedspread, cracked handbasin, no shade on the overhead bulb, mauve carpet, everything stinking of cigarettes. Suttle lay on his back, staring up. There were damp patches on the ceiling and canned laughter from the TV in the next room. Forget the TV and the fags, he told himself, and he might easily have been at home. The dripping tap. The draught through the window stirring the thin strip of curtain. The overpowering evidence that someone didn't care, that someone should have tried harder. The thought sobered him. Lizzie deserved better than this. He reached for his mobile and keyed her number. It rang and rang before going onto divert. He stared at it, perplexed, then tried again. Still no answer. Only on his third attempt did Lizzie answer.

'Are you coming home?' Her voice was cold.

'I've hurt you,' he said.

'You're right. So when are you coming home?'

'Tomorrow,' he said. 'I'll be up first thing. Should be back by—'

He broke off, staring at the phone. She'd hung up. He shut his eyes. For a minute or two he tried to think of nothing. When he opened them again, the damp patches, the canned laughter and the sour reek of a million cigarettes were still there. Rolling over, he hammered on the thin partition wall.

'Shut the fuck up,' he yelled.

Nothing happened. He beat on the wall again. Nothing. Finally he rolled off the bed and went out into the corridor. The door to the adjoining room was unlocked. He pushed it

149

open. The room was empty. He bent to the TV and ripped the plug out of the socket in the skirting board.

Back in his own room, he sat on the bed, his elbows on his knees. Ten to midnight. At length he reached for the mobile again. He'd stored Gina Hamilton's number only yesterday. She answered on the second ring.

'Who is this?'

'Jimmy. Jimmy Suttle.'

'What do you want?'

Her voice wasn't as hostile as he might have expected. He even sensed a a hint of warmth when she asked what he was up to.

'Fuck knows,' he said.

'Where are you?'

'Pompey. This is a room you will not believe.'

'What room?'

Suttle tried to explain but gave up. When he tried to pretend a renewed interest in Tom Pendrick she saw through it at once.

'What are you after?' she said.

Suttle stared at the rain dripping down the window pane. Good question.

'A meet. A drink,' he said at last. 'I need someone to talk to. You call it.'

'You're serious?'

'Yeah.' He'd shut his eyes again. 'I think I am.'

Lizzie lay in bed. Grace's cot was beside her. Lizzie had moved it in as a precaution. If anything happened, she told herself, better that they faced it together.

The last couple of hours the wind had got up. She pulled the duvet closer, buried herself in its warmth, tried not to listen to the noises outside in the garden, but every creak, every sigh, every rustle in the long grass beyond the patio sparked another image. Someone watching. Someone waiting. Someone stealing ever closer to the gaping window downstairs.

Once she switched on the light and risked a look at her watch. 03.17. In a couple of hours a pale grey light would wash through the thin curtains. After that, God willing, she might sleep. In the meantime she had to fight this sense of welling panic, this certainty that things could only get worse, and to do that she had to concentrate on something amusing, something positive, a single image that might keep the busy darkness at bay.

She tried and tried, raiding her memories from Gill's visit. The ducklings in the stream at the bottom of the garden. The horses on the beach the afternoon they'd walked to Straight Point. The expression on Grace's tiny face when her mum had staggered to her feet after the first session on the rowing machine. For a moment or two this worked. But then the images faded and the darkness crowded back in and she flailed around in her mind's eye, looking for some place to hide.

Then, quite suddenly, she had it. She was afloat again, taking her first strokes towards the dock, listening to the big man with the huge hands. He'd told her she could do it. And he'd been right.

Five

Suttle was on the road early next morning. By five to nine he was mopping up the last of a hangover with an all-day breakfast in a café off the Bridport bypass. The rain had cleared overnight and the hills in west Dorset were a vivid green in the fitful sunshine. He stood in the car park, enjoying the taste of the wind, waiting for Lizzie to pick up. After some thought he'd decided to pretend last night never happened. When she finally answered, he could hear banging in the background.

'What's going on?'

'I've got a guy in from down the road. He's fixing the window.'

'Right ...' Suttle wondered who was paying but decided not to ask. 'You OK?'

'We're fine.'

'Grace?'

'She's teething again. Don't forget about tonight.'

'What?' Suttle was fumbling for his car keys.

'I'm rowing. You need to be back by half five. You think you can manage that?'

Suttle's office was still empty when he made it to Exeter. The Office Manager, a resourceful divorcee called Leslie, brought him coffee and a couple of stale biscuits. Luke Golding, she

152

said, was about to be redeployed by Mr Nandy but the lad was still upstairs. She knew he wanted a word.

Suttle nodded. He was looking at the list of messages on his desk. Leslie had already arranged them in order of priority. The first one asked him to bell the CSI at Scenes of Crime.

Mark was en route to an aggravated burglary in Totnes. Suttle heard the *tick-tock* of his indicator as he pulled in to take the call.

'Kinsey's PC,' he said. 'Christ knows how but we got bumped up the queue. They haven't done full analysis yet but they've taken a good look.'

Suttle was impressed. The techies were as hard-pressed as everyone else in the force and the wait for hard disk analysis often stretched to weeks, sometimes months. Nandy's doing, he thought. Has to be.

Mark told him to get a pen. He'd spent a couple of hours with the key data yesterday afternoon and sorted what he thought might be useful.

'The guy's a businessman, right?'

'Right.'

'Building resort hotels?'

'Retirement communities. Top-end stuff. High six figures for a nice view and fancy CCTV.'

'Gotcha.' For once in his life Mark was laughing. 'There's a whole load of emails about a site at a place called Trezillion. It's hard to get the context without more info but I get the feeling this thing's still on the drawing board. He's forever nailing the planning guys to the wall. Telling these people what to do and when. Real fucking arsewipe.'

Suttle reached for a pen. Mark's language always enriched a conversation. Scene of Crimes guys were a special breed but Mark was a one-off. Mr Gloom one minute. Mr Yippee the next. Definitely bipolar.

'Where's Trezillion?'

'Cornwall. North coast. Lovely little bay with nothing but a public lavatory and a bit of car park. Used to be a top bogging spot for gays down from Newquay. You should give it a go before Kinsey gets his hands on it.'

'He's dead, Mark.'

'Fuck me, so he is. Surprise or what?' Another growl of laughter. 'I'll ping you the meat of this stuff. See what you make of it.'

'Anything else?'

'Yeah. We've got a single blonde hair from the floor beside Kinsey's bed. Proves nothing except he might have got lucky.'

Suttle scribbled himself a note. The Viking, he thought. Definitely worth a return visit.

'Is that it?'

'No.' Mark confirmed that Kinsey hadn't belonged to Facebook or any of the other social sites. Neither did he appear to have any close mates worth an email or two. There was, however, one chink in his armour.

'What's that?'

'The guy was a huge video gamer. Played most nights.'

'Really?'

'Yeah. I don't know how much you know about all this gaming shit but there's a service called Steam. It's a deal you sign up to. You buy games through the site and they organise everything else for you, keep your games in the cloud, help you find friends in multiplayer, keep a record of how you're doing, sort out the social side.'

'Social side?'

'Yeah. Most of these games you can either play solo against the computer or with other people. The guys you're playing with have weird screen names. Think cyber handles.'

'Who was Kinsey? What did he call himself?'

'Jalf Rezi. As in you know what.' Mark invited Suttle to picture Kinsey bent over the rail of his balcony, barfing mouthfuls of chicken jalfrezi into the night.

Suttle needed to get back to the video games.

'Kinsey was part of a team? Is that what you're telling me?'

'Yeah. Definitely. Some nights he must have played alone. Other nights he logged into a server and went out with his mates.'

'What kind of games are we talking about?'

'I can only give you names, I'm afraid. Most of this shit's way over my head.'

He tallied some of the games in Kinsey's Steam library: Grand Theft Auto IV, Arma 2, Need for Speed, Shift, Assassin's Creed Brotherhood, Battlefield 2, Civilisation IV, Half Life 2, Left 4 Dead, Left 4 Dead 2, Counterstrike, God of War, Team Fortress 2, Wings of Prey.

Suttle was scribbling fast. He wanted to know what these games were like.

'Haven't a clue. I'll email you the guy's Steam profile. You might need someone younger to make sense of it. These guys live under stones during the day, which is why they've all got such shit complexions. Good luck, eh? And tell him to get a life.'

Kinsey's Steam profile arrived by email within minutes. Suttle could make little sense of it. Luke Golding, mercifully, was still at his desk. Suttle drew up a chair while the young D/C explained that Henri Laffont, the Swiss engineer, had definitely spent the weekend in Shanghai. Another name off the suspect list.

'Sorry, Sarge.'

'No problem. How much do you know about video games?'

'Why?'

'Just answer the question.'

'Quite a lot.'

'OK ...'

Suttle consulted the Steam profile and read out the list of games. Golding wanted to know what this had to do with Kinsey.

'They were on his computer.'

'Really? He was a *gamer*?'

'Yeah. Surprised?'

'Very.'

Suttle wanted to know what you could read into a guy by his choice of favourite games.

'Lots. Show me.'

Suttle gave him the Steam profile. Golding studied Kinsey's list of games, which included the hours Kinsey had logged on each. His head came up.

'Well, he certainly liked his shooters.'

'What do you mean?'

'Kinsey was big on two games, right? Counterstrike and Team Fortress 2. Look, he played 400 hours on Counterstrike. That's serious addiction. Plus nearly 200 on TF2. OK. They're both shooter games but the likeness ends there. TF2 is basically one big party. The action could come straight out of *Looney Tunes*. It's also way more player-friendly than CS, especially when it comes to respawning.'

'Respawning?'

'That's when you're returned to the game after you die. On most games you wait a couple of seconds and then bang, you're back in the game. Not with Counterstrike. When you get killed playing CS, that's it for the rest of the round. You're dead. End of.'

CS, he said, was pure. It had no fancy bells and whistles, no back story, no million-dollar cut scenes, just a very simple premise: beat the other team. To do that, in Golding's view, you had to be fucking ace.

'Plus it's multiplayer only, Sarge. Which means you're always playing against real humans so practising against the computer is out of the question.'

'So you have to play with other people? Is that what you're telling me?'

'Yeah.'

'And the other game? Team Fortress 2?'

'Completely different. TF2 is way too anarchic for someone as hard core as Kinsey. It's a bit tongue-in-cheek.'

'So why would he play it so often?'

'Good question.' Golding's gaze had returned to the Steam page. 'This must have to do with the company he's been keeping.'

The notion of company was intriguing. So far, according to dozens of accounts, Kinsey was the near-perfect definition of a loner. On the face of it, all the guys in Saturday's winning quad had been his buddies, but the closer you questioned them the more obvious it became that Kinsey had bought their friendship, or perhaps just their company. So how come he'd spent most nights banged up in cyberspace with a bunch of gamers? Were relationships simpler this way? No messy stuff like having to talk face to face, or having to cope with the million tiny aggravations that came with having real mates?

Golding was still engrossed in the printouts from Kinsey's Steam page.

'I need to have a proper look at this.'

'Why?'

'Because you're going to ask me whether he had a special friend. And the way Steam works, the answer is yes.'

'So who is he?'

'This guy.'

Suttle followed his pointing finger. Somehow he'd missed the name on the bottom left of the page. He reached for a pen and ringed it carefully. ShattAr. Then he looked up.

'So this guy has to be a mate of Kinsey's? Is that what we're saying?'

'Yeah.'

'So how do we find out his real name?'

Suttle's question hung in the air. What he dreaded was having to go to one of the companies that controlled the servers.

157

Most of them were in the States and in his experience even a routine enquiry could take months to process.

Golding, it turned out, had another idea.

'We join the games, Sarge. We play Counterstrike and TF2. And we pretend to be Jalf Rezi.'

'We? I think not. You mean you.'

'Sure.' He was grinning. 'My pleasure.'

Suttle phoned Nandy from his own office. He caught the Det-Supt emerging from a meeting. A million detectives, he said, had been looking for a head to fit the body at the Bodmin scene of crime and so far they'd got nowhere. He'd like to chalk this up to a superior breed of criminal but his instincts told him it was pure luck. Nandy hated factors like luck. Luck, in his view, had no role to play in a properly run investigation.

'You're going to give me a name?'

'Sorry, sir?'

'For Kinsey?'

'I'm afraid not. Not yet.'

Suttle briefly explained about Kinsey's passion for video games. He needed D/C Golding's help just a little while longer. He'd have asked D/I Houghton for the go-ahead but she wasn't picking up.

'She's gone to Brittany,' Nandy said. 'She's looking for the head.'

'Did she mention Kinsey's bank statements and those phone billings before she went?'

'Yes. It'll be a couple of days yet. Are you sure you need them? The banks are charging us the earth.'

Suttle confirmed he'd need the records for the Coroner's file. Nandy wanted to know how long he'd be hanging on to Golding.

'Couple of days, sir. Max.'

There was a long silence. Suttle was wondering about the

ethics of a police officer impersonating someone else online. Then Nandy was back on the phone.

'Two days it is, son. Consider yourself lucky.'

Lizzie picked up a copy of the *Exmouth Journal* at lunchtime. She'd wheeled Grace down to the village store and only caught the headline on her way out. She stopped beside the rack of newspapers. The story occupied the entire front page. Beneath the headline – MURDER SQUAD PROBE MARINA DEATH – was a colour photo of a bunch of guys in a pub. She recognised the biggest at once, Tom Pendrick. Kinsey, according to the paper, was the little guy centre stage.

Lizzie bought the paper and took it home. The handyman she'd found had finished with the window, hammering the metal frame back into line and reseating the hinges. It was a snug fit now and Lizzie told herself it would resist all intruders. The residue of last night had stayed with her, but she saw no point in letting it spoil the sunshine. The last forty-eight hours had taught her a great deal about her marriage, but the lessons she knew she must draw were still unclear. For the time being, boxed in, she'd simply have to bide her time.

Kinsey's death had spilled onto page 2 of the paper. A reporter looking for another angle had put a call through to the secretary of the rowing club. She'd confirmed that everyone was deeply shocked by what had happened and were discussing what the club might organise in the way of a tribute. Jake Kinsey, she said, had been more than generous in his support for local rowing.

Lizzie went back to the front page, wondering how she'd be dealing with a story like this if she was back in the newsroom. She knew for a fact that the police were treating Kinsey's death as suspicious and all the chatter she'd overheard in the boat and on the beach suggested that the club's benefactor had been far from popular. One of the girls had called him The

Passenger. Another had said he was creepy. Tonight, maybe, she'd find out more.

Suttle was contemplating a sandwich when he took the call from Exmouth Quays. As the last man standing in *Constantine*'s abandoned stockade, all inquiries to the central control room were being routed to him.

Suttle bent to the phone and introduced himself. It was a woman's voice. He didn't understand why she was shouting.

'That Kinsey man,' she bellowed. 'He'd no right. Absolutely no right.'

'No right to do what?'

'To act the way he did. This is enslavement pure and simple. He simply didn't care. No man should be allowed to do that.' She paused. 'Did you get my letter about Prince William?'

'I'm afraid I didn't.'

'His life is under threat. I have the documents, the proof. You should come and see them.' Another pause. 'Are you a monarchist, by any chance?'

'No.'

'Neither am I. Do come round. Number 31.'

'Where?'

'Regatta Court. The name's Peggy Brims. My mother was half-French.'

The phone went dead. Suttle did a reverse number search to check the address. Peggy Brims, 31 Regatta Court. He turned to his PC. A couple of keystrokes took him into the Operational Information System. He needed a couple of checks before he could decide whether to turn this woman's call into an action.

He waited for a moment or two then keyed in her name and postcode. It turned out she had an entire file of her own. It stretched back more than eighteen months, call after call alerting the forces of law and order to a long list of imminent threats. She'd been worried sick about gunrunning in Cuba, about the activities of a gangster called Marc Puyrol in Marseilles, about a bunch of goths in Whitby who were trying to set fire to a hotel on the harbourside.

In every case these pleas for action had been dismissed as crank calls. This woman had form as well as money. She spent most of her waking life dreaming up fictions to keep the police on their toes. But then Suttle's eye was caught by another entry. Back last summer she'd reported a local woman speeding out to sea on a borrowed jet ski. It was Peggy Brims' settled view that this woman had been rendezvousing with one of the huge oil tankers anchored out in Lyme Bay. She'd doubtless returned with thousands of pounds' worth of cocaine or heroin or something equally noxious, determined to corrupt and subvert the nation's youth.

In her choice of language and the sheer force of her indignation, there was absolutely nothing to distinguish this call from any of the others. Except that she'd been right. HMCR had been running an intel operation in the bay for months. And a couple of weeks later, partly thanks to her contribution, arrests had been made. There were difficulties producing her as a witness in court because of her looniness, but the fact remained that she kept her eyes open and had – for once – lifted the phone in genuine anger.

Suttle binned the idea of a sandwich and drove down to Exmouth Quays. Number 31 was on the third floor, served by the same lift as Kinsey's flat. Peggy Brims came to the door the moment Suttle knocked. She was a big woman, nudging sixty, beautifully dressed. She walked with the aid of a stick and was followed everywhere by a small brown dog. The dog's name was Pétain.

'As in Maréchal, young man. How much do you know about French history?'

'Very little.'

'Petain? The hero of Verdun? The saviour of *la belle France*? Went to seed later but a great, great man. Do you drink vermouth by any chance?'

She led him through to the sitting room at the front of the apartment. This was a miniature version of Kinsey's view, smaller but no less impressive. Suttle was watching a yellow kayak crabbing across the tide when he felt a glass in his hand. Dry Martini with a single green olive.

'*Salut*. What shall I call you?'

Suttle had already shown her his warrant card. She wasn't interested in surnames.

'I shall call you André,' she announced. 'We must raise a glass to those imps in the City. Did I mention the Libor rate? I'm deeply, *deeply* concerned.'

Suttle hadn't the faintest what she was talking about. The Martini must have been 90 per cent gin. He wanted to know about Kinsey.

Peggy had settled on a long crescent of sofa. Suttle had last seen furniture like this in a National Trust property he'd visited with Lizzie before the baby arrived. There were pictures on the wall, the frames equally ornate, that oozed money and taste. Dark landscapes in oil. Maritime etchings with a naval flavour that took him back to Pompey. He was beginning to wonder whether she entertained coach parties at the weekend when she reached across and tapped him lightly on the arm. She couldn't get this horrible man out of her mind.

'Kinsey?'

'Of course. He was thoroughly unpleasant, I'm afraid. No class. Absolutely no breeding. Which, of course, is why he did it.'

'Did what?'

'Had those little girls round.'

'I'm not with you.'

'The girls. The oriental girls. The girls in the lift. They belonged on my mantlepiece, some of them. Truly exquisite. A couple, one in particular, I even talked to.'

'Where?'

'In the lift. A pretty, pretty little thing. I was worried about cholera then. They used to call it the flux. I expect you know that.'

The word flux brought Suttle's head up. Milo Symons had used exactly the same term when he was talking about his film. *Flux*, he'd said. Tasha's idea.

'You discussed cholera with the girl in the lift?'

'I did. I think she was alarmed. I *hope* she was alarmed. She didn't say much. One has a duty in this life. Bad news should be shared. Don't you agree, André?'

She emptied her glass and held it out. Suttle refilled it from the cocktail shaker on the sideboard. A line of nicely mounted black and white photos featured a couple in their early twenties. Peggy was watching him in the huge mirror that dominated the wall opposite.

'My ma and pa, André. Pa served in the Diplomatic Corps before the war. A handsome man, my father. Knew nothing of the flux.'

Suttle wanted to be sure about Kinsey. 'These girls were definitely going up to his flat?'

'Of course.'

'How do you know?'

'I accompanied them. Just to make sure they came to no harm.'

'No harm how?'

'En route, André.' Her face darkened. 'Highwaymen.'

'In the lift?'

'Everywhere. *Partout.* Of course they never tell you in the brochure, and there's another thing.'

'What?'

'That man Kinsey. He had twelve fingers, you know. Ten for himself, and two for special pies.'

'I don't understand.'

'What don't you understand? The fingers?'

'The pies.'

'Ah, my poor André, *mon pauvre. Viens.* Come ...' She

163

struggled off the sofa, gathered up the dog in her spare arm and led Suttle through to a bedroom. The window was framed with heavily ruched curtains and offered a view of the dockside and the waterfront beyond. Immediately below was the stretch of promenade where Kinsey had met his death.

'There ...' A quivering finger indicated something in the distance.

'Where?'

'There. Beyond those hideous flats. That's where they're going to build the next one. They call it Pier Head. And you know who wanted to put his snout in that ghastly trough?'

'Kinsey?'

'Of course. My André ... so quick off the mark.' She patted his arm, delighted at this meeting of minds, then led him back to the sitting room.

'I need to be sure about these girls,' Suttle said. 'Would you recognise them again?'

'Of course.'

'If I brought photographs?'

'A great pleasure, André. You'll take care on the way out? After dark is worse, of course, but daylight can be equally un-nerving. You understand my drift?'

Suttle was still on his feet. The interview was evidently over.

'Of course,' he said 'because of the highwaymen.'

'Wrong, my dear André,' she was beaming now. 'Because of the *flux*.'

Mark was still at Totnes when Suttle phoned him. Suttle wanted to know about Kinsey's seized iPhone.

'Did you go through all the pictures?'

'No. There were hundreds,' said the CSI.

'Where's the phone now?'

'Back in the office. I've bagged it for analysis. Mr Nandy's definitely got the inside track with the techies. Shouldn't be more than a couple of days.'

'I need it faster than that.'

'Do it yourself, then. Ask for Lola. She's got the magic key.'

Suttle drove across to Scenes of Crime at Heavitree Road to take a look at the iPhone. Lola wasn't prepared to release it. If Suttle was going to go through Kinsey's pictures there had to be someone else on hand to testify he hadn't inserted any new material. Otherwise there might be evidential problems down the line in court.

Suttle shrugged. More and more these days detectives had to put up with this kind of procedural nonsense but he understood the logic and knew he had no choice.

'Splash of milk, please,' he said. 'No sugar.'

He settled down to await her return before boredom drove him to scroll through Kinsey's address book. He had a print-out of this already but needed to remind himself about Molly Doyle, the rowing club secretary. A single blonde hair had the makings of a serious interview. He scribbled down her number as his coffee arrived. Lola, it turned out, was a busy girl. Time to browse Kinsey's gallery.

The first sequence of shots were trophy views from Kinsey's penthouse. April had sparked a series of sensational sunsets and Kinsey had taken full advantage. Next came photos snapped from an accompanying launch on what Suttle assumed was a training row. He recognised the elfin figure of Lenahan in the cox's seat and the towering bulk of Pendrick rowing behind the stroke. Milo Symons was in the number two seat with Kinsey himself in bow. These were very telling. Only Kinsey ever stole a glance towards the camera. And only Kinsey's blades were ever out of sync with the rest of the crew. Stick insect, Suttle thought. Another of Tasha Donovan's little phrases.

'What exactly are we looking for?' Lola was on the meter. She had another ten minutes, absolute max.

'We'll know it when we see it.' Suttle was looking at a matchless crescent of sand softened on the landward side by a line of dunes. An offshore wind had sculpted the incoming tide into surf to die for, and the blueness of the water was dotted with tiny black figures waiting for the perfect wave.

Suttle scrolled on. There were more shots, the same cove photographed from every conceivable angle.

'Where's that?' He offered Lola the phone.

'Haven't a clue. Are those the ones you're after?'

Suttle shook his head. This must be Trezillion, he thought, the jewel in Kittiwake Oceanside's crown. He scrolled on, finding more shots, a different location this time. Finally, at the back end of last year, came the proof that his afternoon visit to Exmouth Quays had scored a modest result. The date – 24.12.2010 – was the only clue Suttle needed. Jake Kinsey, in his big fuck-off apartment, had bought himself an early Christmas prezzie.

'That's gross. That's horrible.' Lola turned away. 'You'd have to pay someone to do that.'

Lizzie was changed and ready half an hour before Suttle got home. She offered a cold cheek for a kiss, reminded him about a bowl of puréed bananas she'd left in the fridge for Grace and asked him to keep an eye open for the cat.

'Has he gone?' Suttle sounded hopeful.

'I doubt it.' Lizzie got in the car and adjusted the seat. 'One other thing. There's a bill needs settling for the window. It's on the table. I said you'd drop a cheque off tonight. A Mr Willoughby. He's just up the road. Sweetest man.'

She pulled the door shut, backed into the lane and floored the acclerator. In the rear-view mirror she could see Suttle watching her. He didn't wave.

At Exmouth once again a couple of quads were already on the beach. Thursdays, she knew already, was a big night for the juniors, and Tessa was doing her best to organise them. The club captain was due down any minute and wanted to have a word with everyone about Kinsey. Coverage in the local paper had made the club front-page news and in his view, according to Tessa, there had to be ways of turning all this publicity to ERC's advantage.

Lizzie parked, aware at once of Pendrick crossing the road. She got out and gave him a wave. He fell into step beside her.

'Back for more?'

'Of course.'

'Ever thought about the double?'

'I wouldn't know what a double is.'

'Come with me. I'll show you.'

They walked back to the compound. The club's double scull was half the length of the big quads and looked, to Lizzie's eye, a serious challenge.

'I'm a novice,' she said. 'The quad gives me somewhere to hide.'

'You don't need it. Just trust me. We're talking a 1.8 tide tonight. It's low water at half six. No wind to speak of. We couldn't capsize this baby if we tried.'

We? She looked up at him, already half persuaded, wanting the chance to prove she could do it. This guy's probably been rowing for ever, she told herself. And if he thinks I can hack it who is little me to spoil the party?

'OK.' She grinned and dropped a little curtsy. 'As long as you're sure.'

By the time they'd rigged the double and dragged it across the road towards the slipway, a sizeable group of rowers had gathered on the beach. The club captain was an older man, tall, visibly weathered by life. He was already in full flow, talking about what Kinsey had brought to the club, and as she and Pendrick paused to listen, Lizzie became aware of a younger guy with a video camera circling the group. His long black hair was gathered into a ponytail with a twist of yellow ribbon and he panned the camera to catch a listening face or two before returning to the captain.

By now the shape of the club's tribute to Kinsey was clear. Weather permitting, the club would be launching all its boats on Sunday. On an ebbing tide they'd row in line abreast towards the dock. Abeam of Regatta House they'd pause and hold formation before releasing a wreath of interwoven flowers. The specially designed wreath had been guaranteed to float. As it drifted down-tide, the club's boats would form an escort. Molly Doyle, said the club captain, had contacts in the local press. With luck a TV crew might even turn up. The resulting pictures, if they got it right, would do the club no end of good. The flowers, he added, included red camellias. These he understood to be Kinsey's favourite.

There was a mutter of approval. Several of the younger girls were comforting each other. One of the older boys eyed them in disbelief.

'Let's go.' Pendrick jerked his head towards the water.

They tugged the double scull down the beach beyond the quads. Pendrick untied it from the trailer and began to talk Lizzie through the next stage in the operation. Lizzie, still watching the crowd of rowers on the beach, wasn't listening.

'That's a nice thing to do,' she said. 'The wreath should work beautifully.'

Pendrick, steadying the double, shot her a look.

'It's bullshit,' he said.

'Why? How?'

'Kinsey was clueless about flowers. He wouldn't have known a red camellia from a hole in the road.'

'But what about the juniors? Those girlies?'

'They didn't know the first thing about him, probably never met the guy. It's showtime. Cameras. Grief. These days, unless you shed a tear it isn't real.' He frowned, then nodded at the double. 'Are we going to do this thing or what?'

Despite the fact she was teething, it took Suttle less than half an hour to get Grace settled. Before he'd got to the end of her favourite story she was asleep. Suttle returned downstairs. Lizzie had left a pile of vegetables for his attention but he ignored them in favour of a Stella from the fridge. He opened the tinnie and reached for a glass. The bill for the window refurb was lying on the kitchen table – ninety-five pounds.

He went next door and inspected the window before settling in the Ikea rocker beside the ancient telly. By the time he'd left the office, Suttle had secured Carole Houghton's permission to explore Kinsey's affection for video games. He'd explained Golding's suspicions that Kinsey had developed an online relationship. In the young D/C's view there might be a special person in Kinsey's cyber life who would repay a little attention. Maybe, in the vast spaces of the Internet, Kinsey had let slip a confidence or two. Maybe.

Houghton had accepted the logic and checked out the RIPA situation with Nandy. Under the Regulation of Investigative Powers Act, *Constantine* might need a warrant if Golding was to pose as Kinsey. Nandy loved the idea. A warrant, he said, would be no problem. The more proactive *Constantine* became, the better he liked it.

The warrant had been signed off before close of play. Tonight Golding would be settling at his own PC, monitoring both Counterstrike and Team Fortress 2, jumping in as Jalf Rezi and hoping that ShattAr showed up. He'd promised Suttle a call if he struck lucky but was gloomy about his chances of surviving the killing fields of Counterstrike. He'd log on to different servers for a bit of discreet practice but it was years since he'd played the game and he knew how tough it could be.

Suttle swallowed a mouthful or two of Stella, trying to imagine Kinsey at his PC up in the emptiness of his trophy apartment. Tired or drunk, according to Luke, he'd probably take a gentler ride with Team Fortress 2. That way he could rely on being respawned, an endless process of reincarnation, keeping himself from the jaws of death. On screen it had doubtless worked. In real life, alas, it hadn't.

The brutality of this contrast between the make-believe of cyberspace and the lethal suck of gravity was, Suttle sensed, one of the keys to *Constantine*. The more he thought about it, the more he suspected that video games must have offered Kinsey the perfect surrogate for real friendship. Any attachments he formed on the Internet were risk-free. He could expose as much or as little of himself as he chose. And every time he logged on there was the prospect of another hour or so in the company of like-minded loners, busy zapping the next shadow lurking at the edge of the screen.

This was fine as far as it went, an intriguing line of enquiry that might yield a name and even a confidence or two. But what was he to make of SOC's blonde hair retrieved from Kinsey's bedroom? And of Peggy Brims' impassioned belief that Kinsey's interest in real estate extended further than a clutch of picturesque waterside sites in north Cornwall?

The latter had taken Suttle to the East Devon District Council website. These people were the planning authority for Exmouth, and a couple of minutes' research had revealed an application to develop Pier Head, adjacent to Exmouth Quays.

Peggy Brims, once again, had her thumb on the pulse of local life. The architectural drawings showed a towering apartment block that would dwarf everything else in the area. The application was the work of Devon-based property developers. Accompanying the drawings was the usual tosh about gateway locations, iconic structures and local employment opportunities, and Suttle's suspicions that the sheer size of this proposed monster would have sparked local opposition turned out to be spot on. A call to the *Exmouth Journal* confirmed a flood of objections. Many of the locals, said the news editor, were outraged.

But did Kinsey really want to help himself to a slice of the action? Or might his interest be limited to the spec purchase of an apartment or two, something way up at the top of the building, an asset he could flog on when prices started to rise again? Suttle had tried to raise some kind of answer from the developers, leaving a message on their switchboard, but so far no one had returned his call.

He finished the Stella and stole upstairs to check on Grace. She was curled in her cot, a corner of the sheet bunched in her tiny hand, oblivious to the world. Back in the living room Suttle tried to map out the coming days. The key to every live enquiry was the Policy Book. *Constantine*'s had been in the hands of Carole Houghton. She'd now handed it over to Suttle and already he'd drawn on its contents to better understand *Constantine*'s brief history. Houghton, as he expected, had been characteristically thorough, recording and explaining every investigative decision she'd taken. Suttle's next task was to add a sheaf of statements, especially from the winning crew, who'd been the last people to see Kinsey alive.

Andy Poole's statement was already in the file, as was the account *Constantine*'s D/Cs had taken from Tom Pendrick the night he'd come back from north Cornwall. But both Eamonn Lenahan and Milo Symons would need a revisit for statementing, and Natasha Donovan – Milo's partner – had yet to be interviewed at all. These calls would now fall to Suttle and he made a mental note to start with Tash Donovan. The word flux kept coming back to him. His years in CID had taught Suttle to discount the likelihood of coincidence. How come both Tash and Peggy Brims had been so interested in 'flux'?

Suttle was thinking about the single blonde hair and wondering when to make another call on Molly Doyle when his landline rang. It was Luke Golding.

'How's it going?'

'It isn't, Sarge. I got Scenes of Crime to rip Kinsey's Steam password from his hard drive and logged on as Jalf.'

'And?'

'I got zapped within seconds. Total fucking disaster.'

'Counterstrike?'

'Too right. I waited until the game ended and respawned. Survived for a whole minute this time then crashed and burned again. Horrible.'

By now, he said, his performance had begun to attract

attention. He wasn't on headphones for obvious reasons but he'd got a couple of messages. One of the players had asked whether he was pissed. Another, interestingly, thought that Kinsey might have been subbed by his brother. Or more likely his granny. Either way, there was a general consensus that Kinsey had stepped out of his former persona and become someone else. Which was, of course, exactly right.

'Anything else?'

'Yeah. There was a third message. This was definitely kinder.'

'What did it say?'

'It wanted to know what the problem was. You want to guess the sender?'

'ShattAr.'

'Spot on.'

'So what did you say?'

'Nothing. But that's not the point, Sarge. This one used Kinsey's real name. He called me Jake. The guy's in touch. He's out there. He exists.'

Suttle thought about the implications. At last Kinsey might have found someone he could confide in.

'So how do we progress this?' he said at last. 'What do we do next?'

'I log on again. Tonight. Tomorrow. Whenever. Wait for the guy to reappear.'

'But you're still pretending to be Kinsey, right?'

'Right.'

'So how do you handle him? What do you say?'

'Number one, I'm still going to be crap at Counterstrike. So the guy's going to start wondering if I really am Kinsey. So maybe I should go on headphones and have a conversation.'

'Saying what?'

'I could tell him Jake's had a bit of an accident. I could tell him I'm standing in. That way I could maybe get a steer on who this guy is.'

Suttle smiled. A bit of an accident, he thought. He bent to the phone again.

'And you think that might work?'

'It might. It's possible. But there's another way. Maybe better.'

'Like what?'

'Like I log on again as Jalf and wait for him to appear. Then I send him a message asking him to be a Facebook friend.'

'What if he's a Facebook friend of Kinsey's already?'

'He can't be. You told me Kinsey wasn't on Facebook.'

'You're right. He wasn't. Brain-dead, me. So what do we do about that?'

'I get myself a Facebook page.'

'As Kinsey?'

'Of course. Then send this guy a friend request and add a message about Counterstrike so he knows who I am. Fingers crossed, he friends me.'

Suttle nodded in approval. Once ShattAr got in touch, his Facebook profile might give them everything they'd need to have a proper conversation.

'You really think he'll do it?'

'I've no idea, Sarge. Worth a try though, eh?'

The line went dead. Outside, after a decent sunset, the light was beginning to die. Suttle got up and went to the window, peering into the gathering darkness. Lately he'd made an effort to tally the jobs that badly needed doing around the property but knew that lists were no substitute for the real thing. He checked his watch, wondering how Lizzie was getting on. Nearly half eight. Late.

Lizzie's outing with Pendrick was a disaster. Rowing in the double turned out to be a circus act after the comforting embrace of the quad. The slightest wobble, a single mistake with either blade, seemed to threaten a capsize. By the time she and Pendrick got down to the dock, she was ready to give up.

Pendrick was rowing in the bow seat, checking their progress over his shoulder, feeding her instructions as they picked their way through the buoys and moorings. Heavy on green. Go red. Equal pressure. Lizzie tried to process all these commands, turning them into strong tugs on the right-hand oar or the left, but her brain had turned to mush.

In the end Pendrick beached them on the long curve of Dawlish Warren and helped Lizzie get out.

'Useless,' she said. 'Totally fucking hopeless.'

He told her not to be dramatic. Rowing the double after a single outing in the quad was a tough call.

'So why are we doing it?'

'Because I thought you could hack it.'

'Wrong. I can't.'

'You can. You just have to relax. Listen to me.'

With infinite patience he pointed out what she was doing wrong. She had to ride the double like a horse. She had to feel the river through her bum. She had to think of the double as a musical instrument, amplifying the suck and nudge of the tide.

'Listen to your body,' he said, 'and you won't go wrong.'

Lizzie began to laugh. This sounded wildly karmic. She'd tried yoga once and been just as challenged.

A smile ghosted over Pendrick's face. Maybe he'd got the wrong metaphor, he said. Maybe she should start thinking about the *grain* of the river, how to feel it, how to make it a friend.

'That's even worse. We're talking water, not wood.'

'Same difference. It's a living thing. And so are you. Fight it, like just now, and the river will always win. Make it your friend –' the sudden grin took her by surprise '– and anything can happen.'

They tried again. This time, Lizzie was worse. Sheer concentration made her nervous. Nervous, she began to wobble. Wobbling finally brought them to a halt. By now they were back beside the stretch of beach that led to the compound.

At slack tide the water was like a mirror. Downstream, Lizzie could see a couple of quads heading seawards. For a moment she envied them but then she felt the gentlest tap on her shoulder. It was Pendrick.

'Drink?' he suggested.

They went to a pub on the seafront. To Lizzie, it was the sanest decision they'd made all evening. There were benches and tables on the big apron of forecourt and Pendrick disappeared inside to the bar. Lizzie gazed out at the beginnings of a decent sunset. For mid-April, it was still warm.

'Cheers. Here's to your lovely bum.'

Pendrick was back with the drinks. He slid into the bench across the table. The same subtle grace, she thought. The same instinctive sense of balance that had just steadied the bloody double.

'Thanks for putting up with me.' She lifted her glass.

Pendrick shrugged. The double was history. They'd have another go when she was ready. Meantime he'd just remembered what date it was.

'You know what I was doing this time last year?'

'Surprise me.'

'Rowing.'

'I said surprise me.'

'We were a week out from Cape Cod. It was an evening like this. I remember it like yesterday.'

Lizzie was staring at him.

'Cape Cod's in Massachusetts,' she said.

'You're right.'

'You're telling me you were on the Atlantic? For a whole week? *Rowing?*'

'Yeah. And the next week and the week after and ...' his hand closed around the pint of Guinness '... for ever really.'

Lizzie had abandoned her drink. Something in this man's face had been nagging at her since she'd first met him and now she realised what it was. The hair, she thought. He had hair then.

'You're the guy who rowed the Atlantic,' she said.

'Yeah.'

'And lost his wife.'

'Yeah.'

'It was all over the papers.'

'Yeah.'

'Shit.'

'Yeah.' He lifted his glass. 'Happy anniversary, eh?'

Lizzie didn't know where to take this conversation next. As a working journalist she'd have had no problems. There were ways you could get people to open up. But this was different. She felt she'd begun to know this man a little. She'd shared something precious with him. She might have fucked up just now in the double but she'd fallen in love with rowing and that she owed to Pendrick.

'You want to talk about it?' she said at last.

'You want to listen?'

'Of course.' Lizzie fought an urge to reach for his hand. 'Tell me.'

He gazed at her then looked away. For a moment Lizzie thought she'd blown it – too hasty, too blatant – but then he was back with her. He wanted to start somewhere else. He wanted to start in Thailand.

He and his wife, he said, had spent the best part of three years bumming round the world with a couple of surfboards and not much else. They'd spent time in California, in Oz, in New Zealand. He was an electrician by trade, and Kate had nursing qualifications, and whenever the money ran out they'd work for a couple of months then hit the beaches again.

'Is that when you got your scar?' Lizzie had been dying to ask.

'Yeah. I got dumped on a reef down near Melbourne. Place called Suicide Beach. Split my face open from here to here ...'

His finger tracked down from the corner of his eye. 'Thank Christ Kate was there. She stopped most of the bleeding and got me to a hospital. My own bloody fault.'

'It didn't put you off?'

'Never. Surfing's a drug. You can't get enough.'

'Sounds great.'

'It was. Kate and I? We had nothing in the world except the ocean. It's amazing how rich that can make you feel.'

'I'm sure. Did Kate think that way as well?'

'Most of the time.' He nodded. 'Yeah.'

After New Zealand, he said, they took a flight to Bangkok, bought an old camper van from a Scouser heading home and drove south.

'You know Thailand at all?'

'No.'

'The best bits are down by the Malay border. We ended up in a village just inland from the beach, place called Ao Lok. We spent the whole summer there, Mr and Mrs Idle, just surfing, swimming, making friends with the locals, totally lovely people. It was a brilliant time.'

After a while, he said, they'd become part of the village. They were renting a hut from someone who'd gone off to work in Phuket. Pendrick would do the odd wiring job for various neighbours while Kate would help out with the kids when they got sick. In return, families would give them food and invite them along for the party when a daughter was getting married or a long-lost cousin flew in from Europe or the States.

'It was like we belonged.' He was smiling. 'It was a nice feeling.'

'And Kate?'

'She was cool with it. In fact she loved it. I think it gave her something we'd never had before. We both came from broken homes. The last thing these people were was broken.'

Ao Lok, he said, was as perfect as perfect can be.

'Like how? Tell me.'

'You could hear the surf at night through the trees. We lived on fruit and bread and fish and rice. Like I say, we were in the water most days. Kate used to look after this little boy, Niran, and she taught him to swim. Once he'd got his confidence, I'd paddle him out on the surf board. He loved it. Fantastic little kid. Always grinning. Happiness on legs. We wanted to kidnap him. Tuck him in the back of the camper and drive away. But what would be the point? Where in the world would ever be more perfect than Ao Lok?'

Lizzie mistook this as a question. She was trying to offer something similar in her own life but failed completely. Pendrick hadn't finished.

'You know something really strange?' he said. 'For years we'd always been moving on. It becomes a kind of habit, maybe stronger than that, maybe a kind of addiction. You're convinced there's always something better round the next corner, and so you look and you look and then you find somewhere like Ao Lok and you realise you've found it. It's the end of the line. It's where you belong. It's where you want to stay. Maybe for ever. Except we couldn't. Because it became impossible.'

'How come?'

'You really want to know?'

'Daft question.'

Pendrick got up to fetch another Guinness. Then he was back.

'Boxing Day.' He wiped his mouth. 'We're up and about and Kate's taken Niran down to the beach. I've told them I'll be along later. We've sold the camper and I'm trying to sort an old moped we've just bought. Next thing I know, there's this roaring noise, a bit like thunder. It gets louder and louder then there are people running up from the beach through the trees. They're yelling about a huge wave coming. I run down towards the beach and get there in time to see this wave breaking way out in the bay. They're right. It's vast. Kate's down there too. The water is being sucked out to sea ahead of the wave and she's running after Niran. By the time she catches him, the wave's on top of them both. That's the last I saw of the kid. No one ever found him.'

'And Kate?'

'She survived. Sort of.'

Afterwards, he said, he and Kate went to America. They'd made friends a while back with a couple from California, surfers like themselves. Kate was really close to the woman – nice girl, half Sri-Lankan. They picked up casual jobs for a while, then got green cards, which made it all legit. They were still spending time by the ocean, he said, but it was never the same.

'That was five years ago.' He was studying his hands. 'Time's supposed to be the healer, isn't it? Time's supposed to make the difference. No chance. Kate had lost it. She became someone else.'

Lizzie nodded. This, at last, sounded familiar. She was getting to know a lot about strangers in her life.

'Difficult,' she said simply.

'It was, believe me. And it was especially hard because I couldn't see an end to it. There was no way Kate could make peace with what had happened because there was no peace to make. Ao Lok and Niran and all the rest of it had taken us to a place we could never get back to. And once that happens, believe me, you're fucked.'

Lizzie reached for his hand. It seemed the simplest thing in the world.

'So what did you do?' she said.

'In the end, you mean?'

'Yes.'

'I figured we had to do something big, something amazing. Double or quits time. The ocean again. Another crap decision.'

They'd saved like crazy for a couple of years and moved east to Cape Cod. Backers had paid for the boat and the provisions and everything else they needed, and they'd made contact with one of the charities that had sprung up after the tsunami.

They'd put together a support team in a town called Woods
Hole and spent a week or two rowing up and down the coast
to get the feel of the boat.

'And then?'

'We went for it. April's supposed to be kind, and to be fair
the weather wasn't that bad, but what nobody ever tells you
about is the rowing, the routine, the sheer fucking monotony
of going on and on, day after day, just on and on. If you're
not careful, if you're not strong, something like that can break
your heart.'

'And did it?'

'You're talking about me?'

'Yes.'

'No.' He shook his head. 'I more or less survived.'

'But Kate?'

'Definitely.'

'It broke her heart?'

'Yes.'

He looked up. His eyes were glassy. He gave Lizzie's hand a
squeeze and then withdrew his own.

'We had a couple of storms on the way over.' He reached
for his drink. 'In that kind of sea there's no way you can keep
rowing so you get into this shithole of a cabin, the pair of you,
and try and make sure the hatch is watertight, and just ride the
storm out. This kind of stuff can go on for days. The cabin's
tiny, just room for the two of you. Kate had done her best to
cheer the place up. She'd put photos everywhere, places we'd
been, friends we were missing, but it's dark most of the time
because you're trying to preserve the batteries, and the boat's
all over the place and you start to recognise the pattern of the
waves, the intervals before they hit you, and you realise after
a while that you're just helpless, a sitting target, tense as fuck,
waiting for the big one.'

'And did it come?'

'Yeah. Middle of the night. Turned us over. Total capsize.

Kate was crying. She wanted out. She'd had enough. In the end the boat bobbed up again, righted itself, but she cried for hours, really quietly, no big drama. There was nothing I could do, nothing I could say. She'd gone. It was hopeless.'

Lizzie wanted to know if this was when she disappeared. Pendrick shook his head. That happened weeks later. By the next day, he said, the storm had blown itself out. They did their best to get everything back together again, to lash stuff down, to figure out what was missing and what wasn't, but the truth was that the fight had gone out of them.

'You lose heart,' he said. 'Because you keep realising there's something else you've lost, something else you can't put your hand on. It's a bit like being burgled. This stuff's personal. It hurts.'

The worst, he said, was a stone that Kate had kept from the beach at Ao Lok. She'd hung onto it from the day Niran had disappeared, and now it too had gone.

'We looked for it everywhere. We emptied the cabin, shook everything out, looked under the thwarts, tore the boat apart, but it had gone. That did it for her. After that, I knew she'd had enough.'

'Meaning?'

'She wanted to end it all. Slip overboard. Go where Niran had gone.'

'And that's what happened?'

'Yes.'

'Did you talk about it? Before?'

'No.'

'Why not?'

'Good question.' His glass was empty again. Lizzie wondered whether to buy him another Guinness but knew this wasn't the moment. Her hand was back in his.

'You know something about the sea?' He nodded out beyond the promenade.

'Tell me.'

'It puts you to the test. Take on a voyage like we did, day after day, and if there's the slightest weakness in the relationship, the sea will find you out. You set off on a high. You think you're immortal. You think you'll conquer the world. And then it turns out you're wrong.'

'So what happened?'

'We got found out.'

'Because of Niran?'

'Because of me.'

'You blame yourself?'

'Yes.'

'Why?'

'Because I should have been bigger, stronger, more attentive, more loving, more understanding, more ...' He shrugged. 'What the fuck do I know?'

'You know everything. Because you were there. And from where I'm sitting I doubt there's anything else you could have done. We're talking serious depression, right? Depression's a horrible thing. It eats you away inside. You try really hard to get on top of it, you think you've got it nailed, and then you wake up next day and it's *still* there. That's Kate ... no?'

'Yes.' He was studying her. 'So how come you know all this?'

Lizzie held his gaze. Then she lifted his hand to her lips and kissed it.

'Don't ask,' she muttered.

It was dark by the time Suttle decided to make the call. He'd put together a rudimentary stew and boiled a panful of rice. Twice he'd tried to call Lizzie but both times her mobile was on divert. There was no more Stella in the fridge and he couldn't find the remains of Gill Reynolds' Stolly.

'Gina? Jimmy.'

'Hi.' She sounded far away. Non-committal.

'I was just wondering about a meet.'

'Is that right?'

'Yeah. We're still on?'

'I'm not sure.' She paused. 'Do you always call this time of night? Only I might have difficulty getting my head round that.'

'Round what?'

'Becoming your answering service.'

'That's not the way it is.'

'Oh yeah? Tell me more.'

'Like I said last night, I just need to talk.'

'About Pendrick?'

'About me.'

'Why?'

'That's what I want to talk about.'

Another silence, longer this time.

'Tell me something, Jimmy. Are you married?'

'Yes.'

'Kids?'

'A daughter. Grace. She's asleep upstairs.'

'And do you love her?'

'Yes. Very much.'

'I meant your wife.'

It was Suttle's turn to hesitate. The silence stretched and stretched.

'That's a no then,' he said at last.

'No to what?'

'No to a meet. No to a conversation. I just thought … you know … sometimes you meet someone and you think there's something there and you need someone to share stuff with and you lift the phone and … whatever.'

'That someone would be me?'

'Yes.'

'And you think I felt the same? When we met?'

'Yes.'

'Why?'

'Because we're still talking. Because you haven't told me to fuck off.'

'You think I'd do that?'

'I do, yes.'

'Good, because you're right.'

'You're telling me to fuck off?'

'No, Jimmy, I'm not. I'm telling you to sort out exactly what you're after in that lovely head of yours and then pay me the compliment of a decent conversation ...' she paused '... at a reasonable hour.'

'Like tomorrow?'

'Like when you start to make some kind of sense. I'm in bed, by the way. If that's important.'

The phone went dead. Suttle could hear Grace beginning to stir. Within seconds she was crying. Suttle brought her down and settled in the rocker again, trying to calm her.

It was gone eleven when Lizzie finally returned. She stood in the open doorway, framed against the chaos of the kitchen. Both the stew and the rice were cold.

Suttle asked her about the rowing.

'Fabulous evening.' Lizzie was grinning. 'The best.'

Six

D/I Carole Houghton was back from Brittany. She'd been enchanted by Saint-Malo but despite some promising intel she still hadn't found the head.

'So how's *Constantine*?'

Suttle brought her up to date. The Coroner's file was coming along nicely but he thought it a shame not to explore a new lead or two.

'Like?'

Suttle explained about the possibility that Kinsey might have had a gaming buddy.

'Where would that take us?'

'I've no idea, boss, until I bottom it out.'

'And you can do that?'

'Yes.'

It was a bold claim and he'd no idea whether Luke Golding could deliver, but *Constantine* was no longer a mission for the faint-hearted. With everything else falling apart around him, Suttle had decided to pile all his chips on a single square. Shit or bust wasn't a phrase he'd ever had much time for, but just now he told himself he didn't have an option. One way or another, something good had to come out of this new life of his.

'Then there's a couple of other developments.'

He told her about the Scenes of Crime find in Kinsey's

bedroom, the single blonde hair, and about Peggy Brims keeping watch on the lift. Houghton was even less impressed.

'He was a rich man, Jimmy. There's nothing wrong with buying a sex life if he needed it that badly. What's in it for us?'

'Here, boss.'

Suttle handed her the photos retrieved from Kinsey's iPhone. A very beautiful Thai girl was sprawled on Kinsey's bed doing something inventive with an empty bottle of Krug. The little wave with her spare hand was far from convincing.

'You're telling me she did it? She killed him?' Houghton was having a bad day. First the still-missing head. Now her newest D/S trying to turn a probable suicide into something wildly implausible.

'Not her, boss. Not the girl.'

'Who, then?'

'I've no idea. It's just part of the picture.'

'And you think the Coroner will be interested in this?'

'Probably not. But maybe we should.'

'Why?'

'Because Kinsey simply wasn't the kind of guy to top himself.'

'Says who?'

'Me. And pretty much everyone who knew him.'

'Have you talked to Mr Nandy about this?'

'Yeah.'

'And?'

'He doesn't agree. He thinks people are unknowable.'

'Maybe he's got a point.'

'Sure. And maybe he needs to save on the budget.'

There was a long silence. Suttle wondered whether he'd gone too far. Houghton was studying the photo again.

'She's not blonde.' She looked up. 'So maybe you ought to find someone else who is.'

*

Molly Doyle, it turned out, worked as a solicitor at a partnership in Exmouth town centre. In answer to Suttle's phone call, the Viking had freed up half an hour at lunchtime and was happy to help him in whatever way she could.

Suttle found her in an office at the top of the building. She was wearing a black suit, smartly cut. Her nails were carefully varnished and she'd applied a little make-up to hide the shadows beneath her eyes. The only concession to the woman Suttle had met on Sunday morning was a playful pair of black plastic earrings.

'You've heard about the little ceremony we're having for Kinsey?' She told him about the wreath and the escort of boats from the club. The weather forecast, she said, wasn't brilliant, but fingers crossed they'd be able to launch.

She fetched Suttle a coffee from the machine down the corridor. When she got back she wanted to know how he was getting on.

'Fine,' Suttle said.

'You've established what happened?'

'No, not entirely.'

He began to describe the steps they'd taken to understand the kind of life Kinsey had been leading. An obvious source was his iPhone.

'I know about all this. I used to be a criminal lawyer. We're talking intel, yes?' There was a hint of impatience in her voice. She was a busy woman.

Suttle asked about the emails Kinsey had been sending her. Seven in the past month alone, including Saturday night's invite to the party in his apartment.

'Seven?'

'You're surprised?'

'I am. I never kept count. I never answered them either. But you'd know that, wouldn't you?'

Suttle didn't respond. Scenes of Crime had sent him hard copy of all the texts Kinsey had sent her.

'"Loved the way you handled Andy on the beach tonight. When do we get to have another drink?"' he read. '"Bought a couple of pheasants this morning. My place or yours?"' Suttle looked up. 'Are you married, Mrs Doyle?'

'Why do you ask?'

'Because it might be germane.'

'Germane?' She rolled the word round her tongue. She seemed amused. 'You think all this has something to do with his death? You think my husband might have nipped along on Saturday night and chucked him off his balcony?'

Suttle held her gaze.

'Where was your husband on Saturday night?'

'In Hong Kong. He's a pilot with Cathay Pacific.'

'And you?'

'I was at home. With the kids.'

'Have you had any kind of relationship with Kinsey?'

'No.'

'But you *did* have a drink with him?' Suttle gestured at the texts.

'Yes. That was ages ago when we were sorting out the money for the boat he bought us. Kinsey insisted we did it over a drink. His idea, not mine.'

'And?'

'We got it nailed. I had an orange and soda –' her smile was cold '– if that's germane.'

'You've never been in his apartment?'

'Never. He was keen to get me up there but I always said no. If you want the truth, I think he was mad about tall women. Kinsey was a titch. Bedding people like me would make him feel better about himself.'

'So how did you fend him off?'

'I told him I had a punchy husband. And I told him I hated heights. In case you're wondering, neither's true.'

Suttle scribbled himself a note. Molly was watching him carefully.

'My husband and I are going through a trial separation,' she said. 'I'm telling you now because you're bound to find out one way or another but it makes no difference as far as Kinsey's concerned. Of course he pushed his luck. He was that kind of man. But the answer, I'm afraid, was always no.'

'Afraid?'

'If I was that desperate, there are nicer men around than Kinsey.'

'But you're not that desperate?'

'No.'

'So there's no one who might look at texts like these and draw the wrong conclusion?'

'No, Mr Suttle.' The smile again, even chillier. 'Only you.'

Lizzie spent the morning trying to put her thoughts down on paper. What began as a letter to Gill Reynolds quickly became a confessional Q & A to try and fix her bearings in what felt like a gathering storm. Was she still angry with Jimmy? Yes. Did she blame him for everything that had happened to her head since the move west from Pompey? Yes. Was she still determined to make some kind of change to this half-life of theirs? Again, yes. And had the rowing – Jimmy's idea – made any kind of difference?

At this point her faith in the brisk succession of affirmatives began to waver. Twenty-four hours ago, after a night of feeling more alone, more vulnerable, than she could ever have imagined, she'd been ready once again to scoop up Grace and leave. Now, after last night, she hadn't the first idea how she felt. Meeting a giant of a guy who'd lost his wife to the sea was the last thing she'd ever expected. Among the swamp of emotions he seemed to have unleashed – surprise, curiosity, plus a deep, deep sympathy – was something else. Excitement.

At every level, if she had it right, this man seemed to care about her. More importantly he seemed to understand exactly what she was feeling. After the pub he'd taken her to his place.

He lived in an upstairs flat at the back of Exmouth. He'd made her coffee and asked her to sort out a CD for the audio, and agreed that Neil Young could definitely turn a shit day into something altogether more mellow.

For the rest of the evening they'd sat on the sofa and he'd asked about her – who she really was, what she really wanted – and after a while she'd seen no point messing with the truth. She was living with a really sweet guy who was turning out to be different to the man she'd married. He had a job he loved. He adored the countryside. He was crazy about his daughter. But it hadn't occurred to him for a second that his wife was going nuts.

Until now, she said, that hadn't really mattered. Until now, she'd been able to cope. Just. But stuff was happening that she didn't want to talk about and she'd realised, maybe late in the day, that she was living with a stranger.

Pendrick had said very little. The lamp on the bookcase behind the sofa threw his face into deep shadow, hiding the scar, and it was hard to gauge exactly what he was making of this story of hers. When she finally stopped talking, feeling the first twinges of guilt, he drew her towards him and said he'd like to help. When she asked how, he said he didn't know. The most precious relationships, in his view, were based on conversation, on sharing, on those precious moments when a phrase or a memory or even an opinion proved you weren't entirely alone. Laughter mattered, he said. And so did the preparedness to take a risk or two.

'Like rowing the Atlantic?' she'd asked.

'No,' he'd said. 'Like this.'

She'd left shortly afterwards, kissed him in the darkness of the hall downstairs, thanked him for his patience. He'd walked her to the door, told her to take care on the drive home, given her his mobile number in case she wanted to talk more.

'There's more?' She'd been looking at him from the street.

And she'd loved the grin on his face. *He feels it too*, she'd told herself, driving home.

It was early afternoon before Suttle heard back from the Pier Head property developers. The voice on the phone introduced himself as one of the prime movers in the project and enquired as to the exact nature of Suttle's interest. Suttle explained about Kinsey and asked whether he'd had any kind of stake in the development.

'None at all, I'm afraid. It's way too early for anyone to be buying off-plan. I'm afraid Mr Kinsey isn't on our radar.'

Disappointed, Suttle thanked him for his time and struck the Pier Head development off the fast dwindling list of possible lines of enquiry. So far, he'd resisted the temptation to trawl through the local escort agencies in search of Thai lovelies, preferring to wait for sight of Kinsey's financial records. These days, unless they were married and had secrets to keep, most punters paid with their credit cards. On the point of trying Natasha Donovan again, Suttle looked up to find Luke Golding at his door.

'Sorry, Sarge. I got waylaid this morning. Houghton's fault.'

'Has she found the head yet?'

'No.'

Golding took a seat. Last night, he said, he'd stayed up until two in the morning in the hope that ShattAr might appear.

'And?'

'He did. 01.49. I sent him a message through Steam. Asked him for a link to his Facebook profile. Told him I was setting up an account of my own.'

'Did you get a reply?'

'No. But that means nothing.'

'So what do we do?'

'We wait, Sarge. And I get better at playing bastard Counter-strike.'

*

Minutes later Suttle phoned Natasha Donovan. According to her partner, Milo Symons, she should be back from a couple of days with friends in Bristol. When she picked up, Suttle had the impression she'd been asleep. Yes, she'd be happy to see him. Yes, she was at home. But just now, as soon as she'd got her shit together, she'd be out in the open air, trying to establish contact again.

'With who?'

'Come and see.'

'But how do I find you?'

'It's easy. You can't miss me.'

Intrigued, Suttle made a couple of calls to chase Kinsey's financial records then headed for the coast again. The lane to Tusker Farm was caked with mud from the big fat tractor ahead. The air smelled sweetly of dung. He turned in through the open gate and parked the Impreza beside the mobile home. A woman he assumed was Donovan was standing in the middle of the meadow. She was wearing something white and floaty. Her back was arched and her head was up and her splayed fingers were reaching for the sky. The fall of purple hair rippled in the wind from the valley below, and as Suttle drew closer her head came down and she folded her hands across her chest as she sank to her knees.

He paused beside her. Her feet were bare, dirtied with soil, and she wore a thin silver chain looped around one ankle.

'Natasha Donovan?'

For a moment she didn't move. A second later she opened her eyes and looked up at the proffered warrant card.

'Mr Policeman?' London accent. Appraising smile.

She led him to the mobile home. A newish black Toyota sports coupé was parked where the Transit van had been. Milo, she said, was away for the day. Come in.

Inside, the place had been warmed by the sunshine and the musky scent of incense hung in the stale air. Donovan filled the kettle. She was nearly as tall as her partner and she moved with an artful vagueness that, to Suttle, smacked of long practice. He wanted to ask her about the routine out in the field but she was already in full flow.

'You'll want to know about my journey,' she said. 'It begins with desire and it ends with embodiment. You start with simple movement. Then it gets more complex. The important thing is to *connect*. The body is a springboard. Once you understand that, anything is possible. You connect with nature. You connect with the clouds, the trees, the buttercups, the river, the wind. And most important of all you connect with yourself. It's circular, you see.'

'What is?'

'The journey.'

She threw him a look over her shoulder and reached for a couple of mugs. Her nails were the colour of her hair. She wanted to know whether Suttle was spiritual or not.

'I've never thought about it.'

His answer sparked a small, private smile. She decanted hot water into two mugs. She had loads of stuff on non-stylised body movement if he was interested.

Suttle shook his head. He was grateful for her time. As he'd explained on the phone, he was here to talk about Kinsey.

'Jake? He was lost. He could have gone so far if he'd only listened.'

'To who?'

'Me. Jake lived on the fault line between madness and something worse. You like that phrase? Fault line? That's Milo. Sometimes that man can be so fucking *deep*, you know what I mean?'

Suttle didn't. He was looking at the contents of the mug she'd just given him. Hot water.

'Do I get anything in this?'

'No. Hot water's a cleanser. It has properties you won't believe. I drink it neat. The hotter the better.'

Suttle put the mug to one side. Donovan had settled on the

sofa, her long legs folded beneath her. According to Eamonn Lenahan, this woman had really taken Kinsey's fancy and Suttle could believe it. She was probably the wrong side of forty but you'd never guess.

Suttle wanted her to tell him about Saturday. Had she gone to watch the race?

'No. I was doing a workshop with a friend. Movement and dance for the over-sixties. I hooked up with the guys later. Milo had texted me the result. Can you believe that? My lovely boys? *Winning?*'

By the time she got to the pub, she said, the crew were on their third bottle of champagne. She never touched alcohol herself.

'So what were you drinking?'

'Water.'

'And Kinsey?'

'The man was out of his head. And very happy.'

'Was that unusual?'

'Yeah.' She smiled. 'On both counts.'

They'd stayed in the pub for maybe another half an hour before deciding on a takeaway. The best Indian in Exmouth didn't do deliveries so she'd volunteered to drive into town and get the food. Kinsey, she said, had made a list. In the end the curry had been a big disappointment. Not that anyone was in the mood to complain.

'So how long were you in the apartment?'

'Not that long. Jake was ill, poor lamb. And the guys were knackered.'

'How did you get home?'

'By car. I was the only one sober so I drove. It's a little sports car – you probably saw it – just room for Milo and me. I called a taxi for the others.'

'What time did you get back?'

'I don't know. Past midnight but not that late.'

'And then?'

194

'We crashed. Milo was asleep in the car. Never marry an athlete.'

'You're married? You and Milo?'

'No.' The smile again. 'Marriage is a killer. Look at Jake.'

The phrase hung between them. *Marriage is a killer.*

'What exactly do you mean?' Suttle asked.

'I mean that marriage gets in the way. It stops life in its tracks. It makes you lazy. You stop trying.'

'Is that what happened to Kinsey?'

'Big time.' She nodded. 'Big time.'

'He talked to you about it?'

'Of course he did. It was hard to stop him sometimes. I don't know what he and that woman had to begin with, but marriage killed it. Stone dead.'

'That woman?'

'Sonya. He'd show me photos. She was really attractive. Great eyes. He couldn't understand how she'd changed. He couldn't understand what she'd *become.*'

'And you sympathised?'

'Not at all. I told him it was his own fault. Poor Jake never looked hard enough, never listened. He lived in a bubble, that man. He needed to get out more. He needed to *connect.*'

'You helped him that way?'

'Of course. We did sessions together, up in his apartment. It's all about vitality. It's all about awareness, about tapping into your hidden energy. I'd write simple movement scores, and when the weather was OK we'd go out on the balcony so we could reach for the river, for the beach, for the wind. Jake always found it hard to relax. He'd never close his eyes. I remember that.'

Suttle was trying to imagine Kinsey out on the balcony, showcasing this woman to the world at large, an image totally in keeping with everything else he knew about the man.

'Was he good at this stuff?'

'He was crap at it. Like I say, he could never relax. It was

always the next thing and the next thing with Jake. I'd tell him
to stop, to mark time, to slip his life into neutral and park it
for a while. That way he'd be able to give himself to something
bigger, something vaguer, something he didn't necessarily
understand, but I think that was beyond him.'

'You charged for these sessions?'

'Of course.'

'How much?'

'A hundred pounds a go.'

'That's a lot.'

'You're right. I normally charge forty. That was his price,
not mine.'

'And how often would this happen?'

'It depended. Sometimes twice a week, sometimes more
often. Other times he'd be away on business so we might just
meet for a Friday-night session.'

'And this went on for how long?'

'More than a year.'

'And he got better at it? He started to relax?'

'Never.'

'So why did he carry on?'

'Because he fancied me. It was obvious. He wanted to shag
the arse off me, and the only way he could do that was by
getting me up to that apartment of his. A hundred quid for an
hour of dance and movement? A girl could do a lot worse.'

'But was that enough for him? Dance and movement?'

'Of course not. Sometimes I shagged him as well.'

'For more money?'

'Yes.' She yawned.

'How much?'

'Five hundred quid a pop. He was crap in bed too. Five
minutes, tops.'

'That's a hundred quid a minute.'

'Yeah. I tried the oils and everything. I even brought candles
sometimes, but he wasn't interested. Sex was something he

needed. It had to be got out of the way. Then he felt better and he could move on to the next thing.'

'Which was?'

'Work. Always work. He was into property development. He tried to explain it to me one time, tried to get me interested, but I'm useless at all that stuff. Told him not to bother.'

Suttle looked up from his notes. He'd rarely stumbled on someone so recklessly candid. *Constantine*, at last, was beginning to pick up speed.

'Did Milo know about this?'

'Of course he did.'

'He didn't mind?'

'He thought it was funny.'

'*Funny?*'

'Yeah. He knew Jake like we all did, and if you want the truth I think he felt sorry for the man. What you have to understand about Milo is that the guy's a bunny, a child. What we have is brilliant. We fuck like angels. He knows that, and he knows I know it, and it makes him feel very good about everything. So when I come home and tell him about Kinsey, how hopeless the guy is, how rich he's making us, it just makes everything even better.'

'No jealousy?'

'None.'

'And Kinsey? Did it stop with dance and movement and the odd shag?'

For the first time Suttle caught a tiny hint of wariness in her face. She wanted to know exactly what he meant.

'I get the impression Kinsey wanted to own everything,' he said.

'Including me?'

'That's my question.'

'By taking me away from Milo? By moving me into his apartment? Some kind of trophy fuck?'

'Yes.'

'But why would I do that? When I've got Milo?'

'I've no idea. I'm just asking.'

She nodded. Then her head went down and she picked at a nail.

'You're right,' she said at last. 'But he knew there'd never be a way.'

'And Milo?'

'He knew too. Which is why he never even asked the question.'

She got to her feet. Her mug was empty. She needed more hot water. Suttle didn't move. He wanted to know about the film Kinsey was funding.

'That was for Milo.'

'I know. But it was you who got the money out of Kinsey.'

'That's true. He'd give me anything.'

'A two grand down payment and forty-five to come? Have I got that right?'

'Yeah. Jake was minted, though. That sort of money was nothing to him.'

'How do you know?'

'He told me. It was a little boast. He thought it might impress me.'

'And did it?'

'Never. A day with Milo is better than a lifetime with a man like that. He'd want to bang you up. He'd want to own you. I don't want to be owned. I want to be set free.'

'And Milo does that?'

'All the time. And you know something else? He's not even aware of how good he is. There's not an ounce of malice in that man. He's truly beautiful.'

She talked about the film they'd wanted to make and how excited Milo had been at the concept they'd both shaped. The spirit of the river. The ancient ghosts of long-dead Dutchmen haunting the Warren. And a love affair untainted by either time or circumstance.

'We shot a trial sequence. Milo called it a taster.'

'I've seen it. He showed me.'

'Us getting it on?'

'Yes.'

'What did you think?'

'Very impressive. Did Kinsey see it?'

'Yes. It was his idea. He'd read the script and when he asked for a taster we left the choice to him.'

'What did he say when he saw it?'

'He thought it was great. That's why he agreed to fund the rest of the movie. Did Milo tell you about that?'

'Yeah.'

'And the training stuff we're doing for the club?'

'No.'

'Come.'

She poured herself more hot water and led Suttle to Milo's PC. A couple of keystrokes took her into an editing programme. Suttle found himself looking at a bunch of people on a beach, mainly youngsters. They were listening to an older man in a grey tracksuit.

'This was stuff Milo shot yesterday. He's putting together a little movie for the club to help with fund-raising. That was the deal when Jake paid for the camera. You want to see Jake in the flesh?'

Suttle was staring at the screen. At the back of the group was a huge guy in a scruffy blue top. Beside him, dwarfed, was Lizzie. They seemed to be swapping glances. They seemed to be sharing a joke. He remembered the photo Houghton had been preparing to circulate, the mugshot she'd ripped from Kinsey's camera in the pub. On the PC this same face was partially obscured. He had to be sure.

'Who's that?' He touched the screen.

'The big guy?'

'Yeah.'

'His name's Pendrick. Awesome man. Everything Jake wasn't.'

Already she was running backwards through a blur of sequences. Finally she found what she was after.

Suttle bent to the PC. Another view of the same beach hung on the screen. A new-looking sea boat waited at the water's edge. Kinsey's crew were taking their seats, one by one. Suttle recognised the little guy steadying the bow as Lenahan. Big Andy Poole was already in the stroke seat. Pendrick was behind him. Then two other figures stepped into the frame. One of them was Donovan. The other, much smaller, had to be Kinsey.

He was first to the boat. He bent to adjust Donovan's seat, then helped her in. His body language spoke volumes. He was bossy, the authority figure, almost proprietorial. This was his boat, his crew, his woman. Once Donovan was safely seated, he clambered into the bow seat and threw an order over his shoulder at Lenahan, who was knee-deep in the water, holding the boat against the current. Lenahan stowed the rope among a press of life jackets, gave the bow a nudge and stepped into the cox's seat as Donovan and Kinsey eased the quad into the incoming tide. The quad paused a moment, then all four sets of blades were out and the boat was moving quickly upstream.

Kinsey rowed the way he seemed to do everything else. He was choppy, impatient, over-hasty, and as the camera panned the quad into the blaze of sunshine the blackness of the silhouette was unforgiving. Three sets of blades were in perfect harmony. Kinsey, the little guy in the bow, was always half a beat too early.

'Stick insect,' Suttle muttered.

'Too right. Even I'm better than he was.'

Suttle asked her to go back to yesterday's sequence. Donovan shot him a look.

'You won't find Kinsey there,' she said.

'I know. Just do it, please.'

They were on the beach again. The older guy in the tracksuit was walking back towards the slipway. As the camera panned left across the mill of young rowers, Suttle found himself watching his wife and Pendrick easing a two-seat rowing skiff into the water. The shot tightened as Lizzie made herself comfortable. She was laughing now as she leaned forward to tighten something that seemed to hold the blade in the gate. Then Pendrick knelt beside her in the shallows, talking her through some detail or other, and the camera settled on Lizzie's face as she tried to follow him. Suttle hadn't seen this expression for years. There was an eagerness, a hunger for what was coming next, and when the camera eased out again as Pendrick stepped into the bow seat Suttle caught the moment when she reached back to steady him.

'Who's that?' he asked.

'Pendrick. I just told you.'

'I meant the woman.'

'Fuck knows. I asked Milo that this morning. Apparently she's new, just moved into the area, lots of potential. The girls say she responds well to coaching, really quick on the uptake. Definitely does it for Pendrick too. Just look at the guy.'

The skiff was on the move now, silhouetted against the sun, exactly the same effect Milo had conjured for Kinsey's quad. The sheer bulk of Pendrick had wiped Lizzie from the shot and only her flailing oars were evidence that there was anybody else in the boat. The skiff was wobbling badly. The oars came to a halt. Then a cloud hid the sun and detail returned to the shot. Pendrick was leaning forward, his hand on Lizzie's shoulder, his mouth inches from her ear.

Suttle had seen enough. He'd wanted to ask Donovan about the word flux and whether or not she knew Peggy Brims, the woman who lived in the apartment beneath Kinsey, but he no longer saw the point. He gathered up his notes and told Donovan she'd have to attend the police station to read and sign a formal statement. He'd do his best to have it ready by midday tomorrow but clerical staff were under enormous pressure and he couldn't guarantee it.

Donovan was still looking at Milo's shots from yesterday. On the way out, Suttle paused by the door.

'You dye your hair that colour, right?'

'Of course.' She looked up at him, surprised.

'So what colour was it before?'

'Blonde.'

Pendrick phoned Lizzie in mid-afternoon. He'd just finished a rewiring job at a house in Woodbury and wondered whether she fancied a coffee.

'I'm at home,' she pointed out. 'With an infant daughter and no car.'

'You want me to drop round? No pressure.'

Lizzie thought about it for a split second.

'No.'

'Sure?'

'Yes.'

She could hear the disappointment in his voice but knew she had no choice.

'Don't go,' she said quickly. 'Talk to me.'

'About?'

'You could start with last night.'

'Last night was great. You know it was great. Except for the bloody rowing.'

'Bugger the rowing. That was my fault. I meant the rest of it.'

'The rest of it was what it was.'

'Meaning?'

'I'd love to see you again. Talk some more. Get one or two things straight.'

Lizzie giggled. She felt about twelve.

'Nice idea,' she said. 'Let's work on that.'

'How about tomorrow? There's a quad going up to Topsham.

One of the girls wants to be subbed on the way back. It's five miles. Could you cope with that?'

'No problem.' She was laughing now. 'The mood I'm in I could cope with anything.'

Suttle took his interview notes back to the MCIT offices at Middlemoor. D/I Carole Houghton, to his intense relief, was at her desk upstairs. The missing head had finally turned up in a Bodmin wood a couple of hundred metres from the rest of the body, a discovery that had done nothing for her respect for intel.

'This better be good,' she warned as Suttle eased himself into her spare chair.

He took her briefly through the bones of the interview. Tash Donovan had freely admitted having regular sex with Jake Kinsey. She claimed that her partner was cool with this arrangement but Symons hadn't mentioned it in interview. On the contrary, towards the end of their conversation he'd become visibly irritated at Suttle's suggestion that Kinsey might have had some kind of relationship with Tash.

'But he didn't, Jimmy. That's not how it happened. The way you're telling it they danced round together and did lots of hippy stuff and had sex from time to time. He was paying her for it. That's not a relationship. That's business.'

'Not to Symons. Not if you're crazy about the woman. Not if she's older than you and pretty much controls every aspect of your life. The way I see it, the guy's hugely vulnerable. We could nick Donovan for child abuse.'

Houghton laughed. But she still wasn't convinced.

'There's no way she'd have told you all that stuff if he didn't know too. She's putting it on the record before you get there first. That makes her clever, not guilty.'

'Wrong, boss.' Suttle wasn't having it. 'She wants me to believe that she and Symons have a great sex life. I'm in no position to know for sure, but I'll give her the benefit of the doubt. Let's say they get it on loads. Let's accept it's great for both of them. Let's even agree that Symons knows about the deal with Kinsey and is happy to rent out his partner for five hundred quid a pop.'

'It's her decision, Jimmy, not his.' The expression on Houghton's face might have been a smile.

'Sure. Fine. OK. But we're missing something, aren't we?'

'What?'

'Symons is a bloke. He knows about blokes. He knows how territorial they can get. More to the point, he knows Kinsey. And when it comes to territory, he knows that Kinsey has to be top dog. There isn't a lamp post he won't piss on. Including Tash Donovan.'

'That's unnecessary.'

'My apologies. But you see the logic? You see where this thing leads? Symons knows Kinsey can't help himself as far as Donovan's concerned. He knows the guy probably wants every bit of her, for keeps. They win their race. All the guys get pissed in the pub. They go back to Kinsey's apartment. Donovan's the only one still standing. After Kinsey's gone off to bed they all go home. Donovan and Symons are in their little car together. They have a monster row. Maybe Kinsey's said something out of turn. Maybe he's come on to Donovan in the apartment. Whatever. By the time they're back home, or tucked up in some little lay-by, it's got really nasty. Symons has had enough. He's going to sort this guy out. Bosh. Back he goes.'

'How does he get in?'

'She'll have a key. Bound to.'

'So she's part of this? She drives him back? Lends a hand? Gets rid of the guy who's keeping them afloat?'

'I've no idea, boss. All I know is that they're alibiing each other but they've got fuck all corroboration. Plus Symons isn't comfortable with what his partner's up to. All it takes is a night on the piss. That and a decent opportunity. From where I'm sitting, Symons had both.'

Houghton nodded. It was true that booze played a huge part in most murders.

'What about this film of his? Why would he want to kiss all that goodbye?'

'Because there was something else in his life that was even more important.'

'Donovan?'

'Of course. These people are off the planet most of the time, Symons especially. I'm not saying for a moment that his movie wasn't important. It was huge. But you know why? Because of her input. Because she made the running – the idea to begin with, getting the development money out of Kinsey, starring in their little movie trailer so Kinsey could perve over it, all of that was her. She's the driver, boss. She's in charge of this relationship. Without her, Symons would be nowhere. Fuck the movie. When Symons feels under threat, Donovan is what really matters.'

Houghton was silent. Suttle knew she sensed the logic in the case he was trying to make but he knew too that she was under the same cosh as Nandy. In every investigation you think court from the off. So where was the incontestable evidence to pin either of these people to Kinsey's death? First call in any murder lay with the Crown Prosecution Service. And so far, as Houghton pointed out, the CPS wouldn't waste a second on this horse shit.

'It's supposition, Jimmy. It's a nice little fairy tale. It's neat. It sounds more than plausible. But it's still supposition.'

'It's early days, boss. We're not through yet.'

'You mean *you're* not through yet.'

'Exactly. Help would be nice but I'm not complaining.'

'Remind me how long you've got on the Coroner's file.'

'Another week. Give or take.'

'And will that be enough?'

'Sure,' Suttle forced a grin. 'You're spoiling me.'

*

He phoned Gina Hamilton when he got back downstairs. The office was still empty. He could tell at once that she'd been expecting his call.

'How about an early drink?' he said.

'How about supper?'

'Where?'

'My place if you don't mind pasta.'

'I love pasta.'

She gave him a postcode and a street number. He'd never been to Modbury in his life.

'What time?'

'You say.'

Suttle checked his watch. 17.12. He still had a number of calls to make and the rush-hour traffic on the A38 could be brutal.

'Seven o'clock?'

'Perfect. If you're late don't even bother knocking.'

She rang off, leaving Suttle gazing at the phone. He knew he should be calling Lizzie. He knew, at the very least, he should give himself some kind of cover. A couple of late interviews. A squad meet he couldn't afford to miss. But then he was back in front of Symons' PC, watching Lizzie and Pendrick hauling the skiff away from the beach, and he knew he couldn't be bothered. A moment later the office door opened and he found himself looking at the Office Manager. Leslie had taken a call earlier. It was personal for Jimmy and it sounded urgent.

'She wouldn't leave a name but she wants you to bell her,' she laid a number on Suttle's desk. 'It's a Portsmouth number. I checked.'

Pendrick called again as Lizzie was trying to wrestle Grace upstairs for a bath. Thinking it was Jimmy, she hesitated a moment then decided to ignore it, but when it rang a second time she returned downstairs.

Pendrick apologised for phoning so late. He hoped it wasn't a problem.

'It's not. Did you phone just now?'

'Yes. Tomorrow's off. We've got a big front coming in and there's no way we'll be going to Topsham.'

'Oh ...' Lizzie tried to mask her disappointment. 'Never mind.'

'I had another idea.'

'Does it involve rowing?'

'Sadly not.'

'Thank Christ for that.'

Pendrick laughed. He was planning a trip to the north coast. Wondered if she'd like to come along.

'The north coast of where?'

'Cornwall. Just a place I think you might like.'

'Is Grace invited?'

'No.'

'At least you're honest.' It was her turn to laugh.

There was a moment of silence. Lizzie could hear a car approaching up the lane. She very much wanted it not to be Jimmy. The car went past.

'What time?' she said. 'And where?'

Suttle made the call from a lay-by on the A38. As he expected, the number belonged to Marie Mackenzie.

'I've made some inquiries,' she said. 'I don't know why I bothered but there it is.'

'And?'

'It turns out there's very little I can do. Your friend Winter has made some serious enemies. These people aren't as stupid as you might think.'

'I never thought for a moment they were.'

'Then this won't come as a surprise.'

'What?'

He listened intently for the best part of a minute, doing his best to shield the phone from the thunder of the passing traffic. Finally, at her prompting, he reached for a pen. In the absence of anything else, he wrote the number on the back of his hand. Pompey again.

'And you really think they'll leave Lizzie and Grace alone?'

'Yes. As long as you make the call.'

'I have your word on that?'

'It's not my word you need. It's theirs. Make the call. That's my advice. Everything else is down to you.'

Modbury was a small town cupped by rolling green hills south of the A38. Gina Hamilton's house lay in a small estate of newbuilds. Suttle had looked at similar developments in Exeter last year when he was searching for somewhere they could live and knew he'd die in a house like this. Tiny windows. Tiny rooms. And a scrap of threadbare turf instead of a garden.

Hamilton's Golf was parked outside, the tailgate open. The front door to the house was open as well and she stepped into the sunshine as Suttle approached.

'I just got back myself,' she said. 'Give me a hand?'

Suttle helped her carry shopping and a couple of tins of paint into the kitchen. She'd been to Sainsbury and B&Q on the way home. Lots of stuff for the freezer and four bottles of Australian Chardonnay. Suttle gave her a bottle of red he'd picked up on the way over. The galley kitchen was spotless. A wine rack beside the fridge badly needed restocking and there was a National Trust calendar on the wall above a bowl of fruit. April featured a drift of purple crocuses at Lacock Abbey.

'What are the green ticks?' Suttle was still looking at the calendar.

'I go running. The green ticks make me feel virtuous. Anything else you want to know about my social life?'

Suttle looked harder. Not much seemed to have happened over the last fortnight.

'You find the Job knackers you?'

'Yeah. But for the wrong reasons.'

She shot him a look but wouldn't take the conversation further. She nodded at the vegetable basket beneath the work surface and asked him to sort out an onion and some garlic. Tomato paste in the fridge. Olive oil in the cupboard. She also fancied something to drink.

Suttle was looking at the remaining bottles of wine. The red he'd bought had been on offer, a South African Merlot that Lizzie adored.

'You've got a corkscrew?'

'Silly question. Drawer on the left.'

They sat down to eat half an hour or so later. The lounge diner extended the full depth of the house: magnolia walls, a big plasma TV and a line of stuffed animals carefully arranged on the Ikea sofa. This house, Suttle thought, might have belonged to Kinsey. No clutter. None of the chaos of normal life. No photos of family or friends. Just somewhere to crash after yet another day among the performance reviews.

Suttle poured more wine and asked how long she'd been in Modbury.

'Just over a year. John and I went our separate ways and this was all I could afford. We used to have a place in Tavistock. It was sweet.'

'John?'

'My husband. He was a D/C on the drugs squad. The best. The very best. And that's not just my opinion.'

She'd met him, she said, on the operation that had taken her to Pompey five years ago. He'd been driving the intel and she'd fancied him from the off. He was an older man, a grizzly bear of a guy, rock solid. The drugs operation had won her a commendation from the Chief, plus lots of media exposure, and she and John had got married within months.

'That job was a real result,' she said. 'One of those moments when you think you're immortal.'

Suttle nodded, telling her he'd been through something similar himself back in Pompey. He explained about the u/c operation to pot Bazza Mackenzie and all the plaudits that had followed. This guy had dicked them around for years and it was sweet to have finally nailed him.

'Literally?'

'Yeah. It got heavy at the end and the ninjas had to take him out. Incredible evening. He ended up in a shop full of snakes he happened to own. He was about to do something evil to the key informant and we had no choice. Bam-bam. You're right. After that you feel you can do anything.'

'And afterwards?'

'Afterwards I came down here.'

'Good move?'

'The best.'

'You mean that?'

'I do, yeah. But it's not just about me, is it?'

There was a silence. Then Hamilton asked him whether he wanted to talk about it. Suttle told her about finding the cottage, about moving the family down, about living with a woman who couldn't wait to take her life in another direction.

'Why?'

'Because living in the country drives her nuts.'

'You still love her?'

'I do, yes.'

'Then sort it out.'

'I can't. I try and I can't. It just doesn't work.'

'Why not?'

'Because she's become someone different, a different person. Because everything's different. Have you ever had kids?'

'No.'

'They don't help. We've got a daughter. She's lovely. I adore her. But she doesn't help.'

'That's harsh.'

'But it's true, believe me. If there's something wrong in a

relationship, if something's not working, a child makes everything worse.'

Hamilton nodded and reached for the bottle. Her third glass. When she offered Suttle a refill, he shook his head. He wanted to know more about Hamilton's marriage.

'That didn't work either.'

'Why not?'

'Because I couldn't let go of the Job. I'm good. I know I'm good. I'm ambitious too. It's not going to end with D/I, not if I have anything to do with it, but these days that kind of pressure eats you up. You have to watch your back all the time. You have to make the right friends in the right places, walk the walk, talk the talk, make sure there's nothing in your in-tray that's going to come back and bite you in the arse. At the end of every day you're wasted. And since you've asked, there's another problem too.'

'What's that?'

'I'm two people. At work I'm Ms Efficient. Ms Gimme. Ms Sort It. But you know something? It's all pretend. I do pretend brilliantly. Pretend decisive. Pretend organised. Pretend savvy. People look at me and think wow, that woman's got it cracked. But you want to know the truth?' She touched her chest. 'In here it's all mush. I haven't got a clue what's going on. It's horrible. Just horrible. Some days I think I'm going mad.'

'And John? Your husband?'

'He saw right through it. He understood. He tried to make me get a grip, do something about myself, take the Job less seriously, but I never could. He'd got the Job totally sussed. He knew exactly what he was good at and he knew exactly where to draw the line. I don't do lines. Which is why the marriage turned to rat shit. John gave up in the end and I don't blame him. You're right. You become strangers to each other. And after that you're dead in the water.'

In the end, she said, John applied for a job in another force.

She knew that it had been for her sake more than his and the gesture had touched her deeply.

'Where's he gone?'

'Dorset. He works out of Bournemouth. They're lucky to have him.'

'You're divorced?'

'Yes.'

'But you still talk?'

'Yes. Occasionally.'

'And that's OK?'

'It's weird. It's like we were never married in the first place. You know my theory? We've all got a default setting and no matter what you do it'll always reset.'

'So what's yours?'

'Don't go there.'

She went into the kitchen to fetch another bottle of wine. Suttle was looking at the stuffed animals on the sofa. The biggest, the elephant, was pink.

Hamilton had appeared at the kitchen door.

'Red or white?'

'You choose. I'm driving.'

'Yeah?' She lingered a moment, then disappeared again. Suttle heard the pop of the cork. When she came back, Suttle asked her about the running.

'You really want to know?'

'Yeah.'

'That was another drama. There's a bunch of local joggers here and I joined up. They go out a couple of nights a week, decent distances, nice enough people I thought at first, but then some of the guys turned out to be pretty gross. We'd go to the pub afterwards and they'd find out you were living alone and after that they just wanted to get into your knickers. It wasn't anything personal. They were all happily married, or that's what they'd tell you, but then they'd come on to me like it was some kind of favour. It was so blatant. They assumed I couldn't wait to get fucked. Like I say. Totally gross.'

In the end, she said, she'd abandoned the group outings and started running by herself. She had a handful of favourite circuits and lately she'd been wondering about getting a dog for company when winter came and the nights drew in. Either way she felt the exercise was keeping her half sane but there were moments when she doubted even that.

'It's really hard to explain. Some nights when I go out I take me with me. Then other nights I'm running with a total stranger. Does that make sense? Is that *normal*?'

Suttle laughed. Mercifully, he always excused himself serious exercise. He asked to use the loo. She directed him upstairs. Afterwards, drying his hands, Suttle could hear the clatter of plates in the kitchen. Her bedroom lay across the tiny landing at the top of the stairs. The door was open and he could see a pair of running shoes abandoned on the carpet. He stepped inside. The bed was turned down. A Tiffany-style lamp on the bedside table cast a soft light across the whiteness of the sheet. There were more stuffed animals on the duvet, partly covered by a powder-blue towelling gown. Over the bed, hanging on the wall, a framed poster of Amy Winehouse.

Back downstairs, Suttle found himself looking at a plate of blueberries. His hunger had gone but he accepted a spoonful of cream.

'You're big on Amy Winehouse?'

Hamilton was pouring herself another glass of wine. Nearly a bottle so far, thought Suttle.

'You've been in my bedroom.' It was a statement, not a question.

'Yes.'

'Why?'

'I'm curious.'

'About what?'

'About you. About this ...' He gestured around.

She nodded, sipped the wine.

'Are we talking intel here? Or something else?'

'You tell me.'

'You think your luck's in? You fancy a quickie before you go?'

Suttle didn't answer. She was drunk now, something that probably happened night after night, and he sensed her neediness. He very definitely didn't want to hurt her but he understood all too clearly where this might lead.

He reached out and took her hand.

'I'm glad I came,' he said.

'Why?'

'Because I needed to talk.'

'Great. Happy to oblige.' She held his gaze for a long moment, then nodded down at the number scrawled on the back of his hand. 'That's a Portsmouth code. You want to tell me more?'

Suttle shook his head. He had to go. The meal had been great. Maybe they could meet again, his shout next time.

She looked at him, saying nothing, then her eyes went to the bottle and she lifted an enquiring eyebrow.

'No,' he said. 'But thanks for the offer.'

She accompanied him to the front door. He was reaching for the latch when he felt her hand on his arm

'There's something I meant to tell you,' she said, 'about Pendrick.'

'What's that?'

'It turns out he kept half of the insurance settlement. That's three hundred grand.'

'How do you know?'

'I checked on the charity's website.' She offered him a weary smile. 'That's what detectives do, isn't it? You get that for free, by the way.'

Suttle nodded, then opened the door. 'I'll be in touch, yeah?'

'Yeah?'

They both stepped out into the night air. Suttle held her for a moment. She was shivering in the cold. He kissed her briefly, thanked her again for the pasta and headed for the garden gate. The car door unlocked, he turned to wave goodbye but she'd gone.

Suttle was pushing 90 mph on the outside lane of the A38 when, too late, he saw the police car tucked into a lay-by. The road was empty. He throttled back and hoped to God they hadn't tracked him with the radar gun. The patrol car had already pulled out and was accelerating hard. Then came the flashing blue light and Suttle knew they were going to give him a tug.

He was in the slow lane now, still decelerating, trying to play the good citizen. On his side of the carriageway he was the only vehicle for at least half a mile. He had to be the target. Had to be.

The patrol car was beside him now, the pale face in the passenger seat checking him out. He signalled Suttle to pull over. The next lay-by was a couple of hundred metres ahead. At a steady 40 mph, Suttle was trying to work out exactly how many glasses of wine he'd had. Two? Three? Getting pulled for speeding was one thing. Failing the breathalyser would land him with a driving ban, a disciplinary charge and possible suspension. Without a licence, the Job and life in general would become a nightmare. Not good.

The patrol car followed him into the lay-by. Both officers got out and approached the Impreza. The guy in the passenger seat squatted beside Suttle's door. The wind had got up and rain pebbled on his hi-vis jacket.

'Do you have your licence, sir? May I see it?'

Suttle produced his licence. The patrol officer scanned it quickly and handed it back. He was in his mid-forties. He looked unforgiving.

'Where have you come from, sir?'

'Modbury.'

'And you're going to ...?'

'Home. Colaton Raleigh.'

'Are you aware that you were exceeding the speed limit just now?'

'Yeah.'

The patrol officer nodded. He'd caught the sour taint of alcohol on Suttle's breath. Then his eyes strayed to the dash-board where Suttle had left a pass for the MCIT car park at Middlemoor.

'In the Job, are you, sir?'

'Yeah.'

'CID?'

'Yeah.'

'Have you been drinking by any chance, sir?'

'Yeah.'

'Well, well ...' The beginnings of a smile ghosted across the big face. Uniforms liked nothing better than nailing pissed detectives.

'Out of the car if you please, sir.'

Suttle did what he was told. The officer read him the caution and warned him that he faced arrest if he failed a breathalyser test. The rain was heavier now and Suttle was soaking in seconds but he didn't much care. One way or another, the next minute or so might decide the fate of his entire career.

The officer had returned to the patrol car to fetch the breath-alyser. Suttle waited in the rain, wondering whether he should – after all – have stayed at Gina Hamilton's place. Then he put the thought out of his mind. What will be will be. Fuck it.

The officer returned with the breathalyser. Suttle blew into the tube. The PC watched the figures on the readout climb and climb. His mate had joined him by now. Their backs were turned and Suttle caught a mumbled exchange before the officer was back in his face. The reading was just short of the figure that would haul him back to the nick for a blood test and a great deal of paperwork.

'Who's a lucky boy then?' He didn't bother to hide his disappointment. 'Would you step this way, sir?'

Suttle sat in the patrol car while the PC wrote up his details for the speeding offence. Ninety-two mph would probably earn him a three-point deduction and a biggish fine. The deduction was no problem, and though the fine was a pain in the arse it was nothing compared to what might have happened.

Swamped with relief, Suttle closed his eyes and let his head sink back against the restraint. When the officer asked him whether he had anything to say with regard to his excess speed, he said he wanted to get home. The officer turned and shot him a look.

'Little woman waiting up is she, sir?'

Suttle held his gaze and then shut his eyes again.

'I doubt it,' he said.

He was wrong. Lizzie was downstairs nursing a glass of red wine. Dexter was curled on her lap, ignoring the remains of a fish pie beside the chair.

She looked up as Suttle came in from the kitchen. His hair was plastered against the whiteness of his skull and the rain had darkened his suit.

Lizzie studied him a moment. The cat didn't stir.

'Should I ask where you've been?' she said.

'Sure. Why not?'

Suttle told her about his drive out to Modbury. A D/I called Gina Hamilton lived there.

'Alone?'

'Yes.'

'Business or pleasure?'

'Bit of both.'

'Nice evening?'

'Not bad. I got stopped on the way back.'

He told her about the traffic car and the breathalyser.

'And?'

'I passed.'

'Not too pissed then? To come home?'

Suttle knew exactly what lay behind the remarks and ignored them. Lizzie, in the parlance, was after the full account. What was this woman like? How come they'd met at her house? Why hadn't he phoned her earlier? What was so important it couldn't be done in office hours?

Suttle fetched a towel from upstairs. He'd never lied to Lizzie, and now wasn't the time to start. He dried his hair as best he could and hung his jacket over the back of the kitchen door.

'What do you fancy tomorrow?' he said. 'I thought we might go into Exeter. There's a festival thing on.'

'I'm sorry, I can't.'

'Why not?'

Lizzie explained about a call she'd taken from one of the girls at the rowing club. After the wreath tribute on Sunday the crews were returning to the compound for a naming ceremony. The newest boat was to be called the *Jake Kinsey* after the guy who'd so generously signed the cheque. With luck, the media might use it as a photo opportunity.

'Tomorrow's Saturday,' Suttle pointed out.

'I know. We have to sort the compound out. Make it look half decent. A bunch of us are meeting at ten. I couldn't say no.'

'And that takes all day?'

'I've no idea. Judging by the state of the place, it might well do.'

Suttle studied her for a moment, loosening his tie.

'And Sunday?'

'We've got the tribute thing. I have to go, Jimmy. There's no way I can't.'

'OK.' Suttle shrugged. 'Whatever ...'

He turned away, trying to mask his anger, but she knew him too well to be fooled.

'It was your idea, Jimmy.'

'What?'

'The rowing club.'

'You're right. So it's me and Grace then. All weekend.'

'I'm afraid so.' She still hadn't moved. 'Welcome to my little world.'

Seven

Lizzie was out of the cottage by nine o'clock. Suttle was still in bed with Grace, celebrating last night's escape with a lie-in. In truth, he'd no idea where Lizzie was really going but supposed the compound clean-up was at least semi-plausible. Whatever happened, he was certain that Pendrick would be around. Time and again he tried to fight off the image of his wife and one of Kinsey's star rowers on the beach. He'd seen the grin on Lizzie's face. He knew exactly what it meant.

She'd been that way with him once, playful and reckless, happy to surrender to something new and faintly exotic in her life. Suttle was a cop. She'd never fucked a cop before. More to the point, she really fancied him. That's what had taken them to bed the first time and all the times after that, and when he'd recognised there was something really substantial there, something important, the knowledge had been all the sweeter because the laughter and the often brilliant sex had never stopped. Even pregnancy and motherhood hadn't diminished her appetite for that raw enjoyment of each other, and it was only after the move west that married life had begun to seize up. They'd almost stopped talking. They'd definitely stopped laughing. And even the prospect of sex had become strangely awkward, something best avoided in case it sparked a row.

Suttle waited until the burble of the Impreza had disappeared down the lane. The temptation was to have a prowl around the bedroom in case Lizzie had left her mobile. Maybe she'd added Pendrick to her contacts file. Maybe they'd been texting each other. Maybe the other contents of her bag might yield a clue or two. He eyed the scatter of clothes she'd left beneath the window, wondering whether he really wanted to treat his own bedroom as some kind of crime scene, then decided against it. Grace, he knew, would be hungry. Thank God for someone else in his life.

Downstairs, he strapped Grace into her high chair in front of the TV while he went into the kitchen. Lizzie had forgotten to get the puréed banana out of the fridge so he put a saucepan of water on the stove to warm it up. Next door he could hear Grace kicking her legs in time to Horrid Henry. Even with the crap reception, the TV seemed to have become a permanent guest in the house, masking the never-ending drips that penetrated the silence.

Suttle went out onto the patio and put a call through to the Pompey number Marie had given him. The rain had cleared overnight and there was a clarity and brightness to the sunshine that lifted his spirits.

The number answered at once. Pompey accent again but a different voice.

'I know you,' Suttle said.

'You do, son. You do.'

'Dave Fallon.'

'The same.'

Dave Fallon was an ex-6.57 who now ran one of Pompey's biggest cab companies. He'd always been a special favourite of Mackenzie's, a trusted lieutenant in the legendary Millwall rucks in the late 80s and a tactician of genius when it came to laying siege to some of the tastier away firms. Fallon affected a gruff Pompey swagger that led people to dismiss him as a mush, but Suttle had never been fooled. Mackenzie, he knew, had rated Fallon as one of the city's top businessmen.

'We need to meet, son,' Fallon said.

'Why?'

'There's no way I'm going into this on the phone. It has to be Monday night. You decide where.'

Suttle gave the proposition some thought. He didn't want to go back to Pompey again. Not yet.

'How about halfway?' he said. 'I'm in Devon.'

'Wherever, mush. Your call. Have a think and bell me back, yeah?'

The phone went dead. Suttle checked on Grace then stepped back into the sunshine. Gina Hamilton was slower to pick up.

'You,' she said.

'Me,' Suttle agreed.

'Get home OK?'

'No.'

When he told her about the patrol car she laughed.

'Your own fault,' she said. 'You should have stayed.'

She'd decided to turn the memory of last night into a joke, Suttle thought. Better that than more angst.

'I need a favour,' he said.

'Another one?'

'I'm serious.'

'So was I.'

'Your husband ...'

'John?'

'Yeah. You told me he was in Bournemouth. If I asked nicely, would he mind my back on Monday night?'

'I've no idea.' She was laughing again. 'I'll give you his number and you can ask him yourself. Send him my best, eh?'

It was still early when Lizzie got to the rowing club. Tessa was already there with a couple of the other girls and they'd wheeled out the heavy boats prior to attacking the tangle of weeds that threatened to engulf the corners of the compound. A young guy Lizzie had never met was trying to coax some life out of a strimmer while a bunch of juniors lounged on the wooden steps of the Portakabin, enjoying the sunshine.

Over the next hour or so more rowers turned up to lend a hand to sort out the Portakabin, and by late morning the job was done. Tessa took Lizzie to one side. She'd broached an idea to the club captain about tomorrow's tribute on the water and he'd given it the thumbs up.

With the exception of the newest quad, the Kinsey boat, the club's entire fleet would be holding station off the dock. Upstream, meanwhile, the new quad would be waiting with Kinsey's crew aboard. The moment the wreath hit the water they'd scull downstream at racing speed, carving a path through the fleet. Kinsey had been forty-one when he died. Once the quad passed the wreath, they'd put in another forty-one strokes before drifting to a halt and waiting for the rest of the fleet to catch them up. This little piece of maritime theatre, in Tessa's view, would provide a focus for the cameras, the press, and however many spectators chose to turn up.

'Great.' Lizzie was wondering what this had to do with her.

'It's a question of the crew. Kinsey's obviously no longer with us and Tom Pendrick's decided he doesn't want to do it.'

'Why?'

'I've no idea. Ask him.'

Tash Donovan, she said, had agreed to stand in for Pendrick, which left one empty seat at bow.

'So who have you got?'

'You.'

'*Me?*'

'Yeah. Clive and I agreed that we needed the newest recruit in bow. Clive thinks it's symbolic, a vote of faith in the future. It's a nice line for the press too.' Clive Knightly was the club captain.

'But I'm a novice,' Lizzie pointed out.

'That's exactly the point.'

'Racing speed? Are you serious?'

223

'You'll pick it up. Clive's impressed already. We all are.'

'Did you see me in the double the other night?'

'We did. We think you had other things on your mind.'

'Like?'

Tessa shot her a look. 'You think we're blind?'

Lizzie felt herself blushing. This was juvenile, she told herself. She began to protest again, telling Tessa the whole thing was out of the question, that she'd never hack something like that in front of other people, the whole club for God's sake, but Tessa was adamant. The Kinsey crew would be on the water at least an hour before the ceremony. Racing starts were a piece of cake. All Lizzie needed was practice.

'You should be flattered,' she added. 'This is as big as it gets in Exmouth.'

Pendrick turned up minutes later. He was driving a yellow VW van and bumped it onto the pavement on the seafront. Lizzie checked her watch. On the phone they'd agreed midday. It was two minutes past.

Pendrick leaned across and opened the passenger door. He was wearing jeans and a bleached-out T-shirt with a skull on the front.

'You look like a biker,' she said. 'Where are we going?'

'Cornwall.' He was looking down the cut towards the club compound. 'Mystery tour.'

On the way out of Exmouth the weekend traffic was heavy. Lizzie had sneaked a look at the back of the van. Among the clutter of wetsuits and surfboards was a full-size blow-up air-bed and a couple of sleeping bags.

'You kip in here?'

'When I have to, yeah.'

'Cosy?'

'Always.'

She told him about the addition to tomorrow's ceremony. When she asked why he wouldn't be rowing himself he just shook his head.

'What does that mean?'

'It means I've got better things to do. This tribute thing's a joke. Everyone hated the guy. All he had was money. Does that justify all this bollocks?'

'But it's not about him. Not the way I've been told. The club needs the publicity.'

'Why?'

'To bring in new members. To bring in money. Isn't that what it's all about? Profile? Presence?'

'Sure. You're right.' He glanced across, gave her hand a squeeze. 'Maybe I'll help with the safety boat. Just in case you go overboard.'

'Is that in the script?'

'Christ knows.' He glanced at his watch. 'What time do you need to be back?'

Suttle took Grace on a tour of the village, mainly because she was beginning to drive him nuts. She was fretful and upset and whatever he did, however he tried to comfort her, nothing seemed to work. She'd stagger round the sitting room, banging into the furniture, yelling for her mummy, totally inconsolable, and in the end he strapped her in the buggy and set off down the road. Within a minute or so, probably exhausted, she'd fallen asleep.

A tour of Colaton Raleigh was a novelty for Suttle. He crossed the main road down by the store and kept walking. A line of cheerless bungalows led to the church. Beyond the church the road petered out. He lifted the buggy and carried it across a cattle grid. A path led towards the river. The meadows, dotted with cows, were boggy underfoot after the rain and the river itself was the colour of peat. He'd remembered to bring the remains of a stale loaf and he stood on the riverbank, wondering whether or not to wake Grace up. There were ducklings on the river, in line astern behind their mum, and he knew Grace would adore them, but in the end he opted for the rare moment of peace. On the way home, after a brief expedition to the village play-park, she was howling again.

The cottage, after the brightness of the sunshine, felt damp and airless. Suttle opened the windows and put the TV back on. He'd no idea whether Grace had any interest in rugby league but he thought it was worth a try. To his relief, it seemed to do the trick. She sat on his lap, peering at the screen, following the players with her tiny finger. After a while he settled her on the floor in front of the TV and went into the kitchen to sort her out something for lunch. He found a jar of mashed apricots in the fridge and cut up another banana to go with it. Grace gobbled up the fruit with evident relish, losing interest in the rugby.

'You want to come outside? In the sunshine? Help Daddy sort the garden?'

She seemed to nod. Suttle carried the playpen outside and filled it with a small army of cuddly toys. The sight of Grace nursing a stuffed giraffe stirred memories of last night, and he found himself wondering whether Gina Hamilton had ended up preferring the company of stuffed animals to the complications of a proper relationship. Maybe that's what lies in wait for us all, he thought. At least the animals never betray you.

Trezillion turned out to be a perfect cove nestling between two headlands west of Padstow. The tide was out and the blueness of the water stretched unbroken to the far horizon. Gulls were prowling among the hummocks of seaweed on the beach and a lone cormorant was patrolling the creamy froth at the water's edge. It was a magical place, Lizzie thought. No wonder Pendrick had always treasured it.

Out of the wind, among the stands of marram grass on the dunes, it was warm enough to sit in the sunshine. They'd detoured through the outskirts of Camelford and Pendrick had shown her the council house where he'd grown up. Kate, he said, had come off the same estate. They'd gone to school together, learned how to get drunk together, and later – both mad about the rave culture – they'd hitchhiked up-country for festival after festival.

By now they'd both become hard-core surfers, and when the winds were right and a big Atlantic depression brought the heavy ocean swells rolling in, there was no better place to be than Trezillion. It wasn't to everyone's taste. A heavy break on the far side of the cove was tricky to get right and the shape of the bottom at certain states of the tide didn't leave much room for beginners, but the sheer intimacy of the place made it one of Cornwall's best-kept secrets.

'Which I guess is what turned the little bastard on.'

A brown envelope lay between them on the blanket he'd brought from the van. Lizzie had been intrigued by its contents since she'd spotted it on the dashboard. Pendrick extracted a glossy-looking brochure and handed it across. They'd bought tins of Guinness and a cooked chicken from a Spar store on the Camelford estate. Lizzie licked the grease from her fingers and picked the brochure up.

'Right here.' Pendrick gestured at the photo on the front of the brochure. 'That's where he wanted to build. That's the view you'd get. Exactly here.'

Lizzie checked the photo against the real thing. He was right. For £899K you could buy this view for the rest of your life.

'And it's going to happen?'

'No one knows. Kinsey was the driving force, but he's got a partner up north somewhere, and these days it's all about property development. If the sums stack up, if there's a profit to be had, my guess is he'll make it happen.'

'But it's protected, surely. National Trust? RSPB? All that?'

'Big deal. Money talks round here. Cornwall's on the bones of its arse. It's fine if you're minted like Kinsey was. He's pitching to people like himself, people with London property, zillions in the bank, not a clue what to do with it. Kinsey made it easy for them. You get the view. You get peace of mind, 24/7 security, high-end catering, like-minded neighbours, the whole deal. He sells this dog wank to the local planners, promises them a couple of memorial benches or a playground or whatever they want, and the rest is conversation. Thank you, Mr Kinsey. We're grateful, Mr Kinsey. Just sign here, Mr Kinsey, and bung us a few quid to keep the punters happy.'

'Punters?'

'Us.'

Lizzie looked away, surprised by the venom in Pendrick's voice. He really feels it, she told herself. And why not? He grew up here. He fell in love here. He's carried this view to the other side of the planet and he still treasures it. Except it appears to be doomed, tucked into a developer's swag bag and sold to a bunch of rich cardigans for silly money.

She took another pull at the Guinness, leaning against Pendrick, letting her head fall against his shoulder. She felt him stiffen, then relax again.

'So what do you do about it?' she asked.

'You fight it whatever way you can. Not just me, dozens of other guys, hundreds of them. But you know what? We don't have a prayer, none of us, because the whole fucking thing is a game and whoever dreams up the rules gets to win. This country's fucked, Lizzie. You heard it here first.'

'So what do you do about it?' she asked again. Second time round it seemed an even saner question.

He didn't answer. Instead he picked up the brochure and began to leaf through. His fingers left grease marks over the architect's impression of life at Trezillion Oceanside. Finally, he tossed it aside. He was gazing out to sea.

'Do you ever dream of sailing away?' he said.

'Yes. Since you ask.'

'I'm serious.'

'I'm sure you are.' She reached up for him, kissed the stubble on his cheek. 'So how would you do it?'

'I'd buy a yacht. Something that would get me anywhere. I

did the nav stuff for the crossing with Kate. I'd need hands-on experience but that wouldn't be a problem.' He was looking down at her. 'How does that sound?'

Lizzie was stroking his arm.

'It sounds great,' she said. 'What would you do for money?'

'I've got money.'

'Enough?'

'Yeah. Money wouldn't be a problem.' He was lying full length now, his head propped on one arm. 'So what do you think?'

'I think it's brilliant. I think you should do it. Unless ...'

'Unless what?'

'Unless you want to buy one of these.' She nodded at the brochure.

He gazed at her blankly. 'Why would I do that?'

'It's a joke, Tom. Of course you wouldn't do that.'

He looked at her a moment longer, still uncertain, then forced a laugh before popping another tinnie. He took a couple of swallows and then wiped his mouth with the back of his hand.

'How about you?'

'How about me what?'

'Would you fancy it?'

'I'm married. I've got a little girl. I think I mentioned her.'

'She could come too.'

'That's kind.'

'I mean it.'

'Yeah? Do you? Do you really?'

She put her tinnie down and cupped his face in her hands. There was something new in his eyes and it took her a moment or two to realise what it was. Alarm.

'Does this bother you?' Her fingers followed the crease of the scar down his face. 'Because it shouldn't. You want to know a secret? I've got a scar too. Down here. Way down below my belly.'

'How come?'

'It happened when I was a kid. I was climbing some railings with a friend and slipped and got caught by the spike. My mum always said it could have been worse, but the older I got the uglier it made me feel.'

He smiled at her. She kissed him on the lips.

'You're a beautiful man, do you know that?'

'No.' He shook his head.

'Yes. Believe me. You are. Take it from me, people like you are rare. How does that work? You're rare because you take a risk or two. You're rare because you stick to what you believe in. And you're rare because you dare to care.'

She broke off, embarrassed. Rare, dare, care. She hadn't meant it to come out that way. Garbage like that belonged in a Hallmark card.

'You haven't answered my question,' he said.

'I know.'

'So how would you feel about it? Hopping aboard and sailing away?'

They were nose to nose now, the wind fluting through the marram grass.

'I don't know you,' she said.

'You do.'

'No.' She moistened a finger and traced the shape of his lips. 'But maybe we could remedy that.'

'Sure.' He didn't sound at all certain. 'And then?'

'Then we'd be closer. Then we'd get to know each other. Properly.'

He nodded, said nothing. He seemed to have lost focus. He was gazing out to sea again. He wanted to talk about the places they could go, the beaches he could show her, the people she could meet. Simple people. Real people. People who'd never let you down.

'Are we talking Thailand?' she said softly.

'Yeah. And a thousand other places. Think about it, Lizzie. Please.'

The conversation appeared to be over. They lay in silence for a while. The stiffening wind was blowing sand in Lizzie's face. She thought about seizing the initiative, about taking him by the hand and going back to the van and making a space in the back for the airbed. It might work. It might even be wildly successful. But something told her that this was the last thing he wanted and she didn't understand why.

'Do you find me attractive?' she asked after a while. 'Be honest.'

'I love you.'

'That's a big word.'

'I know. I mean it.'

'But how do you know?'

'I just do. It's something you feel. Don't ask me how. It's just there. It's happened. It's real. It exists. It just feels ...' he shrugged '... right.'

Lizzie said nothing. This was a conversation that was fast getting out of control. She closed her eyes. Could you really fall in love that quickly? And if you could, should you ever admit it?

She felt a movement beside her and became aware of his face looming over hers. He was smiling.

'The answer's yes,' he said softly. 'Of course I find you attractive.'

'Do you fancy me?'

'Yes.'

'That's good.' She nodded. 'Good.'

Another silence, longer this time. Pendrick lay back again, his huge hands clasped behind his head, his eyes closed. She wanted to kiss him properly, to unpick a little of the mystery that was complicating something that should have been so simple, but she couldn't bring herself to do it. It wasn't meant to be this way. She'd wanted them to make love, to share each other physically, to get to a place beyond the rights and wrongs of stony-hearted developers and the wickedness of the Western world, but deep down she realised it wasn't going to work. For all his talk of falling in love, something was holding him back.

At length she picked the brochure up and flicked through it again, aware that he was watching her. She looked up at him.

'Where did you get this?'

'Kinsey's apartment.' He seemed to be smiling at the memory. 'If you want the truth, I nicked it.'

It was gone six before John Hamilton phoned back. Suttle had left a message on his mobile asking him to call. Suttle was still introducing himself when Hamilton interrupted.

'I know who you are,' he said.

'How?'

'I got a call from Gina. She seems to think you're all right. Does that come as a surprise?'

'Yes, definitely.'

'Should I know more?'

'There isn't more to know.'

'Ah …' Suttle thought he caught the softest of chuckles. 'Then I think I understand.'

Suttle briefly described the meet he was setting up for Monday night. Bournemouth seemed a good location, but he didn't know the town and he needed a steer on an appropriate rendezvous.

'Is that all you need?'

'No. I want someone to watch my back. Put me down as paranoid but in this kind of company I need to have a back-stop.'

'Sure. That's understood.'

Hamilton said he had a flat in Westbourne. There was a Café Rouge up the road at the end of a crescent of shops. Suttle could get directions from Google or his satnav. The parking was fine across the road and the cafe might do nicely. He'd be happy to ride shotgun.

'That's good of you.'

'Not at all. Blame my crazy wife.'

'You're still married?'

'Yes.' The chuckle again, but louder. 'She told you otherwise?'

Lizzie was back in Exmouth by half six. She and Pendrick had shared the journey back in a companionable silence. He'd reached for her hand from time to time, a form of physical solace that made Lizzie begin to suspect that Pendrick – in some dimly understood way – was damaged goods. When he stopped on the seafront and let her out beside her car, he wanted to know when he'd see her again.

'Tomorrow,' she said brightly. 'I'm the girlie in bow making a fool of herself.'

She drove home, increasingly perplexed. In many respects it had been a lovely afternoon. In others, though it shamed her to admit it to herself, it had been deeply disappointing. On the way up to the north coast she'd rather assumed they'd get it on. She was curious to know whether they'd work together, and to be blunt there was only one way of finding out. Yet it hadn't happened, and the more she thought about it the more she realised that it probably never would.

There was a wariness in Pendrick that seemed to stand guard against the encroachments of the outside world. You stepped towards him and extended a hand only to watch him back off. To begin with she'd blamed herself for being too eager, too pushy, but then she found herself wondering why he and his wife had never had kids. Did they ever screw? Or had the marriage been based on something else?

In truth she didn't know, and as she turned the Impreza onto the parking area beside Chantry Cottage she found herself confronting another surprise. Driving up the lane, she'd assumed that the curl of blue smoke had come from the adjoining farm.

233

Now she was watching her husband circling a sizeable bonfire with his daughter in his arms.

She got out of the car. Suttle met her on the patio. He smelled of woodsmoke. He told her he'd had a great day. Even Grace was beaming. Together, they toured the garden. Suttle, it turned out, had parked Grace in her playpen in the sunshine and taken a scythe to the long grass. He'd hacked away at the dead vegetation along the wall that led down to the brook and raked a small mountain of twigs and assorted leaves into a monster bonfire. A lot of the stuff was still wet, he said, hence the lack of a proper flame, but if the weather held over the coming week he'd have another go.

Lizzie was surprised and impressed. With her eyes half closed the garden resembled a savage grade two. Far more importantly, her ever-distracted husband had at last made a start on the chaos of their domestic life. She lifted Grace from Suttle's arms and gave her a hug. Suttle wanted to know how the clear-up at the club had gone.

'Fine,' she said. 'But it took for ever.'

Later, after Lizzie had put Grace to bed, Suttle made supper and explained about Monday night. Lizzie, who knew Dave Fallon by reputation from her days on the Pompey *News*, warned Suttle to be careful. He said he'd already taken care of it.

'How?'

'The D/I I saw last night? She's got an estranged husband who lives in Bournemouth. He's agreed to keep an eye on me.'

'That's nice of him.'

'Gina's doing. Not mine.'

'She vouched for you?'

'Absolutely.'

'So what's in it for her?'

The moment she said it Lizzie knew she'd kicked open a door she should have left well alone.

Suttle was standing by the cooker, stirring a pan of fried rice.

'How about you?' he said softly.

'How about me what?'

'How about you and all your new buddies?'

'You mean the rowing club?'

'Sure. Unless it's gone beyond that.'

'Beyond what? I haven't a clue what you're talking about.'

'You haven't? A couple of nights ago you're back at eleven. What's going on with these people? Do they row in the dark?'

'We had a drink.'

'Who had a drink?'

'A bunch of us. They're very social. That's nice. Bit of a novelty, if you want the truth.'

'And today? Out at nine? Back at six? That's a lot of sweeping-up.'

'It was a shit heap. I told you.'

'Sure.'

'You don't believe me?'

'No.'

'You think I'm lying?'

'I think you're hiding something.'

'Same thing, isn't it?'

'Yeah.' He nodded. 'It is.'

'Great. You want the truth? Then here it is.' Lizzie stepped towards him. A vivid blush of colour pinked her face. He could feel her anger. 'Just for the record I object to this cop routine. I'm your wife, not some bloody suspect. I'm sure you're great in interview but marriage is a different gig. Have I been fucking some he-man rower ? No. Have I been tempted? As it happens, yes. Why? Because I can't stand living the way we live.'

Suttle nodded. He'd given up on the fried rice.

'So where did you go this afternoon?'

'I'm not answering that question.'

'But you did go somewhere?'

'Yes.'

'Great.' He turned back to the pan and gave the rice a savage poke. 'Thanks for fucking nothing.'

'You spent last night with a woman who just happens to live alone.' Lizzie was in his face now. 'You came home at God knows what time. Good was she? Worth it?'

'She's nuts, if you really want to know. Totally out of her tree.'

'Perfect.'

'What does that mean?'

'It means you could fuck the arse off her and walk away. No commitment on your part. No comeback. A totally risk-free screw. Like I say, perfect.'

'And you think that's what I did?'

'I don't know. Because you won't tell me. And even if you told me, even if we had a conversation, I'm not sure I'd believe you.'

'You wouldn't?'

'No. Not now. Not here. Not the way we are.'

'Great. Then that's it, yeah?'

'That's what?'

'Everything. You. Me. Grace. This khazi of a house you hate so much. Let's just bin it, shall we? The lot.'

'Call it a day?'

'Sure. If that's what you want.'

She stared at him for a long moment. She was shaking inside. She'd never imagined a scene like this. Never.

'I'm sorry.' She reached for the car keys. 'I'll go.'

She drove fast, keeping to the country lanes, swamped by her anger, fighting to concentrate on the next bend and the bend after that. Among the trees on top of the common, she nearly killed a fox. She had time to register the piercing redness of its eyes in the darkness as it turned to face her headlights. Instinctively, she stamped on the brakes and swung the wheel to the right, heading for woodland at the side of the road. The car shuddered and began to slide sideways. Finally it stopped. Lizzie closed her eyes. She was shaking again. Then she opened the door and threw up.

Exmouth was fifteen minutes away. She knew that Pendrick lived in a web of streets near the river and the station. She drove up and down, looking for his van, trying to fix his front door in her mind. There'd been some kind of card in the window of the flat downstairs. A tatty knocker and peeling paint on the door itself.

Finally, she found it. She parked across the road and switched the engine off. The light was on in the upstairs flat and the curtains were pulled back. She stared up at it for a long moment, trying to steady her pulse, trying to regain control of herself. She'd never snapped like that in her entire life, and the knowledge of where it might lead alarmed her deeply. She'd never been frightened of making decisions. On the contrary, especially at work, she'd won a reputation for being on top and ballsy in the trickiest situations.

This, though, was different. She'd pushed married life to the very edge of the cliff and she wasn't at all sure what she wanted to happen next. She needed to talk this thing through. She needed a listening ear, someone who'd understand, someone who wouldn't take advantage. Pendrick, she knew, would give her that kind of space, that kind of attention. If necessary, she could stay over. Whether she slept in his bed or not didn't matter. She wanted to be close to somebody. She wanted to be touched, to be held, to be told she wasn't some ditzy slapper cheating on her husband. Chantry Cottage had never been a great idea. She wanted out.

She rinsed her mouth with water from the bottle Jimmy kept in the glovebox. Then, reaching for the door handle, she paused. There was movement in the upstairs window. Someone was standing there, staring down at the street, a black silhouette against the light inside. It was a woman. She turned her head and must have said something because she was joined by

237

another figure, bigger, broader. It was Pendrick. For a moment or two he and the woman were both immobile, watching her, then Pendrick reached out for the curtains and the tableau was gone.

Lizzie stared up at the window, trying to make sense of this image. Then her gaze lowered to Pendrick's van at the kerbside. Parked in front, neatly wedged into a tiny space, was a small black sports car.

Suttle was asleep when Lizzie slipped into bed beside him. She touched his face, told him she loved him, told him she was sorry, promised it would never happen again. Suttle stirred, grunted something she didn't catch, then rolled over. When dawn broke, hours later, she was still lying there, staring up at the damp patches on the ceiling, the tears cold on her cheeks.

Eight

It was Suttle's idea to drive the whole family to Exmouth for the Kinsey tribute. Lizzie, exhausted, was tempted to phone Tessa and cancel, but Suttle insisted she see the thing through. The way he read it, they were offering her a leading role in this morning's ceremony. If the rowing was doing her good, if she enjoyed it, the last thing she should do was let them down.

Lizzie knew she had no choice but to agree. Last night, to her immense relief, appeared to be history. Suttle was cheerful, positive and starving hungry. Making bonfires, he told her, was hard-core exercise. He made porridge for them all and patiently monitored Grace's attempts to spoon-feed herself in her high chair.

They were on the road by half nine. Suttle dropped Lizzie on the seafront, a discreet distance from the club compound, and drove on towards Exmouth Quays. The porridge hadn't quite filled the hole. He and the *Constantine* team had used the Docks Café earlier in the week and now he decided to share an egg and bacon butty with his infant daughter.

The café was packed. With Grace in his arms he was about to step back into the street when he caught a wave from a table in the corner. It was Carole Houghton. She was with her partner, a tall handsome woman called Jules. He went over, did the introductions. Grace gave them both a precautionary look and then nestled on her father's lap as he took the spare seat.

Houghton insisted on buying their egg and bacon butty. Suttle had mentioned the Kinsey tribute on Friday and she had thought it only proper to make an appearance. A full week had gone by since the investigation kicked off and, in the absence of a result, this was the least she could do on behalf of what remained of the *Constantine* squad.

'Does Grace like brown sauce?' Houghton was already on her feet, en route to the counter.

'Loves it.'

Suttle turned to her companion. Jules, he knew, was a lawyer, and he'd always suspected that Houghton shared one or two details of the more interesting jobs with her. He was right.

'Carole tells me you're the last man standing.'

'On *Constantine*?'

'Yes.'

'That's true. Short straw, me.'

'Coroner's file?'

'You've got it.'

'And it stops there?' She smiled. 'I think not.'

Houghton was still at the counter. Suttle was looking at Jules. He wanted to know more.

'Carole really rates you,' she said. 'I shouldn't be telling you but it's true. She thinks you're shrewd. And more to the point she thinks you're honest.'

'That's nice to hear. What does honest mean?'

'It means you're hard on yourself. It means you don't take short cuts. And I guess that means life isn't always easy.'

'Too right.' Suttle was thinking of last night. 'What else did she say?'

'She said that this investigation of yours, whatever it's called, is still in the balance. That you shouldn't give up.'

Suttle blinked. Houghton, he knew, was a class operator. Was this why she'd volunteered to fetch the butty? So her partner could deliver a discreet message? He voiced the thought as Houghton returned.

'Of course.' Jules was clearing a space on the table. 'You read her well, young man.'

Lizzie met Tash Donovan at the club compound. Tessa did the introductions and said that Tash would be rowing in the number two seat ahead of Lizzie in bow. The rest of the crew, including Tash's partner Milo, were already on the beach helping to rig the boats. God speed, Tessa said, and when it comes to the row-past be sure to give it some welly.

Lizzie and Tash crossed the seafront road and headed down the slipway towards the beach. The tide was falling fast, flooding out of the estuary, and a ledge of high cloud had thinned the sunshine.

Lizzie wanted to know how long Tash had been rowing. She loved the colour of her hair.

'Couple of years. I'm first reserve with this lot.' She nodded at the nearest quad. 'Four of them are bloody good. Kinsey was deadweight.'

'That's what everyone says.'

'It's true. The poor lamb had his strengths but rowing wasn't one of them.'

They joined the rest of the crew at the water's edge. Tash did the introductions. Lizzie recognised Milo from the Thursday session. This was the guy with the camera, she thought. Andy Poole offered her a crushing handshake and a wide grin. Lenahan, the cox, asked whether she was cool with rowing bow.

'I need to be out of the way,' Lizzie said. 'Bow sounds fine to me.'

'A little bird told me that you and racing starts are strangers.'

'Your little bird's right.'

'We can fix that. Leave it to me. No problem.'

He was as good as his word. He supervised the launch, and the quad nosed out into the current. There was still plenty of water over the offshore sandbank and they crabbed away from the beach towards the nose of a distant promontory.

Lenahan was calling the stroke rate, warming the crew up, and Lizzie could feel the power in the boat. Despite her exhaustion, she realised she was beginning to enjoy this. Then came a small dot powering out of the harbour. The dot grew rapidly bigger and Lenahan gave the speeding safety boat a wave as it circled the quad. There were two men aboard. The portly guy at the wheel Lizzie had never seen before. The other one was all too familiar. Pendrick.

Suttle and Grace found a space near the edge of the dock for the tribute ceremony. Houghton had taken Jules for a stroll round Regatta House. Under the circumstances, she thought her partner deserved a proper look at the crime scene. They'd rejoin Suttle later.

The last of the sunshine had gone by now and it was appreciably colder. Suttle bent to the buggy, tucking Grace in. Earlier he'd watched Lizzie's boat out in the far distance, stopping and starting, time after time. Now the other quads from the club were pulling hard against the tide, forming a protective square around a couple of smaller skiffs, slowly closing on the dancing water off the dock. All the rowers were wearing club colours, red and white, and as the boats approached, each crew in perfect time, a murmur of approval went through the watching spectators.

By now a decent crowd had gathered and a second TV crew had joined the BBC South West team who had earlier been prowling around Regatta Court. Suttle had watched the reporter on the phone before doing his piece to camera. He'd stationed himself on the stretch of promenade immediately below Kinsey's apartment, trying to flatten his thinning hair in the rising wind. Suttle was too far away to catch what he was saying, but the cameraman's dramatic tilt upwards towards Kinsey's balcony was all too eloquent. *The dead man fell from here, and still nobody knows why.*

'Mummy!'

Grace had seen her first. She was waving her little arms in excitement. Suttle turned to find himself looking at the Kinsey boat as it passed through the rest of the fleet on its way upriver. Lizzie was at the front and Suttle felt a jolt of admiration at the way she seemed to have mastered the business. He supposed that rowing was difficult. Lizzie had told him so. And yet there she was, perfectly in tune with this strange music, her blades dipping in and out with the rest of the crew, her back straight as she pulled on the oars, her body moving sweetly forward to take the next stroke.

'Which one?'

'At the front there. The small one.'

Houghton had appeared behind them. She pointed Lizzie out to Jules, who stepped forward and cupped her hands.

'Go Lizzie!'

Someone else in the crowd took up the chant. Then another. Then a third. Even Grace was having a squeal. Lizzie had caught the chant. Suttle saw the tiny nod of her head, an acknowledgement. Suttle cupped his own hands.

'Go! Go Lizzie! GO!' he roared.

She recognised his voice. A grin this time, spreading and spreading. Suttle turned to Houghton.

'She's not bad, eh? For a probationer?'

Lenahan had elected to make the turn about 500 metres upstream from the dock. His cue to start would be an orange distress maroon fired from the quad dropping the wreath. Molly Doyle had cleared this through the Coastguard at Brixham late last night and they'd assured her they'd resist the temptation to launch the lifeboat or a chopper.

'Red, please.'

Lenahan had got to the turn point. The crew hauled on their right-hand blades, pivoting the quad around a buoy.

'Next stroke, easy up.'

The crew stopped rowing. Lizzie could feel the tide beneath her, lifting the hull and carrying it downstream. Lenahan was waiting for the maroon.

'Come on,' he muttered. 'Jesus, what's the matter with those eejits?'

Lizzie wanted to glance over her shoulder and watch the maroon go off, but she knew she'd get bollocked. Eyes in the boat. Always eyes in the boat.

'Whole crew come forward to row.' Lenahan had his gaze locked on the dock.

The whole crew came forward, blades in the water, ready for the racing start. The first time she'd tried it, half an hour ago, Lizzie had nearly totalled Tash's oars. Her second attempt had been better and after that she'd started to get the feel of what was required. She was still playing catch-up, though, and just hoped that no one watching had binos.

'Ready to row?' Lizzie caught the muffled bang of the maroon. 'ROW!'

Andy Poole was leader of this tiny orchestra. Rigid in his seat, he took a swift choppy stroke. Then another. Then a third. The quad surged forward. After five strokes, in a blur of scarlet, the crew went to half slide, a foot of movement under their bums, the strokes longer, more power in the water. Another five strokes and they settled into racing speed, thirty-two strokes a minute, every oarsman intent on pouring maximum effort into the churning blades.

To her immense relief, Lizzie was still in one piece. She hadn't caught a crab, she hadn't got in Tash's way, and while she knew she was a minim off the beat she quickly settled down. By now the quad was, in Lenahan's phrase, at battle speed. With the looming orange presence of Regatta House fast approaching, Lizzie concentrated on giving it everything. *Lean forward,* she told herself. *Take the catch. Push back hard with legs. Arms straight. Accelerate the blade through the water. Feel it in the thighs. Go for the burn. Big tug at the end.* Then hands away quickly and do it all over again.

Off to her right she could hear cheering and applause from the dock. She pictured Jimmy and Grace. She hoped they were watching her. She hoped they weren't laughing. Then, much closer, came the other club boats, the rowers keeping station with tiny movements of their blades, and a brief snatched glimpse of Kinsey's wreath bobbing gently in the middle of the formation.

'Forty-one big ones. GO!'

They'd passed the wreath. Lenahan was driving them on. This could have been a race, easily. Tash had already warned her about what to expect. Flat out, she'd said, it's the lungs that seize up first. Keep sucking in the air. Keep pushing hard on the footstretcher. Above all, watch the timing. Catch, extract. Catch, extract. Get it right. Exactly right. Keep on the beat.

'Twenty to go. Own the water, people. Make it yours.'

Lizzie was starting to struggle. Then she remembered her first outing on the rowing machine, how she'd kept the pressure up until the very end, chasing the numbers on the readout, ignoring all the distress calls her body was putting out.

'Five of your best. Your very best.'

Lizzie's eyes were shut. She was rowing on empty. She squeezed every last ounce of effort into those final strokes. Then, quite suddenly, it was all over.

'Easy up, guys. Angels, all of you.'

She barely heard Lenahan. She let go of her oars and reached forward to pat Tash on the back. The boat was still moving at speed. The water caught her blades, smashing both against her midriff and sweeping her overboard. It happened so quickly Lizzie hadn't a clue what had happened. All she knew was that she was underwater, being dragged along by the boat.

She struggled, starting to panic. One of her feet was still trapped in the footstretcher. She must have over-tightened the strap. She shut her eyes a moment, fighting the temptation to take a breath, trying to get her head out of the water. It was hopeless. Her body was twisted and she no longer had the energy or the strength to break free. By now her lungs were bursting. They must have seen me, she kept telling herself. A couple of hundred people can't all be blind.

Desperate for air, she opened her mouth. The water was ice cold. She could feel it in her chest. She began to cough, to choke. More water. Then she sensed hands beneath her arms and her head at last broke the surface, and seconds before she passed out she caught the looming face of Pendrick, treading water beside her, the white hull of the safety boat inches from his back.

'You'll be fine,' she heard him say. 'I've got you.'

A chopper flew her to A & E in Exeter. Wrapped in a space blanket with another blanket on top, she'd managed to stop the shakes. The accompanying paramedic told her it was the shock as well as the water temperature. She supposed that was a comfort but she wasn't sure.

In A & E they put her in a giant suit that looked like a duvet with arms. She lay in a cubicle trying not to relive those final few strokes before she'd gone overboard. It had to be her own fault, had to be, but she simply couldn't work out why. One moment she'd been telling Tash what a star she was. The next she'd been fighting for her life.

Jimmy and Grace turned up minutes later. They squeezed into the tiny cubicle. Jimmy gave her a hug and then found a chair and sat by the bed while Lizzie clung to Grace. Jimmy's boss seemed to have come too. She'd found some change for the machine in the waiting room and returned with teas and coffees, keeping a discreet distance while Jimmy described the scene on the dock.

Most people, including him, had been unaware of the incident. All they'd seen was the safety boat racing to the still-moving quad, and then a big guy going overboard to fish someone out of the water. Only a nearby birdwatcher in the crowd on the quay had the full story. He'd watched the whole episode through his binos. It's the girl in the front, he told Suttle. She seems to have come a cropper.

'That was me,' Lizzie said. 'What a wuss.'

Suttle told her to forget it. Stuff happens. Thank Christ someone had been on hand to fish her out.

'Who was it?' he asked.

'Pendrick.' She found his hand and gave it a squeeze. 'Who else?'

Lizzie was released a couple of hours later. The consultant took Suttle aside and told him not to hesitate to seek help if there were any after-effects.

'Your wife's been through serious trauma,' he warned. 'This can mess with people's idea of themselves in all kinds of ways.'

Suttle was intrigued by the phrase. He'd have liked to find out more but one glance at the consultant's face told him this wasn't the place or the time. Lizzie's GP, he said, should be the first port of call. After, of course, a little home-grown TLC.

'No problem.' Suttle thanked him and returned to the cubicle. To his delight, Lizzie wanted to go home.

'Say it again –' he bent to kiss her '– then I'll believe it.'

That evening, for the first time in months, they felt good with each other. Houghton had offered Suttle a couple of days off to help Lizzie get over her little accident but Lizzie herself wouldn't hear of it. She was embarrassed, and grateful to the small army of folk who'd fished her out, emptied her lungs, strapped her into the chopper and flown her away. Now she'd be grateful for a little time on her own with just the baby for company and the knowledge that Suttle would be back before nightfall.

'That could be a problem.' He was thinking about tomorrow's meet in Bournemouth. 'I'll cancel.'

'Don't.' She put her hand on his arm. 'I'm a strong girl. Stronger than you think. Stick with the arrangements, but nothing silly, eh?'

'You're sure?'

'I'm sure. And you know something else?' She beckoned him closer, kissed him on the lips and nodded towards the stairs. 'I owe you.'

Nine

Suttle was in his office at Middlemoor by eight o'clock next morning. Lizzie had insisted he leave early to beat the rush-hour traffic and had dismissed his offer to return at midday to sort her out a bit of lunch. She had a long list of apologetic phone calls to make. Mea culpa. My fault. Sitting beside the bed, Suttle had wondered whether the list of calls included Pendrick. Given the fact that he'd saved his wife's life, he fancied the answer was liable to be yes. Lizzie was watching him carefully. In certain moods, like now, Jimmy Suttle was an open book.

'Don't worry,' she'd said. 'That man's the reason I'm still here.'

'How does that work?'

'It's complicated.' She'd kissed him. 'One day, if you're good, I might tell you.'

Now, Suttle took a call from D/I Houghton. She had good news and bad. Preferably face to face.

Suttle went upstairs. Houghton had found a traffic cone from somewhere to keep her office door open when she was in the mood for callers. Now she asked Suttle to close it.

He took a seat in front of her desk. A large Manila envelope had his name on it.

'I had Traffic on first thing,' she said. 'About Friday night.'

Suttle owned up at once. He'd been going way too fast. He'd

249

had a couple of drinks. Next time he'd suss these Traffic numpties way earlier.

'That's not what bothers me.'

'It's not?'

'No. I understand you'd just been to Modbury.'

'That's right.'

'D/I Hamilton lives in Modbury.'

'Right again, boss. We had dinner together. I needed to sort
some stuff out.'

'*Constantine* stuff?'

'Partly.'

'Private stuff?'

'Yes.'

She nodded. The more Suttle saw of her, the more he liked
her. It was rare to find someone so astute, so direct, so switched
on, who applied that intelligence to the people around her.
Suttle had never been quite clear about the phrase grown-up
but fancied that it pretty much covered Carole Houghton.

'D/I Hamilton is neediness on legs,' she said. 'You ought to
be aware of that.'

'I am, boss. Believe me.'

'She has a talent for wrecking other people's marriages.
It may not be her fault but it happens nonetheless. She's an
attractive woman. She can talk a good war. But beware, Jimmy.
This job's tough enough as it is.'

'Crime wise?' Suttle was intrigued.

'No.' Houghton was reaching for the envelope. 'Some days I
think the bad guys are the least of our problems. Do we understand each other?'

'We do, boss.'

Suttle took the envelope downstairs. It had come from the force
intel department and contained Kinsey's financial records.
Grateful, once again, to have the office to himself Suttle sorted
the information into separate piles on a neighbouring desk

and began to go through it. Expecting a complicated web of accounts, he was surprised by its simplicity. On the business side, Kinsey had operated two accounts, one for Kittiwake and one for Kittiwake Oceanside. When it came to his personal life, he drew on a single account in his own name.

By mid-morning, after an initial trawl through all three piles, Suttle had enough information to map the shape of Kinsey's growing business empire. Over the past few months the Kittiwake account had been largely dormant. All Kinsey's energies had been spent on the development of a series of sites across north Cornwall. Most of these, as far as Suttle could judge, were no more than a wish list of locations that might, one day, host Kittiwake Oceanside gated retirement communities. Cheques drawn on the Oceanside business account had gone to a range of planning and landscape consultants, all of whom had featured in the business files Suttle had analysed earlier. Only one of the sites, Trezillion, showed any signs of happening, and this was reflected in payments to a Leeds-based firm of solicitors. A couple of these tied in with credit card payments to Flybe for return tickets to Leeds Bradford Airport.

Suttle had hung on to Kinsey's business correspondence in the belief that it might feature in the file he was preparing for the Coroner. Cheque by cheque, he tied the payments to the paperwork. Planning permission for Trezillion was clearly a huge obstacle to the project going forward, but phrases in a couple of the letters to his legal adviser hinted that this problem might be far from insoluble. Hence, Suttle assumed, the £4.5K Kinsey had been prepared to blow on the design and printing of glossy brochures.

He was about to start on the personal bank records when his eye was caught by another large cheque. On 21 January 2011 Kinsey had paid £13,000 to a Mr Waheed Akhtar. The name alone was totally out of keeping with the rest of Kinsey's disbursements. There was no matching invoice in his business records, and no correspondence that Suttle could find. Was this an Asian businessman Kinsey had tapped up for advice? Was he taking the Kittiwake concept abroad? Would elderly couples with a taste for year-round sunshine be spending their twilight years in Oceanside Dubai?

Suttle thought it was worth a note. He scribbled the details on his pad and reached for the pile of personal bank account statements. Most of this stuff was mundane – direct debits on power, water and council tax, card payments for anything from petrol to booze, plus a recent cheque for £607 to the Exeter Porsche dealer for a service. On top of that came regular expenditure that had to be connected to the rowing club. Repairs to the new quad after a collision with an estuary buoy. Hotel and ferry bills for a winter training camp on Lake Garda. Three-figure payments to Andy Poole for 'miscellaneous services'.

Month by month, Suttle went backwards, looking for anomalies that might flag something interesting, but after a full year and a half he'd found nothing. Kinsey seemed to have lived his life exactly in step with everything the intel had already established. He kept himself to himself, didn't go out much, and spent more than was probably wise on his precious rowing.

Only after he'd finished his initial trawl, making himself another mug of coffee in the squad kitchenette, did Suttle realise what he was missing. Where were the payments to the escort agency for his regular Thai girlies? And how come there was no trace of the money he'd spent on Tash Donovan?

Suttle took the coffee back to his desk. His task this time was to revisit all the personal stuff – bank accounts, credit card billings – and look for cash withdrawals. Within the hour he was satisfied that these couldn't possibly have paid for Kinsey's sex life. In terms of ready money, he appeared to live on surprisingly little. A hundred and ten pounds a week was his average spend. How many girlies could you buy for that?

A knock at the door brought Luke Golding into the office. The young D/C had some good news.

'TF2, Sarge. I cracked it.'

Suttle had almost forgotten about Team Fortress 2. Golding, it turned out, had spent most of the last couple of days on the Internet. It happened to be his weekend off and he'd hooked up with ShattAr on three separate occasions. During the third game he'd saved the guy's life, not just once but on four separate occasions, and this had been enough to finally coax a reply from his earlier message. He'd wanted a link to ShattAr's Facebook profile. And he'd finally got it.

'His real name's Zameer Akhtar, Sarge. And as far as I can judge, he lives in Leeds.'

'Zameer what?'

'Akhtar.' Golding wrote it down for Suttle's benefit.

'You've PNC'd him?'

'Yeah. The guy just picked up a twelve months suspended for possession.'

Suttle raised an eyebrow. He'd been expecting a sleek Pakistani businessman, not a lowlife druggie.

'Have you talked to the locals?'

'Yeah, I got through to their intel set-up in Wakefield. They're busy as fuck just now but the woman promised to come back before close of play. I gave her your name and number, Sarge. Happy days, eh?'

Suttle was looking at the pile of bank statements. Kinsey had business connections in Leeds. He made regular visits on Flybe. The recurrence of the name Akhtar had to be more than coincidence. Were these two people brothers or was there some other family connection?

He glanced up. He wanted to know how Golding was getting on with the Exeter escort agencies.

'That was the other thing, Sarge. I think I've nailed the girl in the photo we ripped from Kinsey's phone. She works for an outfit called Twosomes. They operate out of a grungy little room over a Chinese takeaway in Heavitree. Real shit hole.'

'They ID'd the photo?'

'Of course not. But there was a mug shot on a wallboard. I swear it was the same woman.' He paused and shot Suttle a grin. 'Maybe you should take a look.'

By lunchtime Lizzie was nearing the end of her list of thank you phone calls. Tessa had been more than understanding. The girls, she said, were thinking of buying Lizzie a safety belt for use in the boat, while Clive, the Club Captain, was definitely going to nominate her for the Cock-Up of the Year Award. Molly Doyle had successfully kept the details of the incident from the local press and was anticipating great coverage for the tribute ceremony and the row-through. The Kinsey crew, meanwhile, had been so impressed by Lizzie's capacity to hold her breath underwater that she was in some danger of becoming a regular sub.

'Sub? Submarine? Get it?' Andy Poole roared with laughter, wished her well and hung up.

Lizzie's last call went to Tash Donovan. When she admitted she still wanted to row, Donovan told her she must have balls of steel.

'You're coming out again? After something like *that*?'

'Of course I am. If anyone'll have me.'

'You're famous, girl. We talk of nothing else. Invites to row? Shall I make a list?'

Touched by the gentle piss-takes, Lizzie sat down and wrote a semi-formal letter to Molly Doyle. She wanted the club to know that she was sorry for letting everyone down and grateful for all the calls and support she'd received since. She would definitely be keeping her foot straps looser from now on and looked forward to the next outing. Hopefully, she added, she might even make it back in one piece. She signed herself Lizzie Borden in keeping with the pact she'd made with Jimmy.

Sitting at the kitchen table, rereading the letter, she glimpsed a wraith-like presence behind the careful prose. It was like writing to someone about a bereavement. Her old gloomy self seemed to have passed away. All you need, she thought, is a half a minute or so underneath a moving boat with a lungful of seawater sloshing around inside you. Near-death experiences cure anything.

She glanced through the door into the living room. Grace was asleep on a pair of cushions in her playpen. Every day the shafts of sunlight edged down the back wall as the sun rose higher in the sky. At last the house was beginning to dry out. Soon, with a helping hand or two, Chantry Cottage might even feel like a proper home.

The knock at the kitchen window made her jump. For a moment she had no idea who it was, then her blood froze. Pendrick was wearing a pair of blue overalls and a black beanie. He seemed to be tapping his watch. There was no way she could ignore him but her instinct was to pretend he wasn't there, to somehow turn the clock back to this time last week when she'd never heard of the guy. Then she got to her feet, telling herself that this was the man who'd probably saved her life. The very least she owed him was a thank you.

She opened the kitchen door, standing aside as he stepped past her. He looked around the way a buyer might, noting this detail and that, not bothering to hide his curiosity. Lizzie was fighting hard to keep the smile on her face.

'Grace?' Pendrick was peering into the living room.

'Yeah. Don't wake her up, whatever you do.'

'She's lovely.'

Lizzie didn't know what he meant, didn't know what he was doing here. Trespass wasn't a word she would ever use lightly but this felt very close.

'How did you know where we live?'

'You told me Colaton Raleigh. I asked down in the village. Lovely young mum? Sweet little girl? Can't be that much competition round here.'

Lizzie was filling the kettle. Half an hour, she told herself. Tops.

'Tea?'

'Coffee if you've got it.'

He'd disappeared behind the living-room door. Lizzie found him crouching in a corner, examining one of the sockets that was fast parting company with the skirting board. She'd mentioned the state of the place when they'd been up in north Cornwall. Bad move.

Pendrick had moved on to the radiator under the window-sill. The bowl to catch the drips from the leak was half full. He gave it a poke and grunted something Lizzie didn't catch.

'Sugar?' she said brightly. 'I can't remember.'

'Two.' He didn't look round. 'The socket'll take no time at all. The radiator's trickier. I'll have to drain the system.'

'Who said you need to?'

'You'll have a flood otherwise.'

'That's not what I meant.'

'I know.' He was on his feet again, looking down at her. 'We need to talk about Saturday night. Am I right?'

'No. I need to thank you for what you did on Sunday morning. I should have phoned. I should have thanked you. I can't tell you how grateful I am. Without you, I might have drowned.'

'Who says?'

'The people at the hospital. The medics.'

This news put a smile on Pendrick's face. He took a seat at the kitchen table, reached for one of Grace's toys, a squashy rubber ball, and began to play with it. He looked strangely relaxed. This might have been his own home.

'Right time, right place.' He shrugged. 'If only … eh?'

'If only what?' Lizzie was mystified again.

'If only I'd been able to do the same for Kate.'

'But I thought you said she wanted to go overboard. That it was her decision.'

'Yeah. But it didn't make it any easier, did it?'

'For her?'

'For me.' He was crushing the ball now. It had disappeared beneath the whiteness of his huge knuckles. 'You know Tash, right?'

'Yes. I met her yesterday.'

'That was her at my place on Saturday night, in case you were wondering.'

'Fine.' It was Lizzie's turn to shrug. 'And why not?'

'You don't care? You don't want to know more?'

'No.'

'OK. So why did you come round?'

'Because I was upset about something. Because I wanted to talk.'

'Fine. Go ahead.'

'There's no point. It's resolved. It's finished. It's over.'

Pendrick released the ball and watched it roll slowly towards the edge of the table. He seemed to have lost interest in the socket and the radiator.

'Tash and me are friends. Just friends. She comes round sometimes when Milo's driving her crazy. We talk. That's pretty much it.'

'I believe you. You're good at that. You must have lots of practice.'

'Good at what?'

'Listening.'

'Is that what this is about?' He gestured loosely at the space between them. 'Only I had a different impression.'

'I expect that was my fault. I always dive into things. It used to get me into all kinds of trouble.'

'I'm not surprised.' He caught the ball as it fell from the table and gave it another squeeze. 'You wanted me to fuck you on Saturday, didn't you?'

'I wanted us to make love. There might be a difference.'

'And were you disappointed when we didn't? Was that why you got so upset?'

Lizzie gazed at him. There were some men who needed to

put their smell on everything they touched, and Pendrick, she was beginning to realise, might just be one of them. Territorial was too feeble a word. She shuddered to think what might be more appropriate.

She got up to turn off the electric kettle. As she passed Pendrick he reached out for her.

'Don't,' she said. 'Please don't.'

'Why not?'

'Because ...' she couldn't find the words '... stuff's happened.'

'You're right. And I meant everything I said.'

'About what?'

'About this khazi of a country. About arseholes like Kinsey. About getting hold of a yacht and doing something sane for once. You were up for that. I could see it in your face. You thought we could do it. Maybe you thought we *should* do it. Am I right?'

Lizzie didn't answer. She wanted this man out of her house, out of her life. The last thing she needed was a rerun of Saturday afternoon.

She poured hot water into two mugs and added a tea bag apiece.

'I haven't got coffee,' she said. 'I'm sorry.'

'Fuck the coffee. Tell me about Saturday. Tell me you meant it.'

She felt the first stirrings of impatience. She was being as civil as she could. She put the mugs on the table and sat down again. Then she reached for both his hands, removing the ball and dropping it on the floor.

'You saved my life,' she said quietly. 'Twice. I don't know how many times I have to say thank you but I mean it. I really do.'

Pendrick stared at her. He was confused as well as angry.

'And that's it?'

'I'm afraid so. I haven't a clue what it is between you and

Tash, and if you want the truth I'm not interested. All I know is that this – the house, my marriage, even poor little Grace – took me to a very bad place. You helped me with that. You helped in ways you'll never ever suspect. For that, I thank you. And I thank you. And I thank you again.' She bent and kissed his hand. 'Does that make any sense?'

'None at all. I know you, Lizzie. I know what you want. I know what's real to you. I know what really *matters*. I've been around a bit, believe me. And I *know*.'

To this Lizzie had no answer. They were heading up a cul-de-sac that held nothing but darkness. The last twenty-four hours, she thought she'd left all that behind. She wanted him gone.

'I'm due at a clinic in half an hour,' she said. 'Grace is due a check.'

'No, you're not. You're just trying to make it easy for me. I love that about you. Just the way I love everything else.' He gave her hand a little squeeze and then picked up the mug.

Lizzie stared at him. She was fast running out of options. There was a hint of madness in this man. Go for broke, she told herself. Double or quits.

'She stayed the night, didn't she?'

'Tash?' A smile ghosted across his face. 'No way. If you want the truth, she came round to try and get me to row.'

'On Sunday morning?'

'Yeah. She thought we all ought to be together.'

'Because of Kinsey?'

'Yes. That seemed to be important for her.'

'You instead of me?'

'Yes. It was nothing personal. She'd never even met you.'

'And you?'

'I told her I couldn't do it. Why? Because I couldn't stand the guy. I also told her I was glad he'd gone. She had a problem with that. She thought I was totally out of order.' He reached for her hand. 'Are we friends now?'

It was an impossible question to answer. Lizzie just shook her head and turned away.

'Leave me alone, please. Let go of my hand.'

'No problem. My pleasure.' He nodded next door. 'You want me to sort that stuff out or not?'

'No, thank you.'

'Fine.' He drained the mug and got to his feet. 'Next time, eh?'

The Golden Dragon lay at the end of a terrace of shops in Heavitree, a scruffy red-brick suburb to the east of Exeter. Suttle found a parking spot in a lay-by across the road. When he asked at the counter for the Twosomes agency, the woman simply pointed upstairs.

Access was via an exterior staircase at the back of the property. The window in the door at the top had been boarded up after some kind of break-in, and there were fresh-looking chisel marks around the Yale lock.

A youngish guy opened the door. He was pale and thin. His patched jeans hung off his bony frame and his trainers had definitely seen better days. As far as Suttle could judge, he was eastern European.

'Who are you?' Poor English, heavily accented.

Suttle flashed his warrant card. He'd appreciate a word or two. It needn't take long.

The guy spent a long time examining the card. Then he asked Suttle to come inside. The room must once have been a kitchen. A jar of instant coffee and an electric kettle stood on the work surface beside a pile of newspapers. Suttle recognised a shot of Cracow on the front page of the top paper. There were scabs of ageing dog shit on the floor and a powerful smell of drains.

Suttle pushed the door shut behind him.

'I'm investigating a suspicious death,' he said.

'Where?'

'Exmouth. I need your help. We need to trace this woman.'

He laid the shot from Kinsey's phone on the work surface. Golding had been right. It exactly matched the photo pinned to the wall board. The guy peered at the proffered shot, then glanced up. He was looking alarmed.

'You say she's dead, this woman?'

'No. I'm saying we need to talk to her. Is that possible?'

'No.' He shook his head.

'Why not?'

'She doesn't speak English. She's not here. She's gone away.'

'Where?'

'Abroad. I don't know.'

Lies, Suttle thought.

'You're responsible for this woman? You take the bookings?'

'Yes. Me and my partner.'

'Who's your partner?'

'Mr Wattana. He's away too.'

'You keep records?'

'I don't understand.'

'When people pay?'

'Ah ...' He looked thoughtful. 'Does that matter?'

'It might.'

Suttle bent forward, closing the distance between them. He needed to get this man onside. He wanted to offer him a word of advice.

'You need to make a choice here, my friend. Either you let me see your payment records or the whole thing gets much more complicated. The VAT inspector? The tax people?' He sniffed, looking round. 'Health and safety?'

The guy shook his head. He wanted to say no. He wanted Suttle out of his face. Suttle was looking at a filing cabinet wedged into an alcove beside the boiler. Judging by the state of the paintwork, it might have come out of a skip.

'In there, maybe? You want to give me a hand here?'

With some reluctance, the guy followed Suttle across to the

cabinet. It was locked. Suttle stepped back while the guy found the key. The middle drawer was packed with files. The guy looked up.

'You want the same girl?' he asked.

'Yeah. The punter's name was Kinsey.'

He shook his head. He'd never heard of anyone called Kinsey.

'Little guy? Middle-aged? Drove a Porsche? Big top-floor apartment down in Exmouth? Place called Regatta Court?'

Mention of Regatta Court sparked a nod of recognition. Maybe Kinsey used a false name, Suttle thought.

The guy was riffling through the files. At last he found what he was looking for. He took it out and held it close against his skinny chest.

'And after this?'

'I go.'

'And not come back?'

Suttle smiled. His turn to lie.

'Never.'

'OK.'

The guy handed over the file. Suttle opened it and found himself looking at a sheaf of A4 sheets. Each held a scribbled note or two – date, time, name of the attending escort – and stapled to each was a credit-card slip. These were the old sort, letter-box-shaped, bearing the imprint of the card. Suttle lifted out the first one and gazed at the name of the cardholder. Mrs Sonya Jacobson. Kinsey's ex-wife.

The guy wanted the file back. When Suttle said he was taking it away, the guy tried to protest. Then he was struck by another thought.

'Mr Jacobson?' he asked. 'He's dead?'

Lizzie was panicking. The only call she could think of making was to Gill Reynolds. Mercifully, she picked up.

'You've got a moment?'

'Yeah. If you're quick.'

'Later maybe?'

'Later's worse.'

Lizzie closed her eyes. She was in big trouble with someone at the rowing club. The details weren't important but she'd done something stupid, really stupid, and now the man wouldn't leave her alone.

'How stupid?'

'You don't want to know.'

'What kind of answer is that? Just tell me.'

Lizzie did her best. By the time she got to Trezillion, Gill was laughing.

'You're right,' she said. 'You've got to be barking. That husband of yours can be a dickhead sometimes but he's not that bad.' She paused. 'So what's this guy like?'

'He's OK. At least I thought he was OK. Now I'm not so sure.'

'Why?'

'Because he's all over me. Because he won't listen. Because he won't take no for an answer.'

'And are you surprised? After you came on to him like that?'

'I suppose not. But it gets worse.'

'*Worse?*'

'Yeah. Yesterday he saved my life. Major production. Chopper, paramedics, the lot.'

'Shit. Are you OK?'

'I'm fine. No, that's a lie. If you want the truth, I'm terrified.'

Lizzie explained about Pendrick and his wife rowing across the Atlantic, about the morning he woke up and found himself alone. It took a moment for Gill to place the story. Then she had it.

'Big hippy guy? Hair down round his shoulders? Bit of a looker?'

'That's him. He's cut most of his hair off but the rest is pretty much the same.'

'Fuck. I'm with you now. No wonder.'

'No wonder what?'

'No wonder you went to wherever it was.'

'Trezillion.'

'Yeah. Maybe you should have fucked him and got it over with. Most men lose interest after that.'

'Not this one. Not the way I read him.'

'What about Jimmy?'

'Jimmy's being sweet. Jimmy's noticed who I am at last.'

'Sure ... but does he *know*?'

'About what?'

'Yer man.'

'Yes, I think he does. Not the detail. Not Trezillion. He's a detective, Gill. He does this stuff for a living.'

'And if he found out about Trezillion? What then?'

Lizzie didn't answer for a moment. This was the question she'd been dreading. This was the reason she'd made the call in the first place. She needed clarity. She needed to understand exactly where she'd got to in this hideous story.

'I don't know,' she said at last. 'It's been rough these last few days, really horrible. Jimmy was brilliant yesterday, really cool with everything. He sorted me out after the accident. We even got it on last night. I don't want to lose that, Gill. I really don't.'

'And this other guy? Pendrick?'

'That's what terrifies me.'

'Why?'

'Because I'm beginning to wonder about him. And because he won't let go.'

Suttle phoned Carole Houghton from the car. He was still parked across the road from the Golden Dragon.

'Boss? We need to bottom out a credit card. Or it could be a debit card. Have you got a pen?'

Houghton, it turned out, was preparing performance reviews.

In other circumstances Suttle might have been amused. He gave her the details on the slip.

'And the name?'

'Sonya Jacobson.'

'Who's she?'

'Kinsey's ex-wife.'

'Should I be excited?'

'Definitely.'

Suttle's second call went to Eamonn Lenahan In these situations, especially with someone like Lenahan, Christian names often worked best.

'Eamonn? Jimmy Suttle.'

Lenahan remembered the name at once. He was doing a shift as a locum registrar in A & E at the Royal Devon and Exeter. Trade had been brisk all morning but he'd just seized a chance to put his feet up in the staffroom. Tea and biscuits. God's answer to terminal stress.

Suttle laughed. Just the mischief in the man's voice took him back to the hour or so they'd spent in his rented cottage in Lympstone. Interesting guy. Definitely a one-off.

'Something on that mind of yours?' he said. 'Because now would be a good time to talk. Ask for me at A & E. Doors will open, my friend. I'll save you a biscuit.'

Suttle turned the invitation down. The staff might recognise him from yesterday's drama and the last thing he wanted just now was the likes of Lenahan making the connection between him and Lizzie.

'I'm stuffed, mate,' he said. 'But tell me one thing.'

'What's that?'

'The takeaway you all had on the Saturday night, up in Kinsey's place. Where did it come from?'

'Fuck knows. Ask Tash.'

'I've tried.' Suttle was lying. 'She won't pick up.'

'Bell Pendrick then. I think he uses the same place.'

Suttle scribbled down a number, then checked his watch.

Aside from Andy Poole, Pendrick was the one person he'd yet to see.

'What time does he finish work?'

'He doesn't. He's off today. Number 94, Woodville Road. Fella in the flat down below cracks bones for a living. Charming guy. Give him my best if he opens the door. Canes the arse off us mere practitioners.'

Suttle was in Exmouth by half two. He'd called at Woodville Road days ago, but this time a yellow VW van was parked outside number 94. Suttle resisted the temptation to raise the chiropractor in the ground-floor flat and pressed Pendrick's bell. Moments later came heavy footsteps down the stairs and Suttle found himself looking at the figure he'd last seen on Milo Symons' PC screen. The same bulk. The same shaven head. The same scar. The same hint of amusement in the deep-set eyes.

He stooped to inspect Suttle's warrant card. He was wearing shorts and a thin singlet. The singlet was dark with sweat. He didn't appear to be surprised to find a detective at his door.

'You want to come in?'

'Please.'

Pendrick led the way upstairs. The living room was under-furnished but restful. Suttle liked the Moroccan throws on the sofa and the bookcases brimming with paperbacks. A set of weights lay on a folded towel on the polished floorboards. Miles Davis played softly on the sound system. It didn't need much imagination on Suttle's part to put a woman in here, someone maybe a bit stressed, a bit vulnerable. Someone in need of TLC and a listening ear.

Pendrick had departed to the bathroom. Suttle heard splashing. Minutes later Pendrick was back in a dressing gown, towelling his face dry, trailing the scent of shower gel. He wanted to know what Suttle was after.

'I read the account you gave to our guys back last week. You mind if we go over one or two points?'

'Sure. No problem.'

'Let's talk about Kinsey.'

'Must we?' The expression on his face might have been a smile, but Suttle wasn't sure. There was anger in this man. He could feel it.

'Why do you say that?'

'No reason. I didn't much like the guy but you probably know that already.'

'Something happened between you? Something personal?'

'Kinsey didn't do personal. The guy was a robot. If you want the truth, I felt sorry for him.'

'You knew him well?'

'Not at all. That was never on offer.'

'So how did you hook up in the first place?'

'He bought the boat. Then he bunged Andy Poole to fill it with decent rowers. Andy took advice from people round the club. I was one of the chosen ones.'

'Chosen' was laced with contempt. Suttle began to wonder whether anything put a real smile on this man's face.

'And the rest of the crew?'

'They were good rowers. Andy was the best. He had pedigree. But the rest of us weren't bad either.'

'That wasn't what I meant. I'm asking whether they all felt the way you felt.'

'About Kinsey?'

'Yeah.'

'I dunno. We never talked about him really. He sat up in bow and tried to boss us around, but no one took much notice. He should have learned to row properly. That might have helped.'

'What about Milo Symons?'

'What about him?'

'Did he get on with Kinsey?'

'That guy would get on with anyone. He's a nice man, Milo, but he's a child, a puppy dog. Kinsey would give him a pat from time to time, toss him a bone, and the guy would roll over. Quite sweet if you like that kind of thing.'

'And what about his partner? Tash?'

Pendrick gave Suttle a look. Amusement again? Or something more complex? Suttle couldn't decide.

'Tash is a law unto herself,' Pendrick said softly.

'Meaning?'

'Meaning Kinsey fancied the arse off her. Tash knew that. And made him look a complete dick.'

'How?'

'By filling his head with all the hippy crap. By going round there and trying to turn him into a human being.'

'Round where?'

'Round to his apartment. She does this stuff for a living. Touchy-feely. Astral therapy. Getting in touch with your inner self. That could have been ugly in Kinsey's case.'

'She told you all this?'

'Tash tells me everything. Tash tells everyone everything. That woman knows no shame.'

Suttle nodded, remembering how candid she'd been about servicing Kinsey's needs. Five minutes max. A hundred quid a minute.

'You think she had a relationship with Kinsey?'

'That wouldn't have been possible. There was nothing to have a relationship with. Did she teach him to get in tune with himself? Did she shag the man if the price was right? Quite possibly.'

'But you'd know though, wouldn't you? If she tells everyone?'

'I would, yeah.'

'So did she?'

'Of course she did.'

'And was she shagging anyone else?'

'Like who?'

'Like you?'

The suggestion appeared to amuse him.

'Are you serious?' he started to laugh. 'Me and Tash?'

Suttle let the silence thicken. Pendrick gave his face another wipe with the towel.

'Tell me about Milo,' Suttle said at last.

'I just did. Mr Puppy Dog.'

'His partner's Tash, am I right?'

'Yeah.'

'And she's shagging Kinsey and maybe one or two others and not bothering to keep it a secret, yes?'

'It's possible.'

'So how does that make him feel?'

The silence was much longer this time. There was a logic in these questions and Pendrick knew it.

'You're looking for motivation, right?'

'I'm asking a question.'

'Because you think someone *killed* Kinsey? Went up there and chucked him off his balcony?'

Suttle didn't answer. Pendrick held his gaze.

'Kinsey was an arsehole,' he said softly. 'Arseholes some-times self-destruct. Fuck knows why, but they do. Maybe it's God paying debts. Maybe it's in the stars. Maybe Tash gave him the shag of his dreams and he decided to quit when he was ahead. Who cares? All I know is the guy's gone. And good fucking riddance.'

'The shag of his dreams? For winning, you mean?'

'Whatever.'

'But that night? Saturday night? After you'd all gone?'

'I've no idea.'

'You think she might have driven back to Exmouth Quays?'

'How would I know?'

'But she had a key to his apartment? Is that what you're telling me?'

This time Pendrick didn't answer. At length he checked his watch. Time was moving on. He had a couple of calls to make.

Suttle thanked him for his time. He might come back. He might ask Pendrick to attend the local nick for a more formal interview. In the meantime he had one last question.

'The takeaway Tash went to on Saturday night. Which one was it?'

Pendrick was picking at a loose thread in the towel. He looked up.

'The Taj,' he said. 'In Rolle Street.'

Rolle Street was a couple of minutes' drive from Pendrick's place. The Taj Mahal lay between a hairdressing salon and an estate agency. The door was locked. Suttle got the phone number from the menu in the window. When he rang the number he could hear a phone ringing inside. Then came a recorded message. The Taj could take reservations but take-away orders had to be collected in person.

Suttle tried again. This time the phone triggered a stir of movement from somewhere upstairs. Then came the clatter of feet on the stairs and a voice in Suttle's ear.

'What do you want? Who is it?'

'Police. Can you open the door please?'

The guy had obviously been asleep. He was middle-aged, portly. He was wearing loose cotton trousers and an Exeter FC football top. He rubbed his eyes, asked Suttle to come in.

'You own this place?'

'I do, yes.'

'What's your name?'

'Ratul.'

Suttle gave him Saturday's date. He wanted to know whether Ratul could lay his hands on the card receipts from takeaway orders.

'Upstairs,' he said. 'They're upstairs. You've got a name for the order?'

'Either Kinsey or Donovan.'

'Wait please.'

He disappeared up the stairs. Suttle could hear movement overhead. A drawer opened and closed. He picked up a menu, realising how hungry he was. Then Ratul was back.

'Here,' he said. 'It was a lady. I remember.'

He gave Suttle a copy of the order. It was in Tash Donovan's name. In all, the food for Saturday's little celebration had come to £67.49. The debit-card slip was stapled to the order. This time there was no name, just the last four digits of the number on the card.

Suttle had memorised the last four digits of the slips he'd seized from the escort agency: 2865. He checked the numbers: 2865. Ms Sonya Jacobson.

Suttle had time to grab a sandwich from an Exmouth café before he drove back to Middlemoor. He was certain now that *Constantine* should be revived, and that knowledge made him feel very good indeed. Everyone had put Kinsey's death in the wrong box. In the absence of any evidence to the contrary, it had been quicker and cheaper to assume suicide and consign the file to the Coroner's office. Only Suttle had taken the harder path. And now it turned out that he'd been right.

Carole Houghton was still in her office. In less than an hour Suttle needed to leave for Bournemouth.

'This has to be quick, boss.'

She already knew about the card receipt from the Exeter escort agency. Now he told her about the matching slip from the Taj.

'Same account, boss. Has to be.'

'So what are we saying?'

'We're saying that Tash Donovan was charging the earth for all kinds of stuff with Kinsey, including regular sex. That we can prove because she told me. We're also saying that Donovan persuaded Kinsey to bung Milo a couple of grand to help with his movie with more to follow.'

'How much?'

'Another forty-five grand.'

'Why would he do that?'

'To keep Symons sweet.'

'You can prove that too?'

'No.'

'But you're telling me we can evidence all these other payments?'

'Not so far. The two grand he paid Symons must have come out of the Jacobson account. The forty-five was on a promise. I'm guessing that the rest, the money he was paying Donovan, came out of the Jacobson account too. Donovan would have wanted cash. Kinsey must have had ATM drawing rights.'

'But what's he doing with his wife's account?'

'Ex-wife's. So far I don't know. But my guess is that it was some kind of private stash. Maybe he needed to hide money from the Revenue.'

'Sure. Or his ex-wife.'

Suttle nodded. Either way, they needed to access the Jacobson account.

'Donovan may still have the card, boss. And she's obviously got the PIN number.'

'The card wasn't retrieved by Scenes of Crime?'

'No. I checked just now.'

'And you're sure the Jacobson account doesn't figure in his business records?'

'Absolutely. And if he operated it through the Internet, there's no way you'd ever know it even existed.'

'His PC hard disk?'

'That's a possibility. I'll feed the account number through. See if they can raise anything.'

'Did he have a laptop?'

'Not that we've found.'

'Unusual.'

'That's what I thought.'

Houghton pushed the performance review files to one side

and reached for a pad. Suttle watched her making a neat list of bullet points. Then she looked up.

'Saturday night,' she said. 'Walk me through it.'

Suttle left for Bournemouth at half four, phoning Lizzie as he headed for his car. After the dramas of the past week, it was good to hear the lift in her voice.

'You'll be back when?'

'Tennish. I'll phone.'

'Be careful, yeah?'

'Always.'

'I love you. Remember that.'

Suttle grinned to himself. Traffic out of the city was already heavy but he edged into the outside lane as soon as he hit the Honiton road, maintaining a steady 70 mph as he headed east. Houghton had wanted him to hang on and talk to Nandy, but Suttle had pleaded a personal crisis at home. He'd be back first thing tomorrow. If she needed to make contact in the meantime she could always bell him.

As he left her office, she'd been on the phone to Nandy. The Det-Supt was driving the Bodmin job at breakneck speed but Suttle knew there was no way he'd ignore the weight of evidence he'd unearthed. Pausing at the door of Houghton's office, he'd looked back at her. Still on the phone, she'd smiled at him and raised a thumb. *Constantine* was obviously back from the dead. Brilliant.

Lizzie was feeding Grace when she got the call from Pendrick. She glanced at it and put the phone to one side. When he tried again, she didn't even pick it up. Then, moments later, came the beep that indicated a text waiting. With a tiny shiver of apprehension, she retrieved the phone. It was Pendrick again: 'If you don't pick up, I'll drive out to yr place. Yr call. XXX'.

She looked at the row of kisses, angry now. He answered as soon as she keyed recall.

'We need to talk,' he said.

'I can't.'

'We have to.'

'No way.'

'Is your husband there?'

'No. But he's back any minute.'

'We could meet in a pub. Invent an excuse. Bring the baby. Whatever.'

'You're out of your mind. There's nothing to talk about.'

'Wrong. There's everything to talk about.'

'Like what?'

'Like you and me.' He paused. 'And other stuff.'

'What other stuff?'

'Stuff about Tash. I've had the Old Bill round.'

'When?'

'This afternoon. These guys aren't stupid. I'm in a bad place. I mean it. I need your help. Is that too much to ask?'

The phone went dead. Lizzie didn't move for a moment or two. Then she stole into the hall, double-bolted the front door and returned to the kitchen.. She bolted the door from the kitchen out into the garden too, then looked at Grace. The biggest of the carving knives was in the drawer under the sink. She took it out, wrapped it in a tea towel and laid it carefully on the table. Then she reached for the cooling spoon of mashed potato.

'Open wide,' she said.

Suttle was on the outskirts of Bournemouth a couple of minutes before eight. With the help of his satnav he threaded his way through a tangle of streets and found a parking spot round the corner from the main parade of shops. He'd no idea what John Hamilton looked like but was alarmed to note the yellow no-parking line across the road from the Café Rouge. Traffic was still thick, clotted with buses. *This guy's supposed to be good*, he told himself. One way or another he'd have the rendezvous plotted up.

Suttle stepped into the café. Dave Fallon had already arrived. He was sitting at a table towards the back, with another man beside him. Suttle hadn't seen Fallon for a while, not face to face, and the intervening years had done nothing for his dress sense. The same tired leather jacket with the fraying cuffs. The same baggy jeans. The same curry flecks on his once-white shirt. Fallon had put on weight and it showed.

'This is Carlos.' He nodded at the other man. 'We're in business together. Right, Carlos?'

The other man said nothing. Younger than Fallon, he was tall and lean. He had steady eyes and the kind of tan you'd pay a lot of money to acquire. Beautiful suit, thought Suttle.

Fallon didn't want to waste Suttle's time. Carlos, he said, was in the delivery game. His mission in life was to please people who wanted wrong things put right. In this case they were dealing with a German art dealer who'd lost his daughter, a girl called Renata, to some scumbag thug in a botched contract killing near Malaga.

'With me so far, mush?' Fallon was looking at Suttle.

'Go on.'

'This German guy's got money. Quite a lot of money. In fact he's fucking minted. Losing his daughter like that has really upset him, and way down the line he wants to do something about it.'

'He's offering a reward?'

'Yeah. And a big one. Hundred K.'

'Euros?'

'Pounds.'

'Great. And Carlos?'

'Carlos is on the case. He's also fucking plugged in, believe me. Nothing moves along that bit of coast without Carlos being in the know. Good guys, bad guys, local Filth, even the fucking Russians – he's across them all. Right, *amigo*?'

Fallon gave Carlos a dig in the arm. Carlos was doing his best to ignore him. Suttle felt a tiny prickle of sympathy.

Fallon hadn't finished. All this had happened a while back. The contract killer was an animal from London called Tommy Peters. Bazza Mac had hired him to kill a lieutenant called Brett West who'd stepped out of line. Peters had done the job on Westie but had killed his new girlfriend as well for good measure. It was, said Fallon, a witness thing, just tidying up loose ends, and Peters had been good enough not to charge Baz for the extra body. The girlfriend's name was Renata. Hence the £100K from her dad.

'So this guy's after Peters? Is that right?'

'Yeah. But there's a problem.'

'What's that?'

'Peters is dead. Bowel cancer. Which leaves your mate Winter. He was there too. And as far as we can make out, he ain't got bowel cancer. Not yet anyway.'

Suttle nodded. He knew this story by heart. It was the reason Winter had finally decided to turn police informant, grass Mackenzie up and buy himself a new life abroad. Better that than a guy with a European Arrest Warrant at his door.

'So Carlos wants to find Winter? Is that it?'

'Yeah. Me too. We're in this together, me and Carlos. The minute we deliver Winter, you're looking at one happy man.'

A waiter approached. Suttle ordered a coffee. He thought he knew what was coming next but Fallon surprised him. *Never underestimate this man*, he reminded himself. You don't get to own half the cabs in Pompey by accident.

'That nice Marie you've been talking to? She gave us a look-see at Bazza's records. Turns out your Mr Winter made a couple of trips before all that election bollocks. Baz thought it was on business. From where I'm sitting, Baz was wrong.'

'So what do you want from me?'

'You were part of all this, yeah? The way I hear it, you were the guy pulling Winter's strings. So it stands to reason you know where he went.'

'But you know already.'

'Sure. But how about you tell us too?'

This, Suttle knew, was crunch time. From here on in he had to be very careful indeed. In truth, he was fairly certain where Winter had ended up, but the last thing he intended to do was share that hunch.

'He went to Poland and Montenegro,' he said slowly.

'Dead right, mush.' Fallon swapped glances with his friend. Carlos had produced an elegant notepad, leather-bound, and was making notes. 'And where else?'

Suttle studied him for a moment and then laughed. 'There's something we haven't discussed,' he said.

'Like what?'

'Like what do I get out of this?'

'You want money?' Fallon was looking outraged.

'Of course I don't want money. The deal was simple. I help you as best I can and you call the dogs off.'

'Jonno? The fat bastard that came down with the black cunt?'

'Yeah.'

'Dogs my arse.' It was Fallon's turn to laugh. 'That's a bit harsh, ain't it? On the fucking dogs?'

'You know what I mean. I help you. I tell you what I know. And you leave us alone. Not just now. Not just tomorrow. For ever.'

'Sweet. So where else did he go? Your grassing arsehole mate?'

'You haven't answered the question.'

'That's because you haven't told us nothing.'

'Fine.' Suttle stood up. 'There's a spare coffee coming if you're interested.'

It was the Spaniard who reached over. 'Please, my friend. Sit down.'

Suttle didn't move. He looked at Carlos. Then he looked at Fallon. A woman a couple of tables away had started to take an interest. Boots, jeans and a tight grey T-shirt.

Fallon muttered something that might have been an apology. Suttle resumed his seat.

'Carlos? I have your word?'

'Of course.' He extended a hand. Suttle shook it.

'The Ukraine,' Suttle said. 'Winter went to the Ukraine.'

Fallon's head came up. He couldn't mask his surprise.

'That's a big fucking place. We went there once. Away game. Europa Cup. Got stuffed 3–1. Horrible night.'

'Really?'

'Yeah. That's abroad. That's real abroad.'

'You're right. And it's not in the EU. Not yet.'

This, Suttle knew, mattered a great deal. Only EU countries recognised the European Arrest Warrant. Extradition treaties existed with a lot of other states but extradition was often a pain in the arse.

Fallon wanted to know where in the Ukraine.

'I know he bought a train ticket to Kiev. Beyond that I can't help you.'

'How? How do you know?'

'Because he kept dicking us around. In the end we had to have a sort-out. The trip to Kiev was nothing to do with our operation. Neither, as far as I know, did it have anything to do with Mackenzie. So there you go. The Ukraine. Kiev.'

'And that's it?'

'I'm afraid so.'

Fallon shot another look at Carlos. Then he turned back to Suttle.

'He also went to Montenegro, right?'

'Right.'

'Carlos here has been to Montenegro, talked to some people, a Russian bloke in particular, ex-cop, turned out to be a big mate of Winter's.'

'And?'

'Winter went to Croatia after. Took a taxi first. Then a coach. Carlos found the taxi driver too. Apparently your mate

Winter was asking about a place called ...' He frowned, checking with Carlos.

'Porec. Winter wanted to know about Porec.'

'There. Porec.' Fallon turned back to Suttle. 'Ring any bells?'

'Never heard of it.'

'You're kidding me.'

'I'm not, Dave. I've told you what I know. The Ukraine is definitely a runner.'

'Says you.'

'Says me.'

Fallon was giving him the hard stare. Suttle didn't flinch. Finally, it was Carlos' hand on his arm.

'Thank you,' he said softly. 'Thank you for coming.'

Outside the café Suttle checked as best he could for any signs of the surveillance he'd been expecting. Either these guys are as good as Gina Hamilton had promised, he thought, or I've been stiffed. Back in the Impreza, he was picking his way towards Poole and the road home when his phone began to trill. He pulled in, checking caller ID. John Hamilton.

'OK? Are we off the clock now?'

'Fine. Of course you are. And thanks, I owe you.' Suttle paused. 'Where were you, by the way?'

'I was in the pub across the road.'

'How does that work?'

'It doesn't. I was back-up in case anything kicked off.' He chuckled. 'Did you notice the woman a couple of tables away? Bit of a looker?'

'Boots? Grey T-shirt? Don't tell me.'

'Yeah. Class operator. Good on obs too.'

Suttle was back in Chantry Cottage by a quarter to ten. Lizzie was halfway through a bottle of red. She fetched Suttle's dinner from the oven and turned the TV off. She wanted to know what had happened.

It had taken a while for Suttle to tease the real meat out of the encounter in the Café Rouge. Now he saw no point keeping his conclusions to himself. Lizzie was part of this. Christ, if it came to more nonsense from the likes of fat Jonno, she'd be the one in the firing line.

'Dave Fallon's hooked up with a bounty hunter, a Spanish guy. I'm not sure I believe the figures but you're probably looking at the thick end of a hundred grand.'

'To do what?'

'To find Winter, stick him in the boot and take him back to Malaga. The Spanish police would take care of everything else and Fallon and his mate would cash the cheque.'

He explained about the killing of Brett West and the German girl who'd also died. Lizzie was horrified.

'Paul did that?'

'He was there. He could have stopped it. He didn't.'

'And the money?'

'It comes from the dead girl's father. Christ knows what it buys him. Peace of mind sounds nice but it can't be that simple.'

'So what did they want from you?'

'A steer on where Winter might have gone. I told them the Ukraine.'

'Was that wise?'

'It was a lie. I looked at the map this morning. The Ukraine's next to Poland. It's the best I could do.'

'And did they believe you?'

'Not for a moment.'

He told her about Carlos' enquiries in Montenegro. He seemed to have tracked Winter to Croatia. Worse still, he'd got the name of a specific town.

'What's it called?'

'Porec.'

'And you think he's there? Paul?'

'I've no idea. But Croatia makes perfect sense. It's bang next door to Montenegro. It's handy for flight connections. It's full of bloody tourists in the summer. And it's not in the EU. In his situation you could have done a lot worse.'

'So what do you think?'

'I think I did my best.'

'I meant about us?'

'I think they'll leave us alone.'

'You *think* they'll leave us alone?'

'I'm pretty certain. No guarantees but ...' he shrugged '... I'd be amazed if they turned up again.'

'Why's that?'

'You really want to know? Because I think they're a couple of days away from finding the old bugger. And you know what? That makes me fucking upset.'

Ten

Carole Houghton phoned at half past six next morning. Suttle was already up, trying to calm Grace after a fractious night.

'I would have called last night,' Houghton said, 'but I thought I'd leave you in peace.'

'That's kind. What's happened?'

The phone wedged in his ear, he was still cradling Grace. Mr Nandy, Houghton explained, had found a couple of D/Cs who would be joining *Constantine* by lunchtime. She was expecting a response on the Jacobson debit card before noon, and both guys would be deployed on checking ATM withdrawals. In the meantime, Mr Nandy was insisting that Suttle and Luke Golding get up to Leeds and interview Zameer Akhtar. If there was any chink in Kinsey's armour, any hint that he might – after all – have had a mate or two, then this might be the guy.

'When?'

'When what?'

'When do you want us up there?'

'This morning. You're both booked on Flybe. There's a flight at ten past nine. You should be at the airport by eight. That's why I'm phoning so early.'

Suttle met Luke Golding at Exeter Airport. Lines of beige-clad oldies were queueing for a holiday flight to Madeira. Suttle asked Golding to sort a couple of coffees and retired to a quiet corner to make a call. Thanks to Grace he'd spent the whole night awake, obsessing about Winter.

'Lizzie? I've been thinking about Paul. Somehow or other I need to make contact but I'm fucked if I know how.'

'It's not your job, my love. Not your responsibility.'

'He's a mate. Of course it's my responsibility.'

'It isn't. Believe me for once. Just relax, eh?'

Suttle was staring at the phone, bemused by Lizzie's response. What did she know here? What was she hiding? He was about to ask her when he felt a nudge on his arm. Golding had turned up with the coffees. Unless they joined the security queue now, they'd miss the flight.

Suttle bent to the phone again.

'Later, yeah? I'll call you from Leeds.'

The flight landed at 10.15. West Yorks had sent an intel civvy to pick them up. Sue was an older woman, broad Yorkshire, with three grown-up kids and a husband serving out his time on Traffic.

'It seems yer man were a bit of a handful.' She'd given the intel file to Suttle. 'Didn't like being arrested at all.'

Zameer Akhtar, Sue said, had been a sus small-time dealer, working out of premises in an area called Harehills. He'd been pulled a year or so back and got off with a caution. Then, less than a month ago, he was arrested again and this time he was taken to court.

'I blame Harehills myself. It's right kooky. Our Gary's got a mate who once lived there. Listen to Gary and you'd think it were hard not to end up dealing. Third World is what he calls it. Rubbish and all sorts everywhere. Kids, boy racers, you name it. Know what I'm saying?'

Suttle nodded. He wanted to know whether Akhtar had any family.

'Three sisters and his mum. His mum's an alcoholic. White

Lightning, the way yer man tells it. There used to be a dad too, but he's disappeared.'

'You've got a name for the father?'

'Yeah. Waheed.'

She drove them to police headquarters at Millgarth in the city centre. A uniformed inspector had arranged for them to use one of the interview rooms.

Suttle wanted to know about Akhtar. Was he being picked up or what?

'Voluntary attendance, love. If he doesn't show, he's on a nicking.'

At the police station she organised coffees and took them down to the interview room. To Suttle's surprise, Akhtar was already there. He was thin and pale with a mass of jet-black curls. According to the intel file he was twenty-three but he looked much younger. His jeans had been patched at least once, and the Iron Maiden motif on his freshly laundered T-shirt was beginning to wear off.

He got up the moment Suttle and Golding stepped in. Contrary to what the intel officer had said, the last thing this kid appeared to want was trouble. He'd been offered a solicitor but he wasn't being interviewed under caution, nor was he being investigated for any offence, so he'd decided to do without one.

Suttle did the introductions and thanked him in advance for his time. The next bit, he knew, was going to be tricky.

'We understand you knew a man called Kinsey.'

Akhtar looked blank.

'Jalf Rezi,' Golding said.

'You mean Jake?'

'Yes.'

'Yeah, I do. We just became Facebook friends. I'm waiting for a link to his page.' He had a soft voice, broad Yorkshire accent.

'That was us, I'm afraid.'

'What was us?'

'The Facebook message.'

'From Jake? The friending request? *You* sent that?'

'We did.'

Suttle explained what had happened at Regatta Court. They'd retrieved evidence that Akhtar and Kinsey might have been buddies through the video games they played. If that was the case then they needed to talk about Kinsey.

If anything, Akhtar was more confused.

'You're telling me he's dead?'

'I'm afraid so.'

'How?'

'Like I say, he fell.'

'Sure. But why are you here? Why are you talking to me?'

Suttle didn't answer. Akhtar was still trying to work out the implications of the friending request. He was looking at Golding. Then something seemed to dawn on him.

'So you were playing as Jake? As Jalf?'

'Yes.'

'Counterstrike?'

'Yes.'

'You were right crap. You know that?'

Golding shrugged and looked at his hands. Suttle laughed. A smile even crossed Akhtar's face.

'You were right rubbish,' he said. 'I should have sussed you.'

Suttle wanted to know when he'd first come across Jalf Rezi.

'Last year. I were playing Counterstrike for the first time and he wiped me out. I nearly didn't go back after that, but then I thought why not and I went on again. This time I was OK. Better than OK. After that I played a lot. Then he were sending me the odd message, telling me how much better I was getting, you know what I mean? So I texted back and asked him what other games he played. Turned out he was big on Left 4 Dead. That did it for me. You know it? Awesome game. The best.'

He looked from one face to the other. 'Is this OK, like? Is this what you want?'

Suttle gestured for him to carry on. Golding was making notes.

'Left 4 Dead drops you in the middle of this horrible place. It's a bit like where I live. There's just ruins and wreckage and all kinds of other shit and bad people everywhere. There's the Hunter, the Smoker, the Boomer, the Tank ...' He frowned, checking off the characters on his fingers.

'The Witch?' This from Golding.

'Yeah. Right. The Witch. You've played it too?'

'Years ago.'

'Right. So you know you have to get to the safe house? Get inside and like close the door? I was nearly there. I was outside the safe house and I was half blind because a Boomer had puked on me and the other three guys in the game were bleeding out really fast. You know like you watch their health bars? They were gone. End of.'

'Was Jalf one of them?' Golding again.

'Yeah. That's the whole point. I got into the safe house and I knew the other guys were fucked. The nearest one, right outside the safe house, was Jalf. I needn't have done it. I could have just let him die. I was safe in there. But Jalf comes on to me on the headphones, yells for help, really lays it on heavy. And me? I'm trying not to listen but then I think that makes me kinda mean. On the other side of the door I can hear the Boomer just waiting for me to come out so I blew him away with a couple of shotgun rounds through the door and then went out there again and killed a Hunter, and then another one, and then a Smoker, and it ended with me and Jalf back in the safe house. I needn't have done it, I needn't, but I did.' He was still looking at Golding. 'You understand that? You understand what I did?'

'Yeah, I do. Top move.'

'That's what Jalf said. That's when he asked me where I lived.'

Leeds, as it happened, had become a regular part of Kinsey's business life. A big law firm in the city centre handled contracts for something called Kittiwake and next time Kinsey was up for a meeting he invited Akhtar for lunch.

'We met at the Mint. You know the Mint at all? It's a big hotel down by the canal. It were right posh. Fourteen quid for fish 'n' chips. I had the works. It were lovely.'

Suttle was a spectator by now. Akhtar was addressing himself exclusively to Golding. Jalf, he said, wasn't at all what he expected. He thought he'd be meeting someone rough like himself. Instead he found himself sitting with a businessman at one of the city's top hotels.

'What do you think Kinsey made of you?'

'I think he thought I were all right. I told him a bit about myself, where I lived, my family, all that. My dad especially. He were very good about my dad.'

His father, he explained, had been badly injured on a building site back home. He came from a village in Mirpur and after a while in hospital he'd decided he didn't want to live in Pakistan any more and managed to make his way to England.

'Took him two years, that did. It must have been right hard the way he talked about it.'

Waheed settled in the big Mirpuri community in Leeds and took up with a local girl. Four kids came along. Akhtar was the eldest. By the time he was a teenager his mum was out of it on cheap cider and his dad had become a depressive.

'All he wanted to do was go back. He missed his real home. He missed his brothers and sisters. All he'd do was cry.'

'You told Jalf all this?'

'Yeah. We were playing Team Fortress 2 a lot by then, that's a favourite of mine. And Jake were good about my dad. Kind. *Really* kind.'

Listening, Suttle had the impression Akhtar had never come

across much kindness in his young life. With both his parents effectively off the plot, it had fallen to him to look after his sisters. No wonder he'd turned to drug dealing.

'So what did he do? Jalf?'

'He gave my dad some money. A shitload of money, if you really want to know. Enough to get him back to Mirpur and set him up.'

'You knew Kinsey well by now?'

'I knew him OK. We never went to the Mint again but he'd always buy me something to eat.'

Suttle was leaning back in his chair. Thirteen grand, he thought, Not a bad thank you for getting Jake Kinsey into the Left 4 Dead safe house.

'What did Jake tell you about himself?'

'Not a lot. Not really. Except rowing. Boat stuff. He were really keen on that. He had photos.'

'Did he talk about the guys he rowed with at all?'

'Yeah.' Akhtar nodded.

'What did he say?'

'He said they were good guys. He liked them.'

'All of them?'

Akhtar paused. He was looking at Golding again. The young D/C gestured for him to go on.

'He had a problem, did Jalf, if you really want to know. You could see it in his face. I thought he was, like, gay to begin with, but that weren't it.'

'So what was the problem?'

'I think it were to do with a woman and one of the guys in his boat. I don't know. He never gave me names or anything.'

'But what was the problem?'

'I dunno.'

'You do, Zameer, you do.' Golding bent forward. 'Just tell us.'

'But it sounds daft.'

'Tell us.'

'OK.' He shrugged. 'He thought one of the guys were going to kick off.'

'How?'

Akhtar shook his head, refusing to go any further.

Suttle and Golding exchanged glances. Then Golding leaned forward again.

'Are we talking health bars?' he said softly. 'Are we talking bleeding out?'

Akhtar nodded.

'Fucking right,' he whispered. 'And it were true, yeah?'

Suttle and Golding were back in Exeter by half four. Suttle rang Houghton from the airport. She asked him about Akhtar.

'Total result, boss. We need to talk.'

'Indeed. I've got Mr Nandy with me. As soon as you like, Jimmy.'

Nandy was waiting in Houghton's office. He was on his feet by the window, a mobile pressed to each ear. The Bodmin job was coming to the boil. As, it seemed, was *Constantine*.

Nandy finished both conversations. Houghton returned with a tray of coffees and an assortment of snacks.

'You've eaten?' Suttle shook his head. 'I thought not.'

Nandy had fetched another chair from the office next door. Suttle was already halfway through a packet of crisps. He summarised Akhtar's account. Nandy didn't bother to hide his disappointment.

'No names?'

'I'm afraid not.'

'Nothing in the way of hints? The look of the guy? How old he was?'

'No, sir.'

'Nothing about the woman involved?'

'No.'

'Then where does this take us?'

'Surely it establishes that Kinsey was worried.' It was

Houghton. She was frowning. 'And that could be significant, no?'

'Yeah, of course it could. Call me greedy but I'd have liked a little more.'

'There is no more, sir.' Suttle this time. 'The way I read it, the lad Akhtar was the closest Kinsey got to a mate. This was an arm's-length relationship. Most of it happened on the Internet. As it happens, they got to meet. Kinsey was grateful about all this safe-house game shit and Akhtar seems to have taken his fancy. Here was someone with a problem. He'd done Kinsey a favour. Kinsey did him one back.'

'Thirteen thousand pounds? For pressing a couple of buttons on a games console? You call that a *favour*?'

'Kinsey was showing off. He had money. He was a can-do guy. He liked solving problems. Maybe he felt sorry for the boy. Maybe there are bits of Kinsey we'll never know about.'

Houghton interrupted again. She thought Suttle had a point. One of the things about Kinsey's intel profile that had been bothering her was just how locked-down the guy appeared to have been. No one, she said, could be that alone, that cut-off, that solitary. And here was the proof.

'But he told the lad nothing. Except he was worried.' Nandy still wasn't convinced.

'Exactly. Because Kinsey always pulled back. So far and no further. Am I right, Jimmy?'

Suttle nodded. On the flight back he'd been picturing Kinsey up in the vastness of his apartment, bent over his PC, the lone figure blasting the likes of the Boomer and the Witch into oblivion. Video gaming had always been a cartoon world as far as Suttle was concerned but after an hour with Golding and Zameer Akhtar he'd begun to change his mind. Left 4 Dead had taken Kinsey into the no-man's-land between fantasy and friendship. And the rapport with Akhtar was the direct result. That kind of relationship wouldn't have been enough for most people but it suited Kinsey very nicely indeed. No real obligations. Nothing you couldn't settle with a couple of lunches and a cheque.

Nandy agreed to let the issue ride. Akhtar's account was a pointer, he said, an indicator. Nothing more. He told Houghton to brief Suttle about the ATMs. This, it appeared, was proper evidence.

Houghton was amused. The data on the Jacobson debit card had arrived earlier than expected. She ducked her head to a list of figures on a pad. In all the account held £107,638.34. There was a pattern of regular withdrawals going back more than a year, sums that would appear to pay for Donovan's supply of assorted services.

'Great.' Suttle had finished the crisps. 'Perfect.'

'Wait, Jimmy. It gets better. Kinsey's death should have stopped the withdrawals, am I right?'

'Yeah.'

'Then look at this.'

She passed across a list of the latest movements on the Jacobson account. At 23.45 on 9 April £200 had been withdrawn from an ATM in Exmouth. The following day another £200, this time from an ATM in Yeovil.

Suttle looked up. Moments like this, a sudden breakthrough that transformed suspicion into incontestable fact, were all too rare in complex investigations.

'Donovan's still got the card, boss. We were right.'

Nandy wanted to know how he could be so certain.

'Because she was in Yeovil on Sunday. It was her mum's birthday. Symons told me. It's in the notes.'

Suttle returned to the list. There were four more withdrawals: two of them local, one of them in Plymouth, the other in Bude.

Houghton wanted the list back. She scanned it quickly, then looked up. Excitement showed in her eyes. They glittered behind the rimless glasses. Suttle loved her in these moods.

'Symons' father runs an antiques business in Topsham. Right?'

'Right.'

'I sent a couple of guys round after lunch. That Transit Symons uses for pick-ups from auctions? He was down in Plymouth on the 15th. Up in Bude the next day. Bingo. Perfect match.'

'Do these ATMs have cameras?'

'That's what Mr Nandy asked. We're still checking. Most do, some don't.'

Suttle was doing the sums. Since Kinsey's death Donovan and Symons appeared to have helped themselves to £1200.

Suttle looked up, grinning. 'It's a stone-bonker, boss.'

'A stone what?'

'Stone-bonker. Pompey phrase. It means we've cracked it.'

Houghton was scribbling herself a note. One of Nandy's mobiles was ringing again. He spared it a glance then turned it off.

'OK,' he said. 'So we can probably prove theft. What about the rest of it?'

'You mean Kinsey?'

'Yes.'

Suttle nodded. Fair question.

'The way I see it, sir, is this. The guys win their race. They all come back to Exmouth and get hammered. Kinsey retires to bed and they all leave. Donovan and Symons are driving back alone. They stop at an ATM in Exmouth. There may be CCTV as well as an internal camera. We also need to check whether they got a receipt.'

'Why?'

'Because then they'd know how much was in the account. A hundred and seven grand? That sounds like motive to me.' Suttle paused. 'We should also be talking about Milo Symons. Donovan says he knew all about her and Kinsey occasionally shagging and didn't much care about it, but I've talked to the lad and I don't think that's true. I think he cared a lot. I think it upset him. Maybe other people in the crew knew about it too. And that would have upset him more. Either way, you're now looking at two reasons why he might want Kinsey out of his life. Number one, Tash. Number two, the money. This is a guy with big ambitions. He wants to make a movie. Movies are expensive. A hundred and seven K? Perfect.'

'So they drive back to the apartment?'

'Yeah. Tash has a key.'

'How come?'

'Kinsey gave it to her. Part of his fantasy, as far as I can gather. The walk-in shag.'

'And then what?'

'I've no idea. There are two of them. They're both rowers, both fit. Kinsey's probably still pissed. He's not a big guy. Between them, they could bundle him out of the bedroom and chuck him off the balcony. Piece of piss.'

There was a silence. Even Nandy appeared to be impressed. He was about to say something but Suttle hadn't finished.

'One other thing. Apparently Kinsey had a laptop. Symons mentioned it in his account. It doesn't appear on the Scenes of Crime log.'

'Meaning?'

'It got nicked. And that has to be down to Donovan and Symons. It's easy to carry. It's got value. You could wipe the hard disk and sell it on. We're dealing with thieves, remember.'

'As well as killers?'

'Yeah.' Suttle nodded. 'The way I see it, definitely.'

Carole Houghton called a *Constantine* squad meet for six o'clock. She spent ten minutes behind a closed door with Nandy to agree a strategy for the next twenty-four hours before the Det-Supt left once again for Bodmin. He met Suttle on the stairs. By the weekend, he muttered, he was in some danger of closing not just one job but two. He paused for a moment, looking Suttle in the eye. Then he offered a rare smile and gave him a pat on the shoulder.

'Good work, son.'

The *Constantine* squad now numbered three D/Cs plus Suttle and Houghton. In the light of the latest developments, Nandy had decided to keep the investigation paper-based and not bother with a transfer to the HOLMES suite. There'd be plenty of time to reorganise the file ahead of formal submission to the Crown Prosecution Service. Assuming, of course, that *Constantine* drew a cough from Donovan and Symons.

Houghton wanted thoughts on this issue. The more they could put on the table in the interview suite, the likelier they were to score a confession. So where should they look next?

Among the D/Cs there was a consensus for an early-doors arrest tomorrow morning. Bosh the mobile home and both vehicles. Nail the debit card and any ATM receipts they might have kept. Have a good look for the laptop. Keep Donovan and Symons apart – separate police stations, separate interviewing teams – and sweat their accounts until one or both of them broke.

Suttle wasn't so sure. Delay the arrest twenty-four hours, and he'd have a chance to talk to Eamonn Lenahan again.

'Why would you need to do that?' This from Houghton.

'Because he's the brightest guy in the boat. He listens. He watches. If anyone knew about Donovan and Kinsey it would have to be him.'

'How about tonight?'

'That's possible. I'd have to ring him.'

'How about Lizzie?'

'She'll be cool about it.'

'Are you sure?'

'Yeah.'

There was a brief silence. A couple of the D/Cs exchanged glances. Then Houghton nodded at the door.

'You want to bell him now? Then we can frame up the arrest strategy and sort the interviewing teams.'

Suttle made the call from his office. Lenahan, it turned out, had just come back from another shift at A & E. He was eye-balling the beginnings of a stir-fry and had plenty for two.

Suttle smiled. He wanted a chat, not a meal. Lenahan wouldn't budge.

'This is non-negotiable, my friend. Either we break bread together or you might find I'm busy. Give me half an hour. And bring something to drink.'

The line went dead. Suttle put his head round Houghton's door and promised to bell her later. Only when he was in the Impreza, wondering about an off-licence, did he remember to give Lizzie a call.

She was on the point of preparing supper. Suttle told her not to bother. Something had come up.

'Something that involves a meal?'

'Yes.'

'And a lonely policewoman?'

'Do me a favour.'

He was relieved to hear her laughing. He said he'd be back later, no real idea when but it shouldn't be late.

'No problem.'

'Are you sure?'

'Yeah. Another wild night in with my knitting? Bring it on.'

Suttle arrived in Lympstone with time to spare. He parked beside the railway halt and walked down to the Londis in the village centre. He'd already decided to end the day with a modest celebration and bought two bottles of Côtes-du-Rhône, one for Lenahan and one for afterwards once he'd got home.

Lenahan was alone once again in the tiny cottage. His lodger, he said, was doing Christian things at some night shelter in Exeter and wouldn't be back until God knows when. The kitchen formed part of the living space downstairs and Suttle caught the rich tang of ginger the moment he stepped in. When Lenahan broached the wine and offered him a glass, Suttle shook his head.

'You've got tea?'

'Has to be green, I'm afraid. Goes with the meal.'

'Whatever.'

Lenahan returned to his wok.

'We nearly had another body on Sunday. Did you hear about that? A fancy little tribute to our dead leader and this slip of a girl goes overboard. Another minute or so and we'd all be talking to the Coroner. Jesus, am I glad I listened when they taught us all those resus drills.'

Suttle expressed polite interest. One day, when *Constantine* was history, he'd come back and buy this man a serious drink. For the time being, he wanted to find out more about Donovan.

'Tash?' Lenahan was giving his rice a poke. 'That girl's a force of nature. Truly. I mean it. Astral Tash. Forty-plus years old and still at it.'

'At what?'

'Everything. With pretty much anyone. You know the story with Tash? Pendrick tells it best. It's Christmas Day. Pendrick's having a quiet one because he's that kind of guy and there comes a knock at the door and he looks out of the window like you do and there's Santa Claus outside, red coat, hat with a bobble on, funny beard. He thinks it's a piss-take to begin with but Santa's not going away so in the end he does the seasonal thing and opens the door. It's not Santa at all. It's Tash. She's spent half the day with Angel Dust and she's bored to death, and when she opens that red coat of hers it's pretty plain what kind of present she's got in mind.'

'Angel Dust?'

'Young Milo. That's what she calls him when the drink takes her.'

'She's drunk? Christmas night? On the doorstep?'

'Pissed as a rat. Pendrick gets her in, sits her down, gets her a mince pie or whatever treat he's giving himself, but she's not having it. Are we getting the picture here? Pendrick's under the cosh. And what's worse, he can't get rid of her. Took him hours to hose her down. And even then she was still giving him lists of what turned her on.'

'He was complaining? Pendrick?'

'Big time. He thought it was gross, and I think I would too. You could arrest a woman like that for something. Rape's too polite a word.'

'So she went? In the end.' Suttle was trying to picture the scene.

'Yeah. He managed to find a taxi. He stuffed her in the back with a note for Angel Dust. Return to Sender. Happy fucking Christmas.' Lenahan threw garlic and ginger in the wok and gave it a stir. 'So there you go. Astral Tash and Angel Dust. What else do you guys want to know?'

They sat down to eat minutes later. Out of deference to Lenahan's cooking skills, Suttle had changed the subject. The stir fry – prawns with Chinese lettuce – was excellent. His eye, once again, was taken by the scatter of photos on the wall. Some village in sub-Saharan Africa, every shot ablaze with the overwhelming brightness of the sunshine.

Lenahan caught his interest. Winter by the river in Lympstone had been arctic, he said. On Christmas Day, while Pendrick had been fighting Tash off, he'd been trying to get the ice off his crappy old Mondeo in case the call came from the hospital.

'You miss Africa?'

'Yeah, I do. Mid-morning you're talking forty in the shade. By lunchtime it's fifty. You type with tissue under your wrists to protect the circuits in the laptop from your own sweat. Wherever you go, you end up walking in zigzags just to stay in the shade. It takes for ever to get anywhere.'

'You speak the language?'

'No. A couple of words maybe, the odd phrase, but no. And that's a huge barrier. You know why? Because in my trade the backstory is 90 per cent of the diagnosis. A guy turns up at your door and he looks half dead. He probably *is* half dead. But if you don't know what's been going on in this guy's head,

297

if you don't know what he's been up to, the pair of you are probably stuffed.'

Suttle nodded. He said it was exactly the same in his line of work.

'You're kidding.'

'I'm not.'

'I thought it was all forensics these days? DNA? CCTV? Some other fucking acronym? You're telling me you have to *listen* to people?'

'Exactly. And it's often what they don't say that really matters.'

'Right. Good. Excellent.' Lenahan took a long swallow of wine. 'So try me. Any question. Whatever you like.'

'OK. Let's go back to Tash.'

'Anything, my friend. Your call.'

'Was she shagging Kinsey?'

'Of course she was.'

'And did anyone else know? Apart from you?'

'We all did. She made no secret of it. And neither did Kinsey.'

'So what did that do for Symons?'

'Not a lot, the way I read the boy. She's older than him, of course. Maybe that's why he hated the word motherfucker.'

'Who called him that?'

'Kinsey. When he wanted to wind the poor eejit up.'

'You're kidding me.'

'Never. Kinsey never got his head around conversation, simple stuff like talking to people and not giving them a thousand reasons to punch your lights out. It didn't stop with Tash, either. He was a walking boast, that man. We all knew he was rich because he kept telling us, and we all knew you could buy girlies for a price if Tash wasn't enough, but it took Kinsey to treat us to the full à la carte. He was partial to Thai girls. He'd go on about them like it was some kind of meal he'd just had. What they did for him. How he liked them best.

Garlic and ginger and a sprinkle or two of soy sauce. Are you getting the picture?'

Suttle nodded. When Lenahan offered seconds he shook his head. He had enough. He was nearly through. Nearly.

'So when do you go back?' he said.

'To the Sudan? The sooner the better. You know something, my friend? I've spent the last six months trying to find trouble in paradise but it's hopeless. There's no civil war, no bodies by the side of the road, no dodgy situations to talk yourself out of, no so-called drinking water that will probably fry your guts. Everything works, or sort of works, so where's the challenge? Where's the *fun*?'

Trouble in paradise, Suttle thought. Didn't Kinsey's death qualify as trouble in paradise?

'That depends on your definition of paradise. Kinsey had it all, didn't he? Money? View? Girlies? Astral Tash? Us? Jesus, we even won him a cup. But it wasn't enough. Because it's never enough. Kinsey should have taken himself off to Africa. He should have seen the half-open eyes of the starving. That might have done him some good.' He reached for his glass again and then paused, struck by another thought. 'You're asking me for a diagnosis? Is that it? You want a hand here? From your tame little medic? The wild Irish guy from out yonder? You want a steer on what happened?'

'Go for it.'

'Kinsey ended up dead because he had too much. The poor wee guy choked to death on all that stuff. Me? I'd chuck the whole lot off the balcony. The bling. The money. The goodies. The extras. The Thai girlies. The Porsche. All that dinner-party shit. Everything. The lot. I'm with yer man.'

'Yer man?' Suttle was lost.

'Pendrick. He's like me, don't you see that? The guy's been around a bit. He's seen too much.' He tapped his head. 'Think too hard about what we've become and you end up fucking *ruined*.'

Lizzie was wondering about giving Jimmy a ring when she caught the sound of footsteps outside. Puzzled to know why she hadn't heard the Impreza, she got to her feet and went through to the kitchen. It was dark outside. She checked her watch. Nearly half nine. She switched on the light. She sensed a movement beyond the door that led to the patio. Then she heard a noise, a hard metallic noise, a snip. She froze, knowing now that there was somebody out there. She hadn't heard the Impreza because there was no Impreza. Someone else, God help me.

She edged slowly around the table. The door was unbolted. She'd been expecting Jimmy any time. Then a shape emerged from the darkness, someone big, someone clad in black. Black jacket, black T-shirt, black jeans, black everything. The whiteness of a face pressed itself against the glass panel in the door. A hand lifted wearily in salute. Pendrick.

He let himself in. He'd been drinking heavily. She could smell it. He reached for the support of the table, unsteady on his feet. Then he sank into a chair. He wanted to talk to her. He needed to explain one or two things. She wasn't to take offence. She wasn't to be frightened. He'd do her no harm. He'd never do her any harm. He'd treasure her for ever. And that was a promise.

'Where have you been?'

'The pub. Up the road.' He nodded vaguely towards the garden. 'The Otter? I left the van there.'

She stared at him. His eyes seemed to have lost focus. There was a terrible emptiness in his face. He seemed unaware of where he was, of how he'd got here, of what was supposed to happen next.

'Get out of my house,' she said softly. 'Please.'

He lifted an eyebrow. He hadn't heard a word of what she'd said. She repeated it, much louder, letting her anger show. Go. Leave. Now.

He stared at her for a long moment then shook his head.

'I can't,' he said. 'It's just not possible.'

'I'll phone the police.'

'Yeah. Sure.'

'I will. I'll do it now.'

'Whatever.'

She reached for the table, but his big hand had already closed over the mobile. He gazed up at her, trying to remember how to smile.

'I love you,' he whispered. 'I really, really do.'

Lizzie held his gaze a moment longer. When he tried to reach for her she avoided his outstretched arm and darted into the living room. The telephone was on the table beside the fireplace. When she lifted the receiver, she could hear nothing.

'I've done the line.' Pendrick was still at the table. 'Come back and talk to me.'

Lizzie was eyeing the stairs, but the last thing she wanted was Pendrick following her up to a bedroom. Grace was up there too. She couldn't leave the house without her.

She returned to the kitchen. A pair of wire cutters lay beside her mobile. Pendrick nodded at the other chair.

'Please. For me.'

She asked him again to leave. She promised not to breathe a word to anyone that he'd been here and frightened her shitless. She promised to keep it a secret.

'Just us?'

'Yes.'

'I like that. Why don't you sit down?'

The cutlery drawer was directly behind Pendrick. Even if she could grab a knife she knew it would be hopeless. He was far too strong.

With great reluctance she sat down. Pendrick asked for a drink.

'We haven't got any.'

'No?'

He got to his feet, his eyes never leaving her face. There were three Stellas in the fridge. He helped himself and returned to the table. He popped the tag and offered her the can. She shook her head.

'Here's to Kate,' he said.

He tipped the can and took a long swallow. Stella dripped down his chin.

'You remember Niran? The little Thai kid? The one who disappeared? Kate used to see him. Years afterwards, he kept turning up. He was the wind that opened the door. We'd get back home and he'd have put the lights on. We'd go fishing and he was the tug on the end of the line. He was everywhere that kid. And he was here too.'

'When?'

'Just now.' He nodded towards the window. 'He was the cloud in front of the moon. You should have seen it. I should have got you out there. He was beautiful, that child. Still is.'

'Please leave.'

'No.'

'You said you loved me.'

'I do. You know I do.'

'Then go. It's for the best, believe me.'

'For you?'

'For us.'

'You mean that?'

'I do, yes. If you want the truth, I loved being with you. I loved going to Cornwall that day. Trezillion. The dunes. The picnic. I meant everything I said. But it's like your cloud. Your Niran. It's gone.'

'You're wrong. He's still alive.'

'No, he's not. He's dead.'

'But he's here. He's around us. And we've got a second chance. Both of us. That's what we said, isn't it? At Trezillion?'

Lizzie didn't answer. Pendrick, she knew, was talking to himself. Some of her anger had gone. What he'd done tonight was inexcusable. She'd never forgive him. She'd never let it happen again. But way down inside, somewhere deeply private, she was beginning to feel sorry for this big man with the lostness in his eyes.

She got to her feet. He looked at her, suddenly alarmed.

'What are you doing?'

'I'm going upstairs to get my daughter,' she said. 'Then I'm going to put her in the buggy and we're going to take you back to your van. It's in the pub car park, right?' He nodded. 'Is the mattress still in the back? The sleeping bag?'

'Bags.' He was trying to smile again. 'Plural.'

'Whatever. Stay there. Don't move.'

She began to edge round him but he extended a leg, barring the way.

'I want to sleep here,' he said. 'With you.'

'That's not possible. Not now. Not ever.'

'Then when?'

'I just said. Never.'

He was staring up at her, wet-eyed, trying to coax some sense from the conversation.

'I just want you to hold me,' he muttered. 'Nothing else.'

She began to shake her head, to tell him he had to get a grip, to tell him to accept that whatever they had was over, but then came the burble of the Impreza coming down the lane and the glare of Jimmy's headlights reflected in the hedge beyond the patio. The car swung onto the gravel and Lizzie heard a brief snatch of Adele before Jimmy cut the engine. Then his footsteps quickened and his shadow darkened the window and he was pushing on the kitchen door.

For a second he stood there, holding a bottle of red wine, not understanding. It was Pendrick who spoke first. He'd seen this man only yesterday.

'Police?' He looked bewildered. It must be some conjuring trick. His gaze went to Lizzie. 'How the fuck did you manage that?'

303

'He's my husband. His name's Jimmy.'

'Hi, Jimmy.'

Suttle studied the outstretched hand.

'What are you doing here?' he said.

Pendrick didn't answer. He was looking at Lizzie.

'In your heart you know I love you. Isn't that right?'

Lizzie shook her head. Suttle hadn't moved.

'He's pissed,' she said quietly.

'Yeah, I can see. So what the fuck's going on?'

Pendrick stirred. He drained the Stella and crushed the can. His eyes had never left Lizzie.

'Tell him. Lizzie. Just tell him.'

'There's nothing to tell.'

'No?'

'No. There never was and there never will be.'

'Really?' A smile had warmed the big face. 'You don't re-member? You don't remember Trezillion? All that?' His hand sank to his midriff and then crabbed down still further. 'Is it the scar? Is it that? Don't be ashamed, my love. I've seen worse.'

At last he got to his feet and slipped the wire cutters into his pocket. He offered Lizzie a dip of the head, a courtly little bow, then headed for the door. Suttle stood his ground.

'What is this?'

'Ask your wife.'

'I'm asking you.'

'Then I can't tell you. Either you see it or you don't. That's the thing about life, yeah?'

He gently pushed Suttle aside and stepped into the darkness. Suttle hesitated a moment, then followed. When Lizzie tried to get between them, he told her to go inside.

'Leave it, Jimmy.'

'Fuck off.'

He spun Pendrick round. Suttle's first blow caught him full on the mouth, the second put him on on the ground. Suttle began to kick him, driving the point of his toe into the big man's ribs. Pendrick offered no resistance, just soaked the punishment up. Finally, breathless, Suttle stood over him.

'If you set foot in my house again,' he said, 'I'll kill you. Right? You understand that? You hear what I'm saying? Do this again and you're a dead man.'

Pendrick peered up at him. His mouth was bleeding and he was nursing his bruised ribs.

'Too late, my friend.' He spat a tooth into the long grass and struggled to his feet. Moments later he'd disappeared into the darkness.

In the kitchen Lizzie was pale with shock. Suttle eased her into a chair, stood over her. She was shivering, her hands wrapped round herself. She wanted to know whether Pendrick had gone.

'Yeah, he has. You want to tell me what this is about?'

'Don't do the interview thing. Please.'

'OK.' He turned to the sink, trying to control his temper. Cold water from the tap eased his bruised knuckes. 'Just pretend I'm a bit confused. Trezillion? Scar? This is a guy that loves you, right?'

'So he says.'

'And you?'

'I've been stupid.'

'How stupid?'

'Crazy stupid. Stupid like you wouldn't believe.'

'Try me.' Suttle took a seat at the table.

Lizzie said nothing. She'd never felt smaller in her life.

'You want a Stella?' she said.

'You think that might help?'

'Yeah, I do.' She offered him a weary smile and tried to reach for him across the table. He shook his head and withdrew his hand.

She explained about meeting Pendrick, about how helpful he'd been with the rowing, how attractive he'd seemed, and how supportive.

'With the rowing, you mean?'

'With everything. I was in a bad place, Jimmy. And he seemed to understand.'

'Yeah, I bet he did. But you happen to be my wife.'

'He didn't know that.'

'Maybe not. But you did.'

'I was Lizzie Borden. That's who you wanted me to be.'

'Makes no difference. I trusted you. I thought I knew you.'

'Then you'd have known how unhappy I was. How this house ...' She tailed off. They'd been this way too often. There was nothing left to say.

'You went to this place Trezillion?'

'Yes. He drove me there.'

'When?'

'On Saturday. I lied to you, Jimmy. We'd sorted the club compound by lunchtime. Then we drove out.'

'You and Pendrick.'

'Yeah.'

'And?'

'It was lovely.'

'What was lovely?'

'The cove. The dunes. Being there with him. Everything.'

'So what happened?'

'Nothing. Except we talked.'

'He didn't try and come on to you?'

'Not at all. He was very sweet.'

'You sound disappointed.'

'I was.'

'You mean that? You were fucking *disappointed*?'

'I told you. I was crazy. Out of my tree. I didn't know what I was doing.'

'But you'd have ...?'

'Yeah. I would. Definitely.'

Suttle nodded, said nothing. Then he half-turned at the table and stared out into the darkness. *I've hurt him*, Lizzie told herself. *I've really hurt him.*

'The scar?'

'We were comparing accidents. His was a surfing thing. Mine you know about. It was just conversation.'

'Nothing more?'

'No.'

'I have your word on that?'

'Absolutely.'

'But you would have done if you'd had the chance?'

'Yes.'

She reached for him again. She wanted to tell him that fucking wouldn't have mattered. That the truly unforgivable thing was going all that way in the first place. A conversation that intimate, that natural, was the worst possible kind of betrayal. She wondered about trying to put this into words but knew it would only hurt him more. No relationship, she thought, could survive that kind of honesty.

'I love you,' she said. 'It's important you know that.'

Suttle nodded. His face was a mask. She heard the click of the fridge door opening. He popped a can of Stella and tipped it to his lips.

Lizzie told him about the landline. Suttle listened without comment. More Stella.

'Is that why he had the wire cutters?' he asked at last.

'Yeah.' She felt cold again. She began to shiver. 'That man's so damaged, Jimmy. And I never realised.'

Eleven

Tash Donovan and Milo Symons were arrested at dawn. Uniforms took them to separate police stations in Exeter and Torbay. They were booked in by the respective Custody Sergeants and provided with legal representation. Tash Donovan chose a solicitor she'd met at festival last summer. Milo Symons was happy with the duty brief.

Scenes of Crime, meanwhile, went into the mobile home at Tusker Farm. Within the hour they'd unearthed the Jacobson debit card, the associated ATM slips, a decent cache of cannabis resin and just under a thousand pounds in cash. The latter had been stuffed into a Co-op plastic bag and hidden under the mattress, a hidey-hole the CSI thought quaintly retro. By close of play the previous evening, Donovan and Symons had got the credit balance in the Jacobson account down to a shade over £93K.

Houghton chaired a meet of the *Constantine* inner circle at eight. The PACE clock would give the interview teams twenty-four hours before she'd have to apply to a uniformed superintendent for a twelve-hour extension. Under the circumstances she thought that wouldn't be necessary. The Scenes of Crime team had failed to locate Kinsey's laptop but they'd discovered two keys in the glovebox of Donovan's car. The team had the keys seized from Kinsey's flat and – subject to trying the new set in the apartment door – they were confident they had a match.

Houghton had asked Suttle to oversee and coordinate the two interviews. He'd already briefed the Tactical Interview Advisers working with each of the teams and agreed a strategy. Open account first, rapidly followed by the challenge phase. In Suttle's view there was no way either Donovan or Symons could survive the coming hours in the interview suite. They had both the motivation and the opportunity to return to the flat and consign Kinsey to oblivion. It was, he quietly confirmed to Houghton, a definite stone-bonker.

The eight o'clock meet was brief. At the end the interview teams departed to their respective police stations. Solicitors were due at the custody centres at nine o'clock. Disclosure and client meetings would occupy the next hour or so. By lunchtime, with a fair wind, *Constantine* might be close to a result.

Suttle was about to leave when Houghton called him back.

'You look tired, Jimmy.'

Suttle shot her a look, then nodded.

'Rough night, boss,' he muttered, heading for the door.

Both interview teams called a break at midday. Suttle had judged Symons the likelier to break first and had chosen to spend the morning at the Heavitree nick in Exeter. He was able to monitor proceedings via a video link from an adjoining room in the interview suite and had watched Symons explaining the events of Saturday night. His account exactly mirrored the story he'd told Suttle the first time they'd met in the mobile home: they'd won their race, they'd all had a drink or two, they'd walked across to Kinsey's apartment for a takeaway curry, and then they'd gone home. Only next day, when the detective guy arrived at Tusker Farm, did he realise anything had happened to Kinsey.

The two D/Cs on the interview team, both experienced, pressed him on a couple of points of detail and then tabled the evidence seized from Tusker Farm. Watching Symons on the video link, Suttle had the impression this moment came as no surprise. Symons admitted at once that they'd been to the ATM in Exmouth. Tash, he explained, needed the money to buy her mum a birthday present. She still had the card from collecting the takeaway and she definitely meant to pay Kinsey back when she next saw him. One of the D/Cs asked whether they'd got a receipt with the money and Symons said yes.

'How much money was in the account?'

'A lot.'

'How much?'

'Over a hundred thousand pounds.'

'Did that surprise you?'

'Of course it did. We knew Kinsey was minted but that's a huge amount of money to keep in an account like that.'

'Was your partner surprised?'

'Yes. She thought it was crazy too.'

'And did you intend to make more withdrawals?'

'Of course not. I just told you. We thought Kinsey was still alive. We knew we'd have to give the £200 back.'

'That's a lot of money for a birthday present.'

'That's what I thought, but Tash is like that. Always over the top. You get used to it in the end.'

The interview continued. The news that Kinsey was dead, admitted Symons, had changed everything. He'd phoned Tash in Yeovil and told her. She still had the card.

'Did she tell you she was going to make another withdrawal?'

'No.'

'When you found out, were you surprised?'

'Not really.' A tiny hesitation.

'Why's that?'

'Because Tash just gets an idea and goes for it. I was worried, to be honest. I thought there was no way we wouldn't get found out.'

'You were right.'

'Yeah.'

'And Tash?'

'She didn't see it that way. She said the guy's dead so we might as well help ourselves. She also said that Kinsey had kept the account secret so no one would know about it.'

'Why secret?'

'I don't really know. To hide the money, I suppose.'

'To hide the money from who?'

'I don't know. The taxman? I don't know.'

By now, he said, they had £400. A couple of days went by and nothing happened so they made another withdrawal and then another. In the end, he said, it became a kind of routine. Like the money was their own.

'But it wasn't, Mr Symons.'

'I know.'

'It belonged to Kinsey, to his estate. We call that theft.'

'Sure.'

'But you just carried on.'

'We did.'

The interviewing D/C wanted to know how long these withdrawals would have gone on. Rosie Tremayne was a woman in her thirties, one of Houghton's stars, and Suttle admired the cool rapport she so quickly established with Symons. It had been Houghton's idea to put her alongside the man in the belief he responded well to older women, and in every respect it had worked. He told her they'd have kept hammering the ATMs until the account was empty.

'And what would you have done with the money?'

'There's a project I'm trying to get off the ground, a film. Kinsey had helped me already, so in a way I was telling myself it wasn't really theft, just something he might have done in any case.'

'But you didn't know that, did you?'

'No. He'd promised me £45,000 but not that much, not a hundred grand.'

'So it was still theft? Is that what you're saying?'

'Yes. We stole the money. That's what we did.'

It was at this point that Suttle felt the first prickles of apprehension. Milo Symons was playing these questions with the straightest of bats. He wasn't evasive. He wasn't attempting to justify himself. He didn't seem to be hiding anything. On the contrary, there was a naivety – even an innocence – in his willingness to cooperate. From *Constantine*'s point of view, this would be a quick win when it came to a theft conviction. But would this man really have killed someone?

During the coffee break Suttle phoned the Tactical Interview Adviser supervising the other interview. His name was Frank Miller and – like Suttle – was an incomer from another force. After an uneasy start, Devon and Cornwall had definitely grown on him. Not least because major crime investigations exposed him to suspects like Tash Donovan.

'She's nuts, mate. Totally barking. We could have sold tickets for this morning.'

Like Symons, her description of the Saturday night in Exmouth Quays hadn't departed one jot from her initial witness statement. One of the two interviewing D/Cs was Luke Golding. The TIA had told him to press her on the relationship with Kinsey, and when he'd done so she'd happily complied, offering detailed descriptions of the movement sessions they'd shared up in his apartment. Once she'd even got to her feet in the interview room to demonstrate a particular cycle of gesture therapy and it was only her solicitor, in the end, who'd managed to get her to sit down again.

'What about the rest of it?'

'The sex, you mean? We got lots of that too. She had this guy for breakfast, but he was paying good money so he must have got something out of it. Five hundred quid for a quickie? Maybe they were both barking.'

'You think she liked him?'

'I don't think liking came into it. The woman's an actress. She can play a part. Bottom line, Kinsey was a punter. End of.'

Confronted with the evidence from the ATMs, Donovan

– like Symons – had admitted everything. Yes, she'd lifted an initial 200 quid from his account that Saturday night. Yes, she meant to give the money back. And yes, once she knew that Kinsey was dead, she'd seen no point letting all that money go to waste.

'She said that? She used that phrase?'

'Yeah. It was like she had some right to it. The dosh was hers. It was written in the stars. It was the earth giving her a little prezzie. Total bollocks, of course, but quite amusing. You have to hand it to this woman. Second house starts any time now. If you're looking for something a bit different, you should pop across.'

Suttle declined the invitation. He wanted to know how Donovan had been so sure they'd never get caught.

'To be honest, mate, I'm not sure that ever really occurred to her. At one point she told us that Kinsey was always boasting about his money, and how clever he was, making all this moolah. He told her about his ex-wife too, and how he'd managed to dream up some clever scheme to hide loads of dosh from the old dragon. Donovan said he called her the Gobbler. I think she assumed the Jacobson account was part of all that. I guess it was empty when the wife walked out and Kinsey filled it up again and kept it going.'

'She was specific about that? Donovan?'

'Not in so many words, but that was the drift. Like I say, Donovan lives on another planet. I don't think it's ever dawned on her that some of the stuff she does might have consequences. It's all hippy shit, I know, but it seems to work for her.'

'You think she's worried?'

'Not in the least.'

'You think she killed Kinsey?'

'I'm starting to wonder.'

The interviews recommenced at 12.45. This, Suttle knew, was the moment of truth. It fell to Rosie Tremayne, in Exeter, to suggest that Symons' misdemeanours might not have stopped at theft.

'In your statement to D/S Suttle you denied that your partner, Tash, had any kind of relationship with Kinsey.'

'I said he fancied her. Like everyone fancies her.'

'But you also said it ended there.'

'Yeah. That's true.'

'But it isn't, is it? Because your partner, Tash, has told us she had regular sex with Kinsey.'

'For money.'

'Yes. But it happened, didn't it? So it didn't – as you put it – end there?'

'That's shagging. That's all it is. For money.'

'But you knew.'

'Yeah. Me and Tash don't have secrets. The shag money was for the film fund. The one I told you about.'

'Sure. I believe you. But the fact is your partner was having sex with another man.'

'He was crap at it. Why would that worry me?'

'Because it might not end there.'

'What?'

'Because Kinsey might want more of Tash than you thought. The man had money, lots of money. Tash is a professional actress. Just lately, as we understand it, she hasn't done much. She's still attractive. She might still dream about making the big time. Kinsey could help that happen, couldn't he? With all his money? All the support he could give her? And all those doors he could open?'

Symons was staring at her. He was visibly upset. Rosie had touched a nerve. Suttle was tempted to applaud. At last, he thought.

'I don't have to listen to this, do I?' Symons was looking at his solicitor.

'Mr Symons?' Tremayne was waiting for an answer. 'Milo?'

314

Symons, angry now, abandoned his solicitor and turned back to Tremayne.

'You think Tash lied to me? Is that what you think? You're telling me she had something else going on with him?'

'I'm asking you a question. I'm suggesting that might have been a possibility.'

'Then the answer's no. No way. We're like that, me and Tash, always have been.' He interlinked his forefingers and tugged them hard. 'You know what I mean? Tash would never do that to me, never.'

'Why not?'

'Because she wouldn't.'

'But why?'

'Because she knows what it would do to me. How I'd feel about it.'

'And how would you feel about it?'

'I'd feel shit about it. I'd hate it.'

'So what might you do ...' Rosie gestured at the space between them, which had been warmed by this sudden burst of temper '... if you got really angry?'

Symons stared at her. It was beginning to dawn on him where these questions might be going.

'What do you mean?' he said.

'I'm asking you whether you have a temper. The answer appears to be yes. I'm also asking you whether Tash was – is – important to you.'

'Of course she's important. She means everything to me, Tash.'

'So what would you do to keep her? If you thought she might be tempted to go off with someone else?'

'But she wouldn't. Not Tash.'

'But she might, Milo. Or you might *think* she might.'

'Never. I never thought that. Never.'

'I don't believe you. Look at it from our point of view. Tash means everything to you. You've just admitted it. You know

315

she has sex with this man Kinsey. You know that Kinsey has the kind of money that might make a big difference to her career. You also know he's mad about her. Are you really telling me you were never – ever – worried she might leave you?'

'For him, you mean?' He laughed. 'You're mad. This is crazy.' He looked at his solicitor again. 'Tell her to stop.'

The solicitor gestured him closer. Suttle wished he could lip-read. Maybe he's telling his client to relax, he thought. Or maybe he's starting to see it Tremayne's way.

'My client needs to be clear about the precise allegation you're trying to make,' he said.

'Our allegation is this, Milo. That you were drunk on that Saturday night. This we know from your own account. That you had and have a passionate relationship with your partner, Tash. This too we know. That something probably happened that Saturday night, some remark, something inappropriate between Tash and Kinsey that later sparked a row between you both. Are you with me?'

Symons nodded. He looked transfixed. She might have been telling him a story, Suttle thought, about someone else.

'Go on,' he said.

'That you went back to the apartment that night, back to Exmouth Quays, either with Tash or without. That you got into the flat with Tash's key. And that you killed Kinsey.'

'*Killed* him?'

'Yes.'

'But why? How?'

'Why, I think we've dealt with. How has, at this point, to be supposition. In the end he fell from his own balcony. Perhaps you'd like to tell us exactly what happened before that moment?'

Symons began to shake his head. Disbelief had given way to something else. Fear.

'You really think I killed him? Kinsey? Jake? You think *I* did that?'

'Yes.'

'Why? Why would I have done it?'

'I think we've covered that. You were jealous. And you knew he had money.'

'How?'

'Because you'd seen the slip from the ATM. One hundred and seven thousand pounds, Milo. Think about it.'

'So I killed him? You really believe that?'

'Yes.'

From this point on, the interview went nowhere. The two D/Cs came at Symons from every point of the compass. They pointed out how heavily all the circumstantial evidence weighed against him. They thought it entirely reasonable that he would want to remove the threat of Kinsey from his private life. They agreed that one hundred thousand pounds would ease a lot of problems about funding Symons' precious film. Rosie Tremayne even hinted that the idea might have been Tash Donovan's in the first place, in which case Symons would earn himself a much lighter sentence by testifying against her.

The latter suggestion sparked another outburst from Symons. Tash had never said anything of the sort. And even if she had, there was no way he'd grass her up. To think otherwise was totally vile. This whole thing, he kept saying, is sick. He'd never hit anyone in his life, let alone killed anyone. After stopping at the ATM in Exmouth, he and Tash had gone home. Theft? Yeah. Murder? No way.

Mid-afternoon, Houghton called a meet in a borrowed office at Torbay. Donovan and Symons had been escorted back to their respective cells to ready themselves for the next round of questioning. In the meantime Houghton had to assess where *Constantine* might go next.

Suttle had driven over from Exeter with Rosie Tremayne. He was still convinced there was a way to go with Symons.

'We haven't bottomed him out yet,' he said. 'The guy's more

of a firework than I thought. Press the right buttons and we might still be in business.'

Houghton wanted Tremayne's opinion. She said she was doing her best but deep down thought Symons was telling the truth.

'How does that work?'

'He gave us everything on the ATMs. He coughed the lot. Frankly, I think murder's a bit out of his league. He wouldn't have the bottle for starters. Plus he comes over as quite a gentle guy.'

'He was pissed,' Suttle said. 'And that can change everything.'

Houghton turned to Frank Miller. She wanted the TIA's take on Tash Donovan. How had she reacted to the suggestion that she'd been complicit in Kinsey's death?

'She laughed. I think she was genuinely amused. This is a woman who plays a thousand roles before breakfast. I think the killer thing quite appealed to her.'

'But she denied it?'

'Big time. She said Symons was too pissed to manage a shag that Saturday night, let alone kill anyone. She also said that vegetarians try and avoid that kind of thing.'

'She's a veggie?'

'So she says.'

'And that's some kind of defence?'

'Definitely. She says veggies never kill people.'

'What about Hitler?'

'Good point, boss. Maybe we can bring that up in the next session.'

Houghton didn't share the ripple of laughter that went round the room. She and Nandy would be conferencing on the phone any time now. She had to know where this thing was headed next.

It was Suttle who broke the silence.

'We keep on at them both. That's the only option we've got.'

'We've nothing new to throw at them?'

'No.'

'So without a confession …?'

'You're right.' Suttle nodded. 'We're fucked.'

The next session began at half past four and lasted into the early evening. This time Suttle was monitoring the Donovan interview. Sitting beside Miller, watching the video feed, he knew the TIA had called it exactly right. Donovan was putting on the performance of her life. Not because she was trying to hide something but because she at last had an audience. She said she felt sorry for Kinsey. That last second and a half of his life, she said, would have been seriously crap. Exmouth Quays in the rain was a shit place to die. She hadn't the first idea why he'd done it, and if she'd ever suspected him of suicidal tendencies she might have put a lot more effort into keeping him happy.

The latter phrase appeared to offer at least the hint of an opening. Had this relationship of theirs been more substantial than she'd ever admitted? Might he have ended his life because she wouldn't commit to more than visiting rights? To both questions she answered with a flat no. Kinsey, she said, was an impossible man to get close to. No wonder his wife had done a runner.

In his heart Suttle knew she was right. At ten past seven he took a call from the TIA at Heavitree. After consultations with his lawyer, Symons had decided to go No Comment.

Within half an hour both interviews had been terminated. Det-Supt Nandy was waiting with Houghton in her office at Middlemoor. She'd obviously briefed him already. The atmosphere was grim.

'The PACE clock stops at five tomorrow morning,' he pointed out. 'The briefs will kick up if we insist on another session tonight, and to be frank I can't see what we'd achieve. We could try for an extension and start again tomorrow morning but D/I Houghton's right. We've got nothing left to fire at him. We're out of bullets. There's nothing left.' He paused. 'Jimmy?'

Suttle knew the question was coming. This was his party, his idea. He'd led them up this cul-de-sac. How did he propose to get them out?

'Are we talking fresh lines of enquiry?' Suttle asked.

'Yes.'

'There aren't any, sir. Not immediately. Not that I can see.'

'So what do you suggest?'

'I suggest we charge them anyway. And leave it to the jury.'

'You mean the CPS.'

'Of course.'

'Charge them with what?'

'Theft, obviously. Plus murder.'

There was a silence. Bold move. Two of the D/Cs exchanged glances. Rosie Tremayne was looking at her hands.

'But we have no evidence, Jimmy. All we have is supposition, which, if my memory serves me correctly, is where we began.'

'I still think he was killed.'

'By them? By these two?'

'Everything points that way. Motive. Opportunity. You said it yourself, sir. Other people are a mystery. No one really knows. What you see isn't necessarily what you get.'

'That's true. Do you think the CPS feel the same way? We need evidence, Jimmy. And we haven't got it. This is very nice, very tidy. But it doesn't *prove* they did it.'

'No, sir. It doesn't.'

'So what do we do?'

'I don't know, sir. It's your call not mine.'

He nodded. Suttle thought he caught a hint of disappointment in his face. *Maybe I've given up too easily*, he thought. Maybe Nandy was expecting more of a fight. Fat chance.

'Carole?' Nandy had turned to D/I Houghton.

'I suggest we go for an extension, sir. A night in the cells sometimes does the trick.'

'And what are we proposing in the way of fresh evidence? Mr Cattermole will need to know.'

Cattermole was the duty uniformed Superintendent. Without active ongoing inquiries, he wouldn't sanction a custody extension.

Suttle stirred. He was looking at Houghton.

'There's still one call I need to make,' he said.

'On who?'

'Pendrick.'

It was gone nine when Suttle made it down to Exmouth. The light was on in Pendrick's flat, and Suttle's finger on the bell brought him to the door. His lower face was still swollen from last night and when he led the way upstairs he seemed to have difficulty walking.

'Is this personal?'

'No.'

'What do you want then?'

'I need to talk about Kinsey. We made a couple of arrests last night, Tash and Milo Symons. We'll be charging them tomorrow.'

'For what?'

'Theft and murder.'

'Murder?' The word drew the faintest smile. 'You think they killed Kinsey?'

'Yes.'

'You can prove it?'

'We can get a result in court.'

'How does that work?'

Suttle walked him through the evidence: a hundred grand's worth of motivation and the key to Kinsey's door.

'But why? Why would they do it?'

'You know why they'd do it. Symons was jealous as fuck and they both wanted the money. A couple of minutes in the

321

apartment? The two of them? No CCTV? Middle of the night? Job done.'

Pendrick was brooding. Suttle wanted him to say something. Anything.

'Well?'

'Kinsey was an arsehole. He deserved it.'

'What does that mean?'

'It means he's better dead. It means there's one less of his breed to fuck things up.'

'So we owe Tash and Milo a thank you? Is that what you're saying?'

'Definitely.'

'Are you surprised they did what they did?'

'I'm glad he's gone.'

'That wasn't my question. I asked you whether you were surprised or not.'

Pendrick's head came up. He held Suttle's gaze.

'Nothing surprises me any more,' he said.

Suttle was in Colaton Raleigh by half ten. He stopped for a beer at the pub up the road, brooding on the day's developments. He'd rarely felt so knackered. The last couple of weeks seemed to have emptied him of everything. He toyed with the pint for a while, then took a couple of mouthfuls and left it on the counter.

At the cottage the lights were off downstairs. He found a note from Lizzie on the kitchen table telling him there was food in the oven but he didn't even bother to look. Upstairs, he checked on Grace then went into their bedroom. Lizzie appeared to be asleep, her face turned towards the wall. Suttle got undressed in the bathroom, hanging his suit on the door ready for tomorrow morning. He sponged his face, brushed his teeth and spent a long minute eyeballing the image in the mirror. When he returned to the bedroom, Lizzie hadn't moved. He slipped into bed and turned his back on her. *Enough*, he thought.

Twelve

Lizzie waited until she heard the burble of the departing Impreza before she got up next morning. Suttle must have fed Grace first thing because when she went next door she found tiny gobbets of porridge on her daughter's nightgown. She took Grace back to bed, knowing she had to get them both out of the house for a bit. The thin curtains had never met properly in the middle and the broad blue stripe told her it was a lovely morning.

'The seaside, eh?' She gave Grace a hug.

They took a bus from the stop outside the village store. By half past nine they were in Exmouth. It was a five-minute walk to the seafront. The tide was out and the offshore sandbank was busy with gulls and oystercatchers. Heading east, Lizzie could feel a real warmth in the sun. Imperceptibly, her spirits began to rise.

Curiosity took her to the rowing club. To her surprise the gates were open, the door to the Portakabin unlocked. She parked the buggy at the foot of the steps and lifted Grace out. She wanted to sit her on one of the rowing machines, slide her up and down, pretend they were at the funfair. She mounted the steps and pushed at the half-open door.

After the blaze of spring sunshine, she stepped into the chill of the semi-darkness inside. She could hear someone on one of the rowing machines at the very back of the clubhouse, a steady rhythm, pull after pull, but it was seconds before she could make out a shape in the gloom. A face turned briefly towards her. The rate quickened, then fell back again.

Pendrick.

She knew she should leave. Then she changed her mind. Picking her way over the machines, she carried Grace towards him. He was still rowing, still pushing himself up and down the slide. She stopped beside the readout. Nearly twenty kilometres.

'How long have you been here?'

'Since seven. More than three hours.'

'Christ.'

He was still moving, his rhythm undisturbed. He didn't look up at her. Finally, she turned to go.

'Don't,' he said. 'I have to tell you something.'

'Please, no.'

'It's not that. I promise.'

'What then?'

'It's about this Kinsey thing. They've arrested Tash and Milo.'

'What for?'

'Theft ...' the sweat glistened on his swollen face '... and murder.'

'They killed Kinsey?' Lizzie was staring at him.

'No.' He shook his head. 'I did.'

'*You* did?'

'Yeah. I killed the man. It was me who did it.'

She took a tiny step backwards. *Mad*, she thought. Insane.

'Please,' she said. 'You're making this up. It's a story. You're trying to impress me. You're trying to get us back to wherever you want us to be. I don't want to know. There's no point. It's over.'

'I know that.'

'Then enough's enough. You needn't say any more.'

'You're wrong. I have to tell someone. You walked in.

You're here. All you have to do is listen.' At last he looked up at her. 'Will you do that?'

Kinsey, he said, had been getting under his skin for more than a year. The boasts. The money. The big fuck-off apartment. The way he went out and bought himself a crew. Everything. Then came the discovery that he was going to build at Trezillion. And not just Trezillion but other sites up and down the coast. These sites were almost holy. The man was into serious desecration. The man wanted to leave his scent, his smell, everywhere. Why? To make more money. He'd had a conversation about it, warned the man.

'What did you say?'

'I told him to drop it. I told him to go and build somewhere else.'

'And?'

'He just laughed. He told me I didn't know what I was talking about. He said the world had moved on. He told me that Cornwall needed people like him. He said it was time I got real.'

After that, he said, they barely talked at all. Whenever they were together, Kinsey made sure there were other people around – other guys, people like Andy Poole, people he could rely on. Pendrick looked up at her. He knew Kinsey was frightened of him because he could see it in his face.

'And did that make you feel good?'

'Yes.'

'And did he do what you wanted?'

'Of course not. You know that. You've seen those vile brochures he had done.'

Lizzie nodded. Pendrick was still rowing, still pulling hard on the machine: 20,762 metres.

'Is that enough to kill someone? A brochure?'

'Of course not. It was the girls as well. The Thai girls. He got them from an agency in Exeter. He'd boast about that too, in the boat. He'd tell us what they did for him, what he liked most. He had a special girl. He called her Blossom. Apparently she didn't speak a word of English and he liked that because he didn't have to talk to her. What that guy did was unforgivable.'

'To the girls?'

'To everyone. He screwed everyone. He couldn't stop himself. Guys like that don't deserve a life.'

On the Saturday night, he said, they'd all gone back to Kinsey's apartment. At first Pendrick hadn't wanted to be any part of the celebration but Lenahan had talked him into it. Bring a bit of class to the gathering. Give the wee man a shock. And so they'd all walked across to Exmouth Quays and piled into the lift and carried on drinking.

'It was me who first realised how pissed Kinsey was. He'd been drinking like a schoolgirl all night, knocking back the champagne – Christ knows how much he must have drunk. Then Tash arrived with the takeaway and he was shovelling that in too. There was no way he wasn't going to be ill. You could see it coming.'

When he started throwing up over the balcony no one else noticed. Pendrick went out there and got him to bed.

'Why? Why did you do that?'

'Because I'd made a decision.'

'About what?'

'About him, about Kinsey. I'd had enough. I was going to do it.'

'Kill him?'

'Yes. I didn't know how but that's what I was going to do.'

'Why?'

Pendrick's rhythm began to slow and for a moment Lizzie thought he was going to stop, but then he picked up again, ducking his head to wipe the sweat from his eyes.

'He had this laptop. He said it was in his bedroom. And before he started throwing up he'd promised us all a bit of a show. He called it his PowerPoint. I think he meant it as a joke.'

'You took a look at the laptop?'

'I did. I was using his en suite. He loved showing all this shit off. Granite walls. Jacuzzi. The laptop was on his bed. I fired it up and there she was.'

'Who?'

'Blossom. The Thai girl.'

'And?'

'You don't want to know. After that the guy hadn't got a prayer.'

'So you got him in from the balcony? This is later?'

'Yeah. I left him on the bed. All I wanted were his door keys.'

'Where were they?'

'In his trackie bottoms. I just took them. The state of the guy, I don't think he even knew they'd gone. Yeah, sweet ...'

He was speeding up now, pushing hard with his legs against the machine. Tash, he said, had organised the taxi. He'd been the first to be dropped off. He'd waited up until half two and then walked back to Exmouth Quays. He'd approached Regatta Court via the beach. It was pouring with rain and he hadn't seen a soul. The key to Kinsey's apartment also opened the main door to the block. Once inside the apartment, he'd gone into Kinsey's bedroom. Judging by the smell from the en suite, he must have been sick again.

'Was he asleep?'

'Spark out.'

'So what did you do?'

'I unlocked the sliding door to the balcony, went back to fetch him and just tipped him over.'

'Didn't he struggle?'

'Not really. He was still pissed, completely out of it.'

'And that was it? Simple as that?'

'Yeah. Call it waste disposal if you like. Afterwards I went back for the laptop and threw it into the dock. I was back home by half three –' he glanced up at her '– and I slept like a baby.'

By midday *Constantine* had finally hit the buffers. Milo Symons, while admitting the theft charge, had refused to answer any more questions about Kinsey's death, while Tash Donovan was asking her lawyer whether he could make any kind of case against the police for harassment. Why do these people keeping banging on, she kept asking him. Don't they understand about veggies?

By now, with Houghton's agreement, Det-Supt Nandy had decided to charge both Donovan and Symons with theft and release them on police bail. They'd have to attend the magistrates' court on Friday morning, where a decision would be taken about a possible referral to the Crown Court. With respect to any murder charge, Nandy was obliged to accept that lack of evidence put the investigative ball back in the Coroner's lap. *Constantine*'s MCIT squad had done its best to unearth evidence of foul play but had found nothing. In all probability, by accident or otherwise, Jake Kinsey had taken his own life. Case closed.

Houghton insisted on taking Suttle for lunch. They drove to Topsham, a flourishing village upstream from Exmouth, and went to a pub down by the river. It was a glorious day, warm enough to sit at a table by the water. Suttle insisted he wasn't hungry but Houghton ignored him. She knew his affection for ham, egg and chips. She even returned with two sachets of brown sauce.

'You look terrible,' she said. 'Is it Kinsey or something else?'

Suttle wouldn't answer. In one sense it was both. But how on earth could he explain that his wife had been off with a key witness?

Houghton wouldn't give up.

'Are you sleeping OK?'

'Yeah. Pretty much.'

'Grace all right?'

'She's sweet.'

'Lizzie?'

'Lizzie's fine.'

'So what happened to your hand?'

Suttle fought the temptation to cover his right hand. His knuckles were bruised from last night. He said he didn't want to talk about it.

'Some kind of fight?'

'Yeah. My fault.'

'And the other guy?'

'Don't ask.'

'It *was* a guy?'

'Yeah.'

'Not Lizzie?'

'No.'

The food arrived. They ate in silence. Suttle didn't want to talk about Kinsey or Donovan or Symons or any of the rest of it. He didn't really want to talk about anything. On every front his life seemed to have come to an end. Much like *Constantine*.

Houghton had other ideas. She told him that Nandy had been impressed.

'He might not show it, Jimmy, but he thinks you're the business.'

'Great. Didn't work though, did it?'

'That doesn't matter. What matters is you tried. He likes that. He loves people who answer back.'

'Is that how you got to be a D/I?'

'Partly.' She nodded. 'Yeah. He likes people who argue their case. You did just that. He can't fault you for running with it. And he can't fault you for effort.'

He eyed her for a moment. He felt immensely weary.

'Is all this meant to be some kind of compensation prize?'

'That's infantile, if I may say so. You're better than this, Jimmy.'

'Yeah? Am I?'

He held her gaze, then pushed the plate away. He said he

was grateful and he meant it, but she was right. He was going through a shit time and the worst of it was that he didn't know how it was going to end.

Houghton nodded, said nothing. A swan pushed through the reeds at the water's edge. She tossed it a fragment of roll. Then one of Suttle's chips. More swans.

'Crack on, Jimmy,' she said at last. 'That's the only option we've got.'

Lizzie was back at home when she got the call. It was Tessa from the rowing club.

'We have a bit of a situation,' she said at once. 'And I'm wondering whether you might be able to help.'

Molly Doyle, she said, had phoned half an hour ago after a conversation with the Coastguard. The club's single scull had been spotted by a fishing boat a mile off Straight Point. It was upside down in a worsening chop and there was no sign of the rower. Tessa had gone straight down to the club compound and found a pile of clothes inside the Portakabin. She was convinced they belonged to Tom Pendrick. He hadn't booked himself out the way he should have done, but the single's trolley was on the beach, awaiting his return.

'Why are you phoning me?'

'Because Tom might have mentioned taking the single out. Have you seen him recently?'

'I saw him this morning.'

'And he didn't mention it?'

'No. He was on the machine. He'd just done twenty K. Why would he go out rowing after that?'

'Good question.'

Tessa promised to keep her in touch and then rang off. Lizzie sat by the phone. All day she'd been on the point of putting a call through to Jimmy. Given what she'd inflicted on the man, it was the least she could do, but the more she thought about it, the more she realised she didn't know what to say. She imagined the squad must be close to arresting Pendrick. Hence this morning's confession. And hence, she assumed, his abrupt disappearance. The man had too much pride to hang around. Life had taken him to a very bad place. He'd settled his debts with Kinsey, and now, like his wife, he'd chosen the ocean to end his days. Full circle, she thought, reaching for the phone.

Suttle was still in Topsham when his mobile began to beep. He checked caller ID. It was Lizzie. For a moment he didn't want to talk to her but then he thought of Grace. Maybe something's happened. Maybe she needs the car.

'Hi.'

'Where are you?'

'Topsham.'

'We need to talk, Jimmy.'

'About what?'

'Pendrick.'

'There's nothing to say.'

'There is, my love. He killed Kinsey. How do I know? Because he told me.'

It took Suttle less than half an hour to make it to Chantry Cottage. An ugly situation had just got a whole lot worse. How long had his wife known about Pendrick? A couple of days? Longer? Had they been so close she'd decided to shield a killer? Why hadn't she told him before?

He found her feeding Grace in front of the TV. *The Good Life*. Bizarre.

'Just tell me what happened,' he said.

Lizzie told him about the conversation in the clubhouse. She tried to apologise for not contacting him earlier but knew it was pointless. Whatever she said, she was looking at serious trouble. In his current mood her husband was probably contemplating an arrest for perverting the course of justice.

'So where is he? Pendrick?' Suttle hadn't sat down.

331

'He's disappeared. He took the little single scull and no one's seen him since.'

She told him about the call to the Coastguard. By now she assumed they'd have the helicopters out and maybe the lifeboat.

'And what do you think?'

'What do you mean?'

'You know the guy. What's he up to?'

'I think he's had enough.'

'What does that mean?'

'I think he's out there somewhere, probably dead.'

'Why? Why would he have done that?'

'I assume he knew.'

'Knew what?'

'That you were close to arresting him.'

Suttle stared at her, then produced his mobile. Moments later he was heading for the patio, trying to get a signal to raise D/I Houghton. When he left the house he was still talking. He didn't say goodbye.

The club's single was towed back to Exmouth by the trawler skipper who'd made the initial sighting. Molly Doyle and Clive, the Club Captain, were on the dockside to manhandle it out of the water, lash it to a roof rack and take it back to the club compound. An exhaustive search of the clubhouse had discovered no sign of a note from Pendrick or any other clue that might shed light on his disappearance. Neither was there anything in the single to suggest what had taken him to sea.

The search for a body, alive or dead, continued after dark. Two helicopters with infrared gear worked slowly offshore from Straight Point, a couple of miles to the east, following the tidal drift. It was blowing a Force 4 by now and the sea temperature was a bare 13°C. The search was called off at 21.49, to be resumed at first light.

Thursday happened to be club night at the compound. News of Pendrick's disappearance spread quickly. At Lizzie's request

Tessa had driven up to Colaton Raleigh and taken her and Grace back to the club. In the absence of Jimmy, she wanted to be close to people. The thought of an evening alone in Chantry Cottage filled her with dread.

Rumours had been circulating for nearly a week now about Lizzie and Pendrick. No one knew that she was married, let alone that she was wedded to a detective investigating Kinsey's death, and she was touched by the number of near-strangers who offered her words of comfort. He may have made it ashore. He may still be out there. Don't lose hope. Not yet.

Past ten o'clock, still at the club, her phone rang. It was a voice she didn't recognise.

'My name's Dom,' it said. 'I live in the flat under Tom Pendrick's place.'

'You're the chiropractor?'

'The very same.'

He said he'd dropped by to pick up some paperwork and had found an envelope on his mat with her name and phone number on it. A couple of coppers had just been round and he understood that Tom, silly bugger, had gone missing. Maybe Lizzie ought to pop round and pick up the envelope. Sooner rather than later, eh?

It was Tessa, once again, who supplied the lift. Dom was a big man. He gave Lizzie a hug and kissed Grace and told her he was sure everything would turn out OK.

'He's wild, that Pendrick, but he knows the sea. He'll be back. I know he will.'

He gave her the envelope and wished her luck. Lizzie opened it in the car. Two keys, both Yale. Tessa was about to take them back to Colaton Raleigh but Lizzie told her to hang on. She got out of the car and crossed the pavement. The lock on the street door at number 50 was a Yale. Lizzie struggled with the first key but the second was a perfect fit.

Lizzie returned to the car and bent to the window.

'Here's fine,' she told Tessa. 'You've been brilliant.'

Suttle was at home watching the late-evening news when the text arrived. He spared it a glance. It came from Lizzie. She'd be staying in Exmouth overnight with Grace and would be back in the morning. He put the mobile to one side. On his return from Middlemoor, hours earlier, he'd found a note on the kitchen table: '*Gone to the club. Tess is sorting us out. No news yet.*'

No news yet? Suttle was beginning to wonder whether it was worth sustaining a relationship on notes and texts and a great deal of silence. When he'd got back to the office, late afternoon, Houghton had been waiting for him. He'd already given her the bones of Lizzie's news and now she wanted to know exactly what had been going on. Suttle had done his best. Through no fault of his own, his private life had overlapped with *Constantine* and finally been swamped. Lizzie, he said, had hooked up with Pendrick. He'd no idea how far the relationship had taken them both, but no way had it come to a clean end. At this point Houghton had nodded at his injured hand.

'Pendrick?'

'Yes, boss.'

'You've assaulted a prime witness? Who turns out to be the killer?'

'Yes, boss. A couple of good shots, if we're talking detail.'

'Pleased to hear it. So where is he?'

'I've no idea.'

The meet with Houghton had ended soon afterwards. Given the relationship with Pendrick, she wanted Lizzie interviewed under caution. If it turned out she'd been shielding Pendrick, she'd be in deep shit. As far as Pendrick was concerned, *Constantine* had no option but to wait. If his body was found, the file would go to the Coroner. If he'd simply disappeared, the file would remain open. As for Suttle himself, she had no choice but to remove him from the enquiry. Any further input to *Constantine,* she said, would be prejudiced by what she called his 'personal circumstances'.

'You're happy with that? We understand each other?'

'Perfectly, boss. I'll sort out the interview and look after the baby. Happy days, eh?'

Now he was watching the last of the national news. The local headlines followed. Pendrick's disappearance was the top story. Suttle found himself looking at footage from last year. A gaunt figure, barely recognisable, was climbing a set of stone steps at Penzance Harbour. A battered-looking rowing boat was secured to an iron ring beneath him. His hair was long, hanging in tangles around his bare shoulders, and in close-up his eyes seemed to have lost focus. The news coverage cut to a grainy shot of a helicopter sweeping seawards in the dying light, but what stayed with Suttle were the eyes. What had really happened out there in the Western Approaches? Had this man been nursing a serial grudge against the world at large? Had his poor bloody wife gone the way of Jake Kinsey?

Minutes later Suttle's mobile began to ring. It was Gina Hamilton. He got to his feet and went out onto the patio. Even here the signal wasn't great, but he got the gist of what she was saying. She too had been watching the news. So what was the real story?

'We got him,' Suttle said. 'He did Kinsey.'

'And you can prove it?'

'No problem.'

'How?'

'Full confession.' He stared into the windy darkness, his vision beginning to blur. 'Piece of piss.'

It took Lizzie nearly an hour to get Grace to sleep. Pendrick's bedroom was at the back of the flat. There were clean sheets on the bed and even a couple of neatly folded towels on the low table beneath the curtained window. Elsewhere, Pendrick had made a similar effort to tidy up. There were more towels in the tiny bathroom and a new tablet of soap in the shower tray. The kitchen was spotless, the draining board empty of washing-up. A note beside the electric kettle told her where to find tea bags and coffee, and there was fresh milk in the fridge. She might have stepped into a well-run holiday rental. All it lacked was a cheerful note about local must-see attractions.

With Grace asleep in the clean white spaces of Pendrick's bed, Lizzie went back into the living room. She'd half-expected another note – longer, more intimate – but there was nothing to explain the decision he'd taken. She'd absolutely no doubt about what he'd done.

He'd pushed his body to the limits on the rowing machine. He'd wheeled the tiny single down to the water's edge. He'd set off on an ebbing tide with the knowledge that the weather was about to get a whole lot worse. And somewhere out there, maybe at a time of his choosing, maybe not, he'd capsized the single and slipped away. An end like that, she realised, was totally in keeping with the journey he'd made. His wife had blazed the trail. And, after ridding the planet of Jake Kinsey, Pendrick had followed.

Might this be evidence of madness? She didn't think so. In awkward, uncomfortable ways Pendrick was a man who hung together, a jigsaw puzzle that made a kind of hallucinatory sense. His wasn't everyone's view of the world. In many ways it was savage, unforgiving. In others, she thought, it had an almost childlike naivety. He seemed to believe in the simple things – in getting by on very little, in taking people at face value – and when he realised that real life didn't work that way, that people rarely played by the rules, he'd decided to fold his hand and chuck it in. That's what had taken him to sea in the single. And this flat of his was pretty much all that was left.

She prowled around, trying to ignore her emotional investment in his story, trying to play the investigative journalist, not knowing quite what she was looking for. Leaving her the key this way was, she imagined, a kind of apology. Pendrick had brought sunshine and chaos to her private life. He hadn't understood that this thing of theirs was over and he'd made it infinitely worse by turning up pissed the other night. Any man could imagine the consequences of a scene like that, and access to his flat was his way of saying sorry. Thus the clean sheets and the readied towels. You might be hurting. You may need a place of refuge for a while. Make yourself at home.

His PC was on a table in the corner. There were file boxes beneath the table, each file neatly labelled. She knelt on the rug and started to go through the first box. This was stuff that went back years, letters to friends, photos from a thousand beaches, shots of Pendrick and the woman who'd shared all those adventures. Lizzie spread a handful of the photos on the rug. She was struck at once by how similar the woman was to herself – her own slightness, even her own smile. This must be Kate, she thought. No wonder he'd been so eager, so earnest, so committed. Déjà vu was too weak a word. In the sand dunes at Trezillion he must have been talking to a ghost.

She pulled out another box, extracted another file. This one was more recent. Inside she found an appointment slip for an SD clinic in Bristol. Mr T. Pendrick was due to attend on three dates in January this year. Beside each date was a pencilled tick. SD? Lizzie returned to the file, extracting a printout from the Internet: The web address was www.nhs.uk/conditions/erectile-dysfunction. She stared at it a moment, beginning dimly to understand. SD meant sexual dysfunction. Pendrick, poor man, couldn't get it up.

She sat back on her haunches, her gaze returning to the photos of Kate. Was this something that had happened to Pendrick recently? Or had it been casting a shadow for years? If the latter was true, she could only imagine the consequences. SD had never played a role in her life. Far from it. None of her boyfriends had ever let her down in that respect, and even a night on the Stella didn't seem to affect her husband's prowess. Pendrick on the other hand clearly had a problem.

She began to read. Physical causes of SD apparently included diabetes and nerve damage after prostate surgery. Psychologically, you could blame guilt, depression or some kind of unresolved conflict. She gazed at the list of triggers. As far as she could gather, it pretty much summed up the person that Pendrick had become. Guilt about Kate. Depression about the fate awaiting Trezillion and all the other Cornish coves. And the conflict with Kinsey, which, until a wet Saturday night a couple of weeks ago, had defied resolution.

She picked up a photo. It could have been one of a million beaches – the blueness of the ocean, the curl of faraway surf, hints of a palm tree in the corner of the frame – but what took her eye was the grin on Pendrick's face. It was natural, unforced, wholly genuine. This was a man who was happy in his skin. In the last hours of his life had he met that person again? Before he'd slipped under the waves had he found a kind of peace?

She thought about that last question, knowing she'd never be able to satisfy herself with an answer. Then she heard Grace beginning to stir. The tiny cry took her back to Chantry Cottage, and she shut her eyes, trying not to think about the wreckage of her private life.

After a while she got to her feet. Her mobile was in the bedroom. Grace, thankfully, was still asleep. She took the phone back to the living room and scrolled through the directory until she found the number she wanted. After a while she thought she might have got the time difference wrong but then came the familiar voice.

'Lizzie? How the fuck are you?'

'Crap, if you want the truth. We need help. Badly. And so do you.'

Thirteen

The search for Pendrick's body resumed at first light. By now there was no chance he was still alive. Exhaustion and hypothermia would have killed him long before the police chopper appeared once again over the boiling sea.

Suttle went to work as usual. The downstairs office, briefly busy after *Constantine* rose from the dead, was empty. A house fire in Seaton had taken the lives of two kids and their mother was gravely ill in a burns unit in Salisbury. Growing suspicions about the role of her estranged partner had triggered an MCIT investigation. Nandy, as ever, was blitzing the job, but Houghton had tactfully let Suttle sleep in.

'Appreciate it, boss, but there's no need. The last thing I want is time on my hands.'

Lizzie spent the day in Exmouth. She was in regular contact with Molly Doyle, who had the ear of the Coastguard, but by midday the search for Pendrick's body was called off.

Shortly afterwards, she took a call from a voice she didn't recognise. D/C Andy Maffett wanted to interview her with regard to a Mr Tom Pendrick. She parked Grace with Tessa and walked to Exmouth police station. With Andy Maffett was another detective called Rosie Tremayne. Offered the services of the duty solicitor, Lizzie chose to say no.

The interview, conducted under caution, lasted longer than

339

she'd anticipated. Lizzie kept the details of her brief relationship with Pendrick to a minimum, only too aware of the detectives' curiosity. Yes, she'd got quite close to the missing rower. Yes, he'd been more than helpful in all kinds of ways. And yes, he'd finally trusted her with the story of what had really happened to Jake Kinsey. Had she been surprised by his confession? Of course she had. Had she had grounds to suspect anything of the sort earlier? Absolutely not. Had she been shielding him in any way? No.

The interview over, Andy Maffett had fashioned her account into a formal statement which she'd signed. Warned that she might be recalled for a second interview, she had no choice but to say yes. Murder wasn't something anyone would take lightly. Of course she'd assist in any way she could.

Shaken, she'd returned to Tessa's house. The last thing she wanted was conversation and in her heart she wanted to hide away with Grace in the silence of Pendrick's flat but the premises had been sealed off by the police pending a thorough search. For a while she'd thought about contacting her husband but in the end she knew she wasn't up to hearing his voice. The last few nightmare days seemed to have grown darker still. At the police station she'd sensed that the two detectives wanted a lot more. Chantry Cottage, and now Tom Pendrick, had taken her to a very bad place indeed.

Her mobile rang at just gone seven. Gill Reynolds.

'How's life in the country?'

'Crap.'

Lizzie briefly explained about Pendrick. The man had wanted out. He'd taken a boat and gone to sea. By now, she said, he was probably dead.

'Christ. So how does that make you feel?'

'Terrible.'

She described the night that Jimmy had returned to find Pendrick at her kitchen table. Since then, she said, they'd barely exchanged a word.

'Bloody hell. So what happens next?'

'I wish I knew.'

'You have to do something, Lou. You have to have a sort-out.'

'I know.'

'Then do it. Just do it.'

'I can't. I don't know how to.'

'That's pathetic. I'm not hearing this. Of course you can. You've shafted that man, Lou. You've crapped all over him. You've got a child too. Think of Grace. Pull your bloody finger out, kiddo, and *do* something.'

'Yeah? Like what?'

The question disappeared into silence because Gill was too busy to talk any longer. In truth there *was* something Lizzie had done, but since making the call last night she'd heard nothing. It was a long shot, she knew, but just now she couldn't think of anything better.

He phoned around eleven when she was about to join Grace in Tessa's spare bed. There was comfort in hearing the voice she knew so well. He wanted directions to the cottage. He'd meet her there next day. She told him how to find Colaton Raleigh. She had to spell the name.

'What time?' she said.

'Midday.'

'That's great. I'm having to rely on buses at the moment.'

'To do what?'

'To get out to the cottage. It's the back of beyond.'

'You're not even *living* there?'

'No.'

'Fuck. So where's Jimmy?'

She looked at the phone, realising that she didn't know.

'Don't ask,' she said.

The following day was Saturday. It was raining when Suttle awoke. One look at the chaos of the kitchen convinced him he needed to get out. He toasted the last of the bread, piled the dishes in the sink, fed the cat and headed out into the rain. With no particular destination in mind, he pointed the Impreza west. After Exeter he took the A30 up to Okehampton. The word Bude on a signpost seemed to hold some promise but half an hour or so later he changed his mind. By the time he found Trezillion, the rain had stopped.

He parked behind the dunes and set out on foot. The wind was rising and the tide was in, pushing at the line of seaweed and assorted debris at the top of the beach. He skirted the dunes and found a path that led up onto a headland. From here, sitting among the rocks, he could look down on the nearly perfect crescent that was Trezillion. Any decent detective, he told himself, had to be able to get into other people's heads, other people's hearts. That was an early lesson he'd learned from Paul Winter. You have to *become* these guys, he'd always said. You have to see the world through their eyes. Only then can you be sure how to make life tough for them.

So what was Pendrick's story? And how come this place had meant so much to him? The answer seemed all too obvious. Anyone growing up here would have fallen in love with the place. That might explain the start of his quarrel with Kinsey. It might also account for bringing Lizzie out here. Pendrick had wanted to share an important bit of himself, just the way Suttle had once taken Lizzie back to the New Forest village where he'd spent his childhood years. That's what you did when you met someone you fell for. It was a kind of homing instinct, impossible to resist, and it meant that you'd stumbled over someone who really mattered.

He shook his head, not wanting to take the thought any further. Pendrick had brought Lizzie here because she'd suddenly become part of his life. More importantly, she'd gone along with him, conspired with him, borrowed the key and let herself into this secret place of his. He wasn't at all sure that he bought Thursday's story about Pendrick sculling off into oblivion, but in truth he didn't much care whether the man was alive or dead. Either way, it was too late. From where he was sitting, among a scatter of spring flowers in the spongy wetness of the turf, the damage had been done.

He got to his feet and headed away from Trezillion, following the cliff path. The next town of any size was Newquay. Maybe he could get a bus back from there to pick up the Impreza. Maybe he'd even be up for the return walk. But after half an hour he'd had enough. Trekking on for mile after mile seemed purposeless. He'd lost some inner sense of direction. He felt like a piece of debris, useless, inert, adrift in deep space. Increasingly depressed, he turned back towards the cove, his head bent against the first flurries of the returning rain.

For maybe a mile the cliff path zigzagged upwards. Then came a fork beneath an outcrop of black granite. A path less trodden led to the very edge of the cliff. The cove lay off to his right, the whiteness of the beach fringed by the sand dunes. That's where my wife wanted to make love to Pendrick, he told himself. That's where my marriage came to an end. The wind was gusting now, blasts of cold air off the ocean, and he felt the salty prick of moisture in his eyes. He took a step forward, then another, peering over the edge of the cliff. The sea boiled on the rocks below, surging back and forth. Easy, he told himself. A second or two of gathering terror and then nothing but darkness. For a moment he was perfectly still, telling himself that it would be for the best, that it would offer the kindest way out, but then he shook his head, thinking of Kinsey, of Pendrick, of Lizzie, of Grace, glad of the hot jolts of anger that flooded through him, an anger he could almost taste. He turned and headed inland, away from the cove and the roar of the incoming surf.

The path was steep. Minutes later, maybe a quarter of a mile inland, he found himself climbing through torn rags of grey mist towards a single tree bent almost double by the wind. His doubts had flooded back again. Had all this started way back,

343

with his decision to go for Chantry Cottage? Had he bullied Lizzie into coming with him, into sharing this fantasy life he'd promised her? Should he have been a bit more cluey about the signals she was sending him, about her growing sense of lostness? Should he have been a better husband? A better dad? And just as important in another way, should he be making a bigger effort to get a word of warning to Paul Winter? A man he'd once revered? The questions hammered at his brain: three betrayals, three ways he seemed to have got life so comprehensively wrong. Maybe all this wasn't Lizzie's fault at all, but his.

He was still staring at the tree. The way it had shied away from the wind, the way it had given in to the elements, spoke of an implacable force beyond the power of resistance. But then he climbed a little closer, buffeted by that same wind, and stopped again, barely feet away. Despite everything, he realised the tree was still alive. On bough after bough he could see tiny green buds pushing through. Despite the wind, despite the salt off the ocean, despite the mountain of odds stacked against it, the tree was hanging on. Why? Because it hadn't – wouldn't – surrender. Because it had clung to a life of its own. Come back in a week or two, he thought, and it would be in full leaf. Climb up here on a glorious day in midsummer, with the temperature in the eighties, and he might pause a while to enjoy the shade it offered. He found himself grinning, suddenly alive again. The rain was harder now but he didn't care. He'd had enough of chasing the same old questions around and around. Guilt, in the end, took you nowhere. He checked his watch. Early afternoon. Perfect.

He was in Modbury within the hour. A petrol station on the edge of the town had pink carnations in a bucket outside the pay-booth. He bought three bunches and a bottle of Sauvignon. Minutes later he was parked across the road from Gina Hamilton's house. Her Golf was on the hardstanding. He stood at the front door for a second or two, dripping from the

344

rain. She must have the radio on, he thought. Adele. Bless.

He rang the front-door bell, the flowers and the wine readied. When the door finally opened, he barely recognised her. Her feet were bare and she was wearing a pair of blue overalls, way too big. A crimson scarf was knotted over her hair and the brush in her right hand was threatening to drip white gloss all over the doormat.

She looked at him for a moment, then her eyes strayed to the flowers. If she was in any way surprised, it didn't show.

'You've come to give me a hand?'

'Sure,' he said. 'My pleasure.'

He left next morning at five past eight. Lizzie had been trying to get through to him all evening. Finally, he'd texted her back, asking if Grace was OK. 'Grace is fine,' came the reply. 'We have to talk.' But Suttle didn't want to talk. Not yet.

Then, in the early hours, came another text. 'Please meet us in the cafe at St David's Station. We're on the 09.28 to Portsmouth.' Suttle hadn't responded, rolling over and telling Gina it could wait.

Now he slipped into the Impreza and headed towards the A38. He was in Exeter by nine. Driving into the big car park outside St David's station, he wondered how Lizzie and Grace had made it over from Colaton Raleigh. The buses were hopeless on a Sunday. Had she got a taxi? Or had someone given her a lift?

He found her at a table in the far corner of the café. She looked pale and drawn. She'd gelled her hair too, and it didn't suit her. Her coffee mug was empty. Suttle asked her whether she wanted another. She shook her head.

'And you, young lady?'

Suttle had picked Grace up. She was wearing a dress Gill Reynolds had brought down from Pompey and already it looked too small.

Grace wanted cake. Suttle carried her to the counter. Already this little tableau felt surreal. His wife crouched over her empty coffee mug, staring into the middle distance. A rucksack and a bulging holdall on the floor beside Grace's buggy. A retired couple by the window having a quiet ruck about God knows what. Horrible.

Suttle carried the cake and a coffee back to the table and settled Grace on his knee.

'You'll need a hand with that lot.' He nodded at the bags.

Lizzie shook her head. She could manage. She'd always managed. It wouldn't be a problem.

'Don't be silly. I'll give you a hand.'

She shook her head again. She seemed close to tears. She glanced at her watch, fumbled in her bag for the tickets, anything to soak up the silence. Then, for the first time, she met his gaze.

'Is that all you've got to say?'

'Yeah.'

'You don't think we mean it? You don't think we're off?'

'Your decision, Lizzie. Not mine.'

'Going, you mean?'

'Yeah. And everything else.'

She looked at him for a long moment.

'You won't ever let this go, will you?'

'I've no idea. I haven't been here before.'

'But you won't. I know you won't.'

'How do you know?'

'Because all men are the same. Black and white. One strike and you're out.'

'One strike? Is that how you see it? Some kind of game?'

'Don't.' She turned away. 'This isn't helping.'

Suttle shrugged. If she wanted the satisfaction of a full-scale domestic, then he was happy to oblige. Otherwise there wasn't a lot to say.

'Your mum's, is it?' He broke off a chunk of cake and gave it to Grace.

'Yes.'

'So what's the story? What have you told her?'

'I told her the truth. I told her we're sick of living in the country. I told her we need a real home.'

'We?'

'Me. Does that sound selfish?'

'Yes, since you ask.'

'Thanks.'

'My pleasure.'

Suttle fed Grace more cake and then brushed the crumbs off her dress. A voice on the tannoy announced the imminent departure of the Waterloo train. Passengers for Portsmouth should change at Salisbury.

Suttle was nuzzling the warmth and softness of his daughter. At this rate, he thought, he'd be the one in tears.

Lizzie's hand was back in her bag. Then Suttle was looking at two pairs of keys on the table.

'Are they for me?'

'Yeah. They're both for the cottage.'

'You won't be back?'

'No. Not there. I'm through with it, Jimmy. I've had enough.'

'So it's over. Is that what you're saying?'

'That's your call. And in case you're wondering, I've no interest in where you might have gone last night. Yeah? Does that make any sense?'

Lizzie got to her feet. Suttle gazed up at her. For the second time in twenty-four hours he felt totally marooned, adrift in a world he no longer recognised.

He cradled Grace in one arm and picked up the holdall in the other. The guy at the barrier wouldn't let him through without a ticket. Suttle dropped the bag, kissed his daughter on the cheek, held her tight. He'd no idea when he'd see her again.

'Bye,' he said.

Lizzie had readied the buggy. Suttle strapped Grace in. They had three minutes to make the train.

347

'Be in touch, yeah?' Suttle said.

'You've got the number. You know where we are.'

Suttle nodded. He wanted to kiss her but he didn't. He wanted to say he was sorry, that he'd miss her, that it was all some gigantic fuck-up, but he couldn't find the words. She looked up at him, a strange expression on her face, her lips puckered, then she gestured him closer.

'Yellow Fiat,' she said. 'In the car park.'

Suttle found the Fiat minutes later. It looked brand new. It carried a Hertz rental badge and it was empty. He was still stooped beside the driver's window, looking for more clues, when he felt a hand on his shoulder. He straightened up, glanced round.

Paul Winter.

They drove out of the city, Winter visibly nervous, checking the rear-view mirror, braking at the last minute for turns that would throw anyone in pursuit. Suttle sat in silence, ambushed by a million questions. Was this why Lizzie had been so desperate to talk last night? Had Winter spent the night at Chantry Cottage?

They came to a stop in the middle of a trading estate on the outskirts of the city. The acre of car park outside B&Q was nearly empty.

Suttle was looking at Winter. The older man had put on a little weight since they'd last met and he seemed to have acquired an early tan.

'So how come?' Suttle asked.

'How come what?'

'How come you're here?'

'Lizzie belled me.'

'She's got your number?'

'Yeah. She's had it for ever. She sends me photos of Grace from time to time. That's me doing the family thing, if you're wondering. And something else, son. She didn't tell you because I made her swear she wouldn't. All right?'

Winter was angry. Suttle could see it in his eyes. He'd been flattered by Lizzie's invitation to become Grace's godfather and had never taken his duties less than seriously. Hence, Suttle assumed, the enormous risk he was taking.

'She told you about the Pompey situation?'

'Yeah.'

'Dave Fallon? The Spanish bounty hunter?'

'Yeah. She phoned me.'

'And?'

'We're on the move. It's under control.' He didn't go into details.

'So what else did Lizzie tell you?'

'Pretty much everything, as far as I can judge. You're living in a shit hole, son. You should have sorted it out.'

'I know.'

'So why didn't you?'

Suttle stared out through the windscreen. He didn't have an answer. This was like talking to his dad, he thought.

'Did she tell you about a bloke called Pendrick?'

'That's all bollocks. The woman was upset. She'd been upset for months. When that happens, all bets are off. You should have noticed, son. Then there wouldn't have been a problem.'

Suttle nodded. Winter was probably right.

'It's crazy down here. The job's non-stop. There aren't the bodies to go round any more. This isn't Pompey. You work your arse off and then some.'

'Great. Except you happen to have a wife. And a daughter.'

'I know.'

'And that matters?'

'Of course it does.'

'Then sort it, son. Get a fucking grip.' His hand was in his jacket pocket. He produced a bulky white envelope. When he tossed it across to Suttle it landed in his lap.

'What's that?'

'Money.'

'I don't want money. I don't need it.'

'Wrong again, son. You need to get out of that khazi of a place, you need to find somewhere fit to live in, and you need to start behaving like a human being. That little girl loves you. And so does your daughter. So take a few decisions, eh? And make it happen.'

Suttle had never heard Winter like this, so forceful, so aggressive. Twenty-plus years in CID had made him the master of ambiguity, of the hidden threat, of the carefully prepared traps that littered every conversation. Not this onslaught.

'Do I get a say?'

'Of course you do, son. But do me a favour, yeah? Don't tell me you've been betrayed. Don't bang on about this guy Pendrick. Lizzie was out of her head. And that was down to you.'

'My fault, then.'

'Yeah. Fucking right. So like I say, get a grip.' His eyes hadn't left Suttle's face. 'Are you listening or do I have to start all over again?'

Suttle wouldn't answer. He fingered the envelope. It felt like a lot of money. Winter was still watching him.

'Euros, if you're wondering. High-denomination notes.'

'Where did you get it from?'

'None of your business, son. Sell the place. Buy somewhere half-decent. Then she'll come back.'

'How do you know?'

'Because I'm not stupid. Because I watch as well as listen.' He held Suttle's gaze a moment longer then checked his watch. 'I'm off back to Heathrow in an hour. Where can you get something to eat in this town at ten in the morning?'

Suttle took him to a hotel back by the station. They ordered a full English each, and prior to its arrival Winter raided a neighbouring table for a bottle of HP sauce. There were plenty of very good reasons for living in Croatia but breakfast evidently wasn't one of them. Even Misty, he said, was starting to pine for a proper plate of bacon and eggs.

'How is she?'

'Barking mad. It was my birthday last week. You know what she bought me? A set of salsa lessons. Nightmare.'

The thought of Winter stepping onto the dance floor with the high-kicking Misty Gallagher put a smile on Suttle's face. He wanted to know about her daughter, Trudy, the third member of Winter's little ménage. A car accident last year had broken her neck and left her with serious nerve damage. How was she doing?

'Fine. She's got a boyfriend, and you know what he does for a living?'

'Tell me.'

'He's a cop. Mad about her. Nuts. But you know something? He's another one who can't see further than the end of his dick.'

'You think I'm like that?'

'Only you know, son.'

'That wasn't my question.'

'OK, so what were you up to last night?'

'I was with a woman called Gina Hamilton.'

'Shagging?'

'Yes.'

'OK, was it?'

'Very nice, since you're asking.'

'She's a D/I, right?'

'Yes.'

'Divorced?'

'Nearly.'

'And what else?'

'Neurotic as hell.' Suttle was grinning this time. 'Stuffed animals everywhere. Just like Misty.'

The waitress arrived with breakfast. Winter attacked his black pudding with relish. A tiny comma of HP sauce attached itself to the corner of his mouth.

Suttle wanted to know more about Croatia. In a year or so it'd be joining the EU. After which Winter was back in the firing line for a European Arrest Warrant.

'You're right, son. Unless Dave Fallon gets me first.'

'So what's the plan?'

'Serbia. They've got proper gangsters there. Misty thinks she can pull some real animal who can sort out the likes of Dave Fallon. It's a neat idea. I just hope he's good with salsa.'

Suttle had no idea whether he was joking or not and knew – in any case – that it didn't matter. This brief glimpse of the old Winter had revived something deep inside him. They'd finished breakfast. Winter mopped his chin with a napkin and Suttle accompanied him back to the Fiat.

Winter wanted to know how to get onto the motorway north but Suttle had something else on his mind.

'You want out, don't you?' he said.

'Out of where, son?'

'Croatia. Serbia. Abroad. Wherever.'

'What makes you think that?'

'I've been watching. Like you always told me to.'

Winter shot him a look, then extended a hand.

'Glad to hear it, son. Take care of her, eh? And Grace too.'

Winter turned to go but Suttle called him back. He was holding the envelope. There was no way he could take this money.

'Leave it then.'

'Where?'

'Here. Any fucking where. It's not for you, son. It's for them.'

Three weeks later Lizzie was back behind her old desk at the Pompey *News*. The editor had agreed to let her work three regular days a week plus freelance payments for supplementary features she put together in her spare time. This was a blessing for her mum, who found Grace a bit of a handful, and it also permitted Lizzie to kid herself that very little had really changed. She still got her daughter up every morning. She still put her to bed every night. The only difference was that now she had more to think about than dripping taps, elderly neighbours and incessant rain.

Suttle, meanwhile, banked nearly £37,000 in euros. That same afternoon he wrote a cheque for exactly the same amount and sent it to Lizzie. He'd talked to her a couple of times on the phone, prior to nonsense conversations with his daughter, and had managed to avoid a row. Soon, he promised Grace, he'd be down to Pompey to take her out for a treat or two. Whatever else happened, he explained sternly, she wasn't to forget him.

His relationship with Gina Hamilton, meanwhile, appeared to have stalled. Performance reviews had given way to some kind of operational involvement in a long-running corruption case and she was working all hours. For his own part, Suttle was equally under the cosh. A pensioner couple had been found battered to death in their Sidmouth bungalow and to date no one had a clue who'd done it.

Late one night, as knackered as ever, Suttle lifted the phone to Gina Hamilton. Still numb from losing his daughter, he'd begun to hate the silence of Chantry Cottage. Most television these days was for the brain-dead, and conversations with the cat were a poor substitute for real life.

'I miss you,' he said.

'Yeah?'

'Yeah.'

'Really?'

'Really.'

'Be honest, Jimmy. I know exactly what you're missing.' She laughed. 'Me too, as it happens.'

*

Three weeks later, for the first time, Lizzie had a girlie night on the town with Gill Reynolds. Gill had forgiven her for walking out on Chantry Cottage and they were friends again. They went to a bar in Gunwharf, a minute's walk from Paul Winter's old apartment. Lizzie had banked the cheque from her estranged husband and was quietly checking house prices in Southsea. Jimmy would, in the end, turn his back on the West Country. Of this she was quite certain.

For a Friday night the bar was unusually empty. Gill had just booked a holiday in Sri Lanka, a fortnight she intended to share with her latest conquest. This was a guy she'd been dating for less than a month, but already she knew that she'd stumbled on someone who would change her life.

'He's really bright, Lou.' She sucked the last of her vodka and Red Bull. 'And the good news is he loves me.'

'Married?'

'Yeah. For now.'

'Kids?'

'Two.'

'So how's he going to explain a couple of weeks in Sri Lanka?'

'No idea. I've already bought the tickets, though, so there has to be a way.'

It was at this point that Lizzie's mobile began to ring. Not recognising the number, she ignored it. Moments later it rang again. Same number. This time it was a text with an accompanying photo. Gill had gone to the bar for refills. Lizzie stared at the text. For a second or two it made no sense, a message from a distant planet, just random nonsense. Then she forced herself to look again, to piece it together and try and understand. 'She's a beauty, I promise you. Any time you fancy it. XXXX'

Lizzie's finger strayed to the attachment. She opened the photo. It was Pendrick. He looked thinner and somehow younger. He was standing in the cockpit of a sizeable yacht.

The yacht was anchored in some kind of lagoon. Pearl-white sand. A fringe of palm trees. Not a soul on the beach. Pendrick was grinning the way she recognised from the photos she'd found in his file box. And he was blowing her a kiss.

Lizzie stared at the image, at the beach, at the nut-brown figure so carefully posed against the view. This was a face that she barely remembered, from a time she wanted to forget. So far, the police had shown no interest in calling her back for another interview and for that she was deeply grateful.

'Lou?' Gill was back with the drinks. She'd seen the photo. 'Who's that?'

Lizzie didn't answer, shielding the phone. Gill wasn't having it.

'Show me, Lou. Gimme, you old slapper.'

Lizzie shook her head. The image of Pendrick still hung on the tiny screen. She gazed at it a moment longer, telling herself to get a new mobile, then her finger found the delete command and the face was gone.

Acknowledgements

New series. New setting. New police force.

My thanks to Paul Netherton, Russ Middleton, Antonia Weeks, Jez Capey, Alan Barnsley, Mike West, Jane Williams, Larry Law and Jacquie Cox, all of whom opened doors, shared impressions, explained procedures and generally briefed me on the realities of criminal investigation in Devon and Cornwall. And a special thank you to Steve Carey who was extremely generous with his time and his long experience at the cutting edge of CID in south-west England. Top man.

My son Jack guided me through the netherworld of video gaming and, with his partner Hannah, masterminded a memorable stroll through the badlands of Harehills in his adopted city of Leeds. Rob Williams, a good friend, shared his memories of moving into a near-derelict country bungalow in a damp fold of the Otter Valley, an account which sparked Chantry Cottage. Mia Marchant-John from Regatta Court gave me an extensive tour of Jake Kinsey's extraordinary apartment, while Richard Soper offered a thought or two about the realities of life in Exmouth Quays. Most important of all, Deb Graham shared her memories of growing up in Exmouth – a recent past that has shaped a town I've grown to love. Sadly, Deb died suddenly this year and, as a consequence, this book is dedicated to her memory. An inspirational woman, much missed.

I also owe a substantial debt of gratitude to Dr John Maskalyk, whose book *Six Months in Sudan* is a must-read for anyone interested in what happens when one culture collides head-on with another. Eamonn Lenahan grew out of those pages and sharpened what I always felt to be the real thrust of this book: that we in the West live in a bubble of our own making and may be neither the wiser nor the richer as a result.

To everyone at the Exmouth Rowing Club, another sincere thank you. Offshore rowing, to be personal for a moment, has transformed our lives. Lin and I and our fellow Vulcaneers (don't ask) are the luckiest guys.

This is a step away from the Faraday series and represents an act of faith on behalf of my editor, Simon Spanton, my agent, Oli Munson, and – fingers crossed – my readers. Faraday's was a very different journey. Where this one may lead is anyone's guess.

Praise for Ben Blum's

RANGER GAMES

"A labyrinthine, utterly engrossing meditation. . . . An astonishing book, unlike anything else I have ever read."
—Jon Krakauer, author of *Missoula* and *Into Thin Air*

"Finely written and reported. . . . Surprising."
—*Chicago Tribune*

"A triumph of subtle reportage . . . an unsettling dissection of the moral corruptions, small and great, that bedevil the culture of military honor."
—*Publishers Weekly* (starred review)

"A vigorous, empathetic chronicle of a crime."
—*Kirkus Reviews*

"*Ranger Games* is a rare and totally original work of nonfiction. . . . Once you start reading, you won't put it down."
—Anthony Swofford, author of *Jarhead*

Ben Blum

RANGER GAMES

Ben Blum was born and raised in Denver, Colorado.
He holds a Ph.D. in computer science from the University of California, Berkeley, where he was a National
Science Foundation Graduate Research Fellow, and
an MFA in fiction from New York University, where
he was awarded the New York Times Foundation Fellowship. He lives in Brooklyn with his wife and stepdaughter.

www.benblumauthor.com

RANGER GAMES

RANGER GAMES

A TRUE STORY OF
SOLDIERS, FAMILY AND
AN INEXPLICABLE CRIME

Ben Blum

Anchor Books
A Division of Penguin Random House LLC
New York

FIRST ANCHOR BOOKS EDITION, JULY 2018

Copyright © 2017 by Ben Blum

All rights reserved. Published in the United States by Anchor Books,
a division of Penguin Random House LLC, New York. Originally published
in hardcover in the United States by Doubleday, a division of
Penguin Random House LLC, New York, in 2017.

Anchor Books and colophon are registered trademarks of
Penguin Random House LLC.

The Library of Congress has cataloged the Doubleday edition as follows:
Names: Blum, Ben, 1981– author.
Title: Ranger games : a story of soldiers, family and an inexplicable crime /
Ben Blum.
Description: First edition. | New York : Doubleday, 2017.
Identifiers: LCCN 2016058715
Subjects: LCSH: Blum, Alex, 1987– | United States. Army. Ranger Regiment,
75th. | Bank robberies—Washington (State)—Case studies. | Soldiers—
United States—Case studies. | Criminals—United States—Case studies.
Classification: LCC HV6661.W2 B58 2016 | DDC 364.15/52092—dc23
LC record available at https://lccn.loc.gov/2016058715

Anchor Books Trade Paperback ISBN: 978-0-8041-6969-1
eBook ISBN: 978-0-385-53844-2

Book design by Maria Carella

www.anchorbooks.com

Printed in the United States of America
10 9 8 7 6 5 4 3 2 1

FOR OMA

THE RANGER CREED

Recognizing that I volunteered as a Ranger, fully knowing the hazards of my chosen profession, I will always endeavor to uphold the prestige, honor, and high esprit de corps of the Rangers.

Acknowledging the fact that a Ranger is a more elite Soldier who arrives at the cutting edge of battle by land, sea, or air, I accept the fact that as a Ranger my country expects me to move further, faster, and fight harder than any other Soldier.

Never shall I fail my comrades. I will always keep myself mentally alert, physically strong, and morally straight and I will shoulder more than my share of the task whatever it may be, one hundred percent and then some.

Gallantly will I show the world that I am a specially selected and well-trained Soldier. My courtesy to superior officers, neatness of dress, and care of equipment shall set the example for others to follow.

Energetically will I meet the enemies of my country. I shall defeat them on the field of battle for I am better trained and will fight with all my might. Surrender is not a Ranger word. I will never leave a fallen comrade to fall into the hands of the enemy and under no circumstances will I ever embarrass my country.

Readily will I display the intestinal fortitude required to fight on to the Ranger objective and complete the mission though I be the lone survivor.

RANGERS LEAD THE WAY!

CONTENTS

RANGER GAMES

PROLOGUE

Most residents of Tacoma do not think of it as an army town. To visitors it presents as the scrappy kid sister city of Seattle, the coffee and arts mecca forty miles to the north with which it shares an airport. The notorious midcentury "Tacoma Aroma" from the paper mills has long since been filtered into submission. In its place are juice bars, outdoor supply stores, international film festivals. Every civic surface that hasn't been given over to kayaks and totem poles bristles with the spiky, membranous studio glasswork of homegrown sculptor Dale Chihuly. The only sign of Joint Base Lewis-McChord, whose more than 50,000 personnel make it Pierce County's largest employer by a factor of five, is the occasional Blackhawk helicopter beetling across the silhouette of Mount Rainier. In 2005, while Iraq spiraled into civil war and JBLM (then still divided into Fort Lewis and McChord Air Force Base) was dropping paratroopers over Afghanistan from its fleet of big-bellied C-17 Globemaster IIIs, Tacoma's city council entertained a proposal for a 420-foot "Tower of Peace" to rival Seattle's iconic Space Needle. No one dared mention the base. "We want this to be really inclusive," the tower's leading champion told Tacoma's *News Tribune*. "Let a person form in their own mind what the concept of peace is."

Five miles down I-5 toward the giant blank on the map where JBLM nestles into the strip malls of Lakewood, Parkland, and Spanaway, a different America fades in, one that would be instantly familiar to residents of cities with less complicated relations to their servicepeople. Yoga bows down to CrossFit. Puffy North Face jackets disappear under Carhartt work coats and military surplus camo. All those boardroom-ready Dale Chihuly pieces give way to the very different glasswork at Tacoma Pipe and Tobacco. The Patriots Landing retirement home advertises to military personnel: *You served us. Now let us serve you!*

Halfway down a block of auto dealerships and faded clapboard churches on South Tacoma Way stands a fieldstone-clad Bank of America that is popular with soldiers for its ease of access from I-5. The facade is glassy and generic. A bed of purplish cinders houses a row of shrubs as boxy as green Legos. In back is a parking lot accessible from the alley, feeding to a bright red drive-through ATM. It is just a dreary little branch like any other, a squat corporate cipher in an unremarkable neighborhood close to base.

At 5:16 on the afternoon of August 7, 2006, three men ran out of its front door screaming that it was being robbed.

———

Bank robberies come in two essential varieties. In a "nontakeover" robbery, the bandit—still the term used for bank robbers by the FBI, which publicizes monikers like "Snub-Nosed Bandit" and "Surfer Bandit" for as-yet-unidentified repeat offenders—slips a note to a teller explaining in brief that he intends the teller harm and desires cash. Nearby customers may not find out a robbery has occurred until after it is over.

The bank on South Tacoma Way, crowded with the after-work rush, was an example of the much rarer and more profound disruption of a "takeover" robbery. In a matter of seconds the bank left its old function behind. Building security features designed to protect the piles of $100, $50, and $20 bills from theft—thick concrete walls, bulletproof Plexiglas, clear lines of sight throughout the lobby—were now tactical assets for entrenchment and defense. Tellers and managers who had previously spent their days in service to the smooth operation of the bank now found themselves conscripted into its defilement.

Meanwhile, outside the floor-to-ceiling windows, traffic continued to trickle by in the sleepy August sun. Two customers in turn pulled up to the drive-through ATM, inserted their debit cards, engaged in small transactions, and drove away. Those who had fled the bank had already run down the block and crossed South 60th Street to reconvene in the front office of the Mallon Ford dealership, where employees were calling the police.

Two minutes later, long before the police arrived, a group of men in jeans, dark sweatshirts, and ski masks emerged from the alley that led to the bank's rear parking lot and started jogging down South 60th Street, in full view of the group at Mallon Ford. They carried a mix of AK-47 assault rifles with wood stocks and banana clips, pistols, and duffel bags. One witness, who had happened past the bank as the robbery began and pulled her car over so her husband could run into the dealership and report what he'd seen, instinctively started driving after the gunmen, until two of them turned back and made eye contact with her through the holes in their masks. That was when she remembered that her kids were in the backseat.

Though it was not yet in evidence, there was, in fact, a getaway vehicle. A Mallon Ford employee by the name of Don Keegan had been unloading his company truck in the alley two minutes earlier when he noticed a silver Audi A4 turning into the continuation of the alley on the next block. Four men jumped out, pulled on ski masks, and ran toward the bank. The Audi backed out onto South 60th Street and stopped next to a sealed utility shed whose front door bore a warning about tampering with military communications systems. The license plate was unconcealed. In the driver's seat was a nineteen-year-old kid in a T-shirt and sunglasses. Keegan got into his truck and drove around the block. On a residential street behind the bank, he happened to pass the same Audi going the other way. The four gunmen suddenly appeared from around the corner, spotted the Audi, and flagged it down as they jogged toward it. The kid in sunglasses stopped to pick them up.

That was my cousin Alex Blum.

It is hard to convey the depth of the shock my family experienced on learning that Alex had robbed a bank. It hit us like news of alien life. Alex was the most squeaky-clean, patriotic, rule-respecting kid we knew. Four months earlier he had achieved the goal he had been striving toward since he was a boy, becoming an elite Special Operations commando in the Seventy-Fifth Ranger Regiment's Second Battalion at Fort Lewis. In two weeks he was scheduled to deploy overseas to Baghdad, the fulfillment of his life's greatest ambition. Money had never interested him much. His father, my uncle Norm, a successful commercial real estate broker, had offered him $20,000 if he would delay enlisting in the army for a year. Alex politely declined.

The question that obsessed me for almost a decade after his arrest, the question that obsessed my family too, that obsessed even Alex himself, was simple: *Why?* At the time of the robbery I lived in Seattle, a few short miles from Fort Lewis. I had murky, conflicted feelings about the wars in Iraq and Afghanistan. It was hard to tell what I felt about Alex's fate other than a profound and untraceable wrongness. But the deeper I have dug into it over the years, the more it has cracked open everything I used to believe, like a fissure that turns out to go all the way to the heart of the world.

BOOK 1

THE GOLEM OF TACOMA

Just as thieves are not bad soldiers, soldiers turn out to be
enterprising robbers, so nearly are these two ways of life related.
—THOMAS MORE, *UTOPIA*, 1516

CHAPTER 1

SORT OF A HAPPY/SAD DEAL

From the time we were kids, Alex always had a simple dream: to defend his country from the forces of evil and oppression. None of us took this very seriously but him. After school in the suburbs of Denver, he'd run off in his camouflage T-shirt and cargo pants to play Vietnam commando on the canal that wove through the neighborhood, laying booby traps with dry seedpods and hiding behind stands of cattails to watch joggers jump and yip as the ground exploded beneath their feet. He rented every army movie the local Blockbuster carried, played every video game. There weren't many women in the ads back then, just grim-lipped men in high-tech gear dropping down ropes from helicopters to the sound of that unforgettable jingle: *Be . . . all that you can be . . . in the arrmeey.*

Back then Alex and I barely spoke. Our dream worlds did not overlap. By age seven I had become known in the family as a math prodigy. In the fields where Alex saw darting commie guerrillas, I saw fractally branching ferns, Fibonacci-spiraling pinecones, self-intersecting manifolds of swallows. I'd tell supermarket cashiers how lasers worked, give lifeguards introductions to the Navier-Stokes equations for viscous flow. I was, I realize now, completely insufferable. Human relations were not my specialty: too complicated. By thirteen I was taking calculus and physics at the University of Colorado. The only real common ground I had with Alex lay between the tattered street hockey nets in his driveway, where on summer afternoons he would occasionally deign to scurry around my knees and destroy me, smiling up in triumph each time he scored. He was five years younger but already a budding star.

Our fathers had both made their efforts at manly education. Alex's father, Norm, was the assistant coach of Alex's hockey team with the elite Littleton Hockey Association and played adult league with Denver's finest, including a smattering of pros from the NHL during the 1992 players' strike. Al, my own father, was the quarterback coach of George Washington High School's football team downtown. Both raced bicycles competitively in the brutal Front Range of the Rocky Mountains, played pickup street hockey in a warehouse rink Norm had convinced a business associate to set up, skied, golfed, climbed, and pumped inordinate quantities of iron. Summers they took us camping in the foothills, hiking through the canyons, fishing in the tick-infested ranchland of our Texas relatives. They stuck earplugs in our ears, jammed twelve-gauge shotguns against our shoulders, pointed us toward the discarded appliances at the other end of the ravine, and needled us until we squeezed the trigger.

It all took better with Alex than with me. Even when he was still in school, reports of his shining all-Americanness began filtering in: shoveling snow for an elderly neighbor, coaching little kids at hockey camp, defending classmates against bullies at Littleton High School. Though he was flying to tournaments all over the country with his nationally ranked club hockey team, he became more and more serious about the army thing. It seemed to me as if he had bought himself ready-made off a toy store display rack, a G.I. Joe action figure self, and now that he had the basic model, a world of attachments and product tie-ins were available to him. His would be a life of heroic accomplishment—an American life, a Blum life, a triumph.

Alex signed his 11X/Airborne Ranger contract in the final semester of his senior year at Littleton, reserving the chance to try out for the army's elite Seventy-Fifth Ranger Regiment. Many infantry recruits at the time signed contracts exactly like this one, lured by the chance to become an elite commando, but only a small fraction made it through the series of painful trials on the path to Special Operations. The rest were consigned to the regular infantry. Alex knew all this. He didn't care. He shipped off to basic before dawn on the fifth of July. Five months later he graduated from basic and became an infantryman. Three weeks after that he earned his airborne wings. One final stage remained: what today is called the Ranger Assessment and Selection Program. It was a little different in 2006 than it is today. For one thing, it was shorter: a concentrated four weeks instead of eight. For another, it was still called the Ranger Indoctrination Program—RIP.

Private First Class Alex Blum was about to become a very strong argument for changing the name.

———

There were fifty-five letters in the packet Norm put together a year after the robbery for Judge Burgess of the District Court of Western Washington, the man we had been told would decide whether and for how long Alex would be imprisoned in a federal penitentiary. They were from hockey coaches, neighbors, former employers, the Littleton High School guidance counselor for whom Alex had served as a student assistant his senior year, the father of his ex-girlfriend Anna. They ranged in size from a single paragraph hand-scrawled on a dentist's monogrammed memo pad to a four-page bullet-pointed epic. They had an awkward time deciding between past and present tense.

Alex has a great sense of humor and a great sense of honor. He treated my daughter and the rest of my family with the greatest respect.

The words that best describe the Alex I knew and loved were: confident, fun loving, driven, focused, independent, caring and dependable. I cannot say enough about how well liked Alex was here at LHS.

I can only hope my two sons, ages 5 and 9, have the passion like Alex Blum has for the Rangers and for protecting his country. That is one thing you can never teach and it made me proud to know him and made me proud to be an American.

My great-uncle Bernie in Texas, whom Alex used to visit every summer with his family, went on for a whole page of heartbroken reminiscence.

I appreciate your attention to my rambling. In my heart and mind I will never believe Alex was involved in planning this robbery. It just doesn't fit. Sincerely, Bernard Beck

My brother and sisters were there. My aunts, uncles, and grandmother were there. My mother was there, and so was her new partner, Ozi, in one of his first efforts to assert himself as a part of the extended Blum family. My father was there, squirming in formal prose like a jock in a suit, doubling every description.

Alex was almost painfully straight in high school. He was one of those kids that everyone liked and looked up to, because he never used his charisma in cruel or cynical ways, and he was a steadfast defender of the weaker, less popular kids. Now he is the one who is completely crushed and confused: his lifetime dream of serving his country has ended in trauma and disgrace, and he feels that his life is over.

There was a letter from me in there too. I was at that time studying artificial intelligence in the computer science PhD program at UC Berkeley, the culmination of a lifelong career path that would soon come to almost as abrupt a halt as Alex's. The insecure self-importance of those final years makes my own letter painful to read.

I'm five years older, so Alex and I never had much chance to talk one-on-one when we were growing up. In truth, I hardly knew him as more than a simple, friendly guy until the last few months, in which we've exchanged a number of letters. I have been surprised and gratified to find that he has grown into a mature, self-reflective young man, although of course I am saddened that it has taken circumstances as awful as these for me to discover this. He is just as baffled as the rest of us are to find himself in his present situation. The letters he has written me have been, primarily, focused on finding some explanation for how he could have gotten caught up in something like this, something so alien to his ideals and to the way that he thought he knew himself. He is earnestly and almost desperately seeking some kind of answer.

———

When we were kids, Alex's house was so perfectly suburban it almost unnerved me: ranch style, white-shuttered, filled with clubby wood cabinetry and Bev Doolittle landscapes in which patterns of sandstone boulders resolved, if you stared hard enough, into the noble profiles of Native American chiefs. My own family's house was bizarre, a novelty constructed on the model of a Scottish castle in the yard of an eccentric Texas real-estate tycoon who had intended it for use as a guesthouse, complete with turret and crenellated rampart walls. My brother and sisters and I lived there beholden to nothing but our own imaginations, as if in one of the children's fantasy novels our mom read aloud as librarian at our elementary school. Television was forbidden. Going to Uncle Norm's on the Fourth of July for the traditional Blum family barbecue was like going back to America. There were burnished hunks of chicken so greasy they turned our paper plates transparent, glasses of iced lemonade so sweet they made us squint, fireworks so loud they blasted craters in our eardrums. In the living room was one of those massive, shrieking kaleidoscopes of culture that we affected to disdain but actually coveted desperately: TV, TV, TV. Aunt Laura, her straw-haired, clothing-catalog looks undercut by the Jersey burr in her voice, always baked a cake in the likeness of the American flag. She used raspberries for the stripes, blueberries for the stars. Alex and I would hug with brisk indifference and then make our separate beelines to the food, just another pairing in the awkwardly prolonged combinatorial explosion of cousins that preceded every Blum family get-together.

When it came my turn to deliver my annual life update to Uncle Norm, I'd barely manage to get through the background material he would have to learn first in order to understand my latest mathematical factoid before he would clap me on the back, call me a genius for the umpteenth time, and edge toward the yard for Frisbee. *Hey, I wanted to call out, this stuff's actually relevant to your life! The arc of a throw is a parabola! Gyroscopic precession keeps the Frisbee level!* Instead I sat on the patio with the aunts and watched my father and my uncles hurl, pound, swing, bat, and kick Norm's vast array of athletic gear around the yard like hairy-chested mammals in some kind of toy-rich zoo enclosure. I thought I could perceive slight gradations of personality in the shapes of their bald heads. My dad's was flattest on top, like a musk ox or a walrus, some animal that settled doubt with impact. Uncle Fred's was roundest, a meditative egg that harmonized with his warm, smooth baritone, beard, and gentle belly. Uncle Norm's, the smallest and pointiest of the three, was a guided missile that zipped around threatening at any moment to target you for something "fun." All three had segued from the total athletic dominance of their childhood and college years into gracefully attenuated adult versions of same. A third uncle generally watched from the patio: Kurt, whose wavy brown mullet and mustache broke my system entirely. His jokes were menacing in a way hard to understand as a child, as if the punchline might turn out to be him smacking you in the face and laughing uproariously in his gritty, smoked-out bellow. The Blum brothers bought, sold, managed, and brokered real estate, occasionally collaborating on what were only ever described to us as "deals." I preferred conversing with my mother, a more appreciative audience for my spiritualized glosses on chaos theory.

My cousins weren't all like my uncles. Alex's older brother, Max, was shaping up to be an intellectual loner with a sarcastic sense of humor, and Sam and Carly, their younger brother and sister, followed at Alex's heels like shy puppies, heads bent close together, talking in hushed and dreamy tones. But Alex himself was a Blum straight from his father's mold: cheerful, confident, alarmingly muscular for a preteen, already fluent in that jocular male banter I had always felt so alienated by, quick to snag a disk out of the air and flip it back with a grin on his way inside to watch TV.

———

When Norm and I first met to talk about the robbery, I had already been interviewing Alex about his story for six months. I was twenty-eight years old and inching toward a new direction in life, teaching writing workshops at an elementary school in New York City as part of a fellowship at an MFA program and feeling more and more like a grown-up journalist, but being taken out to lunch by my uncle was an exercise in instant regression.

"Hey, handsome!" he said, rubbing his fist into my hair and corralling me toward his black Saab. I was in Denver for two weeks, staying with my mother. Climbing into the passenger seat felt like boarding a roller coaster. Norm accelerated with a smooth, important hum up the on-ramp to Interstate 25, a stretch of highway as ubiquitous in trips through Denver as paintings of stallions rearing up against the sunset are in the steakhouses, stadiums, and sports bars where you inevitably end up. After learning that I had been commuting from Brooklyn to Manhattan on a bike, he grilled me about my helmet usage, then segued into a long, funny tale of sweating each morning through his only two suits, heavy wool Salvation Army castoffs from my dad, while biking to his own first job in Denver in the '70s. Both of us seemed relieved at having found this common ground.

"These things," Norm said, chuckling, "were like *horse* blankets."

He brought the car and the anecdote to perfect simultaneous conclusions in a restaurant parking lot, ushered me through the front door with a cheerful wave at the hostess, and obliged our teenaged waitress to laugh three times with embarrassed pleasure at all his hammy compliments to her fine memory and good taste as she told us about the specials. It occurred to me that Norm was just the way Alex would be if you added thirty years and removed the distorting influences of a bank robbery and a prison term: relentlessly fun, impenetrably cheerful, quick to dispatch all troubling ambiguities with chummy cliché. He ordered the Cobb salad. I went with the spinach calzone. We watched the waitress walk away in silence. Norm's aura of energetic fun collapsed with startling suddenness.

"Okay," he said. "This gets very complex with the dynamics of the family."

By then the differences I saw between my uncles were no longer just geometric. Stories had accumulated on those bald domes, constellations among the pockmarks and divots. Norm, I knew now, had been the chubby, guileless runt of the family, an unplanned addition born two years after their only sister, Judy. Around the house they had called him "Stump." His older brothers once managed to convince him that ears could be trained to wiggle if you practiced enough. Norm worked for years on his jaw pops and clenched eyebrows before shifting his energies to hundreds of sit-ups, push-ups, wind sprints, and squats every morning before the school bus came, striving his whole childhood to match Dad's accomplishments as a high school football star and eventually exceeding them in both hockey and baseball long after anyone was paying attention. By the time Norm was checking wingmen against the boards for the State University of New York, his brothers were hitchhiking west to the dirtbag mountain towns of Colorado for a lost decade of carpentering, ski bumming, low-level pot smoking, and high-level beardedness. When Norm finally graduated, in 1979, and biked two thousand miles in three weeks to join them, they had already descended en masse to Denver, shaved, gotten into real estate, and surprised themselves by making more money than they knew what to do with. Dad picked up his littlest brother outside town in the yellow Toyota that he and Mom called the "rust bucket" and threw his bike into the backseat. He had a room waiting to rent to Norm in a drafty house he'd just bought on Gilpin Street, some friendly local millionaires to introduce him to, and one of those Salvation Army suits for him to wear to an interview at Coldwell Banker, the firm where he himself had gotten started before striking out on his own.

Norm worked there for eighteen years, through a leveraged buyout and two name changes. Dad never quite let go of his rebellious mountain hippie streak, wearing bright orange skater shoes to business meetings and referring in private to the imaginationless investors of his daily working life as "glompers," but Norm went full native, surrounding his sunny grin with slacks, oxford shirts, and tasseled loafers as naturally as with a hockey jersey. The deep, unsatisfiable yearnings that trouble his brothers have never afflicted Norm. The world as he finds it has always been enough. Those Fourth of July barbecues I remember so well were rare spiritual oases for them all, returns to a boyhood order that was possible only with Stump in the middle.

———

"Alex was a lot like I was when I was a kid," Norm began as we waited for our food. "He was a straight arrow. Sort of a protector. He was a class clown, just like me. Very into routine. Very particular about the location of his toothbrush and towel. Just like how pathetic I am—routine keeps me sane. Sports were his guiding light."

Norm's first son, Max, was born five years after Norm's arrival in Denver, when he and Laura still lived in a small house in Aurora that faced an unfinished commercial park and Buckley Air Force Base's looming polyhedral radomes, known around Denver as the "golf balls." When Laura became pregnant again in 1986, Norm knew they needed something bigger and better, with a broad, flat yard out back where his boys could learn half of what they needed to know about life and a nearby ice rink where they could learn the rest. Though he had just undergone knee surgery to repair a torn ACL from hockey, Norm brokered the biggest deal of his life to scrape together the down payment for the ranch-style fixer-upper that would one day unsettle me with its perfection and began hobbling over every weekend to paint, plaster, and shingle. A month before the deal closed, Laura went into labor with their second son.

Alex was born on April 11, 1987. By the time he was four years old, Norm had strapped skates to his feet and swung him out over the ice at the South Suburban Family Sports Ice Arena, a mile from their new house. By the time he was seven, he was charging around under his own power with a stick jammed in his gloves and a helmet the size of his torso for the Littleton Hockey Association's youngest competitive team, the under-eight "Mites," coached by Norm and a family friend named Murray Platt. He loved skating, loved scoring, loved bonking into teammates so both flopped to the ice, though he was smaller than most since his birthday was right after the cutoff.

Norm and his siblings were the product of an unlikely pairing. Al Senior, their father, was the son of Jewish glove makers in New York. Beverly Beck, their mother, was a glamorous Texan belle who met Al on a fashion-buying trip. Norm's best memories of his own childhood were from the Beck family ranch an hour south of San Angelo, where Beverly's brother Bernie raised cantankerous emus and skittish African deer. Starting when Alex was in kindergarten, Norm arranged to take his own boys there each summer to dodge scorpions and cottonmouth snakes and shoot crickets with a BB gun for use as bait to catch bass in the Concho River.

By fourth grade Alex had grown into a rambunctious, sweet-natured boy with blue eyes and straw-colored hair, popular with schoolmates at Greenwood Village Elementary School, loved for his jokes and generous passing by teammates on the Littleton Hockey Association's "Squirts" team, and worshipped by Sam and Carly. Everyone in the family remarked on what a great big brother he was. He got more and more serious about hockey. One day when Norm was doing his daily sit-ups, push-ups, and dumbbell curls in the basement den after work, Alex left his brothers and sister watching TV and wandered over to see how many push-ups he could do, then how much weight he could lift. Soon he was jumping in regularly, just as Norm had once helped his own father push aside the coffee table for army-style calisthenics every weekday at 6:30 a.m.

As Alex's coach on the Squirts team, Norm was putting him through further punishments each day at practice: sprints up and down the ice that left his teammates gasping in his wake. One afternoon at lunch with a friend of Norm's who had just watched Alex play, the man's young son asked Alex if he was going to be on the Colorado Avalanche when he grew up. Alex was just beginning to allow that there were a few other NHL teams he might be willing to settle for when Norm flashed him a sardonic grin that stopped him cold.

Norm likes to describe himself as a "realist." In his coaching days he was unafraid to inform parents that their darling progeny had no future in competitive ice hockey. He intended it as a kindness. When some poor couple from Colorado Springs drove their no-talent hack an hour each day to practice with a Littleton team, Norm always took it on himself to inform them that if scouts were going to be interested, they would have called by now. "Because their kid can skate backward and they can't skate at all, they're thinking he's got something special," he explained to me once. "But just 'cause their kid is ten or twelve and can skate backward doesn't mean he has a ticket to play in the NHL."

Norm was careful to extend his hockey realism to his own children. When Max got to be ten years old, Norm suggested that he hang up the skates. Alex was different. He really loved the game, even if his talent was not world-class.

In the car ride home from lunch, Norm told Alex how it was. The NHL was Valhalla, Mount Olympus, the Forbidden City, inaccessible to mere mortals. Norm himself had been rudely disabused of his NHL ambitions when he got to college and saw what real hockey talent looked like. The only reason he could skate with former NHL players now was that with all the bike racing he did in the Rocky Mountains, his conditioning as a fortysomething commercial real estate broker was unmatched even by young pros. Maybe one guy out of everyone Alex had ever played against had a whisker of a chance.

Was Alex the biggest, strongest kid on the ice? Could he skate backward faster than anyone he knew could skate forward? Did he have "dangles," the talented stick handler's uncanny ability to flip the puck back and forth through wormholes in space that no defender could follow? Alex shrugged, near tears, and guessed he didn't. What he *did* have, Norm hastened to point out, with no little pride, was a phenomenal work ethic. As long as he was willing to keep twice as fit and twice as strong as any other kid and battle twice as hard for every puck, he would keep earning a place for himself as a "grinder": a player who makes up for his mediocrity with toughness, team spirit, and willingness to do the less glamorous jobs on the ice.

———

As is common with Norm's take on the world, his view of Alex's hockey talent was gradually enshrined as common wisdom by everyone in his social universe, including Alex's future coaches. To a man, in their letters to Judge Burgess, they would speak of their great personal love and admiration for Alex while taking pains to point out that he had no great aptitude for the game.

> While not a "star" player . . . most dedicated player on the team . . . caring little for personal recognition . . .

> Not the most skilled player on the team . . . constant pursuit of his personal growth and team accomplishments . . .

> Talent he did not possess . . . had to get by on hard work . . .

You would never guess from their letters that by the end of high school Alex had earned a position on perhaps the best youth squad in Colorado, after consistently racking up team-high assists, and stood a good chance of a college hockey scholarship after a year or two in the junior leagues. Norm intended his "realism" lovingly, as a ward against the pain of disillusionment that he himself had felt, but ten-year-old Alex did not have that kind of perspective on his father and coach. He had always loved hearing Great-Uncle Bernie's stories of training soldiers after the Korean War, but I think Norm's dismissal of any chance that he would ever play professional hockey marked the moment when World War II subsumed the NHL as the arena of Alex's dreams.

At first much of his interest centered on our grandfather, Al Senior, who fought as a sergeant in command of a pair of half-track 50mm machine guns in the army's Fourth Infantry Division, landing in Normandy shortly after D-Day and punching Junkers, V-1s or doodlebugs, and Messerschmitts out of the sky above the hedgerows as the invasion pressed into the continent. The few stories Norm had passed on to Alex electrified him. While his fifth-grade classmates worked their way through *Are You There, God? It's Me, Margaret*, he began devouring Stephen Ambrose's trilogy of military histories *D-Day*, *Citizen Soldiers*, and, his favorite, *Band of Brothers*, about the 101st Airborne Division's elite Easy Company of paratroopers, who dropped behind German lines and assaulted heavily fortified machine-gun nests in advance of the landings at Omaha and Utah Beaches.

Ambrose writes from the perspective of the enlisted men in the field rather than the generals who tell them where to fight. This makes for a lot of suddenly dead protagonists, but the tale never loses its triumphant momentum, because the real hero is always the company itself, of which individual soldiers are like moods that come and go, intervals of complaint or jokes or kindness. Alex soon had his favorites—Dick Winters, the lieutenant who led a stunningly successful capture of a German "Eighty-Eight" gun emplacement, and Bob Guernsey, who applied for early release from the London hospital where he was recovering from a shrapnel wound so he could rejoin the company for its assault on the Ardennes—but what he loved most was the collective spirit that enveloped them. Page by page, he highlighted passages about the skill, perseverance, and heroic brotherhood of American men at war.

Alex began learning the American infantryman's kit in intimate detail. After school he spent hours in the tunnel of interlinked hollows behind the backyard juniper hedge, reenacting battles with a sawed-off hockey stick as a flintlock musket, Browning automatic rifle, or M1 Garand, ending with elaborate death scenes amid the pinecones and dry needles that left him dirty enough to horrify his mom. The Revolutionary War, the Civil War, and World War I all got

their due, but D-Day was his specialty. One summer he built a rep-
lica of Omaha Beach in the sandbox, complete with Belgian hedge-
hogs made of toothpicks and German bunkers on the bluff, and blew
up toy soldiers with firecrackers as they slogged in from the water.

For his daily workouts, Alex began interspersing the sit-ups and
push-ups he had picked up from his dad with a Navy SEAL regimen
he learned on vacation in Coronado, California. All this strength
training gave his hockey game a boost. Norm and Murray had finally
stepped aside as coaches for the Littleton Hawks, where Alex had
taken his father's advice to heart and settled into a strategic place for
himself as a passer and penalty killer who specialized in corner battles. Some of the teammates with whom he had been playing since
he was seven years old were now among the best in the state. What
Alex liked better than anything was watching a close buddy of his
raise his stick in victory after scoring off a puck that Alex had dug
out by grinding away against the boards. He made the most sense to
himself as a member of the team.

It was *Saving Private Ryan*, the $70 million Steven Spielberg epic
released the summer of Alex's eleventh year, that turned him on to
the Army Rangers. Tom Hanks and his squad of Rangers were a unit
every bit as cohesive, deadly, and ready to sacrifice for each other as
the Littleton Hawks. As terrifying as it was the first time he watched
it, Alex came to love the opening sequence of the Normandy landing
on D-Day, whose many graphic deaths took on a mythic grandeur in
repetition. It was the most realistic depiction of battle he had ever
seen, and the message behind it was equally compelling: even in the
vast mayhem of war, every single soldier counted, every sacrifice was
recorded, every hero was remembered. The army was the biggest
team of all. He even recognized the real-life soldier who had inspired
Private Ryan: Fritz Niland, a private featured in *Band of Brothers*
whose three birth brothers were killed the week of D-Day.

Alex was old enough now to roam away from the house on
his own. On weekends he would meet his best friend, Andrew, at
the place where Franklin Street crossed the High Line Canal and
scramble down the embankment to the canal bed, where in the cool,
echoing darkness under the concrete overpass they pulled on their
camouflage and strapped guns over their backs—Alex still had just a

BB gun, but Andrew had a real .22-caliber air rifle. For three hours they would make their way along the winding banks of the canal like Green Beret commandos in Vietnam, slipping without a sound between the cottonwoods whose ribbed gray trunks zigzagged overhead, sometimes tromping for miles through the shallow water of the canal.

D-Day was Alex's, but Vietnam belonged to Andrew, for whom Alex served as the loyal right-hand man who could be counted on for comic relief, a blend of court jester and confidant. In middle school, their duo expanded into a regular group of six. All played competitive sports. All wore mostly cargo shorts, Nike and Adidas T-shirts, and white baseball caps. They got into paintball. On weekend afternoons they would bike together down to Horseman's Park, an overgrown patch of weeds and pines along the High Line Canal where oddly shaped, never-used horse jumps rose from the hollows, and stage daylong battles, dividing up into teams of three and fighting for control of the ridge along the park's eastern border. Alex, with his goofball charisma and encyclopedic knowledge of military history, was the group's tactician, motivator, and comedian. It was paradise for a while, until the old woman who lived in the house atop the ridge saw them out there flanking each other along the canal bed and called the police to inform them that gang warfare had finally arrived in Greenwood Village. A few minutes later, when a bullhorn commanded that they drop their weapons, the boys climbed out of deep cover with their hands raised. The patrolmen rolled their eyes when they found out what the boys were actually packing, but that was the end of paintball in Horseman's Park.

Death in paintball was just a stinging annoyance that meant you were out until the next round. But at night as Alex lay in bed he played a mix CD he had made for himself of climactic orchestral numbers from his favorite war movies and imagined all the ways it might happen: his convoy flanked and ambushed, or a sniper leading him from a high window, or a Messerschmitt churning up the open field too quickly for him to evade. A circle of shadowy platoonmates gathered around his body as the music swelled, as in the death scene in the Xbox game *Medal of Honor*. He liked imagining that his death had saved them all and guaranteed the success of the mission. It helped him fall asleep.

Alex, Andrew, and the rest of their crew started ninth grade together at Littleton High School in late August 2001, dispersing to new coaches for their various sports. Three weeks later, on a sunny Tuesday morning, classes were interrupted by a scratchy announcement on the intercom.

To high school kids in suburban Colorado, the terrorist attacks of September 11 looked like nothing so much as a big-budget disaster movie: slow-motion explosions, mushrooming balls of smoke, insect-sized extras nose-diving from the windows. The mood in the hallways changed instantly. For two weeks the Denver sky was full of nothing but clouds and mountains. Then the planes returned, little metal splinters that dragged a new menace. Weekend paintball sessions suddenly started feeling a lot less like a game. When Alex's guidance counselor, Angela Zerr, informed him at the beginning of fall semester sophomore year that he needed to attend an after-school career counseling workshop, Alex replied politely that this would not be necessary because he already knew what he was going to do with his life.

Zerr estimates that over the remainder of Alex's high school career she tried to talk him out of enlisting between thirty and forty times. She had all the Blum children as they passed through LHS, but Alex was a special favorite of hers. Teachers had been telling her for years that they couldn't believe the clownish, popular Alex was related to Max, who was famous around school for his brilliance, prickliness, and straight A's, but in Zerr's opinion Alex was as intelligent as his older brother—he just had different priorities. She begged him to get a college degree first so he could at least enter the army as an officer. Alex told her he wasn't interested. He wanted to be a Ranger.

———

I had always felt so different from my family that it was strange at that first lunch with Norm to hear him talk about me and my siblings and cousins as a collective.

"You know, you guys were all at really formative ages when 9/11 happened," he said, picking at scraps of lettuce with his fork. "It left an impression on people in different ways. For Alex, I think that's when the wheels really started to turn. In my mind, this was a phase.

I kept saying, 'Alex, that's great, but you should go to college first, do this after.' I was trying to coach instead of preach, 'cause obviously preaching doesn't work too good."

What finally made it click for Norm was that Alex began studying the infantry handbook in the library between classes and doing ten-mile runs each morning wearing boots and a backpack full of free weights to get in shape for basic training. Once he even cut a mole off his back, figuring he'd have to go through worse for SERE torture-resistance training, and bled so badly he ruined a T-shirt.

"It was his senior year when I finally realized that this was real—he didn't care about school because he was going to the army. This academic stuff was all meaningless, this stuff wasn't important. 'I want to do something important with my life,' that's what he kept saying."

Norm did not exactly share Alex's sense of military duty, but it was hard not to admire it, rooted as it was in the father whom Norm had equally resented and revered.

Albert Likes Blum Senior was not a likely war hero. He grew up in Gloversville, New York, his name a joint branding effort of the Norman Blum & Co. glove manufacturer and the Likes, Berwanger & Co. department store of Baltimore, Maryland (their famous catch-phrase: "Everybody Likes Berwanger!"), and volunteered for the infantry in World War II in part to escape his Jewish upbringing. When he came back he had the bloody papers of a teenage Nazi whose head he'd seen caved in by a grenade in the Harz Mountains, a jagged bolt of shrapnel in his thigh, and a fist of untellable stories in his head. Beverly Beck, whose Methodist family had emigrated from Germany in the 1870s, was the most gentile woman he could find.

Norm, Dad, and their siblings never thought of themselves as Jews. The family celebrated Christmas for the sake of form but worshipped no god but success. Beverly managed to talk Al Senior out of the names he had decided on for his boys during the war—King, Prince, and Duke—but Al still raised them to be winners in the striving American mold, shorn of their tribal history of repression and neurosis. Second place was as good as losing. Whining was as good as quitting. Disputes were settled in the basement boxing ring, battles that repeated themselves on ice rinks, baseball diamonds, football fields, and lakes around upstate New York.

For Dad and Fred, the Vietnam War and the Summer of Love cast a more sinister light on Al Senior's military exploits. Norm was born in 1957, just past the draft registration window, too late to be affected in the same way. His older brothers may have found war uninteresting or worse, but Norm had a boyish curiosity. The fact that Al Senior had killed Nazis and possessed the trophies to prove it had always lent authority to his demands that the boys strap on gloves to beat each other senseless in the basement boxing ring, but he never talked about his service at home. On the only occasion he ever took his youngest son out to dinner alone, Norm seized the opportunity to press him about the war.

"I was really interested," Norm explained to me. "He was in Battle of the Bulge, he was in D-Day plus one or two, a lot of the nastiest shit. He got demoted for punching a superior, because he wasn't really good with rules. He said, 'When you're in a battle, most of these pussies wouldn't even fire their rifle. Your fighting force of a hundred, it might be a force of twenty or forty, because most guys shied from the fight.' I guess that's why Dad was exposed on a fifty-caliber machine gun, because he wasn't afraid to shoot and get shot at. There were three stories he told me."

Norm launched them across the table the way his father had, as if daring me to blink.

"He and his best buddy went out for a smoke. It was a pretty active area. They were leaning against this tree, and then all you heard was a machine gun. His buddy got cut in half." Norm traced a diagonal line across his torso.

"Another one: It was early in the morning, before sunrise. Germans, they carry these lanterns, so if you see a lantern outside the perimeter when you're on watch, you don't ask any questions. You shoot. So he saw one, shot, soldier goes down, next morning it turns out it was an African American guy in his own platoon that he had killed.

"Let's see, the next one was . . . Oh. You see it in these old World War Two films, where they've got this farmhouse surrounded and there's a bunch of Germans inside. They're shooting, they're lobbing mortars, they're throwing grenades, and the place bursts into flames and these Germans come running out on fire. They're saying, 'Mama, mama.' You just pick one out and you shoot 'em. He went up afterward and checked their papers, and they were twelve-, thirteen-, fourteen-year-old Hitler Youths.

"Oh, right," Norm said, "there was one more. He and another guy, they killed all these Germans. There's this pit, they're just going to throw all these bodies in. He said it was a hundred degrees out, it was freaking stinking to high heaven. He said, 'I got the arms, my buddy's got the legs. One, two . . .'" Norm mimed swinging. "Both the guy's arms pulled off. Dad was sitting there holding two arms." He dropped the tough-guy act and gave me a look. "How do you relate to *that* shit?"

To Norm, these stories were yet another wall between himself and a father who had taken the whole family to all of Al Junior's high school football games but had never attended more than one or two of Norm's baseball and hockey games. When he passed sanitized versions on to his children years later, it seemed only fitting to burnish them a little, as tribute to the grandfather they would never have a chance to meet. He didn't expect them to become objects of lasting fascination. But Alex thought they were awesome. He told them to any friend who would listen.

———

A recruiter first called Alex in December, having gotten his number from Andrew. Over the ensuing months they met about half a dozen times at the recruitment center in the strip mall across from the Family Sports Ice Arena, where Alex had first started skating so many years before. Soon he told his dad the recruiter wanted to meet him too.

"So we went to the recruiter," Norm recalled, "Sergeant So-and-so, a big studly handsome guy who was Alex's new hero. I tried to be open-minded. I said, 'Okay, Alex's goal is to be a Ranger.' The guy says, 'Yeah, everyone's goal is to be a Ranger.' I said, 'Can you tell us some statistics about what the chances are?' He says, 'No, that's classified.' I said, 'Well, would you say it's very unlikely?' He says, 'Yeah, it's very unlikely.' I'm sitting there thinking, 'Certainly Alex has asked these questions. Certainly Alex knows that this hill is much taller than most people are going to be able to climb.'"

Norm liked Sergeant So-and-so. He has always respected obvious physical fitness, and he appreciated the sergeant's hard-assed realism.

It did not then occur to him that this was exactly the kind of reverse psychology that kids with hero complexes respond to best.

"I thanked the guy. He was candid. He didn't pull any punches. I appreciated that. We went outside. Alex says, 'Dad, are you going to be disappointed if I join the army?'"

At this, something happened in Norm's face that I had never seen before. He was looking to me for recognition of how crushing it was to hear a son ask if you were disappointed in him, an experience I had not yet come close to having myself.

"I said, 'Of *course* not. My concern is just to help you see outside your tunnel vision that this is your calling in life. Maybe you should consider going to school for two years and then joining the army.' He said, 'Dad, I really want to do this.' I said, 'Okay, buddy, look'—we're driving home now—I said, 'I'll give you twenty thousand bucks and you can travel in Europe for a year or two. Get some worldly experience. Come back and see how you feel about joining the army.' He said, 'I have *no* interest in that.'"

Over the next few weeks the full interrogative weight of Norm's social world came to bear on Alex. The results are apparent in their letters to Judge Burgess.

Jeff "Bud" Ahbe, Alex's boss at the hockey camp, where he coached kids between the ages of six to ten: *I questioned Alex personally . . . he said this was what he wanted to do.* Richard Bell, family friend: *During conversations prior to Alex's enlistment it became clear he wanted to serve his country . . . proudly accepted the inherent risks.* Becca Casarez, family friend: *. . . long discussion regarding his future . . . very confident in his decision . . . proud to be a Ranger.* Frank and Barbara Kelley, neighbors whose house Alex tended when they were gone: *Visited us just prior to entering the military . . . determined to become part of the armed forces.*

Norm's final gambit was to arrange for Alex to have lunch with his friend and colleague Bill Hemphill, a retired colonel in the U.S. Army who had commanded an infantry company in Vietnam and gone through Ranger School himself. Hemphill's greatest point of pride was that despite ample opportunity he had never gotten a single one of his men killed. The plan was for him to play the realist for Alex, as Norm could not do himself.

In about a year and a half, Hemphill too would be writing a letter to Judge Burgess of the District Court of Western Washington.

I pointed out that, as a young man, he would be training with soldiers who were physically and mentally more mature and who might have combat experience. I actually tried to dissuade him—or at least delay him—from Ranger Training. I left the lunch convinced that this young man would make an excellent soldier and would uphold the great traditions of the Rangers. I remarked to my wife that Alex was the type of young man one could feel secure was protecting our country and who would make a difference.

By the time April rolled around, Norm had more or less resigned himself to having a son in the war. He had even begun to feel some pride in Alex's determination to serve his country. It was a tough, thankless choice, but it was Alex's to make. When Alex signed the 11X/Airborne Ranger contract the day after his eighteenth birthday, it didn't come as a surprise.

The other big development that April did: Alex fell in love.

———

When I first left a voicemail for Anna Dudow, now a nurse at Children's Hospital Colorado, she texted back a week and a half later to apologize for the delay, explaining that it had taken her some time to get her feelings under control.

She didn't strike me as someone who often struggled with her feelings when we met at a coffee shop a few days later. Brisk, blond, and very small in stature, Anna struck me instead as a woman who had become wearily expert in convincing professors, coaches, salesmen, doctors, clients, patients, and students not to dismiss her as "cute." At Littleton High School she had been just as much a jock as Alex, an accomplished gymnast with perfect side and straddle splits who could pull a layout backflip when they tossed her in the air on the varsity cheer squad.

Alex used to love telling the tale of their meeting. One dreary morning in April, he crawled beneath a table in the school library to catch up on all the sleep he had been missing between hockey practices every night and road marches every morning, then woke up to a sandaled foot six inches from his nose. It had been simple interest, a motion requiring no decision at all, to reach out and circle the ankle with his fingers. The foot jerked in his hand. Whoa: it was *alive!* He bent up each painted toe in sequence. After a few seconds a head peeked down—blond, pretty, shy, quizzical. A flash of a smile and then the head went back up, embarrassed. He began playing with the knob above the heel.

When I asked her about it, Anna remembered it well. "First of all," she said, laughing, "to catch Alex in the library was, I feel, something very rare. And of course he wasn't doing what he was supposed to be doing in a library setting. He was sitting underneath my table being just a total . . . being Alex. I don't know why I even bothered to acknowledge him. I mean, who sits underneath the table at the library? He was just a total . . . he was *funny.*"

At the time, Alex had already asked someone to the prom, just as friends: a deaf classmate named Kathleen who had been assigned as his volleyball and badminton partner in gym class. This was the latest in a series of efforts at teenage good citizenship. The previous summer he had knocked on the front door of a younger kid whom a large group had bullied at a party to apologize to him and his startled parents. In the fall, after discovering an old friend passed out on a toxic blend of alcohol and antianxiety medication in a back bedroom at a hot tub party, he had sucked the vomit from the friend's throat and saved his life, and he continued to pay him visits and check up on him long after other friends fell away. He considered this the gentlemanly conduct demanded of a soon-to-be Army Ranger—"Gallantly will I show the world that I am a specially selected and well-trained soldier," reads the Ranger Creed. When Kathleen told him that he should just take his new girlfriend, he wouldn't hear of it. One of his buddies would take Anna. They would all go together. It would be fun.

"I was like, look, we were just going as friends, I honestly don't mind if you take Anna instead. I can save my dress for my junior prom," Kathleen wrote to me a few weeks later over Gmail chat from Dayton, Ohio, where she recently married and works in accounting. "But he insisted. Wanted to show me a good time."

"Was the night fun at all or just hopelessly awkward?"

"Haha oh gosh. Very awkward. Especially in the limo. I sat next to Alex, and he's chatting away, casually puts his arm around me, and Anna (of course, in the same prom group!) is just shooting death stares at me. They were this popular senior group of kids that I just saw from afar. They were definitely the cool kids that had a good time and here I was just a goody two-shoes tagging along awkwardly. I thought the dancing might be awkward, but Alex spent a lot of time in the bathroom, so I just danced alone."

Anna too looks back on that night with humor, but in the moment her feelings were desperate. She and Alex had so little time.

"Our relationship went from zero to a thousand miles an hour in point two seconds," she told me. "We were psycho for each other. We spent every minute we could together. I don't think it was him going into the army. I think it would still have gone that fast even if he'd been going away to college at CU."

Alex's enlistment was already a fait accompli when they met. After graduation in June, they had only a month until he had to report to basic training. They went for a lot of long drives together in Norm's black Jeep Cherokee, watched a few movies, but mostly they hung out with Andrew and Jenny and Alex's guy friends around fire pits in one or another of their backyards. The group had known each other for years and fed perfectly off each other's energy. Alex was both the most fun and the most responsible, staying sober—he was on a strict no-alcohol, no-sugar diet for basic—and driving everyone home safely from parties. His loyalty to his friends was incredible. Everyone relied on Alex. Anna had dated guys before, but Alex made it obvious she had only ever been playing around. He made her laugh harder than any guy ever had, but he also treated her with more respect than any guy ever had. He was handsome and popular. Up to thirty people from school attended his hockey games; his team was neck-and-neck for top ranking in the state. He had a touchingly close relationship with his family too, especially his father and his little brother and sister.

"It was strange how much my parents trusted him," Anna said. "I'm still not allowed to have boys sleep over when I'm at my parents' house, but for some reason he was allowed to stay, and I was allowed to go over there. I think they fell in love with him as fast as I did. They were totally okay with us not being seen for days, because they knew I was in good hands. It was really nice how well he meshed into my life and my family and how well I meshed into his."

The only hitch was the army. No one in Anna's world knew anything about it. Alex tried to prepare her for what life would be like once he left: weeks at a time without phone calls, months without visits. To show her the kind of work he would be doing, he screened his favorite movie for her, *Black Hawk Down*, about a 1993 operation conducted in Mogadishu by Rangers and Delta Force operators. It was obvious how inspired he was by this display of military expertise, the fast-roping and room clearing and hand signals and jargon, all of which he eagerly explained to her as it arose, but when the bodies started to mount, Anna couldn't help expressing some misgivings. Alex hugged her to him on the couch and told her not to worry. He loved her; he would always come back to her. Though he tried to play it casually, keeping his eyes fixed on the screen, it was the first time either of them had said it. Thrilled, Anna told him she loved him too.

"Everything was so fast and so perfect between us that I just completely ignored everything bad," she said. "I literally ignored it right up until the moment when they came and picked him up."

Years passed. Anna graduated from LHS, made the cheer squad at the University of Colorado, pledged at a sorority, and completed a bachelor's degree in psychology. She coached cheer at a Denver gym for a while, then went to nursing school and landed the job at Children's. Through it all, she continued to think about Alex. Her parents did not want her talking to me. She wasn't so sure it was a good idea either.

"It's hard not wanting to go back to him," she explained. "All of my relationships now, I'm always comparing everybody to him. He was amazing. He made me feel . . . he made me *feel*. If he'd stayed in the army, I don't know if we would have made it, because I'm sure that would have been hard too. That kid probably would have done it forever if he'd been able to. I don't know if I could have handled that. But I might have. So that's hard. Nothing broke us up. It's not like we stopped loving each other, or got mad at each other, or something happened between him and me. He treated me like a fucking princess. You know that stupid movie *The Notebook*? That was our life. We. Were. *Perfect*."

———

Alex spent his final month at home in Greenwood Village giddy with the knowledge that he was army property already, halfway to becoming the man he had always wanted to be. Not only was he about to kick some serious terrorist ass, he was dating the love of his life and planned to marry her. He trained harder than ever for basic, played a last few hockey games, and took advantage of his remaining weeks of freedom to goof off in high style. Many of Littleton High School's students drove to graduation in the BMWs and Mercedes they had been given as graduation presents; Alex drove his dad's ride-on lawn mower. At a final party with his teammates for the Littleton Hawks, while the rest of them drank and smoked and played poker, bragging about the junior hockey teams they would be playing for in Canada next year, Alex charged into the kitchen stark naked and dove under the table to call in pretend airstrikes using his fist as a radio.

"We had a barbecue for Alex the day before he left," Norm recalled near the end of our lunch. "It was sort of a happy/sad deal."

By some quirk of army scheduling, the day before Alex left happened to be the Fourth of July. "Forty or fifty people came by. Some friends, some coaches, some teachers and administrators from his school who had all just taken to him." Norm shrugged. "He was an easy kid to like. Anna and two of his best friends stayed up with him afterward. We watched a couple of movies. Four-thirty in the morning, I think it was, two guys in uniform came and got him. As soon as they showed up, Alex was gone within a minute. Maybe ten words exchanged. You know, 'I'm Alex's dad.' 'We're here to pick up your son.' They don't give a flying fuck."

It was a rare moment of bitterness from Norm. I asked him how it felt to have Alex gone.

"You know, it's like anything else in life. So-and-so is going to die, because they're a hundred years old and they have cancer, and you're ready for it until it happens, and then you realize there's no way you could be ready for it. Anna's crying. His friends are bummed out. Everyone just goes their separate ways."

I nodded. We chewed in silence for a second. The restaurant was empty now except for us and a few dusty shafts of late-afternoon light.

"How's that?" Norm asked.

I thought he was asking about his story. The truth was that I was moved and astonished that Norm was talking to me like this, but I tried to answer with manly restraint. "Pretty sad," I said.

"That calzone," clarified Norm, looking uncomfortable.

"Oh," I said. "It's good."

"I'll tell you what, Ben. Of the people who go into the military, Alex was probably as well prepared mentally and physically as anybody ever is. He did his homework. He read voraciously. He knew what he was getting himself into. But"—Norm gave me a meaningful look—"he didn't know what he was getting himself into."

At the time of Alex's enlistment, the army, confronted by the possibility of a longer-than-expected fight with an overstretched volunteer force, was studying the factors that helped and hindered recruitment via the USAREC Survey of New Army Recruits, a pink form that looked a little like an SAT booklet. Alex diligently filled in the bubbles with a number 2 pencil.

I enlisted because: *(X) I wanted the adventure I will experience. ( ) I wanted the benefits I will receive. ( ) I wanted the skills I will learn. ( ) I wanted the pay I will earn. ( ) I wanted the money for education. ( ) I wanted the travel I will experience. (X) I wanted to serve my country.*

From the statements above, which is the MOST important to you?
I wanted to serve my country.

From the statements above, which is the LEAST important to you?
I wanted the pay I will earn.

Typically, young people considering enlisting for military service experience some concerns or barriers to this decision. How significant were these concerns to your decision to enlist?
Religious or moral beliefs: *Very unimportant.*
Put education plans on hold: *Very unimportant.*
Loss of personal freedom: *Very unimportant.*

Fear of injury or death: *Very unimportant.*
Fear of basic training: *Very unimportant.*
Family obligations: *Somewhat important.*

Who was the LEAST supportive of your decision to join the ARMY? (Mark only one)
( ) Mother/stepmother. ( ) Father/stepfather. ( ) Athletic Coach. ( ) Teacher.
( ) Husband/wife. ( ) Boyfriend or girlfriend. ( ) Friend. ( ) Clergy member. (X) School
Guidance Counselor. ( ) Sister/brother or stepsister/stepbrother. ( ) Extended family
(i.e. grandparent, uncle/aunt, cousin).

———

I wasn't at Alex's farewell party. I was caught up in my own life, reading research papers on complexity theory in Berkeley, California, and spending my nights playing accordion with a group of grad school friends in the basement of our Oakland rental. Norm showed me a few pictures: Anna looking shell-shocked on the patio, Sam and Carly playing some kind of board game on the trampoline. It was incredible how young everyone was. Alex looked happy and playful, horsing around in the yard, throwing his arm over his buddies' shoulders, holding a glass of water proudly up toward the camera. Norm had permitted the other graduates a beer or two from the garage refrigerator, but Alex was sticking to his training diet.

"He had a great personality," Norm summed up with a shrug at the end of our lunch. "He was fun to be around. Just a gregarious kid."

Even then, the blandness of his language unsettled me. It reminded me somehow of that flat suburban sunlight that suffused so many of my childhood memories. Who was my younger cousin really? What darkness, if any, lay under the cheerful smile of the boy in these photographs?

The culture of the Blum family is a patchwork affair. In hacking off his Jewish roots, Al Senior endowed his descendants with the opportunity and the onus of making their own myths. Some of us have found them in sports, others in science, others in war, but there are times when it seems to me that some vestigial connection to an unconscious substrate of Jewish lore must remain. The best model I have found for the way the extended Blum family came to interpret what happened to Alex is the ancient Jewish legend of the golem.

According to Talmudic lore, the first one was Adam himself, who spent an hour as gathered dust, an hour as form, and an hour as *golem*, Hebrew for "unshaped mass," before God infused him with a soul. Later golems, constructed by mere rabbis, never got that far. The best known is the sixteenth-century Golem of Prague, sculpted from river clay by Rabbi Judah Loew to guard the Jewish quarter from attack. The legend is told in different ways. Sometimes the name of God is written on paper and slipped into the golem's mouth. Sometimes the Hebrew word *emet*, or "truth," is carved onto its forehead. Regardless, language is what fills the golem with its mute, unquestioning half-life. Like Frankenstein, Skynet, or the Predator and Reaper drones that now buzz over conflict zones around the world, the golem represents action without agency, force without conscience, a lurch and a boom and no one there to blame. Inevitably it goes astray. In the end the rabbi manages to pull the slip of paper from its mouth or to erase the first character of the word from its forehead, turning *emet*, "truth," into *met*, "dead," and the golem collapses into a pile of inanimate mud.

Our own golem was dissolved by an other-than-honorable discharge from the U.S. Army in early 2007, while Alex was still in prison. What unsettled us most was that buried somewhere in whatever mud pile remained was the little blond kid who still grinned at us from old family photographs, next to younger versions of ourselves with whom we felt no discontinuity. Like the medieval rabbi Maimonides, whose "negative theology" held that God could not be described in positive terms but only in opposition to whatever was imperfect and human, we began talking about that Alex mostly in banalities and negations: loyal, dutiful, patriotic; not experienced, not skeptical, not capable of questioning, not aware. After a while it began to seem as if all we had left of him was a luminous emptiness defined against the shape of what was to come, a sculpture in negative space.

There was one more negation, of course, the most important of all, so well understood in our family that no one had to say it out loud: not guilty.

CHAPTER 2

BASIC

In America we thank our veterans at every opportunity, but we do not presume to understand what they have gone through. The military experience is sacrosanct, tarnished by any effort to assess it with civilian touchstones. The moment the infantry recruit walks down the cinder-block path from his childhood home at 0430 hours and enters a recruiting sergeant's car via the passenger-side door, he crosses over to a new plane of existence. But in Alex's case we had a few glimpses, transmissions from beyond.

As Norm told it, the change came on in strobe. First Alex was sent home five weeks into basic for a surprise convalescent leave. Because he didn't tell anyone he was coming, he found the house locked and empty, the family gone to San Diego on vacation. Norm bought Alex a ticket to join them, then watched him stare for days at seagulls swooping through the mist above the waves, distracted and remote, dog tags dangling against his bare chest. Three months later Alex graduated from basic in a grid of other eighteen-year-olds, then flew home for another short leave. At first his efforts at military posturing—the crisp walk, the flat eyes, the gunmetal tone, all this set against the sprinklers and novelty mailboxes of Greenwood Village—seemed a little silly. He posed for photographs in the backyard wearing his dress uniform with his older brother Max's AR-15 clapped to his chest, lips pinched into a line as crisp and proud as the fold of his beret, then flew back to Fort Benning for the Ranger

Indoctrination Program. Norm looked up Georgia temperatures on the Internet whenever he knew Alex would be in the woods all night on field drills. It was often near freezing, sometimes below. In the rare phone calls Alex was permitted home, his voice was so thick and confused that it was hard to understand him. On his next visit, his affectations had stiffened. This was no act.

It wasn't until months after Alex's arrest that Norm finally learned what had been happening on the other end of those phone calls. Alex spent a total of sixteen months confined at SeaTac Federal Detention Center before being released on bail in November 2007. In that time he experienced a profound transformation in his mind. Norm, who visited him there every single weekend, described it to us as a long, painful, halting emergence from his military identity. In the beginning Alex could not seem to hold on to the thought that the crime had in fact been real. He did hundreds of push-ups every day in his cell to keep in shape for the day when the misunderstanding was cleared up and he could rejoin his battalion on deployment. It was only eight or nine months into his imprisonment, after Norm gave him an award-winning science book called *Brainwashing: The Science of Thought Control* by a British neuroscientist named Kathleen Taylor, that Alex woke up to what had happened to him. He spent the next month composing a 23,000-word manuscript reconsidering everything he had gone through in his training. When he was finished, Norm typed it up and emailed it to the entire extended Blum family.

I still lived in Seattle then, collaborating with a University of Washington biochemist on my dissertation research. I was sitting at my lab workstation in the UW Medical Center when Norm's email arrived. The dedication page that opened the file was an uncanny glimpse of the Alex we all used to know: cheerful, insouciant, warm. He thanked Norm, Anna, and everyone in the family for their love and support, Paris Hilton "for making prison 'hot,'" and his little brother Sam "for giving me the idea of figuring out, as he put it, 'how you turned into such a jerk'!"

The writing that followed was far more reflective than I was expecting from an indifferent student two months out of his teens. I had never guessed there was anything inside that crewcut blond head except sports clichés and wisecracks.

BREAKING POINT:
TEACHING AMERICA'S YOUTH TO KILL
by Alex Blum

Growing up I always saw epic T.V. commercials of marines climbing plateau faces and soldiers rising as one out of conceal-ment in an open field. I picked up a book about Viet Nam when I was five and stared transfixed at pictures of American soldiers patrolling in rice paddies. By the time I turned seven I knew that was what I wanted to do. I wanted to be the All-American kid who grew up and fought against an evil enemy that threat-ened this country. I fell in love with Stephen Ambrose's Band of Brothers and was awed by the incredible sacrifice in Mark Bowden's Black Hawk Down. I saw the events in these books and many more like them as challenges and wondered if I could have made a difference if I'd been there. I read about the men-tal strength and physical struggles that Special OPS groups like SEALs, Rangers and Delta Force went through and wanted to see if I could make it. I wanted to be a part of the military as the country rallied behind its armed forces. I wanted to come back from war, hug my family and say, "I'm home." I got lost in this fantasy often, not realizing it was just that: a fantasy. The United States doesn't have an identifiable enemy anymore. It isn't fight-ing a nation led by a mustached tyrant or a communist oppressor. The country certainly doesn't rally behind its boys like in World War II and no soldier ever comes home from the violence and just moves on with his life, but that's all hindsight.

I grew up in a stable, loving family and lived in a community completely devoid of violence. I had neither the drive nor the mental capacity to kill. So how does the Army turn a kid like that into a killer? It's a process; a long, painful, mind-numbing, perverse process. It is a necessary process but something that I had never read about in detail and never objectively looked at until I was far away from it.

My experience comes from a small percentage of the Army, small but crucial. I was an infantryman, or 11 Bravo in military terms. Our indoctrination is unique to the rest of the Army. It is unique because ours is the only profession within the Army community that is sent directly to kill people. The rest of the Army's recruits go through two schools: a modified Basic Training which is nine weeks and Advanced Individual Training or AIT which varies in length depending on the job. During the modified Basic they learn just that: the very basics of Army life. They learn how to march, how to handle a rifle and other aspects of life in uniform like rank structure and military time. When they graduate from Basic they are sent to AIT and learn in a college-like environment where the Drill Sergeants teach job skills and continue to mentor them. They work days and get nights and weekends off and when they graduate they are sent to a unit where they perform their job. After their training they are a part of the Army but in a sense they are just disciplined civilians. They are not killers. They wouldn't raid a house and put two rounds into each person's chest inside the structure or let loose with a .50 caliber machine gun into a group of people. So why would I? How is the rest of the Army still able to act and think like the people they were as civilians and 11 Bravos come out of Basic Training like a pack of pit bulls? Why is it that a soldier like Jessica Lynch would surrender and be taken prisoner and I would fight to the death? Aren't both of us part of an Army of One? Isn't it our most basic instinct to survive? Aren't we both from a country where as children we were taught to respect and cherish life? It's not because of sex or bravery that our outcomes would have differed. It is because my induction into the Army was completely different from hers.

As sunlight glittered in from Puget Sound across the monitors and glassware of the lab, the dark world opening out behind my laptop's screen made all the molecular twiddling I had been doing for the past year in this room seem suddenly very paltry. Soldiers in Iraq and Afghanistan were dying on our behalf, and killing in far greater numbers on our behalf, and none of us so much as argued about it over lunch.

Our three Drill Sergeants silently paced us from inside the red lines or Kill Zone as it became known. *"All right you fucking shit bags"* one of them said. *"This is my god damn Bay; I own every-*

thing in here including you, so if you fucking piss me off I'm going to make your goddamn lives miserable!" He yelled as he looked at one of the recruit's foot position, *"You are standing in my god-damn Kill Zone! Get your goddamn duffel bags! Hurry the fuck up!"* We scrambled to our lockers and quickly returned to the line. *"Lift the fucking bags above your heads!"* He turned to the Private whose toe had made contact with the red Kill Zone line and yelled *"See what happens when you piss me off you fucking piece of shit, you fuck everybody!"* By this time another Drill Sergeant had joined in; *"You little fuck, your bitch of a fucking mom should have done the world a favor and swallowed your useless ass!"* The first Drill Sergeant was now inches from the kids face yelling, *"You're going to get everybody here killed, you stupid shit! When you go to Iraq I hope you get blown up by a fucking IED so no one else has to suffer from your stupidity!"* The third Drill Sergeant was walking around making sure the rest of us kept our arms locked and bags above our heads. I looked around the Bay at my comrades and thought "what the fuck did I sign up for?"

Alex's drill sergeants were vets. Many had just come back from Iraq, where Zarqawi's singularly brutal branch of al-Qaeda was doing all it could to spark a civil war between Sunni and Shia. Terrorists and insurgents were gunning down patrols, suicide-bombing mar-kets, and firing mortars at coalition Humvees and fortifications by the day. May 2005 was the bloodiest month since the invasion, with 80 U.S. soldiers and over 700 Iraqi civilians dead. Now it was July, and the action showed no sign of slowing. New privates would be launching into a firestorm. The army wanted them hard enough to survive it. The walls of the bay where Alex slept were decorated with large glossy photographs of IEDs disguised as Coke cans, rocks, and teddy bears. In the stairwell was a wanted poster for a recruit who'd gone AWOL.

As recently as the Vietnam War, soldiers would spend the week doing push-ups and bayonet drills and then go into town on weekends to catch movies and blow off steam. Nowadays no steam is blown off. The lid comes down at the beginning of "Red Phase," in which drill sergeants exercise total control over every aspect of recruits' lives in order to initiate the "soldierization process," and does not come up again for three weeks. As far as the family is concerned, the recruit simply vanishes off the face of the earth. Though drill sergeants are forbidden to strike recruits without provocation, Alex's account made it clear that they had plenty of techniques for inflicting pain at their disposal. They seemed to take particular pleasure in forcing recruits into Catch-22s whose inevitable outcome was "getting smoked," the army phrase for punitive physical exercise.

On Friday we were eating lunch chow and our Drill Sergeant was entertaining himself by placing contraband ice cream sand-wiches on recruit's plates and telling them to eat it. When they finished the Drill Sergeant would yell *"You fucking shit head! You're not allowed to eat sweets, you fucking cunt! Go run until I get tired!"* The Private would sprint out to the track and run under the supervision of another Drill Sergeant. The Private was told to run until he began vomiting. Our Drill Sergeant gave an ice cream sandwich to one Private who said "I'm not allowed to eat that Drill Sergeant." "Sure you are fucker, I said you could." "I don't want to get in trouble Drill Sergeant." *"You won't get in trouble shit bird!"* The Drill Sergeant said playfully. *"Go ahead, eat it."* "I'm not allowed to Drill Sergeant." The Drill Sergeant's face grew hard and he screamed *"everybody out of the god damn chow hall right fucking now!"* We scrambled to put our trays away and tore out of the chow hall to our common area where we waited in formation at parade rest. *"Jumping Jacks you stupid fucking pricks! No, you stay out in front. Come here fucker!"* The Private who refused to eat the ice cream sandwich was pulled out of formation and made to watch as we paid for his "mistake". *"See fuckers, when you don't listen everybody suffers! All of you are undisciplined little shits. God damnit! I hate this fucking Platoon!"* He turned to the Private who was watching us and handed him a box of ice cream sandwiches. *"As soon as you finish this box I'll stop smoking these mother fuckers!"* he said. The Private crammed ice cream sandwiches into his mouth and finished them as soon as he could. Our Drill Sergeant yelled at him *"You little fucking pig! You're not allowed to eat sweets, and your fucking fat ass eats a whole god damn box of ice cream!? Holy fuck Shit head! That's all right, we'll pay for that!"* The Drill Sergeant sent the Private to the track and continued to smoke us. When the Private came back he was covered in puke and gasping for air. *"Push with the rest of the fucking Platoon! You fuckers are gonna get fat from all these sweets. So I'm gonna have to help you burn those calories!"* He quickly added the calories in his head and told us that each bar contained 20,000 calories. After smoking us for what felt like four hours, he said we had only burned 1000 calories and that we would pay for the rest later.

For more than 13,000 words, basic training went on and on and on. Belongings dumped in a field, bayonets jammed into straw dummies, teargas pumped into a sealed chamber of trembling recruits, profound and accumulating sleep deprivation, getting smoked, getting tricked, getting insulted, getting threatened, weeping, puking, getting smoked for weeping and puking. *What makes the grass grow? Blood, Drill Sergeant!* As I continued reading, I kept glancing around at my lab mates with that self-conscious lack of expression you see on the faces of people reading pornographic novels on public transportation.

This non-stop, continuous negative reinforcement erases any and all self confidence you once had. You firmly believe that you can't do anything right. At the time, you can't see that they are intentionally and methodically breaking you down, removing all of your self esteem. You just believe that you are incompetent and unworthy of anything. You operate under complete and total fear and try to do anything to avoid more pain, embarrassment and humiliation.

Was all this a surprise? Not exactly. I'd seen *Saving Private Ryan*. I'd seen *Full Metal Jacket*. I was familiar, on a basic cultural-memory level, with the archetypes at play. There was the fat Private Pyle type, so chronically out of shape that he didn't understand that the most he had ever exerted himself in his life was about one third of the baseline he needed to sustain here. There was the Joker type, who could not bring himself to accept the authority of the drill sergeants as legitimate and had to swallow his laughter down to a bitter, festering place whenever they bellowed in his face on the theme of his mother's genitalia. And of course there were the screaming, stomping, cursing, toiletry-scattering drill sergeants themselves, who appeared to have watched all the same movies I had and strip-mined them for material. What I hadn't seen before was a portrait of the interior life of the guys who only ever appeared as extras in these movies, for the obvious reason that they were of zero narrative interest: the ones who *bought* it. Who respected the drill sergeants as heroes whom they desperately wanted to please and live up to. Who overloaded their rucksacks by thirty pounds on marches and met secretly in stairwells on "rest days" for extracurricular physical-training sessions to prepare them for the Ranger Indoctrination Program, which they knew was going to be a whole lot worse. Who viewed the breakdown of their own bodies under all this strain as a shameful mark of weakness. Who wanted to be ready for Iraq.

In the seventh week of basic, after sleeping outdoors through a pounding storm that ended with cottonmouth snakes flopping in puddles in the recruits' tents—weeks later they would learn that this had been Hurricane Katrina—Alex's right leg started to hurt.

The following morning we had a five mile run for PT. Afterwards we marched to breakfast chow and I was in so much pain with my leg that I fell out of formation and was on the verge of blacking out. A Drill Sergeant came up to me and screamed *"Get up you fucking pussy!"* "Roger, Drill Sergeant," I said and painfully tried to catch up with my Platoon. When I couldn't keep up the Drill Sergeant dropped my buddies to do push-ups and made me stand in front of them and watch. *"This little pussy thought the run was too hard and thinks he's better than all of you! He thinks he's allowed to rest while the platoon continues to march!"* I was overwhelmed with guilt and when I tried to join them I was told to stand and watch. My leg progressively got worse as the week went on and by the weekend I was fighting back tears every time I put pressure on it.

The next week was the beginning of "White Phase": weapons instruction. By the time the privates were finally let loose on the long-awaited machine-gun range—they were taught to count off six-to nine-round bursts on the M240 by saying "Die, Iraqi, die"—Alex had chewed a hole in his lower lip to manage the pain. Then came the grenade range.

After practicing with dummy rounds, we marched down to the live range to throw real explosives. We waited under a tin roof and heard debris land above us each time a grenade went off. When it was my turn to throw, I limped to my assigned bunker and listened to a Drill Sergeant review the prep and throw process. When he finished he handed me a grenade and we squatted as I prepped the explosive. I held the spoon with my right thumb, took off the safety and pulled the pin. I stood up and got into my throwing stance. When I put weight on my right leg I felt a POP! and fought through the pain to stay conscious. I managed to throw the grenade before I fell and heard the dim sound of the explosion while on my back. The Drill Sergeant grabbed me by my body armor and shouted *"Holy fuck, Cletus! You almost killed me, you stupid piece of shit!"* He eased up when he saw the pain in my face and told two of my buddies to help me to the ambulance. I hung on to their necks and struggled to the Humvee at the top of the hill.

For two days Alex stood around on crutches watching his buddies march and flutter-kick, begging to be allowed to join back in, mocked by the drill sergeants for his weakness. It was only when x-rays showing a cracked tibia came back that they sent him home. Two months later, when he rejoined another training company, his closest friends, Roman and Kane, the remaining two thirds of the "Battle Bastards" fellowship that had met for extra PT in the stairwell, had already graduated. Alex missed swapping intel with them about surviving RIP (hot tips from those who had made it before included squirting Tabasco sauce in your eyes, snorting chewing tobacco, and bayoneting your earlobes to stay awake and focused), but he made the most of it, getting into the swing of things as training zeroed in on the fine points of the infantryman's arsenal. When he graduated at last, Alex refused to let anyone in the family fly out for the ceremony. This one didn't matter. Next up was Jump School, where he would earn the pin that put the "Airborne" in "Airborne Ranger," a pair of wings on either side of a bulbous parachute.

It turned out to be a cakewalk.

There were no shouting Drill Sergeants or the constant threat of being smoked. Jump School was just that, a school! The Instructors were called Black Hats and its students consisted of privates all the way up to majors, from cooks to infantrymen. The environment was friendly and everyone joked and talked to one another except for the Infantrymen. We stayed together and only talked to each other. We shared a strong dislike towards everyone else and viewed them as inferior in every way. While all the other MOS's (Military Operational Specialty's) complained about the difficulty of the school we viewed it as a vacation and breezed through PT (Physical Training) and our daily classes. The first two weeks we spent practicing exiting the mock Aircraft and landing. We rarely got smoked and tried to piss off the Black Hats to get them to drop us to the ground as often as possible so we could laugh at all the other pussies as they struggled with the pain. This was our first interaction with the rest of the Army and it showed us just how different Infantrymen were from EVERYONE else in the Army.

Alex graduated from Airborne School at Fort Benning in December 2005. I remember that Christmas clearly. At the traditional Blum family gathering, while Anna hovered nervously alongside him, Alex secured a position leaning against the banister that divided Aunt Judy's house in two and commenced squinting around with the facial expression that zombie-slaughtering action heroes must hide behind their aviator shades.

Like everyone else, I tried to talk army with him. He responded with monosyllables and grunts. Only long after he left the army would I learn how much I had been pissing him off. All our blithe, ignorant questions about what guns he'd shot and whether basic had sucked implied that his new life still had some place within the civilian universe of job applications, gas mileage, and adult-league sports where we piddled away our own lives. This was a fundamental error of category. He and his infantry buddies were the shining knights of freedom. For months they had been experiencing levels of physical unpleasantness beyond what any of us could conceive of, learning every day how true all the marching cadences were that said the only ones you could rely on were fellow DICKs—Dedicated Infantry Combat Killers.

————

Basic is in fact a carefully calibrated process. Recruits are both habituated to violence and acculturated into a new family with radically different standards of behavior. Drill sergeants are not sadists—at least not entirely. They are also there to teach, correct, motivate. A faint paternal air suffuses the brutality, a sardonic kind of lovingness expressed through torment. From moments of wryness in Alex's manuscript—"Basic is very 'fucking' and 'holy shit,'" he summed up at one point—it was clear that he was aware of it too. Ultimately the drill sergeants wanted everyone to succeed, qualify, graduate. The war needed soldiers.

The Rangers did not need soldiers. They genuinely wanted candidates to quit. At times they actually seemed to want to kill them.

The final section of *Breaking Point* was broken out from the rest and titled "Ranger Indoctrination Program." The 10,000 words that followed were a scary read. The rigid formal bounds that had contained the violence of basic, from the synchronization of drill and ceremony on the parade ground to the absolute stricture against drill sergeants striking recruits, no longer appeared to apply. The atmosphere was chaotic, alive with threat. Ranger instructors did not yell "Holy shit!" Often they did not yell at all. They darted through the pages like musclebound velociraptors, creeping up behind candidates and saying "cunt" into their ears in intimate, terrifying voices. Smoke sessions in basic had been guided by cadences. "One two three," the drill sergeant would count off. "One!" the recruits would yell back, completing a rep. "One two three," the drill sergeant would count off. "Two!" the recruits would yell back. Ranger instructors would simply bark out, "Beat your faces, cunts," and then the only sound would be the syncopated thumps and grunts of fifty chests hitting the concrete as fast as they could.

The pretense of instructional value that attended activities at RIP was so flimsy as to be a kind of mockery. For the Ranger Combat Water Safety Test, Alex strapped on sixty pounds of gear and climbed up a high-dive ladder, where a sergeant said, "You look like a piece of shit!" and threw him in the pool below. For combat medicine training, he and his fellow candidates were given some cursory instruction, then sent out into a field with hypodermics and saline and instructed to pump the latter through the former into each other's bodies. None had done this before. The needles kept poking through skin and slithering off into muscle as the recruits tried to keep their hands steady and slide them into veins. After dozens of failed jabs, blood was splashed all over the grass. For their incompetence as medics they were forced to crawl on their bellies through the gore.

But all this was just preamble. The carnival really got going in the middle of week two, at the land navigation course on Cole Range. It was January in Georgia and very cold.

At 5:00 am we were bussed out to the land nav course and were told to run across the field to the wood line a quarter mile away and get wood for the Sergeants' fire. We sprinted across the field as fast as our legs would take us. We picked up as much as we could hold and sprinted back to our rucks.

As I got closer to the sand bags I noticed a bunch of gear floating in a nearby body of water named "Just Cause Pond." The Sergeants had been checking our rucks and any that weren't secured properly were torn open and thrown across the pond. We dropped off our wood and were immediately sent back to the wood line. It was 5:30 am Wednesday and Cole Range had just begun.

The temperature was between 38 and 45 degrees and we were wearing only our cotton BDU's.[*] We were sent to the wood line more times that I can remember. We bear crawled, low crawled and buddy carried across the field returning with wood each time. We were given MRE's[†] at 12:30 pm and had five minutes to eat our first meal of the day. I ate as much as possible and put a small Tabasco bottle in my pocket. When we finished eating we were smoked for another hour for eating too slow.

[*] Battle Dress Uniforms, camouflage fatigues
[†] Meals, Ready-to-Eat

We were given coordinates, compasses, maps and were split up into three-man groups and told we had three hours to find our seven points. My group fought through the thick forest to get to our points. Five miles and two and half hours later we had found five points but were too far away from the starting point to risk looking for the rest of them and being late on our return.

My heart sank as we ran up the dirt road to our rucksacks. We saw groups carrying telephone poles and others doing push-ups. I quickly ran to one of the Sergeants and gave him our five points. He looked at my group and said *"You idiots only found five points!?"* "Roger Sergeant." He looked at me and yelled *"Well do push-ups you fucking faggots! You would have found all of your points if you hadn't been sleeping! You shits want to sleep out there then you'll pay for it here!"* We joined our buddies and pushed until we were told to do flutter kicks.

After a while we were sent to the wood line and continued to run until 9:00pm. We were given five minutes to eat our MRE's and after got smoked until midnight. The weather was tolerable until we stopped sweating. It then became evident how cold it was and how quickly we were losing body heat.

We were given more points and told we had three hours to find each of them. We rushed off to plot our points and turned on our red lens flashlights. I was exhausted and poured my bottle of Tabasco sauce into my eyes to keep from falling asleep. We struggled through swamps and rugged terrain for the next three hours. My feet and pants were soaked and I could feel the skin on my thighs and feet rub off with every step I took. By the time we headed back to the starting point my body was racked with pain and discomfort.

As we got close I could see groups pushing. *"You fucking cunts only found two points!? Are you fucking kidding me!? Push-ups you faggots!"* We were smoked until about 4:30am and then told we could sleep. The ground was covered with a light frost and all we were allowed to sleep under was our paper thin ponchos. I could see my breath hanging in the frigid air and my pants and boots were frozen. My Ranger buddy and I clung to each other trying to share body heat. We would shake each other awake whenever we started shivering uncontrollably.

We managed about five minutes of sleep in our frozen stupor and were woken up and told to stand at parade rest. I saw our Sergeants crowd around their fire and heard one say *"Jesus it's cold out here! Good thing we have this fire but I think we need some more wood!"* He turned to us and shouted *"Hit the wood line motherfuckers!"* We scrambled painfully across the field and returned with more firewood. We were told to line up with our rucks in three circles, one inside the other. We were instructed to run in opposite directions with the inside and outside groups running clockwise and the middle circle moving counter clockwise. We ran with our rifles over our heads and shouted "boots!" every time our left foot hit the ground. This exercise was called "mind erasers." We were completely exhausted, freezing and sleep deprived. Ten minutes into this exercise I was on a whole new plane. The world moved slow and fast at the same time. My body was beyond exhaustion, my mind was over loaded and I was unable to put a thought together.

After an hour we were told to hit the wood line again and were smoked until noon. We quickly ate our last MRE of Cole Range and were given new points. As we set out my body was seared with pain in every area. My brain was hardly functioning. I could no longer feel the burn of Tabasco when I poured it into my eyes. I was forced to resort to a more extreme measure to stay awake. I took out my can of Copenhagen and snorted the tobacco through my nose. We were no longer able to think coherently. We easily got lost and confused. We constantly had to back track to re-shoot our azimuth. I snorted half a can of chew and cut my earlobe with my knife and still struggled to stay awake.

We returned with four points and got smoked for sleeping. I threw-up water and bits of chew and was soon covered with it. We were instructed to low crawl through "Just Cause Pond" and then hit the wood line. We repeated this until one of our Sergeants said *"Alright fuckers! Change into your extra set of BDU's!"* We rushed out of the water and put on dry clothing. As soon as I got into my new clothes I felt energized and refreshed. *"Hit the pond you fucking cocksuckers!"* our Drill Sergeant yelled when everyone was finished getting dressed. We ran to the pond, crawled through the cold filthy water and hit the wood line again. We got back and did flutter kicks in the pond and watched five Drill Sergeants urinate in the water. We were told to get up and the five biggest students in the class were told to lay in the Sked-co's the Medic had set out. We secured them to the sleds, picked them up and followed our Sergeant through a stagnant swamp. We fell into the thick mud as we struggled to keep the Sked-co above the surface. It took us two hours to get back to our rucks. When we arrived we were told to drag the Sked-co's to the wood line.

We were smoked until night fall and rushed into the woods in search of our new points. When we stopped to shoot a new azimuth I put a pinch of Copenhagen into my lip and snorted another pinch. I took off my boots and socks to remove a couple of pebbles. My feet were missing patches of skin and my toes were bleeding. The remaining flesh was snow white and wrinkled. I put my socks and boots on quickly trying to function as best I could. The simplest tasks became challenging and at times overwhelming. I had to think about each step and focus to stay upright.

We returned finding only one point and again were smoked for sleeping. I was delirious. Everything was a blur, my feet felt like cinder blocks and my brain was completely numb. We pushed a Humvee around the field and would crash into the back of it when the Sergeant inside would hit the brakes. When he grew bored with his ride he had us low crawl across the field. My fingernails were torn up as I pulled myself across the grass and rocks with my bloody hands. I soon felt the familiar sting of fire ants and started laughing hysterically.

After a blur of time we ran to the tree line and were sent back and forth over and over. One time while running back I saw my girlfriend and heard her say "I love you baby, I'm right here." I started crying and struggled to keep running. We were stopped and told to drink from our canteens until they told us to stop. When I had finished three quarters of my two quart canteen we were told to put our foreheads on the muzzle of our rubber duck* and spin until we were told to hit the wood line. I took my head off and immediately fell to the ground. I tried to stand but the

---

* Waterproof mock rifle

world was spinning too fast. I vomited and fell into the pond where I breathed in the stagnant water. I crawled out and threw up again.

When we got back to our rucks we did mind erasers shouting "Airborne Ranger" at the top of our lungs. We were stopped at 2:00am and given a class on how to tie half hitch, clover hitch, and figure eight knots. I was too far gone to even care or laugh at what we were being taught.

When the lesson ended at 3:00am we were told *"Get some sleep fuckers! The boss will be here soon!"* I was lying under my poncho trying to fight off the unbearable cold holding on to my Ranger Buddy to share warmth. It started to rain. I was shaking from the cold and we began to laugh uncontrollably. The laughter stopped when a Sergeant yelled *"Hit the wood line fuckers!"* We painfully started running and heard *"Low crawl through the fucking pond and then to the tree line goddamnit!"* I crawled through the water and felt like a million pins were being pushed into my body. I struggled to breathe and as soon as I got out of the water it began raining harder. My skin continued to feel the pain of imaginary pins. We returned to our ponchos and were told to sleep. The only warmth we would feel during the two hours is when we would urinate on each other.

It was impossible to sleep for all of us. At 6:00am we were told to put our rucks on and practice patrolling across the field that we had crossed so many times. The rain continued. We were told to take a knee and pull security. We were left like that for an hour in the freezing rain. My brain was numb. I didn't even feel or care when I saw blood pool around my knee. We were still in the field when the bus came and we sprinted towards it. A Sergeant yelled at us as we limped across the field. He came over and began tearing rucks off of Privates' backs, ripping them open and throwing the contents into the pond. We all scrambled to help retrieve their belongings and we were smoked for taking too long.

We finally left Cole Range and slept on the way to the barracks. Upon arrival we were smoked in the puddles on the basketball court for sleeping. When the Sergeants were done with us we were told to change into PT's and be back on the basketball courts for some good news. We returned in four minutes and were smoked for taking too long. As we were pushing a Sergeant said *"You fucking faggots are gonna get the weekend off so get the fuck out of here and be back by 9:00am Sunday, GO!"* We did one more for the Airborne Ranger in the sky and sprinted up to the barracks to change into civilian clothes. We heard a different Sergeant yell *"Bullshit fuckers, you're not going anywhere this weekend! Go shower and be back on the basketball court in PT's at 5:00pm!"*

We disappointedly ran upstairs and crowded into the showers. We stood under the showerheads hugging each other trying to create more warmth as we shivered uncontrollably. For the first 15 minutes I couldn't feel anything. We stayed under the water for an hour and a half and slowly warmed up. We dressed into PT's and sat on our bunks for another hour until it was time to go back down. My feet were raw and I was covered with cuts and bruises. We helped one of my buddies clean and wrap his feet in a ripped T-shirt. When he had taken his socks off he cried out in pain. As we turned his socks inside out the soles of his feet lay on the floor completely peeled away.

That was two and a half days. RIP went on for fifteen more, and so did Alex, in excruciating detail. He and a team of six others raised a telephone pole on their shoulders and weren't allowed to drop it for forty-eight hours, napping two at a time in brief shifts underneath. Afterward Alex found a pair of bumps on his calf. He spent three days ignoring them as the bumps grew wider and began to leak pus, until a sergeant spotted him limping and sent him to the infirmary, where the medic took one startled look and informed Alex that these here brown recluse spider bites were necrotizing fast. This being the Rangers, the medic issued no anesthetic before scraping the dead flesh out with Q-tips, swabbing out the wounds with iodine, strapping on a bandage, and sending Alex back out to be smoked for his laziness.

In the final week those who remained in the drastically thinned class were issued M4s, a shorter version of the M16 which Rangers and other Special Ops units had recently adopted for use in the confined spaces of urban combat. Two hours into the first day of training on this new weapon, a sergeant leaned over a buddy of Alex's whose mother had recently been killed in a car accident and yelled his intention to do a range of graphic things to her body. The recruit stopped firing for a second, and that was enough excuse for the sergeants to halt all shooting drills and smoke everyone for an hour. For another two days they shot at plastic targets. That was the end of RIP.

Thursday we got the day off to clean and pack our belongings. That afternoon my buddies and I went to Ranger Joe's. After four weeks of hell, filled with more pain than I could ever imagine, I was allowed to purchase a $7 Beret and $2 Scroll.

The next day my Dad pinned the Second Battalion Scroll on my shoulder and hugged me. I had made it; I was an Airborne Ranger. After four weeks, our starting class of over a hundred graduated only about thirty students from one of the most difficult courses in the Military. My original Company from basic had 60 Ranger Candidates and only 4 of us had made it through the program.

I left Basic Training looking for a challenge and graduated from RIP with the mental capacity to kill. Before I joined the Army I was vibrant, funny, easy going, loving and independent. When I got my Tan Beret I was a shell. I was an angry, testosterone-driven prick. I was no longer me. I only felt comfortable with other Rangers. When I was with childhood friends I was stand-offish and unable to hold a real conversation or relate to them. I couldn't relate to my family and was no longer the fun and pleasant kid they knew me to be.

I had changed dramatically. My thought process was that of a five year old and when I got to Battalion (next assignment after RIP) I had to be raised again. I was brainwashed. When you arrive at Basic Training you are entirely isolated from the world and your entire life becomes the Army. During the first few weeks I would go to sleep terrified of Iraq and try to convince myself that the Army would not send me. Surely they knew that I was "too young to die!" I also could not imagine being put in a position where I had to kill someone. I was still able to think objectively, but over time your mind gets so used to being controlled it is unable to do anything independently.

You are told when and how to do everything, and when the Drill Sergeants see that you're thinking by yourself or expressing any type of emotion or action associated with free thought or will they punish you severely with the best teacher understood by your brain. They teach you with pain. We got smoked so often I began to doubt every thought and feeling I had. During the fourth week I could literally feel my brain shutting down. I would no longer think "this is unfair" or "I don't want to do this." I no longer had an opinion. I was unable to value human life and could no longer weigh pro's and con's or right and wrong. I was unable to understand emotions. I would feel scared before jumping and nervous while setting a door charge or waiting to enter a shoot house. I felt these emotions but could not understand why or what they meant.

The only exception to all of this was Anna. Every time I got smoked or would be terrified or felt alone I would escape by thinking about her face and the time I had spent with her. She became my strength and sense of hope. The only feelings I understood were toward her. I would be happy and excited when I was with her and it would make sense. She made me feel safe and I felt like the most important person in the world when I was with her. For that I love her more than I have ever been able to express. I felt that no matter what happened I would always be the kid that loved Anna and the kid that Anna always loved. That love was the only thing that linked me to who I once was.

Basic Training turned me into a mindless follower and RIP confirmed it. I used to think RIP was a way to root out the weak. I have since realized that it is used to root out the ones who are still able to objectively think. When things got out of hand they could say, "I am not going to put up with this BS, I don't want to do this anymore, I quit!" The guys that make it through to graduate are unable to quit because they feel there is no other choice but to finish. I never had to fight the urge to quit. In my mind there was no option to quit. I would think, "You'll be dead soon and it will be over. Just go until you die." I never said anything about my leg wounds for two reasons: I didn't want to get anyone in trouble and I believed that how I felt was irrelevant. I waited to be told what to do.

There is a quote from Band of Brothers: "There are no bad soldiers, only bad leaders." This is especially true in Ranger Battalion. Privates are a product of how their superiors raise them. They will do anything their leaders tell them because we are taught to trust and believe them in every way. Kids who join the Infantry don't join to kill. In fact the Army doesn't accept people who are already willing to kill. They want young impressionable minds that join for the adventure. They want kids who see the ads on TV and in magazines who think it looks like a fun challenge.

These kids leave home with the morals and teachings of their parents and society. We emerge from Basic Training wiped clean, lacking any type of objective thinking. We are then re-taught the standards of our superiors. We blindly follow and do as told. Our superiors re-teach us right and wrong and we are no longer able to think about pros and cons. The Army doesn't want us to.

There are no positives or right in what Rangers do as viewed by our society. If we weren't brainwashed the Rangers wouldn't exist. It is our superiors' responsibility to guide us because of our mental state. I was literally unable to understand my emotions and believed everything I was told was the right way to act and think. I had complete faith in my Tabs (superiors at Ranger Battalion) and knew they would never do anything wrong. I was unable to think or question. I was a model Ranger.

There the document ended. I sat back from my laptop. My lab mates had left one by one while I read. I was alone with the hum of centrifuges and agitators in the darkened medical center.

CHAPTER 3

AMURICAN BANK ROBBER

The modern army is mostly support staff. More than 80 percent of servicemen package foodstuffs, install WiFi hubs, repair helicopters: the shaft, in a favored army metaphor, of the spear that drives into the body of the enemy. The infantry is the blade. The Seventy-Fifth Ranger Regiment, U.S. Army Special Operations Command, is the razor-sharp tip, two thousand of the best-trained soldiers in the world. On D-Day, Rangers were the first to charge up Omaha Beach and breach the line of bunkered German machine guns cutting troops down by the thousands before they could even get ashore. "Rangers, lead the way!" was the cry that sent them forward. It is now the first of their two regimental mottos, called out by soldiers of the regular infantry as a gesture of respect whenever they salute a Ranger. The reply to this salute is "All the way!"

To earn the legendary Ranger beret, you have to volunteer three times: for the infantry, for airborne certification, and finally for the process formerly known as the Ranger Indoctrination Program. Those dedicated, crazy, or pain-blind enough to pass up the thousand good opportunities to fail or quit along the way have proved themselves worthy of the Seventy-Fifth Ranger Regiment's second motto: "Sua Sponte," Latin for "of their own accord." They will be assigned to one of three battalions: the First and Third, headquartered in Georgia, or the Second, at Joint Base Lewis-McChord.

"Sua Sponte" has another important meaning to the modern regiment: self-directed initiative in meeting the enemy. Senior Rangers will sometimes joke that an overenthusiastic younger soldier has "Sua Sponte'd it." The people of Tacoma are well aware of this particular virtue of JBLM's most famous tenants. In 1989, at the height of the crack cocaine boom that gave Tacoma the short-lived nickname "Compton of Washington," a Ranger sergeant named Bill Foulk took matters into his own hands when the open drug trade in his Hilltop neighborhood got out of control. After dealers threw rocks and shot BBs at a security camera Foulk had installed over his driveway during a "neighborhood solidarity barbecue," he called a dozen or so of his Ranger buddies from on post and suggested they come armed. That night Sergeant Foulk and his team fought off an hours-long siege by the Crips with pistols, shotguns, and semiautomatic assault rifles, firing hundreds of rounds into the dark. The "Ash Street Shootout" made Foulk a national cause célèbre for the drug war. No disciplinary action was taken against any of the soldiers involved.

Special Operations soldiers have become increasingly central to the way the army fights, a model for the rest to evolve toward as the monolithic battles of the age of industrial war between great powers give way to the ambiguities of rapidly shifting opponents in complex urban environments. In 2001, army chief of staff General Eric Shinseki issued a surprising army-wide order:

> In the United States Army, the beret has become a symbol of excellence of our specialty units. Soldiers of the Special Forces, our airborne units, and the Ranger Regiment have long demonstrated such excellence through their legendary accomplishments and unmatched capabilities. Their deployability, versatility, and agility are due, in part, to their organizational structure and equipment. But more significant is their adaptiveness, which keeps them ready to take on any mission, anytime, anyplace . . . Effective 14 June 2001, the first Army birthday in the new millennium, . . . the black beret will become standard wear in The Army.

Shinseki must have thought the Rangers would be honored. Instead they were outraged. Regular infantry was for bumbling slackers. As for soldiers of the noncombat branches, who steamed broccoli and fixed computers at the FOB (Forward Operating Base) while

Rangers were out raiding houses and getting blown up, the nicknames were various: "fobbits," "pogues," "rear-echelon motherfuckers." The idea of these clowns wearing the signature black Ranger beret was intolerable. Many Rangers road-marched to Washington, D.C., in protest. When that didn't work, they changed their berets to tan.

U.S. Special Operations forces have long been divided into Tier I, comprising the experienced commandos of SEAL Team Six and Delta Force, and Tier II, which includes units like the Rangers, which draw directly from pools of young, unpracticed recruits. In 2003, Brigadier General Stanley McChrystal, a former commander of the Ranger Regiment and "110 percent Ranger," in the words of a close associate, was assigned as commander of Joint Special Operations Command (JSOC). During his time leading the Rangers, he had radically transformed training, upping the tempo, concentrating on nighttime operations, and modernizing weaponry. At JSOC, the tier-based hierarchy did not sit well with McChrystal. He immediately went to work raising his beloved Rangers to the stature of the others rather than just the feeder team for Delta, giving them extensive duties on nighttime raids for "high-value targets." For months at a time during deployment, Rangers slept and lifted weights by day and charged by night into the homes of shocked Iraqi families. Airfield seizures had once been their primary mission, but now that became assaults on homes and small facilities, a skill set McChrystal knew well: at West Point he had once organized a mock assault on a campus building with balled-up socks for grenades and real guns, nearly getting himself shot by campus security.

———

Alex still has his tan beret—on house arrest, he hung it from a nail over his bed in Norm's basement—but he will never be permitted to reenlist in any branch of the U.S. Armed Forces. An other-than-honorable discharge is the most severe discharge short of a court-martial.

We wrote to each other a few times while he was in custody, after Norm had commenced the long process of wiping out his business and bank accounts by flying to Washington State every weekend for visitation hours. After Alex's revelatory experience reading Kathleen Taylor's book *Brainwashing* and writing his long account of his training, Norm took him a number of other books on topics he thought might help him understand what had happened to him. I first wrote to Alex after reading a few of these myself, with some vague hope that my scientific perspective would be of help. When I asked how he felt about the war in Iraq, his reply showed an earnest moral urgency I would never have predicted from him growing up.

My view on the Army is I still respect the hell out of the men and women who make it what it is but have a much better understanding regarding the machine that it is. As for the infantry and its conduct in Iraq I will say this, Ben the men of the infantry are killers nothing more and nothing less. They are designed to kill people and the transformation their minds go through is amazing and frightening at the same time.

After Alex's release, it was hard to see his hurt puzzlement at the failure of each successive effort to turn his new life into something he could be proud of. Even meager civilian approximations of his childhood ambitions—emergency medical technician, fireman, policeman—were closed to him now. For a long time he worked fixing three-hundred-pound lengths of steel pipe into ceilings for a fire-sprinkler installation company before landing a job driving a Zamboni at an ice rink on the decommissioned Lowry Air Force Base southeast of Denver. What Alex really hoped to do there was youth coaching, but to do that in any lasting, official capacity, he would need a coaching license, which would require a background check. Instead he drove in endless circuits on the ice, listening for problems in the hiss of blade and steam as the truck scraped off ridges and filled ruts with boiling water.

I began wondering if I might be of use to Alex and the family. His manuscript about basic and RIP had helped precipitate a career crisis of my own. For a long time I had been confounded by how little my growing technical expertise seemed to help me in understanding the forces that shape our lives. After reading Alex's story, rather than feeding new tasks to the lab's supercomputer, as I should have, I began spending hours in the university library researching the history of U.S. military training. What I found only dismayed and confused me more. Within a year or so of my arrival in Seattle,

I was drinking all night before giving molecular biology talks, doing cocaine in strange apartments, funding a friend's rap album with money from my National Science Foundation grant—more or less deliberately screwing up, seized by a half-articulate hunch that my lifelong impulse toward abstraction and schematization was perpendicular or worse to the real meaning of life, a long march toward, as the poet Philip Larkin puts it, "the solving emptiness / that lies just under all we do." I had begun asking questions I had never thought to ask before. Why does this research matter? Whom exactly does this research help? Decades of scrabbling for grant money to improve the efficiency of algorithms to accomplish things I didn't believe in sounded suddenly unendurable.

———

In March 2009 Alex was finally sentenced to time served. We first got together to talk about his story nine months later, the day after Christmas, shortly after he started working at the ice rink. He drove us to a Denver sports bar in the same silver Audi he once drove to the bank. After having bared our souls to each other in letters, it still felt a little strange to be hanging out in person. The planes of Alex's cheekbones and jaw, which in his army days used to resemble the tilted panels of a stealth bomber, were a little worn down from prison, but his physique was still imposing. I could tell he was nervous by how hard he worked to crack me up on the ride over, going into funny voices for the white supremacists and Mexican gangsters he had mediated between in prison gambling disputes, for the Hells Angels enforcer who bestowed upon him the cell-block-wide nickname "Skinny," for the Gambino crime family boss who bought the burrito bowls he cooked on a stove the guards let him use. "Thees boreeto bowl," he wheezed in a Don Corleone rasp, holding his thumb to his fingertips, "is the beist I ever had. Skeeny, you are a *genios*."

We found a corner table with a small red lamp. After he was done charming our middle-aged waitress, spitting chew into a beer glass, and tilting back his well-rolled baseball cap to ask for a double Jack Daniel's neat—"Cuz I'm an *Amurican*," he said in a fake hick accent whose layers of regret and self-mockery were lost on her—Alex surprised me by lurching into a new, grave register, his blue-gray eyes intent on mine for understanding.

"The way I conveyed it to my mom was, 'What if Jesus Christ came down and told you to do the same exact thing?' Look at all these cults. The people in that Jim Jones cult, they weren't so crazy. They were just at a point in their life where they needed someone to look up to. For Christian people, it's Jesus Christ. For me it was the Rangers. I never did drugs, I hardly drank, I always kept my body pure, because that's what Rangers do. Whenever I was at a party I was always the one who looked out for everybody, because that's what Rangers do. And then finally the one thing happened, and it wasn't like, 'Oh, this is wrong.' It was like, 'If this is wrong, then everything I believe in is wrong.'"

The one thing happened . . . Amid his white polo shirt and clear skin, Alex's new tattoos flashed like false eyes on moth wings: a dotted line with the all-caps instructions CUT HERE across the left wrist, his prison bar code on the belly of the right forearm.

"What's up with those?" I asked.

Alex explained their meanings with an exaggerated enthusiasm that made me suspect he had been getting some pretty ambivalent reactions. They reminded me of the jokes he had been telling for a year at family gatherings: "Felon coming through! Hide the knives!" When he first got out of prison these jokes had cracked us up. *Way to own it, Alex!* was the general sentiment. *Don't let some label get you down!* By now, with the mounting grimness of his job prospects impossible to ignore, the jokes sounded increasingly off. I worried about the tattoos. I knew how seductive it could be, when your personal heroic narrative broke down, to try on its opposite for size. I had gotten tattooed myself while he was in prison, at a parlor on the second floor of a minimall where I would eventually get a job as a bookstore clerk, having befriended a bunch of musicians, actors, and writers who made careless disregard for the future seem revolutionary and fun. Back then I had seen the tattoo as a promise to myself to stop practicing math professionally. I knew that if I were ever to climb into a hot tub full of world-class researchers at some conference somewhere with this dumb, romanticizing thing on my chest—a twelve-sided polyhedron called a snub disphenoid that I had loved and sort of identified with as a kid—I would never be taken seriously again. Since then my views on it had grown more complex. The flamboyant ex-con persona seemed pretty out of character for Alex, but maybe this was just how character formed: by groping whims we had no choice afterward but to commit to as ourselves.

I asked about his favorite army books. Alex told me he had given them all away, $5000 worth, after he got out of prison.

"I was kind of the weird kid in high school. During off periods I would read the army handbook. I knew all the standard operating procedures before I went to basic. Everybody was proud of their acceptance letters to college, and I carried around my Airborne Ranger contract because I was so proud of that. That's all I was known for. I mean, it was everything. It was my life. I saved every piece of newspaper on the Iraq war to the point when I joined up. I got all of Opa's stuff from Oma."

Opa and Oma were the names we had always used for our grandfather and grandmother, an homage to their German ancestry. Family lore had it that Opa had written a memoir of his World War II service, but I had never laid eyes on it.

"The shrapnel they took out of him," Alex ticked off, "his German cross . . . oh, this is funny. Well, it's not funny. It's kind of ironic. Opa killed a German at the point where we were pushing them back into Germany, this blond fourteen-year-old kid from the Hitler Youth. He got his papers. The kid's last name was Becker. Then Opa married Oma—Beverly Beck."

He raised his eyebrows at me. Our grandfather, a New York Jew, killed a teenage Nazi in the country his people left behind, then married a blond Texan Protestant who almost shared the boy's name? I wanted to give Alex the response he was looking for, but I was honestly not sure what I thought of this piece of family trivia. I didn't share his simple fascination with war. I'd never known that deep manly camaraderie he experienced in the army, that unity of violent purpose, although in my own way I'd longed for it.

I realized to my surprise that he was on the verge of tears. Before I could respond, he broke eye contact to look over my shoulder at the TV above the bar, where we had both been glancing periodically at the Broncos game.

Blums love their football. During his coaching days, my father once explained that what looks like a brawl to the unpracticed eye is in fact a complex strategic interplay of formation and counterformation amid a fog of feints and reverses. Big college coaches are as prized as star professors not just because of the fund-raising dollars involved but because the required blend of analytical prowess and charismatic machismo is vanishingly rare. The coach is the general. He has to persuade a group of very tough, opinionated men to put enthusiastic effort into acting against almost any sane measure of self-interest.

I've since learned that the war/football analogy goes only so far. Ever since machine guns and precision artillery blasted close infantry formations apart in the late nineteenth century, armies around the world have had to find new ways to maintain discipline and motivate troops without recourse to the mass choreography that makes football so comparatively precise. How to get soldiers in thousands of private hiding spots to decide, each independently of the others, to leave cover and apply the strategically desirable quantity of violence in situations where the more natural human response is to run away or go murderously insane? This is the problem of battle command. It is a much harder job than coaching. Even leaving aside the vastly higher scale, vastly higher stakes, and vastly denser fog of miscommunication induced by all the explosions and killing and fear, there is also an essential difference between the players on the field: by the standards of professional or even college athletics, war is fought by laughably unpracticed amateurs. Every player on a university team, from the quarterback to the nose tackle, has been staring for years into the eyes of opposing formations through the grilles of their facemasks, learning subtle nuances of stance and shift to draw on instinctively in the grunting crush of a game. In the early years of World War II, by contrast, the average newbie infantryman received only seven weeks of drill on his rifle, none of it against real opponents. In the American Civil War many men went to the front lines with no training whatsoever. Wars back then were fought by teenage farmers, blacksmiths, shopkeepers, and teachers, as clumsy as Little Leaguers forced onto the team by their dads. Now, when most American soldiers enlist directly after high school without first learning a trade, wars are fought by basketball jocks and cheerleaders, by skaters and emo kids, by Harry Potter fans and stoners and jazz band clarinetists. At an age when many parents hesitate to trust children with their own cell-phone accounts, we trust our young soldiers to follow complex rules of engagement in determining when they are supposed to kill.

"Another thing," Alex said, looking back from the game. "When the Iraq war started, I was sitting by the fire in the living room. The power was out. I remember seeing the bombs go off in Baghdad on this little battery-powered TV. I was *so happy* that we were invading Iraq, because I knew I'd get to go to a combat zone when I joined the army."

While Alex was in prison, Norm had offered an evolving series of explanations for his involvement in the robbery that culminated in a version whose principal virtue was that it was less crazy than any of the alternatives: Alex had been so brainwashed by his training that he actually thought the bank robbery plans were some kind of legitimate military operation.

I waited until my second drink with Alex to ask him if my understanding was correct.

"Actually," he said, "I kept thinking that for probably four months in prison. There were points where I was like . . ."

"Wait," I said. "Are you *serious?*"

"Yeah." Alex shrugged. "I was like, there's no way this is *possible.*"

In the months ahead, my disbelief would give way to amazement and outrage as Alex and the rest of the family told me more about the crime. I heard my uncle Fred in North Dakota muse about it in his baritone croon: "I think Alex just had no idea what he was getting into." I heard my uncle Kurt in San Diego growl in disgust: "Ben, that team leader had Alex *completely* freaking brainwashed." I heard Oma brush it off in her mannered Texan lilt: "All Alex did was follow that man's orders." I heard Norm sputter with despairing incredulity: "And this whole time Alex was thinking this was a freaking *training* exercise."

But before all that I heard it from Alex himself, who made time every Monday during his break between Zamboni passes at the ice rink to fill me in over the phone about the day the one thing happened.

CHAPTER 4

ONE FINE DAY AT BATTALION

On August 7, 2006, in Room 321 of Charlie Company barracks, Second Ranger Battalion, Seventy-Fifth Ranger Regiment, U.S. Army, the alarm went off at 0430. Privates Blum, Ryniec, and Martin clicked awake like soldiers, with none of that shell-shocked fog that clung in your brain during the Ranger Indoctrination Program, when all the late-night wake-ups by sergeants screaming at you for your latest failures wore the edge off the self you recognized. They climbed out of bed like soldiers, snapped their sheets taut and tucked them under the mattresses like soldiers, rolled a quick smear of deodorant under their arms. Charlie Company, Second Ranger Battalion: same outfit Tom Hanks's character commands on D-Day in *Saving Private Ryan*. How cool was that?

A few stars still shone out the window over Fort Lewis's Ranger field. Blum swapped a morning nod with each roommate. All down the hall came the muted wooden bangs of wardrobe doors slamming open and shut, the abortive beeps of alarm clocks sounding and just as quickly going dead. The walls of the cramped, dormlike room were papered with the weapons specifications the privates had been studying for their Expert Infantryman Badges as well as an array of bumper stickers: TERRORISM IS A DISEASE; RANGERS ARE THE CURE. RANGERS DON'T DIE; THEY JUST GO TO HELL AND REGROUP. When Blum first arrived here four months ago, it had taken him a moment after waking to see the Ranger memorabilia all over the walls and remember—*I made it.* Now the routine moved through him like a piston through a cylinder, the pride of being a Ranger thrumming deep in his bones. The men didn't shout endless *Hooah*s here as they had in basic training. Rangers leaned more toward a clipped *Roger, Sergeant*: cool, clean, deadly professionalism.

"Cherry" privates like Blum—combat virgins—were at the very bottom of Second Battalion's pecking order. When their platoon's time came on the rotating schedule, they rose an hour and a half earlier than anyone else so they could buff every windowpane and porcelain fold of toilet to the same sheen of purity they strove for in their minds and bodies. If some dusty corner failed inspection, they would all be marched outside and smoked. There were London Towers, Mountain Climbers, Flutter Kicks, Bear Crawls, Iron Mikes. There were TV Watchers, squatting with an invisible TV held in front of their faces. There were Koala Bears, clinging upside-down to telephone poles until they lost their grip and dropped. There were, always and forever, push-ups, which the sergeants liked to order by shorthand: *"Beat your fucking face!"*

It was still dark when Blum and Ryniec pushed open the stairwell door to the concrete apron behind the barracks. The tall firs that ringed the parking lot waved in the early breeze. They circled in opposite directions to pick up all the empty Skoal cans and damp plugs of earthy chew that littered the pavement. Ryniec kept his voice just above a whisper as he and Blum converged on the dumpster with their handfuls of trash, bantering about all the blood they'd spill on deployment.

At 1200 hours today, the entirety of Second Battalion would be released for two weeks of block leave, after which the damp green mountains of Fort Lewis would be swept aside for the blazing dust of Iraq. *Deployment.* Excited speculation about the missions to come had hummed for weeks through every conversation. On Second Battalion's last deployment, they had helped rescue a Navy SEAL named Marcus Luttrell, whose account of the harrowing mission, *Lone Survivor*, would soon become a *New York Times* bestseller and a major Hollywood film. Now rumor had it they would be deploying with Luttrell to Ramadi. For Private Blum, the feeling resembled nothing so much as the anticipation that had built inside him just before a big hockey tournament when he was a kid, that same little bell ringing on and on. This was it: what he had worked for more than half his life.

He and Ryniec ducked to look beneath the benches and pull-up bars of the small exercise area. Behind them, pale beige room lights showed through the windows on the second and third floors, where the privates stayed. Darkness prevailed in the windows on the first, which housed the noncommissioned officers and "tabs," those who had completed a combat deployment and passed Ranger School to earn their Ranger tab, a black arch above the shoulder sleeve insignia with RANGER inscribed in gold thread. One of these rooms belonged to Specialist Sommer, the team leader Blum had taken orders from when he first arrived at battalion and who by now had become a kind of mentor. Also sleeping in Specialist Sommer's room were the two Canadian friends that Blum had driven Sommer to pick up at the Tacoma Greyhound station last night. But Blum's thoughts were not on Sommer or his friends. Even deployment was a little unreal to him on a day like today. All he could think about was getting through the hours that lay between now and his evening flight home to see Anna.

I had been talking to Alex for two months on the phone about every other possible topic before he finally opened up about his ex-girlfriend.

"In basic training," he told me, "you can't control the drill sergeants, can't control what time you wake up, when you eat, when you piss, what you do all day. The one thing they can't touch is Anna."

Before leaving for basic, Alex had arranged for two of his friends at Littleton High to deliver Anna a new red rose every day, accompanied by successive installments of a long love letter. He wrote more letters to her from the barracks, often taking an entire hour from the handful he'd have for sleep to fill page after page of notebook paper.

> I love you baby I love you as far as the universe stretches you are the love of my life and my best friend. Whenever I am surrounded by darkness I see you and all of a sudden I am surrounded by light. Thank you.

Between the body and the signature, some letters contained as many as six pages composed entirely of the phrases "I love you" and "I miss you," modulated with varyingly effusive relatives of "so much."

You are my entire life baby. Marry me. I love you
Alex

During Alex's tenure, a Ranger battalion generally deployed for
three months, then came back for six months of rest and recovery
as the other two deployed in sequence. Rangers trained hard in the
off-season. Their elite standards demanded intensive upkeep, like a
top-shelf Ferrari in racing condition. Because the RIP curriculum
contained precious little in the way of actual instruction, the biggest
challenge was to bring the new cherry privates up to speed on Ranger
tactics and integrate them into combat teams, each of which specialized in one of the two primary zones of urban warfare: inside and outside. A "line" team performed home invasions and secured interiors.
A "gun" team provided cover with M240 machine guns from outside,
shooting "squirters"—those who attempted to flee the building—and
lighting up targets with tracer rounds for the helicopters, known as
"little birds," to hit with the serious weaponry. Although Ranger protocol has changed a little since Alex's time, when he joined battalion the responsibility for training new guys mostly fell to their team
leaders, recently anointed tabs who enjoyed the same gleeful lordship
over cherry privates as fraternity brothers over new pledges.

To PFC Blum, the tabs represented a standard of competence
and achievement he could barely imagine attaining himself. Not only
had tabs actually *taken on terrorists in combat*, they had all completed
Ranger School, a leadership course twice as long and just as brutal
as RIP. The presence of a tab in a room brought in a thrilling after-
scent of Iraqi dust and blood. Cherry privates admired them desperately. The tabs repaid the favor with unrelenting hazing. At any
moment, whether firing rounds at the machine-gun range or shopping downtown on weekend leave, a tab could yell "tab check" and
force a private to do whatever he wanted: bark like a dog, pump out
fifty push-ups in a crowded elevator, chug three beers and run ten
laps around the barracks.

August 7 marked a loosening of the hierarchy. Soon the soldiers
would all fight side by side against a common enemy. Today, Charlie
Company's morning hour of PT was light and fun, a reward for all
the work the privates had recently put in for their Expert Infantryman Badges. The forty-odd soldiers of Blum's platoon gathered in

formation at 0600 hours in the parking lot behind the barracks for warm-up calisthenics and stretches, bouncing on their toes to keep warm. Blum and Ryniec had taken special care not to leave even a stray gum wrapper or cigarette butt. Nearly all Blum's closest Ranger comrades were here, including Specialist Sommer and the other tabbed specialists and corporals who filled out the ranks of team leaders and assistant team leaders—the "E4 Mafia," as they called themselves, referencing their military pay grade. Exercise gear had been dragged through the side door from the gym for a five-station circuit: power military press, box jump, rowing machine, squats, clean-and-jerk. Platoon Sergeant Congdon bellowed the names of five soldiers at a time to sprint up and rotate through, doing as many reps as they could manage in the minute allotted for each station. Privates struggled wildly to outdo the tabs. The whole platoon screamed encouragement and happy threats as the clanks and wet thumps of bodies in motion echoed through the parking lot. After half an hour, the sun cracked over the shaggy silhouettes of the firs, netting the Rangers' chests and faces in pale, orangish light.

When grouped as one unit, the gun teams were known as "MGT Squad." This was short for "machine-gun teams," but it was pronounced, with relish, "Maggot." After everyone had been through the PT circuit, Corporal Roe led Maggot Squad on a run out the Ranger complex gate and around some nearby barracks. The point of this route, the easiest they ever took, was to intimidate regular infantry ground troops. Maggot ran by at full speed, puffing their chests out in an exaggerated goose step, then circled back to the barbed wire fence wrapped in brown tarp that surrounded their complex. Blum and the other cherries had been told that just before their arrival at battalion, a first sergeant from a nearby Stryker brigade had led a daredevil charge of other sergeants through the gates. The tabs who saw them, all outranked, had chased them down, beaten them up, flex-cuffed them, and deposited them outside.

After a quick shower, everyone changed into BDUs—battle-dress uniforms, which the soldiers called fluff-and-buffs because they dirtied and washed them so often. Most days they went straight from breakfast to the morning's training, which was typically dangerous and exhilarating. Today their only responsibility was to prepare their rooms for block leave inspection. Blum went to the gym with his team leader, Corporal Sager, to lift weights for an hour, then returned to his room and started cleaning out his minifridge. In contrast to nearly every other day he had spent at Ranger Batt, the morning was unstructured and leisurely. Privates wandered between rooms to hang out for a minute and chat. All the talk was of how excited they were to go on deployment and shoot people.

The infantry's job is to "close with and engage the enemy," a classic piece of military euphemism that translates roughly to "run up near armed, dangerous men and perforate their bodies until they die."

"Can you sink into that?" I asked Alex that first night at the Denver bar. "What's the back-and-forth like?"

Alex obliged me, making his voice go excited and young. "It's like, *'Dude.* I can't wait to go fuckin in-house. We've been practicing all this fucking time to go take a house down—I can't wait to kill a fucking hajji. Those fucking sand niggers. Fuck those motherfuckers. I can't wait to waste those motherfucking . . . Can you imagine the size of a 7.62 going into those cocksuckers? Kill a little fucking kid with a bomb strapped to him? That'd be fucking sick. I can't fucking wait.' It's like that."

I couldn't help wondering if any of the guys in Broncos sweatshirts at the bar were within earshot. Alex's eyes flicked a little, as they do when he's nervous.

"Is that an exaggeration, slightly?"

"That's literally how it is. It's probably worse."

I asked him where the men had picked up that habit of speech. He told me it came from mimicking the soldiers with combat experience.

"Do they talk that way about people they've actually killed?"

I saw the memory hit in his eyes as he nodded. His voice climbed before he remembered to hush himself. "Oh man. Oh *fuck.* One time we were at this range learning how to set off Claymores. This one sergeant, this was him, I swear to God, his fucking husky voice, he goes"—Alex's voice dropped an octave as he leaned over his tumbler of whiskey—"*'You motherfuckers. When you get over there, I swear to God you don't know shit. When you kill a body, you take their soul.*

You fucking take their soul. But fuck 'em, cause they're going to kill your buddies.'"

He glanced around to see if anyone had heard him, then met my shocked expression with one of his own. "That's what they're like! That's the mind-set! He goes, *'This fucker was shooting at my squad with his kids on his back, so I wasted him and his little shits. I killed a little twelve-year-old girl. I pissed in her bulletholes.'* And we thought he was the coolest guy in the world! Like, 'Holy shit, this guy's fucking *crazy!*'"

Moral outrage sounded a little jarring coming from Alex. In tone it was only a few degrees away from the fascinated awe he used to express for all things military.

"In the infantry," he went on, "you want to be a cold-blooded, detached killer. That's the coolest thing to be."

"So you talked that way to impress each other?"

"I think we said how excited we were to do it to tell ourselves we *could* do it. We can talk hard, we can be hard."

————

It wasn't just the veterans from whom they drew cues. Video games and movies were also full of role models and great lines. Like NFL players squeezing in a game of *Madden NFL* in the locker room or drummers taking on the lead singer in a tour bus round of *Guitar Hero*, the Rangers relaxed after training by sniping each other's heads off in *Call of Duty 2*. Blum and his buddy PFC Anderson from Bravo Company had joint custody of an Xbox that lived in Room 321. If they couldn't muster the energy for the taunts and fights that inevitably followed a multiplayer death match, they opted for cinema.

The movies the privates loved best were big-budget epics that presented a vision of war both accurate enough to believe in and glorious enough for them to want in. Movies about heroic Rangers like *Saving Private Ryan* and *The Great Raid* had inspired a lot of them to go army in the first place, but around battalion, *Black Hawk Down* was the go-to choice. For a Ranger, it played like a two-hour highlight reel. It had been filmed with close cooperation from the regiment and featured real Rangers as extras and helicopters exactly like the ones they trained with. Big-name actors played people they saw every day. Their chaplain, Major Jeff Strueker, a squad leader back then, had dragged an early Mogadishu casualty to safety and demanded to be returned to the action. Strueker was whispered of around battalion as "a fucking killer, man." The running joke was that he had found God only to get his captain's bars.

Campy schlock was good too. Now that Alex and his compatriots were real Special Ops commandos, it never ceased to delight them that all the terrorist-killing, hostage-rescuing, bomb-defusing action heroes America slavered and thrilled over were *doing a Ranger's actual job*. They loved to hoot together at Hollywood's efforts at military realism: the boneheaded tactics of the supposedly elite counterterrorism team scrambling through a shower grate to be slaughtered in *The Rock*, the garbled lingo in just about everything. Their favorite was *Navy Seals*, the 1990 bomb in which Charlie Sheen plays a bad boy in a red Corvette and Bill Paxton plays a sniper code-named God ("Your God does not help you now!" screams a terrorist at his helpless victim just before Bill Paxton puts a bullet between his eyes, triggering convulsive guffaws from every Ranger in the room). Rangers often collaborate with SEALs on critical missions in the Middle East, which causes problems: the rivalry between army and navy gets particularly fierce between their elite units. A few days before block leave, Platoon Sergeant Congdon had gathered all of Charlie Company's First Platoon by the trophy case in the hallway that featured a Mercedes hubcap and a certain prominent Iraqi's bloody uniform to ask that they please, if possible, on the upcoming deployment, refrain from calling SEALs "swim fags" or asking them how Charlie Sheen was doing.

Violent movies, violent video games, juvenile pranks, and porn: the barracks were a lot like what any other dorm in America would look like if you slipped a canister of vaporized testosterone into the air conditioning. Some privates went to frat parties in Tacoma with no other goal than to start fights and steal beer.

When I asked Alex who the big characters at Ranger Batt were—the scary guys, the cool guys, the weird ones and outcasts—I could tell the question grated.

"See, now you're getting down to an individual aspect. You don't have that there. Guys had tabs or they didn't. EIBs [Expert Infantryman Badges], CIBs [Combat Infantryman Badges], number of combat tours. That's what made them them."

There was only one soldier Alex identified as failing in some way to fit in: a private named Chad Palmer in the line team Alex's gun team was paired with. The reasons were various. Palmer had a combat deployment but no tab. Nearly everyone in Ranger Batt chewed Copenhagen, but very few smoked, because it compromised endurance; Palmer was one of them. When he talked he tilted his head back and squinted as if with secret knowledge, a peculiar and off-putting attitude in an environment where every single experience was shared. He just didn't seem as serious about the Rangers as some others—a big deal to PFC Blum, who was as serious as it got. But Palmer's biggest fault was acting too familiar with the tabs. He chatted and joked with them as if he were their equal.

That's what Alex told me. Soon I had developed my own theory: the real problem with Palmer, I suspected, was that PFC Blum couldn't understand why Specialist Sommer liked him so much.

———

The cherry privates were as comfortable with each other's bodies as lovers. This came in part from all the fighting. In the total mutual exertion of hand-to-hand groundwork you had to grab whatever you could to gain advantage. They practiced a lot, in venues both official and otherwise. A favorite tab game was to send a private down the hall to ask for dental floss or some other pointless item from another squad, whose members would invariably drop him to the carpet, wrench his wrists behind his back for flex-cuffs, duct-tape his mouth, and leave him slumped outside his squad room door.

"How often did that happen?" I asked Alex.

"Daily. Literally every single day."

On rarer occasions, tabs would stage free-ranging battles between squads that left everyone in bruised piles by the end. PFC Blum once took a boot to the face that cut halfway through his lip. At times he was spurred by the tabs to choke other privates to unconsciousness. Other times he himself was choked out. When I told Alex that I couldn't imagine how that felt, he offered to show me.

By now it was the summer of 2010. A lot had passed between

us in the six months since that first conversation in the Denver bar: thousands of cell-phone minutes, a growing repertoire of inside jokes, and an increasing undercurrent of subtle verbal jockeying over the sequence of events of August 7, which so far neither one of us had named. We were facing off on a mat in Alex's dad's garage in Greenwood Village, dressed in two worn black sweat suits that Alex had scavenged from his bedroom closet. Mine hung off me in pouches that looked like trash bags stuck on a fence.

"Okay," I said. "Sure."

There is a funny intimacy in the moment when someone's arm is around your throat but he hasn't yet started to squeeze. After some rearranging as he sought the optimal angle, Alex made a fist and expanded his biceps. I felt instantly transparent. Blood and thought rushed back into my head when he let go.

"You okay?" he asked, concerned.

"You're really good at that," I managed to say.

Alex grinned, glad, as always, to be of help.

———

It was just after noon on August 7, when PFC Blum zip-tied his desk drawers and stuffed the last of his clothes into his hockey bag, that the story started to get complicated.

Half an hour after the official release time, Platoon Sergeant Congdon conducted an inspection of First Platoon's barracks that brought him finally to Room 321. As he poked into desks and cabinets and checked off items on his clipboard, Blum, Ryniec, and their roommate, Martin, stood at attention, spines rigid with that electric tension that always accompanied a superior; the feeling when a civilian boss materializes beside you isn't too far off, if your boss happens to exude readiness at all times to beat your ass. In Blum's case, the anxiety was coupled with the private swoon of worship he felt for the Rangers he admired most. Congdon was tattooed and huge, with a shouted-out husk of a voice. His friends in Delta Force all called him Sergeant Congo, a nickname meant to evoke bloody jungle atrocities.

"Don't fuck up on leave," Congdon said. "See you back here in two weeks."

Blum, Ryniec, and Martin slumped into chairs and beds with the extra talkativeness of mild relief.

Next to appear at their door was Corporal Roe, Ryniec's team leader, announcing a soft armor inspection. Although Roe was a tab, the privates had enough day-to-day contact with him to render this a fairly relaxed exchange. Each gathered his soft armor, a butterfly-shaped bulletproof vest that hugged the body without constricting movement, and dumped it in the growing pile outside the squad room door.

Shortly afterward, Specialist Sommer came by, gestured for Blum to follow him out into the hall, and asked him for his soft armor. Blum dug it from the pile and handed it over.

The first time Alex told me about this moment, I asked him how he could possibly have failed to be suspicious. He explained that questioning his superiors was a habit of mind he had long since given up. "What you have to realize," Alex said, "is I never thought it was possible for a tab to do something wrong." He told me that he assumed that Sommer's request had something to do with the inspection—that he gave it no more thought than that.

For all the detailed verisimilitude of Alex's story, it was beginning to seem increasingly strange to me how normal a day August 7 appeared to have been. In the story as Alex told it, he and the soldiers he regarded with such affection did little other than lift weights, watch TV, gobble huge rations at chow hall or off post, and insult each other's chances with women on leave. All the while, though, Specialist Sommer was flashing in and out among them. How many suspected what he was planning for that afternoon? How many knew? Why didn't anyone do something?

CHAPTER 5

YES, SPECIALIST SOMMER

August 7, 2006, was not, of course, PFC Blum's first experience of Specialist Luke Elliott Sommer. Sommer was one of the very first tabs Blum met at Ranger Battalion.

PFC Blum reported for duty about four months before the robbery, in April 2006. After the exhilaration of surviving the Ranger Indoctrination Program and the princely rides in limousines from the airport to Fort Lewis, he and the other new cherries had passed for the first time through the hallowed gate in the brown-tarp-covered chain-link fence and discovered a ghost town. The few tabs in the barracks dumped out all their belongings and smoked them perfunctorily, then ignored them. The rest of Second Battalion was still in Iraq. The new privates' only duties were to clean up the barracks and service gear in preparation for their return. When Specialist Luke Elliott Sommer arrived three days later from Ranger School with a brand-new tab on his shoulder and gathered the new privates to watch *The Great Raid* with him in Charlie Company's bar, they were glad just to have their existence registered. Five minutes into the opening sequence a sergeant strode in, puffed up with displeasure at the presence of cherry privates in the bar. The privates steeled themselves to get smoked. But Sommer told the sergeant that they were with him, and that appeared to be enough.

Even among Rangers, Sommer stood out: over six feet tall, with dark hair, blue eyes of powerful intensity, and a smattering of fierce tattoos. He spoke quickly but reasonably with a mild Canadian accent about his two combat deployments, one each to Afghanistan and Iraq. He laid out his philosophy on the Rangers for the new privates. "Ranger Batt is like no place on earth. You're with the best of the best now," he said. "But you have to play it smart. It's a political game."

Near the end of Ranger School, after weeks of slogging through Georgia swamps, climbing rock faces with numb hands and combat boots, and leading all-night ambushes in which even the intestine-clenching certainty of imminent explosions could barely keep you awake and moving, Sommer had fallen out of formation to administer first aid to a soldier with heat stroke, after which he had been recommended for an award at graduation.

PFC Blum listened in awe. This was the first time an active-duty Ranger with combat experience had treated him like someone worth talking to. Specialist Sommer's birthplace in Canada just so happened to be home to the Kelowna Rockets, an elite youth club that the Littleton Hawks had once traveled up to compete against. Nervous but excited, Blum spoke up to mention the connection. Sommer told him that he had once played for the Rockets, although in a different age bracket. And there was another link between them: the room Blum was staying in now, number 321, had been Sommer's the year before.

The rest of the Rangers returned from deployment, then were released on April 7 for two weeks of block leave. Alex flew home to Colorado to see Anna and his family. When he returned, he found himself assigned to the second of three gun teams with a private named Womack, whose measured speech and prickly shaved head reminded him of Squidward from the cartoon *SpongeBob SquarePants*. Their boss, the team leader assigned to teach Privates Blum and Womack how to do their new job, would be Specialist Sommer.

———

A few weeks later, shortly after Alex's nineteenth birthday, Ranger Battalion held a parents' visit weekend. Norm drove out from Colorado in the silver Audi A4 he had promised Alex for use at battalion.

Alex has always worshipped his father. Back when Norm was playing a charming and tolerant host to his friends, he had been the coolest dad around. On this weekend, though, for the first time in his life, Alex found himself embarrassed by his father. Mortified, actually.

"So what kind of guns do you guys shoot?" Norm asked.

"Guns" was a civilian term. PFC Blum winced.

"Weapons, Dad. They're called weapons."

He introduced Norm to the specialist in the parking lot behind Charlie Company.

"I just remember, 'This is Specialist Sommer,'" Norm recalled to me when I asked him about Sommer on the patio behind his house. "I recognized the name. Alex had talked about him, because this had been his boss for a period of time. He was just a big, thick British Columbia kid. Pretty studly-looking, outgoing, polite. He was bright. Before Alex enlisted, my opinion of army guys was that they had nothing better to do with their lives. 'Alex, you've got all this opportunity, why do something like this?' But the guys I met there were really impressive. Physically, they're in perfect shape. They're so committed to their cause, you have to respect it."

Later that day Sommer showed up again, joking his way into a room full of privates and launching his big frame up Alex's back like an extension ladder. Norm was puzzled by his son's kowtowing formality in response but soon learned that cherry privates and tabbed E4s were strictly separate castes. "There was such a divide between private and specialist, tab and nontab," he told me.

Ranger Battalion had been set up as a kind of war-themed day camp, with several activity stations to choose from. Sommer asked Norm if he and Alex would like to join him for the walk to Range 7, where parents would have the opportunity to fire automatic weapons. He told Norm to call him Elliott. Norm was happy to oblige. While they chatted about Sommer's childhood, swapping jokes and hockey lingo, Alex cringed in silence.

"I liked him," Norm recalled. "I like Canadians. I like hockey guys. I'm thinking, 'I'm glad Alex has a hockey guy in addition to these Ranger guys. The hockey relationship's a deep bond.' I'm thinking, 'Alex is really comfortable here. This isn't all bad. So my kid lost his personality, but at least he's around quality guys. He's going to learn a lot about life.'"

At the range, Sommer took Norm into a pitch-black tent and strapped goggles on his head that popped the room into the horror-movie depth of night vision, then set him up outside with a squad automatic weapon, the same M240 model Alex trained with. The barrel climbed uncontrollably as Norm shot bursts at the metal targets fifty yards away. Sommer went next. To illustrate, Norm leaned forward in his patio chair, holding an imaginary assault rifle to his shoulder and taking aim at the lawn mower parked beside a broken planter across the grass.

"He's just, *boom boom boom boom*. Just, *ding ding ding ding*. He was right on the fucking target. He didn't fucking miss. You're thinking, well, you don't want to be on the other end of this."

By the time the trio walked back from the range, crammed into the shoulder of a busy four-lane road with troop carriers whizzing past, the dynamic between Sommer and his son had begun to bother Norm. They were just a couple of kids—Alex was nineteen, Elliott only twenty—but Alex almost seemed to enjoy playing the role of subordinate. It made normal conversation impossible.

"Every time with Alex it was, 'Yes, Specialist Sommer. Yes, Specialist Sommer.' So we're walking back, and I go, 'Alex, do you guys have to do this? It's just the three of us. Why don't you relax a little? His name's Elliott. Just call him Elliott.' That's when Sommer says, 'Uh, Mr. Blum, that's not how it works around here.'"

Sommer turned to Alex and barked a command. *"Private Blum! Get out in that road and beat your face!"*

Alex turned without hesitation and charged into traffic. Norm stared in disbelief as his son pumped off push-ups with his bare hands flat on the hot black asphalt, Specialist Sommer yelling counts from just above. Armored trucks rocked to a halt on either side of them. Alex's form was perfect, eager, proud. His chest dropped over and over to within a millimeter of the double yellow lines. When Sommer finally called him off, Alex sprang to his feet and both jogged to join Norm on the shoulder. Traffic rumbled back up to speed.

"Sommer goes . . ." Norm wrinkled his forehead in an effort at recall. "'He does whatever I tell him to do and he has no vote or say about it. He's my . . .' I don't think he said 'bitch.'"

Before Norm flew home at the end of the weekend, leaving the Audi behind, Specialist Sommer told PFC Blum to see if his father would loan him $200. Norm agreed. Two weeks later, Sommer paid him back.

———

A few days after my conversation with Norm, Alex and I met in his father's driveway to talk about his training.

"Hope you're ready to get smoked," Alex said, hauling up the garage door.

The next two hours were the most animated I had seen from Alex since his arrest. He rolled around on the cement of the garage floor shouting synchronizing codes to demonstrate a "talking guns" drill he had practiced on the quad with Womack, swapping in and out at Sommer's command and cycling bursts to keep the barrels cool. He grabbed printer paper and pens from Norm's home office to draw diagrams of the bullet-riddled live-fire shoot houses that had to be rebuilt every few months, remembering jogging excitedly back to the barracks alongside buddies who had once more succeeded, through a mix of professionalism and luck, in not killing each other. He dug cardboard boxes and soup cans out of the recycling bin to build a three-dimensional map of a company-wide training mission, pointed out breach points to each building with a golf club. He slipped into voices for sergeants and tabs with theatrical relish as he issued commands down the chain. I could almost see his gear-laden teenage form in digital-print fatigues and combat boots floating at twilight into the mock city in the hills where they staged the exercise, mind compressed inside his helmet by the pulse of chopper blades. He talked me through the sequence as if it were a favorite movie: dropping to a hover with dozens of other black helicopters over a dark field, leaping from a cabin packed tight with men and gear into open air on a thick black rope that charged up through your thighs and gloves like an animal, watching the grass beneath you widen, ripple in coiling eddies, hit through your boots with the total shock of body woken to itself. It was as close to battle as PFC Blum ever got. Hours later, as they flew home through the dark, Corporal Sager, a friend of Sommer's from British Columbia who had taken over as Alex's team leader after Sommer moved to a line team, let him sit in the helicopter's door with his legs dangling in the wind.

"The moon was full," Alex intoned. "We were flying along the highway. I was strapped into the Black Hawk with the 240 hanging between my knees. The wind was pushing my right pant leg across my lap. Sager leaned over. He said, 'I wouldn't let you sit in the door if you hadn't done a perfect job.'" Alex paused for a moment to savor the memory. "I was so happy that I'd made him proud. I knew if we'd been in Iraq, he would have trusted me to be in the door to engage the enemy. The highway cut through mountains covered in pine trees. We were eight hundred, nine hundred feet up. I remember watching a lone car weaving through them, the faint lights on a Honda or a Toyota or whatever it was, and thinking it had no idea we were up there, no idea what we'd just done."

––––––

Those months were transformative for all the cherry privates. At night and on weekends, they ventured into Tacoma with new eyes. Every door was a potential breach point, every bar counter a red zone concealing hidden gunmen, every Denny's dining room partitioned into lines of fire. Civilians looked more and more like another species entirely. Cherry privates watched in bemusement as men and women with giant poofs of hair puzzled over menus, smoothed napkins over their laps, wiped their children's mouths. One night after raiding airplane hangars, Alex and his buddies went out to see the new X-Men movie at the AMC multiplex near the highway, and all they could talk about, lined up there in the dark among teenagers who had no idea they were surrounded by Rangers, was how simple it would be to take down the theater. They all tried to outdo each other in assessment of the tactical problem, which was almost identical to that of a hangar: three exits, red zone in the projectionist booth, big interior space with a bunch of sheep to herd. Piece of cake.

Talk of hitting spots around Tacoma was a reliable way to show off knowledge and sound hard, a real-world application of their classroom sessions planning raids on satellite photos of al-Qaeda complexes. Whenever they watched heist movies, they laughed at how much better they could do the job themselves. Tabs were fluent in the lingo of tactical planning, but the sharper of the privates were already picking it up. In this PFC Blum was lucky to enjoy the special mentorship of Specialist Sommer.

Even after his replacement as Blum's team leader, the specialist popped in once in a while as Blum broke down M16s or shined boots to ask him for a ride into town. He was friendlier to the privates than other tabs were, taking more than a few of them out to facilities around Tacoma to war-game, but Blum seemed to be a favorite of his. Sommer thought the silver Audi was cool, nicknaming it "the Transporter," after one of his favorite movies, in which a disillusioned Special Forces operator runs criminal errands in an Audi A8. Blum tried to hide his nervousness about the stick shift. No matter where Sommer wanted to go—Chili's, Starbucks, Quiznos, Dairy Queen, the supermarket, a porn shop—he made a little lesson out of it.

"Where's our infill?"

"Side door by the booths."

"Right. Red zones?"

"By the counter. From the kitchen. Behind that soft-serve thing."

"You forgot the bathroom, Blum. Bang. You're dead."

As they ate, Sommer would regale him with tales of Iraq and Afghanistan and of his youth in Kelowna, a city of several hundred thousand east of Vancouver. His mother was a Royal Canadian Air Cadets instructor, but since Sommer had dual citizenship, he had chosen the U.S. Army, because Rangers were the ones who scoured the world of the vilest bad guys. He singled out one group in particular for his venom: the Hells Angels Motorcycle Club, a gang that Blum was surprised to learn maintained a stranglehold on Kelowna. Sommer detailed their offenses: drug dealing, extortion, squatting in houses and ejecting their elderly inhabitants. He fantasized about gathering a team of Rangers to take them on.

"These guys are like the insurgents of Canada. A few Rangers would wipe these motherfuckers out, easy."

"Hell yeah they would."

Hooah. *Get* some. Blum was thrilled to be included by a tab in this kind of swaggering banter. Specialist Sommer impressed him: funny, experienced, highly motivated to stamp out evil wherever it might be found. Of course, in Blum's heart of hearts, he was a little more into defending America from freedom-hating jihadis than Canada from some aging biker gang. But he wasn't about to say that. The range of Sommer's expertise in tactics, weaponry, and politics was formidable, and he was drilling PFC Blum on the skills he would soon need to perform flawlessly in Iraq: securing sight lines, covering hostages, taking quick charge of the package. The package might be a terrorist leader, a stash of guns, a hard drive full of enemy plans, anything. If you didn't get out with the package, the mission was a failure.

When I asked Alex how it felt to complete these extracurricular exercises, he emphasized their similarity to the work Rangers did every day. As a nineteen-year-old private, he had simply been grateful for the chance to improve his skills. He was dreaming of heroic feats in Iraq. It seemed clear enough, though, that he had also found them profoundly exciting—like a video game you got to play in real life. Not that this distinguished them much from the rest of his training. Blowing the heads off plastic terrorists with assault rifles was another real-life video game, and Alex and his comrades played a lot of others on their Xbox, especially a game called *Hitman*, whose Mafia storyline dovetailed with a real-world game they called "Sommer Syndicate."

By July, Sommer's vigilante fantasy had expanded to include building a team of Rangers that would take over Kelowna and keep the Hells Angels out for good, sustaining themselves with protection money from local businesses and living by a strict code of honor. Once in a while he would toss a pistol to Blum, Palmer, or one of the other privates he was tight with and call "suicide check." The requirement then was to point it at your head and pull the trigger. To examine the chamber first was an insult, forbidden. The godfather, "Don Terrino," commanded absolute trust. In return, he was available to help out when it really counted. Once, when Blum pulled charge-of-quarters duty after two straight sleepless nights of field drills, he passed out at the desk and woke to a furious sergeant demanding to see his supervisor. Blum went upstairs and instead got Specialist Sommer, who somehow managed to calm the guy down and keep Blum out of trouble. The import of this anecdote didn't sink in for me until another soldier told me about a friend of his who, after being caught asleep on CQ duty in Iraq, was court-martialed and stripped of his rank, becoming an instant pariah in his unit. His girlfriend broke up with him. A week after he got out of the brig he committed suicide.

In civilian life back home in British Columbia, where Sommer had gone by Elliott, his near-poetic facility with wild tales had earned him the nickname "B.S. Elliott." Among his close associates at battalion, his bullshitting and over-the-top craziness was known as the "Sommer factor." He liked to pop his dental retainer—one false tooth lodged in the middle to fill a gap he'd earned in a fight—in and out as a joke. Other tabs played along with his games. One day at the 240B gun-mapping range, Corporal Sager gave Blum his keys and asked him to move his truck so he wouldn't get a ticket. Blum came back glowing from the trust that this personal errand implied and discovered Sager talking to Sommer on the curb. Sager raised his eyebrows at Blum with an air of jokey conspiracy. "You planning to take out some Hells Angels, Private?" he asked.

"Definitely, Corporal."

In late June, Blum drove Sommer to a casino off I-5 along with PFC Palmer and an older tab named Byrne whom he had never met before. After Byrne made a recon run, they all brainstormed the tactical problem of taking it down: breaching the vault with plastic explosives, escaping in Humvees. As usual, Sommer took the normal Ranger chest-beating one step further, going so far as to diagram the mission on Google Earth satellite images in the same way raids were marked up in the classroom. But whenever PFC Blum started to think this was all getting just a little too real, Sommer would throw in some crazy detail about bringing Bravo Company along to fast-rope in from Black Hawks while Maggot Squad covered them with 240s, and soon it was all laughter and comfort again.

Now that they were spending more and more time together, Specialist Sommer told PFC Blum that he could begin to call him Elliott. Blum was flattered by the offer but found himself too uncomfortable to accept, sticking instead to "Specialist Sommer" as regulations required. Sergeants cracked down hard if they saw a private fraternizing too closely with a tab.

"He kept it in military-speak," Alex told me. "It was always, 'This is the infill, and I need you to map this out for me, and this and this and this.' I was like, 'Okay, okay, okay.' It was just like homework for me. Maybe in his mind he was like, 'Yeah, he's in on it, he's good with it.' But at the same time . . . This is actually the main question I have. Was he like, 'I have to keep this power over him'? Or was he like, 'We're actually equals'?"

On the afternoon of Thursday, August 3, just after PFC Blum successfully completed the rigorous multiday testing phase for the Expert

Infantryman Badge he would need for combat duty in Iraq, Sommer asked him for a ride to the Bank of America branch on South Tacoma Way, where he had a checking account. While Sommer engaged in a lengthy transaction with a teller, Blum sat in a plush chair in the lobby and gave the place a once-over. Afterward, at a nearby Quiznos, he charted out on a napkin how a Ranger team would hit the place, trying his best to impress the specialist with his tactical acuity.

For PFC Blum, the morning of August 7 really was in many respects no different from an ordinary day: a long series of more-or-less arbitrary orders from superiors, some making sense, some not. Sergeant Congdon came by to release them for block leave. Corporal Roe came by to announce the soft armor inspection. Specialist Sommer came by to pick up PFC Blum's soft armor. Blum and the other privates wandered into each other's rooms to kill time until their flights. Two hours later PFC Blum was in the squad room watching TV with a few other privates and their squad leader, Sergeant Waterhouse, when Specialist Sommer leaned in the door and gestured for him to come out into the hall.

"My grandma just died," he said.

PFC Blum had no idea how to react. Was it his place to give comfort? In fact, as Alex would learn years later, Sommer's grandmother had just suffered a botched biopsy that would soon lead to her death but had not yet passed away. The story Sommer had given to superiors was that his Canadian friends were here to ride north with him and visit her in the hospital.

"I'm sorry, Specialist," Blum ventured, which was how he truly felt.

"I need your car keys," Sommer said.

"Sure."

As he watched the specialist walk away with his keys, Blum realized to his dismay that he was now in danger of missing his evening flight. His buddy Anderson from Bravo Company was supposed to drive him to the airport in the Audi. Back home in Denver, Anna was waiting. But there wasn't anything Blum could do about it. He returned to the squad room.

Around 1500, Privates Anderson, Ryniec, and MacDonald decided to take Ryniec's old Ford Explorer into Tacoma for an afternoon snack at Applebee's. From there they would drive MacDonald to the airport to catch his flight. Anderson planned to go in to the airline counter to see if he could switch his own flight to tonight. If he managed to do so, Alex's ride would evaporate. His best bet was to load his hockey bag in the Ford and go with them to the airport now.

"You sure you don't want to come, Blum?"

"Nah, I have to wait for Specialist Sommer."

They all slapped hands with him, pulled it in for the clinch, exchanged a few last words of excited anticipation for deployment, and disappeared down the hallway.

PFC Blum received two phone calls in the next hour from friends carpooling to the airport and offering rides. He was forced to decline both offers.

By 1610 he was all by himself in the squad room, slouched in a pile on the sofa, alternating his attention between the TV and the clock. His cell phone lit up again: Specialist Sommer.

"I need you to come downstairs and drive," Sommer said. "We're going to the bank. We're going to take care of it."

———

It was a warm July afternoon a few days after the mock mission in Norm's garage when Alex and I drilled down to the deepest level yet on these crucial few minutes, in a conversation on my mother's balcony that would resonate with me for years. A brigade of storm clouds were bearing down in slow motion from the Rockies.

" 'We're going to take care of it,' " I repeated.

"Yeah," said Alex.

After months of army talk and job commiseration and, more recently, exultation at the conquering prowess of the five-year-olds he had been granted permission to coach at the rink despite his lack of a license, Alex and I seemed to our mutual surprise to have entered the ranks of each other's closest friends. His loyalty, I had discovered, was hard-won but immense. He called regularly, kept up with the details of my life, told me stupid jokes when I seemed down, even grew a beard to match my own. But for all his efforts to explain how he could have believed the robbery was a training exercise, I still kept getting hung up on small details. In his lawn chair he was sunk into a very different slouch from the kind in the squad room years ago, his hat pulled low over his eyes, his lips popping on and off the mouth of his beer bottle to hide his nervousness. He had only recently begun trusting me with the more difficult details of his story.

"But," I said, "I mean . . . you know what that means. You guys have talked about the bank."

Alex made a pained noise through his teeth. "Well . . . I think he didn't specifically say it, so it was kind of like—and I think that's where the mind-set goes, where it was like—and I, like I said, I . . . You're always under the impression that he wouldn't do something wrong."

Within a few months, after driving Alex to frustration by repeating the same questions over and over, after asking as many other people as I could think of, after reading thousands of pages of court documents, I would begin to see all the arguments about what Alex "knew" at each stage as serving mainly to illustrate that our conventional sense of "knowing" one thing or another was absurdly insufficient as a representation of the humongous junk wad of partially contradictory beliefs tangled in layers of self-justification and denial that constituted a mental state.

Law, I realized, had to file these wads into bins labeled with categories of knowledge and intent on an industrial scale that forbid unlimited attention to each one. I began almost to envy those who could just call Alex guilty and stop thinking about it. For them, arguments about his state of mind were pointless quibbles. What really mattered was what his nineteen-year-old Ranger incarnation now did: flip the phone closed, shove himself into the couch for the spring-launch to vertical, walk through the empty hall with flip-flops smacking his bare soles, and jog down the stairs—mad at the specialist, even more certain now that he would miss his flight, but outwardly unprotesting.

PFC Blum pushed through the stairwell door to the parking lot behind Charlie Company. The asphalt wavered in the heat of the August sun. PFC Palmer was already in the back of the Audi with the two Canadians. Blum climbed into the driver's seat, next to Sommer.

It was a beautiful Pacific Northwest afternoon. Thin clouds pushed into the satiny blue sky as if through slits from another world. The road from battalion took them past the Stryker brigade barracks, the PX, the commissary, to the line of departing cars at the main gate. After the wave-through by the MPs, they were off Fort Lewis grounds. The freeway ran along the barbed-wire perimeter fence before leaving the forest that obscured the base interior. Barns and small trading posts drifted by on either side. Traffic thickened and slowed. Every minute that passed Blum counted against his chances of making his flight.

Sommer too was growing impatient. "Exit here," he said abruptly.

The Audi swung off the freeway into a maze of side streets.

It was hard to keep up with all the specialist's sudden orders to turn at approaching stoplights. PFC Blum worked at the clutch with his sandaled foot as he hunted with the stick for the invisible slots between gears. He feared stalling. Palmer and the Canadians were doing things in the backseat that he was too busy to pay attention to, even as he caught glimpses while whipping his head around to check blind spots and palming the wheel to cut across lanes.

"Most of the time," Alex said as the first raindrops rattled my mother's balcony's pine boards, "people are like, why didn't you notice what was going on in the back? But A, I didn't know my way around Tacoma. B, there was a ton of traffic. C, I'd only been driving a stick shift for five months and was still learning. D, we were going on back roads to a place where I was absolutely lost. I was with someone who I totally respected and didn't want to get lost with, so that's another factor."

"When you say people are always asking, what kind of people do you mean?"

"FBI guys, prosecutors."

"What *was* going on in the back?"

"See, I don't really know."

In South Tacoma they hit a patch of construction that backed them up half a block. This neighborhood looked a lot like Denver: box stores, grassy medians, strip malls with dirty stucco walls. Hot wind blew through the open windows. Long-armed balloon men bowed and waved outside a string of car dealerships festooned with plastic flags. Road crews in orange vests ushered cars through one by one. Finally they emerged onto a clear stretch of frontage road. Beside them on the freeway, tankers lurched and braked above a glimmering ribbon of cars. Specialist Sommer directed Blum to cut left under the big green highway signs giving miles to Seattle and Portland. A block of warehouses and loading docks went by before the neighborhood turned residential. Telephone lines splayed overhead in the blue. Sommer thought he recognized a church he had flagged earlier as a landmark, realized he was mistaken, then recognized the right one.

Was it really possible that PFC Blum never noticed what was going on behind him?

As Alex talked, I found myself grasping for the kinds of analogical scientific explanations that had always served for me as reflexive responses to mystery. Rather than young men inside that silver Audi A4, maybe it was better to imagine five entangled waveforms, three struggling to pull on bulletproof vests and hooded sweatshirts below the sight of people in adjacent vehicles, one yelling commands, one stomping frantically at the clutch in flip-flops and flower-print shorts. Maybe it was only when the humongous junk wads of quantum probability inside their heads were measured, again and again, by prosecutors and judges and psychologists and cruelly adamant cousins, that they collapsed into the simplistic points that endured. Measurement changes what it measures; questions commit us to the answers we give. But maybe this was just a complicated way of saying that all Alex remembered, or all he could admit to himself that he remembered, was that he never saw the guns.

"There's the alley," Sommer said, pointing to a strange blue shed with a gabled roof and no windows. "Right up there."

Gravel pinged under the wheels. On the left was a chain-link fence woven through with beige vinyl. On the right was a series of lean-to garages. Blum and Sommer stared through the windshield at the bank's rear parking lot. The time was 5:11 p.m.

"That's a lot of people," observed Specialist Sommer.

Even now, Alex told me, whatever part of his mind did more than follow dumbly along had halfway managed to convince itself the game ended here.

Of course he's not really going to do this. Sommer would never do this.

"What do you think?" Sommer said to the space behind Blum's head.

"Maybe we should take a lap around the block and get a better idea of things," came a voice from the back—PFC Palmer's.

"Yeah," added the voice of one of the Canadians. "We could look through the windows. See how many people are inside."

In the parking lot, a steady trickle of civilians walked out to their cars, pushed buttons on keyless entries, climbed in. The bank was probably closing. Nothing, Blum felt certain now, was going to happen. He could go home and see his girlfriend. He could sleep in his own bed. He shifted the car into reverse.

PFC Blum did not know that all four of the others had stayed out late the night before practicing dry runs by flashlight on Noble Hill.

"Fuck it," said a new voice from the back. "If we don't do it now, we never will."

There came the sound of a door unlatching, a small melodious chime.

PFC Blum's gaze was directed toward Specialist Sommer, so his first glimpse into the strange new world pouring like gas through the opening rear door was of Sommer's expressionless face. The specialist's hands fumbled in the front pocket of his sweatshirt to pull out a laser-sighted pistol, then something black and flexible: a ski mask. Past him, through the right passenger window, the unmistakable barrel and wood stock of an AK-47 assault rifle accelerated into view, followed by a dark-clad body. Specialist Sommer pulled the mask down over his eyes. There was a flurry of shouting and movement. Doors slammed open, doors slammed shut. Blum was alone with the luxuriant hum of the still-running Audi.

Say your father takes you deep into a dangerous foreign country, then abandons you there with no means of getting out. Everything you believed is wrong. The sun does not rise. Jesus Christ robs a bank.

"When you were little," Alex asked me, "did you ever get lost in the mall?"

The specialist was no longer beside PFC Blum to assure him that this was all okay. The specialist had crossed over into someplace else. Four figures in sweats and ski masks ran down the alley in ragged formation, empty duffels flapping, two with AK-47s held across their chests and two with dangling pistols. The last of them—Luke Elliott Sommer, soon to be distinguished on security-camera footage by his gray shirt—waved at an approaching pickup truck before running on. The truck braked hard. Behind the steering wheel, the terrified eyes and mouth of a middle-aged woman shrank away down the alley as the truck wove off wildly in reverse, bright red in the afternoon sun.

It was then that PFC Blum realized that he was in the strange position of deciding for himself what to do next. The sob of helpless remorse called up in him by the sight of this unfamiliar woman's fear had triggered one thought I recognized as coming from the guy I knew: *This is all wrong. I have to get out of here.*

CHAPTER 6

THOSE WHO ARE VERSED IN THE SCIENCES

Alex and I don't much resemble family. As a kid I was skinny, angular, and odd, a classic math nerd. Alex was lantern-jawed, fit, and popular, a classic hockey jock. The more we talked about his story, though, the more we discovered unexpected affinities between us. It began to seem that at the far extremes of nerd and jock there was some kind of strange convergence. After a lifetime of pursuing our childhood dreams with single-minded focus, he and I had both ended up as naive tools of forces far beyond our ken, two very different kinds of muscle.

Growing up, I had always been so daunted by the complexity I saw laid out in the face whose voice I was listening to—twitching nostrils, forced smile, tongue folding back over withheld laughter, secrets and simplifications and lies—that eye contact felt like two live wires touching. Math was safer. Massive shapes interlocked in the darkness with comforting impersonality. Evangelicals like to offer up the intricacy of the eyeball as evidence of intelligent design. For me, mathematical order so far surpassed the haphazard mess of the body that biological typologies struck me as arbitrary, ugly, absurd. Math was simply true. Like antennae poking out of a fogbank, surface facts always suggested deeper purposes, buried cities. Diving for their hidden interconnections was as much a form of prayer as anything I've heard my religious friends describe. But unlike religious faith, mathematical faith was rewarded with concrete affirmation: after plunging for hours through the gloom, going so deep your breath ran out over and over, forcing you to retreat back to the light gasping and confused, you would suddenly *see* it—perfect, glorious, gigantically indifferent to the mind that had stumbled on it. Paul Erdös, the itinerant, speed-addicted Hungarian who pioneered modern combinatorics, said of particularly pretty proofs, "That's one from the book." He meant the book of God.

Adults reacted to my talent as if I had a fabulous occult power. Soon I too was seduced. I'd peer down from the Mile High Stadium bleachers at 70,000 Broncos fans dropping off in murmuring tiers, or squeeze into the mall escalator's infinite extrusion of perfumed blouses and curls, or cut between skiers under pine trees fat with oblong pads of snow, and out of nowhere glory would fill my whole throat: a web of field lines and force vectors shimmered out through everything, and no one could see it but me. *"Statistically speaking,"* I would think, *"I am probably the smartest person here."*

Whenever Alex told me about his preparations in high school for basic training, I recognized the loneliness and glory of my own childhood self-absorption. Like me, he perplexed those closest to him. Like me, he sustained himself with fantasies of a world that would celebrate his idiosyncrasies—in his case, Ranger Battalion, where he was sure he would finally encounter true believers like himself who stood ready to give up their lives for the people and the country they loved. The culture he encountered there may have frightened him at first with its frank, relentless focus on killing, but it also gratified and expanded his sense of myth. He is lucky never to have faced the reality of war, which I imagine does for military idealism approximately what grad school does for the pure love of knowledge as an end in itself.

———

The most important mathematical results of the twentieth century concerned the limits of mathematical knowledge. Gödel's incompleteness theorem showed that not all true theorems could be proved; the Church-Turing thesis led to the understanding that not all problems could be solved algorithmically. The rest of the world shrugged—of course there were some things you couldn't do with math. One look at the spacey, stuttering basket cases who were good at it suggested that interpersonal communication, fashion, and hygiene were among them. But for mathematicians and scientists of all stripes, the blow to their faith in the descriptive power of their language was shocking. The relation of scientists and nonscientists to the inexplicable is very different. What Keats called negative capability, "when a man is capable of being in uncertainties, mysteries, doubts, without any irritable reaching after fact and reason," is a daily necessity for social beings. We won't ever understand why people make the crazy choices they make, love the awful music they love, believe in astrology or baseball or God, but having good manners entails accepting these mysteries. Art entails producing them. Scientists are often bad at both. After leaving the University of Colorado for an abortive two-and-a-half-year effort at a normal high school experience, I started at Stanford as a shy seventeen-year-old with a suitcase full of Nine Inch Nails T-shirts and combat boots and a schedule full of graduate seminars, utterly baffled by actual human beings, utterly confident in my ability to model them algorithmically.

I wasn't the first to overestimate myself in this way. After the wild enthusiasm of the field's early years in the 1950s—the efforts at representation of the world's entire store of knowledge in logical form, the gradual comprehension that logical propositions were too rigid and inflexible to have much predictive use, the blind alley of "fuzzy logic," the probabilistic models of belief that grew to dominate the field—artificial intelligence researchers came to understand that the big problems of memory, reasoning, language, and consciousness were much more complex than they had imagined. By the time I went knocking on those researchers' doors, breaking naive undergraduates of their hazy dreams of programming themselves a computer friend had become a distasteful but necessary part of the job. The fundable problems were the kinds you could get traction on: recognition of handwritten zip codes on envelopes, the parsing of Internet search queries, automated flight control of helicopters. The first major project I was invited to participate in sought to compute Nash equilibria in structured strategic scenarios. Funding came from the Department of Defense.

It was an exciting time to be in Silicon Valley. Google's first server, scaffolded on rainbow-colored Legos, rested in a display case in the Gates Building basement. Movies and magazines were awash in romanticized hacker imagery. We few undergrads who had bulled our way into research were a club every bit as proud, in our way, as the Rangers. When we put together presentation slides for the yearly funding meeting with a stodgy, uncomprehending naval officer and a few of his staff, we all laughed together at how shamelessly we were using clip-art icons of tanks and soldiers instead of the usual abstract blue circles as nodes in our directed acyclic graphs. The joke was on the military: we were a bunch of apolitical nerds funneling away their bomb money to do awesome mathematics, all of which was far too theoretical—practically aesthetic in its aims—to have any chance of military application.

Eight months into the war in Afghanistan, when the legendary Defense Advanced Research Projects Agency (DARPA) announced a $1 million prize for the winning robotic vehicle in an unmanned race across the California desert, I watched hundreds of casually pacifist nerds like me in computer science departments around the country leap into an excited spasm of whiteboard sketching, number crunching, and microcontroller programming. I wasn't surprised. I wasn't even bothered, aside from feeling a jealous pang or two at how much cooler their projects were than my own. If you have ever done technical research, you know just how *right* an idea seems if the math works out.

No one made much progress that first year. Toppled Hummers and Jeeps punctuated the Mojave, radar antennae spinning in the dust. But the year after that, with the prize now doubled, a blue Volkswagen Touareg traversed more than 130 miles of treacherous desert terrain and roared across the finish line. Printed on the hood was the logo of the energy drink Red Bull, two bulls charging head to head in front of a yellow sun. Printed on the sideview mirrors were the pine tree and collegiate-fonted *S* of Stanford University. Behind the steering wheel was nothing at all.

By then we had occupied Iraq.

———

Ours is not the first age to dream of a war without soldiers. Pushing tokens across a map to mark the deployment of troops and matériel to tactically optimal locations has always been a happier task than sending actual human beings there to be killed. Military commanders struggled for centuries with problems of troop psychol-

ogy, those half-mystical "moral elements" that made the difference
between ranks that fought bravely and ranks that panicked and scattered to certain death. "In war the moral is to the material as three
is to one," said Napoleon, attempting with characteristic grandiosity to quantify the unquantifiable. Clausewitz, the great nineteenth-
century Prussian general whose work forms the foundation of the
modern theory of battle command, was humbler. "Moral elements
are among the most important in war," he wrote. "Unfortunately
they will not yield to academic wisdom. They cannot be classified or
counted. They have to be seen or felt."

Our contemporary elevation of science over the humanities as
the standard-bearer of truth has changed the conversation dramatically. That grand old distinction between moral and material is not as
distinct as it used to be. Today's commanders think of Clausewitz's
"moral elements" simply as "morale," a psychologized enthusiasm
with no moral component at all.

In the early twentieth century, as America contemplated entering the Great War, no one yet knew if the promising new discipline
of research psychology had anything to offer the war effort. On the
occasion of the American Psychological Association's twenty-fifth
anniversary in December 1916, its first president, G. Stanley Hall,
issued a call to arms, reprinted four months later in an issue of the
Journal of Heredity amid such unfortunate company as "A Decrease in
American Intelligence" and "America's Fighting Stocks: Half a Dozen
Races Available for War, Each Valuable in Its Way." Hall's title was
"Psychology and the War: Emergency Stimulates Practical Work and
Application of Science Rather Than Development of Theory—New
Views of War—Probable Changes in American Institutions—Need
for More Research on Man's Inherent Traits." His tenor was opti-
mistic.

I believe we are quite ready to meet this call in the field of
both pure and applied psychology, provided only we escape the
obsession of finality in either method or result and realize that
psychology is just beginning, the best things are yet to be found
out, and that its difficulties and obscurities are the twilight of
dawn and not that of evening.

Two and a half decades later, Hall's view was the convention. Alongside all the brave young infantrymen who volunteered for battle against the Japanese and the Nazis, a skinnier army of slide-rule warriors also marched to their nation's aid. Everyone knows about the physicists of the Manhattan Project, who pioneered explosive new ways to split the atom, but few are aware that a cadre of equally pathbreaking social scientists made parallel gains in cracking war's "moral elements." The Research Branch of the army's Morale Division was established in 1941 and surveyed over half a million soldiers under the leadership of the sociologist Samuel A. Stouffer. His 1949 opus *The American Soldier* is charged with the pioneering energy of a man with exactly the new intellectual tools the frontier demands. Its central finding, so surprising that it forced a major shift in research efforts midway through the war, was that combat effectiveness depended less on what officers had always assumed—patriotism, moral authority, and most of all good officers—than on small networks of friendship between individual soldiers, what sociologists called the "primary group." In a series of surveys about what "helped a lot" when "the going was tough," two activities consistently encouraged the majority of infantrymen: "thinking that you couldn't let the other men down" and "prayer." Two didn't: "thoughts of hatred for the enemy" and "thinking of the meaning of what we are fighting for."

The most powerful force driving men to fight, it seemed, was peer pressure.

This was a painful discovery, threatening the treasured patriotic narrative of unflinching sacrifice for country and principle. Follow-up studies enfolded it in the comforting neutrality of jargon. But no such tact was practiced by World War II's renegade hero of sociological analysis, an eccentric brigadier general and former newspaperman named Samuel Lyman Atwood Marshall in the Historical Branch of the General Staff, who liked to introduce himself by his initials: S.L.A.M. To form his historical accounts of battles, Marshall broke with the tradition of relying on the recollections of officers and spoke directly with the troops, in bull sessions that he called "after-action reviews"; like Stouffer, he found the story by going straight to the source. In 1947 he published a short treatise titled *Men Against Fire* summarizing his observations, most of which were instantly forgotten amid the clamorous reception of a single chapter, "Ratio of Fire," in which Marshall attempted to quantify for the first time exactly how large a problem the breakdown of combat discipline really was. His numbers were shocking: over the entire span of an average engagement in World War II, only 15 to 25 percent of infantrymen ever fired on the enemy.

This insult to our brave American boys was almost insupportable. Even worse was Marshall's explanation for *why* soldiers weren't shooting at the enemy: in the increasing social isolation of the modern battlefield, where forces had to spread out to avoid mass annihilation by shells and machine-gun fire, soldiers couldn't pressure each other to overcome their innate human aversion to killing. "The fear of aggression has been expressed to him so strongly and absorbed by him so deeply and pervadingly—practically with his mother's milk—that it is part of the normal man's emotional makeup," Marshall wrote. "This is his great handicap when he enters combat . . . At the vital point, he becomes a conscientious objector, unknowing."

"Ridiculous and dangerous assertions—absolute nonsense," responded General Bruce Clarke, a prominent war hero who had commanded U.S. forces in the Battle of the Bulge. Others—General James M. Gavin, commander of the Eighty-Second Airborne Division throughout World War II; Harry W. O. Kinnard, later commander of the First Cavalry Division in Vietnam—were equally aggrieved.

Marshall himself was ambivalent about his findings. His efforts to rescue the spirit of war from the encroaching jaws of amoral analysis were sometimes torturously backbending:

> I imagine that those who are versed in the sciences would see in these statements simple proof that the ego is the most important of the motor forces driving the soldier, and that if it were not for the ego, it would be impossible to make men face the risks of battle. From that point, one could go on to say that social pressure, more than military training, is the base of battle discipline, and that when social pressure is lifted, battle discipline disintegrates. But I would prefer the simple statement that personal honor is the one thing valued more than life itself by the majority of men. The lips of the dying attest how strongly this force influences individual conduct in battle. A young company runner, hit

by a shell at Carentan, collapsed into the arms of his commander, and with his life swiftly ebbing, said: "Captain, this company has always called me a f—-up. Tell me that I wasn't one this time." The captain replied: "No, son, you sure weren't," and the boy died with a smile on his face.

Stouffer and Marshall are the fathers of what the sociologist Charles C. Moskos, 1987–1988 S.L.A. Marshall Research Chair at the U.S. Army Research Institute for the Behavioral and Social Sciences, identifies as the "two grand traditions" in American military sociology: quantitative and qualitative. He might as well have called them nerd and jock. Stouffer had the broader academic influence; Marshall addressed himself first to men of war. His grandly heroic sentiments still inspire the young infantrymen who read him today—an excerpt from *Men Against Fire* appears in the *Soldier's Handbook* that serves as the bible for all new recruits, in the chapter on army values. Marshall's love for the common fighting man booms from every page he wrote. His defense of the courage of retreating infantrymen in a notorious Korean War defeat earned him a mention in *The New Yorker* as "spokesman for the rabbits." He was bothered by the postwar attitude of fetishistic awe for the atomic bombs dropped on Hiroshima and Nagasaki, decrying the tendency "to magnify the role of the machine in war while minimizing the importance of large forces of well-trained foot soldiers." The key phrase, of course, was "well-trained." We were sending our boys into combat like bent, rusty rifles, as likely to jam as to fire. Marshall found himself in the thrilling position of having uncovered an enormous problem hidden in plain sight, which gave him first crack at the solution. If a weapon malfunctioned three quarters of the time, it would demand a major effort of refurbishing. Didn't our soldiers deserve the same?

Many took Marshall very seriously indeed. After *Men Against Fire* was bootlegged in Hebrew, the Israeli Defense Forces smuggled him into the Sinai to consult in the defense of Israel, which would soon be at the forefront of the military use of computers too, bringing its first mainframe into service in 1969 (the rabbi who blessed it and begged for its peaceful use dubbed it *"Golem Aleph"*). In the United States, the abstract circles that had always been used for target practice were replaced with man-shaped outlines. Drill was deemphasized in favor of realistic battlefield scenarios, saturated in the sounds of real gunfire and the smell of cordite, with thorough repetition of stereotyped actions like firing at a suddenly appearing plastic enemy. The "battle buddy" system was introduced to ensure that no soldier or trainee would ever spend a moment alone. In the 1944 infantry handbook, two-man foxholes had been presented as an option "when men must work in pairs or when, for psychological reasons, battlefield comradeship is desirable," but one-man foxholes were given more emphasis, partly because of the common German practice of aiming tank treads for the former and spinning in place: "Since it is longer than the one-man type, the two-man foxhole offers somewhat less protection against tanks crossing along the long axis, as well as against airplane strafing and bombing and artillery shell fragments." Marshall recommended larger foxholes on the grounds that soldiers would be less apt to run away under attack. The 1968 handbook presented more advantages than drawbacks: "In a defensive position, the two-man foxhole is generally preferred to the one-man emplacement . . . The psychological effect of two men together permits positions to be occupied for longer intervals."

In the Korean War, Marshall repeated his after-action reviews (newly acronymed and increasingly ubiquitous in army practice) and reported that 55 percent of servicemen were now firing their weapons in any given engagement. In Vietnam, the rate was up to 95 percent. In accounts from that era, soldiers described shooting at a sudden moving figure in the trees without any conscious awareness of what they were doing.

It's hard to measure one man's impact, especially on an institution as enormous, secretive, and tradition-shackled as the army. Marshall's trace is everywhere, a faint scent in the pages of deprecated field manuals and doctrinal manifestos, but how much is directly attributable to him? In *SLAM: The Influence of S.L.A. Marshall on the United States Army*, from the Training and Doctrine Command (TRADOC) Historical Monograph Series, Major F.D.G. Williams writes: "His ideas affected many military issues, but none so significantly as those relating to combat at the small unit level. In this area alone—had he contributed nothing else—Marshall could claim to be one of the most influential men of his century." Williams cites references to Marshall in the Trainfire I system in the 1950s, Realtrain in the 1970s, and Chief of Staff Edward C. Meyer's efforts in the early 1980s to build loyalty and unit cohesion with the COHORT unit replacement system and the reestablishment of historical regiments (the program that named the Ranger Regiment "Seventy-Fifth"). But it is probably most accurate to say that Marshall's thinking folded into an intellectual current much larger than himself: CIA experiments with mind-control drugs, fear-resistance tests on recruits, the development of increasingly sophisticated virtual-reality combat systems. The revolution continues today, though Marshall is no longer a part of it.

Men Against Fire still appears on mandatory reading lists for officers in multiple branches of the American military, but even as Williams wrote, evidence was materializing that Marshall's numerical methods were fuzzy at best. The ARI research chair established in his name just a few years earlier for his "immense contribution in the introduction of the 'human factor' into the systematic consideration of military effectiveness" is no more. Many anecdotal accounts of officers and soldiers corroborate his findings, including those of my own grandfather, but Brigadier General S.L.A. Marshall appears to have pulled his exact firing ratios more or less out of his ass.

Marshall had no more fondness for the cold functionalism of the engineer than for the cold empiricism of the scientist.

> We like to pretend an intellectual maturity which refutes the passions that have shaped the destinies of other nations . . . A note of smugness was not missing from the remark all too frequently heard during World War II: "We go at this thing just like it was a great engineering job." What was usually overlooked was that to the men who were present at the payoff, it wasn't an engineering job, and had they gone about their duty in that spirit, there would have been no victory for our side.

The great irony of the life of "SLAM" Marshall is that it was precisely his extraordinarily compassionate insight into the spirit of fighting men that made him such an effective engineer—though not up to the standards of the world he helped create, with its still further progress in the annexation of the moral by the material, the quantification of every quality. Stouffer went on to wide acclaim as a pioneer of public-opinion polling. The nerds have had their revenge.

In 2012, as the Iraq war drew down and drone strikes escalated in Pakistan, more active-duty American military personnel died of suicide than in combat. Napoleon and Clausewitz would have understood perfectly: after a century of subsuming the moral to the material, material danger had finally been outpaced by moral danger.

———

It is hard to know exactly how much Marshall's work influenced the army's Basic Combat Training course, which has a cultural inertia all its own. But basic too has received its share of research attention.

In 1967, Captain Peter Bourne, an army psychologist posted at Walter Reed Hospital, decided to measure the stress levels of incoming recruits. After taking blood samples over the course of the first few days, he found that "the severity of [the] shock on each recruit in terms of acute psychological stress . . . is reflected quite dramatically in the 17-hydroxycorticosteroid levels . . . From the start the stunned, frightened behavior of the men in this situation bears a striking resemblance to that seen in physical disaster situations such as bombing raids, fires, or earthquakes." This was during in-processing at the Reception Battalion, where teenage recruits encountered nothing more physically painful than vaccination.

In all the hours I spent at the University of Washington library during Alex's imprisonment, I discovered that scholars had found a lot of ways of looking at basic: as a forger of boys into men; as a brainwasher of men into robots; as a warrior initiation ritual akin to the facial tattooing of the Maori, the ritual circumcision of the Masai, and the solo lion hunting of the Zulu; as a very intensive employee training program; as an extended theatrical production. Numerous journal articles proposed or endorsed each, with titles like "The Military Academy as an Assimilating Institution" and "Rehearsing the War Away: Perpetual Warrior Training in Contemporary US Army Policy." The problem with these perspectives—at least for someone trying to understand what the hell a recent graduate might have been thinking while robbing a bank—was that they belonged to reflective adults, whereas the people who actually went through basic were mostly unreflective teenagers, for whom the experience appeared to bear about as much resemblance to academic or military studies of it as a freshman fraternity mixer bears to pedagogy articles in journals of education or the brochures that colleges hand out to prospective parents.

I did find that some soldiers had written about basic online, though not often at length. The tone was invariably of rueful appreciation for the drill sergeants who had then seemed sadistic tyrants but were now recognized as having tried their best to prepare recruits for the unendurable. A combat veteran who told tales about training seemed to be a little like a young professional with a job and two kids who still crowed about college hookups and brutal premed midterms. Ducking bullets on the streets of Baghdad while your best friend hyperventilated beside you with his shinbone shattered by a 7.62mm round tended to reveal all the tears and high drama of basic as having been essentially synthetic, without real stakes.

Very few graduates had written about basic while it was fresh. It takes a special kind of recruit to journal diligently throughout training for the future edification of the civilian friends, family, and colleagues whom drill sergeants are daily denigrating as broke-dick pansies or worse. Hence the aspiring actor Monroe Mann's self-published *To Benning and Back* from 2002: "Some folks are already breaking down, crying. I'm happy I'm not one of them. I'm trying to encourage them the best I can. The mental torment doesn't bother me too much. It's sort of funny when they yell at me, especially the Korean DS. No one can understand him. 'Hey you! You no eat! No EAT! I SAID NO EAT!' Ha ha!" Or John W. Bornmann's 2009 doctoral dissertation, "Becoming Soldiers: Army Basic Training and the Negotiation of Identity": "The civilian world is frequently portrayed as feminine, the abode of girlfriends and wives, who 'will fuck you over.' This dynamic between the feminine civilian and the masculine soldier serves to enforce the identity of the privates going through Basic Training, further separating them from what they once were in preparation for assigning them new roles as masculine soldiers."

Both Mann and Bornmann held college degrees when they enlisted. Both went through the army's generic nine-week course rather than the infantry-specific fourteen-week One Station Unit Training course that Alex attended. Perhaps this goes some way toward explaining why Alex left Fort Benning without any similar ability to put quotes around what he'd experienced. His professional, social, and political aspirations converged on the same target: becoming an Army Ranger. He had no interest whatsoever in communicating with the world he'd left behind.

To Benning and Back shares a few choice drill sergeant quotes from bayonet training: "OK, this is the butt smash to the groin, thrust, and when he's begging for mercy in some language you don't understand, crack his head open and spit on him: MOVE!" Private Mann, one imagines, reacted with less than perfect enthusiasm. "We're really learning to kill people," he recorded later in his journal. "How sickening."

Alex, of course, reacted in exactly the way he was supposed to. He moved. Hard.

CHAPTER 7

SOMETHING YOU WOULD SEE OUT OF A MOVIE

August 7, 2006, had for a long time meant just one thing to Norm: the first day of Alex's final trip home to Colorado before he stuffed his rucksack full of underwear and body armor, flew halfway across the world, and clambered off a military transport plane into a real live war zone, happy as a kid on his birthday. But two hours before Norm was supposed to drive to Denver International Airport to pick him up, Alex called to inform him that he had missed his flight.

Norm didn't ask why. Alex's tone, curt and flat, did not encourage it. The family had learned in the past months that you couldn't get any more out of Alex than the brittle shards he offered—if you ribbed him about his hard-boiled commando attitude, he just retreated further into the persona. Norm offered to help him book a new flight for the next day. Alex replied that he had already taken care of it. They said goodnight. They hung up.

It's difficult to know exactly what was going on in Alex's head.

Millennia ago, Plato imagined the mind as an aviary, in which memories were birds we had to leap to catch. On the other side of the world, Chuang Tzu pictured it as a "mirror of heaven and earth," which the sage kept clear and still. In the centuries to come, with a growing pantheon of complex mechanical systems for metaphoric use, the carousel of comparisons sped up considerably: a clock, an engine, a factory, an electromagnet, a telephone switchboard, a digital computer. Spurred on by the military's ancient dream of machinelike humans and humanlike machines, cognitive modeling has become one of the great intellectual frontiers of our time. Representations of the mind have exploded in their diversity, sophistication, and scientific rigor. Few have so far proved much help in understanding the people we love.

The legal battlefield in which the prosecution and defense staked out their claims of willfulness or obliviousness was contained almost entirely inside PFC Blum's mind during the weeks leading up to August 7, 2006. There has never been much question of bodies and their placement. On the morning of August 8, Alex walked across Denver International Airport's glass Skybridge and brushed off his father's hug as Norm tousled his sandy hair. Half an inch away from Norm's fingertips, through layers of skin, bone, and meninges, was something none of us would try to characterize until much later. A shaken aviary. A mirror effaced by clouds. A clock, a computer, an influence diagram in which belief propagation had so far failed to incorporate new evidence. A house toward which the wrecking balls were already descending.

"Hey, handsome!" Norm said to his second son.

All the way home, Alex stared out the passenger-side window as fields of tan prairie grass slunk by in prickly undulations, answering Norm's cheery questions about battalion and Iraq with monosyllables obviously intended to discourage more. In his hockey bag was an envelope containing thousands of dollars in cash. The other three Blum kids met them at a sushi restaurant for lunch. Sam and Carly, initially excited to see him, soon retreated into uneasy conversation with each other. The caring, funny big brother who had been their guide to microwaves, malls, cars, and other big-kid privileges barely seemed to register their existence.

Alex told me on my mother's balcony that it wasn't the envelope in his bag that had him so preoccupied. What he was worried about was his enormous screw-up in trying to drive away from the bank before the operation was complete. The Rangers around battalion whom Sommer had crowed to afterward had all seemed pretty impressed, but once the other tabs got wind of PFC Blum's unreliability under pressure, who would ever trust him on deployment in Iraq?

Norm took Alex to Anna's after lunch so she could drive him up to Boulder to see the campus where she would start school in the fall. He was oddly quiet.

"I just thought he was tired," Anna told me. "I thought he needed the day to get back to being him, you know?" They met up with a few of her girlfriends. All day Alex followed her mutely, half a step behind. "Which was just so *weird*," she said. "We were always glued at the hip."

The next morning at Norm's office, a call from an unrecognized number popped up on his cell phone. Norm let it go to voicemail. He was rushing through paperwork so he could get home and prepare for that night's big welcome-home barbecue. At the white-shuttered house in Greenwood Village, meat was marinating in the refrigerator.

"A seven-and-a-half-pound beef tenderloin from Costco," Norm added at this point in the story, apparently helpless not to. "I like to slow-cook it. It's the best. Feeds fifteen people."

A few hours later, he finally listened to the message.

" 'Mr. Blum, this is Agent So-and-so from the FBI. I need to talk to you.' I go, Yeah right. They've got the wrong Norm Blum. I dismiss it. Erase it."

———

The man the FBI first sent to the Bank of America on South Tacoma Way was Special Agent Monte Shaide of the Pierce County Violent Crimes Task Force, a former nose tackle for the University of North Dakota whose button nose, boyish eyes, and imperceptible head-neck transition lent him a pit bull's air of friendly ferocity. He arrived twenty-five minutes after the robbery was over and received a sheaf of hand-scrawled witness reports from the Tacoma police. *"I was sitting at my desk w/ a client . . ." "I was in the middle of a transaction when I heard someone scream . . ."* Next Shaide huddled with the local Bank of America VP of corporate security to review the digital surveillance tapes from the bank's eight security cameras.

"It was something you would see out of a movie, the way they planned it," he would testify a week later to a Seattle grand jury. "The military-style precision and planning and timing all immediately stuck out to me as these were guys that were not amateurs."

One detail, however, was puzzlingly amateurish: the uncovered license plate on the getaway vehicle. Shaide called in a trace. An hour later the results came back from the Colorado Department of Motor Vehicles. There was a silver Audi A4 with license plate 420NNA registered to one Norman M. Blum of 1475 Greenwood Lane.

———

Norm categorizes his gigantic DVD collection by frequency of viewings. He watches his twenty or thirty favorites at least once a year. His children, raised on his movies, all developed their own preferred genres. Max liked the brainier stuff. Alex liked war movies and cartoons. Carly, the youngest, liked mysteries and crime dramas. Sam was the odd one out—gentle and sincere, more inclined to quiet talks with Carly than to sports, he never identified as strongly with the onscreen characters as with the actors bringing them to life. For years the chatter around the extended Blum family was about how sorry everyone felt for him, tucked like a little stuffed lamb in the sweaty gym bag of Norm's household.

I met with Sam in his father's living room. He was home for the Fourth of July from Hollywood, where he lived now in the pool house of a famous screenwriter, waiting tables, taking acting classes, and carefully swooping his hair for head shots. He told me that the day after Alex's return to Denver, he and Carly had spent the afternoon watching MTV, then decided to drive to the nearby Chipotle for a lunchtime burrito. Onscreen they had just watched a dramatic reenactment of an impostor policeman telling a kid on spring break to throw his keys out the window as a pretext for stealing his car.

"That's *ridiculous*," I said. Sam shrugged helplessly.

"So we're driving to Chipotle," he said. "We turned left on Franklin before I realized that a car was following me. I made sure that I stopped at the stop sign really well, because it kind of looked like an unmarked cop car. The car turned its lights on. The guy got out and came up. He was like, 'Please put your hands on the steering wheel and then take the keys out and put them out the window.' I was like, 'Oh my God, Carly. We're getting carjacked.' Because this guy—I don't remember him having a cop suit on. He was just in all black. I was like, 'Carly, just stay quiet. I'm going to get us out of this.' The guy was like, 'You need to stay right where you are.' I was like, 'I didn't do anything wrong. You have no right to be pulling me over.'

I put the car into drive. He took his gun out. I was about to floor it when all of a sudden probably six other cars circled us. Probably ten guys in all black jumped out with automatic machine guns or whatever. At that time, I was like, 'Okay.' I turned the car off and put my keys out the window. I remember them grabbing me by the neck and shoving me up against the car with a gun to the back of my head. Then I saw Carly. They had a gun to the back of *her* head."

Sam looked into my eyes to see if I understood the gravity of this.

"The guy was like, 'Alex Blum, you're under arrest.' I was just like, 'I'm not Alex Blum.' Right at that moment, that's when my dad drove up."

————

I asked Norm about this moment at our lunch. It was around 2:30 on the afternoon of August 9 that he turned into South Franklin's entranceway on his way home from work, threaded the long row of big new houses that clomped their way to the horizon, circled the new brick roundabout, crunched across the spray of gravel dragged into the road by joggers on the High Line Canal trail, and crested the final rise.

"There's a fucking *scene* there," Norm recalled to me. "I'm going, My God, the speed limit is twenty miles an hour, it couldn't be that bad a crash. I get a little closer. Another two or three seconds, my mind—*There's a black Jeep. Holy fuck, that could be Sam and Carly.* And it is. Guns are pointing in the windows. Carly's in the front seat going—" Norm made a terrified face, opened his hands out in baffled perplexity, and whispered in a tiny voice, "*Daaad!*"

The agent who seemed to be in charge approached Norm's open window. "Are you Mr. Blum?" he asked.

"Yeah. What the fuck is going on here?" Norm replied.

The agent, wearing body armor and an all-business expression, gave an explanation that sounded to Norm absolutely ridiculous.

"Okay," Norm allowed. "Can you just leave—that's not Alex. That's his brother. Can you just leave him alone?"

The guns retracted. Norm climbed out of the car. Standing everywhere were men in black helmets with SWAT printed on their jackets. The agent asked if Alex was really an Army Ranger. When Norm affirmed that he was, the agent grimaced.

"All right," he said finally. "There's a lot more ways for this to go badly than for this to go well. Situations where you have some of these high-powered military guys, all of a sudden you get in a high-speed chase and they end up getting killed."

He seemed to be appealing to Norm's understanding. Gradually it became apparent that the FBI wanted Norm's help in arresting his son.

In the next hour, police cars shuttled Norm, Sam, and Carly around as FBI agents trickled through every cranny of their lives, chunky with guns and gear. Two accompanied Norm around the corner of Greenwood Lane to search Alex's room in the basement: grown men like himself, all responding to the acts of a nineteen-year-old boy. It was a little hard for Norm to take seriously.

"God, this is a nice house," one said.

"I tell you what," Norm said. "You can have the house if you give me my kid back."

They laughed. Norm told them Alex was at his girlfriend's house. On the way there, one of the agents didn't wear a seatbelt. "You know," Norm said, "if I was driving around without a seatbelt, you guys would probably give me a ticket." This time the agents barely chuckled.

"Does Alex have any weapons on him?" one asked.

"Are you kidding?" replied Norm. "He's probably in board shorts and flip-flops, like always."

"We just don't want this to turn into something else," the agent said. "It won't be a good ending for anyone."

Norm realized the agent was referring to the possibility that he would try to escape with his son.

The SWAT team and the Greenwood Village Police Department set up three blocks from Anna's house. Norm drove on alone. Outside he called Alex's cell phone and rang the doorbell. Anna came down first. Norm told her he needed Alex's help with the barbecue. It was then that Anna knew something was wrong.

"That man is Superman," she told me. "He doesn't need help with *anything.*"

Alex appeared at the front door a few minutes later in board shorts and flip-flops. "Hey, Dad," he said.

"Hey, handsome," said Norm.

Alex seemed confused as to why his father needed him but finally followed him to the car. Anna watched them drive away. After a few minutes she called Alex's cell phone. There was no answer.

———

There are moments for a parent when vast new vistas open up in someone you had gotten in the habit of thinking you knew well. Beside Norm in the car were the high school hockey star, the elementary school movie buff, the toddler zooming trains around the Playmobil village, but there was someone else too.

One story Norm told me about Alex during that lunch has stuck in my head forever. It took place at Great-Uncle Bernie's ranch in Texas.

"Alex was absolutely enthralled with the little lizards out there," Norm began. "They're about this big"—here he held his hands six inches apart, then darted them around—"and they move about five feet at a time, really fast. Once in a while he'd get one by the tail, then the tail would break off. Bernie always had BB guns out there. So one day Alex stumbles on this lizard. He wants to see it *so bad*, up close and personal. In his six- or seven-year-old mind, he decides the best thing to do is to shoot it and then he can finally get a good look at it. So he shoots it. He hits it, doesn't kill it. Wounds it. He's so mortified it almost kills *him*. He's crying, sobbing, all upset. The thing isn't dead yet. I say, 'All right buddy, here's what we'll do. We'll put it in a zip-lock bag, we'll freeze it, and we'll bring it to the vet when we get back.' That saved his day. And his week. And his trip."

In the three blocks he had left before the intersection where the SWAT team was waiting, Norm asked Alex about Boulder. He watched the intersection approach. The red octagon of the stop sign grew in the windshield, slid up trees and houses toward the sky.

"Whoa!" said Alex. "Dad! You just drove through a stop sign right in front of that cop!"

The patrol car pulled out behind them with a whooping bark of the siren. Norm eased over to the curb.

"I think our problems are bigger than that, buddy," is what Norm told me he said then.

It jarred me. Maybe it was true that military training had transformed Alex's personality, but how could Norm have allowed himself as perfect a line as that, which might easily have sent the rogue commando fugitive the FBI thought they had on their hands fleeing out the door to be hurt or killed, if he hadn't at heart felt that his same old Alex was there beside him in the car, settled into his seat for one last action movie with his dad?

The patrolman approached the driver-side window. The neighborhood was quiet. Bare yards and empty windows repeated into the distance.

"Sir," the patrolman said, "could you please step out of the vehicle?"

To explain to me what happened next, Norm brought his hands together over his empty plate with a loud whooshing noise.

"Guns, everything. On his face, handcuffed. He's got this look, like—I don't know—like this is not right. They lift him up. He goes, 'Dad, I might have fucked up.' That was all. That was it. They took him away."

CHAPTER 8

FEDERAL VACATION

Blum by Blum the news began to spread, catching us in kitchens, dorm rooms, offices, and libraries around the country, interrupting dinners and homework and toothbrushing, sending us all scrambling to the nearest computer to Google the crime.

Alex's arrest did not yet stand as the pivot it would come to seem, the beginning of a broad downturn in family fortune. Many of the recurrences that would soon be obvious patterns were already taking hold—Oma forgetting a name here and there, Kurt no longer returning calls, Dad disappearing for weeks on silent meditation retreats, Norm evading questions about the days he had spent in the hospital for what he claimed was just the flu—but in most respects the family appeared to be on the ascent, crackling with centrifugal energy, cousins launching off to college and careers around the country. The disaster of Alex's imprisonment exerted a tremendous tribal gravity. Despite years of doing everything I could to distance myself from the family, even I experienced the sudden pull of Blumhood. The feeling was, there had to be some mistake here. We would clear up the misunderstanding, fight the injustice, win.

They call it retroactive consolidation, the way every trivial detail around a great shock is seared into your memory. We all have it around Alex. The stories amuse us now with the way they reflect the petty family grievances his imprisonment blasted into irrelevance. My own is of seeing my dad's name come up on my phone and steeling myself for another of his efforts to share a fact that had lately amazed him and that he seemed to think we might bond over: two millennia ago, Tibetan monks had discovered that what we experience as fixed reality was actually no more than an ever-shifting dream—*the very essence of quantum mechanics*. As he elaborated with the enthusiasm he used to reserve for describing a great football play, I had paced through the big, dark, wood-floored bedroom I had rented for the summer in Seattle, nodding with an exaggerated smile, biting my fingernails down to the quick.

Tonight was different. I still remember the pause on the line after I said my usual, "Hey, Dad, how's it going?"

"Not too good, actually," Dad said, in a voice I had never heard before, high and strangely soft.

A week later Norm and Dad flew into Seattle and met my sister Beth and me for dinner at one of those downtown grills he and his brothers always ate at when traveling, rich with mahogany and brass, branded for men like them. For twenty minutes, as we studied our menus and talked about everything but Alex, I tried not to steal glances at Norm. Throughout my childhood he had never had more than an uncle's existence to me, a looming grin machine whose primary functions were shoulder clapping, Frisbee throwing, and barbecue chicken flipping. Now he looked gray and unwell, his grin teetering under eyes that went in and out of startled focus. A smug, overcoiffed waiter about Alex's age came over in his vest and bow tie to detail the specials for us at elaborate length. Norm looked on with desperate fascination.

"Wasn't that kid great?" Norm said after he was gone. "Boy. That kid is going places."

"Well," said Dad, "should we tell them about the depressing day we've had?"

All morning they had met with defense attorneys. All morning they had heard the same story. The driver was just as liable as the guys who ran in screaming and waving guns around and shoveling cash into sacks. Via 18 U.S. Code §2, *"Whoever commits an offense against the United States or aids, abets, counsels, commands, induces or procures its commission, is punishable as a principal,"* Alex would even be indicted for *"Brandishing a Machinegun During and in Relation to a Crime of Violence"*—minimum sentence, thirty years in a U.S. penitentiary. Best case with a plea bargain was five to seven years. More likely was eight to ten. For the first time in our lives, my sister and I saw Uncle Norm grope for a silver lining and miss.

"There's just no positive side to it," he said incredulously, having evidently given this some thought. "If your kid gets his arm cut off, at least you can say, 'Okay, we'll just get you a new arm.'"

———

It was a long time before Norm was able to see Alex. After dozens of unanswered voicemail messages over the following days, he finally found someone at Englewood Federal Correctional Institution who would explain the necessary procedures: "Well, you've got to fill out the paperwork, then it's about a week delay."

"A *week*!" Norm recalled to me at our lunch, still outraged four years later. "A fucking *week*! That's a fucking *lifetime* right now. Who knows what he's going through? My son is in fucking prison!"

But when Norm and Laura, who had recently separated, finally got approval to visit their son at Englewood FCI, they did not find the hopeless, traumatized teenager they expected. They found Private First Class Alex Blum of the Seventy-Fifth Ranger Regiment.

"The first visit," Norm said, "he comes out in jumpsuit and shackles. Laura starts crying. He goes, 'Mom, don't cry. This isn't that big a deal.' His biggest concern was Corporal Sager. It must be six times he says, 'Dad, you need to get hold of Corporal Sager.' He goes, 'We deploy in two days. I have to get back there. He might not even know I'm *here*.'"

From Englewood, Alex was transferred to San Bernardino Central Detention Center, the West Coast hub where federal prisoners are gathered from all around the country, warehoused for a week or two under twenty-four-hour-a-day fluorescent lights, and redistributed to more permanent berths in the jurisdictions where they will be tried. In Alex's case, that was SeaTac Federal Detention Center, a pretrial facility jutting off the side of a wooded ridge just south of the airport like some kind of rebel fortress from *Return of the Jedi*.

Norm visited him there every single weekend for the next year and a half. Laura never once went along.

———

By the time of our lunch, it had become apparent just how much Norm's devotion to Alex had cost his health, his business, and the rest of his family. It drove a further wedge between him and Laura. Sam and Carly were in high school and very much in need of their dad. But for Norm, as long as he was able to afford plane tickets, there was not really much choice. Alex's imprisonment was a sickness in his heart that never for a minute released its grip.

In the first weeks he wasn't even able to swallow solid food. He lost so much weight his old clothes hung off him. The lifelong train of hockey games, bike trips, barbecues, and other adventures that he had always organized for friends and business colleagues came to a dead halt. What little spare time he had, he spent riding the stationary bike at the gym and watching movies with Sam and Carly before passing out at the one-bedroom apartment he was renting near the Denver Tech Center. Whenever yet another business contact turned out to have heard about Alex's arrest, Norm brushed it aside as best he could. *It's a tough break,* he'd admit. *Now about that cap rate . . .* It was almost a relief to get on the plane every Friday at 10 a.m., rent a car at Sea-Tac International Airport, and drive to the one place where his abjection could unfurl in all its enormity.

Since inmates at SeaTac never saw the light of day from the moment of their arrival, there was no need for a concertina-wire perimeter fence, no need for guard towers, no need for a gate into the parking lot. Like a giant concrete dragon, the central tower spread its seven-story wings to either side of a trapezoidal waiting room that was one part futuristic airlock and one part dingy post office branch. Inside, the angled concrete walls funneled toward a pair of one-way mirrors with circles cut out for the faces of the prison receptionists, whose attitude toward the tide of visitors who flooded in every weekend was one of wary disdain.

The wait was often four hours long. There were never enough seats. Overhead roared a procession of planes taking off from the runway just half a mile north. At any moment a face might appear in one of the mirrors to announce without explanation that further visits for the day had been canceled, prompting a muttering exodus to the parking lot and a chorus of slammed car doors. There was no solidarity among visitors. Turnover was fast. Inmates were here because their families could not afford bail or because their crimes were so severe they hadn't been granted it. Most were brought to trial within a month or two. Alex's case was different. Sommer had been captured in a Canadian supermarket but then released on bail to his mother's house in the mountains of British Columbia, from which he seemed likely to stage a prolonged extradition battle. Since Alex might have to testify against him, the U.S. government was keeping him in custody until they managed to bring Sommer to trial. As summer gave way to a long, wet autumn and then a record-breaking snowstorm that turned the access road from the top of the ridge into an icy chute, Norm saw wave after wave pass through: tattooed gangster types, teenage mothers with five screaming children in tow, a few sad old geezers like himself. Most were black or Hispanic, with a sprinkling of Southeast Asians and whites. Norm outlasted them all.

It got to be second nature to deposit his belongings in the lockers, to file shoeless through the metal detector, to submit to the patdown for drugs. In the visiting room, some long-ago work detail had painted a wobbly outline of Seattle's famous Pike Place Market on the white cinder blocks, complete with a stall selling fresh salmon. Four long rows of chairs were laid out down the center of the room, two back-to-back for the prisoners and two others facing them at a safe remove. After all the visitors had been seated, a stream of truly alarming men filed through a far door, most in khaki jumpsuits and laceless white sneakers, a few sex offenders in neon orange.

It never stopped being a shock to see Alex come out with them. He crossed the room with a satiric air, as if the jumpsuit were a joke between him and his father.

"Hey, handsome," Norm would say.

"Hey, Dad," Alex would reply, taking a seat.

For Norm, the heart of the matter was this: Alex didn't belong here. It appalled him to imagine that day after day Alex was breathing the same air as these scumbags. Norm had never had much patience for criminals. Like all his business buddies, he had been a Reaganite in the eighties, a firm believer that the best way to deal with a violent felon or dope dealer was to lock him up and throw away the key. After a few months, though, Alex started to change his mind.

"Some of the stories that he was telling!" Norm told me, "I mean, people are going across the border with a little bit of pot and they get *ten years*. Are you shitting me? I have a whole different view on the system now. There's a lot of people in prison that shouldn't be in prison."

Norm could tell how well liked Alex was by the way everyone nodded to him as he made his way down the aisle, not just the white guys but the black and Hispanic guys too. That was unusual. Even in the visiting room, races stuck to their own. One time a black man whom Alex had previously pointed out to Norm as one of his cell-mates, nicknamed "Clips" because he was known for cutting other inmates' hair, walked by and exchanged a quick head tilt with Alex.

"Hi, Clips!" said Norm, giving him a big wave.

"Dad!" Alex hissed. "Don't do that!"

Alex's lawyers had arranged for him to cooperate with the government in his case. That usually brought an indelible stigma in prison culture, but being known as a trained commando earned him leeway that no one else got, as did his jokey personality and air of unconcern, which floated him above all the grievances and rivalries of long-time convicts whose fates depended on their reputations. Strength training and military exercises were forbidden at SeaTac, so inmates quickly went to flab, but Alex was doing secret workouts in his cell to keep in shape—the real story behind the nickname "Skinny." His entire focus was on getting back to battalion.

This presented Norm with a quandary. He wanted nothing more than to share his rage with Alex at how the army had used and abused him, but this delusional fantasy of still being a Ranger was all Alex had to cling to. Norm did not tell him that the estimable Specialist Sommer was now fighting extradition by claiming to have staged the bank robbery to gain a platform to publicize war crimes he had witnessed in Afghanistan and Iraq. He did not tell him that his beloved Ranger brothers at Fort Lewis had all dropped him like a bad date, nor that Charlie Company's commanding officer, Captain Fuller, had already submitted requests for Sommer, Palmer, and Blum to be separated from the army with other-than-honorable discharges. Instead Norm chatted about the latest hockey games, about how Sam and Carly were doing at school, about a new ice rink under construction on the decommissioned Lowry Air Force Base. When the hour was up, he would drive to a nearby Marriott, where everyone knew his name by now, work out, walk around for a while racking his brain for new ways to help his son, and watch hotel TV all night for material to fall back on during the next day's visitation hour. Saturday evening he would fly back to Denver. Next Friday he would come back and do it all again.

Winter gave way to the long pissy drizzle of a Pacific Northwest spring. Norm began feeling markedly more sympathetic toward his fellow visitors in the waiting room, especially the young mothers. He would watch them applying makeup from cheap plastic cases while their kids ran around screaming and think to himself, God, *I'm* barely surviving this. How do *they* manage?

Whenever he asked Alex how he was holding up—if anyone was pressuring him to do things he didn't want to do, if he felt endangered in any way—Alex would brush off his concern. "Compared to the army, this is like a vacation," he'd say. "I'm just bored."

All Alex's frustration was reserved for his attorneys. Why was he even dealing with these civilian bozos? They didn't know anything about the Rangers. Why hadn't they gotten in touch with Corporal Sager yet?

His attorneys were equally frustrated with him. He answered their questions with that dead-faced politeness he reserved for civilians who had nothing to offer him, declining to elaborate beyond the basic facts. The lead attorney, Jeff Robinson, told Norm that the first proffer meeting with the government had been a near disaster. How did you get a client to help you defend him when he didn't believe there was anything to defend?

———

In Norm's eyes, the reality of Alex's situation was simply beyond his ability to grasp. Alex saw his time in prison as a test he had to pass to get back to the Rangers. For eight months, the only thing keeping his spirits up was this illusion.

"Those were the *easiest* eight months in prison," Norm recalled to me at our lunch, "because he thought he was passing this test with flying colors."

I was glad to hear Norm address the hardest part of Alex's story for me to understand. By this point I knew that Alex was more fragile than he looked. After his arrest, the leader he respected most in the world had abandoned him, his Ranger brothers and high school friends had united in shunning him, the woman he hoped to marry had started dating other guys at her parents' insistence, and his mother had declined to visit him a single time in prison. Now he worked every day among people who, if they ever found out about his past, would consider him a threat to their children. He had some understandable issues with trust. It was painfully obvious that he was in need of a friend who would value him unquestioningly, and a big part of the him that needed valuing was his story. I had been careful to respond with outrage when required and astonishment when required, tendering my reservations in private.

"This is the stuff that's hardest for me to get a handle on when talking to Alex," I told Norm tentatively, "because his brain is so . . ."

"Mush." Norm chuckled.

". . . locked into things that, um . . ."

"Totally mush. Over and over, it was, 'Corporal Sager can explain it. Can you just ask Jeff and Amanda'—his attorneys—'to call Corporal Sager?' And I already knew, obviously, that that was a fruitless endeavor. But I didn't tell him that."

"On the other hand, Corporal Sager might have been useful to the defense in explaining the amount of influence Sommer had over Alex."

Norm shook his head in exasperation. "No. That wasn't it."

"That wasn't why Alex was asking for him?"

"Absolutely was not it. No. Alex was asking because he wanted someone to explain that he wasn't really in all this trouble. 'This was set up. This was approved way above Sommer. This was approved above Sager. I know so because Sommer *told* me. Look, Sager's an ally, he was grooming me, he picked me for all the best assignments. He understood the value I brought. If you just *talk* to him, he can explain what's going on here.' I was sort of torn. How far do I try to relate the fact that you were just involved in what the prosecutor is calling one of the worst crimes in the history of Tacoma? My whole goal was to help him survive prison and not melt him down mentally and emotionally in every way. I remember when he finally realized this was not a training mission—it took him *that long*, Ben, to figure out. He starts crying and he finally realizes that he just got worked as bad as anyone in history by this guy Sommer."

Norm told me then that the instrument of Alex's enlightenment was Kathleen Taylor's book *Brainwashing*. With the shocking new perspective this book gave him on the crime, Alex was able to help his lawyers construct a daring legal argument that resulted in his release on bail after sixteen months and subsequent sentence of time served, the first steps on the long, hard road to recovering the person he used to be.

———

Or so the story went.

To explain to me how he could have talked himself into believing this was all still part of his training even after his arrest, Alex himself had referred me to the memoir of former Delta Force operator Eric L. Haney, *Inside Delta Force*. Alex read it dozens of times in high school. Haney describes how in the final stage of training, new operators had to make it to a meeting with a contact in Washington, DC, without being apprehended by local FBI agents, who had been given their identifying information and told they were dangerous criminals. But how could Alex's attorneys have failed to notice that their client was in the grip of a severe delusion? How could they have failed to devote all possible resources to restoring his hold on reality before setting him in front of a prosecutor? How could Norm himself have failed to do so, even if it was making Alex happier to believe the lie?

At our lunch, it seemed obvious that Norm believed everything he was telling me.

"So I imagine when you first saw Alex," I tried again, "you assumed that he, like any other ordinary human being, knew exactly what was going on. How did you come to understand that that wasn't the case?"

"Well, he was still defiant. He'd do sit-ups and push-ups for a long time each day because he thought, 'I gotta be in shape when I get the fuck out of here and get back to battalion. I just want to get back to battalion. I don't know how long this is going to last.' I started to see the picture here that he really was that deluded. That he really thought this was a mission that was approved way above Sommer. And then he told me about how Sommer made him point the gun at his head and pull the trigger, the 'suicide checks.' Just all of Sommer's mindfucks. The Rangers don't have any idea what's over that next cliff they're going to jump over each day. Whatever it is, they're going to have to do it. You don't ask questions, you just know they've got your back because you're part of this elite group. Who the fuck robs a bank when you're a Ranger? It. Never. Happens! There are no bank robbers in the Rangers!'" Norm was picking up steam, increasingly agitated.

"So obviously this *wasn't* a bank robbery. 'They're throwing me in here, this is my test. I wonder what Palmer's doing. I wonder what the other ten guys from Ranger Batt are doing that had to go on some other mission.' He couldn't get his head around it that this was totally outside the army and he was fucked. Couldn't understand it. And again, for me, my sense was, the longer that he believed that this was a military mission, the easier his time in prison was going to be, so I didn't go out of my way to try to explain it to him. And he was defiant to his attorneys, because they were outsiders and he didn't believe that they had his back. He wasn't allowed to talk about the mission or anything else with them. The military had his back. So when he met with these FBI interrogators who were ex-military—there's some inconsistencies there that I don't really know how to explain, but I just know for the first eight to nine months when Alex was in prison, he didn't think he was in prison for a bank robbery."

"Okay," I said. "Okay."

"I'm absolutely *convinced* of that. And then there were two or three visits in a row after I got him the book on brainwashing when the lights started to go on. It was incredible. All of a sudden he started to see through all this mind control he'd been under and get his brain back a little bit. I remember the tears just started welling up in his eyes and dripping off his cheeks. He realized he was now officially all alone. But the most heartbreaking thing was, he wasn't a Ranger. All he cares about is disgracing the Rangers. And I kept lying to him, telling him, 'Alex, we have no idea what's in front of us right now. Don't sit here and torture yourself, telling yourself it's over, because we don't know how this thing's going to end.' Of course, *I* know it's over."

Norm promised to send me all the documents he had from the case. Thirty forwarded emails arrived a few hours later. I worked through them one by one. Many were correspondence between Norm and Alex's attorneys: forwarded news articles, ideas Norm had for the defense, letters of support from old friends, bits of research he had done on his own, countless examples of his tough-love brand of cheerleading. "Great work, guys," many of the emails concluded. "Don't fuck it up." I'd had no idea he was so actively involved in the case. He took it on himself to ask Kathleen Taylor to submit expert testimony on Alex's behalf. When she replied that she wished she could help but did not have enough experience with the U.S. legal system, he refused to take no for an answer: "If I was a normal person I would drop it and move on . . . but I am not a normal person. I have an innocent kid in prison and am trying everything to free him."

The reports I had hoped to see of the FBI interrogations were not here, but as I neared the end of the batch, increasingly fatigued by all the frustration, heartbreak, and administrative complexity, I came across something surprising: an email to Norm from Luke Elliott Sommer himself. It was dated February 5, 2007, six months after the robbery, when Sommer was still fighting extradition from Canada.

> !!Warning!! The following is a harsh reality check:
>
> You honestly believe that your son, who you have known for his entire life, never dreamed of being involved in this? He helped me plan it Norm. Your [sic] are so naive because you want to believe in your heart the best about your son. The truth is I never intended to get your son compromised, but when I shot it out in the dark, he didn't slap it down, he helped me recruit. Your son is not the stupid naive kid that you make him out to be. He is [a] charismatic, intelligent Ranger.

I shrank back involuntarily from my laptop. My mind groped for all the reasons this had to be a manipulative attempt by Sommer to dodge responsibility for involving Alex, but for a long, disorienting moment, the mysterious inconsistencies in Norm's and Alex's stories that had been puzzling me for months snapped together with a brutal neatness that almost felt like truth.

BOOK 2

THE PRODIGY OF PEACHLAND

Loyalty is the big thing, the greatest battle asset of all.
But no man ever wins the loyalty of troops by preaching loyalty.
It is given to him as he proves his possession
of the other virtues.

—S.L.A. MARSHALL,

AS QUOTED IN THE U.S. ARMY'S

INITIAL ENTRY TRAINING SOLDIER'S HANDBOOK

CHAPTER 9

SOLDIER

On June 27, 2003, the day after Luke Elliott Sommer's seventeenth birthday, Christel Davidsen drove her oldest son three hundred kilometers from their home in Peachland, a lakeside town in the mountainous Okanagan country of British Columbia, to the U.S. border. She might have made him drive himself if she had trusted him more on the curves, but Elliott was unnerving behind the wheel, his intense blue eyes flitting everywhere but the road. He had never gotten his license. Instead, with characteristic boldness, he had taken up hitchhiking, soon acquainting himself with half the residents of their small town. When the customs agent asked what the purpose of the trip was, he leaned over his mother to explain that it was so he could enlist in the U.S. Army. An hour later Christel pulled into a Bellingham strip mall beneath a big red plastic sign reading ARMED FORCES CAREER CENTER, parked, and followed him inside.

For the next hour, she watched her son blast through the ASVAB, the U.S. military IQ test, and the DLAB, a linguistic aptitude test, and waited for the fireworks to start. Christel was a sergeant in the Canadian Forces reserves who taught survival skills for the Royal Canadian Air Cadets youth training program and could bench-press more than you might expect from a petite platinum blonde, so she knew the strength of her son's specifications better than anyone: six feet one inch tall, 195 pounds, accepted by Okanagan College at age fifteen, repeat winner of citizenship, leadership, and best cadet awards from his Air Cadets squadron, expert in karate, jujitsu, boxing, rifle marksmanship, and computer programming, evangelical Christian. Though Elliott had been born in Canada, Luke Senior had registered a Consular Report of Birth Abroad for him, making him a U.S. citizen, before moving the family to his hometown of San Jose, California, for a 1988 congressional bid. Two-year-old Elliott had served as Luke's star campaign prop, reciting the pledge of allegiance from memory in his toddler's lisp at fund-raising dinners and answering "Wonald Weagan!" when chuckling real estate tycoons asked him who was president. He was a lot bigger now, with close-cropped hair, boa constrictor forearms, and a handsome jawline, but just as precociously talkative, holding forth in rapid-fire military lingo about his desire to join America's War on Terror.

Recruiters from the U.S. military branches that shared the office were starting to get the picture that Luke Elliott Sommer was not their typical slouching Bellingham skater with no other prospects for escaping town. They began hurrying over, one after the other. Elliott entertained them all for a while, clearly enjoying the feeding frenzy, but Christel knew his mind was already made up. He wanted to be a Ranger.

It surprised Christel a little that none of them subjected Elliott to any kind of psychological screening. Elliott was the oldest of five and the bright star at the center of her universe, but he had always been different. Headstrong, hyperactive, given to grandiose plans and proclamations, he could turn a peaceful classroom upside-down in thirty seconds if the teacher wasn't savvy enough to handle him, which led Christel to home-school him from first grade on. Then, at age eleven, he walked out of his bedroom and told her he had been hearing voices saying his name.

There was schizophrenia on both Elliott's mother's and father's sides of the family, as well as at the Christian rehab clinic where Christel volunteered, so she had long been familiar with the symptoms and alert to their possible appearance in her own children, but Elliott had never given her that sense of disconnect she felt from schizophrenics, who tended to blindside you with casual remarks from a different universe altogether. Everything Elliott said sounded reasonable—too reasonable. It wasn't so much that he was out of touch with reality as that he made you a part of *his* reality, which could be a very extreme place. At get-togethers with fellow mothers at her church, Christel always found herself telling the wildest stories. There was the time Elliott somehow extracted the personal phone number of Richard Marcinko, first commanding officer of SEAL Team Six, from U.S. government computers and called him to say hi, getting him to agree to fly out and speak to Elliott's Air Cadets squadron before Christel explained gently that this was not in the budget. There was the time he launched an international computer-game-development project at age twelve that had foreign partners calling at all hours in hard-to-understand accents and shrink-wrapped packages of expensive software showing up at the front door; he told Christel that when a call came in from an unrecognized area or country code, she should just pretend she was his secretary. A typical family stay at a hotel in Fairmont had him convincing his little sister Karis to swim three pool lengths on one breath and then diving in to save her when she passed out underwater.

Back then, Christel thought of Elliott's more extreme characteristics as deriving from his father: the ambition, the self-confidence, the knowledgeability. Luke and his namesake had butted heads from the day Elliott, at three years old, first started telling him he was wrong, until Luke moved to nearby Westbank when Elliott was sixteen, after Christel demanded a separation and started dating Elliott's commanding officer in the Air Cadets, letting a breath of long-stifled liberalism into the house's cloistered air. The way she saw it, Elliott chafed against his father's authoritarianism, much as she always had, because he was a born leader himself, pairing all Luke's talents of persuasion and oration with firmer abdominals, better aim, and mesmerizing blue eyes. With Luke gone, Christel could finally wear something other than drab calf-length dresses, and Elliott too began to blossom—in fact, he and his good friend Tigra were so successful with the local girls that Christel and Tigra's mother began referring to the two as "man-whores." Elliott often hitchhiked as far as Kelowna, the town of 100,000 across the lake. When people questioned Christel's wisdom in allowing him to ride with strangers, she joked that it wasn't Elliott who had to worry, it was the guy picking Elliott up.

What did make Christel anxious was imagining her firstborn son leaving home on his own for a culture that was slightly but definitely foreign. People didn't always recognize Elliott's tremendous leadership potential without his mother there to translate his idiosyncrasies and draw out the kernel of truth at the heart of even his most outlandish tales. He was, after all, only seventeen. She hoped the U.S. Army would provide him the structure he needed to thrive.

The first warning sign came before he ever deployed. Elliott reported for basic training at Fort Benning, Georgia, in the fall of 2003, graduated in winter, and progressed immediately to Jump School, where, as the youngest candidate in his Airborne class, he was designated keeper of the wings. On the class's final training jump, the jump master pulled him out of line and set him up as the last man in the chalk, then waited for all the other trainees to drop out the open hatch before screaming, "Good news! You're a dad!" and booting him into the wind. Elliott called his girlfriend, Angela, from HQ after he landed and learned that he had a son, Landon Michael Sommer-Rose. After a short leave home, he proceeded to the Ranger Indoctrination Program in late spring 2004, where he survived a brutal winnowing of the class and joined the Second Ranger Battalion at Fort Lewis in June 2004 as one of their youngest members. It was then that Elliott wrote an email of threats to his father so violent and alarming that his grandmother, Margaret Sommer, contacted his chaplain at Ranger Battalion to express her concerns. The chaplain told her that older Rangers at battalion would give him all the mentoring he needed. A few days after his eighteenth birthday at the end of the month, Elliott flew to Baghdad to join First Platoon, Charlie Company, as part of a machine-gun team.

Within a year Private Sommer was a combat veteran of two foreign wars. It was a time of rapid change for the Ranger Regiment, whose primary mission had become to extract high-value targets in platoon-level "direct action raids" on houses, offices, and other small facilities rather than the more traditional companywide light infantry operations that had been their historical purview. This put Rangers at the forefront of some of the most dangerous, violent, and high-stakes combat in both Iraq and Afghanistan, but it is hard to know how much of it Elliott saw.

Five years later, in November 2010, with Elliott now locked up in a high-security U.S. federal prison with a sentence measured in decades, Christel would begin campaigning for his transfer home to Canada on the grounds of undiagnosed mental-health issues.

"I still to this day do not know the details of what horrific things happened there but I know they triggered PTSD," she would write to Canada's minister of public safety. "When Elliott returned from Afghanistan he was traumatized. I was working at my job as a CIC* Officer at CFB† Comox when one evening I talked to him on the phone; I knew something was wrong. He had come back to Peachland and had talked with my dad, brother and cousin who all told me he was not in a good headspace. I used the military phone system and had Chief Warrant Officer Bradley connect me to Elliott's First Sergeant. I told him that I was very concerned about his state of mind and that I thought he needed a good debriefing and possible PTSD counseling. The Sergeant assured me that he would be looked after and then promptly told Elliott to tell his 'mommy' not to call and threatened him with extra work etc if I did it again."

Late one night after his return from Afghanistan, Elliott called her to say he was about to go AWOL and sneak across the border into Canada. "Bad idea, dude," said Christel. They discussed the possibility of him training as a medic. Christel's mother, Denise Fichtner, was a nurse, and Elliott was very close to her, having traveled with her to Singapore, Hong Kong, and Indonesia on an extended missionary trip as a boy; he still called her Nana. He floated the idea of pursuing a civilian career as a pediatric cardiologist. "Or I could just rob a bank," he said. Christel laughed. "Really bad idea, dude," she said.

Shortly thereafter, the army sent Private Sommer to Ranger School at Fort Benning, the notoriously difficult leadership course whose average participant loses twenty-five to thirty pounds in three months of sleep deprivation, stress, and extreme physical exhaustion. This was the kind of challenge at which Elliott had always excelled, and it reinvigorated his interest in the army, but he was recycled twice to the beginning before graduating, first when he fell ill with bronchitis and then again because he hadn't yet fully recovered his fitness. In all it took him seven months, preventing him from joining Second Battalion's next deployment. He graduated on April 4, 2006,

---

* Cadet Instructors Cadre
† Canadian Forces Base

with Christel and Nana in the audience, received his promotion to specialist and his long-coveted Ranger tab, and flew home with them for leave in Peachland. It was the longest time he had spent with his son, Landon, who was now more than a year old, since just after he was born. He and Christel and Nana had many conversations about his future before he returned to the Ranger compound at Fort Lewis. The battalion was still a week away from returning from deployment, but a fresh crop of cherry privates had just arrived from RIP, including one who had once traveled to Kelowna to play hockey. Though Elliott befriended a few of them, he wasn't planning to stick around: from his barracks room, he made an April 18, 2006, post on his private blog, "Exploits of the Dangerously in Love," describing his relief at completing Ranger School and adding that although he "would love to lead men in a more immediate time frame," he planned to head instead to San Antonio for medic training, because "being able to heal them in a physical way while providing spiritual guidance is something that intrigues me."

The rest of the battalion returned a few days later and congratulated Sommer on his promotion and Ranger tab. After talking to his sergeant about what would be involved in a switch to the medic track—essentially beginning his career again—he made an abrupt change of plans. In the past couple of weeks he had blown through his entire savings at Chips Casino in Lakewood. He needed money. Instead of requesting a transfer, he reupped in the infantry, spending a good chunk of his reenlistment bonus on a custom-built desktop computer with a large monitor and a black Cooler Master chassis. As team leader of a gun team, he was given command of two of the cherries he had met just the week before: Privates Womack and Blum.

For a few weeks the new-minted Specialist Sommer trained Blum and Womack in a skill he had practiced on both deployments, manning an M240B machine gun and shooting "squirters" who emerged from buildings that line teams were assaulting. Then he was reassigned as assistant team leader of a line team so he could broaden his capabilities and prepare to breach buildings and assault interior targets on the upcoming deployment. As spring turned into an unusually hot Pacific Northwest summer, he spent his spare time completing a medical technician course at the Fort Lewis clinic.

In June, a month and a half before the battalion was scheduled to deploy to Iraq, Denise Fichtner was diagnosed with advanced pancreatic cancer. A few days later, on June 25, Elliott's last day as a teenager, he wrote a letter for his two-year-old son expressing his undying love in case he did not live long enough to see him grow up.

> I am a Ranger, a specially selected, specially trained US Military Commando. It seems more glorious than it is. It translates as follows: I volunteered for the hardest, most demanding job on the planet when I was seventeen, and immediately got thrown into a war I had nothing to do with. I do long hours with little recognition and it has cost me time away from you, time I can never get back. I guess in light of my expression of love this may confuse you as to why I chose this life and why I continued to serve after you got a little older. I chose to because there are those in life who can fight and won't, and there are those who can't fight but will. Those who can fight and commit themselves to the protection of those whom they love are rare, and the honor for those men is irreproachable.

On July 12, Hezbollah fired rockets from Lebanon at Israeli border towns as cover for an assault on two Israeli patrol vehicles. Three Israeli soldiers died and two were captured. Forty-four Lebanese civilians died in Israel's response, which included an air strike on the runways of Beirut's airport. Ranger Battalion scrambled into emergency readiness, canceling leaves and upping the tempo of their training as the conflagration expanded into what would soon be called the Lebanon war.

Shortly afterward, an emergency biopsy of Denise Fichtner at Kelowna General Hospital resulted in punctures to both her lungs. Her doctor advised Christel against authorizing the procedure to drain them of fluid. "She's got fourth-stage cancer," the doctor said. "Why would you do that to her?"

On August 3, Elliott published a long screed about the oppressive overreach of American power on a newly created blog, awokendreamer.blogspot.com. "I am a traitor," the post read. "America must fail."

No one in the family saw it. Christel was making frantic arrangements to get her siblings together for their mother's passing, tracking down her sister and her family, who lived as missionaries in a remote part of Indonesia, consoling her little brother, who was a mess, and handling the day-to-day needs of her four younger children. On the morning of August 7, 2006, she called Elliott to say that Nana was fading fast but would be kept alive long enough for him to say goodbye. On Tuesday, August 8, Angela picked him up from the Greyhound station and took him to Kelowna General. Christel met him at the elevator.

"I robbed a bank," Elliott said to her as they hugged.

She rolled her eyes and hurried him to Denise's room in the palliative care ward, where the extended family was already gathered. It was approximately the five millionth absurd declaration Elliott had made to her in his life, from "I'm on the phone with Bill Gates" to "I got a job with NASA," and just this once she didn't have the time or emotional energy to deal with it.

Denise was hooked up to a complex tangle of tubes and wires and had begun to swell from all the fluid. She was far past consciousness. As soon as Elliott saw his grandmother's condition he started crying. The family sang a few hymns, prayed together, and said their goodbyes. Christel told the doctor he could disconnect her from life support. Elliott bawled through her final minutes. Afterward the family regathered at Christel's house in the Peachland hills. It was late evening now, purplish light hanging low along the lake. Elliott pulled Christel aside and said, "Mom, I can't stay here."

She didn't understand what he was talking about.

"It wouldn't be good for me to stay here," he spelled out, as if she were being willfully obtuse.

"Why?"

"Mom," he said impatiently, "I robbed a bank."

It wasn't until Christel saw a security-camera video clip on the news the next morning, long after Elliott was gone, that she believed him. He was wearing a ski mask and a bulky gray sweatshirt, but she knew the way he moved.

———

On the morning of Friday, August 11, Sergeant Ross van den Brink of the Royal Canadian Mounted Police issued a confidential safety alert to all officers of the Kelowna Rural Detail that an elite

U.S. Army commando named Luke Elliott Sommer, wanted for armed bank robbery in Tacoma, Washington, by the Federal Bureau of Investigation, was suspected to be in the area for his grandmother's funeral, possibly hiding out at Christel Davidsen's house in the hills above Peachland. The FBI considered Sommer "armed and extremely dangerous." A provisional arrest warrant was in the works under the Extradition Act, but in the meantime officers were advised to exercise extreme caution when approaching Davidsen's address. The most viable opportunity for capturing Sommer might be at the funeral, scheduled for Monday, August 14, at the Westside Alliance Church at one in the afternoon. Most of this information had come from Sommer's own father, Luke Sommer Senior.

Detective Constable Bruce Singer spent the morning of the eleventh surveilling Davidsen's house in an unmarked car and visiting several other locations that Sommer was reported to frequent. Near the end of the afternoon, shortly after Van den Brink radioed to say the warrant had just come through, Singer made a second pass by a house of interest down near the water on Buchanan Street and this time observed a man who matched Sommer's description walk across the lawn and climb into a black Ford truck containing three unidentified individuals.

Kelowna is the largest by an order of magnitude of the towns nestled between the hills on either side of Lake Okanagan, a fifty-mile-long mountainous rift in the approximate shape of a left curly brace. This August, like most Augusts, had been paradisal, pairing tropical temperatures with pine-scented air. It had also seen an unusually high amount of gang activity. Earlier that very afternoon, in fact, another Mountie had pulled over a Toyota SUV near the marina and discovered a kilogram of cocaine in the backseat, the biggest payoff so far of a summer-long surveillance operation of a large local drug ring. There were also gangsters in Peachland, a beach community ten miles south on the lake's opposite bank, whose main tourist draw was the floating dock at Swim Bay, complete with diving boards and zip-line. All summer you could see the beefy drug lords spilling out of their black Chevy Blazers, sunburned to a crisp, spiky tribal tattoos encircling their steroidal biceps, with a brood of baby drug lordlings charging after them into the water. Hells Angels roared openly up and down Main Street.

A bank-robbing U.S. commando, though: that was something else. In Denver, Colorado, three days earlier, local police had coordinated with the FBI to stage an elaborately choreographed arrest of a young commando named Alex Blum in which a swarm of patrol cars surrounded him and a dozen officers and SWAT team members jumped out pointing assault rifles at his head. It was the FBI's subsequent interrogation of Blum that had identified Luke Elliott Sommer as the ringleader of the robbery. Sommer was a combat veteran of Iraq and Afghanistan with extensive Special Ops training and access to military-grade weaponry and explosives, some of which he had used in the robbery. "Convalescent skills" that Rangers studied between deployments included hot-wiring vehicles, picking locks, and field-dressing gunshot wounds.

Singer was a fortysomething Mountie alone with his service revolver in an unmarked patrol car. Nonetheless, he decided to follow. He had military experience himself, in the Canadian Forces.

The black Ford truck drove about fifteen minutes north along the contour line that Highway 97C carved above the lake, cruised between the towering board stacks of the Gorman Brothers mill, a teal-roofed complex that employed a lot of local boys, and descended into Westbank, the long stretch of fast-food franchises and hotels that served as the gateway to the floating William R. Bennett Bridge. Rather than continuing across the lake to Kelowna, though, the truck turned off into the parking lot of the Westbank Mall. Singer pulled in just as the suspect was climbing out of the backseat, and then the man was off and running toward the sliding glass doors of the Extra Foods supermarket, where he went inside.

Clearly the man was being cautious, but Singer remained confident. When the backup he had called for finally arrived, in the form of a uniformed Mountie named Jones, Singer brought him up to speed on the situation and made the call to surprise the suspect inside.

Thirty seconds later they had him facedown on the tiles in aisle 13 with his hands secured behind his back. Constable Jones pulled a black balaclava and several thousand dollars in U.S. bills from his pockets and located a U.S. military ID.

"Boy, you guys are good," said Luke Elliott Sommer. "You got me. I was the ringleader for the whole thing. I was the one who got the AK-47s."

CHAPTER 10

INTERROGATION

The RCMP was still waiting on details about the crime from the FBI—they didn't know exactly what the other suspects had said. Still, Constable Singer felt he had established a real rapport with Sommer while transporting and booking him. They both had military backgrounds. He thought he could get through to the guy. So it was that at three the next afternoon he collected Sommer from the jail room where he'd spent the night, set him up in shackles in an interview room, said a few preliminaries, left to fill out some paperwork, and came back to find his hulking, muscular prisoner fiddling with something in his fingers.

"What have you got in your hand?" Singer asked, settling into his chair on the opposite side of the table.

"Drinking straw," said Sommer.

"A straw? Is it from the dinner I bought you last night?"

"Mm-hmm."

"How was that?"

"It was good," Sommer said. "Thank you."

The guy certainly had poise. That military crispness.

"You know what?" Singer said. "You're not a bad guy, okay? Just some bad things, you've made some bad choices. And you even said to me yesterday when you were arrested that you made some bad choices."

"I did say that, yes," Sommer acknowledged.

There were rights to read and extradition procedures to explain, and Sommer indicated at each point that he understood, but Singer's further efforts at establishing rapport didn't get him very far.

"So your grandma, are you close to your grandma?"

"We traveled to Indonesia, Hong Kong, Singapore, the Philippines, et cetera, when I was a younger kid, and she raised me for a significant part of my preteen and young teen life."

"Oh. Okay. And when, uh, she passed away, did she have any sickness? Or just old age? Or . . ."

"Pancreatic cancer, liver cancer, two punctured lungs, pulmonary embolisms in both lungs, pneumonia, and hemothorax."

"Oh my God," said Singer.

They moved on to military topics. Usually this provided an easy basis for male bonding, but Sommer seemed less interested in finding commonalities with Singer's Canadian Forces background and personal favorite handguns than in lecturing him on Army Ranger weaponry and organizational structure. Finally Singer gave up and got to the point.

"We know that this happened. Okay? I'm not gonna bullshit you, saying I think that, well, maybe he didn't do it. I know that he did it. Okay? And you know that you did it. I'm not here to dispute that with you. And you know what? Everybody else is on the raft here. They're all on individual rafts," Singer corrected himself, "but they're goin' down the river, and they've all given their versions of . . . of . . . of the events. How they saw it and their perceptions about what was goin' on in their mind and all that kinda stuff. You don't have to tell me. 'Cause you know what? There's gonna be consequences in this. Guarantee it, there's gonna be consequences. I'm not threatening you," Singer clarified. "But these guys have sold you down the river. So you don't have to tell me one thing, but I'm here to get your version of the events. To hear it from Mister Sommer." Singer sat back and waited for the haul.

"They were instructed to," Sommer said.

"They were instructed to what? Tell the police?"

"The purpose of everything is to create an equal reaction. People don't get the opportunity to say what needs to be said if they're not given the spotlight."

"You got the spotlight right now."

Sommer held his eyes for a second and then laid it on him. "I watched thirteen people get bound in Afghanistan by members of the American forces, executed, and then a bomb dropped on the village to cover it up. I didn't do anything for financial benefit or for the capability of demonstrating how much of a badass I am. I know that. This can open handcuffs. You know?" Sommer held up the drinking straw he had been playing with.* Singer's stomach took a little plunge. "I don't need to show you. I don't need to try and escape. I don't need to be the resistant futile loser that ends up in prison for the rest of his life. I needed a way to demonstrate to the world that a government that has done so much to so many people with no reason will get treated, tried, and convicted just like the person on the street who does the exact same thing. I don't care if I go to prison for the rest of my life as long as what I have seen, and those around me have seen, is accepted as truth and processed. I saw a woman raped in front of her husband to extract information about the location of someone the guy didn't even know. I'm twenty. I left Canada to join the United States Army to defend a nation that was a beacon for freedom for the planet. Not to go slap a swastika on my arm and be their little enforcer. Britain, it's the same thing. I've worked with the SAS, the SBS.† I'm not saying that they've done things like that because I've not witnessed them. I am saying that the Crown is very closely connected to America. I'm also saying that Canada is the only place that's willing to stand up to America in a political way and look out for the interests of the world without taking a side. So why did I come home and stay in the only place where anyone could find me? So I could be found. This was never about fifty-one thousand dollars."‡

———

In seven months, Sommer would email Norm to tell him that Alex was a "charismatic, intelligent Ranger" who had "helped [him]

---

* Make a slit in one end to form a three-inch-long plastic sheath, slide it over the teeth into the locking chamber of the handcuffs, and push past the point of resistance to raise the spring-loaded ratchet. The straw now forms a smooth plastic track atop the teeth for the ratchet to slide over. Hold it in place as you pull the handcuffs open. With practice, it takes about three seconds.

† Special Boat Service

‡ The true total was closer to $54,000.

recruit" for the crime. But his answers to Singer's questions hint at a different story.

"Who drove?" Singer asked early on in the interview.

Sommer hesitated. "Well, you already know that," he finally said. "It was Blum."

"Was it his vehicle?"

"His vehicle."

"Okay."

But Sommer was not satisfied to leave it at that. "Now," he said, "for the most part, even though he knew, or had a general idea, I mean, the details of what exactly went on, you know, he didn't know. And that's honestly the truth. Like, essentially he knew that it had happened, but his involvement was fairly limited compared to everybody else."

Alex "essentially" knew that it *had* happened—was Sommer suggesting that Alex didn't know in *advance*? Singer didn't pursue it.

"So was that in design by yourself because his job was a driver?" he asked. "He didn't need to know about the other stuff?"

"Right. Plus, whether this is understandable or not, he's . . . although slightly misguided, he's probably . . . If you think I'm a good dude, that kid is solid."

The rest of the interview contains almost nothing about Alex. After Sommer revealed his intention to publicize U.S. war crimes as part of a secret organization of military whistleblowers called Black Cell, whose leader was an incognito U.S. senator intent on exposing the National Security Agency's domestic spying program, he spent three hours explaining in exhaustive detail how every feature of the robbery, even those that might at first have appeared haphazard or blundering, had in fact been an essential step in a paramilitary plot so intricate it was worthy of a Jason Bourne film. The target and hit time for the operation had been chosen after extensive war-gaming and statistical analysis of criminal activity in the area to maximally delay police response. Sentries had been paid $200 apiece to watch for police cars at distances of five hundred meters from the bank. A nearby decoy target had been "burned" to direct police attention elsewhere. If the police did arrive, instructions had been to surrender peacefully. It was of course impossible to avoid frightening innocent civilians during an operation like this, but extensive steps had been taken to ensure that no one was hurt. Intimidating suppressive weapons had been necessary to ensure compliance, but Sommer had made it clear to every man to whom he supplied one that if he went "nuts" and hurt a civilian, he would "get put down." The team brought a medical kit along in case they needed to provide emergency care to hurt bystanders. A deliberate trail of clues had been left to lead investigators to Sommer's barracks room, where they would find a hard drive full of evidence which would take the NSA about six months to decrypt, "which is probably my version of a joke."

Sommer manifested indignation at the idea that Singer might ever have suspected anything else. "I placed two ATF-illegal, fully automatic, foreign-procured weapons in the tile rafters of my room," he scoffed. "For Christ's sake, my little brother would look there if he was lookin' for weed."

Singer told Sommer that he had gotten the Kelowna RCMP pretty worried there for a while. He asked why Sommer hadn't just turned himself in. Sommer replied that he had always intended to but had hoped to wait until after his grandmother's funeral. When he noticed Singer tailing him, he realized the time had come and asked his friends to drop him off in a public place.

"I'm more inclined, because of my training, to react to a situation hostilely if I'm alone," he explained. "So I went to a place where there were people so that my first reaction would be to protect them."

"Well, I appreciate that," Singer said.

One of the suspects who carried AK-47s in the bank was still at large: Nathan Dunmall. Sommer refused to name him, and Singer exerted himself at length fishing for clues to his identity. Alex came up again only when Singer asked about the team's departure after the robbery. Rather than reporting, as most other conspirators had, that the Audi was nowhere to be found when they emerged from the bank, Sommer explained that Alex was, as planned, on "roving patrol" between two grid points, which Sommer identified by numeric codes. Three lines from this section have been redacted in the transcript because the techniques Sommer described are U.S. military secrets.

"At that point in time," Sommer said, "the car pulled up, weapons were fairly well concealed, and we got in the vehicle, and the driver still was kinda, 'What the hell?' You know, 'What's going on?' He

had agreed to do this with very limited information and, uh, like . . .
I mean, don't get me wrong, he knew."

"Mm-hmm," said Singer.

"But to what end was—"

Singer, however, was not very interested in Alex Blum's mental
state. He interrupted to get Sommer back on track. "So where'd you
guys go then?"

———

Of all the things that irk me about this interview—Sommer's
freewheeling lies, his self-aggrandizement, his calling Alex "slightly
misguided" without any apparent awareness of who might have done
the misguiding—it is this simple question from Singer that still drives
me up the wall.

There are only three occasions in the entire interview in which
Sommer directly quotes another speaker. First, after U.S. forces
allegedly bomb a house full of executed Taliban to cover up the murders but forget to take the zip-ties off their wrists, a fellow Ranger
recounts the tale to Sommer, telling him, "Yeah dude, we had to
clean up after," belying Sommer's claim to have witnessed the action
himself. Second, when Sommer is considering the question of turning himself in, his father advises him, "If you're ever in significant
enough trouble where you have to question it, just go in," belying not
only Sommer's claim that he had always intended to do so but the
broad sense that he didn't consider himself in "trouble" at all. Finally
there are Alex's words on picking the bank robbers up: "What the
hell? What's going on?"

Like the others, this quote leaps out at me with the raw, authentic oddity of memories that have not yet been tamed into narrative.
Might these be Alex's actual words—unpolished data from that brief
period after the crime when truth was not yet lost forever beneath
layers of interpretation and deceit? Sommer immediately interpreted
them for Singer: "I mean, don't get me wrong, he knew." But why
would it even have *occurred* to him that Singer might arrive at a different interpretation, the utterly absurd one that the driver hadn't
known he was participating in a real bank robbery, unless on some
level *Alex really hadn't?*

I don't blame Singer for failing to push on this. Alex wasn't his focus. For three hours he had been firehosed with unfamiliar American military acronyms, elaborate logistical information about the planning process, false names for Nathan Dunmall, rants about American imperialism, and hints about shadowy paramilitary organizations with revolutionary agendas, all of it expressed in that impatient, commanding register that comes at you so fast there is no attentional capacity for anything more critical than temporary suspension of disbelief. He had heard vivid, disturbing scenes of military atrocity that would soon keep the U.S. Army's Criminal Investigation Command busy for weeks and the press busy for much longer. With a few pleas here and there to slow down and explain, he had succeeded in flattering Sommer into further revelations—"I'm not gonna sit here and blow sunshine up your ass, but I've talked to a lot of really bad guys, and you're probably one of the most intelligent people that I have ever had the pleasure of sitting across the chair from"—and he had scored some clues to the identity of the missing coconspirator, whose last name Sommer finally revealed as ending in two els (he claimed not to remember the rest of it). The transcript runs to 158 typewritten pages, 95 percent of which have since been revealed as horseshit of truly epic shamelessness and scope, albeit so persuasively delivered that someone who cares enough about Luke Elliott Sommer to consider the distinction meaningful might wonder if it sprang less from a cynical master scheme than from a compulsive, pathological defense of his delusional self-image as infallible—narcissistic personality disorder wrapped up in a cloak of Army Ranger authority, Canadian amiability, and an uncanny facsimile of self-awareness.

But none of this really matters to me. What matters is that if Singer hadn't interrupted him, Sommer might have provided my first piece of evidence from someone other than Alex himself about what exactly Alex had been told about the robbery in advance.

Instead Sommer described what happened shortly after Alex drove the team away from the bank: dropping Nathan, Chad, and Tigra off at a Tacoma movie theater.

"What movie did they go to?" Singer asked, chuckling. "*Bourne Identity?*"

"Nah," Sommer replied, "that's too Hollywood for me."

"Well, this is Hollywood to me."

"Well, look at it from this perspective. People that listen to conspiracy theories, people that watch crazy movies, have an unrealistic portrayal of reality. Reality is this: if you're going to do something like this and your goal is financial, don't do it."

Singer chuckled again, more quietly this time, perhaps in disbelief.

"You know?" Sommer said. "There are only two reasons, aside from being a complete crackhead and an imbecile, to rob a bank. One is to make a statement and expect to be caught. The other is to be so goddamned good that you can't get caught. And I've never seen that outside of a movie."

CHAPTER 11

FREEDOM FIGHTER

It wasn't until late November that the story really blew up. After being granted bail with surprising ease, Sommer holed up in silence for three months at Christel's house. Then a grand jury indictment revealed that investigators had a new theory: the purpose of the robbery had been to fund a mob-style crime family of Army Rangers who would drive the Hells Angels out of Kelowna and take over selling drugs and racketeering. The front cover of the next *Seattle Weekly* featured a full-page Photoshopped image of a black-and-red Ranger scroll that had been altered to read ROBBER in white stitching with dollar signs on either side instead of the battalion number. Inside was another bombshell: under cover of anonymity, one of the conspirators now claimed that the robbery had been an act of political protest.

Anonymity did not suit Sommer for long. Shortly after the *Weekly* story ran, he called David Bowermaster at the *Seattle Times* to tell him the government's story was preposterous. Would an elite U.S. commando be so stupid as to take on a well-entrenched outlaw motorcycle gang with a handful of soldiers and a little over $50,000? Bowermaster and a cameraman drove all the way up to the Okanagan to hear him out.

"Ranger's Defense: If I Did It, It Was Political," read the headline of the story the *Seattle Times* ran on December 7.

It was the first sally in a media blitz. From all over the continent, reporters for *Rolling Stone*, NPR, *The New York Times*, the *Los Angeles Times*, the *Army Times*, and countless Canadian publications called in for interviews, many making the trek up the snowy hillside and rutted dirt road to Christel Davidsen's house above the lake to meet Sommer in person. To say they approached him skeptically would be a drastic understatement. At best, he had traumatized a bank full of innocent people in order to gain the publicity that the press was now queasily complicit in granting him. At worst, he was using them to promulgate gruesome lies that dishonored his fellow soldiers and had the potential to stoke further outrage and violence in Iraq. Still, Sommer cut an interesting figure: charismatic, intense, mercurial, very possibly possessed of some crucial information.

Christel would serve reporters tea in the bustling top-floor kitchen while Sommer played with his now almost three-year-old son, and then he would take them down to the dank unfinished basement, where he had set up his "command center" around a desktop computer with multiple screens. There he would talk of the bombing of thirteen executed Taliban fighters in a hut and the rape of an Iraqi woman by Delta Force operators in a white semi trailer, sometimes tossing in a tidbit or two about rigging a car bomb to assassinate a Sunni political candidate or watching helmet-cam trophy videos of sport killings set to heavy metal soundtracks. As he talked, Sommer would bring up Google Earth satellite photos of the locations of the alleged crimes—a violation of OPSEC, or Operational Security, he would point out—and hint that he had documentary evidence, though he refused to release it until his extradition hearing.

The Army's Criminal Investigation Command released to the press the results of an internal investigation it had conducted in October, concluding that Sommer's claims had been investigated and proved baseless. Sommer, incensed, said that CID had never even interviewed him. He played a taped phone call for reporters with an officer at Joint Special Operations Command who sounded genuinely alarmed by Sommer's accusations.

It wasn't hard to guess why. Reports had been trickling out for two years of extensive detainee abuse by the shadowy contingent of Special Operations soldiers known as Task Force 6-26 in Iraq, whose mission had become to hunt al-Qaeda leaders after the surprising collapse of Saddam Hussein's army. The most egregious documented abuses had taken place at Camp Nama, the improvised Special Ops detention center which had been the first stop on the way to Abu Ghraib for many of those rounded up by U.S. forces. Placards posted on walls read NO BLOOD NO FOUL. The "High Five Paintball Club" used detainees as targets for sport. Interrogations took place in a windowless former Iraqi government torture chamber known as the Black Room, with pitch-black walls and hooks in the ceiling. Delta Force operators had been seen taking detainees into a soundproofed shipping container and taking them out hours later looking much worse for the wear. A handful of Department of Defense officials had spoken to reporters about Camp Nama under conditions of anonymity, but Task Force 6-26's operations remained classified, and in contrast to the far better known incidents at Abu Ghraib, photographic documentation of abuses was nonexistent. Not even the Red Cross had been permitted inside. Two Navy SEALs spotted taking photographs from a roof had been arrested and expelled from the base. Of twenty-nine allegations of abuse since 2003, only five had yielded sufficient evidence to prove misconduct, resulting in the disciplining of thirty-four task force members. The camp had been shuttered in the summer of 2004, the time of Elliott's first deployment, and the unit's headquarters had been moved to Balad, with even tighter restrictions on information leaking out, but abuses continued: five Army Rangers were convicted of beating detainees in September 2005. Now here was a witness who seemed ready to provide an inside look into one of the darkest corners of the American war effort.

When I asked David Bowermaster about it over coffee, he turned out to be just as sympathetic to Alex as everyone else involved in the case, from the Pierce County detective who investigated the robbery to the prosecuting attorney.

"Sommer is so confident in the certainty of whatever he's talking about," Bowermaster told me. "It can be persuasive. With the war crimes stuff, my main takeaway was, 'That's fucking absurd.' But he weaves his tale in such intricate detail, you start thinking, 'Maybe he *does* have some evidence.'"

The creepiness came on bit by bit. Though Sommer approximated the tone of a wounded warrior haunted by what he'd seen, some reporters thought the way he phrased things seemed at times to show unseemly pride in his own cleverness. Others thought he had something of the pornographer in him, recounting the bloodiest moments with especially vivid detail.

Bowermaster had his own theory about the key to Sommer's character: his DVD collection. "Sommer is *obsessed* with movies," he told me. "*V for Vendetta* was a huge fascination when I talked to him. He saw himself as the V guy. There were Google Earth satellite photos up on the screens in his 'command center' of the federal penitentiaries where his coconspirators were imprisoned. He and unnamed cohorts were going to do an assault and get them out. The robbery always made me think of *Point Break*—five guys with assault rifles. And the notion of taking on Hells Angels—it's a movie-style motivation. He would come up with these really fantastical scenarios, leaving out all the possible things that could go wrong, since he was so smart he'd always be able to figure out a way around them."

Despite having already confessed outright to Constable Singer that he had planned and led the robbery, Sommer insisted on speaking to reporters in hypotheticals—"*If* I did it," he kept saying—and scoffed at any suggestion that the crime had failed to go according to plan.

"We get trained how to avoid capture, specifically on things like license plates and telltale signs on vehicles," he spelled out for Martin Kaste of National Public Radio.

Kaste asked if Sommer meant that he and Alex Blum had deliberately left the license plates on the car so they would be traced.

"I convinced him," Sommer said. "Yes. *If* that's the case."

When Bowermaster asked him if the other defendants had known about his political plans, Sommer said they hadn't. Alex and the other participants in the robbery had been "developed as assets." "As much as that totally made me into a jerk," Sommer said, "it's totally true."

Bowermaster asked if Alex had been a gung-ho Ranger.

"He was gung-ho, but at the same time I think one of the things he felt was a necessity to protect me as well. Because even though he didn't know exactly what was bothering me for the last few weeks and months, you could see it on my face that something was wrong. A lot of those guys, because of the respect I had gained from them, banded to me like my knights and protected me. Very, very dedicated."

Bowermaster published his final article on Sommer's claims in February, likening conversation with him to "enduring a commando raid." By then he had consulted an expert on extradition law at the University of Washington Law School named Gary Botting, who pointed out that while the Canadian Extradition Act disallowed political arguments against extradition for a variety of serious crimes like murder and sexual assault, there was nothing preventing Sommer from attempting it for armed bank robbery. It made, in Botting's words, "a certain amount of screwball sense." The photographs accompanying the article showed Sommer swigging champagne from a bottle in the snowfield behind the house and playing with Landon on a bed next to an alarmingly realistic toy gun.

The Canadian press was more sympathetic. Participation in America's wars had only grown less popular after a 2002 incident in which an American fighter pilot dropped a five-hundred-pound laser-guided bomb on a Canadian Forces training exercise near Kandahar, Afghanistan, killing four and wounding eight. Sommer's claims were front-page news in the *National Post*, which ran the all-caps headline NOW THAT I HAVE YOUR ATTENTION above a head shot of Sommer smoking a cigarette and staring intensely into the distance against a backdrop of snowy pines. "I'm a Canadian," read the quote that concluded the article, "and I was raised with a different sense of liberal leanings and moral and ethical standards."

Eventually even the Canadian coverage tapered off. The *Rolling Stone* feature never ran. The *L.A. Times* reporter lost interest. Everyone would now, it seemed, have to wait for Sommer's extradition hearing, when they would finally see whatever actual evidence he possessed.

They never got the opportunity. On June 27, 2007, the day after Sommer's twenty-first birthday and the fourth anniversary of his enlistment in the U.S. Army, he vanished, leaving behind a note of explanation and an accompanying CD of data that surprised pretty much everyone.

———

No one had paid much attention to it at the time, but Luke Elliott Sommer's brief confinement at the North Fraser Pretrial Centre after his August 11 arrest had coincided with a stay by one of Canada's most notorious criminals: a diminutive, chubby, chain-smoking financier of Indian descent named Rakesh Saxena.

Saxena is of that class of shadowy international supervillains who seem to come straight out of a James Bond film. Wanted by Thailand for helping to defraud the Bangkok Bank of Commerce of an amount estimated as high as $2.5 billion, triggering its collapse and a global financial crisis that the *Wall Street Journal* called Saxena the "Mrs. O'Leary's cow" of, he spent more than a decade fighting an extended extradition battle while on nominal house arrest at his luxury condominium outside Vancouver, watched by guards he hired himself as he wheeled and dealed on the phone, helped fund a countercoup in Sierra Leone that led to diamond concessions for his Africa Resources Corp., bought nightly rounds of Indian food for his employees/captors, and hosted occasional journalists. The wealth in his various Swiss accounts was unknown but assumed to be vast. David Baines of the *Vancouver Sun* described him as "immensely intelligent—one of the smartest people I have ever met." Saxena justified his Sierra Leone plot to the Toronto *Globe and Mail* by saying that although he was now operating as a capitalist, he held true to his old socialist ideals by funding resistance movements around the world. "I was a Marxist in my student days," he said, chuckling. "I still am at heart. I'm trying to destroy the system from within now." In March 2006, with a palpable sigh of relief, the British Columbia Court of Appeals denied his final appeal and ordered him jailed at North Fraser as a flight risk pending extradition to Thailand.

Five months later, a loquacious twenty-year-old Army Ranger who also appeared to have an interest in destroying the system from within arrived.

Christel learned from Elliott soon after his arrest that he had a powerful patron who saw in him a potential protégé. Saxena set him up with his own high-priced lawyer, getting him released on $40,000 bail. Two days later a military coup toppled the Thai government. Saxena argued that this constituted a material change in the conditions of his extradition that required starting the proceedings over again, as his safety under the new military government could not be guaranteed. The court reluctantly accepted his argument, this time permitting his confinement to take place in a new and plusher environment, his own house in the Richmond suburb of Vancouver, under the same security arrangement that had obtained at the condo.

Saxena took Sommer on as a business associate shortly afterward. Christel got used to daily phone calls from Rakesh. The note that Sommer left behind when he skipped bail revealed that through all the months in which reporters had been making the trek up his mother's rutted driveway, he had been helping Saxena conduct penny stock scams on the poorly regulated OTC Bulletin Board exchange and facilitating the sale of shell companies to foreign investors for use as tax havens. Though Saxena would later claim that Sommer's involvement had been restricted to computer programming, the dozens of emails between them that Sommer packaged on the accompanying CD showed that he had been involved in many other facets of the business.

The other revelation in Sommer's note was even more peculiar. It seemed (or so he claimed) that he had been collaborating with a major Indo-Canadian gang on an international heroin deal, all the while informing on them to the RCMP through a handler code-named Lone Wolf.

"To the ghost team," Sommer wrote, "you guys were awesome to work with and I never broke my promise to you to keep your names out of the light."

———

Two weeks later Sommer was recaptured at a phone booth in Richmond on a phoned-in tip from a friend. Reporter David Baines was the lone press representative at his next appearance in a Vancouver courthouse, during which a dark-haired woman waved at Sommer and called out a few words. Baines followed her outside and learned that she and Sommer had become romantically involved after meeting on the Internet. She introduced herself only as Chenoa and described Elliott as lethal but tender, a "highly trained killing machine" who would never hurt an innocent. The point of the robbery, she insisted, had been to protest the United States' willingness to prosecute crimes at home while ignoring greater crimes abroad.

"This is an intellectual leap I cannot make," Baines wrote for the *Vancouver Sun*. "I just find the whole thing sad."

Canada's enchantment with Luke Elliott Sommer, dissident hero, appeared to be at an end. But Sommer's own enchantment with this incarnation of himself also seemed to be waning. In November he waived his right to an extradition hearing in favor of a direct appeal to the minister of justice. After another seven months in Canadian custody, he short-circuited the deliberations by voluntarily surrendering to U.S. authorities and submitting a plea of guilty. On December 12, 2008, he was taken to the historic copper-domed Tacoma Courthouse for sentencing. Teller Jessicah Stotts and bank manager Stephanie Ness testified to the terror he had caused and the lasting damage to the community at their workplace. Assistant U.S. attorney Mike Dion spoke at passionate length about the "moral defect" Sommer had exhibited time and again, especially in fabricating stories about his fellow service members, and recommended a sentence of twenty-four years.

The judge accepted Dion's sentencing recommendation. Sommer was removed from the courtroom in shackles. The Bureau of Prisons would soon arrange permanent quarters for him in a high-security U.S. penitentiary. In the meantime he would have a few more months to think things over at SeaTac Federal Detention Center, the same facility where Alex had been held for sixteen months.

Though no one paid much attention to it at the time, SeaTac happened just then to be housing perhaps the biggest drug kingpin in British Columbia, a heavily tattooed martial arts champion named Clayton Roueche, who had been arrested on his way to a wedding in Mexico.

A tae kwon do champion born of a scrap-metal dealer in Chilliwack, a poor farming town in the Fraser River Valley halfway between Kelowna and Vancouver, Roueche got into marijuana through connections to the Vietnamese underworld and revolutionized the industry by forging a relationship with the Mexican Sinaloa cartel, exchanging BC Bud for cocaine, which he then resold in bulk throughout British Columbia. Weed soon evolved from a small-scale hippie pastime in the Kootenays to a $7 billion industry, bigger than agriculture or mining. British Columbia was suddenly a world-class player in the international drug trade, with professionalized chains of production and distribution and open gang warfare in Vancouver.

Most of the big players shooting each other in the streets over control of the BC drug trade tended to be racially exclusive, like the all-white Hells Angels Motorcycle Club and the all–South Asian Indo-Canadian mafia. Roueche's gang was different. One day an old friend surveyed his extensive, expanding grow operations, full of Vietnamese, Laotian, Thai, Chinese, and plain old white Canadians, and likened it to the United Nations. Thereafter they became known as the UN Gang. Initiation rites involved drinking the blood of a decapitated rooster under crossed swords and reciting the "thirty-six oaths" common to Chinese criminal organizations. Roueche, a practicing Buddhist with Chinese character tattoos and a taste for designer hoodies and Prada man-purses, presided as a ruthless guru king, like some burly, spray-tanned mash-up of Tyler Durden, Bruce Lee, and the cast of *Jersey Shore*.

It's easy to see why he and Elliott got along. Still, given the interpersonal savvy it must have taken to survive as lord of the BC Bud trade for nearly a decade—identifying credible threats, reining in extravagances, deciding whom to trust in a business with no recourse but violence for even the pettiest contract disputes, distinguishing fake-crazy from dangerous-crazy from useful-crazy in a population of enthusiastic drug users who manifested creative blends of every personality disorder in the books—it's a little surprising that Roueche too managed to get himself burned by the Army Ranger bank robber with the big ideas.

According to documents filed by the government, a jailhouse informant notified SeaTac officials in January 2009 that Roueche had told him he expected a few events to occur in the very near future: the assassinations of the warden, the district attorney, and Roueche's prosecutor; Roueche's escape from SeaTac with the help of UN Gang members using machine guns and other weaponry supplied by one Luke Elliott Sommer; and the assassination of Sommer's own prosecutor, assistant U.S. attorney Mike Dion.

Though neither Sommer nor Roueche ever confessed to any involvement with the other, Roueche was ruled a security risk and transferred to the United States Penitentiary in Marion, Illinois, to await sentencing at the relatively safe distance of two thousand miles from Luke Elliott Sommer. Two weeks later, Christel inadvertently confirmed on Vancouver's *CTV News* that Sommer and Roueche knew each other by saying that Elliott had scarcely even talked to her about Clay, then inadvertently confirmed the plan's existence by scoffing at the possibility that Elliott would actually have gone through with it. Later, in an interview with the *Chilliwack Times* seeking to contain the damage, she explained with motherly exasperation that Elliott had always been prone to grandiose schemes that had to be taken with a grain of salt. "I think every time he opens his mouth, people take him, like, dead serious," she said. "He possibly could've sat down with Clay and said, 'Hey man, let me tell you, I can probably help you.'"

In the end the government did not pursue charges for the alleged conspiracy—jailhouse informants are notoriously unreliable, and no other firm evidence came to light. Roueche's motion that he be granted a new judge who didn't know the reason for his transfer to Marion was denied. He was sentenced to thirty years. Two new charges were brought against Sommer. One was for soliciting the murder of Mike Dion. The other was for an attempt on the life of his codefendant and erstwhile friend Nathan Dunmall, the man with the last name that ended in two els, who happened to hail from the same little farming town as Clayton Roueche.

CHAPTER 12

THE FOURTH MAN

It's hard to imagine how a scrawny, eager-to-please eighteen-year-old Canadian stoner with no criminal record ended up carrying an AK-47 in a bank robbery with U.S. Special Ops commandos, but that is what happened to Nathan Dunmall in the summer of 2006. Elliott billed Nathan to the other conspirators as a rock-star car thief and getaway driver—"He is from a place called Chilliwack, and it's evidently a kingdom of car thieves," Sergeant Todd Karr testified to the grand jury, to general snickering—but in fact the closest Nathan had come to criminal experience was getting himself kicked out of Chilliwack Senior High School for being caught with marijuana, after deciding to quit via the ill-conceived expedient of giving his whole stash away to a friend on the school bus. He first met Elliott through his ex-girlfriend, Tasha, who had known Elliott and his fellow "man-whore" Tigra since they were all eleven. She saw the boys every summer when she and her friend Vicki traveled up to Peachland to go camping. On their 2005 trip, Nathan followed Tasha to try to persuade her to get back together with him. The gesture was a success. Shortly afterward, when Elliott traveled down to Chilliwack to visit Vicki and Tasha, Nathan was invited along.

At the Abbotsford Police Department a year and a half later, he would recall to Special Agent Gary France of the FBI that as the four of them drank and smoked on Vicki's porch and camped out at the beautiful Cultas Lake in the shadow of the Cascades, Elliott regaled them all with thrilling tales of parachuting into combat in Afghanistan, from which he had just returned.

Nathan ate it up. Skinny, mildly learning-disabled, and bad at sports, with only 150 pounds on his five-eleven frame, he had bounced from school to school across Canada as his father's sales job forced the family to move, and had been bullied and teased wherever he landed. His greatest joy in life was driving around in his electric-blue 1988 Mazda pickup truck with customized engine, rims, and hood intake, into which he poured every spare cent of his wages. Elliott had traveled even more than Nathan, and he was an order of magnitude more badass than any of the guys who called Nathan a loser and a faggot at Chilliwack Senior High, but he didn't talk down to Nathan at all. They worked out together. They went for runs on the high school track. Elliott taught Nathan a Ranger training routine and gave him some exercises to do to enhance his tactical awareness. Nathan began to consider enlisting in the U.S. Army. He didn't take Elliott's crazy speculation about smuggling guns across the border and robbing casinos very seriously. It just seemed like another facet of Elliott's over-the-top Ranger persona, the kind of fantasy scenario you played out in conversation to pump everyone up.

The next year was not kind to Nathan Dunmall. First Tasha, with whom he was deeply in love and whom he had told was the only good thing in his life, broke up with him. Then he got into a minor traffic accident which necessitated repairs that put him in serious debt. His job at Boston Pizza didn't pay well enough to cover a mounting cell-phone bill. By the time the next summer rolled around he was lonely, depressed, and badly in need of money so he could move out of his parents' house. Tasha's family had recently moved back to Chilliwack, but she seemed ambivalent about spending time together.

On July 20, 2006, Elliott got in touch with Tasha over MSN Messenger to see if she and his now ex-girlfriend Vicki would be vacationing in Peachland again this year. Tasha said they were headed up there in four days to go camping. After the two made vague promises to hang out once Elliott came home on block leave, he asked if she had seen Nathan recently. She said that she had, at her surprise welcome-home party. He had invited her sailing on nearby Harrison Lake, but she wasn't sure whether to accept. It was hard, she confided, to spend time with someone she still loved but didn't want to lead on. "b/c nathan and i are very different and in a lot of ways he used to bring me down and i just feel scared almost to do it again, i guess vulnerable is the right word," she wrote.

"true," wrote Elliott. "I see the problem. Do you know his email? does he use msn?"

"hes not a bad guy elliot im just not so sure anymore that hes the right guy for me"

"Its kind of like me and everyone I have ever known," Elliott wrote. "I am a good guy, just not the right one ;)"

Tasha told Elliott she'd look for Nathan's contact information, then got so wrapped up in talking about her feelings for him that Elliott had to prod her again.

"did you find his msn?"

"lol sry," Tasha said. "lowrider_mags. he doesn't go on ever. i dont even know if he still uses it"

"damnit," said Elliott. "you have his cell number? lol"

"why do u need to get a hold of him so bad?"

Elliott said that he just wanted to tell Nathan hi. After some hesitation, Tasha finally gave him the number.

"ok cool thanks hun," Elliott said.

"no problem," said Tasha. "but hey elliot, remember what i asked u when it comes to nathan right?"

"actually no I dont"

"plz dont give him any ideas and get him into any kind of trouble. i think u kno what i mean"

"I just want to say hi"

"u promised u wouldnt"

"I will keep him out of trouble," said Elliott.

"okay," said Tasha. "lol k"

After signing off, Elliott emailed Nathan to say he had an opportunity available for a talented driver. All the job required was parking at an unguarded position along a road in Tacoma, where a bag would be thrown over a fence to him, which he would then have to transport to a secure location. Elliott assured him that the plan would put no heat on him and that he would not require a weapon. He would be paid a minimum of $20,000.

A few days later, drunk at a party with his friend Kaela, Nathan got a call on his cell phone from Elliott. He wanted to know if Nathan had thought his proposition over. Nathan had been thinking about little else for the past few days, but he hadn't decided anything yet. Well, he told Elliott, fine, okay, sure—he would do it. Elliott said he was very pleased to hear that. Unfortunately, certain complications had arisen which necessitated minor changes to the plan he had previously discussed. The changes were not serious, but Nathan would now be required to stand outside the facility and make sure no one entered. The operation was slated for August 7, a week away. Elliott would give him the full details when he arrived in Tacoma.

In the next week, Nathan felt more and more hopeless. He knew he wasn't prepared for what Elliott wanted him to do. Though he didn't let on that this might be goodbye, he tried to see as many friends as he could before he left. Then, because Elliott told him that a round-trip ticket would cause less suspicion at the border, he bought one for $80, and on Sunday, August 6, he boarded a Greyhound bus to Vancouver. He kept thinking back to something Elliott had told him the previous summer, in a spirit of what had then seemed harmless bravado: if an accomplice were to freeze in the middle of a crime, Elliott would shoot him himself.

A friend of Elliott's named Tigra, whom Tasha had told Nathan about, met him at the Vancouver bus station. They made small talk as they waited for their connecting bus to Tacoma. Tigra was about five inches shorter than Nathan but far more muscular, with military experience as a Canadian Forces reservist. They avoided discussing the purpose of the trip except obliquely.

"This is some crazy stuff," Nathan ventured.

"Definitely out of the ordinary," Tigra said.

It was near sunset by the time the bus left Vancouver. As they descended the Pacific coast, Tigra tilted his seat back and napped. Nathan couldn't sleep. For five hours he stared out the window at the giant cedars going by, the darkening sky above the Olympic Mountains, the black expanse of Puget Sound, the blinking lights atop the cranes at the docks.

———

At the Tacoma Greyhound station, Nathan and Tigra found Elliott with two other Rangers, who Nathan would learn later were named Chad Palmer and Alex Blum. It was near 11 p.m. The stars were out above the giant silhouette of Mount Rainier, which dominated the skyline. They loaded their luggage into the trunk of a silver Audi A4, which Nathan thought was nice and complimented the driver on. Elliott gave them a paper bag full of food from Taco Bell to eat in the backseat as they drove to Fort Lewis. There was an uncomfortably long interaction with the uniformed MP manning the guardhouse at the edge of the base, requiring Nathan and Tigra to dig their IDs out of their bags in the trunk of the car, but then the MP waved them through into the dark, tree-lined roads and mysterious military structures of Fort Lewis. Elliott pointed out a barracks complex where soldiers of the regular infantry lived. If any of these losers entered the sacred ground of Second Ranger Battalion's walled compound, he explained, the Rangers would beat the shit out of them.

The driver dropped everyone off inside the compound and said goodnight. As the group approached the barracks, Elliott told Tigra and Nathan what to say if challenged: they were Elliott's cousins, visiting for the night before traveling together to Kelowna to visit their sick grandmother. They pushed through the door into the faceless, three-story concrete block of Charlie Company.

Dozens of America's best-trained killers caromed through the hallway in a spirit of high hilarity, leaning into each other's rooms, spitting chew into cups, going outside to drink and smoke, hooting about their upcoming block leave. Elliott introduced Tigra and Nathan using the agreed-upon story several times on their way down the hall, including to his sergeant, then ushered them into his room and shut the door on all the noise. He dug two AK-47 assault rifles and two handguns from under the cushions of his couch. Amid all the oohing and aahing and gun chatter, Elliott casually explained to Nathan that now he would be holding one of the AK-47s and entering the facility. This, Elliott said, holding up one of the rifles, would be Nathan's. He demonstrated how to load in a fresh magazine and charge it. Both rifles were fully automatic, he explained. They would empty all thirty 7.76mm rounds in the magazine in three seconds flat.

Elliott handed the rifle to Nathan. The wood was old and gouged and the shoulder stock was missing. It looked like a weapon that had killed human beings in myriad uncomfortable climates. Elliott said that this and the other AK-47 had been smuggled into the country by another Ranger and were untraceable.

The party in the hallway quieted down. Elliott led Nathan and Tigra back outside into the night, where they met up with Chad Palmer. The group walked a long way through crunching underbrush in the summer darkness. When Elliott finally allowed them to turn on their flashlights, they were standing in a hollow on the side of a hill. Silhouettes of shaggy cedars rose high overhead toward the stars. Lines of sandbags marked an imaginary room in the dirt.

The target, Elliott said, would be a Bank of America branch in South Tacoma. He began detailing each of their roles in the robbery. His own job would be to leap over the bandit barrier and clear out the cash drawers in the teller line. Tigra's job would be to find the bank manager and get the cash in the vault. Chad's and Nathan's jobs would be to enter the bank and guard the two entrances with the AK-47s, throwing down any customers or employees who tried to escape.

"If police show at the bank," Elliott said, "whip them out."

That got him on the subject of the 1997 North Hollywood shootout, in which a pair of well-armed bank robbers in body armor wounded eleven policemen and seven civilians with about 1100 rounds from their arsenal of fully automatic assault rifles and pistols. After forty-four minutes of mayhem that turned a Los Angeles parking lot into a war zone strewn with blood and shattered glass, both were dead, one by a self-inflicted gunshot.

Those guys were amateurs, Elliott explained. Their own team was better trained, better armored, better armed, and twice as big. They would have had even more firepower available if a friend of Elliott's hadn't just been called away to sniper school, leaving a bunch of Elliott's guns and grenades locked in his truck and storage unit. If police arrived at the bank, no one should hesitate to open fire. Nathan would carry eight additional magazines for the AK-47s and a medical kit in case one of the team members was wounded. However, Elliott added, in case of a shootout, Nathan should pass his AK-47 to Elliott, who was better qualified to operate it.

They ran through the plan inside the rectangle of sandbags with Chad counting down the minutes. Elliott drilled them on a few tacti-

cal essentials. Then they walked back to Elliott's room in the Charlie
Company barracks and played Xbox. Nathan and Elliott took occasional smoke breaks in the parking lot. Once they ran into a Ranger
out there whom Nathan hadn't seen before, a blond guy who was a
little shorter than either of them. He chatted with Elliott about tattoos for a while and then started talking openly with him about the
operation. He said they were crazy to be thinking of robbing a bank,
totally nuts. Then he wished them luck and went inside.

After everyone got tired of *Call of Duty* and *Hitman*, Elliott
put on a movie titled *3000 Miles to Graceland*. They all watched in
silence as five Elvis impersonators robbed a casino to pounding electronic dance music and subsequently betrayed and slaughtered each
other one by one in an endless, grinding postscript that made up the
bulk of the film, until only the two leaders were left for the grim
finale. Tigra was the first to go to sleep, on Elliott's bed. Nathan lay
awake a long time on the couch. When he finally drifted off, around
4:30 a.m., Elliott was still working at his expensive-looking desktop
computer, bathed in the icy blue glow of the enormous monitor.

————

When Nathan woke up four hours later, Elliott was still there,
now dressed in a workout T-shirt, tennis shoes, and the short black
shorts known as "Ranger panties." He turned briefly to explain that
he had already finished cleaning duty and physical training with his
platoon and had been released for block leave.

Tigra was the last to wake, an hour after Nathan. Chad joined
them as they spent the morning training on the weapons and medical
supplies. Elliott showed Nathan how to apply a tourniquet from the
medical bag to stop bleeding. He gave him the AK-47 to hold again
and showed him the safety and the rate-of-fire lever that switched
between semi- and fully automatic fire. Nathan and Chad were supposed to enter the bank with bolts open and full magazines loaded,
then drive the bolts forward to charge the rifles so all the customers
and employees inside could hear the click of bullets sliding into the
chambers. Tigra and Elliott would contribute to the atmosphere of
terror by shining the flashlight and laser attached to their pistols into
everyone's faces.

The AK-47 proved a tricky piece of machinery. The steps required

to charge it, disengage the safety, eject a round, and release the magazine were confusing. After Nathan had practiced a few times, Elliott
told him to put the weapon away before he got someone shot.

The rest of the day they spent going over the plan and staging the
gear. Elliott pulled up Google Maps and pointed out a church near
the bank that they would use as a landmark to find the alley they
would enter from. He played some inspirational YouTube videos of
Special Forces soldiers on his computer. Nathan showed everyone
pictures of his truck on a car enthusiast website. They all tried on the
jeans, hooded sweatshirts, skater shoes, ballistic vests, and balaclavas
Elliott had acquired for them, then stuffed them all into two black
garbage bags to avoid suspicion from other Rangers and took them
down to the Audi. After the car was loaded, they waited ten minutes
in the hot afternoon sun before the driver finally showed up in board
shorts and flip-flops.

This, Nathan would soon be telling Special Agent France, was
the first time he had seen Alex Blum since the night before, when he
had dropped them all off at the barracks. They had been able to load
gear into the Audi because Elliott had previously acquired his keys.

————

FBI reports of interviews with suspects, known to prosecutors
and defense attorneys as 302s, are usually so dry they might as well
have been written by robots. But in the 302 summarizing Nathan
Dunmall's statement to Special Agent France and ATF agent Brice
McCracken in March 2007, after all the other conspirators had agreed
to cooperate, an unmistakable wryness peeks through the Bureau-
ese. Although the robbery was now seven months past, Nathan came
across like a half-stoned first-time X Games competitor who had just
skidded on his face out the bottom of the hugest, scariest terrain
park of his life and wanted everyone present to know that he was
never, ever, ever doing that again. France began sprinkling his report
with bemused little excerpts of Nathan's phraseology. Of the summer camping trip when Nathan was so enthralled with Sommer's
tales of combat jumps in Iraq and Afghanistan, France wrote, "DUN-
MALL advised at this stage in his life he was a 'thrill seeker' and
desired to participate in similar adventures which would bring about
a 'rush' and 'adrenaline.'" Of Nathan's skepticism regarding Som-

mer's criminal plans, he wrote, "DUNMALL believed SOMMER was 'full of shit' regarding the possible crimes and assembling a team. DUNMALL believed SOMMER only talked about committing such crimes in an effort to further excite DUNMALL." Of the scene in the car on the way to the bank, he wrote, "DUNMALL described the process of retrieving the bags from the rear, putting on the vests, and handing out the weapons, as a 'circus.'"

The backseat of Alex's Audi folded down to provide trunk access. It was through this narrow passage that the weapons, vests, and clothing had to be extracted while Alex drove the team north on I-5 in full view of surrounding cars, with Tigra sitting on Chad's lap to make room. They distributed and pulled on the sweatshirts and jeans while squirming around in the cramped backseat. It was very hot. The radio had been broken ever since a fellow Ranger spilled tobacco juice into it weeks earlier. Elliott gave Alex turn-by-turn directions but got them lost for a while after identifying the wrong church. When they finally pulled into the alley behind the bank, the parking lot was swarming with customers. Elliott asked the team what they should do. Chad and Nathan suggested taking a lap around the block to get a better sense of how many people were inside. That is not, of course, what happened.

Two minutes later, when the team raced back out to the parking lot, the Audi was gone. In a panic, they ran all the way to the end of the alley without seeing it, then turned left and started jogging into the residential neighborhood that contained their landmark church, trying to remove the balaclavas and hide the weapons without slowing down. Just as Elliott suggested that they commandeer one of these houses for use as a "fortress," they entered an intersection and saw the Audi driving down a cross street.

Back in the safety of the car, everyone began talking excitedly about the robbery. In between directing Alex through a series of rapid turns, Elliott crowed about having reentered the bank after the others ran out, to thank everyone inside for their cooperation. He said that the tellers, four pretty young women, had been so cooperative as to suggest they had been attracted to him, even flirting with him. Nathan thought this was one of the most ridiculous things he had ever heard in his life.

As the Audi turned onto a stretch of road that pointed them

briefly back toward the bank, the mood abruptly changed. A patrol car from the Tacoma Police Department was racing up behind them with siren wailing and lights ablaze. Elliott ordered a left turn into the next cul-de-sac. If the policeman followed, he said, "we get out of the car and waste him."

The five conspirators had only a few seconds, then, parked at a suburban curb with the sound of one another's breath filling the car, to consider, each in his own way, what role they might play in whatever happened next. They stared out the rear windshield at the mouth of the cul-de-sac. When the policeman roared past moments later, he had a taut expression on his face that certain team members took, in the relieved chatter that immediately followed, as a grin. A silver Audi A4 bearing four men in sweatshirts and one in a T-shirt in the vicinity of a recently robbed bank on a hot summer day had not been enough to divert him from his course. Perhaps eyewitness descriptions of the getaway vehicle had not yet been broadcast. Elliott said he was probably smiling because he finally had some excitement in his life.

The Audi nosed out of the cul-de-sac and headed toward I-5. Everyone began tearing off their sweatshirts and jeans and stuffing them back into the trunk with the weapons. Nathan couldn't stop thinking about how suspicious they all looked. He couldn't believe the policeman hadn't followed them. He decided he wanted out.

"DUNMALL stated 'just drop me off' and 'I'll meet up with you guys later,'" wrote Special Agent France. "DUNMALL was ignored by the other team members as they were busily discussing what to do next."

It was decided that Chad, Tigra, and Nathan would lie low for a few hours at a movie theater while Elliott and Alex, the driver, returned to Fort Lewis. The three of them climbed out at the curb of a big Tacoma multiplex, where they bought tickets for a movie titled *The Descent* and took their seats in the darkened theater just as the opening credits began.

The Descent turned out to be about a race of pale, cannibalistic half-men who inhabit a deep cave system and prey on a team of female explorers.

"DUNMALL described the movie as a horror film," wrote Special Agent France. "DUNMALL does not like horror films. DUN-

MALL was already feeling a great amount of emotion and adrenaline from robbing the bank. DUNMALL stated he felt like he was going to 'pass out' several times during the movie because of the horror film content coupled with his heightened emotions."

———

They called Elliott from the sidewalk outside the theater after the movie was over. It was still light out. Elliott said that unfortunately he would not be able to pick them up, as Alex had already left for the airport. Nathan had to withdraw $20 from an ATM at the movie theater to pay for his share of a taxi to the Ranger barracks.

When they got to Elliott's room, another Ranger whom Nathan had never seen before was standing inside chatting casually with Elliott about the robbery. Cash was spread all over the bed. After the man left, Tigra, Nathan, Chad, and Elliott took the cash to another room to count it. The total came to about $53,000. They took $10,000 apiece for themselves, set aside $3,000 for those unnamed associates of Elliott's who had supplied the equipment and weapons, and carried the final $10,000 up to Alex on the third floor; he was back from the airport, having missed his flight. Then Elliott, Tigra, and Nathan took their bags downstairs to the parking lot, where yet another Ranger whom Nathan had never seen before, a thirtyish man with brown hair, met them in a brand-new Honda Accord, which Nathan thought was nice and complimented him on.

As the older Ranger drove them to the Greyhound station, Elliott yet again talked openly and in depth about the robbery, including details of the planning process, which the man had apparently been involved with. He dropped them off at the station. The three Canadians boarded the bus together, transferred to a different bus in Seattle, and crossed the border around 1:30 a.m. into the dark, verdant farmland of southern British Columbia. As they neared the point where the route veered north into the mountains, Elliott invited Nathan to continue with him and Tigra to Kelowna and from there on to Elliott's mother's house in Peachland. "However," wrote Special Agent France, "DUNMALL did not desire to travel and stay with SOMMER or TIGRA. Consequently, DUNMALL exited the bus in Chilliwack, BC."

Special Agent France asked if Elliott had ever spoken to Nathan about crimes or atrocities committed by the U.S. military.

Never at any time, Nathan said.

———

Elliott Sommer's arrest for armed bank robbery and Tigra's subsequent surrender at the border were big news in Chilliwack. Nathan's ex-girlfriend Tasha couldn't believe it. Elliott and Tigra weren't anything like the kind of guys you pictured doing something like that. Elliott was a little different, sure, and he had changed a lot since joining the U.S. military, but nobody had believed for a second that all his wild talk the year before would actually amount to anything.

She talked to Nathan about it. He seemed just as shocked as she was.

By the Monday after Elliott's arrest, the day of Denise Fichtner's funeral, four of the five bank robbers had been identified and apprehended. One remained at large. Tasha was discussing the robbery with a group that included both Nathan's parents and her own when she happened to mention that it had taken place in Tacoma, Washington.

Nathan's mother seemed startled. She said she had recently found a bus ticket stub to Tacoma.

It took a little sleuthing to find out more. Tasha and her friend Kaela discovered that Kaela's ex-boyfriend had been on the same Greyhound bus as Nathan out of Chilliwack. When they drove to his house to ask him about it, he told them that he had debarked outside Vancouver to visit his new girlfriend but that Nathan had continued on. He hadn't said much about the purpose of the trip—the two of them barely knew each other—but he had said he would be visiting family in Tacoma.

Kaela and Tasha drove from there straight to Nathan's house. Nathan was sitting outside. Tasha jumped out of the van before it had even finished moving. "What did you do?" she screamed as she ran up to him. She hit him square in the face. "Was it you?" she demanded. "Was it you?"

Finally Nathan nodded his bowed head. Tasha hit him again and again.

In the recordings of their statements two days later to a very sympathetic-sounding RCMP constable, Jennifer Cook, which last about twenty minutes each, Kaela and Tasha weep without pause.

"Nathan's manipulated very easily," Tasha insists brokenly. "He's not the person to want to come up with it or to dream about it or anything. Elliott's very *convincing*."

"All right," murmurs Constable Cook.

"Elliott's the smartest person I know. *Honestly.*"

"Okay," murmurs Cook. "Okay." She asks what Nathan told Tasha about his role in the plan.

"He was just supposed to drive. And then it changed to he was supposed to stand by a door and make sure that nobody came in. And then it changed to have him actually being there. The plan kept changing, and before he knew it, he was part of it, and he didn't back out. He knew he should . . ." Tasha takes a minute to get herself under control. "He knew he should have . . . he, he wanted to . . . but he didn't."

She is crying so hard now that all she can get out is a whisper. "I don't know why."

Nathan spent seven months in Canada before the extradition process was complete. After giving his statement to Special Agent France in Abbotsford, he was transported to SeaTac Federal Detention Center, where, like Alex, he spent more than a year in custody. In May 2008 he learned through ambient prison chatter that Elliott had arrived. He would be housed in a different unit, with a separation order in place to keep him and Nathan apart at all times.

Still, Nathan began glancing over his shoulder in the cafeteria and the common areas, even after Elliott pleaded guilty and was sentenced to twenty-four years. He redoubled the efforts he had been making to bulk up and get in shape. A little past three in the afternoon one Friday late in January 2009, just after he had finished a set of bar dips to exhaustion in his cell, he looked up to see another inmate standing in his open doorway.

Two and half years had passed since they had last seen each other, but even in prison khakis, Elliott was unmistakable: the POW MIA tattoo on his arm, the tall, muscular frame, the smoky blue eyes. He looked puzzled at first, as if he didn't quite recognize Nathan, and then he stepped across the threshold and charged.

Nathan felt a sharp pain in the upper left side of his chest. When he tried to pull away, he saw the knife in Elliott's hand, a spike of sharpened gray plastic with a fabric-wrapped handle. He knew then that he was fighting for his life. Elliott was taller, trained as a killer, and armed. Nathan's only chance, he decided, was to force the fight out of the cell so a guard might hear it and intervene. He shoved Elliott back against the wall by the toilet. Elliott laughed.

"You've gotten bigger since the last time I saw you," he said, then charged again, locking Nathan's head under his arm and stabbing at the back of his neck with the knife. Nathan managed to get his hands on Elliott's arm and pull him off, dragging him toward the door. Elliott grabbed Nathan's throat in his other hand and squeezed. Nathan felt his windpipe clamp shut before he managed to rip the hand away and burst into the hallway, where he and Elliott got in a few punches apiece before a screaming corrections officer dove between them. Elliott kept shoving the CO out of the way to leap at Nathan, but suddenly knelt and interlaced his hands on his head. Nathan felt a sudden certainty that he was about to be attacked from behind. He whipped around to look, but no one was there. He got down on the floor too.

It took only a few seconds for backup to start running in. As they knelt side by side amid the commotion, Elliott told Nathan that he knew his registration number and what he'd said to the FBI and that no matter where he went in the U.S. prison system, he was a dead man.

Soon a whole circle of prison staff surrounded them. The knife was recovered from the floor of a nearby broom closet, where it had slid during the fight. Elliott proudly informed the crowd that he had shaped it from a piece of plastic broken off from the black-and-gray stair-stepper exercise machine in his unit, sharpened it with a razor, and dulled it on Nathan's head. He also informed them that he had nearly ripped out Nathan's Adam's apple during the fight. While

Nathan was being led off to the medical unit, Elliott yelled after him, "You won't even be safe at the ADX.* You can't hide anywhere."

Nathan's medical checkup revealed multiple lacerations on his head, neck, and finger and a shallow stab wound on his upper left chest. He told investigators that he believed if God had not been looking out for him, Elliott Sommer would have killed him, and that he was thankful for God's intervention.

———

It did not prove necessary to investigate how Sommer had gained entrance to Nathan's cell block. With Nathan's blood still drying on his shirt, he bragged about it in detail to the counselor who escorted him away from the scene of the fight. Earlier that afternoon, just before the guards' shift change, he had asked to be taken to the pharmacist. Then he had waited for a guard who didn't recognize him to arrive so he could tell the new guard to escort him back to Nathan's unit rather than to his own. The shank had been hidden in his shoe. He claimed to have been planning the attack for sixty days.

Nathan Dunmall was sentenced by the Honorable Judge Robert J. Bryan on March 20, 2009, to ten years in a U.S. penitentiary with credit for time served. His lawyer pointed to psychiatric evaluations and bountiful letters of support from Nathan's Chilliwack community that declared the bank robbery was a bizarre aberration in Nathan's life that wasn't likely to repeat. Since surrendering himself to the RCMP, he had taken every opportunity to do the right thing. He had earned high honors in studies toward his unfinished high school degree, cooperated fully with U.S. authorities, and expressed remorse to his family, friends, and church, all of whom vowed to help him rebuild his life.

"In looking at Nathan's history and background," Judge Bryan said, "it is clear that this was very much out of character for him. One can only speculate, even after reading all of the information about Nathan's background and psychological make-up and so forth,

———

* The maximum-security facility in Florence, Colorado, known as the "Alcatraz of the Rockies."

one can only speculate about how someone like Nathan would get so involved in something so serious."

Judge Bryan lent his endorsement to a treaty transfer to Canada.

"I am sorry that you got involved in this," he said to Nathan. "You are not the only one that was taken in by Mr. Sommer, but somewhere there needed to be that internal voice that we all have that needed to tell you 'no' instead of allowing you to go forward with his scheme."

BOOK 3

THE GOOD PERSON

Reality is that which, when you stop believing
in it, doesn't go away.
—PHILIP K. DICK, "HOW TO BUILD A UNIVERSE
THAT DOESN'T FALL APART TWO DAYS LATER," 1978

CHAPTER 13

THE B-WORD

PFC Alex Blum, combat cherry and hapless criminal accomplice, was never the U.S. government's top priority. The authorities wanted to put Luke Elliott Sommer away for a very long time. The legal position in which Norm found his son was delicate, presenting both opportunities for lenience, if Alex agreed to testify against his old team leader, and opportunities for self-sabotage, if he failed to make a clear distinction between his own role and Sommer's. Norm and my father flew out to Seattle a week after the robbery to find a lawyer with the skill to handle it. In the course of a day they interviewed three candidates, settled tentatively on one, packed their bags, and were about to leave for the airport when Jeff Robinson, the final name on their list, called to say a defendant he was representing had just settled and he might have time to squeeze them in.

Robinson, a 1981 Harvard Law graduate, was one of *Black Enterprise* magazine's top hundred black lawyers in the country and the King County Bar Association's 2003 Lawyer of the Year. Within fifteen minutes, he had impressed Norm and Al as one of the most engaging, compassionate, brilliant men they had ever met. But unlike the other lawyers they had spoken to, he did not work alone. He had a secret weapon: a genius researcher and former honest-to-god rocket scientist named Amanda Lee, who he said would be doing much of the legwork. "My strength is collaborating with Amanda Lee," Jeff told them. "When it's time to get in front of the judge and make the case, that's where I come in."

A week later, on August 24, 2006, Amanda was peering through the window of a descending airliner at the thin blue meniscus of atmosphere that lay atop the foothills west of Denver.

Englewood Federal Correctional Institution, when approached from the direction of the airport, rises against the mountains on the horizon like a sprawl of concrete warts. Amanda pulled through the Cyclone fence into the parking lot shortly after noon. The correctional officers at the detention center sprang to immediate attention when she named the detainee she was there to see. *Oh! Right! Okay!* The bank-robbing Army Ranger from Tacoma was clearly the biggest fish they had.

Amanda had seen a lot in her fifteen years of practice in criminal law. Back in Seattle, she had been spending much of her time on Daniel McGowan, an environmental activist who had been charged as a terrorist for a series of arson attacks with the Earth Liberation Front. But it was immediately clear when Alex Blum walked into the visitation room in prison khaki that he would be no ordinary client.

———

When I met Amanda at her office at Schroeter Goldmark & Bender in downtown Seattle in September 2010, two months after my lunch with Norm, her memory of meeting Alex was still vivid.

"Almost his very first words to me at the detention center in Colorado were"—Amanda shifted her low, dry voice, which had reminded me all afternoon of an expensive briefcase handed across the glossy wood slab of her desk, into a small, confused register—" 'Is there an AAR? Where's the—is there an AAR?' "

I looked at her uncertainly. I felt a little intimidated by Amanda's droll intelligence. The last time I had seen her was at Alex's sentence hearing, where she was pantsuited and commanding, shepherding us all into a Tacoma courtroom to hear Jeff argue a version of Alex's story confusingly different from the one Norm had been telling us in private. She peered over her eyeglasses at my perplexed expression.

"I said, 'What are you talking about?' " she continued. " 'An *after-action report*,' he said. 'Have they done an *after-action report*?' "

Oh: because Alex still thought the whole thing was a training exercise.

"His affect was so flat that it was hard for me to tell whether he was fabricating or whether he really believed it, but once it became clear that he was wondering why I wasn't accompanied by a person from his unit, once he started asking where some military person was and if I had talked to his sergeant, his CO, and I just had to keep saying, 'No, no, no, this doesn't have anything to do with the military,' and he just kept at it . . . He couldn't wrap his mind around the idea that it was a civilian lawyer coming in to talk to him."

I couldn't believe what I was hearing. Many difficult conversations with Alex had passed since Norm had forwarded me the "harsh reality check" email from Luke Elliott Sommer. I had come here today half dreading, half hoping that Amanda would deal Alex's improbable tale a final death blow of pitiless logic. In the halls of Schroeter Goldmark & Bender, I had heard, her nickname was "the Robot."

"Now," Amanda said, evidently noticing my excitement, "I've long since given up any notion that I can tell when someone's lying to me or not, because so many people have lied to me so capably. So to this day I don't have an opinion on whether what he was saying to me was genuine. You know what I mean?"

"Yeah," I said. "I do."

"But he stuck with these stories long enough that I came to believe that it was very likely true that he really was expecting military people to come in and . . . *relieve* him"—Amanda shook her head in disbelief at the absurdity of the idea—"from this situation somehow. I never had the sense that there was any sort of overt planning going into some elaborate deception or anything like that. It was more like a real, a true, a deep, deep difficulty coming to terms with what was happening to him. There were several phases. And then at a certain point, months and months into it, I had a sort of an epiphany: you know what, he's—for lack of better language for it—he's *deprogramming* himself. But in the worst possible place and way. I've seen young people who've gotten sucked into Hari Krishna or some of those ultra-isolating cults, and when they are led out of that there's an elaborate process of reorienting their view. But usually there's someone helping them. Right? And they're in a safe place. He didn't have any of that. He was doing it all by himself."

That first hour with Alex at Englewood FCI, Amanda told me, she had intended only to get her new client up to speed on what came next. The blip of alarming jurisdictional confusion at the beginning barely registered.

"I didn't ask him to explain it to me because it sounded so *crazy*," she said. "And if he was crazy, I didn't want to get into his craziness."

Instead she brought the conversation back to ground, trying her best to penetrate his military demeanor and make sure he understood some basic facts about his case. First and foremost, they would not be going to trial. Alex would have to continue cooperating fully with the government in order to secure the 5K motion that would allow the judge to depart below the minimum sentence guideline. She warned him that he was looking at years, not months, but that even after five or so—just to throw out one possible number—he would still be a very young man, with much of his life ahead of him. She thought she saw him tear up a little at this, but if so, he quickly recovered his expressionless detachment, accepting everything she said with a curt nod.

During Alex's initial interview with the FBI, an hour after his arrest, he had first claimed that Sommer had coerced him into the robbery. When the agents expressed skepticism and asked if Sommer had pulled a gun on him, Alex said yes. On being told that this story was absurd, he immediately recanted it. He readily admitted as much to Amanda, shrugging it off as if it were no big deal. His total lack of curiosity about his own defense was unprecedented in Amanda's experience. It suggested some unique challenges ahead. She mentioned it at the very beginning of her memo to Jeff about the meeting.

> He seems somewhat restrained in his communication—he answers questions quickly and directly, but does not volunteer any information and did not ask any questions at all about how we would approach his case. He comes across as very young, very committed to being an Army Ranger.

The biggest response Amanda got was when she pushed him on the role of rank hierarchy at Ranger Battalion in getting him involved in the crime. He told her that above all, neither the Ranger Regiment nor his own unit at Fort Lewis should be disparaged. This was obviously important to him, but the speech struck her as theatrical, like something out of a bad war movie.

A week later Alex was transferred to San Bernardino Central Detention Center. A week after that he was transferred to the place he would spend the next year and a half: SeaTac Federal Detention Center.

It was at SeaTac that Alex had his first proffer meeting with the prosecutor, assistant U.S. attorney Mike Dion, and the lead investigator on the case, Special Agent Shaide, the former defensive tackle from the University of North Dakota. Amanda was worried that Alex might not be ready, but Jeff, after a preparatory meeting of his own with the client, drove down to the prison to see him through it.

It did not go well. Jeff came storming back to the office, furious: despite all Norm's assertions about what a good kid Alex was, it seemed that he had not been wholly honest with them about Sommer's criminal plans. Agent Shaide, whom Jeff described as "an extremely macho, take-charge personality," joined forces with Dion to hit Alex hard with how much they already knew. Half the questions were about a casino robbery plan that Alex had never mentioned, either to the government or to his own lawyers. Jeff tried to hide his shock as Alex readily admitted knowledge of the plan—and then, to make matters worse, tried to dismiss the whole thing as some kind of a game, volunteering that he himself had suggested stealing cars for the robbery, using their Ranger "convalescent skills." It was only after Shaide and Dion pressed him repeatedly that Alex finally relented and agreed with them that joking about it was one thing, but actually driving to the facility you intended to rob was a different thing entirely.

Jeff called Norm to advise him that his son was not living up to billing. A few days later, he and Amanda drove to SeaTac FDC together to read Alex the riot act. In the dingy little visiting room, Jeff explained in no uncertain terms that Alex needed to tell them every incriminating detail before it came out with the government, that Dion would never cut him a deal if Jeff could not trust his credibility as a witness, that it was time to take responsibility for his participation in the crime.

———

The Alex that Amanda described to me at her office in September 2010 was not the same as Norm's. Amanda's Alex was not so deluded as to truly believe that his imprisonment was part of some elaborate military training exercise. But the insane new reality of his legal situation was so much less substantial to him than Ranger Battalion, where Sommer's plans had been no more than a sideshow of harmless tactical exercises among elite brother warriors on the road to Iraq, that his mind couldn't seem to keep a lasting grip on the truth.

"It took at least a couple more visits before Alex even sort of accepted that the people he was going to be dealing with were civilians," Amanda recalled. "I remember having a couple discussions with him that were just very, very basic."

He continued to plead with her to get in touch with Corporal Sager or his commanding officer at Fort Lewis, insisting that battalion had to be conducting some kind of internal review of the "operation."

"Look," Amanda would say, "you guys robbed a bank. And now you're being prosecuted. By federal prosecutors, in federal court."

"Okay," Alex would say. "All right. I hear you. Okay. I get it."

But from the way he retreated into sullen detachment, she could tell that he didn't get it, not really. It was a little maddening; also a little frightening. But Amanda was surprised to find how gentle and sweet he could be on the other side of the tough-guy persona. He talked to her about hockey, about his girlfriend, about the food he missed, about his favorite movies. He asked after her family. It took a few months, but by the time he finally began interacting with other detainees at SeaTac, Alex and Amanda were enough at ease with each other that his pitch-perfect reconstructions of the conversations he was having inside often had her laughing so hard that tears streamed down her cheeks. As their meetings drew to a close he would be desperate to keep her from leaving, telling one after another funny anecdote just as she was gathering up her things to go.

"The more I got to know him, the more I realized he was just so naive and so young," Amanda said.

Most defendants commit their crimes in their home state, so it is relatively easy for family to visit. Norm was visiting Alex often enough to astonish Amanda, but his mother wasn't even talking to him, and his girlfriend, Anna, who had just started her freshman year at the University of Colorado, was in the long, slow process of breaking up with him.

The challenge was getting him to accept responsibility for his actions. Element by element—casing the bank, buying gear for the robbery, picking up the Canadians the night before, giving Sommer his soft armor, giving him the keys to the Audi, driving him to the bank—she had to push him to acknowledge that he had participated knowingly in Sommer's plans. But each time Amanda thought they had made progress he would suddenly backslide, sometimes to his old, discredited claim that Sommer had coerced him, sometimes all the way to arguing that the bank robbery must have been a legitimate Ranger action.

———

Though Alex was pleading out, arguments for leniency in sentencing often appeal to the categories of innocence that judges are familiar with, replicating in miniature the kinds of arguments that might be used in a full defense. Alex's case had the unusual property of tracing a long, winding path along the ridges between the various categories recognized by criminal law without ever quite falling into any of them. In the Biblical era of "an eye for an eye," harm alone was enough to prove guilt, but today a criminal is generally convicted both in body and in soul: the criminal act, or *actus reus*, must derive from some species of criminal intent, or *mens rea*. In cases of total mindlessness—sleepwalking, hypnotism, spasm, seizure—the court may rule that no *actus reus* occurred at all. Case law is littered with tragic tales of somnambulist murder and unconscious car accidents. As one legal scholar puts it, "Talk of excusing here seems to make no more sense than would talk of excusing a rock for falling on one's head." But it was clear from the start that this would not be Alex's fate. He was awake and aware at the time the robbery occurred. Defense had to hinge on *mens rea*.

Could Alex be said to have participated "knowingly" in the crime? Did he *will* that the robbery occur, or was he merely *willing* that it occur? Accomplices are subject to the same charges as principals, but there is a profoundly knotty doctrine of complicity in joint criminal action, rife with case studies of landlords renting to known hosts of illegal gambling and gun merchants selling to known gangsters. Alex was in the strange position of having provided far more material support for Sommer's crimes than these examples with— apparently—less awareness that crimes would occur.

An equally knotty doctrine governs "mistake of fact." Many of the precedents are statutory rape cases with defendants who believed their partner to be of age. In various ways, at various times, Alex tried to claim to Amanda that his participation in the robbery had indeed been a mistake: he had thought that Sommer was only asking him to drive there as an exercise, or a joke, or a test, whether of loyalty to the Rangers or to Sommer himself wasn't always clear. Amanda tried not to show her impatience. No judge or jury would ever in a million years buy that Alex had driven Sommer to the bank without knowing it was for a robbery. If Sommer had outright deceived him, that would have been one thing, but after Alex helped him case the casino, appeared with him on the bank's security cameras four days before the robbery, took him to the sports supply store to buy sweatshirts and jeans, picked up the Canadians from the bus station, and lent Sommer his soft armor, it was hard to imagine arguing that anyone had deceived Alex other than himself. "Willful ignorance" is identical in criminal law to full knowledge.

———

The hardest part was impressing on Alex that Specialist Sommer had brought him in for the specific purpose of committing a crime.

"He was very reluctant to think that Sommer had intentionally wronged anyone in any way," Amanda said.

At times Alex would hypothesize that the specialist must have had some misunderstanding. Some commander must have told him that the bank was going to be used to stage an operation, that there would be fake civilians inside.

"There was a lot of talk at the beginning about the Rangers collectively, including Sommer. 'You don't understand. We don't do crimes. You civilians are unappreciative of what the Rangers do.' Just spouting the stuff he must have heard a million times. I couldn't tell whether he was saying that to try to suggest that they *hadn't* committed a crime or whether he was just seeing the horror of it: 'We don't do crimes, and yet here I just did one.' I couldn't really wrap my mind around that."

Instead Amanda asked in as neutral a tone as she could manage about Sommer and Alex's initial relationship. He told her how Sommer had taken him under his wing and taught him the ropes at battalion, how Sommer had taken him to his barracks room to show him a few treasured belongings: private weaponry, mementos from combat.

"He wasn't supposed to have that, was he?" she asked.

"No, but everybody had that shit. Everybody brought stuff back."

Even as Alex rationalized away Sommer's every little transgression, it was easy enough to read between the lines: the more experienced soldier befriending him, grooming him, implicating him bit by bit, normalizing each stage before moving on to the next. Amanda asked what he and Sommer would do when they hung out. Alex told her about their adventures in Tacoma: doing tactical breakdowns, casing the casino and the bank. When he described Sommer preparing him for involvement in the robbery, Alex always called it "the mission" or "the action" and framed it as a legitimate thought experiment. " 'Cause when you're overseas," he explained to her, "and you're in an undercover situation in a little town, you might have to do that, you know? Get local currency to use."

She did not point out to him how ridiculous all this was. "You couldn't just say it to Alex," she told me. "He had to come to it on his own."

This wasn't all for Alex's benefit. Amanda really needed to understand what had happened. The newspapers were starting to publish stories about Sommer that made it seem as if something very strange indeed was afoot in Peachland. Little by little, she tried to get Alex to see Sommer not as a Ranger and mentor but as a criminal architect; to talk about all their interactions not as ordinary Ranger banter and gamesmanship but as preparations for a crime.

They did not have the luxury of endless time, because the government wanted Alex's cooperation immediately. Mike Dion called Amanda over and over to complain that Alex kept minimizing his involvement. Amanda insisted over and over that he was fighting through some "very intense psychological drama." This did not thrill Dion, though he at least seemed ready to accept that Alex was not just a scheming criminal out to cover up his involvement.

What Alex failed to understand in all his desperation to be believed was that the pressure from the government was less about him than about locking down the case against Luke Elliott Sommer, who was already making rumblings about going to trial rather than pleading out. What the government needed was to prove that Sommer's crime had been heavily premeditated, and for this they needed Alex and the other cooperating witnesses to attest to a long planning process with clear criminal intent.

Though other defendants too had tried to bring it up, it had occurred to no one at this point—not the government, not Norm, not Amanda, not Alex himself—that Sommer had encouraged his fellow Rangers to think his plans were just a game as a deliberate ploy to get them involved.

———

In January, a fellow inmate at SeaTac FDC called Alex over to listen to Sommer claim on National Public Radio that he had robbed the bank to protest war crimes. After that Alex was somewhat less apt to think of Sommer as an upstanding Ranger who would somehow fix all this and restore his place at battalion. Alex had long maintained that he never saw anything wrong with the robbery—that it had just been business as usual for a Ranger—but he now confessed to Amanda that in the alley behind the bank he had locked eyes with a woman in a truck whose fear shocked him into realizing, at least for a moment, that what they were doing was wrong. Then, Alex said, he had tried to drive away, but got only a block or two before the conspirators burst into sight and flagged him down, so quickly that he assumed the operation had been canceled. When Amanda dug through the witness reports, she found Don Keegan's observations of a silver Audi driving away during the robbery before picking the conspirators up, consistent with Alex's story.

Eventually Alex broke his reticence about his former team leader and wrote Amanda a letter.

> When [Sommer] started talking about killing Hells Angels and drug dealers in Canada it was just a way of him teaching me about how we operate anywhere in the world and it was the same when we talked about taking down banks or casinos, it was just going over options and strategy because we took our profession seriously . . . Even after the robbery it made more sense to me that it was an exercise rather than something wrong. I actually apologized for driving away because I felt stupid for thinking they robbed the bank. When I got arrested I was waiting for the FBI to be like, "We know this was just training, so hang tight, we just need the AAR." To be honest with you I'm still confused because none of this makes sense to me. When people ask "What were you guys thinking?" I tell them I'm still trying to figure that out.

Amanda contacted the *Seattle Times* reporter David Bowermaster to suggest he ask Sommer if Palmer and Blum had been led to believe that the robbery was not really going to happen, or that it was "one more training exercise."

"Absolutely not true," Sommer told Bowermaster. "[Blum] drove there. You get that? He made the trip there. And instead of running away once we were out of the vehicle, stayed to pick us up."

Shortly afterward Norm wrote Sommer an email.

> Elliott, when I met you at parents day I was impressed by your seemingly grounded and levelheaded demeanor . . . a buddy for Alex to play hockey with.
>
> If only I knew what was really in your head. You fooled a lot of people. I wonder if you understand the grief and pain that your misguided plans has [*sic*] caused for so many people . . . none more so than Alex and I.

Sommer, of course, wrote back immediately, with the "harsh reality check" email that would appall me three years later: "You honestly believe that your son, who you have known for his entire life, never dreamed of being involved in this? He helped me plan it Norm."

In March 2007, Alex apologized to Mike Dion and Monte Shaide for having originally claimed he was coerced at gunpoint. In fact he tried to explain—to Amanda's horror—that at the time of that interview he had still believed this was all a training exercise organized by Sommer, and that this was what Sommer had instructed him to say.

In April 2007, Alex wrote Sommer a letter.

> I know this letter isn't going to matter to you, but this isn't for you, it is for me, this letter is my redemption.
>
> I looked up to you. I trusted you. You were like a brother to me. I relied on you to guide me through my time at BAT until I got my Tab. Instead of being a man and leading your little brother through his first steps of life you betrayed me, you used me and put me in an unimaginable life situation.
>
> I dreamed of being a Ranger since I was 5 and you took it away. Obviously you forgot what it is like to be a new private at BAT. If you told me the world was flat I would have believed you. If you told me to run until I fell off the face of the earth I would have. I guess at some point when you were at school you thought you were God. I'm going to tell you something, you will realize over time you are not God, you are not some iconic figure out to do good. You are a small insignificant person who took advantage of someone who loved you. You are a person who shamed his Ranger family. I hope you have taken off your scroll with a cheese grater. You let me down and you have ruined a lot of lives. I hope your son turns out much better than you have.
>
> I was a good Ranger and I thought you were a great Ranger. Obviously I was wrong. It has taken me 8 months to figure out that you never cared about me or the Rangers. You only cared about yourself. You got a cherry to do what you wanted . . . congratulations. You could have been something great and you had a lot of people who needed you. I was one of them and you threw it all out the window.

Norm sent it to a friend of Sommer's. Sommer wrote back to Norm:

Mr. Blum, my friend received the letter and summarized for me.

Here is a response to you. Whether you pass this on to your son or not is on you. I am not allowed to communicate with your son.

If I were given the chance to say anything to your son it would be this.

I love you and I failed you as a friend and as a superior. You are one of the best men I have ever known and I was not worthy to be your friend, and for all you looked up to me, I looked up to you far more.

Getting angry at Sommer was an important step for Alex, but he was still apportioning blame in legally unproductive ways. What changed that was reading Kathleen Taylor's *Brainwashing*. Suddenly there was a word for the enormous gulf of incomprehension that Alex had felt for so long between himself and everyone else. Suddenly there was a way to explain his involvement in the robbery to Amanda, Jeff, and his family without trying to convince them that Sommer had deceived him or lapsing into haughty lectures on what made Rangers so different. In the first shock of discovery, he fixated on "brainwashing" with a certain excess of enthusiasm. He now seemed to think that having been brainwashed explained not just his inability to say no to a Ranger superior like Sommer but all other unpleasant behavior since his enlistment. He spent a feverish month writing *Breaking Point*, the account of his training that would electrify me when I read it at my lab in Seattle.

For Norm, this was no less than a deliverance. Now that Alex saw once and for all that the Rangers did not have his back, he and Norm could finally be angry together. But for Amanda, relief at Alex's progress was tempered by her innate scientific skepticism. She saw this epiphany as merely another stage in a complex psychological process that had been ongoing for months. "Brainwashing" might have wrapped everything up in a tidy little package for Alex and Norm, but in the eyes of many Americans—and, more importantly, of U.S. criminal law—it had about as much credibility as alien abduction, demonic possession, and golems.

As Taylor's book tells it, the term was first introduced to the West by the journalist and undercover CIA operative Edward Hunter in his sensational, propagandistic 1951 book *Brain-washing in Red China*, which purported to explain why some American veterans of the Korean War who had spent time in Chinese prison camps refused even after liberation to give up the Communist principles they had been forced there to adopt.

Taylor's *Brainwashing* is both a readable introduction to a very complex topic and an impressive work of scholarship, diligent and measured. It was shortlisted for the 2005 Mind Book of the Year Award. Though offering strong empirical support for the psychological phenomena that underlie the techniques of coercive persuasion practiced in the last century by cults and totalitarian regimes, Dr. Taylor argues that the brainwashing concept tends to emerge in pop culture in response to "events which seem to admit of no other explanation: a last-resort concept, a veil drawn over one of the many gaps in our understanding of ourselves." She likens it to a secularized version of demonic possession.

It has not always been so ill-regarded. After the conclusion of the Korean War in 1953, there was broad public sympathy for the American prisoners of war who espoused Communist ideals after undergoing "thought reform" in Chinese camps. The authoritative text on Korean War–era brainwashing is *Thought Reform and the Psychology of Totalism*, by the Harvard psychiatrist Robert Jay Lifton, who built detailed case histories of forty people who underwent it. Lifton documented with exacting compassion the painful stages of identity breakdown and reconstruction that he saw in common among his subjects, distilling the conditions they encountered in their various camps, discussion groups, and hospitals into eight "totalist themes": milieu control, loading the language, demand for purity, confession, mystical manipulation, doctrine over person, sacred science, and dispensing of existence.

It was one of Lifton's students, Margaret Singer, who pioneered the application of his theory to the many cultic groups that began springing up in America during the widespread social unrest of the 1960s and 1970s. As her study of social influence in the United States brought her into increasing contact with the distraught families of children who had joined cults, she began to notice that certain charismatic leaders were using techniques to recruit and retain new followers that bore striking resemblances to those pioneered by the Communist Chinese.

At first both public and academic sympathies were very much on Singer's side. Thousands of middle-class parents saw their sons and daughters pay their life savings to Hari Krishna, the Church of Scientology, or the "Moonies" for lives of destitution, isolation, and servitude. The tide began to turn in the 1980s as cults opened themselves up to certain sympathetic academics, whose research they subsidized through cult-sponsored conferences and other perks. Cult-friendly academics began referring to cults with the value-neutral phrase "new religious movement," or NRM, which soon became the accepted term as the cult-friendly position took over as the mainstream one. By the millennium it was so entrenched that when the Rutgers sociologist Benjamin Zablocki called in 1997 for a reinvestigation of whether cults in fact used coercive indoctrination techniques, it was received as a radical polemic from the fringe.

The legal attack on Singer's stance began with a 1980 fraud and emotional-distress suit filed by former Moonies against the Unification Church. Cult-friendly academics fought Singer's participation in the lawsuit by lobbying various professional organizations, including the American Psychological Association and the American Sociological Association, to take the unprecedented step of signing an amicus brief to the court declaring "brainwashing" to be an illegitimate scientific concept with inadequate empirical grounding. Both the APA and the ASA agreed at first, but eventually withdrew their signatures after protest from their members. The Unification Church finally settled out of court, an apparent victory for Singer, but the specter of scientific controversy over brainwashing stuck—the legal standard at the time called for scientific consensus before expert testimony could be ruled admissible, and that consensus was no longer secure.

The final blow was dealt in the 1993 trial of Steven Fishman, a former Scientologist who claimed that the church had forced him to file a series of fraudulent claims under various class-action settlements. The judge ruled Singer's testimony inadmissible, citing the controversy over brainwashing, a precedent that made it hard for Singer or other "anticultists" to intervene again in criminal law. Singer lived out her days hectored by cult operatives who tapped her phones, stalked her in airports, and left threatening messages on her doorstep.

———

The case that springs immediately to mind for any lawyer who hears about Alex is the bank robbery trial of Patty Hearst.

Hearst, a wealthy heiress, was kidnapped in 1974 by the Symbionese Liberation Army, a radical cultic group. Four months later she appeared on security-camera footage brandishing an AK-47 in a series of SLA-led bank robberies. Because no criminal defense that remotely approached this situation existed, Hearst's defense attorneys attempted to argue that she had committed her crimes under "duress." Margaret Singer testified on Hearst's behalf that extreme isolation and deprivation had induced unnatural sympathy for her captors, the so-called Stockholm syndrome (though the phrase was not used at her trial). Hearst garnered such broad public sympathy that President Jimmy Carter later commuted her sentence, but a successful duress defense would have required proving that she had acted under imminent threat to her life; she was found guilty.

Thirty-five years later, despite occasional clamoring from legal scholars, there was still no accepted brainwashing defense in American criminal law. But unlike Patty Hearst, Alex was not pleading innocent. He would accept legal responsibility for his part in the robbery. Amanda had a hunch that the court might be ready to hear an argument for leniency in sentencing rooted in coercive social influence.

Sommer would not be the focus. It wasn't as if Norm and Amanda took everything Sommer had told them about Alex at face value, but there seems little question that Sommer's "harsh reality check" email and comments to David Bowermaster helped reframe their understanding: after his flat denial of having manipulated Alex, he began to occupy a smaller place in their explanations of Alex's involvement. Instead of an active deceiver, he became a dark abstraction, a "bad apple" in a hierarchy that Alex respected and to whom he subsumed his own will. The real focus of the defense would be the psychological effect of Ranger training. Jeff and Amanda needed to show that Alex had lacked free will. For that they would need expert witnesses.

Norm made the first approach to Kathleen Taylor. She declined, arguing that having Luke Elliott Sommer tested for psychopathy might be a more fruitful approach, but suggested that if Norm was set on the indoctrination argument, he should get in touch with a certain American psychologist whom he had never heard of. Norm duly copied and pasted the opening letter he had written to Taylor, changed some proper nouns, and sent it to the email address that she had given him. On receiving a sympathetic but skeptical response from the psychologist in question—Dr. Philip Zimbardo, professor emeritus of psychology at Stanford University—he handed the reins to Amanda.

Amanda, astonished, was happy to take them: Zimbardo was perhaps the most decorated research psychologist in America. In the 1971 Stanford prison experiment that had made him famous, volunteer subjects had been assigned to prisoner and guard roles at the flip of a coin. Guards sank so deeply into their roles that they began abusing prisoners almost immediately. Amanda thought it seemed possible to link this result to Alex's case. And Zimbardo had intervened in criminal cases before, most notably on behalf of Chip Frederick, ranking noncommissioned officer on the night shift at Abu Ghraib.

At first Zimbardo told Amanda that he was too ill to help, and besides, the case was hopeless, a rehash of the Patty Hearst case. Amanda wrote back explaining all the ways in which Alex was different from Patty Hearst—principally, in accepting responsibility for the crime—and then laid on the guilt trip with a trowel: "Alex is going to cry, I kid you not, when I tell him you've turned him down." Finally Zimbardo's armor showed a chink: "What is your best-case scenario? I'm out of the hospital."

She was thrilled. This was the first stroke of good fortune she had had in a while. Then she managed to secure another expert opinion from Thomas Blass, the leading authority on the work of Stanley Milgram. Milgram's famous experiments on the willingness of ordinary people to deliver painful electric shocks to strangers had laid the groundwork for Zimbardo's own. It was beginning to look like Alex might have a chance.

———

For all its therapeutic importance, Alex's new understanding of his training as brainwashing marked a disorienting upheaval in his sense of himself. The extraordinarily painful trials he had overcome on the way to Ranger Battalion had not made him a hero; they had made him a patsy. The U.S. Army had used and abused him. Not one of the brother Rangers that he had been pining for so much in prison had made any effort to contact him. In fact, Amanda discovered that after his arrest, they had gone into his barracks room and stolen most of his stuff.

Alex wrote the final page of *Breaking Point*, gave the stack to his father to type up and send around to the family, and went into an immediate emotional tailspin. For the first time since elementary school, the daily regimen of push-ups and sit-ups that formed the core of his routine began to fall apart. His phone calls with his girlfriend filled up with heavy silences. Anna was leaving him.

CHAPTER 14

JUST AN INEXPLICABLE EVENT

A year into Alex's detention, Norm reached the point of crisis. His son was sinking further and further into depression, and Norm himself was running out of money.

"Hi Amanda," he wrote in September 2007. "I imagine it was not too hard for you to feel Alex's complete exasperation, anxiousness and anger during your meeting. He is so frustrated; since in his mind he is completely innocent and such an obvious victim of Sommer. It took me a full hour to calm him down so that we could have a useful visit today . . . It is becoming more obvious to me with each visit how critical it is to get him out of there now!"

The plan Norm proposed was to get Alex out on bail right away, then to try to persuade Judge Burgess not to give him any more time at sentencing. Amanda and Jeff were skeptical.

"What they were asking for was, from our objective perspectives, unattainable," Amanda told me. "Absolutely unattainable. Jeff was like, 'There's no way. It's a fucking armed bank robbery. They had assault weapons. Nobody's going to let him out.'" Jeff finally agreed to Norm's request, but his doubts did not disappear.

"Jeff still didn't believe in it. He was like, 'It's going to be a fucking disaster. He's gonna have to go back in and it's gonna be heartbreaking. He'll be set back so far. It'd be better if he just stayed in.' And then Norm would yell at me and I'd go back to Jeff and say, 'No. They want him out.'"

The challenges were many. Chad Palmer, the Ranger private who had counted out time in the bank, had shocked everyone by pleading guilty and accepting the government's suggested sentence of eleven years. Against this baseline, how could Alex hope for much less?

To get Alex released on bail over the government's objections, Jeff and Amanda had to file a motion for conditional release. I drove down for the hearing from Seattle. After I took my seat with Norm in the back of the courtroom, federal marshals ushered in what appeared to be a used-car salesman in his forties, fish pale, balding, and fat, with stringy hair halfway down his neck. It took me a few long seconds to realize that this was Alex. Because federal detention centers are designed as temporary waystations, they are not required to make provisions for exercise or recreation. Alex had not been outdoors since his transfer from San Bernardino.

Bail was granted. Norm paid with a lien on his house.

———

For the next year and a half, Alex lived in Norm's basement with an electronic monitoring band around his ankle, copying recipes from cooking shows he watched with Carly and finding work wherever he could. After a byzantine series of delays, setbacks, and false hopes, his sentence hearing was finally scheduled for March 6, 2009. Despite Jeff's doubts, Amanda was still pressing him to ask for time served.

From all around the country, we made plans to fly to Tacoma: Norm's siblings Al, Kurt, Fred, and Judy, each with spouse and children; our grandmother Beverly from Colorado and her brother Bernard from San Angelo, Texas, whose army stories had entranced Alex as a boy; seven of Bernard's brood that Alex was close to, spanning three generations; Alex's entire immediate family; about a half dozen other friends and supporters. The total came to forty people. My brother and sister were flying in from California. Another sister was driving down from Seattle. I myself had a ticket from New York, where I had recently begun teaching workshops for my creative writing fellowship. It would be nine more months before Alex and I officially began collaborating on our book project at the Denver bar the day after Christmas, but I already had it in the back of my mind.

After we had all made our arrangements, the hearing was abruptly postponed until March 13. Much of the family, including most of the Texas side, held nonrefundable tickets and couldn't afford to buy new ones or had other obligations they could not avoid. The rest of us rearranged our schedules as best we could. On the afternoon of Thursday, March 12, an inverse starburst of eighteen Blums and Blum affiliates began crossing the continent at 30,000 feet.

Then, with most flights still in the air, Amanda and Jeff received word that Judge Burgess had fallen ill and would not be able to hold the hearing after all.

Our grandmother Oma, Norm's beloved sister Judy, and her son Ryan landed, heard the latest, found a flight back to Colorado, and departed within the hour. But by the time my own flight landed there had already been another shocking update: the hearing would proceed as scheduled, at nine o'clock the next morning, with a different judge.

For two years Jeff and Amanda had been sending material to Judge Burgess. He had sentenced Luke Elliott Sommer and was intimately familiar with the case. Now Alex's fate rested in the hands of someone we had never heard of, Judge Robert J. Bryan, who had recently sentenced Nathan Dunmall to ten years. He would have only a single night to read the sentencing arguments from the government and Alex's defense team, the expert opinions from Dr. Zimbardo and Dr. Blass, the letters of support from all of us Blums, and the voluminous evidence from the case.

———

I stayed with friends in Seattle and drove down on the morning of the thirteenth in a borrowed car. My mother and her partner, Ozi, met me at the courthouse steps. We walked in together under the great dome with its dangling cluster of Dale Chihuly glass, passed through the metal detectors, and found the court case printed on a placard of others scheduled for the day: *U.S.A. v. Blum*. Amanda escorted us up a narrow flight of stairs to the landing outside the assigned courtroom, where we found Alex with Norm, Sam, Carly, and what remained of the family.

Though Alex was the principal player, we all knew this was Norm's show. My uncle gave me a distracted hug before moving on to the others. Alex shot me a tight smile. The doughy, vulnerable kid who had taken me by surprise a year and a half before was no longer in evidence. He was almost back to his military physique, trim and muscular in slacks and a blue dress shirt with a *V* of blond hair shaved close to his forehead.

He nodded toward my shoes, a beat-up pair of leather slip-ons that were the nicest I owned. "*Those* are what you wear to my sentencing?" he asked.

I smiled back uncomfortably. The doors to the courtroom swung open. We filed into the wooden benches.

———

"This is United States versus Alex Blum, Number 06-5528," said Judge Bryan from his elevated position at the center of the room.

The government was represented by Mike Dion and John Doty from the district attorney's office, both in dark suits. Judge Bryan reviewed with them the sentences received by previous defendants he had not sentenced himself: twenty-four years for Luke Elliott Sommer, twelve and a half years for Tigra Robertson, eleven years for Chad Palmer, and only a few days of pretrial detention for Richard Olinger, the Ranger friend of Sommer's who had given him the use of his truck and storage shed, whom the government had been unable to prove knew about the bank robbery in advance.

Doty stood to ask for a sentence of four and a half years. "The government's recommendation of fifty-four months generously takes into account the mitigating factors that are present in this case," he said, "including, as mentioned, the defendant's lack of criminal history, his ultimate acceptance of responsibility, and so on. But it also sends an appropriate message, Your Honor, that these people who are trained by armed services to essentially be the best of the best should not receive special treatment after the fact when they so egregiously breach their duty, as the defendant and his coconspirators did in this case."

Jeff stood up next. In his mesmerizing voice, a rich baritone with a little nasal pinch at the top like a burr in mahogany, he described everything that made Alex's participation so baffling: his lifelong history of patriotism, community service, respect for neighbors, and care for peers and family. "Why does a young man like that end up driving his own car in broad daylight to transport four people to a bank robbery? Your Honor, don't we have a responsibility to at least try to answer that question with the truth if what we are here about is to impose a sentence that actually equates to justice?"

I listened with increasing puzzlement to the answer Jeff proceeded to sketch out. For all his eloquence, he was not telling the most important part of the story: that Alex had done it because he *hadn't known the bank robbery was real*. Was Jeff just saving this for the end? Instead he began belaboring the point that Alex accepted responsibility.

"He accepted responsibility on the day he was arrested when he talked to the officials and told them of his involvement. He accepted responsibility on the day of his initial appearance when, despite substantial evidence that would have justified his release, he refused to allow me to argue for his release primarily because the government told us, 'It would be a lot easier for us to work with your client if he agreed to remain in custody so that we could meet with him to try and figure out this very, very serious crime.' And he has showed acceptance of responsibility in the way he has behaved since his release, a way that has made his family and should make this court proud of the decision to release him pending sentencing."

Jeff called on two speakers: Bill Hemphill, the family friend and former Ranger who had met with Alex in 2005 to advise him about enlisting in the army, and Norm. Finally Judge Bryan asked to hear from Alex himself.

"Thank you, Your Honor," Alex said, taking his place at the podium. "Thank you for being here and taking this on such short notice. First I would like to start by expressing my deepest regrets and sorrow for taking part in a bank robbery."

Even with two years to get used to the idea, these words still sounded to me like no more than another of Alex's jokes. But there was no trace of a joke in his voice.

"I am sorry beyond explanation. It's hard for me to describe how terrible I feel knowing that I took part in such a cowardly event. I accept full responsibility for my part in the robbery and I will never lose sight of the harm and fear it caused those people at the bank that day. My one dream growing up was to serve my country, and even give my life, as a Ranger. I dreamed about living the life of a Ranger and making my family and country proud. I'm constantly reminded that I sacrificed my lifelong dream and a profession I was passionate and proud of. I feel the shame of letting down all of the Rangers of the past and present, from Roger's Rangers in the Revolutionary War to the brave men currently fighting in Afghanistan and Iraq. I failed them and put a terrible mark on the pride and heritage of the lineage of these great warriors."

At this a full sob burst out of Alex, a strange and unfamiliar sound. By the time he got himself under control, most of us were crying too.

"Now when I walk in a bank I can't help but imagine the fear and helplessness of the unsuspecting patrons who were there because they had to be. They were not combatants; they were civilians, the very people I took an oath to fight for and protect, not to terrorize. I do not see this as a case of them being in the wrong place at the wrong time, but as a case of stupidity and a cowardly act on our part that put them there. I am also very ashamed of letting all of my family and friends down and for putting them through financial hardships and emotional distress. I lost the love of my life because of this and have hurt her beyond any repair. I'm fortunate to have the support of all the people that have written to you or tried to come to court today and many more back home. I want to thank each and every one of you guys for believing in me. And I apologize for disappointing all of them, and I will never let you down again."

Alex bowed his head and gripped the lectern.

"Excuse me, Your Honor," he said. "I'm sorry." He swallowed several times and went on. "I have been and will continue to be a law-abiding citizen just like I was the day before this happened and every day after. I know you have a hard choice ahead of you, Your Honor, and I want you to know I will serve any time or any sentence you give me in this matter with honor and I'm ready for it. All I can ask is that you understand what my lawyers and others have presented to you and also believe me when I say that my participation in this terrible event does not represent who I am. I hope in my actions over time going forward from this I will demonstrate to everyone who is affected by my conduct that I sincerely regret it. Thank you, Your Honor."

"Thank you, Mr. Blum," said Judge Bryan.

There was some debate between Jeff and Mike Dion about leeway in the sentencing guidelines. Judge Bryan asked for some time to think things over. Finally he indicated that he was ready to address the court.

"This is very interesting from a legal standpoint," he said, "a very interesting question, because the laws direct that courts consider the offender and the offense when you go to sentence someone. 18 United States Code, Section 3553, says that the court shall consider the nature and circumstances of the offense and the history and characteristics of the defendant. If you follow the first part of that, you get to one answer in this case; if you follow the second part, you get to a separate answer, and it's hard to put those two things together.

"I found it interesting reading Dr. Zimbardo's report. It was interesting, I guess, to a judge who's been sentencing felons for just a few months short of forty years, to have a psychologist tell me how I ought to do my job."

Something close to a gasp of horror arose from the Blums. Judge Bryan cited a few lines from Zimbardo's report in support of the opinion that Zimbardo's call to take situational factors into account was little more than a restatement of 18 United States Code, Section 3553.

"Now, as to the offense," Judge Bryan said, "this is a most serious crime. It carries with it a maximum of life in prison. If somebody had pulled a trigger during that robbery, you might be looking at life in prison, Mr. Blum. Congress determined that it was a serious enough offense that it should be a minimum of seven years."

Judge Bryan opined that all the various numbers under consideration—seven years, as mandated by federal sentencing guidelines before the motion for downward departure; six years, as recommended by the probation officer; four and a half years, as recommended by the government—would be reasonable, given the seriousness of the offense.

"Now, that's half of the consideration," he continued. "It's a very serious crime. The other half is to look at the offender, the history and characteristics of Mr. Blum. Your uncle Fred—I guess he's here. Uncle Fred says, if I can quote from his letter, 'Alex is not a criminal.' Well, on the seventh of August of 2006, Alex was very much a criminal. I've said before that we have two kinds of offenders that come through here. One is good people that do bad things, and the other kind are bad people that do bad things. It appears from all of

the showing made that you are basically a good person who did a very
bad thing."

Judge Bryan was not done. He mulled about Nazi Germany. He
mulled about the Kate Winslet film *The Reader*. He mulled about
soldiers going "off the deep end."

"Now, that's kind of a philosophical or psychological background
for this," he said, "but what is really important here is determining the history and nature of Mr. Blum. The entire life that he has
spent before this and after this has been entirely commendable, a life
devoted to public service and a life that was crime-free. So when we
look at the history and characteristics of Mr. Blum, we see that you
come to a very different answer than if you look at the nature and
characteristics of the offense. One calls for a high sentence, one calls
for a low sentence, and that's what I have to resolve here."

Judge Bryan was still not done. He mulled about the four purposes a prison sentence is meant to fulfill: retribution for society,
enrichment of the criminal's character, deterrence of others from
committing similar crimes, and protection of the public from further
crimes by the defendant. He concluded that only the first of these
purposes would be served by giving Alex a long prison sentence.

I looked around at my family weeping quietly in our hard wooden
seats.

"Well, here's what I come down with," Judge Bryan said finally.
"I'm sorry to make you listen to me so long before I get to the bottom line. I think I should sentence Mr. Blum to hard time of sixteen
months with credit for time served."

As Judge Bryan carried on with a whole series of technical rid-
ers and additions—eight months of home arrest, five years of probation, restitution of whatever stolen funds were not recovered, two
hundred hours of community service—we all whipped our heads
around at one another in confusion. Hadn't Alex *already* served sixteen months?

"You will be subject to electronic monitoring to be sure you're
not cheating on the home detention business, but you will be able
to continue to work and go to school and do community service
and those things, though your other freedoms will be substantially
restricted. I guess that's about all I have to say about this. It's just an
inexplicable event that you participated in. What you need to know

is that if you make good on all these requirements that are going to be placed on you, you can go ahead with your life and put this behind you, and I hope you will."

We all collapsed, sobbing with relief. Uncle Fred reached forward across the space between benches and grasped Norm's shoulders, banging the limp body of his youngest brother again and again into the wood.

———

That night we went out as a family to a seafood restaurant in Seattle to celebrate. Fresh bread steamed in baskets all down the table. Fish came on white platters. Lamplight gleamed in scattered constellations off the brass fixtures. Norm raised his wineglass to Jeff and Amanda.

"You guys did above average," he said.

Everyone laughed, clinked their glasses together.

Alex made the rounds as we ate, squatting beside each of us in turn to say hello. Though Norm put on a good approximation of his old self, grinning and backslapping and chatting about all those banal family details that suddenly seemed relevant again, every once in a while I would catch him glancing at his second son with a look of startled wonder on his face, as if he had just seen Alex knocked down by an onrushing semi only to get up with a shrug on the other side.

I too kept glancing at Alex. On our way out of the Tacoma court-house a few hours earlier, he had backed through the doors with his hands held behind him in a pantomime of the handcuffs in which he had once entered it, calling a sardonic goodbye into the echoing dome. The gesture had left a strange taste in my mouth. Still, I could understand Alex's pique—his lawyer had just won his freedom with an account of his involvement that we Blums all felt to be a profound misrepresentation.

"Who is this hack?" my father remembers thinking as Jeff's rich baritone ascended in preacherly cadences through the courtroom. "Why isn't he just explaining it like Norm does?"

I think most of us Blums in those rows of wooden benches must have wondered something similar. I know I did. A fizz of puzzled rationalization filled the gap between my limited understanding of Alex's story and the story Jeff Robinson told. But when Alex stood up at the podium to perform the guilt that legal expediency seemed to require him to perform, when he told the judge he took full responsibility for his participation in the robbery and broke down crying at the podium—how to say it? His performance shocked me with its failure to be fake. Amid the overwhelming courtroomness of the courtroom, with its grave hardwoods and federal seal and dispassionate judge in robes beneath the gold-fringed American flag, I watched Norm's head stiffen on his neck, Sam's bony shoulders convulse in a harrowing sob, Carly's hands fly up to cover her face, and found that hot tears were streaming down my own cheeks. Later we would find explanations for this mass outburst, safe ones that erased the awful realness of that moment, but there had been no room in us for explanation at the time. We wept with our guilty son, cried out from our very souls for his absolution.

At my first meeting with Amanda, she was adamant that there really was a period when Alex was delusional in prison.

"It was right in the very beginning," she said, "when he was still like, 'I'm part of the Rangers. You're part of the outside.' That was partially why I didn't want to do that first proffer meeting with the government. He was still saying these things that exhibited an unawareness of what was happening to him. And then it cropped up again just for a brief period of time a month or two in. It was kind of crazy. I was like, 'What the fuck are you talking about, Alex? I thought we'd got through that already.'"

I asked her if she still had her notes from that first meeting with Alex—the one where she remembered him asking about an AAR, or after-action review. She told me they were in storage, though she still had an electronic copy of the memo she had written up from them for Jeff. She printed it out for me to read alongside her.

Alex explained that in the Rangers, a private such as him takes orders from anyone of superior rank. So even though Sommers [sic] was not currently his CO, it was all the same. I asked why he could not have gone to another superior officer and report what Sommers was directing him to do. Alex said he thought about it.

He said Sommers would have denied it or said he was just fucking with Alex, and Alex's reputation would have been destroyed. No one would have believed him over Sommers. So he knew that wasn't an option. He didn't think there was any other option.

There was not a single sign in this memo of Alex asking about an AAR, believing the military would come to his defense, or failing in any other way to grasp that the robbery was real.

> Alex is incredibly remorseful. All he has ever wanted to do is be a Ranger. At one time he thought about the Navy seals [sic], but he decided, after looking into both, that being a Ranger was really the thing for him. He really believes in it. I asked him what he believed was going to happen to his military career as a result of this, and he said "dishonorable discharge."

I watched Amanda's eyes scan back and forth, her head tilted back so she could look down her nose through her glasses. It was hard to imagine what was going on in her head. How was it possible to reconcile the distraught prisoner who still occasionally argued that the crime must have been a training exercise months into his imprisonment with the remorseful, self-aware young man in this memo?

"Huh," she said finally. "I'm very surprised to see this." She looked out the window for a moment at the sun glinting off all the skyscrapers. "One thing I have to say," she went on, "is when I type notes, I'm somewhat strategic. I do intentionally leave certain things out, out of concern for what might happen if the file had to be produced to another lawyer or something like that. I'll want to see my handwritten notes to see if there's anything about—because I *distinctly* remember him asking about an after-action report. I had never heard the term."

The next morning she sent me an email.

> Just talking about the case yesterday threw me off balance for the rest of the day. It was emotionally difficult at times to represent Alex. Talking about it brought it all back to the surface.

A week after that, when her handwritten notes came back from storage, there proved to be no trace in them of Alex asking about an AAR.

Why had Amanda failed to record the incident? Because it was irrelevant to Alex's case? Because it was too bizarre to place, its meaning apparent only after the fact? Or because Alex's question about the AAR was no more than a figment of collective imagination, remembered back into that meeting as confirmation of the story that Amanda, Norm, and Alex all came to believe?

CHAPTER 15

THE COMPLEXITIES

From the start it was clear that Alex's story was a little myopic, slanted away from certain touchy details, but for a long time I felt nothing but compassion for his painful efforts to come to terms with what had happened to him. It was only when I encountered Sommer's "harsh reality check" email that the possibility occurred to me that Alex was lying to us all.

> You honestly believe that your son, who you have known for his entire life, never dreamed of being involved in this? He helped me plan it Norm.

By the time I read these words, Alex and I had already spent six months talking about the robbery, after which I spent weeks drafting a first chapter of our book, proudly emailing it to him in May 2010. "Nailed it," he wrote back, then immediately forwarded the draft to Norm, who in turn forwarded it to numerous extended family members, many of whom soon got in touch to tell me what a wonderful thing I was doing for Alex. I was startled and flattered. It made me uncomfortable to have such a rough draft so widely distributed, but its reception was so much warmer and more comprehending than any I had met with for my past scientific work. A family, it seemed, was as much a web of shared myths as of shared DNA. Uncle Fred selling half the mountain town of Frisco on a shipment of marijuana that sank in the Gulf of Mexico, Uncle Kurt buying Ernest Hemingway's old sailboat in Key West, Uncle Norm moving from New York to Colorado on his bicycle one snowy November—these were the stories that the Blum brothers had been weaving through the hearts of their families for years, uniting us across the country as a clan. And now I was weaving myself in too, with the thrilling tale of a heroic soldier duped into robbing a bank and the ex-prodigy cousin using science to clear his name.

It was that tender new connection to Blumhood that wrenched in shock with the impact of Sommer's words. I sat for a while in the dark of my mother's spare bedroom trying to control my breathing, then spent the next two hours composing a long, careful email to Norm.

Late the next morning, just after my mother, Ozi, and I had finished watching a World Cup soccer match, Norm pulled up outside and bustled into the living room with his usual cheeriness dialed up to a higher pitch than I had ever heard it. He had a few choice words to share with us about international soccer.

"These European guys, they're down on their backs like *turtles* looking for the call!" Norm's eyes scrunched up in mock agony as he swung his head back and forth while he spurted fey European grunts. *"Uuugh! Aaagh! Uuugh!* This guy Duncan Keith on the Chicago Blackhawks gets nine teeth knocked out by a slap shot and he's back on the ice in five *minutes*!"

With a round of chuckles, back slaps, and hugs, Norm followed me outside. We split to either side of his Saab. As soon as we slammed ourselves shut into the leathered silence of the interior, Norm turned to me in his seat with all the enthusiasm fallen off him and a new intensity in its place, stark and almost relieved.

"This is very complicated, Ben," he said, starting up the car.

———

Back when I was a scientist, subjectivity had been a manageable irritant, mere grease on the microscope lens that you wiped off as best you could before getting on with your measurements. This kind was new to me. It was hard to express to Norm just how disturbed I felt to see no possible reconciliation between all the perspectives I now had on Alex's story.

"Listen," Norm said as we pulled away from my mother's house,

"I have all these uncertainties and questions too. I can't tell you how many times I went and visited him and said, 'So you didn't fucking *know* this was a bank robbery?' For months, he was like, 'You can't understand that I couldn't say no. You can't understand that a Ranger leader, a tab, would *never* do this.' "

"He would say things like that explicitly?"

"Yes! Yes!"

"So he was acknowledging—"

Norm glanced over with a startled look. "No," he said, shaking his head.

"—like, 'Okay, this *was* a crime, but I couldn't—' "

"No. No! He said, 'You *never* questioned what was going on.' "

We parked in the driveway of Norm's house in Greenwood Village. This was the same house I used to visit as a kid, white-shuttered and hyper-suburban, but Wells Fargo was now threatening foreclosure and Norm and Laura were in the middle of a messy divorce. Norm's girlfriend, Tami, had recently moved in with her two young children. We took glasses of iced lemonade outside and sat in matching deck chairs in the middle of the sunlit yard, where a toppled planter decayed in the bushes next to the carcass of the rideable mower Alex had driven to his high school graduation years ago.

For the next three days Norm and I threw our heads at the problem of what exactly had been going on in Alex's mind in the hours surrounding the event that broke every natural law of his universe. I still treasure this time as the closest I have ever felt to one of my father's brothers. For the first time in our lives we were not uncle and nephew but two puzzled guys, comparing evidence, swapping theories, joining forces to figure out how best to care for someone we both loved.

The trouble, of course, although I could barely admit it to myself, was that I was beginning to wonder about Norm's mind too.

———

"Alex always sounds so *normal*," I said on that first day. "But then you go back and look at the transcript and you realize he's talking around certain issues. I think it's so important to his sense of himself to have this understanding of his coercion at the hands of Sommer."

"I think you're exactly right," Norm said. "In his own mind he can't allow himself to think that he was complicit. I'm not sure exactly how I feel about it."

Ever since his release, Alex had been living in his old bedroom in Norm's basement. Norm told me about how protective he was of the kitchen knives he had earned by saving coupons from Albertson's, how carefully he chopped ingredients for the gourmet cooking he had taken up as a hobby in his final months in prison, how neatly he kept his clothes all rolled up army-style in the drawers.

"In my mind," Norm said, "however Alex deals with it where he keeps his sanity for me is a good thing."

He told me how painful it had been during Alex's imprisonment to hear people offer their magnanimity, their forgiveness, as if Alex were an ordinary criminal who had willfully done something wrong. Laura's parents said only that they hoped Alex would take the right path from now on.

"My best and closest friends," Norm recalled, "who loved Alex, who coached Alex, who knew him off the ice and adored him, they go, 'God, what was he *thinking?*'"

He clutched his head in agonized disbelief at the memory. This was, in his mind, exactly the wrong question, though of course it was also exactly the one I was asking, albeit in a different tone of voice.

"The amount of humiliation you go through with something like this! Knowing you have to face every one of your friends. Your kid, who's this superstar, or a good kid anyway, who they know and love, and he fucking robs a bank? How do you deal with that for the next year? It's been a long, bumpy road. There were maybe five or six close buddies in my inner circle who I could talk to. But it wasn't until Alex got out that I really explained to them that he had no idea until eight months in that he was screwed. When people tried to understand that, it made an impression on them."

The weather never changed, a long hot breath of blue. Each day, after we wore each other out with questions, I pedaled fifteen miles home to my mother's house on the red Italian racing bike Norm had lent me for the trip, staring down at the rust patch on the top tube where sweat had been dripping off his chin for thirty years.

By the end of day three, Norm and I had developed a term for the stubborn inconsistencies in Alex's story that refused to go away: "the Complexities." There was a measure of relief in this act of linguistic quarantine, as if the window of time surrounding the bank robbery were some kind of narrative Bermuda Triangle, a vortex of interpretive subtleties where any effort at stable meaning was doomed to fail. Still, I was desperate for some model of PFC Blum's mind that would explain it away.

"Let's say there were two parts of his brain," Norm finally offered. "Probably this yin-and-yang tug of war between his different thoughts. One part goes, 'They're really going to rob a fucking bank here and you know this is wrong.' Maybe in his own mind he can't let that one part of his brain be disclosed. He's sort of resisting it. If it exists. Ben, that's as far as I . . . I can't . . . I don't know if we're ever going to get too much more than that."

————

The next time I biked to Norm's house, Alex's little sister, Carly, had just come home from a lifeguard shift at the pool, where she was working hard to save up money for her first semester at the University of Colorado. We sat under the big spreading locust tree in the far corner of the yard and talked about her brother. Carly and Alex had become very close since his release. During his house arrest, when his ankle bracelet kept him inside a tight perimeter, they had lifted weights together in his room and watched a lot of movies. But at the time of his arrest they hadn't really been getting along. Two weeks afterward, Carly had to start as a freshman at his alma mater, Littleton High School, where his name was still well known.

"Was it weird talking to your friends about it?" I asked.

"Oh, I didn't tell anybody," Carly said. "I told everyone that he was away at school or something. It was just too complicated to get into. It's hard for people to understand the details of it, how he really wasn't . . . His involvement in it is really hard to explain to people. It was easier for me just to make up some excuse."

I asked her what her first clue was after the robbery that something was wrong. She told me that at the sushi restaurant where they went out for lunch the day before Alex was arrested, he had flashed a lot of money in front of her and Sam.

I tried not to show how stunned I felt. A few moments later, Norm came out the back door. Carly and I both fell silent as he took a seat beside us in the grass and leaned back with leonine ease, his bare chest flecked with hairs of gray and gold, smiling indulgently at us. After a few minutes, I forced myself to mention what Carly had told me about Alex flashing money around. Norm looked taken aback.

"I didn't know about that," he said. "Carly, is that right?"

Carly repeated a far less committal form of what she had told me, so fragmented with ditziness and self-questioning that I could barely understand her. Norm nodded with pursed lips.

"I heard some of this money banter," he mused. "I don't remember what day, but I remember Alex telling me he had received a bonus for completing RIP. So if there was any talk about money, the way Alex probably explained it was, he had gotten some of his bonus. And, you know, maybe Sommer had told him, 'Here's part of your bonus.' "

"Yeah," Carly said, visibly relieved. "I think that was—"

"What Alex said it was?" Norm finished for her, nodding.

"Yeah."

They both turned to me. I looked back uneasily. The sun was hot on my face. I felt like a scientific instrument programmed for the wrong units, something sensitive and elaborate whose readings were meaningless.

Norm saw my expression and grinned. "There's more complexity for ya," he said.

I grinned back instead of screaming.

On July 3, Alex called me from just south of Castlerock. He had been in Texas for the last week, staying at Great-Uncle Bernie's ranch with his old army buddy Kane.

"Hey, bro," he said, "how's it going? Been having fun with my dad?"

We agreed to meet at a coffee shop my mother had recommended to me the next afternoon.

———

I had picked a coffee shop because I didn't want Norm or anyone else to walk in while Alex and I were hanging out. It had not occurred to me that Alex might never have been inside one before, nor that he might be in particularly rare form on the Fourth of July.

"I'm an *Amurican*," he said, looking at the hand-lettered menu on the chalkboard behind the cash register. "I don't know any of these fancy terrorist drinks."

He was wearing his usual board shorts and sandals. The coffee shop was filled with dramatically lamp-lit wood booths occupied by lone men with iPads and expressions of defiant self-sufficiency. Its name was the Tibetan word for a liminal state of consciousness.

"What's the fanciest thing you guys make?" Alex asked the barista in a belligerent hick accent.

"The Blond Caramel Latte is pretty fancy," she said.

Alex drawled that he would go with that. The barista smiled at him. She was about Alex's age. As far as I knew, he hadn't dated anyone since having his heart broken by Anna.

"So what are you doing for the Fourth?" she asked, tamping down the grounds.

"Nothing much. Probably drinking a fifth of Jack Daniel's alone, wrapped in the American flag. Probably screaming the national anthem a few times."

"Sounds fun."

She first noticed his forearms when she rang us up at the register. "Nice," she said. "What are they?"

The hesitation was microscopic. Alex, doing his best to maintain his casual grin, flipped his arms over to show the dotted line and scissors over his right wrist, the prison barcode on his left. The barista leaned in closer. When she understood what she was looking at, something happened to her face that made me think of a jabbed sea anemone.

"That's the saddest tattoo I've ever seen," she said.

"I think it's hilarious!" said Alex. "Because I'm not actually like that at all. So I think it's a hilarious tattoo!"

She handed him his Blond Caramel Latte, a huge beige drink in a pint glass with whipped cream and chocolate shavings on top. Her professional warmth was almost indistinguishable from the personal warmth she had showed earlier. Alex left her a two-dollar tip. In the back room, he pulled out a printout of the chapter I had emailed him several weeks before. As we flipped through the pages, he put a dip in and spit tobacco juice into a paper cup he had picked up on the way back.

"You got this mostly right," he said. "A few hang-ups on the military terminology, but that's to be expected."

We went through page by page. He had highlighted all the problem spots—little details I had gotten wrong, like which Ranger Battalion was stationed at Fort Lewis, how many of his family members were present at his graduation from RIP, the precise tonal register in which soldiers insulted each other's penises—but as the moment of the crime approached, the highlighting dropped off. At the point where Sommer asked him out of the blue for a ride to the bank, I saw that Alex had highlighted nothing whatsoever.

"So this part was okay?" I asked.

"Yeah," said Alex. "This stuff was all great."

———

It was after our coffee-shop meeting that Alex and I had our conversation on my mother's balcony while watching a storm roll in from the Rockies. It was there, after two beers apiece, that I finally got up the courage to confront him about what Norm and I were calling the Complexities, by means of a fumbling lecture about narrativization, reconstructive memory, and the irreducibility of truth that by the end had him slumped nearly horizontal in his chair, muttering "yeah" and "right" and "okay" and "I hear you" at least two dozen times in five minutes.

"So I guess the question is, was it clear you guys were going to go to the bank?"

"When we were driving there?"

"Yeah."

Alex squinted at me and drank from his beer. "Yeah," he said. "I mean, that was the point of destination."

His face was half in shadow from the brim of his cap, suspended in a stagnant, greenish light from clouds that seemed to bulge with indrawn breath. Somehow he had rendered my question tautological.

"Okay," I said. "So you knew you were going to go to the bank?"

"Yeah."

His eyes were steady on mine. I decided to push it.

"Had there been talk before with Sommer about going to the bank on that day?"

Alex pursed his lips.

"Uh, he brought it up. Yeah, he said, 'I'm gonna have to go here, and this is what's gonna happen, so—'"

"And it was in terms of hitting the bank."

"Yeah. Yeah, yeah—"

It was expanding already in his face, the frustrated fidget that meant I had forced him into a statement whose interpretation by a non-Ranger didn't accurately reflect reality as experienced by a Ranger and which he therefore needed to qualify and explain. And just like that the doubt in me crumpled before his obvious distress. This wasn't feigned. It caused him actual pain to think about this.

"Of course, you're not thinking of this as a robbery," I said.

"*Exactly*," Alex said, relieved that I got it. "He *never* referred to it as a robbery."

Then he was off on how Sommer had used nothing but military terminology and military tactics in planning the robbery in order to keep Alex on board, and how all the same techniques had come into play during the plans for hitting the casino that they formulated before the bank but never went through with, which, incidentally, was one more reason Alex thought the bank plans were just a tab game, which pointed again to just how thorough and effective Sommer had been in his manipulation, and etc., etc., etc. It had always made me a little impatient to hear Alex paint Sommer as some kind of comic-book mastermind. But he wasn't done. He told me about the way Sommer would riff with other tabs in front of him about going up to Canada to kill Hells Angels, all jokey and well within the bounds of standard battalion bravado, then pull Alex aside and tell him they were all relying on him. He told me about how Sommer would intersperse their planning with wild speculation of going into the bank with a helicopter and Humvees, which made the whole thing seem like the tab game Alex thought it was. I was glad at least that Alex had stopped claiming that he was so brainwashed that he had truly thought the robbery was a legitimate mission approved from above. He began to seem uneasy, though, increasingly defensive. The gray-green sky came at us like a landing ship. Raindrops spattered the balcony.

"So you've picked up the Canadians at the bus station the night before. Was there any part of your mind, however small, that was thinking, 'Huh, maybe tomorrow we're actually going to hit the bank'?"

"No," he said. "I wasn't even stressing about it. My main thing was get through the day and then go home and see Anna."

"And at what point do you know for sure you're going to the bank?"

"That afternoon."

"When he comes and asks you for a ride?"

"Yeah."

"He's like, 'I need a ride to the bank.'"

"Yeah."

"Does he say, 'We're going to hit the bank'?"

"No. He just says, 'I need a ride.'"

"To the bank?"

"Yeah."

"Do you—"

"Or you know what, I think he actually phrased it, 'Okay, we're going to go to the bank, and we're going to take care of it.' Like that was probably how he phrased it."

I scrutinized his forcibly nonchalant expression, mouth twitching around the massive bulge of chewing tobacco that pushed out his lower lip and made his whole face a squinting, back-tilted slope.

"'We're going to take care of it,'" I repeated.

How could this possibly be the language of a superior deceiving PFC Blum into thinking this was all a training exercise?

Hours later, long after we had run out of conversation, an occasional muffled thump continued to remind us that it was the Fourth of July. Then our glances swung past each other toward the gushing rivulets webbed across the dark windows as rain plinked into the new acuteness of the silence. We were both drunk. Across the back court-yard, Mom and Ozi had curled up in the den and put on a movie. Cool white patterns shifted across their expressionless faces.

I had already asked Alex about Carly's memory of him flashing money around, about the money Sommer gave him from the rob-bery, about all these things I already knew the answers to, a kind of running in place that went on for hours: *no recollection of that, never thought of the money as mine, held on to it for him and awaited further instruction.* I had half expected all this opening up to bring us closer. Instead it had just made eye contact difficult. Sommer's exclamation marks kept jangling in my head.

!!Warning!! The following is a harsh reality check.

———

A few days later I visited Alex at Big Bear Ice Arena on the decommissioned Lowry Air Force Base. He had opened the facility two hours earlier, but at 6:30 a.m. it was still dark and chilly outside. He showed me around. The warehouse was as high-ceilinged as a hangar, with grids of spotlights overhead in the gloom. From the north rink came the muted cries and bangs of a scrimmage in progress. The lights were still off in the south rink. Alex flipped a bank of switches and they stuttered into harsh fluorescent brilliance as we wandered out into the white. After a tour of the basement den where the Zambonis were parked, we returned to the front desk. Players trickled in over the next hour for the morning's free skate session. Soon we heard their blades on the ice.

I had never seen Alex in a place where he so clearly belonged. He looked so normal here in his baseball cap and plaid pajama pants, so young. As the players signed in, he joked about little details of their lives, asked if they had brought an extra coffee for him. It was clear that everyone liked him, but in the Rangers he had been surrounded by comrades he knew would die to save his life, united in a cause that filled their days like wind driving a sail. Here it was mainly a question of putting in the time and remembering to take customers' needs seriously.

"The captains of the rec teams are always complaining," he confided to me in a down moment. "About the refs, about the schedules. I'm like, for real? You think this is important? It's a recreational league. I mean, I understand, you paid money. But do you have any idea what it sounds like to me when you complain about shit like this?"

I went back a few days later to watch his team of four- and five-year-old Pre-Mites play a tournament game from the glassed-in viewing booth between the two rinks. They had become so dominant in their own age division that this time Alex had signed them up to play against seven- and eight-year-olds. It wasn't pretty. Alex's players looked like chihuahua puppies yipping at the heels of Labrador puppies who lacked the fine motor control to avoid stepping on them. The crowd in the viewing booth gasped every time one went down. When his players skated in for line changes, Alex picked them up one by one from the ice and set them in their assigned places on the bench, squatting in front of each to squirt water into his mouth with a squeeze bottle through the grille of his enormous helmet. One after another nodded in response to whatever he was asking. He gave them a familiar slap on the top of the head.

Around me a knot of parents were arguing.

"They're getting crushed out there," protested a middle-aged father.

"Alex says they learn faster this way," said a young mother with a Russian accent. "It's better they don't always win."

––––––

Alex's brother Sam arrived from L.A. for a short visit. I drove over to find him wearing jean shorts and high-top Chuck Taylors, his hair as swoopy as ever. Norm and Tami were puttering around the kitchen. Alex was not home. Sam made no bones about his disappointment.

"I'm only going to be in town for two days and Alex is nowhere to hang out with me," he said. "If he's got nothing better to do, he'll hang out. But if anything's going on, I won't hear from him."

I felt for Sam, but I knew how confounding it was for Alex when Sam asked him for a closer relationship. Guys like Alex got close like pit bulls do, by stopping just short of snapping the other guy's neck. Guys like Sam got close by hugging it out. I followed him into the living room, closed the glass doors to the kitchen behind us, and asked what life was like after Alex's arrest.

"I didn't know how to talk about it," Sam said, shrugging. "And no one really knew how to talk to me about it. Basically I lost most of my friends. It was just impossibly hard to live the life that we had previous to that day. Everyone at school knew. Carly was a freshman. We were the brother and sister whose older brother robbed a bank and was in jail."

Sam's best friend at the time was the younger brother of Alex's best friend, Andrew. They stopped hanging out.

"Whenever I went over to their house, Alex was all anyone wanted to talk about. Everyone had their own opinion on the subject. No matter what you said, you could just feel them judging you, and at the time I was too fragile to be judged like that. My mom, she wouldn't talk about Alex being in prison. She said he was in camp. She said it was a luxury paradise camp. It was so obvious, in my view, that she wasn't on his side. The way my grandparents talked about the subject to her was, 'Your son is a felon.' She wouldn't leave the house. She went a little crazy because she didn't have anyone to talk to."

———

I look back on what happened next as one of those rare pivots around which everything changes, subtly and forever. It began when, in describing the conversations I had been having with Alex and Norm about the robbery, I found the phrase "party line" coming out of my mouth, as if from another dimension. Sam had never heard it before. I had to define it for him.

"So where would you say you fall in all that?" I asked, already regretting having framed it this way.

"I don't quite understand what you mean," Sam said carefully.

Through the glass doors, Norm and Tami were visible, eating chips at the butcher block. A few seconds passed as Sam took my measure from across the coffee table.

"Well," he said finally, "I think the thing that stands out most to me is how I told the story to people. When I told Alex's story, I told the truth about what I knew about it, which is basically the first chapter of your book, except—you know how he was new to driving manual? So I told the story like when they got out of the car and took the guns out of the trunk, Alex stalled his car. Because why the fuck couldn't he have gotten away? You know? They were in and out of the bank in, what, two minutes? That's plenty of time to leave the bank. So I told people he stalled his car and kept stalling it. Then the other part was I never said that he left Tacoma with money. It's like, 'Why the fuck would you take that money, Alex?'"

"So there were bits that didn't quite make sense to you, and you kind of filled them in to have the whole thing make sense?"

"I filled them in to make Alex . . ." Sam scrunched up his face in thought. "As innocent as I wanted him to be."

At that unnerving word "innocent," whose opposite was never far behind, my eyes flicked involuntarily to Norm and Tami.

"I've never asked Alex about it," Sam said.

For a moment, I caught a glimpse of how Alex must have been for Sam: every year harder, every year further away.

"Part of the complexity here," I tried to explain, "is that I think, fundamentally, Alex had no reason to do this thing and would never have done this thing if it had been his own—well, say it."

"Well," said Sam, "this doesn't sway my judgment at all, or change what I think happened, but when you look back on his relationship with Sommer—I know what it's like when your hero wants you to know something that not everyone else knows about. Even if it was just the *idea* of a bank robbery, even if Alex was just going along with it for the fun of it, somewhere in the back of his head it had to be such an honor that Sommer wanted him involved. If Sommer never brought it up to Alex, then totally—the story makes sense. But if Sommer ever said, 'Hey, we could get a lot of money, would you be interested in doing this . . .' It sounds like Sommer is really good at pitching stuff. If he got all those guys to rob the bank with him, hell, why wouldn't Alex? And then Alex did it and he took the money. You know? It's perfect. I mean, I don't want to believe that, and that's *not* what I believe, but when I look back on it now, it's like, 'Alex, what's going on in your head in those two minutes when they were in the bank?' Because that's a long time."

"That *is* a long time," I admitted.

"That's a long time to be, like—you're interrupting our interview."

Puzzled, I followed Sam's eyes to see the man we had been talking about taking a seat in the armchair in the corner, crossing his thick, tattooed forearms over his chest. He had come out of Norm's darkened office. There was no telling how long he had been in there.

"Red light is on," I said, pointing to the recorder, where a small LED indicated a recording in progress.

"I don't care," Alex said. "This is my interview."

In the second of silence that followed that flat proclamation, something strange rippled through the fabric of this room I had been passing in and out of all my life.

"This is the golden stuff right now that no one else is saying," Sam said, his voice going pinched and hysterical in an effort to make this sound like a joke.

I forced a grin into my voice. "Oh man," I said. "We're getting emotional, Alex."

His body shifted in his seat. "I know how much you love *that*," he said to Sam, then got up and walked through the door to the basement stairs. On the sofa, Sam looked stunned, his left sneaker frozen atop his right knee in a parody of relaxed composure.

"That was *movie* timing," he whispered.

Alex emerged again and sprawled in the armchair, one leg swinging over the arm.

"Alex, *you can't come in here right now*," said Sam.

"Just continue with the interview," he said.

The impasse went on. I couldn't think of anything I might say that would stop it. Finally Alex got up again and walked into the office. Seconds later he appeared in the kitchen, joining Norm and Tami at the butcher block. Sam and I made a few jittery, stilted efforts at proving to each other that we were fine to continue, then went and joined everyone else. Norm popped open a beer for each of us, then spent an hour dragging us through a conversation about the way we all used to play together as kids. Sam took every occasion to bait Alex with barbs of aggressive touchy-feeliness. Alex snapped back with increasingly gruff wariness. Norm produced pained grin after pained grin, telling them both to ease up a little. Tami looked on uncertainly, still parsing the familial codes and trying to figure out how to situate herself. I didn't speak much. Every word I said I had to plan in triplicate, fanning out three meanings for the three Blum men around me whom I had been talking to all week. I began to feel as if we were clinging here by our elbows as the lit wood square of the butcher block slid down the face of some huge, invisible wave, fighting for stakes that no one could acknowledge out loud. Sam and Alex may have appeared to be sniping at each other, but I knew in part they were performing for me, fishing for the raised eyebrow that would confirm our private understanding. Alex wanted to believe

I was just indulging Sam in his emotional bullshit. Sam wanted to believe I was just indulging Alex in his macho bullshit. They were both right, but they were also both wrong. Indulging bullshit, I was beginning to suspect, was the only thing I knew how to do.

"Ben looks pretty beat," Norm said after a while.

I was so grateful I had to hold back tears. "Yeah," I said. "I've got an early flight tomorrow. I better get home."

Alex walked me out to the car. As soon as we were alone together in the driveway, all the tangled allegiances were behind us, locked up behind the fragile squares of light that shone through the windows of the garage door. The night was warm. Juniper hedges rose into the darkness around us.

"Fun time with Sam?" he asked.

"So emotional."

"He's a needy little fucker." Alex chuckled, relaxing visibly.

We stood for a while by the car talking about all the progress we had made this week. Alex told me I should get some rest, that I worked too hard, that he didn't envy me the job I had to do. We shook hands repeatedly, clapped each other on the shoulder. His loneliness was palpable out here.

"Talk to you soon, bro," he said. "Have a safe flight."

We shook hands one last time, pulled it in for the clinch. As I backed my car onto Greenwood Drive, I watched his silhouette recede into the stars, his shorts and bare feet and lifted hand, and then I turned onto Franklin Avenue, where four years before an FBI agent had pointed a gun at the back of Sam's head.

———

Two months later, in September 2010, I was riding to the Seattle bookstore where I had begun working as a clerk when my phone buzzed in my pocket. I straddled my bike, pulled it out, and saw my cousin's face beneath a red baseball cap.

"So, uh, hey," Alex said, "no big deal, but Dr. Z just gave me a call." His star-struck voice suggested that this was a very big deal indeed.

"Dr. Zimbardo? The Stanford prison experiment guy? What about?"

"Ah, you know, nothing much. He, uh, wants me to appear with him on *Dr. Phil*. A special episode he's putting together called 'When Good People Do Bad Things.'"

The taping was at Paramount Pictures in Hollywood, California, in two and a half weeks. The anxious, crabwise dance that Norm, Alex, and I were performing around the truth was about to be staged on national television.

CHAPTER 16

THE PHABULOUS PHILS

There's a certain useful fiction one tells oneself when watching a show like Dr. Phil's: every person onscreen knows exactly what they signed up for. They too have watched their share of American television. They too have chuckled at the vast divide between the genre of "reality" and capital *R* Reality. No one expects a television psychologist to actually solve their problems. Right?

Dr. Phil McGraw used to be a middle linebacker for the University of Tulsa Golden Hurricane. After receiving a Ph.D. in clinical psychology from the University of North Texas, he got his start in show business on *The Oprah Winfrey Show*, where his six-foot-four-inch frame, bald dome, squirrel-tail mustache, baby-blue eyes, and tough-love Texan advice regularly had Oprah leaping out of her chair to cry such things as, "*Oooh*, that's good, Phil! That's a good Phil-*ism!* Somebody write that down!" His own show spun off in 2002. McGraw turned out to be even better at tackling deep clinical pathologies in hour-long time slots than quarterbacks on passing plays. In the episode that aired the week after I learned that Alex would soon be a guest, Brandon, the former drug addict for whom six years before Phil had orchestrated "one of the first interventions on national television," reappeared to help intervene with a new addict, Nick.

"Let's start with you," Dr. Phil said to Nick's mother. "You are an enabler. You got that, right? You have no idea how many thousands of letters we get here. But we chose yours. We chose Nick. And so we come to you, we do this intervention, we provide the rehab for him at what I believe is the *singular best facility in the globe*." Phil held up one beefy forefinger for emphasis as Nick's mother wept and nodded. "And you've been to two meetings in two weeks. You've got no sponsor. What the hell are you doing? What the hell are you thinking? I just have to tell you the truth, 'cause this ain't my first rodeo."

"This ain't my first rodeo" is one of Dr. Phil's favorite catchphrases. He has a lot of catchphrases. It is possible to confuse yourself by thinking too hard about some of them, like "No dog ever peed on a moving car" or "No matter how flat you make a pancake, it's got two sides," but Dr. Phil's favorite catchphrase of all is fantastically simple: "Get real."

I have no doubt this is good advice. Millions of people have found it valuable enough to purchase McGraw's best-selling book, *Dr. Phil Getting Real: Lessons in Life, Marriage, and Family*. But let's imagine, just for the sake of argument, that you are a convicted felon who believes that he was capable of committing armed bank robbery only because he *didn't* think it was real. And let's imagine that Dr. Phil McGraw, a wealthy, famous, six-foot-four-inch former linebacker who happens to be seated two feet away from you on the stage of his very own studio, filmed by the cameramen he employs, edited by the editors he employs, watched by a live audience of hundreds who waited in line to be here because they love and trust and believe him—let's imagine that this imposing figure listens to whatever tiny sliver of your story you can convey in two minutes, cocks a big Texan eyebrow, and tells *you* to "get real." Whose idea of "real" do you think is going to prevail in this interaction?

That is the question I pondered in the week after Alex called me with the news that he was about to be a guest.

———

I called Norm first. He sounded unworried. In fact, he sounded as giddy as a schoolboy. Dr. Phil's stamp of legitimacy, he seemed to think, would finally do the trick of convincing everyone of Alex's innocence.

"It's not some attack show," Norm assured me. "This isn't *Jerry*

Springer, where they bring out the bank manager to tell him what a scumbag he is. Dr. Phil is actually a pretty insightful guy. And Zimbardo will be there to make sure the right message comes through."

I wrote to Amanda next. We had just had our first meeting. I was still waiting to see the handwritten notes from storage where she expected to find some record of Alex asking for an AAR. I told her I thought it would be better for Alex to face a harsh reality check from me in a Hollywood hotel room than from Dr. Phil in front of 3.3 million Americans.

"I just got the boxes of materials from archives today, and I'll go through them sometime tomorrow," she wrote back. "I hope you don't confront Alex in a big way prior to the interview, if it's possible to avoid it. I urge you to think about whether you can caution him to stay away from certain specifics, rather than getting him to back off entirely on whatever version of the truth he believes. This whole thing is going to produce a lot of anxiety and it would be awful if he feels his confidence eroding right now."

A few days later, after I had spent hours at Amanda's office going through three crates of archival papers without finding anything helpful, I called my father.

"It's just—it's very complex," I said after explaining the situation.

"It's very complex," Dad repeated ruminatively. "You know, Ben, I think the human mind is completely capable of holding two contradictory thoughts at the same time . . ."

There followed a fifteen-minute disquisition about this crazy dream we call reality. By the end I was crawling out of my skin. How could he be so blasé about this? I told him that all Norm's explanatory shorthands for translating Alex's bizarre experience into terms other people might be able to understand—"superior giving orders" for the relationship between Specialist Sommer and PFC Blum, "training exercise" for tab game, "brainwashing" for Alex's acculturation into Ranger Battalion, "deluded in prison" for all his fantasizing and rationalizing at SeaTac, "figuring out the bank robbery was real" for accepting that he needed to reconceptualize himself as having known the bank robbery was real—had carried Norm so far away from the facts that I was not sure anyone could say he was telling the truth at all anymore.

Or at least that's what I wish I had told him. In fact I was still so confused at this point—I had only had one day with the archival materials—that all I really managed to articulate was that Norm's and Alex's story appeared to have some serious holes. What if Dr. Phil tried to "get real" with Alex? What if Alex, with his usual prickly defensiveness, pushed back so hard that he ended up implying less involvement than he'd really had?

Instead of answering my concerns, Dad changed the subject. "How's Norm's health?" he asked.

"He seemed pretty energetic when I saw him in Colorado this summer. Why?"

"When did you see him?"

"I saw him in June. Late June, early July."

"July, August, September," Dad counted off to himself. "So yeah, you saw him—yeah, okay. So about four years ago, just before all this happened to Alex, Norm had this flu. I remember vaguely he got more and more tired. More run-down. I was up in Boulder, and so who knows what I was doing, but anyway it turns out that he had a virus in his heart, and by the time he got to the hospital, because he couldn't get out of bed anymore, his heart was eighty-four percent destroyed."

———

The Blum brothers have a complicated relationship to illness, injury, death, and other admissions of weakness. Their father, Al Senior, was so enraged by the sudden-onset Guillain-Barre syndrome that paralyzed him when our grandmother was pregnant with Kurt that he refused to allow her to visit him in the hospital, simply vanishing from family life for the year it took until he could come home walking again. Six months before I was born, he developed stomach pains that he felt sure heralded a further bout of medical incapacitation. Instead of going to the doctor, he committed suicide with saved-up barbiturates.

"Eighty-four percent destroyed," Dad repeated.

His own philosophy on seeking medical attention has been a little different ever since the aching testicle that he sneered at for months in his midforties turned out to be a cancerous tumor.

"The only reason he's alive," Dad went on, "is because he was in such good shape. But part of what happens with myocarditis is it screws up the electrical system so the heart goes out of rhythm. So with his heart already going out of rhythm, Norm decides what he needs to do is go work out. He leaves a message for his cardiologist saying, 'Listen, I'm gonna go work out,' and he goes to the gym, he gets on a stationary bike, and he has a massive heart attack."

Thanks to the extraordinary efforts of a cardiologist who happened to be working out nearby and who revived him with chest compressions, Norm survived after open-heart surgery. But the whole time he was visiting Alex in prison, his heart was going in and out of a two-hundred-beat-per-minute arrhythmia which required an electrical shock treatment called cardioversion to reset. It has recurred ever since. Just after I saw him in Denver, Dad told me, Norm's heart had started into another bout of arrhythmia. He didn't have the money for the cardioversion, so he simply toughed it out. Soon he was so weak he couldn't get out of bed. The only one who knew was his sister. Finally Judy called my father in tears and told him the whole thing. This was the first that Dad or anyone else in the family had heard of Norm's condition.

"His heart was like a fish," Dad said. "You could see it leaping in his chest. He was turning green. You theoretically can't live when your heart beats that fast for two months. I mean, it's ridiculous."

Dad finally convinced Norm to go to the hospital for the cardioversion. When he asked why in four years Norm hadn't told anyone, even his own children, Norm produced one of those dismissive head-jerking *Ehhh* sounds all the brothers use.

"There's nothing they can do," Norm said. "I don't want 'em to worry."

———

I got off the phone in a daze. My entire trip to Colorado rushed back through my head: Norm's mocking pantomime of injured European soccer players, his exasperated account of Alex's theatrics after getting spattered with hot grease in the kitchen, his self-satirizing show of spinning his index finger back and forth in front of a look of mild puzzlement to demonstrate how he himself might react to a chopped-off fingertip. I remembered my aunt Judy talking to me in her backyard about all Norm's biking, hockey, and weightlifting. "If he didn't exercise, I don't think he'd be here," she had told me, smiling oddly. "I mean that." At the time I had thought she was talking about suicide.

Suddenly I felt disgusted with myself. I thought back to that long train of weekends when Norm visited Alex in prison: buttoning his shirt each morning over his fluttering heart in a Marriott hotel room, waiting for hours at SeaTac, seeing his son. Who cared what verb tense they were using? The "deluded in prison" story might not have captured the full complexity of an eight-month psychological progression, but what possibly could? Norm and Alex gave every appearance of believing it sincerely, and shouldn't that be enough for me? This was *U.S.A. v. Blum* all over again, except this time the court was public opinion, the judge was a mustachioed former linebacker from Wichita Falls, Texas, and the jury was millions of Americans whom Norm understood a lot better than I did.

For a whole week I repeated all this to myself while ringing up customers at the bookstore, at times even managing to believe it. Then I talked again to Norm, who told me he had just put Alex through a dress rehearsal in front of a room of his business buddies.

"Ben," Norm said, "it went perfect. Alex was absolutely great. He was very sincere, very open, none of that defensiveness crap. He absolutely took responsibility. His answers were very, very convincing. My buddy Harry goes, 'Now did you *really* think this was a training exercise?' Alex goes, 'For eight months in prison I *still* thought it was a training exercise.' I think that's a very important detail."

———

"Welcome to Los Angeles!" said a cheery voice from the airplane's overhead speakers a few days later. "Where the temperature this afternoon is a record-breaking one hundred and thirteen degrees!"

I made the hour-long trip to the Renaissance Hollywood Hotel & Spa in a taxi with broken air conditioning. Unlikely mansions went by in the hills above the highway, Italian villas and pink Miami beach houses and glassy Scandinavian lodges all snug up against each other, with flower gardens dividing their immaculate lawns. A bus crept up next to us with Phil McGraw's head grinning on the side of it, that same friendly promotional photograph I had begun seeing everywhere: crinkled eyes, sandy mustache, pads of ginger hair above each ear, wedge of in-tilted teeth. Then it drifted away into the dingy understory of duplex apartments and taquerias.

Alex opened the hotel room door a few seconds after my knock wearing bright orange board shorts and an Ultimate Fighting Championship T-shirt with bloody claw marks printed across the chest. We gave each other big hugs. He showed me around the small room, which came compliments of *Dr. Phil*. Through the window I could make out the distant white letters of the HOLLYWOOD sign in the hills above the city.

"Not bad, right?" said Alex.

He poured us a pair of whiskeys. I hurried through the pleasantries, fairly bursting with eagerness to get to work. I had a new weapon in my back pocket: a probabilistic model of PFC Blum's mind drawn from my past training in artificial intelligence that I thought just might be able to reconcile the "Complexities" with my deep sense of Alex's fundamental honesty.

"So," I said, once we had finally settled ourselves on the bed with my laptop. "I have some new ideas."

Two hours later, Alex and I met Norm; his girlfriend, Tami; and Amanda in the hotel lobby bar for a pretaping powwow with Dr. Zimbardo. As we all hugged and caught up, a frail older man hobbled down the grand staircase, relying heavily on a cane. It was impossible to mistake the signature jet-black goatee that has made Zimbardo, as the host of PBS's multipart *Discovering Psychology* series, the "face of contemporary psychology" for thousands of high school and college students in the classes where the series has been screened.

"So this is Alex!" Zimbardo said. "He doesn't look like a bank robber!"

Alex hugged him carefully, beaming. "Hi, Dr. Z!" he said.

It was the first time Zimbardo had met any of us in person. We all shook his hand in turn. He explained that it had been while he was stuck watching daytime television during a recent hospital stay that *Dr. Phil* came on and gave him the idea for this special episode.

On its face, a collaboration between America's two most famous psychologist Phils seemed an unlikely proposition. McGraw's perennial theme was that everyone needed to get real with themselves and take personal responsibility for their problems. Zimbardo had premised his whole career on the claim that things were a lot more complex than that: rather than making choices in a vacuum, individual actors were constrained by a social and political web in which they had surprisingly limited autonomy. This message had so far failed to resonate much with America's deep individualism, but now Zimbardo hoped to convince Dr. Phil's audience that blaming evil deeds on the individuals through which systemic forces work would be a simple mistake of cognition—that abuse was latent in the chain of command at Abu Ghraib and in the tab checks at Ranger Battalion.

Zimbardo listened with real curiosity to Alex, giving him space to talk in his own terms about his story, and then opened up a little about himself, telling us of how his early interest in what led certain kids from the rough streets of the Bronx into gangs and others into productive lives helped inspire his later interest in social psychology. While still a junior professor at NYU in the 1960s, he had led one of the first teach-ins to protest the Vietnam War and organized a walkout of more than two hundred faculty and students when secretary of defense Robert McNamara was awarded an honorary degree. After the conclusion of the Stanford prison experiment, he had become an outspoken advocate for prisoners' rights, testifying at two congressional hearings on prison reform. He had recently launched the Heroic Imagination Project, an educational nonprofit that developed curriculum materials to train young people to speak up for what they knew was right despite social pressure to conform.

Zimbardo told us he had lent his assistance to several other criminal cases over the years that involved defendants who acted under the influence of powerful systemic forces. The first was Johnny Spain, one of the prisoners involved in a San Quentin riot that occurred the day after the Stanford prison experiment was shut down. The second was Larry Layton, a lieutenant of cult leader Jim Jones who was charged with the murder of a visiting congressman at Jonestown in Guyana. The third was Chip Frederick, the ranking noncommissioned officer in charge of the "hard site" at Abu Ghraib prison outside Baghdad at the time of the infamous abuses there, who had only recently been released from the brig with time off for good behavior. Of these, Zimbardo told us that Alex's case was his "only success."

By the end of an hour I was ready to believe that the next day's episode might make some kind of a difference, however small. Maybe it was just Zimbardo's tough Bronx upbringing, but he and Alex were getting along famously. Alex seemed thrilled that all his own efforts at explaining what he had gone through were finally being heard not as self-serving excuses but as evidence for psychological theories which served a higher purpose. He was obviously glad to be able to repay Dr. Z for his help. Norm too seemed more at ease than I had seen him since the robbery. What a relief it must have been to have an adult outside the family believe him about Alex, especially an authority as eminent as this.

"You know," Norm chimed in during a conversational lull, "Alex was so fucked up—excuse me—so effed up in prison he still couldn't wrap his mind around the fact that this wasn't a training exercise. It took him eight months before he really started to figure out, okay, this wasn't a training exercise, this was a real bank robbery."

I looked at Zimbardo, one of the world's leading experts on human nature, a man who had decades of experience working with both soldiers and the criminal justice system. Surely he would balk at how unlikely this story was. But that's not what happened.

"Really!" Zimbardo said, just as enchanted as everyone else always was when they heard it for the first time.

I looked at Alex. In our conversation earlier, he had agreed to try to make the point that his belief that the robbery wasn't real had been only partial, with some high but nontotal level of confidence—I felt this helped explain how he had managed to come across as rational in high-pressure conversations with lawyers who insisted on the opposite.

"Well," said Alex, "it was eight months before I could sit there in a cell *by myself* and say, 'Okay, I robbed a bank.'"

"I mean, did you see money?" Zimbardo asked.

"Yeah, I saw money. Sommer handed me a big wad of it. But every time I thought something was wrong, I'd go back to that Ranger mind-set."

Amanda stepped in with her own attempt at clarification. "For months in prison," she said, "Alex vacillated between a Ranger mind-set and grasping what was really going on. It took him a very long time to come to terms with what he'd done."

"Wow!" said Zimbardo, clutching his head in astonishment, as he had a few times before in the conversation at moments of great surprise or moral outrage.

Was this my chance to bring up all those crackpot theories I had just subjected Alex to a few hours ago—me, a guy who had never so much as taken a psychology course at the university where Zimbardo still taught? I had a sudden need to use the bathroom. As Norm and Alex continued telling the story to Zimbardo, I excused myself and walked away, alternately muttering and laughing all the way to the stall.

CHAPTER 17

GETTING REAL

Blum by Blum we gathered from around the city. My sister Leah, who lived with her property-developer boyfriend in Beverly Hills, picked me up in his car, decked out in a dress and high heels. We parked in a row of candy-colored BMWs and Mercedes in the Paramount Pictures lot just as Dad and his new partner, Sari, pulled into the spot next to ours. Their interpretation of the business casual attire requested on the invitation was fraying blue jeans, untucked shirts, and the lumpy orthopedic bricks that served all their footwear needs now that they had transcended the fake demands of fashion. It was another extremely hot day. At the back of the parking lot, below a sky tufted with big white clouds, a three-story wall had been painted to look like a sky tufted with big white clouds.

We walked down a long alley past a series of hangars full of half-built plywood deli counters and spaceships. Above the *Dr. Phil* show's exterior holding pen for audience members, the studio's massive air compressor sprawled against the wall like a roaring beige octopus. Alex's older brother, Max, arrived, then a friend of Norm's who had been at Alex's Denver dress rehearsal. Sam and his girlfriend were supposed to be here any minute. People started filing inside. We deposited our electronics in ziplock bags for safekeeping, passed through a metal detector, and entered the Church of Phil.

The ceiling, when you looked up, simply failed to occur. A web of black scaffolding and unidentifiable gear rose into the darkness.

That familiar promotional photograph of Dr. Phil's face looked out from flat screens all over the stage, which was much larger than I had expected from the cozy living-room vibe it projected onscreen. Above center stage hung a tilted rhombus of wood and glass intended to evoke a skylight.

"I'm going to put you guys in the second row," said a bald guy with a headset to the Blums. "You should all get to be on camera." He sized us up over his shoulder as we followed him down the aisle. "Look at all those blue jeans! Wow. People in blue jeans, unfortunately I can't put you in the second row. So let's see. You, you, you for the second row. The rest of you . . ." He led the rest of us to the back of the section, took laminated handicap placards off a row of widely spaced chairs, and pushed them closer together.

A few minutes later, Norm, Alex, Tami, and Amanda followed a different escort into the front row and craned their heads around to find us. Alex and I made faces at each other that I recognized from our fathers, stiff grins with comically terrified eyes. He looked a little awkward in his blue dress shirt, like some loose cannon of a best man whose wedding toast everyone was secretly terrified of. So young. I kept forgetting that. Then we all turned to the front, where something was happening to the lights.

———

We were as ready as we were ever going to be for *Dr. Phil*. But instead something even scarier happened: a man in an expensive-looking suit with sleek hair tucked behind his ears and a cordless microphone in one hand burst out of the wings to the opening keyboard stabs of "Billie Jean," clapping his hands over his head with such overwhelmingly infectious enthusiasm that the entire audience was on its feet clapping in under five seconds.

"Are you ready to make the world a better place and help people change their lives?" he yelled into the mic, panning his eyes across the crowd.

"Yes!" everybody yelled back.

"Because that's what we're all here for!" yelled the man. "Now I'll tell you what I want: I want you to dance for me. Think you can't dance? It's easy!"

"Ooh, baby!" Dad muttered from a place of deep anguish as the applause swelled around us and Michael Jackson started in on the vocals. "Billie Jean is not my lover . . ."

The man with the cordless mic—in the industry, I would soon learn, guys like this are known as "fluffers"—kept it up for twenty minutes. It was hard to ignore the waves of mounting existential horror radiating from my father, whose spiritual immune system appeared, in its efforts to reject this whole experience, to be eating itself alive. Dad had clearly missed the last three decades of American memos on how to relax and enjoy a profoundly fraudulent spectacle. Each of the successively sillier things we were now called upon to do jerked another little blurt of bitter sarcasm from his mouth, exclamations like *Can you dig it?* and *Wowee zowee* that made me shrink into myself with the hope that no one around us could hear. These were the first echoes I had heard in years of the gleefully superior father I used to know as a kid, the one who would have called a crowd like this a bunch of "glompers."

"Now I'll tell you what *I* want," the fluffer said, pointing to the left edge of the risers. "I want to see a little thing called the waaave. Do you know how to do the waaave?"

We did the wave. Out of the corner of my eye I saw my father's body lurch up and down, his stubby hands flop listlessly into the air.

"Oh, that's gorgeous," said the fluffer, overcome. "That's just gorgeous. I wish you could see what I'm seeing right now."

After extracting three successively louder full-audience exhortations of "Dr. Phil!" he left us standing on our feet with instructions in no uncertain terms to go absolutely apeshit when the man himself appeared.

This was not going to be a problem. We were ready. We were seriously fired up. When a crew member escorted Dr. Zimbardo onto the stage, we almost pulled the trigger prematurely but caught ourselves just in time. He hobbled to one of the two very high chairs placed side by side at the center and allowed himself to be helped up, then divested of his cane. You could see the realization cross his face that he was stranded there. When "Billie Jean" came on again, those irresistible opening chords, we knew exactly what to do, breaking into spontaneous, synchronized clapping and dancing. Zimbardo danced along in his chair, doing an adorably creaky old-person shuffle. He waved to Alex and Amanda and Norm, then caught sight of me in the handicap section and gave me a finger-gun salute.

The music built in intensity. A hush fell over the crowd as we realized that the man, the myth, the legend, the reason for every electron zipping through every wire in this building, was walking down a corridor into this very room.

And there he was.

People always say the same thing about celebrities: "He looked exactly like he looks on TV!" This turns out to feel a lot more profound in person than it sounds. The sheer animal power of Dr. Phil's onstage charisma swamped us like a tide. He interrupted his approach and our applause to issue an introductory monologue in the new bright on-air silence toward a wheeling camera manned by a hunched and attentive crewman, accompanied by the fantastically baroque repertoire of hand gestures with which he punctuates his speech—a kind of Realness kung fu, in which the left hand takes the role of probe or scold while the right serves as the object of palpation or reprimand.

"Now, Dr. Philip Zimbardo is the author behind *The Lucifer Effect: Understanding How Good People Turn Evil*. Now, he is hugely famous in the world of psychology and someone that I have admired for many, many years."

Dr. Phil looped his left hand's fingers into a Pecking Peacock of Subdivided Truth and counted off Zimbardo's accomplishments in a crescendo of encomiums, culminating with a double-lapel grab that raised his entire Volkswagen-sized frame onto the balls of his feet. Zimbardo, hunched in his chair, ducked his head in periodic mock embarrassment.

"He's done some of if not *the* most famous experiments in the history of psychology, including the Stanford prison experiment. Please welcome Dr. Philip Zimbardo."

Amid a storm of applause, Dr. Phil McGraw descended to the frail, birdlike figure of Dr. Phil Zimbardo with the hulking inevitability of a sacking defensive end.

"Keep your seat. Good to see you, man," he said, voice muffled on the chest mic by the manly hug that surrounded it.

And we were off.

The arc of the show was very smart. Zimbardo had explained it to us last night over martinis, nuts, and pretzel sticks. The goal would be to convince us two hundred or so Regular Folks in the studio, as stand-ins for the 3.3 million across the country who would eventually tune in to the show, that we ourselves were capable, if put in the right situation, of violence, crime, and atrocity. The plan was to lead us up to it in stages.

For stage one, Zimbardo and McGraw craned their heads around to the giant screen behind them to watch an experiment taped the morning before, the results of which Zimbardo had summarized for us last night while cackling in delight and munching on a cashew. A man in a vaguely policeman-like uniform (*No badge, though*, Zimbardo had told us, cackling) walked to the front of one of the studio's waiting rooms and gave all the soon-to-be audience members a series of increasingly pointless orders, culminating in a demand for blond women to move to the back of the room because "gentlemen do prefer blondes, but Dr. Phil doesn't." As the unwitting experimental subjects bumbled around obediently onscreen, invisible speakers throughout the studio played the kind of carnivalesque jingle meant to evoke donkeys in red hats trotting quickly in circles.

Three female audience members from the video walked onstage to be grilled by Zimbardo and Dr. Phil about just what they had been *thinking* in there—the guy had *no badge*! We all laughed along. What kind of nincompoops would sleepwalk through a bunch of foolish, borderline humiliating activities just because some guy dressed a certain way got up in front of the room and told them to?

We cut to commercials. We came right back. And with a pronounced upward click of the atrocity meter, we were on to stage two, a riff on perhaps the most famous twentieth-century psychology experiment other than Zimbardo's own.

———

Stanley Milgram designed his 1961 experiment to answer a riddle that still perplexed the world: how had so many ordinary Germans committed Nazi atrocities? Through the kind of deceptive wizardry much more kosher in psychological experiments at the time than today, Milgram's subjects were led to believe that they would be playing the "teacher" role in an experiment whose real subject,

the "learner," was in the next room. The teacher's job was to punish the learner with escalating electric shocks for failures at a simple
word-association task. The learner was in fact an actor trained to
yell in pain and beg to be released when the "shocks" reached certain
thresholds, but under prodding by a stern man in a lab coat, 65 percent of teachers shocked the learner all the way up to the maximum
intensity of 450 volts, by which point the learner was pretending to
have been knocked unconscious or worse.

The videos of the Milgram subjects are terrible to watch. Some
"teachers" wince at each audible moan from the "learner" and shake
with reluctance before flipping the switch; others beg the experi-
menter for permission to stop, earning only the icy response, "The
experiment requires that you continue." But the ones who stick with
you most are those who greet each fresh eruption of agony with
laughter: desperate chuckles, grimacing barks, hysterical giggles that
leak out of their mouths like bile. Men like that make me think of the
moment in Mark Bowden's *Black Hawk Down* when a woman's body
comes entirely apart in the street under a volley of machine-gun fire
by a squad of teenage Rangers. The Rangers laugh in shock at the
zombie-level horror of it. Impossibly, the woman tries to stand up.
They fire more, laughing harder. Delta Force operatives, older and
more experienced, look on in scorn.

Milgram's results are so counterintuitive that it is next to impossible to watch the videos without concluding that there is some
essential cruelty in these people's hearts. When a psychology graduate student named Günter Bierbrauer showed a taped reenactment of the experiment with a fully obedient "teacher" to his own
experimental subjects, they estimated that only 10 to 20 percent of
Milgram's "teachers" would behave as the one in the reenactment
did—in other words, they inferred that the disturbing behavior they
had just watched was best explained by the individual rather than
the situation.

Zimbardo was hoping to do better. The small-scale version of the
Milgram experiment that he had devised for today's show involved
another of those no-badge "policemen," this time walking around
outside the studio with a shady Bad Guy in tow. The "policeman"
cornered a passing Regular Guy, handed him a very real-looking
taser, and asked him to watch over the Bad Guy and shock him with

40,000 volts if he tried to escape. The "policeman" then hurried away to "find backup," too quickly for the befuddled Regular Guy to protest. Bad Guy tried to walk off. Would Regular Guy tase him?

We Blums knew from Zimbardo that the taping yesterday had gone swimmingly. The prize subjects were a man and wife who worked as facilities director and youth pastor, respectively, at a Baptist church in Kentucky. The wife had clenched her eyes shut and held the taser as far away from herself as possible.

"'Run away, Bad Guy! Run away, Bad Guy!'" Zimbardo acted out for us, cackling in delight and flapping his hands in the air of the lobby bar.

The real prize, though, was her husband. He had not only chased after the Bad Guy and tased him to the ground but had actually proceeded to bend over his prone, twitching form and tase him again in the ass.

The husband's clip played first on the back-of-the-stage screen. At the ass-tasing, Zimbardo gave a convulsive hiccup of joy in his chair. And here he was being led in from the wings—Regular Guy himself!

Dr. Phil, who had brought the fake taser with him onstage, had some real fun with this one.

"And then when he was down, you thought you'd just give him one for good measure?" Phil jabbed the taser into an imaginary ass, pushing a button to invoke the lights and zapping sound as the audience guffawed.

"I wanted to make sure he didn't get up, right?" mugged Regular Guy, with the hunted flicker in his eyes of a little boy in the principal's office who can't quite tell whether the principal's good humor is a trap.

"'Make sure he didn't get up,'" echoed Zimbardo, chortling.

Phil sat back in satisfaction, grinning at what a good time everyone was having. "So some guy with a hat on just walks up and says, 'If he moves, hit him with forty thousand volts.' And you gave him eighty thousand!"

I shrank into my seat as the audience laughed. If I were up there, I'd have been pointlessly pointing out that a second shock doesn't double the volts—all it does is double the joules.

They played the next clip. The woman, blond and sweet-faced, really did say, "Run away, Bad Guy!" Afterward she was escorted onstage and seated beside her husband. They didn't look at each other.

"I just don't think I could inflict pain on someone else," she said by way of explanation for her own reaction.

We all had a good chuckle as her husband winced. She told Dr. Phil to a fresh burst of audience laughter that no, she wasn't really surprised that her husband had acted differently. I scrutinized the boyish face and silky hair of the desperately smiling Regular Guy. In truth there was something a little unsettling by now about his permanent grin, his wood bead necklace and striped purple shirt, his efforts to laugh the whole thing off.

"Do you find this interesting?" Dr. Phil asked the audience. "I find this really intriguing."

———

Stage three was the Stanford prison experiment.

After a percussive crash that made everyone jump in their seats, a nervous cello gnawed away as grainy black-and-white footage of an institutional hallway appeared on the screen behind McGraw and Zimbardo atop a backdrop of computer-generated prison bars that looked straight out of *Wolfenstein 3D*. The camera jerked across images of long-haired young men in a grayish murk, some wearing shapeless white sacks and stocking caps, others wearing guard uniforms and sunglasses. Prisoners lined up and chanted. Guards dragged their mattresses out of their cells. The cello escalated in intensity. Each shot disappeared in a jolting burst of distortion, as if all this evilness kept actually incinerating the videotape. With a giant cymbal crash, the camera performed a two-stage horror-movie stutter-zoom onto a prisoner with a thin bare chest and a paper grocery bag over his head.

"Okay," said McGraw to Zimbardo. "Now, that is disturbing."

"Yeah, really," said Zimbardo. "It was disturbing then. It's disturbing now when I look at it."

The Stanford prison experiment has so thoroughly permeated academic lore that Zimbardo himself has referred to it as "virtually an urban legend." The version of the story that most people are familiar with—the one Zimbardo was telling Dr. Phil now—is essentially as follows. After answering a 1971 ad in a Palo Alto newspaper offering $15 per day for two weeks to participate in a "study on prison life"—a generous wage at the time—twenty-four college-age men were assigned to "prisoner" or "guard" roles with the flip of a coin. With three of each held out as alternates, the prisoners and guards took up residence in the "Stanford County Jail" that Zimbardo had constructed in the basement of the Stanford University psychology building. Within five days the guards were subjecting the prisoners to such horrendous psychological abuse that three prisoners had broken down under the strain. By then Zimbardo was so caught up in his role as prison superintendent that it was only his girlfriend, Dr. Christina Maslach, an outsider visiting the prison, who was able to recognize that the experiment was spiraling out of control. Fortunately, Zimbardo listened to her. Shortly after that, he married her. They have been together ever since.

———

Next came Abu Ghraib.

Stage four began with another bang-bang montage intro, except this time the orchestral wailings were louder and darker, synched to blasts of those familiar awful images: tiny, crop-haired Lynndie England clenching a jaunty cigarette between her teeth as she pointed a finger gun at the penis of a naked prisoner with a bag over his head; mustachioed Charles Graner grinning like a demented architect behind a pyramid of naked inmates; the famous Hooded Man on a cardboard box with a blanket over his shoulders and wires clamped to his outstretched fingers. I had never seen them anywhere but on a computer screen or a sheet of newsprint. It was uncomfortable to see them blown up to human size. After the video concluded, McGraw squared the blunt tips of his fingers together in a Granite Wall of Increased Skepticism and peered at Zimbardo from under his fleshy brows.

"Is what you're saying here," he asked, "is that any one of us, put in that situation, under those circumstances and dynamics where we believe these are the enemy, these are evil people, we believe we're doing the righteous work of the military in serving our country, could have been subject to doing exactly what these guards did?"

"I would say almost any one of us," Zimbardo said.

Zimbardo didn't get very far into Abu Ghraib, managing to slip in that "nakedness was a dehumanization technique promoted by Secretary of Defense Rumsfeld" before Dr. Phil called him off with a gesture and climbed from his chair. We seemed to have traveled a little far down the road to atrocity for his comfort. With a surge of anxiety, I realized that he was about to address a question to us in the audience.

"Okay," Dr. Phil said. "Let me ask you this. If you think in this situation, 'No way would I torture someone,' raise your hand."

Nearly every hand in the auditorium flew up. I felt a telepathic gulp of simultaneous realization among everyone in my family that in just a few seconds, when Dr. Phil named the next category, it would be our duty to raise our hands.

"Wowww," said Dr. Phil. "You know what? I want to see people standing up."

Most of the nontorturers who had just raised their hands now stood up, although a few seemed too shy to. In the front row, Amanda got to her feet next to Alex, who looked up at her in surprise and then shook his head, grinning in disbelief. She gave him a pinched, embarrassed smile in return, then faced forward with the smile still stuck on her face. I thought I knew why she was standing. Some of the men she knew through her pro bono work at Guantánamo Bay had been tortured by U.S. interrogators. Across the aisle, next to his standing wife, Regular Guy stood up too, somewhat extra-emphatically.

"Wowww," Dr. Phil said again, looking over the mostly standing audience. "Okay. Y'all sit down. If you think, 'Yeah, I can see how I could get sucked into that,' stand up."

All the Blums stood up. McGraw checked us out, looking surprised at our numbers.

"Okay," he said. "Bring me a microphone out here."

It all took a long time to arrange. Seated people craned their heads around to gawk at us openly as a crewman slunk up the aisle with a mic. McGraw's gaze roved around, coming close enough to tighten my stomach before stopping on Max. There was no way for him to know this was Alex's older brother. On the transcript he would be listed as "Unidentified Man #9." The mic guy crouched beside him and held the microphone to his face.

"Tell me," Dr. Phil said from the stage, "why do you think you could fall victim to this?"

"I think," said Unidentified Man #9, "if you're in any sort of group situation, especially if there's repercussions for not following the group leader of everybody else—" The nervousness Unidentified Man #9 had been suppressing until now finally caught in his throat. He swallowed and went on. "—you could definitely fall victim to something like that."

Dr. Phil's attention shifted to the person next to Max. My little sister is adopted from South Korea. McGraw probably assumed she and Max were married.

"And how about you?" asked Dr. Phil.

"Well," Leah said, and even from the sound of this one syllable I knew she was paralyzed by fear. She embarked on a long paragraph about authority and influence whose syntactic exit ramps she repeatedly veered toward and missed. Dr. Phil nodded absently. He asked the same question of two more people, a young woman and an older man who turned out to have served in the military, and eventually it seemed okay for us to sit down, and we did, and the brief Q&A was over.

I was a little nervous to think that Alex's segment would have to follow this one. How could being the driver for a bank robbery where no one got seriously hurt compare to supervising the torture of dozens of detainees? Wouldn't it have made more sense for Chip Frederick to play the final stop along the road to atrocity? As an Abu Ghraib prison guard who went knowingly if reluctantly with the pack, he seemed a much better exemplar of Zimbardo's theories than PFC Blum, for whom Specialist Sommer was at least as important as "situational factors."

It suddenly occurred to me that Zimbardo might well have asked Chip Frederick first. And that Chip Frederick might have had the good sense to say no.

———

"You really want to be liked," Zimbardo was saying onstage. "You want to be liked by strangers." The topic now was teenagers, in-groups, the desire to be accepted. "And so the problem is when that group begins to veer in a certain way, to begin to do things that violate your conscience or morals, you don't even make an active decision, you just begin to do the thing. You act in—"

"But it's not an active decision," Dr. Phil repeated, nodding.

"Yeah," Zimbardo said, leaning into the syllable as if to say more but then sitting back in defeat, because Dr. Phil was already talking directly across him toward a large wheeling camera, having employed one of his most effective techniques for graciously shutting up a guest. He executed a Spreading Double Lotus of Maximum Welcoming.

"Right now we're having a discussion about this on DrPhil.com, the message boards. You can go to Twitter, you can go to my Facebook page."

He cocked his head inquisitively to the side. This display of enormous personal interest was directed at a saucer-sized lens. In the televised version it catches you right in the face.

"I want to know if you think you *do* have kind of an *inner demon*, some evil inside that could be unleashed, could be unlocked situationally."

At the mention of "inner demon," an expression passed over Zimbardo's face that suddenly made the world's most Satan-bearded psychologist look a whole lot like Faust. Dr. Phil had just bent his thesis so far around into the language of folk wisdom that it had ended up facing almost exactly backward. The whole point of this episode was supposed to be that the demon was *outer*, not inner, that evil derived from systems and situations rather than from disposition. Zimbardo's smile widened and hardened, his eyes sliding out to the audience.

"I thought that was stupid," he would tell me point-blank when I visited him later at his house in San Francisco. "Especially since they used it in the promos. This notion that we all have this evil creature inside ourselves that usually gets suppressed, almost like Doctor Jekyll and Mister Hyde, and then under some circumstances it comes out . . . I mean, what is the likelihood that Alex would ever have done anything like that had he not been in the Rangers and met Luke Sommer? Zero. Can't imagine it. Was he the class bully in tenth grade? Did he kill cats when he was young? There's not a single bit of inner demon in his record."

"Tell me what you think about that," Dr. Phil continued musingly. "I find this really intriguing. Now, coming up, you won't believe what happened to one military Ranger who says he was just obeying orders."

Just obeying orders? Oh no.

———

McGraw cut to commercial. My father and I raised our eyebrows meaninglessly at each other. Crewmen strolled back and forth across the stage, stopping once in a while to fidget with gear on Zimbardo's chest, paying him all the human attention that might be afforded a tree stump. McGraw walked into a corner and began mumbling to himself, perhaps practicing for his upcoming monologue. Alex was escorted onstage and seated alongside Zimbardo. McGraw walked over to his favored direct-address camera. In a mild conversational voice, he asked, "Ready?"

Lights. Action. Dr. Phil emitted another gorgeous clopping gout of Texan grammar, sentences that galloped off through tilting ranchland to the horizon.

"Now, I have a world-famous psychologist and renowned author Dr. Philip Zimbardo is here with us and we are discussing his book *The Lucifer Effect: Understanding How Good People Turn Evil*. Let me tell you something, you need to read this book and you need to read it twice. Then you need to give it to your kids."

Zimbardo chuckled in a heroic effort at impersonating someone who had not just made tens of thousands of dollars. Alex was sitting stiffly in his chair, one shoulder higher than the other, eyes alternating between McGraw and the audience.

"I mean, it really is very, very insightful," continued Dr. Phil. "Today we're talking about when good people do bad things. Now, obeying authority is rule number one in the military. But I want you to look what happened when one former Ranger says he thought he was following routine orders."

Zimbardo and Alex turned in their chairs to look at the screen on the back of the stage, where, in place of the swirling Dr. Phil logo, an eight-foot-tall Alex stood in his tidy basement bedroom, head bowed, digging an old camo fluff-and-buff out of his closet. The drumbeats started up almost at once. What followed was a short series of edited-together sentences in Alex's voice, each of which I had at one time or another heard him saying to me, not one of which was individually untrue, though the only possible unifying interpretation was of some kind of bizarre military delusion that none of us civilians could begin to comprehend.

The music finished. There was a big pause.

"Okay," said Dr. Phil, with a kind of a sigh. He leaned forward in his chair and scrutinized Alex from underneath skeptical, inward-pointing brows. "Having not been in this situation, all of us right now are saying, 'Now, wait, what?'"

Alex went through one of his patented full-body fidgets.

"So what you're telling me," Phil continued, spreading out all ten of his fingers in an unprecedented *double* Let's Get Real Hands, a motion somewhat akin to Emperor Palpatine shooting electricity from his fingertips into the spasming body of Luke Skywalker, "is that you did not know"—Phil now began actually *slapping* his clenched fist with the palm of his other hand to punctuate each word—"that you were involved in an armed. Robbery. Of a bank."

———

For many forms of violence, we have different words for the moral and material senses of the act. When a UFC fighter punches another fighter inside a chain-link octagon under the supervision of a referee licensed by the UFC Federation, we do not call it "assault." When a soldier kills an enemy combatant on terrain defined as an active war zone under the Geneva Convention, we do not call it "murder." Unfortunately for Alex, there was no such dual vocabulary for "armed bank robbery," for the simple reason that perhaps never before in the history of the English language had there been a need for it. The phrase he kept trying to use, "hit the bank," had barely any resonance for civilians, who were so used to conflating the moral and material senses that they could barely conceive of them as separate. Dr. Phil might as well have been slapping the two together between his big, meaty hands. The image came to me of McGraw interviewing a shaman who had served a year and a half in state prison for helping conduct a peyote ceremony. *What you're telling me*—slap, slap, slap—*is that you did not know*—slap, slap, slap—*that you were involved in distributing two. Pounds. Of narcotics.* How was the shaman supposed to answer a question like that? How was Alex?

I realize this is a slightly unfair comparison. The shaman comes from a special class of citizens with legal sanction in certain jurisdictions to perform ordinarily unlawful rituals. So, of course, do the Rangers, but there is a significant difference: although twenty-two states still forbade peyote usage in Native American religious ceremonies as recently as 1996, Congress has since enacted a federal law legalizing it nationwide. No law will ever be passed legalizing domestic building takedowns for Rangers. The only ceremony during which their defining ritual is lawful is war, and war has not yet come to Tacoma, Washington.

Still, I do think it is fair to say that by the time of the robbery, PFC Blum was a member of a radically different society, with radically different norms. I don't mean the society of the Rangers. I mean the society of Luke Elliott Sommer, which Alex and a number of other young soldiers *mistook* for the society of the Rangers but which turned out to differ from it in certain crucial ways having to do with the fact that Sommer's Ranger tab, specialist ranking, and goofy personality were little more than decorations on a shockingly successful facade.

The remarkable thing is how similar Sommer's society and the society of the Rangers really were. Both dressed up violence in myth and ritual. Both served a higher law that civilians were too weak to understand. Both normalized killing, bloodthirstiness, ruthlessness, and domination with jokes and staged habituation. Both drew heavily on movies and video games. Little wonder, then, that Sommer raised no eyebrows talking openly, if lightly, about his plans. They were in close enough accord with Ranger values and norms that everyone at battalion could dismiss them as abiding in that narrow margin of play that extends, for all of us, just past the limits of what we're actually ready to do.

Despite all Alex's personal growth since then, that society left an unmistakable imprint on his language and attitudes. I had a pretty good idea of how he was about to respond to Dr. Phil: the same way he always responded to questions like this from me. "Yeah," he would say, as if it were the most obvious thing in the world, staring back with a challenging shrug, like, *What, you don't get that?* Only after a painful second would he explain. "What you have to understand is, in the Rangers . . ."

But he surprised me. He bobbed his head in good-natured frustration. "At the time when it happened," Alex said, "there was . . . there was definitely that tension that I was thinking about, the whole, it's . . . 'Something's wrong here.' But ultimately, my entire mind-set, it was conflicting between there's something wrong but a tab would never tell me to do something wrong."

"What's a tab?" Zimbardo prompted.

Alex ventured gladly off into this lower-stakes conversational territory. After he wrapped up his explanation of the power tabs have over privates, with a little assistance from Zimbardo, both turned proudly to Dr. Phil, awaiting the royal gesture of approbation.

"You said it took you eight months to realize that this was actually a bank robbery," said Dr. Phil.

Oh no. Where had he gotten this from? Zimbardo? Norm? By the rapid series of contortions in Alex's face, I couldn't imagine it was Alex himself.

"Yeah . . ." he said finally. "When I was—when I went through prison, went through all that, it was eight months before I was able to sit there *by myself* and finally say, 'I robbed a bank. We were part of a bank robbery,' and get away from that Ranger mind-set of 'This is who I am. We wouldn't do anything wrong.'"

Well, hell. At least he tried. Unfortunately, like everyone did when confronted with this sincere young man saying puzzling things, Dr. Phil made his own good-natured effort to bridge the explanatory gap. "Because they told you, 'We're doing this as rehearsals because we might have to rob banks behind enemy lines,'" he said matter-of-factly.

Alex gave a quizzical half-nod.

"So you pull up to the bank that day. This is just a bank on a street in civilian land. I mean, this is just—all of a sudden you've pulled up, people are getting out, they're putting on masks, they got machine guns, they're going into this bank, and they come out with big bags of money."

"Absolutely," Alex said. "Yes. When I pulled up, I still had that sense of comfort. And there was—there was a thought in me that said, 'This isn't going to happen. It's just, you know, Specialist Sommer playing these Ranger games, doing what he always does just to push it to the limit.' And as soon as they got out, I locked eyes with this woman in a cherry-red Dodge Durango, and right then and there I saw how scared she was, and right then I just said, 'Something is wrong here.' So I backed out of the alleyway, turned my car around after sitting there trying to analyze and make sense of it, and all of a sudden I went with the thought that something's wrong. So I left. I come back around to try and head back towards base, and all of a sudden I see Specialist Sommer come out into the road and—"

"He pulls you back in," said Zimbardo. While Alex turned and nodded to him, Zimbardo rotated one fist next to the other, the universal mime for reeling in a fishing line.

It was a strange moment. I thought I understood why Zimbardo had cut Alex off before he could say too much more about Specialist Sommer: as Alex well knew but had a hard time staying on-message about, Zimbardo's narrative was that the power dynamic between tabs and privates was responsible for PFC Blum robbing a bank. The "Lucifer effect" made no room for anything so dispositional as a psychopathic Svengali of a superior. For Zimbardo, Sommer was a lunatic embodiment of the situational forces of Ranger Battalion, just as Superintendent Zimbardo was an embodiment of the situational forces of the Stanford County Jail. This view fit Jeff and Amanda's defense strategy, but it never sat easily with Alex himself, who asked his lawyers from the start not to impugn the regiment. Although he eventually accepted their view after his "brainwashing" epiphany, in the time since then he had lapsed into placing much of the blame back on Sommer.

———

For the next ten minutes, the two Phils pushed all the most exciting buttons on their animatronic Army Ranger bank robber doll.

I burrowed deeper and deeper into my seat. I was aware that Dr. Zimbardo had been doing this kind of thing for a very long time. I knew he understood his audience better than I did. Still, I couldn't help wondering if all the pageantry was really necessary. I got that this wasn't a Stanford lecture hall. I got that his first obligation here was to entertain. But was it really too much to hope that he might seize this opportunity to teach some admittedly nerdy but also kind of fascinating and important findings from his field?

He could, for instance, have gone into more depth on conformity, one of the most well-developed research topics in social psychology. Four main dispositional attributes have been demonstrated to influence the likelihood that an experimental subject will conform to a group's behavior: self-esteem in general, task-specific confidence, security within the group, and culture. Alex had always had pretty good self-esteem, but in the other three dimensions PFC Blum was off-the-charts vulnerable in the directions predicting conformity. His task-specific confidence for deploying to a war zone and engaging in live-fire gun battles with insurgents was about as high as you could expect under the circumstances—that is, nil. As a cherry private, he had trained a lot but lacked the real-world experience that a specialist with two deployments like Sommer had gained. He clung to whatever tips Sommer could give him for how to stay alive. His security within the group was likewise abysmal. Cherry privates were the bottom of the totem pole, utterly at the mercy of the tabs. If they so much as turned and grabbed a rope at the wrong moment during a fast-roping exercise, as a roommate of Alex's had once done, they were in danger of permanent ostracism.

As for the culture factor: on the grand spectrum of global cultural attitudes toward conformity, Ranger Battalion in 2006 existed somewhere between a medieval order of samurais and a radical death cult.

Which of course raised the question of how a naive Greenwood Village boy managed to fit in there at all. Here too the Phils might have offered some interesting insight. Though certain aspects of infantry and Ranger culture bothered Alex at first, he had gone through the deepest agony of his sheltered young life to become a part of the regiment, and numerous experiments demonstrate that we tend to cling to what we've worked hard to obtain in order to justify how much it has cost us. When Harold Gerard and Grover Mathewson admitted subjects to a discussion group only if they agreed to undergo a painful electric shock as an initiation ritual, subjects later rated the group as more interesting and worthwhile than subjects who had been allowed in without any ritual. I could imagine few shocks as painful as the Ranger Indoctrination Program.

I realized this was a tall order for a ten-minute television segment. But there had to be a better option than what we did get, which felt an awful lot like a circus, with Zimbardo in the role of lion tamer and Alex in the role of lion, called on to roar so often that it was easy to forget we were supposed to view him as a lamb.

"And this indoctrination, I mean, they clearly had a hold on you," said Dr. Phil. "What are suicide checks?"

A frustrated look crossed Alex's face. He hated casting aspersions on the regiment. "Suicide check, that's not something that everybody in the military does," he said. "It's something that Specialist Sommer specifically used to test my willingness to follow him. So the first time he handed me a nine-millimeter pistol and he said, 'Suicide check,' I said, 'I don't know what that is, Specialist.' He said, 'You put it to your head and pull the trigger.'"

"You show us," said Zimbardo.

Alex looked to Zimbardo to see if he meant this. "Yeah," said Zimbardo, showing him a finger gun. Alex put his own finger gun to his head and pulled the trigger, an image that would soon show up in the promos for the episode.

"You had dinner last night with Alex," Dr. Phil said to Zimbardo. "Tell me what happened."

"We're having dinner," said Zimbardo, "and he's a really sweet, lovable guy. And at some point you say, 'Alex, give me the Ranger Creed.'"

"Do it," said Dr. Phil.

This part, I knew, Alex was actually looking forward to. He hadn't had a chance to recite the creed for an audience in years. With the shy smile of a kindergartener who has been asked to sing his special song in front of the class, he hopped off his stool, snapped to attention, and started yelling at top speed. Unfortunately, top speed proved a little overambitious. You could see the train wreck coming long before it arrived, mental habit creeping out ahead of his civilian mouth millisecond by millisecond, until finally the syllables piled up on his tongue and flopped out in a tangled heap. The panic in his eyes was feral. He was ready to be dropped and smoked. He rushed through the rest, then walked back to his seat with a big self-disgusted roll of his head toward the ceiling.

"So the question is," said Zimbardo, "what was the limit? I mean, so you robbed a bank. If Luke said, 'Kill somebody'—and you're back then now. You're a different guy now, obviously. But you're back then in that mind-set, and Luke Sommer, your tab, says, 'Kill that woman.'"

Even Alex looked taken aback at that one. "If I was in Iraq?" he asked.

"Yeah," said Zimbardo, shrugging.

It almost seemed at first as if Alex might find a way to dodge this question. But thirty seconds later, after some floundering and further prodding that would mostly be cut in the final edit, he was using his trusty finger gun to mime the execution-style murder of a kneeling woman in front of 3.3 million Americans, not one of whom was going to understand the spirit of helpfulness to Dr. Z in which he was doing it. If anything, his cheery attitude would only make him look scarier. Perhaps this answered my question about how Alex's segment was going to avoid being a letdown after Abu Ghraib.

I knew, of course, that Alex was up there of his own accord. He was genuinely glad to be helping Dr. Z. But that was beginning to seem to me exactly what was most insidious about obedience: the way our little expressions of personality within it gave us the illusion that we were free. From the perspective of the guy in charge, did any of it really matter? I thought back to the fluffer's commands. Whether with Alex's cheery helpfulness, Norm's proud optimism, Dad's grudging sarcasm, or my own hapless efforts at post-ironic excess, when the wave circled round to our place in the crowd, we all had put our hands in the air.

"All right," said Dr. Phil. "Well, we got to take a break, but there's more to this story. Alex's father was shocked at the difference in his son after Ranger training. We're going to talk to him next. Plus, how Dr. Zimbardo saved Alex from a thirty-year prison sentence. We'll be right back."

CHAPTER 18

REAL REAL

A few days after the episode aired, my father and I talked over the phone about it. He pointed out that there had already been two more episodes of *Dr. Phil* since "When Good People Do Bad Things"—more public trauma, more quick fixes, more life lessons.

"There was a flattening of emotional impact for me," he said. "Here was this thing that took up years of our family's life, and it was just five minutes between deodorant commercials."

I called Alex several times in an effort to learn what reactions he had been hearing from people in person, but all he seemed capable of talking about was how annoyed he was at himself for botching the Ranger Creed. It didn't matter when I told him it was an understandable mistake. It didn't matter when I told him it had only made him look more human. He stubbornly repeated that he was never going to watch it.

It wasn't until late December, just before I was due to fly out to Colorado for Christmas, that Alex admitted to me casually and dismissively that four days after the episode aired, a group of parents had sent a letter to the owner of Big Bear Ice Arena. I asked him to forward it to me. A few hours later he did.

Vassily,

As with all things in life problems happen and circumstances change. While it's with regret the following families are requesting the return of their remaining equipment in the locker room, and also that you sign the financial releases . . . the unfortunate facts are simple, you currently have a convicted felon on your staff that works with children, and you can't guarantee that he will never interact with our children in a way . . .

If the above is incorrect please provide this to all the families in writing, that the felon is gone and you'll unconditionally agree that the kids and families will have Coach Andrei Krivokrasov, and he'll remain for the entire season.

After that came a long list of names.

I spent most of the flight with my forehead against the window, thinking about that hour I spent with Alex before the episode, coaching him through all those subtle nuances of knowledge and intent that had seemed so crucial to me then, so essential to get right.

I dropped off my bags at my mother's house and drove straight over to Norm's in Greenwood Village. Scraps of packing tape were stuck to the floorboards. They expected to be evicted around New Year's. The landscape paintings that used to fascinate me as a kid, full of hidden faces in the pine knots and boulders, were stacked against bare walls. I found Norm cooking his famous Christmas fudge in the kitchen.

"Hey, buddy!" he said, giving me a big hug.

Alex and I went downstairs to his room in the basement, where his Ranger beret still hung from its nail above the bed. His voice was hoarse. He had spent two months on paperwork and "zamming" the ice with the rink's Zamboni machine, but today, he told me, had been his first back as a coach. He seemed as proud and relieved as I was.

"The day after *Dr. Phil* happened," he explained, "Vassily comes up to me and says, 'Look. CAHA, the Colorado Amateur Hockey Association, which you have to register with to be a coach, they're doing an investigation on you.' He's like, 'Honestly, it would be best if you take a step back from coaching and wait to see what the final verdict is.' But the parents of the Pre-Mites, the little guys, they fought with the facility, tooth and nail. They were like, 'Why isn't Alex out there?' One kid came up to me and gave me a card: 'Thank you for all the hard work.' These parents said to me, 'You're tattooed up, you were on *Dr. Phil*, you robbed a bank, we don't give a shit. Our kids love working with you. Our kids have learned more in nine months working with you than they have anywhere else. Everybody makes a mistake.' And, I mean, you know, I was *manipulated*, but that means a lot to me." Alex gave me a loopy half-smile.

"I play a tough guy on the exterior," he said, "but a kid gives me a card, I hang it in my office. He signed it himself, in his little retard writing. Sometimes the other guys make fun of the little ones. I'm like, 'Man, you don't know what it's like to watch a kid go from not being able to skate to being the fastest kid on the ice.' It's a huge accomplishment for me. You want to look at me as a bank robber, as a scumbag? I don't care. These kids listen to me, they love working with me. And I love working with them. I didn't realize how much I missed it until I got out there today. As soon as I was like, 'Guys, we got a fucking tournament coming up . . .'" He stopped, looked embarrassed.

"I mean, I didn't cuss at them. I'm like, 'Guys.' They stopped, they looked at me. I said, 'Guys, we have two practices and then a tournament this weekend. Do you want to get better?' Every single one's like, *'Yes, coach!'* Just—*loud*. There's kind of a sense of military discipline. I mean, these are five-year-olds. How many guys can get five-year-olds to stand still?"

I tried to suppress my smile. "So what was the result of the investigation?" I asked.

"They haven't responded. CAHA said to send in my background check, and I did. It's been three weeks now. Vassily's like, 'They don't want to do the investigation? Fuck 'em. If they come back with this, we'll sue 'em.'"

———

Christmas came, and the drab day after. We played video games all evening at Norm's house. Threadbare snowdrifts sagged against the dark windows. Long into the night, I finally got up the courage to ask what I had wanted to since July: whether Alex found it difficult to live up to what his father wanted to believe of him. After all this time, I still couldn't tell whether Norm understood how aware Alex had really been of his situation in prison. Alex stiffened in his chair, then tried harder and harder to cut in, as if to erase the question before it arrived.

"I think he understands. I think he understands. Look," Alex said. "The only thing I can say about my dad is that he *saved* me. He's the only one who was able to help me tell the story. That's the biggest thing: he helped me grow to understand it. He might not have had that plan. His plan was probably just to keep me positive and make sure I didn't kill myself. But it made me function again. He was the perfect personality at that moment, in that place. To be as harsh as he was but at the same time as understanding and compassionate as he was—that's more impressive than Beethoven's Ninth Symphony, to nurture me through that. How many vets do you know, and how many guys who have been to prison, who are able to adjust back to life? If you look at me, you'd never guess. It's so subtle you have to watch *Dr. Phil* to know I've been to prison. I still struggle with lots of shit, but it would have been a whole lot worse if he'd been anyone else. I can't look at what he did and analyze it. He saved who I am. I can't analyze anything on that point."

For the second time in my experience, Alex was near tears. "Do you know about his heart?" he asked quietly.

"Yeah," I said after a moment.

"He *died*." His voice was so strange and wondering that I felt suddenly afraid. "He was riding the bike at the health club and *his heart stopped*. He woke up on his back. He *just told me*. I knew about the financial strain when I went to prison—I told him, 'Look, I'll take a public defender. I'll take six years to help the family out.' But he came up every weekend and he never said a word. It was all about me. When he says, 'I was in there with you,' I really believe that. If I hadn't been in there, I don't think the stress would have worn him down. Literally part of his heart was breaking because of where I was."

Alex was weeping openly now. "He might not see sixty. If there's a hero in this story, it's him. I want people to know that. Even if I had gotten twelve years, he'd still be coming there every single weekend. I hope he sets an example for anyone who thinks of leaving their kid. I hope he inspires people."

Two weeks later, Alex was out of a job.

———

The next years were not easy, either for Alex or for the Blums. Leaving the ice rink hit Alex hard. He spent a few months trying to start a private hockey school with a former coworker, unwilling yet to accept that he would never be able to coach. As a stopgap, an old linemate of his named Scott Beech from the Littleton Hawks, one of the few friends who hadn't abandoned him after his arrest, got him a job at the distribution center for a sports supply store, slinging boxes full of kneepads and sticks in a warehouse just as cavernous as the one where his Pre-Mites used to play.

My long obsession with modeling PFC Blum's brain looked more and more to me like exactly the sort of cold-hearted scientific investigation I had tried to leave behind. I did my best to get back in touch with the core emotional truths of the family story, digging through legal documents for further evidence of Alex's innocence and rewriting the draft of the book in an effort to frame the "Complexities" that made Alex's tale so hard for me to understand as merely one more example of that unbridgeable chasm between two minds that you had to leap over by faith in order to love another human.

A few months in, I fell into a severe depressive episode. My relationship with my girlfriend disintegrated. I set my writing aside and began looking for software development jobs, trying to keep myself from dwelling on the Facebook profiles of old colleagues from grad school, many of whom had gone on to prestigious professorships and research awards.

One bright spot emerged: Norm managed, for a time at least, to hold on to his house. When Alex saw my condition the following Christmas, he insisted on dragging mats out to the garage. "Fighting always cheers me up," he assured me. "There's nothing like a roundhouse kick to the head to make you feel like whatever you were worrying about is stupid."

I still remember that first afternoon we rolled: the wintry light slanting through the windows of the garage door, the evaporating outlines of our footsteps on the freezing concrete as we laid out the mats, the tens of thousands of black streaks on the walls and ceiling from all the stray pucks Alex had shot there over the years. He ribbed me a little for my nervousness, but once we got down to the elementary stances, guards, and bars, I was suddenly in the presence of a man I had seen across a rink but never met firsthand—not a friend but a coach. Alex was kind, patient, gentle with my clumsiness. Soon I was actually having fun for the first time in months, amazed at the way the moves seemed almost preordained in the geometry of the body, as if we were not fighting but dancing. As he led me through a sequence of left-right jabs against pads strapped to his forearms, nodding in approval with each strike, it occurred to me that if Alex had never met Specialist Sommer, he would by now have been a team leader in the Rangers himself. Maybe even a squad leader.

I finally got a job in New York designing routing and scheduling algorithms for a green transit startup. Alex kept working at the warehouse. We saw less and less of each other. When we talked, the topics now were his efforts at finding a landlord who would rent to him so he could move out of Norm's basement, our nonexistent love lives, his hopeless efforts to stop dwelling on Anna. The seriousness of his drinking was becoming obvious even to me. In order to make extra money toward paying off his $19,000 restitution, he began working a second job as a bouncer at a Denver bar and bowling alley, where drunk belligerents tried to head-butt him and puked all over his shirt, and where he once had to extract an obese, half-naked, feces-smeared seventy-year-old woman from a bathroom stall. His few free hours he spent training at the mixed martial arts gym, gravitating more and more toward the kinds of friends who weren't fazed by his criminal past. The brief openness about the robbery that I had felt from him before the *Dr. Phil* show hardened into an angry crust.

Without a meaningful goal to aim at, all Alex's old strengths—his drive to excel, his humor, his goofy charisma—began turning in on themselves. It was becoming clear that he would never be able to incorporate a violent felony into his old social identity as the jokey, friendly do-gooder whose heroics justified his cockiness, but rather than play the chastened criminal, which seemed the only role his Denver community offered, he retreated from public view, deleting his Facebook account and all but eight contacts from his phone. It became more and more unpleasant to listen to him rant about slow drivers, customers in the checkout line who miscounted their change, and employees who slacked off at the warehouse. At family gatherings he reverted to his army-era braggadocio, piling up empty beer bottles as he recounted Ranger feats and showed off his hand-to-hand combat skills on whichever unlucky cousin strayed too near. The rift between him and Sam deepened. Finally Sam changed his last name to his mother's and stopped visiting Colorado at all.

The burst of the housing bubble took a toll on everyone. My father's best friend and lifelong business partner, a gregarious eccentric from California, shot himself in August 2011. His death was hard for me. He had been a constant presence in my childhood, daffy and maniacally fun, like an overgrown ten-year-old. I flew to San Diego for the memorial service and watched my father nod gravely as a procession of aging businessmen made their offers of pat wisdom: *such a shock, never would have guessed, chemical imbalance, happens to the best of us, fought his demons, lost to his demons, unique, special, what a loss.* Later that afternoon, my uncle Kurt, whose chronic depression and painkiller addiction after a debilitating motorcycle accident had long kept him at a distance from Blum family life, drove me to the airport. My father had told me that this would give Kurt a chance to feel useful, but after taking a minor wrong turn near the airport, he was stricken, lambasting himself over and over no matter how many times I told him it was fine. To get him off the subject, I asked him what the story was with Hemingway's boat.

"Oh, Papa's boat?" Kurt asked, wheeling hard through the parking lot of a strip mall, his gravelly voice regaining some of its old expansiveness. "Yeah, I owned Papa's boat!"

He spent the last few minutes of the drive detailing the specifications and contents of the *Pilar* (named after a character from *For Whom the Bell Tolls*), including an old typewriter that had belonged to Hemingway himself, and telling me how proud and excited he was that I had become a writer. We shook hands at the curb with real warmth. It was the closest I had ever felt to my gruffest uncle. Norm and my father had both suggested to me that Kurt might be in possession of Opa's mysterious war memoir, but I had been putting off calling to ask. I resolved to do so before too long.

I never got around to it. Soon Kurt had killed himself too, spending his last month on Norm's couch talking military history with his favorite nephew. When I went to a memorial gathering of Blums one year after his death, Fred had set up a table full of photograph albums and mementos excavated from Kurt's belongings. I leafed through pages and pages of Blum brothers posing in various stances of playful combat until I found what I was looking for: Kurt in sunglasses and his trademark mustache, holding up a glass of champagne on a dock next to a gorgeous natural-wood yacht. Painted on the back in bold yellow letters were the words PILAR—KEY WEST—HAVANA.

I gazed at it for a minute in quiet communion. Then I read the accompanying news clippings and found out that the *Pilar* had not, in fact, been Hemingway's boat. Hemingway's boat had rotted at dry dock after his suicide. The boat Kurt had invested in was one of two sister ships that had been built to the same specifications, refurbished and styled as Hemingway's own by a Key West business partner of Kurt's for use as a tourist attraction. I soon learned that the family tale about Uncle Fred's boatload of marijuana was even more apocryphal.

After Kurt's death, Alex hardened further. One Christmas I went home to find that he had gotten a new Ranger tattoo on his biceps, a green-and-blue crest shot through by a red lightning bolt. I stared at Alex's defiant smile in shock. If I had heard someone outside the family express the thoughts playing inside my head, I would have bristled and disagreed, but the truth was, I felt that this betrayed the moral seriousness I had been trying for so long to attribute to him. Like everyone else in the family, I was still defending Alex at every opportunity—chuckling indulgently at his unkind remarks, submitting to his self-congratulatory stories, explaining away his abrasiveness as soon as he roared out of the room—but some kernel of resentment that I had not felt before lay beneath it now.

One day I called Scott Beech, the friend who had gotten Alex the job at the warehouse, to get a read on how Alex was doing. A fast, powerful, six-foot-three-inch forward, Beech had been a big goal scorer for the Hawks, though he insisted that all he had ever done was "feed off Blum's hard work": knocking pucks into the net after Alex dug them out of the corner. He told me that as soon as Alex started at the warehouse, the robbery had begun coming up. Everyone wanted to know the story, including Beech himself, but Alex was touchy about the details. It culminated in what Beech described to me as a "heated argument."

"Basically how it went—" Beech began, then broke off. "I was never in the military," he said, starting again, this time in that careful, formal tone I knew so well from having used it myself. "I was never an Army Ranger. I will never experience what he went through, how he even felt during the situation. I'll just never know. So even though he could say a hundred million times, 'I was brainwashed, brainwashed, brainwashed,' it's going to be really tough to try and relate to that unless you're somebody else who went through it, right?"

Despite the years I had now devoted to the book about Alex, I fantasized often about abandoning it. My old family rationale was gone. Though Alex still felt that his story had not been told right, it had become obvious after *Dr. Phil* what effect even sympathetic publicity had on his life. But something in me just couldn't let it go. It rankled that the family I had finally begun to feel close to seemed to have no stomach anymore for my difficult, hairsplitting questions. For them, a Blum myth sufficed that I no longer subscribed to in my heart. It reminded me of the days when I had felt driven to disenchant the world of that gloss of social meaning which I had always felt so excluded from, bitterly but compulsively explaining away everyone's so-called feelings as no more than cascades of electrical impulses.

It was at the height of this impasse that I fell into something like friendship with a man to whom I could speak far more openly about Alex's involvement in the robbery than anyone in my own family: Luke Elliott Sommer.

BOOK 4

THE DUNGEON MASTER

Those who can make you believe absurdities
can make you commit atrocities.
—VOLTAIRE, *QUESTIONS SUR LES MIRACLES*, 1765

CHAPTER 19

WHEN BAD PEOPLE DO GOOD THINGS

I first considered making contact with Inmate 38474-086 of the Federal Bureau of Prisons just a few months after the *Dr. Phil* episode aired, with the goal of trying to extract some final proof of Alex's innocence. Amanda seemed surprised and a little alarmed when I told her that I was thinking of writing to him. "He'll definitely want to talk," she said. "He'll assume he can control the narrative. Let him believe he's smarter than you."

I also asked for advice from David Bowermaster, the *Seattle Times* reporter who had covered the case. "It's easy when you're in the midst of conversation with Sommer to lose sight of how absurd and doubtful what he's talking about is," Bowermaster told me. "He's very manipulative. He was able to figure out what buttons to push with people. He passed the story differently to each. He'll think he can convince you that he had no culpability in Alex getting involved."

Finally I alerted Alex to my plan. "That psychopath?" Alex said, with the aggressive shrug he generally presented in response to confusing or distressing information. "Be careful."

Amanda had also used the *p*-word in reference to Sommer, as had Kathleen Taylor, the author of *Brainwashing*. But something about him intrigued me. I knew he too had started college early, at the tender age of fifteen. And I had discovered a post on his personal blog, dated a couple of weeks after he emailed Norm while fighting extradition from Canada, that might as well have been addressed to me at that age—casually atheist, reluctantly nihilist, intensely questioning.

SEARCHING FOR A MATHEMATICIAN

I am looking for someone to help me convert a concept into a mathematical proof. I am attempting to prove that morality and ethics are based on a list of factors including society, personal conviction and environment. If you have the math skills to present this equation with all the axioms factored I would appreciate your time. I can pay a limited salary, and I am willing to relinquish publishing rights to the mathematician.

Thanks.

I began strategizing my approach, feeling as if I were preparing for one of those math contests I took so seriously as a kid, where you sit across from another wiry, fierce-faced nerd with your hand over the buzzer and think viciously at him while the audience looks on. Finally I typed up what seemed safe to include of my contact information and mailed it to U.S. Penitentiary McCreary in Pine Knot, Kentucky. Three days later, while I was out walking near the University of Washington with my mother and Ozi during a short visit of theirs from Denver, a call from a blocked number showed up on my phone. *"This is a call from—"* said a recorded female voice. "Elliott Sommer," said a cheerful male voice. *"—an inmate in a federal prison,"* said the recording. *"Dial five to accept the call."*

"Is this Ben?" asked Luke Elliott Sommer.

The exchange that ensued was so friendly and normal that I was left with a foolish sense of anticlimax, as if I had cocked my arm for a swing at a giant, monstrously distorted reflection only to turn and find the real guy walking up behind me with a wry smile on his face that indicated he had seen the reflection too. In conversation, the man who had destroyed Alex's life was not Specialist Sommer. He was not even Luke. He was Elliott. Elliott had a Canadian accent. He explained that he had only a few cents left on his phone card, so this would have to be fast, then informed me that he had been diagnosed by Bureau of Prisons staff with post-traumatic stress disorder and rapid-cycling bipolar disorder, whose symptoms he encouraged me to look up, and was now medicated to the gills, totally transforming his perspective on life. He described his past criminal activity as "crazy." He said he felt terrible about what had happened to Alex. A

U.S. senator was supporting his treaty transfer to Canada, where he would likely be paroled in two to three years. "I got incredibly lucky," he admitted, chuckling ruefully. He said the clicks I had just heard meant we were about to get cut off but promised he would email me soon. With a string of casually accelerating pleasantries, his voice disappeared back to Pine Knot, Kentucky, as if already heading to his next appointment.

I got off the phone with a strange floating feeling. It was a beautiful afternoon in Seattle, brisk and bright, with seagulls swooping off the masts of docked sailboats to harvest scraps from Lake Union. About a third of the way through the phone call, I had instinctively dropped back from the group to avoid being heard conversing on a first-name basis with the Blum family's personal bogeyman. Now, as I caught up and summarized what he had said, I found myself referring to him again as "Sommer," and the stunned, wary look on Mom's and Ozi's faces made the conversation feel retroactively dangerous. The news that he would be out in two to three years—"I just thought you and Alex should know that," he had said, in the solicitous Canadian voice I still heard ringing in my ears—came out of my mouth sounding suddenly like a threat.

The next day three emails arrived through a Bureau of Prisons webmail service called CorrLinks. One was addressed to Alex. One was addressed to me. One described various materials Sommer would be willing to provide if I sent $3000 to his mother, Christel Davidsen.

In his letter to Alex, Sommer apologized for getting him involved in the robbery. He said he hoped for but did not expect forgiveness one day and that there were no hard feelings for testifying against him. "In any case," he concluded, "I hope you are doing well, and I am sorry I killed your dream. I know that it was important to you, being a Ranger. I know that I took something away from you that you can never get back. Believe me, I think about it every day. Elliott."

"Hey," began the letter to me. "I have mixed feelings about Alex. On the one hand he lied about me repeatedly (largely because he was scared of what his friends and family would think) and on the other, he IS my friend . . . I have a lot to say, much of which will make a lot of sense out of this convoluted story, though none of it will attempt to put the blame on Alex's shoulders. He was/is responsible for his own actions, but I was his superior, and while at the time I did not consider that as a factor, time has lent me a different perspective."

How, if everything I understood about Ranger Battalion was true, was it remotely possible that Specialist Sommer had not considered rank a "factor"? Elliott's long account of his own motivation for the bank robbery passed in a blur as I hunted for more on Alex. "Mentally ill . . . direct result of combat duty . . . went off the rails . . . hypermania . . ." Finally, near the end, I found it. "This I am adamant about, but I will acknowledge I cannot prove: I did not threaten, order, or manipulate your cousin. I asked him to come with me, and he agreed. Period."

Never before had I felt so furious a desire to explain just how wrong someone was. After hitting CorrLinks' 13,000-character limit with my reply, I had to go back and compress earlier rants so I could fit in more. It was both liberating and frustrating to be forced to argue against Alex's guilt rather than in favor of his innocence. For the first time since the Complexities of the previous summer, I found I could believe wholly in what I was saying, but I didn't have enough hard evidence to say as much as I wanted to.

Elliott's reply was quick and conciliatory but expressed no deeper understanding of Alex's psychology than he had showed at the outset. It wasn't just frustration that I felt. It was confusion. On the phone, Elliott's voice had been compelling enough, but on paper, his language was riddled with war-movie truisms and clichés, so crude in their moral categories that they might as well have been written by a hyper-articulate ten-year-old. Could this really be the psychopathic Svengali figure Alex kept describing, the brilliant criminal mastermind I had been gearing up to outsmart? He sounded exactly like what he said he was: mentally ill.

The next day I called Christel Davidsen for the first of what would prove to be many times.

———

The robbery had not only upended Alex's life and career but had similarly affected all three other accomplices directly involved in it: Chad Palmer, another private from Ranger Battalion; Nathan Dunmall; and Tigra Robertson, Elliott's closest friend on the team and principal coconspirator. A strange fellowship had developed between the Blum family and theirs. Norm had spoken over the phone with Chad Palmer's parents and Nathan Dunmall's mother. I would soon exchange emails with Tigra Robertson's mother and send her some documents about the case.

Christel was in no way part of this fellowship. In our first phone call, neither of us sounded overly comfortable to be talking to the other. I did my best to convince her that I hadn't called just to berate her. What Elliott had done to Alex trembled between us like an over-full glass we had to hold very carefully.

"How's Alex doing?" she asked.

"He's doing pretty well," I said, then gave her the update in brief. "And how are things going for you? I've seen how tough all this has been on Alex's dad."

Over the phone came a low-res digital sigh. "There's been a lot of fallout. Tigra and Elliott grew up together. His mom and I were close all their lives, and we don't talk anymore. I've had a lot written to me about Elliott. Horrible stuff. I expected that, I'm not offended by that. Don't ever think I don't believe my son deserves consequences for his actions. But I try to explain to people that there was a context for what he did. I want these boys to be able to come to an understanding of what happened to them. The sum total of their lives is not that one decision."

I don't know what I was expecting of the woman who gave birth to Luke Elliott Sommer—maybe a horrified Rosemary rocking Satan's baby to sleep in helpless maternal thrall, maybe a cynical, half-snake Echidna—but Christel wasn't it. Within ten minutes of conversation I had to admit to myself that I sort of liked her. After another few phone calls I even sort of admired her. Thoughtful, warm, and frantically busy, she somehow scraped together enough to support her four other children (and now in part her grandson, Landon) by working full-time for the Royal Canadian Air Cadets, teaching music, cooking for a local summer camp, and doing various other odd jobs I couldn't keep track of, meanwhile volunteering for a local Christian substance-abuse clinic, presiding over the Peachland Arts Council, leading prayers for her evangelical church, taking recovering drug addicts into her home to engage them bit by bit in the tremendous cheerful engine of her Protestant industriousness, and helping men that Elliott came into contact with in the prison system land on their feet after release—"Three for three so far!" she chirped in her winning lilt. I could not detect one iota of bitterness from her about the Sommer family's trials and tribulations, nor of self-righteousness about her borderline superhuman efforts to keep it going. The only way all the hardship in her life showed through was in the occasional quavering strain that underlay her upbeat pronouncements. Every dollar she could spare (and, I began to suspect, many she couldn't) went toward Elliott's legal bills.

The treaty transfer was no sure thing, I learned. Christel forwarded me the letter she had composed to the minister of public safety, signed by scores of supporters in Canada, but it was the U.S. side she was more concerned about. She was doing her best to keep her hopes up, and Elliott's, as she petitioned various senators for support. No one in the family had yet been able to afford a visit to him in Pine Knot, Kentucky. International phone calls were expensive. They wanted him home.

Still, Christel appeared to harbor few illusions regarding her oldest son. "I understand how persuasive he can be," she said. "He's always been a leader. At the same time I always knew there was something terribly wrong with him."

She told me that Elliott had been impossible to discipline as a child, because he never understood the effect his actions had on others or the repercussions they would bring down on himself. Every punishment came as a surprise and an injustice. Once, when he was around ten years old, his father caught him with cigarettes and scolded him for smoking, which sent Elliott into a rage because he had not actually been *smoking* them at the time. But instead of confronting his father, which he was still too young and intimidated to attempt, he left an anonymous, convincingly adult-sounding note threatening to blow up the house of the neighbors from whose foster children he had acquired the pack. When one of the neighbors brought the note over, ashen-faced, to show Christel, she recognized the handwriting immediately. Elliott denied everything with his usual calm facility until she bluffed that the police were going to dust the note for fingerprints.

"It didn't dawn on him that he had scared the crap out of somebody. His whole worldview was all about him. He had no real ability to have any compassion for someone else or see their perspective. He would have moments where all of a sudden he would see something clearly, start sobbing, and apologize to me. Then, bang: he was the king of the world again. There was a saying among family and friends: 'Well, that's just Elliott.' Can't expect anything more or less."

When she tried to tell me about his propensity for grandiose fantasies and schemes, Christel ran out of words. "From the time he was little, my whole family, we just constantly—it was beyond imagination. It was almost like he lived in a book. You know? Like he was writing storylines but never really attaching them to consequence."

She confirmed that Elliott had been diagnosed with rapid-cycling bipolar disorder and post-traumatic stress disorder by the Bureau of Prisons and placed on a regimen of psychiatric medication. She was baffled that his mental illness had gone undiagnosed by the army.

"I'm in the military myself, but part of my frustration is the fact that the military itself uses these kids. In a sense, it has trained them not to use their brains, not to be critical thinkers. Nowise do I say Elliott is blameless in this thing. He is totally guilty of committing a crime. The crime of involving other young men was the worst part of it for me. But had the United States military screened him for mental illness, they would not have let him in. They loved the fact that he was as manic and crazy as he was, because that's the kind of guy they want jumping into trouble. They like 'em slightly psychopathic, to do the work they do."

She said she thought his youth had had a lot to do with it too. "In the Canadian Army we don't send our seventeen-year-olds to the front lines. We send our thirty-year-olds with experience, and the seventeen-year-olds do supporting work."

Christel also told me I shouldn't worry too much about Elliott's request for money. He felt guilty, she explained, about being a drain on the family, and was always looking for ways to take care of her. When I admitted that I had felt a little scared to contact Elliott at first, she told me she understood perfectly.

"I get that," she said. "But I don't think you have anything to fear anymore. There's two reasons. One is that he's being medicated and it has totally connected him to reality. Which is important, but in so doing, it has also connected him back to his moral compass. The other is that . . . I don't know how else to put it, but I woke up one night and God told me to pray and pray and pray and pray, and I did and I did, and miracle after miracle happened that weekend, and by Monday morning he was a new man. His whole existence has changed. His whole purpose has changed. He runs a small church in the prison now. Everybody that comes in new gets a whole set of stuff so that they're not without toothbrush and paste and toilet paper and clothes and shoes. Another example: a guy ripped him off twenty-five hundred dollars and he just said, 'You know, Mom, part of me wants to go scare the crap out of him, because I know that's your money that he just ripped off'—because it was, and I can't afford it—'but you know what? I'm a Christian now, and I am not going to do that. I used to be the tough guy, and everybody was scared of me, and if I said to give me the money back or else, they'd have done it, but I can't do that anymore. So I'm sorry to do this to you, but you're going to have to suck that up.' So I really don't think that there's too much to worry about."

"Well," I said, "that's good to hear."

"If you're ever having problems with Elliott," Christel said, "just call me. He listens to his momma."

The possibility that there was some depth to Elliott's character seemed to reside in the philosophical questioning that his military service had apparently inspired in him. In his first email to me, he wrote that he had been just as idealistic about the military as Alex had been on enlisting, but that his experience deploying with the Rangers had been deeply destabilizing, forcing him to question everything he once believed.

I had come across a peculiar moment in Constable Jennifer Cook's interview with Nathan's ex-girlfriend Tasha, who camped with Nathan and Elliott during that fateful summer trip to Cultas Lake in 2005, just after Elliott returned from Afghanistan. Constable Cook asked if Tasha had ever heard Sommer talk about his plans.

"He had talked about getting back at America because of all the bad things America's done," Tasha said in a tearful gush. "He was going to plan something and we knew where his head was at but we didn't know that it was actually going to happen. The military changed Elliott. Like, he's always been kind of different, but when we met him . . . We've known him from the time before he was in the military, and he's changed completely."

"What had he said about how he was going to get back at the United States? What types of things was he talking about?"

"I don't know. He just wanted to plan something big and I . . . I always maybe thought that if he did, it would actually be something *big*, you know, like, not . . ." Tasha fell silent. When she spoke again, her voice was warier. "I don't know," she said.

Cook let it drop.

Elliott readily admitted to me that after his arrest he had tried to turn what he had seen abroad to his own advantage. "I saw, and did, things overseas I did not like," he wrote. "Contrary to what I have said in the past, the only thing that those events triggered was a profound sense of apathy. I did not do this because of a profound sense of moral outrage, I did it because I had no sense of morality at all." Still, he insisted that the specific incidents were genuine. When I asked for details over the phone, he told me it wasn't just the war crimes that had bothered him. When he first deployed to Iraq, two soldiers in his platoon had just stolen thousands of dollars from an Iraqi family on a raid of their house and had been punished with kitchen duty.

"That was the first day I got to Baghdad," Elliott said. "These two assholes were on KP duty for doing it the night before. So when I came back, having just seen everything that I had seen, and then people would make comments like, 'Man, we should rob a bank,' the thought process stopped being 'Man, that's crazy,' and it started being like, 'You know what, let's do it.' You know, like, 'Who the hell cares.' There is no right, there is no wrong, you know what I mean?"

The next incident Elliott described by email.

I was on a prisoner transport mission to a black site at BIOP. One of the prisoners I took off the chopper sat down on the tarmac and resisted me moving him. I tried pulling him, pushing him, yelling at him . . . nothing worked. The chopper blades were spinning and nothing I could do would make him move. So I became angry, and began beating him. It was dark and things were, as they often are in combat environments, chaotic. The warrent [sic] officer in the chopper got out, and came to help me. After he asked me why I hit him, I explained. He pointed out a tourniquet around his leg. The truth was, he wasn't fighting me . . . he had been shot, and was mortally wounded. He was the enemy, but to this day the fact that I hurt a man in his dying moments, alone and seperated [sic] from his family and friends, being screamed up under the cover of darkness in a language he couldn't begin to comprehend . . . it haunts me. I was 18. I am not a cruel person, and I was not built for war.

After a year of Alex's endless, shifting excuses, it was at least refreshing to talk about the robbery with someone who seemed interested in looking inside himself for reasons. But these incidents, if true, seemed alarmingly insufficient to account for the change in Elliott. Many soldiers had seen worse. How could the path from disillusionment to an intricate, months-long preparation for a violent crime be as simple as "Who the hell cares"?

———

Two more years went by—the housing crisis, Uncle Kurt's death, Alex's new Ranger tattoo—before I felt stymied enough in other avenues of research to get back in touch with Elliott. First I checked in with Christel, who told me that her son's journey of reform and self-discovery had culminated in writing a book-length memoir, which she promised to pass along as soon as she had it. She was happy to report that the last year had brought further big developments in Elliott's life. The first was that he had a girlfriend. The second was that he was pursuing an advanced degree in mathematics.

"The head of the math department at San Francisco State University is helping him out," she explained. "He's waiving the residency requirement. Elliott's into . . . what's it called . . . number theory. He likes an Indian mathematician who had no formal training and only lived to twenty-seven but who discovered all these things that no one else could understand. Srini . . . uh, vasa . . . Ramoo . . . Rama . . ."

"Ramanujan." I couldn't help laughing at the bizarreness of hearing his name in this context. "An English mathematician named Hardy took him over to England from a rural town in India. No one at Cambridge understood how he was arriving at these crazy theorems."

"Right! That's the situation Elliott's in. He's asking professors these questions and they're like, 'Well, wow. Nobody really knows the answer to that.' He's interested in primes, minimal 3D numbers, the idea that there can't be an infinity in 3D . . . I don't understand it, really. I just listen."

I look back on everything that followed with unresolved bafflement. Is it really possible, despite all the intellectual safeguards I thought I had put in place, that I too succumbed in some way to Luke Elliott Sommer's mysterious charisma? How else to account for the fact that I became more open with him about my doubts about Alex's story than I was with any of the Blums, that I grew increasingly complicit in his ongoing deceptions of his own family and wife-to-be, that I began to hold Alex's every exaggeration and misrepresentation against him even as I found reasons to excuse Elliott's own, that I ended up trusting Elliott more than Alex himself?

I can't quite bring myself to attribute all this to deliberate effort on Elliott's part. In our conversations about Alex, he positioned us as peers, looking down together on Alex with pity and compassion for his inability to tell the truth, but was it clear to Elliott how desperate I was to connect to someone who appeared more capable than my cousin of sincere self-reflection? Could he sense how alienated I increasingly felt from a Blum family that seemed more interested in defensive myth-making than in scientific truth-seeking? Did he understand how seductive it was to me to be respected as a mathematical authority in this time of severe career disruption and nostalgia for my prodigy past?

What seems unlikeliest of all is the possibility that Elliott undertook a year-long study of number theory just to get closer to me.

Still, there is a story every math kid knows about Ramanujan. It takes place toward the end of the First World War, an event whose duration matched Ramanujan's years of greatest mathematical productivity but whose only effect on him appears to have been to frustrate his access to the vegetarian meals his Hindu faith required. Everyone at Cambridge was astonished by the raw eccentric force of Ramanujan's genius, but the climate did not agree with him, and he soon fell ill with tuberculosis. G. W. Hardy took one of London's black cabs to visit him in the hospital. Knowing that numbers were Ramanujan's greatest comfort, he opened the conversation with the license plate number of the cab, 1729, which Hardy described as singularly uninteresting.

"No," said Ramanujan. "It is a very interesting number—it is the smallest number expressible as the sum of two cubes in two different ways."

This is easily verified: 1729 can be written as either $1728 + 1$ or $1000 + 729$, the sum of 12^3 and 1^3 or of 10^3 and 9^3. Ramanujan is not exactly correct, however, that this makes 1729 interesting. The reason this story fills the skinny chests of math kids everywhere with a glow of amusement and fellowship is that being the sum of two cubes in two different ways is so arcane and pointless a distinction, so tangential to any serious line of mathematical inquiry, that it implies a whole lifetime's worth of rambling through the solitary landscape of numbers to have been ready with it the moment Hardy asked, and what this says to the skinny-chested math kid is, *You have never been alone there.*

Ramanujan was my favorite too. He has probably been the favorite of every backwoods prodigy for a century. He makes kids want to be mathematicians the way Kafka makes them want to be writers, standing as proof that genius springs from the oddest of origins, that being perennially misunderstood is evidence of true originality, and that to succeed all you have to do is be your weird, impossible self. Number theory, Ramanujan's specialty, is for a budding talent the most seductive and the most dangerous of fields. Many of the greatest unsolved problems involve only elementary concepts, can be stated in a sentence or two, and have swallowed some of mankind's profoundest thought as far back as the ancient Greeks. They stand like unlocked houses on well-traveled streets whose labyrinthine basements contain the bones of thousands.

What Christel had conveyed of her son's mathematical insights was not very promising, but it did mean something to know that Elliott had been in those houses too. When I emailed him with some new questions about his relationship with Alex, I slipped in a postscript asking what he was working on. Elliott wrote back with a reiteration of the position he had stated two years before, that he had simply seen Alex as a good friend who agreed to help out—in fact, Alex had been such a cool kid at battalion, and Elliott such an outcast, that Specialist Sommer had actually seen himself as striving for

PFC Blum's approval. Far more text was devoted to a very famous unsolved mathematical problem known as Goldbach's conjecture. The language surprised me. It was more sophisticated than any I had seen from him before—in fact, as I read it, I felt for perhaps the first time with Elliott that I was in contact with a human being whose interior life I could relate to. The strange thing was, even after three paragraphs of brisk, elliptical, jargon-dense mathematical prose, it somehow managed to remain completely unclear to me whether he had any idea what he was talking about.

———

Elliott's new girlfriend turned out to be a cocktail waitress from Westbank named Mandi Chmelyk, with whom he had been involved off and on since he was fifteen. After Christel gave her my email address, Mandi sent me a copy of the book-length memoir Elliott had just finished writing. It was not, as I had hoped, a deeper and more searching account of his motivation for the robbery. It was about hacking. The technical language was so convincing that even an experienced dabbler like me couldn't help reading with some degree of belief, at least on the paragraph level, although the plot rang a few alarm bells: learning the trade from an online guru code-named "Cyph3r," joining the hacktivist group Anonymous, then building up from scamming Peachland soda machines to running a team of underlings from a hotel room that cleared $40,000 per month from Kelowna ATMs in a nonstop bacchanal of drugs and code. Midway through came a glancing encounter with a younger girl named Mandi, whom teenaged Elliott had not at the time recognized as his destiny (Angela and Vicki, among others, were presumably also in contention for that honor) but whom he now saw to have been his beacon of hope and purity all along.

"I'm biased," Mandi's email read, "but I think it's really good."

I wrote to Elliott to see if he could put me in touch with his hacker friends. He replied with great regret that they were too publicity-shy to speak to me.

I called Mandi. She sounded very nice, very young, very much in love.

"Ever since he kissed me when I was thirteen years old," Mandi said, "I've never been able to see my life without him. He was just always the end result for me. I was with someone else for the entire six years that we were apart, and I tried really, really hard to get over him. I tried really, really hard to be in love with the guy that I was with. And it wasn't that I didn't love him, but I just couldn't stop loving Elliott. The entire time that I was outright refusing to speak to him, he was still sending me love letters from jail. They would show up and cause these fights. There's actually a street in Westbank called Elliott Road, and my ex couldn't even—I'm still getting used to calling him my ex—he would flinch every time we drove past it. He was so jealous of all things Elliott. I couldn't go up and see anyone in Elliott's family. But in the past year, I finally just started doing it. Christel is such a phenomenal woman. She is amazing. She's wonderful. I get all my advice from her. So I finally broke up with my ex about a month ago, and two days later I was like, 'All right, well, I guess I better write him back now.' So I did."

She told me that when she had started high school, two years after Elliott, she had rolled her eyes at all the rumors about how tough and scary he was. I asked her if she had personally observed anything resembling the computer hacking escapades that appeared in Elliott's book.

"No. I knew he was really, really smart with the computer, but it was never something that I excelled at so it wasn't something that we shared. He didn't keep many secrets, but that was one of them. All that stuff that he did, I had no idea about it until I actually read about it in the manuscript. I was pretty shocked."

I asked what her thoughts were about the future for her and Elliott.

"The future is that—people think I'm totally nuts—I am going to marry him one day. I'm making him wait until he's out of prison, but he's the only person that I want to be with. I'm a giddy little girl when he calls. My whole world just lights up. I have a smile on my face for hours. I just can't—I tried—I just can't be with anyone else. He's my happily ever after, in a really, really weird way."

Mandi, Christel, and I made arrangements for me to drive up from Seattle to Peachland to meet them in two weeks.

CHAPTER 20

SPACE STATION SOMMER

On the concrete median between the lines of traffic approaching and departing from the Sumas customs station on the border between Washington State and British Columbia sit a pair of black marble towers about the height of a man. They were erected six months after September 11, 2001, by Canadian law enforcement officers in honor of "those who fight and sacrifice in the war on terrorism." Few stop for a closer look. The moment of international goodwill toward the United States in which they were born has by now so thoroughly evaporated it is strange to think it ever existed.

At the window, a leather-jacketed customs agent took my passport and asked me in a flat Canadian accent what the purpose of my trip was.

This struck me as a good question. Two days of rest and relaxation with the mother and girlfriend of my family's arch-nemesis, who just might be telling me more truth about my cousin's involvement in his bank robbery than my cousin himself?

Like much else in British Columbia, Okanagan Lake turned out to be monstrously huge, deeper from lake bottom to the twilit peaks that surround it than the Grand Canyon. The turnoff for Peachland took me all the way down to the waterfront, then climbed back into the hills beyond through a pine grove full of ramshackle houses with pickups and ATVs in their driveways. The first sign after the paving ran out was polite: black type on a white background reading ROAD CLOSED. The next two were more strident as they flashed through my headlights: neon orange and yellow type on black backgrounds reading NO TRESPASSING and PRIVATE DRIVE. The road leading up to the final sign got steeper and bumpier. This one was a sandwich board leaning against a decaying wooden fence with six-inch-tall plastic letters stuck on at erratic intervals: NO PUBLIC ACCESS.

I let the car roll to a stop and got out. Tucked into the tree line at the top of a grassy slope was a house with a wraparound deck. A tiny figure with hair that looked vaguely aglow in the moonlight was leaning on the railing. I called Christel's number on my cell phone. A few seconds later, the figure lifted her hand to her ear, and a second after that I heard the voice I had come to know.

———

At nine the next morning, we sat out on the deck where I had seen her standing the night before, perched high above the ten-mile squiggle of lake between Peachland and Kelowna.

"Is there a moment you remember when you first recognized that Elliott was special?" I asked. "Or . . . different?"

Christel gave me a wide-eyed, open-mouthed, rotating nod, like *You better believe it.* "I knew from the time he was a year and a half old. Most kids at a year and a half say 'daddy' and 'mama,' but he was *quite* well-spoken. One night, after trying to coax him to brush his teeth, I said, 'Well, then, *don't* brush your teeth,' and all of a sudden he looks at me and goes, 'I hate you.'" Christel clutched her hands to her heart and fell back in her chair as if shot, then laughed. "You know, I hadn't been a mother long. Now I look back and go, 'No big deal. They all hate you at one point or another.' It wasn't so much the behavior as it was the age of the behavior. I knew right away that he was smarter than the average bear."

I glanced away from Christel, who was smiling in anticipation of the answering smile I felt forming reflexively on my face, and back toward the pine-covered peaks that overlapped into the distance on either side of the lake. The house was less grand than the view, not so much squalid as given over in certain quarters to the forces of chaos that had blown through it for years. Under the deck, a descending meadow was littered with scrap wood, tools, and wildflowers. Behind the kitchen, clumps of yellow foam insulation spilled from an upended hot tub near a sagging hay-bale archery target. In the half-finished basement, hanging blankets marked off a warren of alcoves for the gaggle of recovering addicts, paroled convicts, and distraught wives of reoffending former tenants who passed two or three at a time through Christel's care.

I was still trying to figure out what to make of her in person. Instead of the beleaguered Christian matron I had pictured, she was tanned, toned, and vivacious, with a biker babe's platinum-blond hair all the way down past the shoulders of her patterned sundress. Her wit and charm were manifest, but a certain unhinged energy flickered around the edges of her body language. Over the phone to me, as in her petitions to authorities, Christel had always taken pains to describe Elliott as profoundly unwell and guilty of grave crimes. Here, in the house he had played in as her brilliant, challenging first child, it was becoming clear that a different Elliott lingered.

"Do you have anything from his childhood?" I asked. "Photographs, school papers?"

"Oh, sure," she said. "There's a whole box of his old awards in the basement."

Downstairs, Christel dug them out one by one. There was an award for highest aggregate points in the Jr. Section "M" Boys category of the Peachland Fall Fair when Elliott was eight, three "READ THROUGH THE BIBLE GEN. 1–REV. 22" awards presented to him ages nine to eleven by his father, a review of *Toy Story 2* he wrote that was published in the *Peachland View*, judging it "arguably the best Disney film ever created and by far the best sequel." There was a stack of handsomely engraved plaques from Squad 902 of the Royal Canadian Air Cadets: one each for recruitment, leadership, and best third-year cadet, two for citizenship, and three for best dressed, featuring mounted photographs of a teenaged Elliott standing at attention in his uniform, sitting in the cockpit of a small plane, and striking a stance in a belted white karate gi. There was a letter on Peachland government stationery congratulating him for his volunteer activities, signed by Mayor George E. Waldo.

Christel reminisced a little over each photograph before handing it over. I stared into each for a while, trying to see what she saw. Then we went upstairs again, where she blended a smoothie for herself and told me the story of her marriage to Luke Sommer Senior in a way that made it sound like a long, surreal nightmare.

"I went to the Moody Bible Institute in Chicago at age seventeen. Luke had come out of the San Jose wannabe gangster scene, seventies bad-boy stuff, and then had become a Christian after he got in a fight where he felt like he had almost killed somebody and it scared him. He was very charismatic. He'd go to the campus coffee shop and all these students would go like this"—Christel fluttered her fingers under her chin and batted her eyelashes—"as he was debating theology."

Christel liked his dynamism. She shared his political ambitions. She agreed to his strictly Biblical model of marriage, which included head-covering at worship in accordance with 1 Corinthians 11. But the reality of it turned out to be what she called a "twenty-year journey of complete ridiculousness." Suddenly Christel was expected to be a demure stay-at-home wife and mother, restricted from the leadership roles she had grown accustomed to in church, choir, and community service. After a short stint in Peachland so Luke Junior—Elliott—could be born with Christel's health insurance, the family moved to San Jose so Luke Senior could pursue his political career. He had trouble finding work, but that didn't slow him down. When he won the Republican nomination to run for Congress in 1988, against a field that included a World War II veteran, he was thirty-two years old and nominally a real estate agent but in fact eking out a living as a paper boy for the *San Jose Mercury-News*.

After losing on Election Day to the popular incumbent, Norman Mineta, Luke took Christel and two-year-old Elliott back to Peachland, where he again ran into trouble finding work. Over the next decade and a half of intermittent poverty and marital discord, as the family grew by three more sons and a daughter, Christel chafed more and more under Luke's rigid strictures. Elliott's resistance gave voice to her own suffocation. The younger children lived in the shadow of endless clashes between their father and their doggedly rebellious elder brother. Then Christel separated from Luke, started seeing Elliott's commanding officer in the Air Cadets, and became pregnant, all before Luke granted her a divorce. It was a shocking development for devout, hardline Christians like the Sommers. Elliott took it all especially hard, at one point even writing to Luke's mother, Margaret, to see if he could move in with her in California, though he mostly sided with his mother.

———

"The ramifications of Elliott's choices—behavior, whatever— have flowed down the line to my other kids," Christel said. "Maybe some of the same genetic mental-health issues too. Reagan is a perfect example. The tattoo on his arm, which is a drawing Elliott made in prison, is the side of Elliott that none of us want to ever have to see. When Reagan's had behavioral issues—and he's been arrested a few times; he went out and robbed a liquor store with his face all covered up, blah, blah, blah—it is just purely copycat behavior. There are just certain behaviors that—"

"Wait," I said. "*Reagan* robbed a liquor store?"

"Yeah."

I was so startled I didn't know what else to say. Christel was talking on as cheerfully as ever.

"I mean, they're not bad kids. It's just this whole emulating Elliott thing."

I genuinely liked Christel. It impressed me the way she had endured the calamity of her family life with her good humor and optimistic spirit intact. But it was a little unnerving to see her tremendous resources of forgiveness, faith, and pluck directed at explaining away her children's crimes. For all Elliott's lies over the years, her fundamental stance toward him seemed unchanged. She did not doubt pending reasons to believe, as others did; she believed pending reasons to doubt.

"When he was nine, ten, eleven years old," Christel told me, "he'd be on the phone with game companies and game developers and the president of this company and that company and they'd have no idea. Then, once he turned twelve, his voice changed, and his whole world opened up, because nobody knew how old he was."

She told me about software development partners who had called at all hours in strange accents and sent software packages worth $250,000 (in Elliott's valuation, presumably) to her door. She told me that Elliott had once hacked into Kelowna's streetlights and caused accidents by switching them at random. She told me that he had called up Richard Marcinko, founder of SEAL Team Six, and invited him to speak to his Air Cadet squadron.

"I lived with this kind of thing constantly," Christel said. "His ideas were so huge. What was I supposed to do with all this? There were parts of me that didn't believe half of what he was saying. Nobody else would believe me because it was so outlandish. My own brother was one of them. Anything I said, I'd be told, 'Oh, he's just snowing you.' But that's how he lives. Nothing is small with him. There are no limits. He's always felt that anything is possible and he's always loved a challenge and if people said you couldn't do it, he would say, 'Of course you can.' Now, you have to imagine as a parent trying to raise a kid like that. On the one hand, you don't want to be stomping on his dreams, but on the other hand, they're so huge you have to wonder, are we really talking reality here? Or are you just way off in delirious land? I can say, without a doubt, that even though I didn't know about everything he's written about, I know that most of it is extremely *possible*, because of the things I *did* see and *did* know. The fact that I did see $250,000 software delivered to my door, I did talk to people in Hungary, I did talk to people in—you know what I mean?"

When Elliott began complaining of army abuses while he was on house arrest, Christel felt immediately that there was substance to what he was saying. She had heard him talk about this from the time of his very first deployment to Iraq in 2004. Still, a lifetime with Elliott had at least led her to be skeptical about the details.

"I'm sitting there going, 'Okay. There's got to be a root of truth in here. But how much of it is real and how much of it is an extension of that reality?' What got me was within hours of him making national news, we were getting calls from a general of the Joint Chiefs of Staff. I'm thinking, 'You know what? If he was a bag of wind, they wouldn't be calling. They wouldn't be sending a Homeland Security helicopter from the United States illegally into my yard.'"

"Wait," I said. "A *helicopter* landed in your yard?"

Christel painted a vivid scene: the general of the Joint Chiefs making so specific a reference to the weather in Peachland that it sounded as if he were right above them; the black Homeland Security helicopter landing in the field behind the house; Elliott informing the family that the U.S. military might be staging an extraction at any minute. She told me a local journalist named Dave Preston saw the helicopter too.

————

Something was beginning to unsettle me about Okanagan Lake. It was so giant and still and elemental that truth here seemed independent of whatever lay beyond the encircling mountains. As Christel and I walked side by side along the water toward the town center, she waved and shouted hello to shopkeepers and introduced me to a series of swimsuited middle-aged women under beach umbrellas.

"I'm going to take you to meet Tim," she said. She steered me into an Ace Hardware store in a building on the waterfront, which she explained was owned by her father. Behind the register stood an ageless man with pale, fleshy skin and an aura of having held many heavy materials firm in one hand as he punched sharp metal implements through them with the other.

"Ben is writing about Elliott. He wants to know what you think of him."

Tim turned his mineral gaze on me from across the narrow countertop. There was a long silence.

"It's okay," Christel said. "You can trust him."

Trust me? With *what*? But Tim was already talking.

"I know Elliott," he said. "I taught him in Sunday school. I know his grandfather, I know his brothers, I know his sisters, I know his mother. I know Elliott. What do you want to know?"

"I hear he was very bright," I said finally.

"Oh, he was bright," Tim agreed. "As bright a child as I've ever seen. But he was beaten down at every turn, beaten down and beaten down."

No further words turned out to be required from me. Tim began a sermon on the life of Luke Elliott Sommer that wound through God, heaven, Satan, America, and everything in between, forces so grand and shadowy that I could barely make out the quotidian particulars upon which they impinged. His hard, weathered face was close enough to mine that I had to pick which eye to look into. They were milky pale and unblinking as a cobra's. I kept inadvertently switching between them. His voice got softer and lower as the cadence grew more driving.

"He thought of himself as a hero," Tim said. "He sought to become a hero. But it was not his to become. The American government taught him destruction. They taught him to take life. He turned that destruction back upon them, and they could not accept it, and they incarcerated him for it."

Beside me, Christel abruptly pounded the countertop. "Yes!" she said.

Tim's eyes did not waver from mine. "This one will find a way forward, a way to raise her other children, with Jesus. She's a survivor. And one day in the untold future, if enough attention is brought to his story, maybe he will be seen as a figure like Nelson Mandela, and he will be freed."

"Yes!" cried Christel, pounding the countertop again. "Yes!"

His handshake nearly crushed the bones in mine. I hurried outside to take what felt like my first breath in ten minutes. Christel joined me shortly afterward. We walked half a block in silence past the window shoppers in flip-flops and sunglasses and the slate expanse of the lake, where a massive nimbocumulus was hanging like an anvil over Kelowna. I was not exactly sure what I had just been allowed a glimpse of. For the first time since arriving, I felt something that rose above the level of mere incredulity, something closer to fear.

"He's an intense man," I said.

"He speaks what he feels. If you talk to the people who knew Elliott, that's the way a lot of them feel. When I started a petition to send to the minister of public safety, I got a hundred signatures, easy."

———

Back at the house, a crowd had assembled in the living room. Reagan was on Facebook at the kitchen table. Christel joined her daughter, Karis, and Elliott's girlfriend, Mandi, in preparing a big salad behind the counter. Sitting on the sofa were a squat middle-aged woman with a childlike smile, some friends of Karis's who were staying in the basement, and a good-looking kid with a shaggy mop of brown hair who turned out to be Elliott's son, Landon, as courteous, charming, and intelligent a nine-year-old as I have ever met. Laughter flew around the room. There was a decorative cabinet full of china, a wingback armchair with a paperback titled *Tortured for Christ* draped over the arm. The shared conviction beneath all the strange conversations I had been having since arrival was finally starting to come into focus: in this little town on the lake, Elliott was a very different person than the rest of the world knew. Here his crime-family plan was just a trumped-up misinterpretation by U.S. investigators of one of those nonsense fantasies that he had always been so famous for and that those close to him could have told you wasn't real from the start. Here the robbery was an act of protest against the American abuses that had disturbed his profound sense of justice, though unfortunately he had gone about it in the wrong way, as medication had since helped him see. The tattoo that covered Reagan's arm featured an eight ball, a syringe, a screaming head with its scalp planed off, and a horned human skull holding a scroll in its teeth with the initials L.E.S., but now Luke Elliott Sommer was what Reagan referred to as a "completely changed person": a "father figure," a "role model," and a "very good life coach."

The disorienting thing was how familiar so much of this was. The Blums too had united around an unconventional interpretation of their hero's participation in a violent crime. But while Sam and Carly also went through high school known by their peers as the siblings of a bank robber, their response was not to romanticize Alex's role; it was to hide it. The Sommers lived with far less shame. Talking to the Blums about Alex was like slogging around on a planet with terrible gravity, each tiny adjustment in the truth bearing immense emotional consequence. Talking to the Sommers was like being in outer space, Bibles and robberies and war crimes and salad greens all bumping around free and loose in the moral and epistemological antigravity field of Luke Elliott Sommer. His little brothers could descend into Peachland for what Christel called "copycat behavior" amid all the teenage girls here on vacation from Calgary and Vancouver, and then they could just come back up here above it all and float.

For the first time in a long time, I missed my family.

———

The next morning I met Dave Preston, the reporter whom Christel had referred to several times as having special knowledge about

Elliott. Preston had been one of Peachland's most prominent journalists for years, a mainstay of the weekly *Peachland View* who had gone on to launch his own news website, peachlandnews.com. He turned out to be a genial middle-aged man in shorts, sandals, and a baseball cap over light buzzed hair, with a kooky smile and a bit of a potbelly.

"Elliott's arrest caused quite a stir," Preston recalled. "He was a local boy, a Christian boy, homeschooled. People thought he'd been raised right. They were quite shocked about it. Three days later, when he was in the detention center in Kamloops, I got a telephone call. 'Hi, Dave, this is Elliott Sommer—would you like to talk to me?'"

Preston first met him in person at Christel's house, when he was released on bail and confined there on house arrest.

"He was a ripped Army Ranger like something right out of the movies. He had these big eyes. He was so wired. His brain was always going, always going, always plotting something new. If someone yelled boo, he would have killed them first and asked questions later. I found him to be just about the strangest guy I had ever met, but on the other hand he was kind of *likable*. Over the course of the eighteen or twenty-four months while he was awaiting extradition, I spent probably a couple hundred hours with him. I have to admit I did get quite friendly with him. He'd call me up at eleven-thirty and say, 'Dave, I need a pack of smokes.' His mother wasn't such a believer in smoking. So I'd bring him a pack, we'd have a smoke, I'd pump him for information, he'd make up a few things, and it was all good."

"How much of what he told you did you buy? He's notorious for spinning tales."

"Oh God, yes," said Preston. "Point zero zero one percent, when it comes right down to it. He certainly had the press up here going for a while. The guy is, I'd say, close to brilliant. But I think the most interesting part of Elliott is his psychological makeup. What makes him tick."

"What does make him tick?"

Preston blew air through his lips like a horse. "I haven't quite figured that out. I know he's been diagnosed with fast-cycling bipolar and PTSD. He was raised by a really strange father. Luke Sommer was absolutely pro-Republican, pro–American flag, pro the U.S. Army. He'd line the kids up for inspection every day, check their fingernails and grooming habits, weird stuff like that. He got Elliott at age seventeen or whatever going across the border and joining the army. Then he became a Ranger, which for him was the pinnacle. 'Yeah, I'm going to kick some butt.' I think what he experienced over there was very different from what he'd expected."

I asked him about the helicopter.

"Oh, so it's landed now?" Preston said, chuckling. "Last I heard it just flew overhead. Apparently a cousin of his saw it."

"You didn't see it yourself?"

"No."

Preston did confirm that he possessed a recording of a phone conversation with Special Operations Command, but it was a colonel, not a general.

"Elliott was really big on the intrigue at that time. 'SOCOM's really terrified,' that kind of thing. In private he blasted the Rangers, the U.S. military, he had a 9/11 conspiracy thing going, but the second he got on the phone with the colonel, it was 'Yes sir, no sir, all that and a bag of bread, sir.' Instant changeover into military grunt."

"So it wasn't a general of the Joint Chiefs?"

"It was a SOCOM colonel."

This is approximately the difference between a Supreme Court Justice and a district judge.

"Did he take him seriously?"

"He certainly heard him out."

Preston talked about his time with Elliott Sommer with wry humor and a certain wistfulness. The story seemed to be for him the big one that got away.

"I have a stack of notes two feet high, but I don't know how to write about it," he said. "It almost works better as a novel."

My most important question for Preston was simple: whether Elliott had ever talked to him about Alex. Preston nodded immediately.

"I kept asking him, 'Why, why, why? Why did these guys do it?' He'd say different things. In the beginning, he'd say, 'Everyone had their own reasons.' But he did say, as far as Alex was concerned, he thought it was a training mission. As far as Alex was concerned, it wasn't real."

My hand clenched tightly around my coffee. Preston sipped mildly from his. The feeling this time was not so much of relief as of whiplash.

"When was this?"

"While Elliott was on house arrest. He felt the worst about Alex. The impression I got of Alex was that he was an energetic puppy dog, willing to do almost anything to fit in. I got the impression that Elliott had a kind of mystical power over him. Of all the guys, it seemed like Alex was the most misled."

———

Preston promised me that as soon as he found the time, he would dig through his two-foot-tall stack for documentation of Elliott's statements about Alex. I spent the afternoon going through the Peachland Museum's archive of old newspapers during the period when Elliott's memoir claimed a three-part series of articles about his spree of soda-machine hacks. All I could find were features about wildfires, roving bears, a solidarity parade after September 11, and a plane that crashed into the hills above Peachland because of an "optical illusion," many of them penned by Dave Preston. By one in the afternoon I was on the road.

I had one final task before going home. Just across the border, I stopped at a small café to call Professor Matthias Beck at San Francisco State University, whom Elliott and Christel had told to expect my call.

"Yes, hello?" answered Beck, in a surprising German accent.

I asked him if he wouldn't mind telling me about his relationship with Luke Elliott Sommer.

"It seems somehow he got hold of a book that I coauthored," Beck said. "This was in January, I believe. He wrote a letter to me asking some questions that he had. I'm vaguely aware of programs like the university prison project here at San Quentin, and I support them— not directly myself, but I've sent students to teach there before—but the reason I responded is that the kind of questions he asked, he clearly had talent. This was someone with a knack for higher mathematics. An interesting case. I was curious to see how much I could help him."

"Is there any chance of his being granted a degree?"

There was a long pause. "That's tough," he said. "He's asked me that, and I've looked into that a little bit, and basically all options involve money, and that makes it hard. Um . . . um . . . hard. It's hard."

"How much do you know about Elliott's criminal record?" I asked.

"Basically nothing at all," Beck said breezily.

———

The interview with Elliott at U.S. Penitentiary McCreary in Pine Knot, Kentucky, suddenly came through. I would have a single seven-hour session with him in November. I wrote to inform him. A few days later he called, excited to be having a visitor, and told me about his first stop after SeaTac FDC, USP Victorville in California, where he became addicted to drugs, had an altercation with a guard, and ended up in the hole.

"I think that was what saved my life," Elliott said. "When you're forced to spend that much time alone, you're forced to confront who you really are and whether you want to change it. Are you a liar, are you mean, are you an asshole? It all comes to the surface. The people who go crazy don't like what they find and don't know how to change it. If you're not an intelligent person and you're cruel, you focus on your anger. Guys come out of there angry and join gangs and stay angry. When I went in there, I didn't like what I found, in any capacity. I was basically a complete waste of human space. Sometimes you come to a point, a precipice, and you have to either jump and fall or roll back. In the hole I realized you have to make that choice to survive. And this has to stay between us, because it would crush my mom, but I am not a Christian. I am agnostic. I haven't been a Christian for a long time. But I had a moment where I was very Christian. I lapsed in the hole. Somebody, possibly a law enforcement officer, did something he shouldn't have done. He hit me. I started carving a knife. I was going to kill him. Then something happened right before I did it. I had one of these semireligious moments. Serendipity or . . . whatever it was. I was days away from getting this twelve-inch knife cut out of the door—it was massive, a fucking sword—when my case manager comes to the door. 'Hey, do you want to go back to Canada?' Apparently a bunch of people were working for me. There'd been a congressional inquiry. All of a sudden I had hope. I stopped and made the choice not to. After that I was very dependent on Christianity for six months. I started falling into the Christian trap, allotting glory to that, to the Christian God, et cetera, and then I weaned myself off. Logic does not do much to support Christianity. But it was the thought process that mattered, it wasn't the Christianity. It functions a lot like a drug. It gives you peace. I've helped my mom convert my brothers and sisters because they were animalistic savages and if they hadn't pursued that path, they'd end up here."

As usual, fifteen minutes had passed without me getting more than a word or two in edgewise. The Bureau of Prison phone system cut us off with a series of clicks. I was still thinking about the vivid way he had described the knife when, half an hour later, Elliott called back. I asked him if he had been medicated during that incident. To my surprise, he said he had been.

"At that point in time," Elliott said, "the decisions were all mine, including the one to go after that guy. So had I committed—had I gone through with it, that would have been all me. But I didn't, you know what I mean? That was the difference. Had I not been medicated there wouldn't have been that choice. I would have just followed it through until I butchered him. But once I got medicated, once I started talking to people and sorting through my issues, it was like there was no pressure at the gate. It's actually gotten to the point now where I've had guys come and, you know, hit me and whatever and I've just basically walked away, which is not something that you're supposed to do in prison culture. I've managed to walk away and have other people politely inform those people that they would not want to do that again. I won't get into that too much. But I just—my goal, I guess, is to help people get out, help them be successful, try and do the same thing myself. I teach. I'm a GED teacher. I've been helping guys get their GEDs and graduate."

Elliott told me that when he was twelve years old he made the conscious decision to live his life as if he were in a movie. When I emailed him to ask what movies he had based his life on, he sent me the list: *Punisher*, *Black Hawk Down*, *V for Vendetta*, heroic tales of vigilantism, soldiering, and terrorism, whose moral clarities he found comforting.

Here is something you need to understand about me, that unfortunately I never did . . . I have almost zero ability to judge right and wrong, from a moral standpoint. I am completely cognizant of legal right, and legal wrong. But questions of morality have always been a mystery to me. For many, this next insight would be bizarre, but I am hoping in your case, you understand. I have, throughout my life, had to base how I feel about certain things off of how I perceive other people responding to them. If I lacked the ability to empathize, I would conclude I was psychopathic, but the truth is that I can, and therefore, am not. However, because I had such little insight into morality, I would attempt to keep a running tally on the morality of any given action in my head. Literally, an equation.

By now it seemed likeliest to me that Elliott's hacking memoir was mostly made up. I had spoken to an urban planning expert who told me that hacking a city streetlight system in that era (as in the famous scene from the movie *Hackers*) was a technical impossibility, and even if Elliott had managed to hack a soda machine or an ATM once or twice, operations on the scale he was describing would not have gone unnoticed. But Elliott prickled when I pushed him on his truthfulness.

Your comment about 60% bullshit got to me, because on the one hand I do know what you mean. A lot of my life is exaggerated. But never on purpose. Do I lie? Without a doubt. But always WITH purpose. What purpose is served by anything I have done in the last ten years? Who calls a hundred and one reporters and dumps on them repeatedly the things I was saying to Dave [Preston] and the others, most of which was patently nuts . . . what benefit is there?

Not long afterward, Elliott informed me that he had just suffered a full-blown manic episode. Over the phone he told me it had gotten bad enough that by the end he was experiencing auditory hallucinations, along with a host of other symptoms. "I was like, 'It's time to go back on the drugs,'" Elliott concluded.

I was flabbergasted. "How long have you been *off* them?" I asked.

"Well, whenever I get supermanic and in one of my 'I'm a genius and I have a million great ideas,' I usually kick off the drugs because I can't make those decisions. But, you know, so . . . about a year."

"You've been off for a *year?*"

"At least," said Elliott.

I got off the phone in a disoriented stupor. Just when I was starting to get a handle on when I could trust Elliott and when I couldn't, he threw a wrench like this into the machinery. Was I to take his hacking "memoir," then, as a manic delusion to be pitied rather than a fabrication to be condemned?

Mandi did not end up making Elliott wait until he was out of prison. In fact, she beat me to Kentucky, marrying him there in October, surrounded by a squad of federal corrections officers in the visitation room of USP McCreary. The closest I had come to warning her had been to ask, in as pointed a tone as I could muster, if it would matter to her if Elliott had not in fact robbed the bank to protest war crimes. Her answer was that she loved him for exactly who he was.

Shortly afterward, I received a CorrLinks email from Elliott informing me that Preston had been indicted on child pornography charges after an online sting and an investigation of his house by the RCMP.

"Weird world," said Elliott's email. "I would be interested in seeing the forensic trail on that one. Anyways, later bud."

I never heard from Dave Preston again. The charges were later dropped.

———

A long time passed before I finally called Luke Sommer Senior at his real estate office in Idaho. Intimidated by the aura of menace with which Elliott and Christel had painted him, I was surprised to find him polite, open, and searching, though his speech patterns were uncannily like his oldest son's, torrentially fast and peppered with hyper-specific digressions which he seemed helpless to rein in. He told me that it had been he who had notified the RCMP when Elliott was hiding out in Peachland just after the robbery, hoping to avoid the death of his son or an officer or both. He told me that he still struggled with guilt over Elliott's crimes, that he felt great remorse for losing his temper with his children when they were young, that he regretted losing solidarity with Christel in the way they disciplined Elliott, that he now thought it better to compromise with one's partner and raise children more "liberally" than to allow the family unit to break apart. When he told me that the "handwriting was on the wall" with Elliott, he made sure to point out that the phrase came from the Book of Daniel, citing chapter and verse.

It was one Biblical explanation of many. I kept thinking of the guys I used to know in the electrical engineering department who, when you asked them how they had spent their morning, would compulsively explain every pin function in their latest integrated circuit. In Luke's case, though, the detail fixation was on the specifications for a Christian life as laid out in the Holy Bible. It was my first encounter with a scripture geek. It occurred to me that it might have been just as upsetting for Luke to see his precisely researched commandments bent, tweaked, and fudged by his new family as it would have been for one of my electrical engineering friends to see a team of junior lab techs wire up his circuit incorrectly. Christel had told me she felt suffocated within their marriage, but Luke saw the power dynamic differently. He still seemed a little dazed by his long brush with that talented, sexy, vivacious, ambitious, hopelessly irrepressible, endlessly prodigal-son-enabling woman.

"While we were still together and happy," Luke told me, "I used to compare falling in love with Christel to being a gazelle chased by a cheetah on the African savanna. She got a claw in and bagged me."

It was a strange new perspective on the dynamic that had given rise to Elliott Sommer: a geek and a cheetah locked in a permanent battle for control.

CHAPTER 21

TOTAL DATA

U.S. Penitentiary McCreary is one of seventeen high-security federal penitentiaries in the United States. It is located in Pine Knot, Kentucky, a town of two thousand in the Appalachian hill country where almost 40 percent of the population is below the poverty line. The closest airport is in Nashville, Tennessee, 250 miles away.

They aren't easy miles. In November 2013, three months after my visit to Sommer's family in Peachland, I flew to Nashville, rented a little Kia, and drove to Kentucky. In the clefts between wooded ridges, rusty pickup trucks decayed in the garages of boarded-up service stations with single pumps and hand-painted signs. For the final hour I could see only as far as the next bend, where bare white aspens rose on an endless procession of graded slopes in the chilly November sun. Pine Knot appeared as little more than a lumberyard, a dollar store, an array of brittle lawns, and a handful of American flags ruffling in the wind on its way back into the trees. My car was the only one in the motel parking lot. The front office was locked and empty, with an envelope holding my room key taped to the door. I had to kick through a pile of oak leaves to get into the room.

When I had informed Alex of the interview, he had told me he wanted to know just two things from Sommer: Did he really play hockey for the Kelowna Rockets? And did he ever even *believe* in the Ranger Creed? I had to suppress an eye-roll. My own questions for the guy I was now forced to rely on more than Alex himself for accurate details about the robbery were a little different: How aware had

Tigra Robertson, Nathan Dunmall, Chad Palmer, Scott Byrne, Richard Olinger, Alex Blum, and various others been of Elliott's plans? Most important, why did his fellow robbers all say yes?

My first impression as I pulled up to McCreary at seven-thirty the next morning was of some kind of Disney palace hacked out of the wilderness. A vast expanse of manicured grass draped over rolling hillocks and edged up to the shorelines of ponds harboring gaggles of geese. Along a driveway curving into the woods stood a redbrick Colonial mansion whose porch was fronted by Grecian columns. Farther on, a dozen gleaming Mustangs and Corvettes fanned out in a cul-de-sac beside a small cottage in which the shadowy figures of guards passed back and forth behind curtains made gauzy by the slanting morning sun. Racks full of riot gear were visible through the open garage door. These were clearly the prize jobs in Pine Knot.

After an elaborate series of security checks involving invisible ink, an ultraviolet light, and a board full of numbered tags to mark who had entered the facility, an escort led me into the no-man's-land between the outer Cyclone fence and the inner concrete walls. We walked along a windy grass corridor to a door on the far side, which turned out to lead into the empty visitation room. Against one wall stood a raised guard station. The opposite wall housed a row of private meeting rooms, each with a table fixed to the floor and two small stools on either side, all of it built of worn plastic the approximate color and texture of ancient, chewed-out gum. I had expected Elliott to be here already. Instead my escort led me to one of the rooms and vanished, leaving me to decide which stool to take: one in the back, facing outward, or one in the front, facing in.

I squeezed past the table and took the far stool. I've always felt more comfortable against the wall. Then, as I was spreading out my papers and legal pad, it occurred to me that this position would put a violent, mentally ill felon between the guards and me. Just as I was considering gathering up everything and switching, a large figure in khaki appeared in the open doorway, escorted by two guards, who ushered him in and then fell back.

Elliott settled himself on the stool across from mine and gave me the quick, false grin of a barroom seducer. "What do you think?" he said. "Do I look like you expected?"

As he was no doubt aware, the truth was, not in the slightest.

Elliott's appearance had transformed dramatically since his army days. He was tattooed everywhere I could see: playing cards, skulls, the seven deadly sins, a Celtic armband, the Ranger unit insignia, POW/MIA, Alice in Wonderland, a beaver shaving itself. Landon's name was printed across his neck. On his ring finger was a black band and the date of his wedding the previous month. Beside one of his famous blue eyes was the outline of a teardrop.

"In here, this earns you respect," he explained. "It means you've killed someone.* For an Iraq veteran, it's like, 'Well, that's easy.'"

For a while we talked about Peachland, about his family, about his wedding, about his son. Though Elliott was larger than me and his voice was the same commanding surge I had grown used to over the phone, there was a delicacy to him, a boyish fragility, that I hadn't expected. He had strange tics, a goofy smile. His knee jumped under the table. He pulled at the skin of his forearm, cracked his knuckles. Once in a while, with no provocation that I could discern, he bent over and clutched his head as if in great pain, a meaningless but oddly endearing gesture.

"Neuromuscular agitation," he explained when he saw me staring at his hand tapping away on the tabletop. "I've always had it."

No one had ever described Elliott to me as having tics, but over the next seven hours, as he tapped, rattled, tugged, clenched, and pulled a Styrofoam cup into tiny white pieces, it would become impossible to imagine him any other way.

He asked about Alex. I told him he was doing well.

"There's little I feel worse about than what happened to your cousin," he said. "He was living his dream. We only get so many chances to touch what we want. To have stripped that from him, it's hard to live with. I'd take another ten years if he could go back and have his dream. It's kind of an empty sentiment now."

On the table between us lay a stack of paper full of quotes from a Luke Elliott Sommer that seemed like someone else altogether.

———————

* In fact, as I learned later, an outlined teardrop generally means an attempted murder. It is only if the murder is successful that the teardrop is filled.

Specialist Sommer's troubles with the law actually began in May 2006, three months before the robbery, when he took a handgun across the border to Canada. After a sordid imbroglio involving high school girls and freaked-out parents, it looked like Sommer might have to face charges for it. His father wrote him an email of advice with six bullet points referencing different passages of the Bible, concluding with "(6) Let your lawyer do ALL your talking in legal matters (1 Jn 2:1–6)."

Sommer sent his father a short response full of cheery exclamation marks assuring him that for now he was "chilling."

On June 6 the boyfriend of one of the dozen or so women whose emoticon-heavy exchanges with Sommer made up the bulk of the material the FBI recovered from Elliott's computer wrote to express his discontent: "u fuckin fagget u talk 2 my gf like that agian ill take ur life."

This time Sommer responded with his own bullet-pointed list, ending with "4) If you even respond to this email, after I speak with J———— and talk to her however the fuck I want, I will cripple you. Not figuratively, not in an exaggerated manner, but paraplegic, 'you-will-never-walk-again-you-hippy-piece-of-shit' crippled. I have more friends in your little hick excuse for a town than you do, and some of your friends even have had the privilege of experiencing what a 'persuasive' individual I can be."

On June 13, Sommer wrote an email to the UN in support of Benjamin Dhunigana and John Dai, Christians held in Bhutan under a charge of illegal proselytization: "I request that these men be assessed not simply by the laws of a reasonable government but also by the compassion of those who understand the drive that powers men to go forth against what may seem an impossible task; to stand against something that is not reasonable and to seek the glorification of a God whom these men are obviously willing to suffer for with dignity."

On June 14 he emailed himself a black-and-white logo of a man with a pistol in a dashing black suit above the words "Neighborhood Watch," the name he would soon give to his Ranger-staffed "security firm."

On June 26, his twentieth birthday, he worked a shift at the hos-

pital. He wrote about it shortly afterward to Angela, the mother of
his son: "Just remember life has its moments when it sucks, but not
all the time! I have been working in the hospital a lot lately did a five
hour shift on my birthday and handled three geriatric patients with
Pulmonary Embolisms and other acute syndromes which was pretty
cool since we managed to save their lives which was nice. Anyways I
miss you tons and I hope your [*sic*] doing well!!!"

The day after his birthday, Sommer messaged an uncle back
home in British Columbia who owned a web hosting service: "So
in theory if I needed to set up a secure server with restricted access
I could get some of your bandwidth? what would that run me? I
only need fairly simple data transfer capabilities, mostly text with
the odd photos." In the coming days he would explain to his uncle
that there was a new push in the army to decentralize communications. The site he was building, onecharlie.com, would be the intel
hub for Charlie Company's First Platoon, "a direct profile of all recon
elements working undercover in the AFGHAN IRAQ area, used for
liasson [*sic*] communication with them without having to try using
the phone or radio."

The U.S. Army does not, of course, outsource secret battlefield
communications. In fact onecharlie.com would be the online hub for
Sommer's "security firm."

Later on the evening of June 27, Scott Byrne, an older Ranger
in Charlie Company's Third Platoon whom Specialist Sommer had
known since Jump School, messaged him to say hello and to relate
the sad fact that he was eating an MRE alone in his room. "everyone
in 3PLT went out for dinner," Byrne wrote, "and i mean everyone"

"why didnt they see if you wanted to go?" wrote Sommer.

"dunno"

"crazy"

In 2006 the official "don't ask, don't tell" policy made it illegal
to be openly gay in the U.S. military. Though superiors were not
permitted to ask directly about the sexual orientation of a soldier,
they were required to open an investigation if there was evidence
of homosexual activity or proclivities. Gay soldiers fought for their
country in fear not just of the enemy but of being exposed.

"Scott's platoon kind of knew he was what he was," Elliott told me. "They didn't care, but he wasn't the most popular. He wasn't the guy you were going to snap on the ass with a towel when you were in the head."

"What first drew you together?"

"We met at Airborne. I was seventeen, in amazing physical shape, running around with my shirt off all the time."

Scott Byrne was more than a decade older than Sommer, lanky and tanned with a receded hairline. He was a tough, fearless fighter who drove a pickup truck and had a strong appreciation for guns, but according to Elliott, he made only three real friends at battalion. They were a benighted bunch. One was killed in a 2005 parachute accident. Another happened to fire the round that penetrated a wall and killed a fellow Ranger in a live-fire shooting exercise. "That was a cool motherfucker," Elliott said of this latter, "but he lost it after the accident. Lost his confidence."

The third was Private Luke Elliott Sommer. Though Byrne did not come out of the closet until after the robbery, Elliott told me he had long ago figured out that Byrne was gay. One time when he was returning Byrne's car keys to his room, he happened to see a chat window open on his laptop with a girl whose profile picture matched the photograph on Byrne's keychain that he had been letting people assume was of his girlfriend. The chat made it clear that she was in fact his sister.

"Scott was my go-to for movies," Elliott said. "I loved watching movies and he never did anything."

On the night after Byrne told Sommer he was stuck in his room eating an MRE, Elliott's own sister Karis messaged to tell him that Denise Fichtner, their nana, might have pancreatic cancer.

"what the fuck," wrote Sommer.

"she doesn't know for sure but she is in so much pain and they did an ultra sound and there is a lump in her pancreas and they told her that her pancreas isn't doing so good or something"

"crazy," wrote Sommer.

Half an hour later one of his young female correspondents messaged to ask what he was up to.

"just watching the godfather," he wrote.

A few days later, while waiting for a ride with Byrne after watching a movie together at a Tacoma multiplex, Sommer pointed out Chips Casino across the street and started brainstorming tactics for taking it down. He told Byrne he needed funds to start a Ranger-staffed business that would pick up extra money between deployments by running security for clients in Canada. Byrne laughed along and contributed a few ideas. Later that night Sommer messaged him, "check this shit out," and attached a photograph of himself having sex with one of his young female correspondents. After following Byrne's shocked, uneasy reply with graphic banter, Sommer wrote, "Anyways dude I am going to finish a movie and I need to catch some sleep but think about what I was talking about. We are starting to get a full crew. I need a consigliere."

"Haha," wrote Byrne, "OK. Nite man."

"gnight bro," wrote Sommer. "eat more your looking thin."

"haha. i know. I lost 10 pounds last weekend. from that stomach flu."

"gay. Well get over it and watch over my ass ;) I am getting in deep . . . keep your mind out of the gutter."

The next day, July 7, Sommer asked again if Byrne had considered it. "So what are your thoughts on everything?" he asked.

"haha," wrote Byrne. "i dunno brother. haven't thought much on it, actually."

Byrne told Sommer he was suffering from a sore throat. Sommer told him not to "deepthroat" so much, then waited for the chuckles to subside before sharing the names of three soldiers he said had agreed to be involved.

"geez," wrote Byrne.

"What?"

"nuthin ;)"

"well i need to try and determine critical mass"

"haha," wrote Byrne, "of course you do"

These are the first of about a dozen Ranger Battalion names on Sommer's hard drive. One private from Bravo Company even sent an unsolicited email asking to be involved. "I think you will find me to be one hell of an asset," he wrote. Sommer replied within hours: "I am aware you are determined to operate for me, and I am also very pleased with your enthusiasm. I have some work for you. Keep in touch, email me after block leave."

I asked Elliott if he had anything to say about the soldiers he had mentioned to Byrne.

"Did they get indicted?" Elliott asked.

"No."

Elliott grinned. "Then no," he said.

In future conversations Byrne tried repeatedly to laugh the whole thing off and change the subject, telling Sommer "ur nuts boi, absolutely nuts." After the plans grew more elaborate, he said, "ur startin to make me think u might actually make this happen."

Sommer wrote, "I knew you would look out for me but I don't want to expose you to what you dont want to see."

Byrne replied, "haha. the only thing i don't wanna see is u getting ur ass in trouble, in jail, or SHOT the fuck up."

It is unclear if Byrne ever grasped that Sommer was serious. Though he ended up pleading guilty to a felony conspiracy charge, his lawyer argued at sentencing that despite the government's characterization of him as knowing and willful, Byrne had never intended to get involved with a real robbery. He had considered the brainstorming session outside Chips Casino mere chatter.

"Scott Byrne describes this conversation, in his mind, as role playing, filling time waiting for a ride," argued Byrne's lawyer. "Scott Byrne indicates that these type of discussions went on all the time, not necessarily relating to robberies, but other 'what if' plans. This was part of their training and was a regular occurrence during 'B.S.' sessions while they were in Iraq, and elsewhere."

"Scott was morally ambivalent," Elliott told me. "I needed to find a way to appeal to him. He liked the idea of being the older, wiser mentor. Whereas Tigra liked the idea of being this powerful, popular mob-style gangster."

———

Tigra Robertson, the close friend with whom Elliott first discussed the robbery, was a short, athletic volunteer fireman in the Canadian Army Reserves with a Superman tattoo on his shoulder.

"We never broke the law together, me and Tigra," Elliott said, then laughed. "Well, let me rephrase that. Prior to breaking about forty of 'em. We were good kids. We went to church together, did a lot of community service."

He told me that as teenagers they had participated together in bottle drives, picked up trash from the streets in road vests with their Air Cadets platoon, fantasized together about joining the U.S. military.

"We were just really interested, really obsessive. Tigra wanted to be a Navy SEAL. He should have been eligible, his father was from the States, but he never signed the birth certificate because he didn't want him to go, so Tigra wasn't able to enlist. He was bitter about that. I think unfortunately that might have been what undid our friendship. I got to live my dream, he didn't."

After a year in the Rangers, Elliott gave Tigra $2,000 for a business venture involving a third British Columbia man, Paul. The money somehow disappeared. Elliott told me he considered this a betrayal by Tigra.

"Tigra started treating me differently when I left," Elliott said. "He made moves on Angie [the mother of Elliott's son], took my money. I went to basic, Airborne, RIP. He desperately wanted to do those things. My life was starting and his was stagnating. If I were doing it over now I would have helped him get what he wanted out of life. He was my friend."

Instead, Elliott told me, he exploited him. After several unanswered messages to Tigra over the same period when Sommer first began recruiting Byrne—Tigra was away at Edgefest, a Canadian music festival—Sommer finally got in touch with him on July 9, sending him a photograph titled "mystuff.jpg" of the beginnings of his illegal arsenal, which already included flashbangs, pistols, and fragmentation grenades and would soon grow to include automatic AK-47 assault rifles.

"wicked," wrote Tigra. "i still want a pistol so bad"

"well I have a shit ton," wrote Sommer.

"niceee"

"so what you willing to do for a pistol? cause I brought one home I have a way of doing it now"

"umm" wrote Tigra.

Sommer wrote that he was looking for help with a "legit" security business. "just be aware that the people we are protecting are shady," he wrote, "but the business is on the level."

"don't need the details," Tigra wrote. "u say it ill do it."

"ok well i will brief you in august on the 8th when I am home."

For all their efforts, the FBI failed to uncover the source of Elliott's weaponry. When I asked Elliott about it, he told me that he was never going to reveal it. "I don't want to ruin someone's career," he said. "You know the name, though. I just thought it would be torturous to know it's within your grasp." He laughed maniacally. "Make sure you write 'laughs maniacally,'" he said.

I did so, smiling along, then looked up at him carefully: in point of fact I did know the name I suspected he was referring to, but there was no way he could have known that—which meant he was trying very cleverly to throw me off the trail.

———

A criminal investigation is a complicated thing. The prosecution and defense weave only a minuscule portion of the evidence into their opposing narratives for presentation in court, calling on witnesses to present their few small threads. Far more is excised than kept. Legal scholars like to pretend the operation is bloodless.

"The event itself comprises unlimited detail," wrote Richard Markus in his 1981 "Theory of Trial Advocacy." "Manifestly, the recited data are a fraction of the remembered data, which is a fraction of the observed data, which is a fraction of the total data for the event."

Back then, "total data" was just an abstraction for the sake of argument. Now the discovery for a criminal case will as often as not include a stack of CDs. In one sense, Elliott was unusually savvy about the danger of leaving a digital trail: he made Tigra and Nathan download encryption software to communicate with him online and wiped his whole hard disk clean before fleeing to Canada. In another sense he was puzzlingly sloppy. His rules about encryption were only occasionally enforced, and his effort to erase his hard disk was only partially successful, leaving behind an enormous jigsaw puzzle of corrupted fragments from hundreds of emails, thousands of Internet browsing hits, and tens of thousands of text messages on MSN Messenger.

Modern tools and techniques might have made it a little easier to sort through it all. Examiners in the FBI's computer forensics lab did run a few global analyses, such as a diskwide text search for "bank robbery," but otherwise mostly threw up their hands. The less-corrupted chunks of MSN Messenger transcripts were so encumbered by XML tags, often with a character or two corrupted or missing, that they were virtually unreadable:

```
<Log FirstSessionID="1" LastSessionID="45"><Message
Date="7/5/2006" Time="4:07:14 PM" DateTime="2006-
07-05T23:07:14.750Z" SessionID="1"><From><User
FriendlyName="Elliott"/></From><To><User
FriendlyName="Tigra- 864-2585- i got text messaging again . . .
text away . . ."/></To><Text Style="font-family:MS Shell Dlg;
color:#000000;">sup dude</Text></Message>
```

The more-corrupted chunks were even worse:

```
Microsoft\MSNMessenger\PerPassportSettings\1513921866
GET /msnvideo/interviews/colinfarelljamiefoxx.jpg HTTP/1.1
i dotn have any time to go to the fucking doctor mind? ts
and Settings\Elliott\Application Data\Microsoft\MSN
Messenger\1513921866\DynamicBackgrounds\map.dat k here
to view your entire conversation history with this
```

Eight hundred pages of this stuff were simply printed out and entered into evidence. The rest of the recovered files and data were delivered to defense and prosecution in raw form on a CD that Amanda then passed along to me.

About a month before flying to Tennessee, I finally threw out the paper version in disgust and came at the CD exactly as if it were a trove of disorganized experimental data at my old biology lab. For two weeks my life was nothing but Python scripts to assemble and clean fragments, hours-long scrolling sessions through endless teenage conversations about sex, violence, and guns, and interlinked Post-it notes on my bedroom walls. By the end I had a remarkably clear timeline of the planning of the crime.

There were also a few surprises.

First was the Microsoft Word document in a back corner of Elliott's hard drive titled "Business plan for Marcus." It seemed little more than a skeleton, a template copied from the Internet, but then

I discovered an email in Elliott's inbox from a fellow Ranger named Marcus Cobb[*] inviting him to a gun show and suggesting that it might be a good time to make "a payment." At the bottom of the email was a phone number, which came up twice in the call log for a cell phone Elliott had borrowed from another Ranger. The time stamps were in UTC (Coordinated Universal Time), nine hours later than Pacific Daylight Time, so it took a few seconds to realize that they occurred at 5:30 and 5:33 p.m. on August 7, 2006.

The robbery took place at 5:13 p.m. Marcus Cobb, it seemed, was the first person Elliott called after it was done.

Cobb was never indicted. He was never even interviewed. I could find his name nowhere in relation to the robbery. Granted, it had taken me a full week of wading through gigabytes of data to find him buried in all the noise, but still, it was hard to fathom how the FBI had missed this. Investigators expended considerable effort on identifying the source of Elliott's arsenal, going so far as to offer Scott Byrne a plea deal if he would wear a wire on their principal suspect. Byrne agreed, but the Ranger in question said nothing incriminating and was never indicted.

When I looked into what Marcus Cobb was doing now, I discovered that he was working for a U.S. congressman.

[*] Not his real name.

CHAPTER 22

THE SOMMER FACTOR

It seemed too early to risk a confrontation with Elliott about Cobb. Instead I moved on to the next step in the inexorable buildup: Tigra getting back in touch on July 11 to say he had a new prospect for their business, a friend named Jeff with whom he played airsoft games in Kelowna. Sommer had by now changed his MSN handle to "Don Terrino," telling a young female correspondent who asked about the new alias that it was nothing, "just some stuff from a movie."

"cool?" asked Don Terrino.

"yeah hes kinda like us when it comes to military stuff," Tigra wrote.

Don Terrino allowed that he could use a few more guys for the security business, then nudged things a step further toward overt criminality. "you know this isn't all on the level right?" he asked.

Tigra assured him that Jeff was down no matter what.

Finally Sommer sent him a Microsoft Word document titled "The Law.doc." "this is an idea of how I want to run shit," he wrote.

After he and Tigra had geeked out for a while about all the weapons in Sommer's arsenal, Tigra asked, "so who's the top man in this? im guessing u. or are you working for someone?"

"thats complicated," Sommer wrote. "I have to kick up to some guys who I am running money through, jewish mob."

I had been wondering about this for a long time.

"Jewish mob?" I asked Elliott.

"I was totally making that up," Elliott said. "He was looking for something, I provided it. It's like D&D, man. I go into this room, what do I find? It's got blue walls, a musty old chest in the back."

"D&D?"

"You never played Dungeons and Dragons?"

"No."

"Well, the dungeon master is running the game. He builds the world, tells you what you find."

"So this world has musty old Jewish mobsters in the back."

Elliott laughed. "Exactly. Old men in the back who I gotta kick up to. And obviously, you know, this strains credulity. It's so bizarre. But that's part of the beauty of it."

Wait—the *beauty* of it?

"Looking at it in retrospect," Elliott clarified before I could break in, "and cringing, and rolling over in my soon-to-be grave."

When Elliott used a canned phrase like this, he looked up at the ceiling and spoke in the corny, apologetic singsong of a dad repeating lame old saws he knew his kids would groan at, a shift so bizarre that for a second my mind just went blank with perplexity. Then he switched immediately back to normal.

"Did I really *say* that?" he went on. "What was I *thinking*? The only true thing guiding me was anger. My whole life seemed invalidated."

"Are you *aware* you're making this stuff up?"

"No. That's what gets me, man. I've always been very good at exploiting people, but very rarely have I made the conscious choice to do it. I'm aware I have to answer a question, and there's this period where I'm racking my brain, and then . . . There were a few times I deliberately manipulated him, but mostly you look back on it and it's like, what was I thinking? I don't remember any of this shit. I remember general themes but not coming up with the details. I can see the things I did and think, 'That was crazy,' but I can't even remember having done them, practically. Other people tell me they're crazy, and I know they're right."

At the time, I felt for Elliott. Mental illness had clearly devastated his life. Only months later would it occur to me how convenient it was for him to be able to write this kind of thing off as a symptom. The "Jewish mob" may indeed have been "crazy," but it served more than just the purpose of persuading Tigra. After wrapping up their conversation, Sommer emailed Paul, the Kelowna connection whom Sommer and Tigra had dealt with earlier, to say, "I have been pretty lenient on that money you owed me so I hope you will get in touch with me and repay the favour."

Paul messaged him later that night.

"So," Sommer wrote after a few quick pleasantries, "I got moved up from enforcer to made guy, they gave me the commission's blessing to work out of kelowna, so I wanted to settle old debts and create the opportunity for people to make themselves a little better situated in my memory. So are things in a good enough position for you to make a gesture toward what you owe me"

"probably in a few weeks," Paul wrote a minute later.

Sommer asked if Paul knew "Abe." Paul indicated that he did not.

"Who was Abe?" I asked.

"That was just an invented Jewish-sounding name. My authority in that town came from my ability to craft this legend—whether I intended to or not."

"So the 'commission' wasn't real either?" I asked.

"No. I was presenting a fantasy so it would get back to Tigra. He thought there were these powerful mob backers and I wanted to reinforce that fantasy for him and at the same time send him a message about how serious I was at having my money stolen. I wanted him to be a little afraid."

Elliott's assertion that he had been deliberately taking advantage of Tigra confused me. I knew that their planning conversations over the month of July had been lengthy and explicit. They had sworn themselves to each other as "brothers in arms," chortled over each new addition to Sommer's arsenal, affirmed many times how excited they were to be doing this together. Christel and others in Peachland had been telling me that they viewed Elliott's plan to take on the Hells Angels as ridiculous, implausible, just a smokescreen—why would he have set out to provoke a gang as large and powerful as that? Now Elliott seemed to be going a step further: not only was his frustration with the U.S. military the real motivation for the robbery, but his crime-family plan was just a fabrication to get Tigra involved.

"Okay," I said, "but later there's a conversation with Tigra in which the two of you decide together to *pretend* to the other guys that there's a mob boss above you. How is that compatible with you trying to trick *him*?"

"I wanted Tigra to think he was in on it, but then also to suspect there actually *was* someone higher," Elliott said. "That seems rather complicated, but"—his voice went corny—"I have never been simple."

"If he had betrayed you, why did you trust him to found this enterprise with you in the first place?"

"The enterprise was always secondary. I had one thing in my mind: I was angry, and I wanted to lash out. Sometimes I wanted to just bomb shit. Well, that sounds too terroristy. But I had this roiling rage I had no outlet for. I needed help, and as much as he had pissed me off and betrayed me, Tigra was still loyal to me in some ways. I knew he would be there if I asked him."

"Did you get him involved *so* he would be busted?"

"No, no, no," Elliott said, looking genuinely offended. "I never wanted anyone to get hurt. But he had moved from the sphere I wanted to protect. It was like, 'If you're willing to do something stupid, I'm not going to stop you.'"

Late at night after his conversation with Paul, Sommer messaged Tigra again to tell him to register an account on the website he had been boasting of having built for some days now, onecharlie.com. Tigra signed up. Sommer made him a captain, with administrative privileges. After they reminisced for hours about their former conquests with women in Kelowna, Sommer told him the plan was to charge local businesses for the service of clearing drug trade from their area. Tigra sought to clarify whether other people in the "family" would be able to see his log-in name. Sommer affirmed that they would.

"can i sign up with a different name," Tigra said. "instead of superman"

"yeah actually that sounds like a good plan," said Sommer.

Sommer told him he had talked to Paul. It would be Tigra's first job to "do some footwork" to make sure Paul was ready to pay back what he owed. For this Sommer would be sending up "a soldier."

"who?" asked Tigra.

"Chad," said Sommer, "hes my bodyguard."

———

Sommer first took notice of PFC Chad Palmer after spotting an Indonesian-language tattoo on his calf. A missionary sister of Christel's lived in Indonesia; that country had been a month-long stop on Elliott's trip with his nana at age nine. He struck up a conversation with Palmer, forged a connection.

Palmer wasn't popular at Ranger Battalion. Though he had already deployed, he hadn't yet been sent to Ranger School to earn his tab. Alex had told me there was a rumor around battalion that Palmer had made a minor error with a .50-caliber machine gun, which amid the high standards of the Rangers was enough to threaten a career. Elliott told me the same.

"They were trying to RFS [release for standards] Palmer," Elliott told me. "He was on CQ [charge of quarters] a lot. People didn't like him. He was a missionary kid who'd just moved back and was still adapting to life, kind of awkward and stilted. Whereas awkward and stilted is my thing. I felt bad for him. If people didn't like you at battalion you were not going to have the political clout to cover for your mistakes."

"How does 'awkward and stilted' fit with your reputation as a ladies' man?"

"I'm very good at picking up how people feel, because that's how I understand my situation," Elliott explained. "That's how I gauge morality. Underneath I'm not a *complete* asshole." He grinned and rolled his eyes toward the ceiling. "And then the panties fall off," he said in his corny voice.

Sommer promised Palmer that if he came to Kelowna, he would find a fantasyland of money, respect, and willing women.

"whats up dude this is chad the body guard," Chad messaged Tigra from Sommer's account in the middle of July. "elliot went out to find a movie. I'll be up in canada on the 18th of august"

"wicked," wrote Tigra. "stoked for the trip?"

"fuck yeah. cant wait"

"yeah it will be good. we will have to hit up some of the clubs and ill show you what kelowna has to offer as far as prime pussy goes"

"i've heard alot already," said Chad. "thats just another plus. a big one. elliott told me alot about that."

They talked about how each had gotten "into business" with Sommer. Tigra made it clear that he had the stronger claim. "we started planning this at like age 14-15," he said. "i dunno me and him are pretty much blood."

Chad allowed that he had only met Sommer after joining the army. "we're good friends though," he said. "along with aaron. i don't know if you've heard of him yet."

———

Only one Aaron appears in the discovery from the case: Aaron Figel, a sergeant in Elliott's platoon. In a sworn statement to the FBI on August 22, 2006, Figel wrote of walking into Sommer's room on the morning of August 6 and discovering him there with two men whom Sommer introduced as his cousins. "Other than the room being slightly messy with dirty clothes laying on the floor," Figel wrote, "nothing seemed out of the ordinary."

Elliott once claimed to me that he had verbal agreements from "most" of the privates in Charlie Company's First Platoon. At first I suspected this was exaggeration or even outright fabrication, but when I dug into the evidence, it began indeed to seem that more soldiers were complicit than were indicted. For a long time I couldn't understand what they were thinking. These were some of the United States Army's most promising young soldiers. A few may have been disgruntled, a few may have been unpopular, but to have made it this far they had to have had big dreams, noble ambitions, families they didn't want to disappoint. Why risk it all for an insane criminal scheme?

I understand a little better now. If you were 99 percent sure Specialist Sommer wasn't serious, why risk your career by snitching on a fellow Ranger for a wild, implausible fantasy? Amid the unrelenting stress of wartime Special Operations training, Sommer was, I think, more than anything, *fun*. Like some living cartoon from *Who Framed Roger Rabbit*, he operated under a separate physics, madcap and consequence-free. With him you could become Donkey Kong or Cobra Commander or Wile E. Coyote, swallowing a pound of TNT and exploding and reconstituting again in time to pant so hard at a passing pretty girl that your tongue spilled out onto the floor. And even if you laughed inside at his Canadian weirdness and over-the-top imagination, even if you dismissed his most gleefully violent speculations as mere adolescent posturing, maybe some adolescent part of you lapped it up—and maybe the nascent adult part of you thrilled at having license to lap it up, because Specialist Sommer was an authority in a culture whose laws you respected, a graduate of Ranger School, a veteran of two foreign wars, a team leader in the best light-infantry fighting force on earth, and how could he have gotten where he was if he was actually a psychopathic, homicidal maniac?

"found our first offensive target," Elliott wrote to Tigra on July 14. "we are hitting a house owned by HA [Hells Angels] they threatened the local neighborhood so we are going to take it down. mass tactical"

"explain," said Tigra.

"how? or why?"

"how. i dont care why."

"knock," said Elliott. "explain our bitch. watch them talk shit. open their door once they go in. and toss in a frag. game over."

Tigra knew what Elliott meant: one of his fragmentation grenades.

"haha," he said. "this is soon?"

"august."

"haha," said Tigra, "so much for your idea of moving in slowly haha"

As Elliott went on and on with the details, elaborating that they would be wearing expensive tailored suits as they killed everyone in the house, Tigra finally stopped laughing.

"u sure you want to do this one right away," he wrote, "not work up to it?"

"we will obviously discuss it in the meeting," Sommer wrote, "but I would like to make a blatant statement, so that we can use it as leverage. the neighborhood wont care there gone nor will the city"

As with Scott Byrne, it is hard to know at what point it became clear to Tigra Robertson that his old friend was not just playing around. A month later, when the FBI asked why he had committed the robbery, Tigra would sound genuinely perplexed: "I really don't know. When, uh, at first I thought it was just for the fun and everything and I didn't actually think it was for real. It was over the computer and it was just a big idea that we kind of had and I didn't think it was actually serious."

"dude," he messaged Sommer on July 16, "ive been having a weird dream lately"

"me too," wrote Sommer.

"i keep dreaming about those guys that took on those cops when they robbed the bank"

"north hollywood shootout," wrote Sommer.

"just going full on assault against them," wrote Tigra. "yeah"

"yeah?"

"yeah. i dunno why"

"and how does it end?"

"it doesnt"

"well we arent robbing a bank lol," wrote Sommer. "it doesn't?"

"just a big shoot out. and then i usually wake up," wrote Tigra. "and i dunno if we were robbing a bank"

"Well I am sure you dont want out," wrote Sommer, "but if you did, all you have to do is say something"

"i dont. lol"

"I know. lol"

"thats not what I was saying," wrote Tigra. "im just saying ive been having dreams like that"

———

Sommer and Tigra really weren't, as far as I can tell, planning at this point to rob a bank. But Sommer may already have been looking for tactical guidance on a takeover robbery—and perhaps someone over age twenty-one who could scope out the interior of a casino—because he continued to hound Scott Byrne. On July 19 he tried once more to bring him into the family.

"I have nine guys going home on block leave with me," Sommer wrote, "someone investing 10K and three guys providing close tactical recon on the city prepping us for ops"

It was in this conversation that Byrne told him he was "absolutely nuts."

"What was that 10K investment?" I asked Elliott.

"That was someone I knew back home who loaned me money. I'm not saying who. And it was more like $3,600."

"What about the three guys doing close tactical recon?"

"That was just some guys from battalion who went to Chips

Casino, got drunk, spotted it out, gave good notes. They never knew it was going to be real. They probably saw the robbery and were like, 'Oh shit.' "

"Who exactly were the nine guys who were supposed to go to Kelowna with you for block leave?"

"There were actually two more guys from battalion who were there outside the bank that day who never got arrested. They were there as extra ammo. They didn't think I was actually going to show up. One of these guys, I showed the money to him when we got back to battalion and he was legitimately freaked out. They wouldn't have participated if they thought it was real. They wanted to see me not show up and say, 'You pussy.' "

There was absolutely no evidence for this in the record. I was sure of that. But how was I to challenge Elliott on it without flatly calling him a liar?

"Chad was the only one who was really planning to visit me," he went on before I had time to think it through. "But the guys I meant were me, Chad, Scott, Tigra, Nathan, those other two, who will remain unnamed, and the guys I got weapons from."

After Byrne called him nuts, Sommer wrote that he wanted him involved "but you need to be willing."

"ugh," wrote Byrne.

A minute later, after laughing off a few more of Sommer's advances, Byrne wrote, "hey . . . off the subject a bit . . . u still have those movies u borrowed? lol"

Sommer said he would bring them up when he was done cleaning his room. It was becoming clear that he couldn't count on Byrne.

"I knew I needed another dude," Elliott told me.

There were a few obvious choices for a driver. First was his good friend Corporal Tom Sager, Alex's team leader, who happened to hail from the same area of British Columbia as Sommer.

"Tom was a big reason I got along in battalion," Elliott said. "I wasn't that popular with the other tabs, but Tom was a cool kid. He was a pockmarked motherfucker, but he could charm everyone."

Sommer and Sager first met just after Airborne, in the Fort Benning barracks where recruits waited to begin the Ranger Indoctrination Program. Sager had already been there for a while when Sommer arrived.

"Have you read *Ender's Game?*" Elliott asked out of the blue.

I looked up warily from my notebook. *Ender's Game*, by Orson Scott Card, was my favorite novel as a kid, a bildungsroman about a sensitive preadolescent genius named Ender Wiggin who was mankind's great hope against a race of aliens. I have since encountered a few others who grew up equally obsessed. We talk about it like a childhood heroin addiction. There seemed no way Elliott could possibly know this.

"Well," Elliott went on, "Sager was like the Nose of RIP hold. He knew all the tricks, knew how the place worked." The Nose was the sole Jew in the brutal military training program where Ender was groomed to command Earth's fleet.

"When did you read *Ender's Game?*"

"As soon as I could read and I found that book. I've read it probably thirty, forty times. I have it in my room right now."

Elliott told me he knew that Sager would never have participated in real criminal activity. "If I had told him about the robbery he would have turned me in," he said. "He would have said, 'Let's go play paintball. There are other outlets.' He's legitimately one of the best people I ever met."

Another possibility was Sommer's good friend Corporal Richard Olinger, who was storing some of Sommer's weaponry in his truck and storage unit and with whom Sommer planned to rent an off-post apartment. Sommer did bring up the casino robbery with Olinger over beers but decided not to force the issue. Olinger was interviewed afterward by Special Agent Shaide and detective Todd Karr of the Pierce County Sheriff's Office.

OLINGER advised that soldiers in the Ranger Battalion frequently joke about robbing a bank. OLINGER mentioned Rangers are trained in interior tactics and have all the necessary skills and equipment to efficiently rob a bank. OLINGER advised they would routinely joke about how easy it would be to commit bank robberies. OLINGER does not recall SOMMER discussing the specifics of any bank robbery. OLINGER was then asked if he had any part of a plan to rob a casino. OLINGER was surprised that the investigating agents knew about a plan for a casino robbery in Tacoma. OLINGER admitted he and SOMMER had discussed robbing a casino over beers. SOMMER talked about the security cameras, getting the money out of the safe, and using multiple vehicles with switched out license plates. OLINGER thought SOMMER was just kidding and didn't think SOMMER would ever go through with a robbery. OLINGER could not provide the location of the casino but thought it was along I-5. OLINGER was asked if SOMMER had planned on using him as the getaway driver for the casino robbery. OLINGER once again became very nervous and stated his nickname over in Iraq was "the getaway driver" because he often times drove the Striker armored vehicle during missions. When OLINGER and SOM-MER joked about the casino robbery, SOMMER told OLINGER he could be the getaway driver. SOMMER told OLINGER he was planning on putting together a "family". The family was to be a group of people involved in criminal activity. SOMMER wanted OLINGER to be a leader of a crew. SOMMER stated PALMER and some other soldiers, holding private ranks, would also be members of a crew. SOMMER also told OLINGER that some of SOMMER's Canadian friends would be members of a crew. The crews would work in Canada providing a "security business". The crews would assist groups in moving illegal drugs. OLINGER told SOMMER he wanted nothing to do with a crew or the family. OLINGER thought SOMMER was just talking "bull shit".

It was on July 22 that Sommer messaged Nathan Dunmall's ex-girlfriend Tasha to ask for his contact information.

When I asked him about their meeting in Peachland, Elliott remembered Dunmall coming up to chase Tasha. "Nathan was all burned out," he recalled. "I big-brothered him."

It was later that summer that they all went camping together at Cultas Lake outside Chilliwack.

"Did you tell them back then that you were planning things?" I asked.

"Oh yeah. 'I'll hit this bank, this casino.' I was angry. Then I went to Ranger School and got distracted."

In Dunmall's own statements to authorities, of course, he spoke mostly of Sommer's thrilling tales of combat at Cultas Lake. When it came to Sommer's criminal plans, Dunmall thought he was "full of shit."

―――――

According to Christel, everyone in her family noticed how disturbed Elliott was by what he witnessed on deployment. Like many others after the robbery, Nathan's ex-girlfriend Tasha believed unquestioningly that Elliott's motive had been political, writing him a letter in which she expressed disgust with Nathan for having done it for the money but understanding that Elliott had followed his conscience. And indeed, Elliott's lengthy post on awokendreamer .blogspot.com three days before the robbery gave the impression that he had been thinking along these lines for quite some time.

> I am a frontline fighter in one of our nations most elite units. I have been in the areas of conflict, fought along side the bravest men our nation has ever produced and seen what we are capable of. I have chased after Zarkawi, seen our enemies and conducted ground combat operations in both theatres of our "war". I am not an outsider, I am as close to the fight as it gets, and yet, with every reflective thought I realize just how far away from this I really am.
>
> America must fail.

On the other hand, his Internet history in the month before he fled to Canada included no news, no political forums, no antiwar literature, no philosophy—just a lot of guns and porn. The closest I had been able to find to a political qualm came at the tail end of a series of Google searches that hinted at somewhat different priorities:

> private islands
> purchasing property in mexico
> purchasing property in columbia
> purchasing property in columbia the fucking country
> buying armored vehicles
> buying weaponless attack helicopters
> becoming rich illegally
> american cocaine

extravagant homes in bc canada
200 million dollars
cost of war

Tigra wanted to come down around July 19, but Sommer told him that what with the recent unrest in Lebanon, it might not be a possibility. "we have a meeting on thursday for joint strike operations, so even if we aren't locked down I will be at a security briefing," he wrote. "gay dude. fucking israel"

"yeah," said Tigra.

"and hezbolla"

Tigra and Sommer spent no more time on politics. Instead they discussed which Kelowna bar would be most hospitable as a family clubhouse, whether an Uzi or a shotgun was more useful in close combat, how to let the city know there was a new operation in town. Both understood that, as Sommer put it, "we are using a legit security company as a front." On July 26 Sommer told Tigra that if he found a worthy "job for our crew" in Kelowna, he would bring him a $2,000 laptop with a fingerprint scanner and webcam. They talked about getting "family ink," a cross with their names in Latin script, and began discussing possibilities for the first operation.

"what about a gas station just to break the ice?" suggested Sommer.

"cameras and not alot of money," wrote Tigra. "and over done"

"whats a good ice breaker?"

"ummm the drug dealer thing," Tigra said, presumably referring to the existing plan to expel dealers from a commercial district. "then hit a business. a bank would be fun but it would take alot of planning. casino would be crazi. haha"

"casino then . . ." wrote Sommer.

This, less than two weeks before August 7, was the first mention I found of a robbery plan. Sommer and Tigra seemed to be talking about Kelowna, but within a few days Sommer had cased out Chips Casino in Tacoma and drawn up plans on a Google Maps satellite image. He was scheduled to take a driver's permit test on July 24, but as it happened, he came down with a severe fever and couldn't take it.

Even if he had taken it, Elliott told me, there would not have been much chance of him being the driver for the robbery. He had been given punitive desk duty in Afghanistan after crashing a truck. "No way was I driving," he said. "This would have gone from a tragic version of *The Town* to a comedy."

Around July 30 he finally made the call to Nathan Dunmall's phone number and got him to agree to be the driver.

"hey dude," Sommer messaged Tigra shortly afterward. "we have the job its crazy and its going down in nine days. can you make it down? I need you and your boy"

Sommer explained that they were going to hit a Tacoma casino for a "250K plus" payoff. "so I hope your ready to fucking rock and roll," Sommer said.

"fuck yeah. wut day"

"chance it might go north hollywood so I really hope your in the mood. alright the target day is monday the 7th"

Tigra indicated that he was in and that he was sure Jeff, his friend from Kelowna, would be too.

"perfect," wrote Sommer. "we have the whole team. Nathan is going to drive, Chad me, you and jeff are going to be running the inside and were all going to be fucking buzzing once we rack in the fucking money"

The casino plan involved clipping a fence with bolt cutters, crossing a broad open field, and killing an employee who patrolled the grounds in a golf cart. But shortly after Sommer told Tigra that the job was on, Scott Byrne accompanied him, Alex, and Chad Palmer to the casino and talked Sommer out of it.

"Mr. Byrne agreed to go into the casino, and believed that his entrance and observations would give force to his recommendation that robbing the casino was a bad idea," Byrne's lawyer would argue at sentencing.

Elliott told me that Byrne's objection was that the casino was a "logistics hassle," but assured me that it wouldn't actually have been as hard a job as Byrne was making out. "After seven years in crime school, I could tell you a million ways to do it," Elliott said.

At the time, however, Byrne's qualms prevailed. Just a few hours after telling Tigra the plan was on, Sommer informed Tigra and Jeff that the casino job was "on hold" due to his "investor's" concerns.

CHAPTER 23

FORCE OF PERSONALITY

As the date of deletion approaches, the readable messages on Elliott's hard disk grow fewer and farther between. Files crumble into increasingly distorted fragments. The initial proposal to rob a bank never appears, but at some time on August 1 a message from Sommer pops out of the noise: "remember the issues I was having with the other job? none with this one."

"kool lets do it," wrote Tigra.

On August 3, a sunny Thursday afternoon in Tacoma, Sommer's little sister Karis messaged to say that Nana was bleeding internally after an operation on her lungs and that the extended family was hurrying home to see her before she died.

"what the fuck man suing the shit out of the doctors," Sommer replied.

It was about an hour later that Elliott appeared for the first time on the security cameras at the Bank of America on South Tacoma Way. In the recording, he walks through the rear glass door at 3:56 p.m. Half a second later, a handsome young man in a white baseball cap follows him in: nineteen-year-old PFC Alex Blum. As Sommer walks through the empty line to Jessicah Stotts's teller station, holding a small cup into which he occasionally spits tobacco juice, Alex takes a seat in a plush armchair in the lobby, his biceps straining the cuffs of his polo shirt. After taking in the view in front of him, he fakes a yawning stretch that looks almost comically obvious, like a teenager sneaking his arm around a date, and scopes out the view behind.

"soo," Sommer wrote to Tigra at 8:35 that evening, "I got the fourth. we are good. plan is concrete."

It is the last surviving message between them. There is no indication of why they needed a fourth. Tigra's friend Jeff from Kelowna simply vanishes from the record. When I asked Elliott about this, he told me that he didn't know why Jeff backed out. In fact, he didn't remember a Jeff being involved at all. "Who is Jeff in that context?" he asked, peering in apparent puzzlement at my page of notes.

―――――

Nowhere on Sommer's hard drive, in all the thousands of megabytes of recovered data, is there a single mention of Alex's name. The closest is Sommer telling Tigra "I got the fourth," although what he appears to have meant is the fourth man inside the bank, which would have been Nathan Dunmall after Alex took over as driver. According to Alex, Sommer originally asked him to go inside the bank. Alex declined, informing his old team leader that he wasn't trained for that yet—he was on a gun team, not a line team.

"Most of the times I spent with Alex were just hanging out," Elliott told me at McCreary. "The robbery didn't come up for a long time. And then once it did, things escalated very quickly." He paused, then asked what appeared to be an earnest question. "Does it ever strike you as strange how quickly people fell in line?"

"Yes," I said, "it does."

"I mean, I know that I'm nice, but the force of personality that would require, I just don't think I have it. So why did they all say yes?"

"I think your military credentials played a role," I said. "Both for the guys under you in the Rangers and the guys outside."

"Partially, yeah," Elliott agreed. "But I had the same ability outside the military. I am just *so convinced of my rightness*, everybody goes along. I could call a friend up at two-thirty in the morning and within half an hour there'd be a party at his house. Or if it was October and freezing out, I could say, 'Let's go swimming at Swim Bay,' and everyone would run down there, jump in, come back, and take a hot shower, no question."

In an interview with David Bowermaster while Elliott was on house arrest in Peachland, he offered a somewhat different explanation: "I knew they wouldn't do it if they didn't have their own reasons. A man can only lead people who believe in their own heart that what they're doing is the right thing. There is one language that speaks to everybody, and that is: fulfill their own personal desires."

"Do you remember going out with Alex to Dairy Queen, Applebee's, Quiznos, and other spots like that and asking how he'd hit the place?" I asked.

"Oh yeah," Elliott said. "I did that with a lot of people. It was not unusual. My own team leaders had done it with me back in the day. For SEALs, how you would hit an oil tanker is a daily question. For us it was how to hit buildings. It was a kind of a game. I guess in a way that's one of the things that got me thinking about it for real: 'By God, I could do it *that* way.' The best for gaming purposes was big insurmountable stuff, because it forced you to think about the worst possible hostage situation: malls, movie theaters, places with lots of people and complex structures. More fast-food places than restaurants, because fast-food places have more interesting layouts. There's a dining area, a bar, an open kitchen—kinda like a bank, actually."

Like Alex, Elliott emphasized that the planning and preparations they went through for the robbery were very close to standard operating procedure around battalion.

"That's part of what made it hard to slow down," he said. "No one around me was objecting. Usually when you're doing something wrong, people point it out to you. 'What are you doing? Are you fucking crazy?' But nobody was saying that."

I asked him if he remembered an incident in which Sager gave Alex the keys to move his truck, then Alex came back to find Sager talking to Sommer about the crime family. As Alex recalled it, Sager said to him, "So, Private, you going to head up to Canada and take on some Hells Angels?" to which Alex replied, "Hell yes, Corporal!"

"That might have happened," Elliott said. "Just in a facetious way. Tom didn't know I was serious, but I probably joked about it with him." A moment passed. "Dude," he said. "That makes me sad to hear. Comments like that make me realize he was just trying to be as good a Ranger as he wanted to be."

It was the closest I had heard from Elliott to an acknowledgment that PFC Blum's understanding of the crime-family plans might have been in any way out of joint with Specialist Sommer's. Despite all

his stunning candidness about his manipulation of the other participants, especially the control he exercised over how real they took the
robbery to be, Elliott still maintained that he had never deliberately
manipulated Alex. As far as he was concerned, they were just good
friends—simple as that.

"There's two sides to every story," he said. "It took me a while
to get over it, but then I realized he wasn't the one who was wrong
about how he felt. I looked up to him. He was cool, popular. My
peers, other tabs, didn't like me, didn't hang out with me. We were
both looking uphill at each other, but the truth is his side is weighted
heavier. I had the rank. The reality is I was holding all the cards, so I
have to accept his perspective."

———

Nathan and Tigra arrived around 11 p.m. on Sunday, August 6.
Alex, Chad, and Elliott drove to the Greyhound Station to pick them
up. Now, for the first time, the whole team was together. In a few
weeks everyone there would be in jail, closely followed by Richard
Olinger and Scott Byrne.

"No one was talking anything heavy," Elliott recalled. "There
were light introductions."

Alex dropped everyone off at the barracks and then left. "He was
just like, 'I got something to do,'" Elliott said.

Sommer took the others to Noble Hill for a run-through. It didn't
take long.

"Tactically speaking, come on, it's simplistic," he said. "It's completely and utterly linear. Four guys through one door, first guy controls the far door, last guy stays on the first door, I go up and over the
bandit barrier. The plan was easy, but you still want to go through it.
Even Delta Force does mock-ups."

The next morning, after PT, Elliott got the call from Christel
telling him that Nana was in a coma but would be kept alive until he
arrived home to say goodbye.

Elliott told me that this served to concentrate his energy. "That
was the moment it became very, very real. 'I'm going to focus all my
attention on this instead of thinking about that.'"

Before the men were released for block leave, there was a platoon-
wide body armor inspection. Alex had of course told me several

times that Sommer came to ask him for his body armor right after the inspection, but on this day Elliott told me that Alex gave him his body armor the night *before*.

"So did you give it *back* to him for the inspection?" I asked.

"I don't know," Elliott said. "Either way. He came and picked it up, or I brought it up and gave it to him. Either way, we got it sorted out."

Before loading the car, Sommer, Palmer, and the two Canadians reviewed the bank's location on Google Maps and watched a six-minute tribute video to the U.S. Army Rangers on YouTube, set to mournful Celtic music. As each tenet of the Ranger Creed displayed in turn, heroic shots of Rangers fast-roping and room-clearing faded in and out on the screen.

There are two calls to Alex's phone number from Sommer's borrowed cell phone on August 7: one at around 2 p.m. and one at around 4 p.m. Elliott said he didn't remember what the 2 p.m. call had been about. The 4 p.m. call was to tell PFC Blum to come drive them to the bank. From that point on, the story was familiar: the commotion, the heat, the pulling on of vests, the broken radio and AC from when another Ranger had spilled his cup of tobacco juice into the Audi's vent, the whoosh of the road under the tires. Like the others, Elliott remembered pulling up to the parking lot and seeing it full of people. Like the others, he remembered hesitating there.

This moment haunts me. I have found echoes of it everywhere, from Truman Capote's *In Cold Blood* to the atrocities at My Lai. It nudges final responsibility for the robbery away from its more comfortable resting place in Luke Elliott Sommer's dark imagination and into that murky, complicated space between two friends and rivals.

Though I have never spoken to Tigra, he appears by all accounts to be quite different in person from the way he sounds in his flamboyantly violent MSN Messenger conversations with Sommer. In the transcript of his interview with the FBI on the day he surrendered himself at the border, he comes across as stunned and chastened, like an Internet john who has met the woman in real life and found her not quite what she seemed online. At the end of the interview, Tigra claims that he really went to Tacoma only to swap his old laptop for the new one Sommer had promised him, that he thought the robbery was scheduled for Tuesday afternoon despite the fact that his return bus was scheduled to depart early Tuesday morning, and that he took this as a sign that it wasn't actually going to happen.

> I thought that this was one of Elliott's big . . . Elliott's been known to be full of shit for most things. And, um, since he was full of shit, I didn't think he would actually go through with anything. And I thought, "Hey, I'll go visit him, hang out with him for a couple days and go bring the laptop back to him." Then, uh, that day when he had everything all planned, I just—and I still thought it was Tuesday—we went down and when I woke up in the morning, it was, I was explained that it was actually Monday and that we were gonna go for it. And by that point, uh, I was just going along with it.

Can self-deception really run as deep as this? If only because Tigra has spent a lot more time than I have inside Elliott Sommer's peculiar unreality field, I am inclined to give him the benefit of the doubt. Maybe in his heart of hearts he still clung to the rationalization that this was all a game. Maybe in his heart of hearts he still believed he was just playing a role. But if so, it was by now so binding a role that it could take over his voice, could move his hand to the door handle, could commit his body to irrevocable action, because the fact remains that in that delicate, teetering moment at the fantasy's furthest extension, when the pull was strongest to snap them all back into their lives, it was Tigra who tipped it over.

"Fuck it," said the smallest man in the car to the team of U.S. Army Rangers that surrounded him. "If we don't do it now, we never will."

And then he opened the door.

CHAPTER 24

THE LADY IN THE STRIPED SHIRT

August 7, 2006, was a special day for nineteen-year-old teller Jessicah Stotts: instead of borrowing her army friend Kevin's Chevy Blazer, she would be driving her very own car to work, an ash-gray Ford Taurus she had bought just the day before at the Mallon Ford dealership down the street. The excitement of it got her out the door of her parents' house ten minutes earlier than usual, with her long wavy hair hanging free down her back instead of cordoned into a high ponytail. After stopping at the Starbucks on the corner for her usual Asiago bagel and morning chat with the barista who kept trying to convince her to come to his metal band's shows, she pulled into the back parking lot around 7:30. The only other car at this hour was branch manager Stephanie Ness's, webbed in reflected sunlight from the glass panels of the bank's rear facade. Steph tilted the blinds in one of the rear windows, the agreed-upon signal that it was safe to come inside.

Theirs was just a little neighborhood branch of the Bank of America, but Jess loved her job. After fleeing home at sixteen to bounce around between the couches of Safeway coworkers in Idaho, moving back to Tacoma to complete her GED, and working a series of thankless retail and food-service jobs, she was starting to think she had finally found her place. It had taken her only a year to work her way up to senior teller, responsible for overseeing the teller pit and signing off on all large transactions, which made her feel very adult. Friends all wanted to know what it was like to hold hundreds of thousands of dollars in her hands, and the truth was it never stopped being terrifying, but the extreme care with which she logged and ordered it all gave her a priestly thrill of sacredness.

By now Jess knew most of her customers by name. The lobby was full of personal touches: a carafe of free coffee for customers to drink while they waited, a play zone in the corner for their kids. Across the lobby floor from Jess's teller station, in a cubicle with her own desktop computer and ergonomic chair, sat a bright, pantsuited vision of the future: Bonnie Mottley, a twenty-eight-year-old personal banker who had started as a teller herself. Bonnie was training Jess as a sales and services specialist, which meant that when things weren't too busy Jess could leave the teller pit to pitch credit cards and money market accounts to customers in line. On weekends they sometimes walked to Port Defiance to play with Bonnie's dog.

August 7 was shaping up to be a very hot day. Jess took her time setting up teller station five the way she liked it. The other girls arrived one by one to set up their own: Virginia on Jess's left, in station six; Heather on her right, in four; another Jessica, from a different branch, in three today because they were understaffed; and in station two the new girl, Elva Navarro, who had just completed the two-week training course downtown. This was Elva's first day in the pit, which meant she would be doing what everyone did their first day: bonking her hand over and over on the three-inch-thick Plexiglas bandit barrier as she tried to pass money or documents to a customer. Steph kept it so crystal clear it was easy to forget it was there, but it was reputed to be impenetrable. On the final day of training they showed a video of a guy shooting a bandit barrier with a sawed-off shotgun from point-blank range. Nothing happened at all.

Jess enjoyed the rhythm of the workday here: the early-morning rush, the drifting noon hour, the gradual pickup until closing. All the girls took a moment at some point during the day to peer out the back windows and admire Jess's new car. It looked good out there in the sunlight. She was looking forward to driving it home after work for a family barbecue in honor of her visiting grandmother. Later perhaps she'd go longboarding around the neighborhood with her little sister. Her favorite sensation in the world was of wind and speed, the fresh smell of cedar blasting her hair back.

At 5:15:48, the man in the baseball cap and gold chain whom she was helping with an $80 withdrawal leaned back from the counter and craned his head around to peer toward the parking lot, as if he had spotted something there he didn't quite understand.

———

What three inches of Plexiglas can't stop is a teller's fear. Among FBI agents who work bank cases, mistrust of the bandit barrier is the subject of an oft-repeated witticism. I first heard it from a twenty-year veteran in the New York field office. "You have these robberies where you have a bandit barrier and the teller just shovels money underneath," the agent explained, chuckling. "I think it was my first supervisor who told me, 'The only thing that can penetrate a bandit barrier is a demand note.'"

Jessicah Stotts had, of course, imagined this scenario. If she was ever so unlucky as to find herself being robbed, she did not intend to shovel money underneath. Like Virginia, Heather, Jessica #2, and now Elva Navarro, she had been instructed that a modern bank robbery was a terrifying but ultimately dangerless widescreen action movie. She knew where to find the silent alarm button, tucked away in easy reach under the counter, which would make the movie stop. It did, however, seem a little strange to her—to all of them, in fact—that in this particular branch there was a narrow gap between the Plexiglas and the ceiling.

At 5:15:53, a man in a ski mask ran through the entrance from the parking lot, planted one foot on the countertop in front of Elva Navarro, and leapt for the barrier's lip.

Elva's cry was more of surprise than of terror, quickly modulated down to an embarrassed yelp. Later she would tell them all that everyone had been so friendly and welcoming to her all day that she figured this was some kind of initiation prank. It was only when the other girls looked over to see the dark figure rising above their heads that panic telescoped through the stations in a crushing surge. They all leapt back as one from their desks and stampeded toward Jess and Virginia's end of the teller pit. Jess dove under the last desk with Virge, striking her shoulder blade hard on the thick iron door of the merchant deposits safe as she went down. Heather and Jessica #2 dogpiled on top of them. Elva burst around the corner a moment later and dove in too.

"Is this a drill?" she murmured. "Do they test us on this kind of thing?"

Jess had to suppress a wild giggle. "I think this is a little extreme for that," she said.

"If this is a drill, I'm quitting," announced Jessica #2.

———

U.S. Army Field Manual 90-10-1, *An Infantryman's Guide to Combat in Built-Up Areas*, describes the army's doctrinal room-clearing procedure: a flashbang or fragmentation grenade followed by a four-man breaching team. "While the team members move toward their points of domination, they engage all targets in their sector," reads FM 90-10-1. "Because the soldiers are moving and shooting at the same time, they must move using careful hurry. They do not rush with total disregard for any obstacles."

Obstacles in the present facility included a promotional display for mortgages with a faux gable roof standing in the middle of the lobby, a water cooler and a carafe of hot coffee on a credenza at the head of the line, a fat-legged play table covered in rainbow blocks in the corner by the printer, and an array of polyester belts paid out between waist-high stanchions, within which thronged a sizable afternoon crowd. The four men in ski masks and sweatshirts now breaching the bank's rear door had been dissuaded from grenades by Scott Byrne, who had assured Specialist Sommer that even if he was crazy enough to do this thing, a flashbang was just completely insane, but they did move toward their points of domination with careful hurry: Chad Palmer to the far door with his fully automatic AK-47 and banana clip of thirty 7.62mm rounds held at his shoulder, Nathan Dunmall to the near door with another AK-47 and a duffel bag full of spare ammo clips and bleeder kits, and Tigra Robertson to the personal banker cubicles with a Springfield XD 9mm pistol bearing an underslung flashlight.

According to a conventional tactical breakdown, the bandit barrier was not an obstacle. It was architecture, dividing the lobby in two. The only entrance to the teller pit behind it was a locked, reinforced door at the end. After breaching at this point, FM 90-10-1 dictated a two-by-two leapfrog pattern from entry to terminus. Infantrymen were not supposed to clear a corridor-shaped space like the teller pit without sufficient manpower.

For Rangers, however, regular infantry field manuals read the way freshman geometry textbooks read to a mathematics graduate student: rife with simplifications chosen for teachability, blind to the way in which axioms might usefully bend.

The man whose body was now twisting sideways to soar through the gap between Plexiglas and ceiling, one gloved hand planted for purchase, the other holding a 9mm Glock 19 with a red laser sight, was Specialist Luke Elliott Sommer.

———

In the lobby, meanwhile, were a dozen or so customers, two managers, a big steel door for access to the vault, and three other masked gunmen rapidly fanning through the space. Bonnie Mottley and a customer had just sat down in the personal banker's cubicle when a noise from the teller pit drew their attention. They looked over to see a wave of startled comprehension sweep through the line of customers. Behind the bandit barrier the tellers abruptly vanished. Three customers shot out the front door to the street as if cracked off the end of a whip. Others, slower, were caught in corners or dove under counters. In the cubicle next to Bonnie's, Stephanie Ness, famous around the bank for going strictly by corporate protocol, was already dialing her phone.

"Drop the phone! Get on the floor!" yelled a sprinting gunman with his pistol held in front of him in a professional-looking two-handed grip. Seconds later the gun was up in Bonnie's face, a ski-masked head cocked diagonally behind it. "Get on the floor!"

Bonnie and her customer, an elderly woman, fell out of their chairs and flattened themselves on the carpet. The man demanded to see the floor supervisor.

"I'm the branch manager," said Steph's clipped voice through the divider between her cubicle and Bonnie's. The gunman strode out. For a few seconds Bonnie couldn't see him, could only hear his voice through the divider.

"I need you to open the vault."

"The door is dual control," Steph said. "It takes two people to open."

"I don't care what it takes. Just get it open."

Steph's head appeared above the divider. "Bonnie," she said. "Come with me."

When she got to her feet, Bonnie saw another man in a ski mask make his way down the empty teller line—*behind* the bandit barrier. The bank was now a strange kind of double spectacle, with witnesses on either side helpless to intervene in each other's fates.

———

Jess Stotts, flat on her back amid the smell of carpet and computer wires under Virginia Bradford's desk in the teller pit, kept feeling that same urge to giggle. The trappings of her new professional life loomed at unreachable heights: drawers, office supplies, sallow fluorescent lights, the underside of Virginia's stool. Someone's legs lay across her chest. The breath of the tellers she was supposedly supervising came fast and close all around her. Seconds pulled out like taffy. The lobby rang with scuffs, cries, thumps, shouts, and then a loud metallic bang which sparked a flurry of desperate looks throughout the pile and then a tentative consensus that there was no way that had been a gunshot. Virge caught Jess's eye and nodded toward the silent alarm button under the counter above their heads. Jess stared at it for a short eon. All she would have to do was pull her arm out, reach her hand out across space, extend her finger up, and—

A pair of giant legs turned the corner into their station. The pile compressed with a gasp. A man in a bulky gray sweatshirt and a black ski mask crouched on his heels to stare at them. His eyes were a blue of such intensity that they seemed to glow through the eyeholes. Laser light spiked from the barrel of the gun in his right hand, dancing in grainy red jags through their torsos and limbs. The image of herself with her arm outstretched toward the button reverberated in Jess's mind with such insistence that she could barely think. She had almost done it.

"Get up," the man said.

Nobody moved. The red bead exerted a tingling force, like the fingertip of a ghost.

"I said, *get up*."

One by one they scrambled to their feet. The man was large and muscular. As he made the bead dart over the fabric of their bare arms and shirtsleeves to pause on each of their chests in turn, his voice went suddenly personable. He explained that he wanted his canvas shoulder bag filled with fifties and hundreds, no dye packs, no bait money, no serialized bills. Jess had not been familiar with these concepts before working at the bank and wondered where he had learned them. He sounded like a guy her age, calm and cocky. She felt suddenly sure she knew him. Had he come in before? None of this was quite real yet.

"Time!" he called out toward the lobby.

"Thirty seconds!" shouted a hooded figure with an assault rifle by the front entrance.

"If this bag isn't full in one minute, you're all gonna get wasted," the blue-eyed man explained to the tellers, emphasizing the point with his gun.

Now it was real.

———

The vault door in the lobby required both a combination and a key. Stephanie Ness knew the combination; Bonnie had the key. But halfway to the door Bonnie realized that she had left it behind at her desk.

"Get it," ordered the gunman, taking an impatient half-step beside her before turning on his heel and striding to the vault after Steph. Neither was able to see Tigra's boyish face or Superman tattoo. They didn't know if he was young or old, experienced at this or a rank beginner. All they knew was that he was unusually short. Bonnie retrieved her key ring and hurried to the vault, her knee-length jacket fluttering behind her. Steph and the man were waiting. By their feet, the woman who owned the tobacco store around the corner and brought her receipts here lay curled in a fetal ball, her bare white calves sticking out. Beside her on the floor a middle-aged man cried audibly. Bonnie unlocked the grate and led the way through the giant metal vault door, past the wall of safe-deposit boxes in the entryway, and into the closet-sized room in back, jammed with a filing cabinet, a stack of logbooks, a spray can of air freshener, and a greasy Diebold safe the size of a small refrigerator. Bonnie inserted the key and Steph set to work on the combination, her hands shaking visibly. The mechanism clicked. Bolts retracted.

The door swung open on its thick metal hinges. Inside was more than $200,000.

The gunman stared. "I need a bag," he said.

There was a yellow mesh sack right on top of the safe. Bonnie's and Steph's eyes met. Should they mention it to him? The protocol was total cooperation.

The man turned on his heel and strode out of the vault.

"But there's a bag right there!" Bonnie said.

"Shh!" said Steph.

———

The teller pit was in a state of pandemonium. Jess and the others scooped up piles of loose cash from the subdivided trays in their drawers and shoveled it into the blue-eyed man's shoulder bag as he went by. It wasn't anywhere near full.

"One minute, guys!" called the rifleman by the front entrance.

"You have thirty seconds to fill this bag or I'm going to blow you all away," said the blue-eyed man. "Twenty-nine. Twenty-eight. Give me your reserve cash if you have any. Twenty-seven. Twenty-six."

They were throwing money at him now, great wads of it from under their trays, arms rubbery with panic. To Jess's left, Virginia looked down at her hand, which was bleeding for some reason, and dropped a whole load of bills on the floor. Elva fluttered helplessly at her station, pleading that this was her first day. Jess saw the blue-eyed man pause beside her and rub her back. Bills flew against the bandit barrier and fluttered over the dividers between stations. A banded stack of fives hit her in the face.

"Ten. Nine. Eight."

The blue-eyed man's shoulder bag was now so full that the tellers had to shove cash down to pack more in. Still he counted and paced. Jess's drawer was totally empty. She crouched and started spinning the dial as fast as she could on the merchant safe, where she had $22,000 more.

"Six. Five. Four."

The rifleman in the lobby called out again. "Come on, guys! A minute and a half!"

The blue-eyed man stopped counting and walked to the end of the hallway. "Could you get this for me?" he asked Virginia.

She leaned over and turned the handle of the door.

"Thanks for your cooperation," he said, then walked into the lobby.

———

I have watched all this happen many times. It is not a comfortable experience. Six of the eight security cameras are located high on the wall behind the teller stations, casting the viewer as some kind of crouching gargoyle voyeur. By 5:08 p.m. a swarm of strangers from the future had already begun staring over the shoulders of the tellers as they worked. The compound image that flickers into being late at night on my laptop at a rate of one grainy black-and-white frame per two seconds is of a kind of a shadow bank, airless and cold. In the workplace Jessicah Stotts liked so much, customers were individuals with names, stories, and distinguishing habits. Here they are a semi-compressible fluid subject to pressure waves and vortices as it surges toward exits and clots up in corners. For Jess, cash was a sacred locus of relationships between institutions and human beings. Here it is an object like any other, governed in its motion only by laws of energy and momentum. It flutters around her head like silent confetti.

The shadow bank is a lot like the world I used to inhabit in my math days. Because I do my best not to see things that way anymore, I have stared at this branch from every possible position on Google Maps, trying to find some glimpse of the humanity Jess experienced inside. But no matter what angle I look from, the white stone facade pulses with malevolence, the shrubs look exhaust-choked in their bed of purple cinders, the Bank of America sign hangs plastic and impersonal against the sun-streaked Tacoma sky.

Everyone tells me how lucky Alex is that no one got hurt. This is true, of course, though it seems a little crass to view the safety of others as mere good fortune for Alex—one of the many insidious ways in which criminality condemns you to a radically self-interested outlook. He is equally lucky that the team stole only $54,000, right at the cutoff past which federal guidelines mandate harsher sentences. We have Elliott Sommer to thank for that. When Tigra charged out of the vault in search of a bag, Sommer told him they had to stick to the timeline, open safe or no. He led the team to the back of the lobby, held the rear doors open as everyone jogged through, then followed them across the parking lot toward the alley, pausing first to wish everyone inside the bank a nice day.

About thirty seconds later, the four of them burst out of the alley onto the sidewalk of South 60th Street with balaclavas still on and handguns and assault rifles in plain view, craning their heads around for the silver Audi A4 that was supposed to be there to pick them up.

Everyone has heard tales of ordinary people taking refuge in the anonymity of the crowd rather than intervening in some violent spectacle, a tendency known in the social psychology literature as the "bystander effect." But the bravery of bystanders in situations like these is just as often incredibly inspiring. Shannon Macleod is the name of the woman who was driving by the bank with her boyfriend and children when the first wave of customers burst out screaming. She was twenty-four years old.

"I circled the area and was gonna try to follow as much as I could," she wrote in jagged handwriting in her statement for the Tacoma police. "But there was five* and when I headed down the street towards them 2 turned around and looked at me and I saw the rifles they had and I have my kids in the car and didn't want to risk my children so I had to stay in the area until my boyfriend and that car lot guy came back. So I just stopped and was directing the cops where to go. Sorry I couldn't do more."

The team jogged down South 60th Street into the residential neighborhood behind the bank, pulling their balaclavas off and obscuring the weapons as best they could. Just as Sommer was informing them all that if they couldn't find the Audi they would have to commandeer one of these houses for use as a "fortress," the team passed through the intersection with Puget Sound Avenue and caught sight of the Audi half a block away.

Alex saw the specialist waving him down. He could have kept driving. But he did not. He stopped to pick up the team. It is one of the many strange ironies of his case, what the philosopher Bernard Williams might call "moral luck," that if he had succeeded in driving away, Elliott might well have killed someone, in which case Alex would have faced a murder charge.

The bank was in full lockdown by now, but someone new was

---

* An oddly common mistake. There were four.

inside. While Sommer and the others were still running down the alley, the last customer of the day, a stylish older woman in a tight striped shirt, had pulled into the bank's rear lot, parked, and entered the same doorway through which Sommer and the team had exfilled less than thirty seconds earlier.

I have replayed this moment over and over on my laptop. The room the woman walks into resembles a functioning bank in many ways. The tellers are more or less at their stations. The belts between stanchions are undisturbed, customers having mostly confined their panicked bolting to the designated pathways. A rectangle of early evening sun creeps across the carpet from the skylight. As the woman in the striped shirt traverses the empty lobby, Bonnie bursts out of the vault just a few feet in front of her—to the great relief, incidentally, of Jessicah Stotts, who has been stealing glances through the Plexiglas for Bonnie's reappearance ever since that unexplained metallic bang—and runs to lock the front entrance, losing a shoe on the way. This does not appear to strike the woman in the striped shirt as sufficiently strange to alter her trajectory. She passes an alcove where customers are still huddled on the floor, picks up a deposit slip from a chest-high counter, considers it for a moment, then gathers her purse and, as Bonnie runs across the lobby in the other direction, wanders toward the head of the line. Bonnie locks the back entrance and hurries toward the teller pit. The woman in the striped shirt moves to intercept her with an expression of puzzlement and concern. The security camera footage shows her mouth move around a series of questions. "Excuse me?" she appears to be saying. "Excuse me?" Her hair is stylishly cropped, her pants sleek and flowing, her sash belt tied at the side. Bonnie, barely slowing down, gives her a look of incredulity so powerful it borders on fury.

I guess the reason I keep coming back to the woman in the striped shirt is that I feel for her. I walked into this the same way. First I was clueless. Then I assumed that whatever had happened here was over. Then the doors were locked and I was part of the evidence.

I have spent a lot of time now on the phone with Jessicah Stotts. At first I wasn't sure whether to approach her. "So," I imagined saying, "my cousin feels really terrible about that bank robbery . . ." I knew the media had bothered her and her coworkers for weeks after the crime, ambushing them on lunch and coffee breaks to probe for the evocative detail. Bank of America offered trauma counseling but no time off in which to pursue it. Though Jess and Virginia were both temporarily one-handed, Jess with her right arm in a sling and Virginia with a bandage around her palm, everyone had to work the next day. Virginia quit immediately, others shortly afterward. Jess held on for a year, but with all the staff shortages there wasn't time anymore for sales training outside the teller pit. All day she would find herself staring at the place on top of the bandit barrier where Sommer's gun had knocked out a chip. A counselor told her that she was exhibiting signs of PTSD. Eventually she quit, got a job at Mallon Ford, and started training as a boxer. In her first amateur fight at a Puyallup boxing gym, she won by decision after three three-minute rounds.

When we did finally talk, she surprised me with her low, gentle voice. There was a determined wryness to the way she described the robbery that gave me the sense she had worked hard to achieve it. Pits of silence opened up between her sentences. Without my asking, she volunteered that she didn't feel any anger toward Alex, that the only one she blamed was Luke Elliott Sommer, and I wanted to correct her but didn't know what to say. A lot has changed for her since 2006. Not long ago, she and her girlfriend, Alyssa, got married at the center of a bridge outside Tacoma while strapped into a tandem bungee harness, leaping off together as soon as they said "I do." For this occasion, and this occasion only, each was wearing the jersey of the other's favorite hockey team.

The thing I can't get over about Jessicah Stotts is that she is an enormous hockey fan. The first time Alyssa treated her to rinkside seats at a game, a slap shot rattled the Plexiglas right in front of them and gave her a flashback to the way the bandit barrier had moved under Sommer's weight. In some other, better Tacoma, she and Alex might have been friends.

CHAPTER 25

THE P-WORD

Nathan Dunmall and Luke Elliott Sommer experienced very different bank robberies than Jessicah Stotts did. As recounted by Dunmall to Special Agent Gary France, Nathan's resembles nothing so
much as a Three Stooges routine. Once through the door, he tried
to control his breathing through the hot black fabric of the balaclava,
"just standing inside the bank almost in shock of what was happening
around him." It was hard to see out the eyeholes, especially toward
the sides, where he dimly perceived large men crouching. He forgot
to rack a round into his AK-47. Tigra forgot to turn on the flashlight
attached to his pistol. Chad forgot to call out the time, though he
remembered once Elliott prompted him from behind the teller line.
Just behind Nathan's back, a woman in a truck drove past the floor-
to-ceiling glass, stopped at the drive-through ATM, and inserted her
debit card, oblivious to what was going on inside. Nathan shuffled
out of sight behind a promotional display for low-interest mortgages.
Tigra disappeared for a minute inside the massive stone-clad vault,
then ran out again saying he had forgotten the bag for the money. "At
one point," wrote Special Agent France, "DUNMALL remembers
SOMMER hugging one of the tellers."

Elliott's robbery was an altogether grander affair. During his first
weeks of house arrest in British Columbia, when family and friends
were latching onto his story of having robbed the bank as a political
protest, a close friend of Christel's named Leah Jewall began collabo-

rating with the young revolutionary on a book that would intersperse his autobiography with her recollections of him as a boy. Chapter One begins with a misquoted epigraph from Benjamin Franklin: "They that can give up essential liberty to purchase a little temporary safety deserve neither liberty nor safety."

I looked over at Tigra and watched as he "persuaded" a manager to help him open the safe, exhibiting the same cold professionalism I had come to expect from him. Palmer was watching the far door, carefully out of sight in the window, nervously checking his watch, waiting to call the next time back. I half expected Nathan to be in the wrong area but as was planned and rehearsed, he calmly sat by the entrance we had stormed through moments before, and had an almost bored attitude in his body language. I turned towards the door that led out of the teller cage and stopped in my tracks. The tellers I had so thoughtlessly misplaced moments ago were huddled into a small group on the bottom of the floor. Sighing heavily, I took a squat and turned to the young woman who was shielding the others with her body. "50's and 100's; no bait cash, no silent alarms, no recorded serial numbers. Your help is appreciated." It's hard to say if it was the incredible intensity of the moment, the robbery training or innate leadership, but the woman acted with an incredibly professional speed. She got the others organized and began moving around the cage in a hurry. One woman however remained standing, and did not move. Smiling, I moved towards her.

After a section break, Leah Jewall takes over the narrative with an anecdote about Elliott as a boy.

Elliott always loved animals, and even though he would sometimes talk about hunting them, he hated to see them suffer. When he was about 4 yrs. old, the family lived at the foot of Mt. Boucherie, a small mountain in the town of Westbank, a few miles north of Peachland. There were rattlesnakes on that mountain, and black widow spiders, which Elliott enjoyed catching with his bare hands. He had no fear of hurting himself; it was an adventure for him.

And on the chapter goes: surgical professionalism, lordly beneficence, folksy Okanagan asides. Elliott does not mention that when the team exited the bank they could not at first find the Audi, nor that he considered commandeering a house.

> We left the parking lot the way we had come, and ran full tilt into the alley way we had pulled into mere minutes before. As we came to the end of the alley the darkness afforded us by the relatively high walls and shade of the local houses gave way as the alley ended.
> And then we entered the light.
> The masks came off, the weapons were slid into our clothing, and we WALKED around the corner and into the awaiting vehicle. Now, nothing is ever perfect, but for what we had set out to do, we had gotten as close as possible to that unattainable goal.

By the time of my interview with him at McCreary, though, Elliott was evincing a very different perspective on the robbery. Over the phone he had told me that we should refer to it only as "el fiasco." When he talked about the tellers, it was to express remorse for their suffering rather than satisfaction with his gentlemanly charm. It wasn't as if the turnaround were flawless: once, in the middle of confessing how awful he had felt when he saw how frightened they all were, Elliott said of his own jump over the bandit barrier, "I gotta admit, it was pretty darn sexy," then chuckled. But I appreciated his remorse. After years of Alex's excuses and increasingly dubious denials, Elliott's open declarations of personal culpability were immensely refreshing.

So it was that I felt no qualms about buying a meal for the man who had traumatized Jessicah Stotts and a dozen other innocent people and sent Alex and five others to federal prison. After a morning of conversation about all the ways he had manipulated and corrupted his coconspirators, I ventured into the visiting room to select a tray of Paleolithically frosted buffalo wings from one vending machine and a can of Pepsi from another. One of the guards, bearded and sad-eyed, cracked open the Pepsi and poured it into a Styrofoam cup for me as we watched the pinkish sauce melt in the microwave's buzzing glow. Cans, he explained, could be made into knives.

"We don't get too many visitors out here," the guard said. "It's remote. But a few months ago one guy had his mom bring in a bag of drugs and hide it with the food. Now she's incarcerated too. How low can you get?"

I carried it all back to the room where Elliott was waiting, thinking about how frustrating it must have been for him to be stuck among the common run of criminals here. As we ate—he insisted on sharing the buffalo wings—we made small talk about math, hacking, and the glorious weather in Kelowna.

———

There is something uncanny to me now about my notes from McCreary. The quotes I scribbled so furiously retain none of the aura of wry warmth and shared understanding that they had for me when I first heard them. At the distance of a small table from Elliott, there was a strange double quality to my consciousness, one half telling myself I could see right through him, the other half helplessly interacting on his terms. Some false note would occasionally jar me out of it, so that for a while I would find myself floating above the conversation at an analytical remove, going through the motions of smiling and responding while a little voice inside me said *Wait wait wait*, but then he would say something oddly relatable again, clear-eyed and vulnerable, and with a little lurch the gears of human connection would reengage. I don't know how to explain this now other than to say that his crimes seemed profoundly unreal to me. I just couldn't integrate my moment-to-moment experience of him with the Luke Elliott Sommer who had robbed, attacked, betrayed, threatened, and manipulated multiple victims and coconspirators. It was all just too awful, too cartoonish, too out of joint with how normal he seemed.

I no longer doubt that Elliott is capable of violence, that he has somewhere inside him what his mother calls the "Sommer switch." What are the odds that the guy who seemed relatable enough to my cousin to rob a bank with should be equally relatable to me? It is clear now that all I ever saw of him was a careful construction. The reflective earnestness I found so compelling was no more the core of his character than the humble Christianity, skeptical atheism, sarcastic hilarity, military idealism, or violent ruthlessness that have made him so compelling to others. Only a year and a half later would the spell finally break—not because of his criminal record, but because of the way he did math.

————

When I first started discussing number theory with Elliott, he had already been corresponding for eight months with Professor Beck, who told me he based his assessment of Elliott's talent both on the insightful questions he had asked and the advanced exercises he had completed. My own experience had been puzzlingly different.

"Sommer's Theorem (oh the cheek of me)" read the subject of one typical email. Inside was a proof that a prime number could always be found between two successive square numbers—an open problem known as Legendre's conjecture that has resisted every effort for two centuries. Elliott's technique made use of differential calculus, Gauss's prime-counting function, and Hadamard's famous proof of the prime number theorem, was conveyed in amazingly sophisticated and portentous mathematical jargon, and relied at its core on a failure to invert the direction of an inequality after negation, the kind of mistake a high school freshman might make on a quiz in Algebra I.

Over the phone, on the other hand, I was surprised to find that Elliott was so fluid and creative with his growing repertoire of technical concepts that I felt that excitement you get only with someone who truly loves numbers.

"Hey, man," he said as soon as I dialed 5 to accept the last such call, "do you know if the twin primes conjecture has been proved?"

The twin primes conjecture, one of the most famous open questions in mathematics, holds that there are an infinite number of pairs of prime numbers that are separated only by 2. Early examples are 5 and 7, 29 and 31, 101 and 103. I assured Elliott that the conjecture still stood, then began to describe some of the progress in the past few years as leading mathematicians had begun closing the gap.

"Awesome," he said, cutting me off, clearly uninterested. "Because I have a proof so stupid simple that I can't believe no one's thought of it yet. I'm sick to my stomach it's so easy."

As he explained his "proof," I listened anxiously. It seemed an act of sacrilege even to suggest that a great problem like this might yield to some minor mathematical trick. I was relieved when I spotted the flaw.

"Okay," I said when he wrapped it up. "I hate to burst your bubble here . . ."

"No, go ahead. That's why I called."

I tried to give him an intuition for the error in his reasoning by showing how it failed for numbers larger than the ones he had so far checked. But I have never been particularly quick at calculation, and as I fumbled my way through the mental arithmetic required to generate the counterexample I had in mind, he cut me off again.

"Listen," he said, "I've checked this all the way out to thirty-six digits."

I was taken aback. His tone wasn't unfriendly—he just sounded excited to share the discovery with me, if a little impatient with my slowness. But it would have been impossible to accomplish this on pencil and paper within a human lifespan.

"You mean out to the first thirty-six *primes*?" I asked.

"No, thirty-six *digits*. On a computer."

"How do you have access to a computer?"

"One of my friends in here got out and I gave him the instructions for coding it in JavaScript. Which I know is not the fastest platform, but it's something he can handle. He wrote me to say, 'It seems to be working. I mean, it filled up the Web page with numbers . . .'"

I listened in amazement as he elaborated further about the application's structure and functioning. Nothing distinguished this story from a hundred others Elliott had told me about hacking or military exploits or prison, all equally thick with offhand detail, except that this time there was no way to rationalize it away as anything but bald fabrication, because of the mathematical fallacy at its core: the algorithm he was describing would have failed within milliseconds. That possibility did not appear to worry him. His voice was just as eager as before. I was too unnerved even to be angry. This fabricated story, like his faulty proof, seemed to be no more than a means to convince me of what he knew to be true on his own unassailable authority. It was as if "proof" and "story" had exactly the same epistemological status for him, as if he thought he could talk his way out of the *laws of mathematics themselves*.

———

When I talked to Elliott at McCreary, I still believed he had essentially the same relation to reality that I did. I thought that with greater trust and harder effort we would come closer and closer to the truth. As the buffalo wings ran out, I edged up to my most important questions of all: the ones about Alex. This topic continued to be painful. Though I felt increasingly persuaded by Elliott's flat insistence that Alex had known about the robbery in advance, it sometimes felt as if we were discussing two completely different soldiers. My PFC Blum was naive and credulous, kept as far as possible from all the overt criminality because Specialist Sommer understood he was too idealistic a Ranger to go along with the plan unless it could be rationalized away as normal tab high jinks. Elliott's PFC Blum was loyal and motivated, kept away from the criminal preparations only out of Specialist Sommer's fatherly magnanimity, in order to give him a legal out in case they all got caught.

"When I introduced Alex to the other guys," Elliott told me at McCreary, "I said, 'He's going to be driving, but if we get cragged, he's going to roll on me.'"

"Why did you do that just for Alex?"

Elliott paused to think it over. "He was the youngest," he said finally. "Tigra I expected to roll with me. He and I were road dogs. Chad, Nathan, Tigra, and I were all—we're very similar. We had the same kinda demeanor. I don't know. For some reason I had this instinct to protect Alex. Chad owed me loyalty for standing by him when he was a pariah, and these other guys were my friends, the ones I wanted by my side. Actually, Nathan was younger than Alex, wasn't he?"

"Yeah," I said.

"But Nathan wasn't the innocent Alex was. We'd been through a lot together. Alex had all the same feelings I had when I enlisted but just hadn't had a chance to be rudely awakened yet. I kind of wanted to suck him into this vendetta. But the consequences of that were not anything I wanted."

"In Dunmall's testimony, he said he didn't see Alex from the time Alex picked them up at the Greyhound station until you left the barracks for the bank. Is that accurate?"

"Yeah, that'd be about right."

"Where was Alex supposed to be when you guys came out of the bank?"

"For all my planning, I wasn't very specific about that. I just said get turned around."

"In the interview with Bruce Singer, you claimed the vehicle was patrolling between two grid points and that's why you couldn't find it immediately. Was that just a fabrication?"

"I don't know," Elliott said, wiping off his fingers on a napkin. "That might have been true. There's a lot of shit I said to Bruce where I was just fucking with him, but then again there was a lot I believed."

"Alex says he freaked out and started to drive away. Do you think that's possible?"

"I can't read his mind. Maybe he had a moment of crisis. He probably did. I can't see any reason a person wouldn't have one."

I could already tell this conversation wasn't going the way I wanted it to, but I still read Elliott the lines from his interview with Bruce Singer that had always driven me crazy.

At that point in time, the car pulled up, weapons were fairly well concealed, and we got in the vehicle, and the driver still was kinda, "What the hell?" You know, "What's going on?" He had agreed to do this with very limited information and, uh, like . . . I mean, don't get me wrong, he knew.

"And then Bruce goes 'Mm-hmm,'" I said, "and you start to say something—'But to what end was'—before he cuts you off—"

Elliott, nodding, cut me off. "I was going along with the mythos of what I told Alex," he said. "So I could play into it if Alex used the story. Then Singer's like, 'They all told on you,' and that's why I turned down the crazy at the end. No point trying to cloud it with bullshit anymore."

I stared at him, helpless. I was pretty sure Singer had told Sommer that the others had informed on him long before this moment—later I would discover I was right—but I didn't have the interview in front of me to prove it.

"What did you mean when you told Singer that Alex was a good kid but 'slightly misguided'?" I asked.

"Joining the army," Elliott answered immediately.

"Did you ever make an effort to disillusion him?"

"A couple of times. But you can't be told. You have to see. But then you see and people don't believe you. Then it becomes next to impossible to tell what's real, because no matter what you think you've seen, everyone else tells you you haven't."

I knew what he was referring to: the rape, the massacre, the war crimes he had been insisting he had seen since the first day we began talking, that shadowy horror in Iraq that had sometimes appeared to me to be the final link in the chain of responsibility for what happened to Alex.

"You said a lot of what you told Singer was bullshit," I said.

"Not about that."

———

How did I allow myself to be deflected away from Alex, just as so many journalists had been deflected away from the bank robbery while Elliott was on house arrest? I knew the treaty transfer to Canada would depend in part on the plausibility of his war-crime claims. The argument was that because of his undiagnosed rapid-cycling bipolar disorder, the things he saw and did abroad dismantled the fantasy of crusading American heroism that had served for him as a guiding moral principle, rendering him temporarily insane. Every bad act he had committed between then and his transformation into the friendly, caring math whiz and family man he was today had to be understood as a symptomatic outburst of a traumatized, unmedicated, out-of-control victim of war.

The core of the argument was mental illness. Of course, if some of us wanted to see something more behind Specialist Sommer's actions, a deeper political cause that gave meaning to what otherwise looked unbearably senseless, Elliott wasn't going to stand in our way.

"What pissed me off the most is that not a single thing I said I saw was a lie," he told me at McCreary. "Only the Public Affairs Office was involved in responding to the allegations. They released a statement before there had even been an investigation. No CID guys got involved until afterward. But this is CAG.* You think investigating

---

* Combat Applications Group—Delta Force

Army Rangers is tough? Try investigating Delta Force. Army MPs don't even have clearance to enter Ranger Batt. We have to give them permission to come investigate. You think there's going to be a fair, thorough investigation of claims involving Delta?"

He told me about the black U.S. helicopter that hovered over Christel's house shortly after he was released to house arrest. It happened at dusk, he said, not long before the call from what he described as a "four-star general and a sergeant major from SOCOM."

"Dave Preston says it was a colonel, not a general."

"It might have been a colonel," Elliott said, with no change of tone or expression, then segued into a secret plan he had heard of among soldiers in the Ranger Regiment to sneak across the border and snatch him back.

The brief statement released by the army's Public Affairs Office in response to Sommer's accusations stated that the rape he claimed to have seen in a white tractor-trailer was impossible, as there were no trailers in the area he described—a difficult assertion for journalists to verify, since the location of Delta Force's headquarters was a closely guarded secret.

Elliott traced out a broad curve in the air over the plastic tabletop. "This is the Tigris River through Baghdad," he said. "There's one big loop in it." He pointed into the weak fluorescent glow above our heads, then slid his finger left. "Saddam's big palace is over here."

One thing I'll say for Elliott: he's got a sense of theater. I think it might be humanly impossible not to feel a shiver down your spine when a disgraced Special Ops commando buried deep behind penitentiary walls in the Appalachian hill country draws a map in the air to a secret military base where he claims the U.S. Army covered up war crimes. There is no question that Elliott has experienced things I can't fathom. He deployed to Afghanistan, deployed to Iraq, fought on America's side at an age when I faced no greater danger than choosing the wrong major in college. His torso is covered with tattoos of giant screaming skulls for the soldiers close to him who died, two in training—Scott Byrne's old friend Blake Samodel, who died in a parachuting accident, and Devon Piguero, who was hit by a bullet in the shoot house—and one in combat. On the invisible screen rising from the table between us, where Elliott's intense blue eyes flitted from place to place as he traced out his map, were two very different images. My side showed a Baghdad of sunbaked firefights and camels, a crudely animated mash-up of *Three Kings* and *Aladdin*. His side showed the real city he patrolled and assaulted every day. As he spoke, it was almost possible to see Elliott as Christel and Mandi did: a victim of history, a squandered resource, an eccentric, brilliant teenager who enlisted in the U.S. Army planning to become a hero and came back something else.

"The next one over is where Delta Force set up," he concluded, tapping firmly in air as his eyes fixed on mine. "I was there June to October, 2004. Look for tractor-trailers on Google Earth."

What did it really mean to Elliott, I wonder now, all that dust and bloodshed? He may well have seen atrocities. Plenty happened in that war, hundreds of thousands of innocent civilians dying in the streets he was tracing his forefinger through. But by the time we spoke at McCreary, the war was long over, the investigations were done, the American people had wrung their hands as much as they were going to, and the sad truth is that Elliott wasn't telling me anything I didn't know. His stories were, in fact, remarkably similar to some that had broken just before his arrest. Tales of torture by Delta Force operators in a white trailer filtered out of Camp Nama, the secret Special Operations detention center, in February 2006. Iraqi police reports of ten civilians being handcuffed and executed by U.S. forces who then dropped a bomb on the house to cover it up first appeared in March 2006. Elliott's Baghdad might be a higher-resolution assemblage of tropes than my own, but does that make it any less a cartoon?

———

It took me a long time to seriously consider the possibility that Sommer really might be a psychopath. There is no known treatment—some evidence suggests that therapy only provides such people with opportunities to learn how to simulate emotional connection better and thereby manipulate victims—and I did not like thinking of Elliott that way. I wanted to believe in the sincerity of his desire to grow and change. I wanted to believe in Christel's conviction that her son had regained his moral compass. I wanted to be able to trust whatever he might reveal to me about Alex and the robbery. Most of all, I wanted to avoid the mistake I had made with Alex, to be a compassionate writer rather than a coldhearted scientist, open to the mystery that lies in every human heart.

Other journalists, I felt, had erred by framing their subjects as inherently evil. In her masterful takedown of one such writer, *The Journalist and the Murderer*, Janet Malcolm, one of my literary heroes, mocked "the fanciful notion that the people who commit evil acts are lacking in the usual human equipment—are not 'real' human beings at all but soulless monsters." As Malcolm saw it, "the concept of the psychopath is, in fact, an admission of failure to solve the mystery of evil—it is merely a restatement of the mystery—and only offers an escape valve for the frustration felt by psychiatrists, social workers, and police officers, who daily encounter its force." I did not want to fail Elliott in that way. But was it possible that refusing to apply a label might be just as grave a failure of understanding as applying it?

Finally, about a month before I was due in Kentucky, I called my brother, a therapist in San Francisco, to ask what he knew about the condition. He put me in touch with an old friend of his from grad school who worked at one of Tacoma's better-kept secrets.

You can make out McNeil Island as a line of cedar-topped cliffs half a mile offshore from the Chambers Bay golf course at the southwest tip of Tacoma, but few discuss it around town. Approximately three hundred "sexually violent predators" are confined there under a 1990 law that allows the State of Washington to hold them indefinitely after their criminal sentences expire. Employees outnumber the inmates: the island has its own security force, its own fire department, its own dedicated ferry.

If I had met Amy at a party, I would never have guessed that psychopathic predators were within her purview. If anything, I might have pegged her as a middle-school teacher, her smart, California-inflected voice bolstered by the gentle firmness of someone good with the young. We met up on a foggy Thursday night at a sports bar on the shore of Commencement Bay and took our beers to a private booth. Amy listened carefully as I detailed Elliott's history of crimes and explanations: armed bank robbery with team of Army Rangers as political protest, penny stock scam with Marxist supervillain as business development opportunity, violent assault as obligatory fulfillment of prison honor code, hit on prosecutor as FBI entrapment; PTSD, rapid-cycling bipolar disorder.

"I don't put a lot of stock in that bipolar diagnosis," she said right away. "Rapid cycling is very rare, and it just doesn't explain these behaviors to me. Setting up a hit is not the kind of thing people do when manic. Mania mimics methamphetamine use. They don't sleep, they ramble, they feel like they're accomplishing great things even though they're almost totally unproductive. It sounds like he was actually able to execute these big projects."

It was strange to hear her take him seriously. I'd expected to be told that compared to the guys she worked with, Elliott was a mere kitten.

"But his schemes were always sort of flimsy," I said. "They eventually fell apart."

"That's very psychopathic. They're so grandiose, they believe they're much more capable than they are. They don't understand consequences."

We began going over the Psychopathy Checklist—Revised, or PCL-R, the forensic instrument that, though not without its detractors, has transformed the field of psychopathy research by providing the first halfway reliable diagnostic test. I tried to explain to Amy why I was hesitant to view Elliott through this lens. For me, at least, there seemed to be a kind of interpretive switch that got thrown when I started thinking of Elliott as a psychopath. Suddenly all his friendliness and relatability were just glibness and faking. Suddenly all his efforts at improving himself were just manipulative ploys to seem good in order to get things he wanted.

"Doesn't everyone manipulate?" I asked. "Doesn't everyone do good partly out of self-interest?"

Amy looked at me strangely. "Well, it's all on a spectrum," she said. "If you look at these various psychopathic traits and how pervasive they have to be, it's pretty hard to score high. There's a really different feel to how psychopaths present."

We started going over the twenty items that make up the checklist.

Factor 1 was about personality:

Glibness/superficial charm. Grandiose sense of self-worth. Need for stimulation/proneness to boredom. Pathological lying.

Conning/manipulative. Lack of remorse or guilt. Emotionally shallow. Callous/lack of empathy.

Factor 2 was about behavior:

Parasitic lifestyle. Poor behavioral controls. Sexual promiscuity. Early behavioral problems. Lack of realistic long-term goals. Impulsivity. Irresponsibility. Failure to accept responsibility for own actions. Many short-term marital relationships. Juvenile delinquency. Revocation of conditional release. Criminal versatility.

I kept laughing to myself in startled recognition, then questioning my laughter—it was like reading Elliott's horoscope, with all the attendant dangers of projection. Amy was careful to point out that she could not make a diagnosis without testing Elliott in person, but it seemed clear which way she was leaning.

"Lots of the guys at our clinic have been diagnosed with ADHD, bipolar, conduct disorder," Amy said. "People want to see other explanations than just 'This is who this guy is.' Especially when they're young and haven't done much yet. But eventually, after they've done enough, someone will say, 'This is just him.' Mania is such a different thing from empathy and morals. Those are a part of your character. Grandiosity can be a part of your character if it's there all the time."

"He used to be very grandiose, but now he's actually really hard on himself. He's always talking about how he hasn't finished anything he's started and how he's mentally ill."

"It doesn't have to be so obvious. Once they get more experienced, they learn how to say the right things. He's trying to relate to you."

"What about all the self-reflectiveness and insight into his own condition that I've been seeing?"

"Ehh," she said. "They find themselves very fascinating."

"But I think there's some genuine interest in figuring out more about himself. He has these surprisingly articulate things to say about his own moral deficits."

"His ability to do that is probably correlated with his intelligence. It could be genuine, but the intellectual understanding of it isn't necessarily a genuine desire to change. Of course, you can't say anything as fact—you can't say he's lying—but there's a clear external motivation to act as if he's changed. You just have to wait and see how he behaves. You see these guys who behave impeccably for fifteen years in prison and then a month after they get out they assault someone. He could be a guy who had an awakening, but that's not what we know about how change happens. It doesn't come from epiphanies. This is someone who has such a pattern of bad behavior, he's not just going to wake up and be a different person."

I was beginning to feel obscurely frustrated. How could Elliott ever hope to get out from under a prophecy as self-fulfilling as this? An alarming suspicion had begun sneaking up on me during my conversations with him over the phone: maybe the only real difference between Elliott and me was that he had gone to war and I had gone to college. My own mechanistic view of morality during my math days had shared more with his than I liked to admit now in literary company. After graduation, it had taken a painful, years-long project of self-socialization and education in the humanities to remake myself, during the course of which I had experienced a number of what felt like transformative realizations. Why couldn't something similar happen for Elliott? Talking to him was so much easier than talking to Alex—calmer, more intellectual, less fraught with emotional damage and transparent self-contradiction.

"His family really seems to think he's changed," I said. "They talked to him before he went on medication and they talk to him now and they say the difference is night and day."

"I hate to say this," said Amy, "but families are pretty poor sources."

"Because they want to think their son is a good person?"

"That's one part of it. The other—gosh, I don't know how to put this. People who end up in these situations, there's often something a little . . . *off* . . . about their families."

Amy had, of course, never met the Sommers. For her they were more scientific objects than human beings, possessors of correlated personality metrics and risk factors rather than of personal histories complexly interwoven with character and culture. I knew that this analytical remove of hers was a product of real experience with violent criminals—I admired it, even envied it—but in that moment, having spent a lot more time talking to the Sommers than to her, I couldn't help feeling on some level as if *Amy* were off, not them. Had all her work with a population ruled legally unreformable hardened her against the possibility that Elliott was different?

To give me a sense for daily life at McNeil, she told me a story of one of her patients. "He was sixty-something," she said, "nice enough, a rapist of teen girl runaways. For fifteen years his rationalization had always been 'They were dirty, naughty girls,' but when I met him he was really trying hard, doing voluntary walk-in therapy. One day he comes in and makes a big announcement to the group. He's had a breakthrough. He understands now that just because these girls were out late in short skirts, they were not in need of being raped. He's realized—this is his big epiphany—one of them could have been a *virgin*."

I looked at her, horrified. She gave a rueful laugh.

"It was *such* a good try," she said, in the voice you'd use to tell a three-year-old who has pooped on the lip of a toilet seat that he's coming along really well. "That's how slow it is. Fifteen years to get *there*."

———

Psychopathy has a two-century-long history of definitional disputes. Dr. Robert Hare, the Canadian psychologist who developed the PCL-R, may be responsible for lending it the empirical armature we have come to expect of modern clinical constructs, but the text that he cites as his main inspiration, Dr. Hervey Cleckley's 1941 magnum opus, *The Mask of Sanity*, operates on an older principle. "We must concern ourselves," Cleckley writes, "not only with their measurable intelligence, their symptomatology (or, rather, lack of symptomatology) in ordinary psychiatric terms, but also with the impression they make as total organisms in action among others and in all the nuances and complexities of deeply personal and specifically affective relationships . . . Only when the concrete details of environment are laid in, as, for instance, in an honest and perceptive novel, can the significance of behavior be well appreciated."

The Mask of Sanity reads like a darker, flatter, far more repetitive

Winesburg, Ohio, all its small-town episodes of disaster and squandered promise building to the same disheartening conclusion. Its ten exemplary patients, chosen from hundreds Cleckley encountered at a large psychiatric hospital in Georgia, do not much resemble the sensational Hollywood killers and con men who might first spring to mind as typical psychopaths. Most are charming, friendly, intelligent, superficially trust-inspiring men and women who lead lives of impulsive exploitation and petty criminality, lie as lightly as breathing, and drive their loving families to despair with their repeated vows to change. In the preface to the second edition, Cleckley writes of the hundreds of letters he received after the first edition was published. "Interest in the problem was almost never manifested by the patients themselves," he writes. "The interest was desperate, however, among families, parents, wives, husbands, brothers, who had struggled long and helplessly with a major disaster for which they found not only no cure and no social, medical, or legal facility for handling, but also no full or frank recognition that a reality so obvious existed."

As with many sensitive subjects, the military view has occasionally been franker. In an influential 1948 study of psychiatric casualties among British soldiers in World War II, what today we would call post-traumatic stress disorder, Swank and Marchand found that the 2 percent of supereffective soldiers able to endure sixty days of continuous combat exhibited "aggressive psychopathic personalities." Other evidence, including the observations of Colonel Ardant du Picq in the Napoleonic Wars and S.L.A. Marshall in World War II and the shooting records of Allied fighter pilots, suggests that the majority of killing in war is accomplished by a small minority of soldiers. In a 1999 article in the U.S. Army journal *Military Review*, Major Michael Pierson addressed the question of how to identify and make best use of psychopaths in an infantry unit.

> We tend to shun the concept of the willing killer because it offends our kinder sensibilities, but a controlled psychopath is an asset on the killing fields. Those who possess such a temperament are natural killers and many have served this country well. The problem lies in identifying these individuals and positioning them where they can be most effective.

The loudest champion of psychopathy in contemporary civilian life is a British psychiatrist named Kevin Dutton. Possessed of a winking delivery, an arresting gaze, and a flamboyant taste in suits, Dutton is a frequent public speaker, the author of *The Wisdom of Psychopaths*, and the coauthor, with decorated Special Air Service commando and verified psychopath Andy McNab, of *The Good Psychopath's Guide to Success*. Dutton and McNab argue that controlled psychopathy might be an advantage in fields that require focused reasoning in morally fraught situations. Dutton has surveyed hundreds of anonymous psychopaths in Great Britain. Among the top ten jobs he has found them to hold are police officer, clergyperson, CEO, and journalist. As the saying goes, though, if you're worried you might be a psychopath, you're not a psychopath.

Other scholars seek to distinguish psychopathy from related conditions. The psychologist Simon Baron-Cohen notes in *The Science of Evil* that "empathy is not the sole route to developing a moral code and a moral conscience that leads a person to behave ethically." Lack of empathy manifests for him in two ways: the "Zero-Negative" psychopaths and narcissists and the "Zero-Positive" people on the autistic spectrum, including those diagnosed with Asperger's syndrome. Those in the latter class can't read or predict emotions well because an overactive "systemizing mechanism" leaves them at sea amid such inherently messy, unsystematic phenomena as human feelings, but they are no more prone to criminality than anyone else and feel terrible when it is pointed out to them that they have hurt others.

If lack of empathy wasn't a sufficient explanation, what made Elliott's behavior so dramatically far from "Zero-Positive"? Had he always been that way? The breakup of his parents' marriage when he was a teenager seemed to me to have been at least as great a shock to his moral system as his experiences on deployment. At the height of the conflict, he had written his grandmother, "I miss being the rebellios [*sic*] kid in the stable home . . . At that time it felt like my problems were 'bigger' than my parents. Not now." Back in Peachland, I had spoken to the former computer store owner, a large, shy gamer named Jamie, who had employed Elliott as a precocious twelve-year-old repair specialist and who told me that, if anything, Elliott had been too strict about moral behavior. Customers would occasionally call for networking help when what they really wanted was help pirating software. Young Elliott was invariably indignant. "He got into trouble because he wasn't able to say to the person gently, 'Sorry, we don't do that,'" Jamie said. "We lost a customer or two. His realm was computers and how they work, not necessarily people and how they work."

Since then, of course, Elliott's realm appeared to have expanded.

———

Seven hours go by surprisingly quickly when you're working through a hundred-page stack of instant-message transcripts. As my time with Elliott wound down, we talked briefly about the additional sentences he had received for his final two offenses, stabbing Nathan Dunmall and trying to put out a hit on his prosecutor, Mike Dion. He corrected me about my understanding that he had received ten years apiece: that was just the way it was structured, he said. Really it was two twenty-year sentences which he was serving concurrently, part of a plea deal in which the government knocked down the charges to assault with a deadly weapon and solicitation to commit a crime of violence. I asked why the authorities were willing to do that.

"I think my prosecutor finally realized I'm bat-shit insane," he said. "But he sent me to prison anyway. That's still got me hot."

On the last phrase, Elliott's voice dropped into a menacing register so cartoonish that I couldn't help interpreting it as playful, like a ten-year-old threatening to blow up his school. He sounded just the way he had a few hours before, when, illustrating the intensity of his family feeling, he had painted a vivid scene of killing everyone in the room if Landon was ever threatened. As we waited for his unit manager to collect him, I jotted a few last notes and tried to massage some life back into my writing hand. Elliott asked me how I was planning to represent him in the book.

"Luke Elliott Sommer, world-famous psychopath," he offered, grinning.

"Well, I don't know about that."

"I almost wish I could be a Dillinger-type character. A rough bank robber type. Alas . . ." He switched for the last time into his corny singsong voice, rolling his eyes up to the ceiling in a way that reminded me for some reason of the animatronic mouse at Chuck E. Cheese. "It is not to be," he said.

The guards fell in on either side as we were escorted out to the still-empty visitation room, its industrial beiges and grays interrupted only by a kids' playroom in the corner with grinning cartoon characters painted on the walls, the rough texture of cinder block showing through their faces. Elliott pointed out the small marked zone on the floor next to the guard's station where he had been permitted to stand and kiss Mandi when they were married the previous month—barring a treaty transfer, the only intimacy he would be allowed with her for the next thirty-seven years. By reflex I reached out to shake his hand, asking if this was permitted only after it was too late for the surrounding officials to tell me it wasn't, and then with quick efficiency Elliott was being led to the secured door on the far side, carrying on a friendly, jokey, totally one-sided conversation with the guards, and then the concrete bulk just swallowed him, and he was gone.

———

Five seconds out of his presence, it was already beginning to seem as if the conversation had happened in an alternate universe.

Was that really the guy who had started it all? Who spent months planning a crime family over MSN Messenger, who sent tellers and customers diving into the sheltered crannies of the Bank of America and policemen swarming through the streets of Tacoma, Peachland, and Greenwood Village, who sparked the years-long chain reactions of trauma that tore through a workplace and half a dozen families? Sam and Carly plastered against Norm's Jeep with guns to the backs of their heads, Tigra Robertson's mother trying to hold back her tears during our one face-to-face meeting, Jessicah Stotts quitting her job and learning to box in Tacoma, Mandi Chmelyk pronouncing her wedding vows under the gaze of armed guards, Alex sleeping each night under the Ranger beret hanging on a wall in his father's basement—and that wasn't even to mention Nathan Dunmall's family, Scott Byrne's, Richard Olinger's, all the other tellers and customers at the bank that day: so many people knocked out of their orbits, so many lives twisted, trapped, or shattered by their pass through the gravitational field of Luke Elliott Sommer, and now I came to the center and found nothing but a man-shaped absence, a friendly surface with no interior, just a faint iridescence of whatever once fell in.

I found myself blinking dumbly in the afternoon sunlight, startled by how far the shadows had swung. The counselor who had been managing my stay, a brisk, professional woman who clearly had other things to worry about than me, locked the door behind us. All down the corridor of blazing concrete and grass, guard towers rose at intervals into the sky. Floodlights clustered on slender stalks like metallic grapes. The two-story-tall concertina-wire fence coiled in perfect cylindrical rows into the distance, pulled taut by metal ratchets at the fence posts. Every square inch had been designed to tear into the flesh of the bodies held inside—young and old, tall and short, wrinkled, tattooed, scarred—but unless a cascade of other systems failed, none of it ever would. It would all just sit here and glitter, a vast machine hidden deep in the wilds of Kentucky for the slow extinction of human life.

The sight made Christel's pain very real to me. How could a mother help but want the best for her son? How could she help but view all the harm he had caused as little more than broken plates thrown by a toddler on the way to becoming his true self? From a mother's perspective, Elliott was as much a victim of his unusually persuasive fantasies and rationalizations as anyone else was. I did not envy her and Mandi the continuing project of identifying what counted as the real Elliott and what didn't.

———

Mandi sent me a portion of Elliott's Bureau of Prisons medical record a few weeks later. I had asked for it in order to confirm his diagnoses. Instead it profoundly undermined his family's claim that medication had turned his life around. I learned that Elliott had been diagnosed with and medicated for both rapid-cycling bipolar disorder and PTSD within two months of surrendering himself to the United States—five months *before* the sentence hearing that preceded his final crimes. His subsequent psychiatric history was, in the modern fashion, mostly represented by a long string of diagnostic codes, but four years in, after endless reassessments of dosage and fluctuating Global Assessment of Functioning scores, a chunk of bona fide English popped out: "Extremely intelligent. Possessing extreme command of language, cognition, dialect and intellect. Has ability to control mental health symptoms and 'hide' his mental health symptoms."

I wasn't at that sentence hearing, but Jessicah Stotts was, along with her old manager from the bank, Stephanie Ness. The prosecutor, Mike Dion, invited them along to make victim impact statements.

Jess remembers well her reaction when she learned that rapid-cycling bipolar disorder was going to be the focus of Elliott's defense. "I was like, *really?*" she told me over the phone from Idaho, where she now lives with her wife and dogs and works at a retirement home. "You're going to make an excuse out of that? I've had so many bipolar friends. I worked with a girl at Safeway who was bipolar. Sometimes she wanted to be the center of attention, sometimes she was really withdrawn. She didn't rob a bank."

CHAPTER 26

PROBABLY SOMETHING I'LL NEVER UNDERSTAND

The hearing took place on December 8, 2008, a dry, cold, overcast Monday. Two and a half years is a long time to have to wait for the guy who robbed you at gunpoint to be sent away to prison, and Jess was glad to be getting it over with, though terrified of having to speak in front of a crowd. She was working at Macy's then, behind the fine jewelry counter. Her whole family came with her to the big downtown courthouse with its heavy copper dome: mom, dad, sister, both grandmothers.

Their first glimpse of the Sommers was in the ornate hallway outside the courtroom. Jess didn't know who they were at first—a middle-school-aged boy with pale blue eyes, a woman with platinum-blond hair, a handful of others—but then Maggie, the FBI witness protection counselor, leaned over and told her sotto voce. Finally the door opened and they all filed in and took seats on opposite sides. Muttering voices echoed through all the hardwood and grandeur as others poured in behind them to wedge into the benches and stand along the back wall. Jess, dressed in her formal best, sank a little further into her seat with each new arrival.

Much of the hearing was a blur to her. Mike Dion spoke first, going through the familiar details of the crime and addressing the question of mental illness. He seemed baffled at what Sommer was hoping to achieve with these diagnoses. A criminal insanity defense can succeed in cases of schizophrenia, psychosis, or profoundly delusional thinking, but even Jeffrey Dahmer, who kept body parts from his victims in a refrigerator for later consumption, was found legally sane by a jury. In the eyes of the law, knowing that what you are doing is "wrong" is more or less the same as knowing that it is Wrong.

"Nobody is claiming that he was legally insane when he committed the crimes, and the evidence and his conduct show that he wasn't," Dion said. "He was legally competent. Of course, he still could have problems, mental problems that just fall short of legal insanity. But while we don't know whether or not Luke Sommer has some kind of mental illness, we do know that he has a moral defect, a moral problem."

Though Jess knew Dion was on her side, he intimidated her, looking like a wall of steely professionalism in his suit and dark tie. But Dion definitely got one thing right: the weird way Sommer seemed to think he could be a badass and a nice guy both at the same time.

"I thought one of the tellers that we interviewed summed it up very well," Dion said. "She told us about the robbery and about how—she was actually working behind the teller counter, and Luke Sommer came and he jumped over the big bandit barrier that separates the tellers from the public. He pointed the gun at the tellers and traced the laser sight across their bodies and he told them that he would waste them if they didn't do what he said. Then as the robbery went on, he started to act a little differently; he started to try and act friendly. One of the tellers got really, really upset. She started crying. She was starting to break down, and Sommer actually went up to her and sort of gave her a little pat as if to reassure her. On the way out of the bank, he actually turned back and waved to everybody as if to say bye-bye. The teller told us how she felt when she saw Sommer trying to act friendly. She said what went through her mind was, 'Don't try and be polite. There's nothing polite about this. There is nothing friendly about this. You are robbing us.'"

That, Jess thought to herself, would be Virginia. After Sommer had thanked them for their cooperation and waved goodbye on his way out of the teller pit, Virge and Jess had exchanged a disbelieving look with each other, like, who the hell did this guy think he *was*?

Then Judge Burgess addressed Sommer himself. "Anything you would like to say?"

Sommer stood and approached the stand.

"Yes, Your Honor. I have spent two years trying to figure out what

I was going to say today. Mr. Dion said it. In fact, I think to a degree he was more accurate than even what we put forward." He sounded calm, composed, reasonable. "I am probably the most arrogant person I know, and I think I used it a lot as a shield for my own insecurity. I hurt a lot of innocent people in this, and those people didn't deserve it from me, and my family has supported me through this, and I don't think I would have made it through without them. The one thing he said about the two minutes being a long time, it is, and I was the one with the gun. I know what it is like to have somebody point an automatic weapon at you, and I know what it's like to get shot at and I know what it's like to get blown up, and I know what it is like to lose people that are close to you, and I put people that did not deserve that in that same position. When he's talking about how on the one hand I went in like a badass and on the other hand I tried to comfort her it is because when I saw those people being scared, it was the first moment in the whole ordeal that I realized that I was the one scaring them."

It had begun to seem a little odd to Jess that although she and Stephanie Ness were right behind him, Sommer was talking to Judge Burgess as if he were the only one in the room.

"It doesn't change what I did," he went on, "and I understand that I have a very, very harsh penalty to face, and that is fine. It is one of the things about being a man, is that when you screw up as badly as I have, you either whine like I did for the first six to eight months of my time down, or you make up for the fact that you acted like a punk and you try and do something about it. That is exactly what I did. I acted like a punk. I dishonored my unit, my country, and my friends, and I hurt these people. So I hope that one day they will forgive me. I don't expect them to. They didn't look very happy when they walked in, that is for sure. But I do hope that they will know that this is something I am not going to walk away from either, because I won't let myself. That is all I have got to say."

He took his seat again. He still hadn't looked at her. A few seconds later, lost in thought, Jess was startled to hear her own name.

"So I will ask Jessicah if she is ready to come forward," Mike Dion was saying.

Trying to write out her remarks the night before, Jess had determined to make two points. First, this was no ordinary robbery, with a guy flashing a gun and demanding money over the counter. This was as violent as it could have gotten short of Sommer actually shooting people. Second, what had made it all so creepy to her was finding out that the culprit hadn't been a stranger. Sommer had come in often enough for her to think of him as a regular, even to know him on sight as Luke, the name on his account.

But as Jess crossed the silent courtroom and took the stand, passing directly in front of Sommer and his lawyer in the front row, her planned remarks evaporated from her head. What bothered her more than anything about the robbery was the gulf it opened between herself and other people—even the people here in this courtroom. How could she possibly convey the living terror of those hundred-odd seconds in this hushed and ceremonial place?

She gripped the sides of the stand and faced Judge Burgess, a grandfatherly man whose kind face reassured her.

"I was sitting thinking about this last night," she started, "and thinking about how it is finally going to happen today, because it's been canceled so many times. I was thinking about what I wanted to say and I just started writing, so I will say what I was thinking."

Judge Burgess gave her an encouraging smile. She felt eyes boring into her back.

"Like most people," she fumbled on, "I never thought anything like this robbery could or would ever happen to me. Unless it's happening to you personally, it is impossible to imagine what it is like to have a gun pointed in your face and your life threatened. During the robbery, my adrenaline was pumping like crazy, and all I could think of was, 'Oh my God, I can't believe this is happening.' It was like . . . surreal to me."

Jess kept groping after it, describing the aftershocks she had felt while sitting on the floor once Sommer was gone, realizing again and again that she might really have died, might never again have seen the faces of family and friends that were flashing through her head, but the gulf was still there, impossible to bridge or even name, her voice just echoing back to her off all that hardwood paneling.

"I just thank God," she said finally, "for not letting anything worse happen to any of us in the bank that day."

She walked back and took her seat, relieved to have gotten it over with.

Stephanie Ness went next. She was tall and magnificent, turning on Sommer with that imperious boss-lady poise that Jess had once bridled at but had since come to adore as they weathered the press and the FBI together. After that came a little wrangling between the lawyers. The sentence length had already been settled in the plea deal, so the only real question was whether or not Judge Burgess would make some extraordinary departure. Richard Olinger would soon be sentenced to time served; Scott Byrne, to eight months with credit for time served; Alex Blum, to sixteen months; Nathan Dunmall, to ten years; Chad Palmer, to eleven years; Tigra Robertson, to twelve and a half.

Burgess gave Luke Elliott Sommer the recommended sentence of twenty-four years.

"You said it was arrogance," he said to Elliott, "and I am hearing something about bipolar conditions and all of these things that don't create any defense to these things. Somehow you just wonder, what could take place that could bring somebody to this extent? It is probably something I'll never understand."

And that was all. Sommer turned to say goodbye to his family, saying something that sounded to Jess like "Don't worry, I'll be seeing you" to the brother who looked so much like him, and then they took him away. Jess and her family left the courtroom by a different door. Never again, it occurred to her with some relief, would she have to enter a room with Luke Elliott Sommer.

The Sommers too had submitted their letters of support to Judge Burgess, just as heartbroken and hopeful, in their own way, as the Blums'. Karis's letter declared that her older brother was her hero for standing up for what he believed in, relating an anecdote about how he had once mercifully and unhesitatingly euthanized a favorite puppy that had been hit by a car. Leah Jewall's letter argued that her erstwhile coauthor's actions were "not without good intent, as he expressed to me atrocities he had witnessed against the Iraqi people while he was overseas, and wanted to bring these to the attention of the American public." Christel's father Archie's letter described a recent visit to SeaTac Federal Detention Center, where he had observed that medication and treatment were helping Elliott to "relax and look at the situation more objectively," to "make good decisions."

It was exactly forty-five days later that Elliott assaulted Nathan Dunmall in his cell at SeaTac FDC, boasting to the counselor who escorted him away that he had been planning the attack for sixty days. And it was a month and a half after that, during a pair of meetings with an undercover FBI agent in the visiting room of the special housing unit, that he offered between $15,000 and $20,000 for a hit on Mike Dion, telling the man he thought he was hiring that he had no preferences regarding how the hit was effected but that he did not want to see Dion's death reported on the news as an accident. He wanted to see it reported as murder.

———

I think back once in a while to something Mike Dion said in that sentence hearing.

"When you plan a crime family," Dion told Judge Burgess, with Elliott directly behind him, "and you rob a bank and you point guns at people and you build up an arsenal of weapons and explosives, people aren't interested in your political philosophy. They don't want to get to know the good side of you. They want to be protected from you."

Two months later Dion was a target himself.

I am a little incredulous at the memory of how unthreatening Elliott seemed to me at McCreary. Every once in a while I will hear his cartoonishly evil voice—*That's still got me hot*—and wonder how Mike Dion and his family felt when they submitted to federal security arrangements, what Nathan Dunmall thought when his old camping buddy appeared in his cell with a knife. Did Nathan too dismiss this as laughably over the top, another corny performance? Or was he too busy fighting for his life?

I did finally confront Elliott about Marcus Cobb. As I laid out my evidence, no expression crossed his face—not a twitch of the eyebrow, not a flutter in the neck, nothing. Feeling almost embarrassed to have brought it up, I waited for him to tell me he had never heard of the guy. Instead, after a stretch of placid silence, he smiled in a way that involved neither eyes, lips, nor body, gave a half jerk forward, said, "Off the record?" and waited for my reply.

I pushed him on the Kelowna Rockets too. It turns out that Elliott never played for them. His connection was that a couple of guys from the team used to show up once in a while for pickup roller hockey games at the Peachland Community Centre.

"Weren't they really good?" I asked.

"Yeah," he said. "They beat our asses every time."

The moment I have come to view as the most important of the interview came earlier, though, when Elliott likened himself to a dungeon master, conjuring the "Jewish mob" from thin air. "And obviously," he told me then, clearly enjoying himself, "this strains credulity. It's so bizarre. But that's part of the beauty of it."

It stuck in my brain, then and long afterward. Elliott hastened to change the subject before I could ask any follow-up questions, but what *was* the "beauty" of "straining credulity"? I thought of it two years later as I watched a supercut on YouTube of news anchors chuckling condescendingly over Donald Trump's buffoonish insults and proposal to deport 11 million illegal immigrants, dozens of expensively coiffed heads repeating the phrases "Trump is gonna be Trump" and "classic Trump style." I thought of it as I read about how past demagogues across the world had been greeted at first as clowns. I thought of it when a friend showed me a series of YouTube videos of bikini-clad girls approached by a pair of men with a camera at the beach. Each girl was wary at first, skeptical, but one after another they laughingly relented to the shorter man's plea for a kiss if he performed a certain impossible-seeming stunt. Then, when he accomplished it with a sudden trick, I watched one after another yield, startled, to his surprisingly strong arms. You could see it in the bend of their naked backs: the tension between the mind's perplexed concession and the body's freer assent, their mouths pushing open like slits in the membrane between game and reality. Thirty seconds later they were stumbling back, dazed and aroused, writing their phone numbers in his little black book.

And obviously, you know, this strains credulity. It's so bizarre. But that's part of the beauty of it.

I think of it now when I imagine all the Rangers at Fort Lewis who dismissed Elliott's crazy schemes, dozens of crew-cut heads chuckling over the "Sommer factor." I think of it when I imagine a nineteen-year-old kid from Greenwood Village, whose young life had never been much more than a long suburban daydream of hockey and Xbox and paintball, perched finally on the precipice of doing something real.

BOOK 5

FREEDOM

The unconscious wants truth. It ceases to
speak to those who want something else more than truth.
—ADRIENNE RICH, "WOMEN AND HONOR:
SOME NOTES ON LYING," 1977

CHAPTER 27

MATRIX OF LIES

So how are you and Alex *doing*?" asked Amanda Lee in December 2014, a month after my return from Kentucky but a full year and a half before Elliott's phone call about the twin primes conjecture.

We were sitting in a Seattle coffee shop on a rainy, blustery afternoon. Amanda's hair was longer, a densely undulant mass of auburn, streaked now with a tide of gray.

"When's the last time you talked to him?" I asked.

"I haven't heard from him at all. I figured—I mean, for one thing, I'm a reminder of a lot of bad stuff. I didn't think it was necessarily realistic for us to continue to be close friends."

There was so much to say that I didn't know where to begin. I told her about Alex's warehouse job, his new Ranger tattoo, his increasing isolation.

"So what's his next step?" Amanda asked.

"He's maxed out the warehouse. There's no real next step for him there."

"Yeah, but there's a whole field of logistics. I don't know where you go to learn more about it, but I know there are people who do that in operations departments. I have a connection very, very high up at Costco." Before I knew it she was offering to pass on Alex's name.

Amanda and I first became close in the months after "When Good People Do Bad Things." I came to know her husband, Bob, too, a tall, elfin vaudeville performer and world-renowned stereographic photographer, and their house in West Seattle, with its framed circus posters, its prizewinning shade garden full of hostas, hydrangeas, and Korean firs, and its elaborate play structure for their leopard-spotted cats, Edison and Tesla. Amanda and Bob had no children. There was something youthful but also a little melancholy about their affection for each other.

We have stayed in touch ever since. Beneath Amanda's dry, logical exterior, I know now, is a subsonic thrum of compassion so powerful you feel it in your stomach more than in your ears. Over drinks, we once got embarrassingly honest with each other about the shock we each went through in our early twenties while coming to terms with the likely course of environmental degradation in our century.

"So many people of my generation were having kids," Amanda said. "These were lawyers, scientists—educated people. I'm just looking around going, 'What are you *thinking?*'"

Something clicked for me in that moment. Maybe Amanda's defendants were her wayward boys: the soft-spoken environmental activist who burned down a string of lumber mills, the Guantánamo detainee picked up in a random sweep and held without charge for a decade, the patriotic Army Ranger who fell in with the wrong superior. She had told me several times that Alex's was the most emotional case she had ever worked on. All the tension behind the scenes played a significant role in her parting ways with Jeff Robinson once it was over. Amanda and I were friends in part because we shared an intuition of some basic, incorruptible goodness in Alex's soul, in part because for years now we had been locked in a strange kind of dance, helplessly disenchanting each other, helplessly doubting.

The reason for that day's meeting was that I wanted to ask her advice about everything Elliott had told me—off the record—when I confronted him at USP McCreary about Marcus Cobb.

Her first piece of advice was not to trust him. "In my world," Amanda said, "with someone like him, I would put everything in the category of attempts to manipulate until it was demonstrated to me otherwise."

She seemed a little more amenable once I explained the data analysis I had performed on Sommer's hard drive and the evidence it had turned up.

"Wow," she said. "The FBI would have been all over that."

But as I went deeper into the details of Elliott's response, Amanda began to look impatient.

"So what did he say about *Alex*?" she finally asked.

It was a jolt to remember where my sympathies were supposed to lie. Amid all the drama of seeking Sommer's weapons supplier, I hadn't been thinking much about Alex at all. I told Amanda about PFC Blum's total absence from the recovered data on the hard drive, about how late in the game Specialist Sommer seemed to have brought him in.

"Sommer really resists the idea that Alex was in some way his subordinate," I said. "He has been very, very insistent that they were 'buddies.' The way he puts it is, 'I'm gradually coming to realize how much of a role rank played here, but I wasn't like the other tabs. I took pains to reach out to the privates. I didn't punish them the way the other tabs did. I connected with them.'"

Amanda was skeptical. She had told me before that all her contact with soldiers at Guantánamo, both regular forces and Special Ops, had led her to see the Rangers as embodying a categorically different standard of military discipline. She found it hard to imagine that the rank hierarchy at battalion was ever less than obvious to all.

"Don't get me wrong," she said. "I don't disagree with the idea that he and Alex were also buddy-buddy. I saw signs of that. Alex talked about talking hockey with him and BS-ing about all kinds of crap. Alex's character is very engaging, always ready to talk to people, so I can imagine it. I'm sure we played up the superiority angle in our legal case. But . . . how should I say it? There were certainly enough indications of the superiority issue that I could milk it for all it was worth."

I gave her the surprising new portrait of the conspirators that had emerged from Elliott's telling: a band of outcasts among heroes, lonely, thwarted, and insecure, whose vulnerabilities Specialist Sommer had expertly exploited.

"Alex was, by Sommer's account, kind of a cool kid," I told her. "He was this up-and-coming guy, very promising, very good. He had this cool car. He was funny and popular. Even though Sommer had rank on him, he considered it an asset to be friends with Alex."

"Even apart from the robbery, you mean?"

"It seems so, yeah. He also said that Alex was incredibly naive and that he liked the idea of getting Alex involved in this vendetta of his."

"That makes me want to bash his head against the wall and break it open until the brains leak out," Amanda said.

I smiled faintly, surprised by her vitriol. It had not yet occurred to me to wonder why I hadn't felt it myself.

———

For the next two weeks, Amanda and I alternated meetings at my office and her house to work through the details of Alex's case all over again. The conversations between Alex and the FBI were particularly unpleasant to revisit. Like Amanda, I had long been trying to interpret the little shifts and jitters in Alex's story as a kind of narrative static, mere artifacts of his traumatized brain's desperate efforts to understand what was happening to him, but Elliott's calm certainty that Alex's misrepresentations were more willful had been working on my mind like a poison.

"There's this recurring theme," I told Amanda, "of people telling Alex the proper frame for looking at what he did and what his actions meant, and Alex not really liking any of those versions. You can see him sort of realizing he's going to have to accept some authority's narrative of what he's done even though none of them quite fit."

"Yeah," Amanda said, "but it didn't seem to me as though *he* had a narrative that explained what he'd done at all."

Finally I decided that a more systematic effort to log Alex's inconsistencies was in order. For every disputed detail I could think of in the buildup, execution, and aftermath of the bank robbery—when Sommer first began talking about the crime family, when Alex was brought on board, when Alex gave Sommer his soft armor, whether there was a moment of hesitation in the car, whether Alex tried to drive away, a few dozen more—I picked out every relevant sentence from all the thousands of pages of interviews of Alex and other defendants, whether by FBI agents, Amanda, Jeff, or myself, and gathered them in chronological order under separate headings: CASINO PLAN, SOFT ARMOR, MOMENT OF HESITATION.

It took about three weeks. Though I had once vowed to approach Alex's case with empathy and storytelling rather than with cold-hearted analysis, there was a satisfaction in this work that I had not experienced in years. I felt finally as if I had found a way to apply mathematical reasoning to the search for human truth—not through some grand theory that abstracted all details away, but through recombining the raw material of experience. The result was a huge grid. Each interview was a row; each disputed detail was a column. The next step was a kind of a matrix transposition. Rather than reading row by row, experiencing each conversation with all its emotional complexity intact as Alex came to terms with his involvement over time, it was now possible to read column by column, each moment in the lead-up to the robbery splayed open like a specimen for dissection. Alex's personal journey receded into the background. Broken out from its social context of confusion and pain, the static no longer looked like static. It was too patterned for that.

Amanda seemed as surprised as I was by the detail that jumped out most: when exactly Alex gave Sommer his soft armor.

"Huh," she said.

It was another late night at the office, overhead fluorescents cold and flickering on the table where we had spread out our papers. The last years, I knew, had not been easy ones for Amanda either. Business was thinner without Jeff and harder without the administrative support of Schroeter Goldmark & Bender. A concussion from a horseback riding accident two years earlier had left her with migraines and memory damage. Shortly afterward, a viral infection had triggered a heart condition very similar to Norm's. I could hear a different tone in the way she and I had begun talking about Alex over the past week, a bitter humor in my own voice and a new formality in hers, as if he were just one more client.

"It sounds like at the time you were very persuaded by the sincerity of Alex's efforts to figure out what had happened," I said.

"Totally persuaded. Yes."

"And it seems now that you are slightly less persuaded?"

"Yes," she said, shuffling papers, "quite a bit less persuaded."

Compiled into a single document, my grid was 280 pages long. In the privacy of my own head, I had started calling it "the Matrix of Lies"—something like a joke, something like an amulet against the very danger it named. The last thing I wanted to do was send it to Alex. There had been a few recent signs of his turning a corner. He had amazed us all by placing a down payment on a small house north of Denver, thereby solving forever the problem of suspicious land-lords, and amazed us further by adopting a puppy, a joyous female pit bull named Pickles, on whom he doted with a physical exuberance that would have killed a lesser dog.

After days of putting it off, I finally emailed him a copy, telling him only that I wanted him to read through and underline any state-ment that he wasn't completely confident was true.

Two days later I got a text message from him on my phone. "This is rough stuff, kid," it said.

————

A week later I was watching my breath at the curb of Denver International Airport's passenger pickup zone, waiting for Alex to arrive. The texts were his usual grunts: "Late." "Fucking traffic." Finally the Audi pulled up, looking salt-streaked and bedraggled, with a cauliflower ear of blackened snow caked around each wheel well. Sixty thousand miles had elapsed since this was Sommer's dream car. It was beginning to seem a little pathological that Alex continued to sink money into it. His beard was as burly as I had ever seen it under his baseball cap.

"This fucking moron back there," he said, turning around to point out the back windshield as I climbed in with my bag, and then for ten unbroken minutes he elaborated at length, his voice hard and sloppy in that way I had come to recognize. He informed me that he had just come from an all-you-can-eat Indian buffet with one of his fellow bouncers, who had taken a whole case of beer along for the occasion.

"How many did *you* have?" I asked.

"Only one, actually," Alex said, glancing at me and then looking away. "I actually couldn't even finish it."

Ten minutes later he pulled into a 7-Eleven to vomit. "Sweet Jesus," he said, pawing at the door to get it open. "Yep. We're doing this. I'M ABOUT TO VOMIT, EVERYONE," he yelled, crossing the parking lot.

A few minutes later he lurched back into the driver's seat. As he turned the key in the ignition, a little boy of eight or nine emerged from the bathroom across the parking lot, dressed a lot like I used to dress at that age: cargo pants, sneakers, moose-print sweatshirt. He stared through the windshield at Alex as if at the rampaging grizzly he was amazed to have survived.

"That kid was in the next stall," Alex said. "Probably scarred him for life."

The undercurrent of self-loathing in Alex's belligerent humor over his own misbehavior was as obvious to me as ever, but for once I let a bolt of hot rage shoot through me. I had been defending Alex for so long. These days it was not always Alex that I wanted to defend.

———

In the den of his new house, he had set up a display case showing Opa's Nazi artifacts, some with visible swastikas.

"A friend of mine from the gym, a black guy, he was here the other day, and he suddenly saw that and was like, 'Wait a minute,'" Alex said, snorting with laughter. "He was about ready to dive out the window."

I managed a chuckle. Alex poured himself a tumbler of whiskey and took a seat across from me. On his lap was an inch-thick stack of printer paper: the Matrix of Lies.

"This is a lot harder to read than I thought," he said. "It's been a struggle. Every time I open it my skin just crawls. The hardest part of all this is seeing what a shithead I looked up to. I keep reading and thinking it can't get worse and then I just read some more. I've only done forty pages or something like that. It was hard to remember to stay on point about deciphering the plausibility of what's true. I would just be like, 'Oh fuck, I need a drink.'"

He flipped to a spot about a fifth of the way in.

"You're only up to *there*?"

"Yeah."

"Okay," I said. "Let me see . . ."

I took the packet from him and started flipping through what he'd read: pages and pages of Sommer's MSN conversations with Scott Byrne and Tigra Robertson, marked up with outraged marginal notes next to the parts where Sommer had exploited Byrne's homosexuality (Alex has been a staunch champion of gay rights ever since his older brother Max came out to him and the family hours after his sentencing). When Alex had texted me about "rough stuff," he had apparently meant only Sommer's planning. He had read none of his own statements. My whole plan was shot.

From the next room, Pickles banged in her cage. "Oy! Come on!" Alex shouted, getting up and leaving the room. I shuffled frantically through the pages. He strode back in with Pickles leaping up at his hand.

"I guess what I was hoping for," I said with desperate casualness as he plopped into his armchair, "is for us to be—"

Pickles surged up at Alex's face. He swatted her down, saying, "Hi! Hi! Hi!"

"—on a level of trust like we were when we first began talking—"

"Hi!"

"—four years ago."

"Yeah," Alex said. "*I* think we are. Sit! Good girl."

"But as I put all this together, I kept coming across these interviews where . . . I don't know if you got to these parts yet—"

Alex cut me off with a gesture at the pile of paper in my lap. "I just figured if you have specific questions about specific things, that'd probably be easier. I can't read through all that shit."

My heart sank. I already knew Alex's answer to every possible specific question. We had rehearsed them so many times, a giant endless muddle as the mood between us soured. But what was I going to do, come back some other time?

I flipped to the "Soft Armor" section, which began with excerpts from Jeff Robinson's first interview with Alex at SeaTac FDC.

"Okay," I said. "Let's start with this one."

I watched him as he read, so big and soft in his sweatshirt, shoving Pickles down with his left hand. Little blurts and half words mumbled out of his lips as he scanned down the page.

"Let's see, *Blum provided either Nathan or Rhyder . . . because he was not coming in the bank* . . . Let's see . . . *had T-shirts on* . . . Okay, so yeah, they *did* have body armor on in the car . . . *put it out in the hallway* . . . Hey! Pickles! Stop! Sit! Um . . . okay . . . wait."

He looked up at me with an expression of outrage. My heart skipped a beat.

"Is this stating that soft body armor holds *hard* plates?"

"This is just Jeff's statement about his first meeting with you at SeaTac."

"Yeah yeah yeah," Alex said. "I just wanted to make sure. Mmm . . . *after he ordered* . . . uh-huh . . ." He put the pages down. "So *that*, Jeff's statement, is true," he said definitively.

At Alex's first meeting with Jeff, I knew, he had told him exactly the same thing he had told me four years ago: Sommer had asked for his soft armor shortly after a platoon-wide inspection on the morning of the robbery. PFC Blum handed it over thinking the request must have had something to do with the inspection.

"Okay," I said. "Keep going."

Alex raised his eyebrows at me and picked up the packet. I knew exactly what came next: the FBI 302 from his subsequent meeting with the government, when he confirmed the version they had put together from the testimony of other defendants, in which Alex gave Sommer his soft armor the night before—a detail so buried in others that no one paid it much notice, not even the government.

"Mmm . . . uh . . . *bus stop* . . . *Canadians* . . . *Blum set out his soft armor for Sommer to pick up* . . ." He looked up at me in puzzlement. "Are they claiming that this happened that night? *10:30 p.m.* . . . . So they're claiming *that night* they picked it up?"

"They're not claiming. They're just reporting what you told them."

"But that would indicate that I'm saying they picked it up that *night*."

"Yeah."

"Which is *not* true at all."

"Okay," I said. "Keep going."

I knew what was next too: excerpts from the testimony of three other conspirators corroborating that Alex's soft armor was picked up the night before the robbery.

"Uuuuukay . . . *Blum gave Sommer* . . . dadadadada . . ." Alex whipped his head up from the page, his eyes big and strange as he shook his head sharply. "Um, uh-uh," he said.

"This is a record of what you told them," I said. "It's also what everyone else has told me."

"Yeah, no, I'm . . . no."

In the silence that followed, Pickles butted her head into my lap and began licking my knee. Neither Alex nor I broke eye contact. We both knew why this mattered: if PFC Blum really handed over his soft armor the night before the robbery, then when the surprise inspection came the next day, he must have gotten it *back* from Sommer in order to pass. This seemed a tiny sticking point, but once you imagined your way into PFC Blum's head, the difference was stark: the story Alex had been telling us all for years was of a PFC Blum who was such a stickler for battalion rules that his superior's request for his soft armor made sense to him only as part of the inspection. The story in the document in his lap was of a PFC Blum who had already knowingly broken the rules the night before, and who now, under threat of exposure, colluded further with Sommer to avoid being found out.

When Alex spoke again his voice was the small, baffled whisper of a nineteen-year-old boy. "I gave him the body armor that fucking *night*?" he said. And then, just like that his full voice was back, booming with false bonhomie. "Um, you know what, if that's what everybody's saying, then that's probably what happened. I mean, I might have tried to deny it a little bit, but, uh, dude, honestly, what I remember is I dropped it off, asked Sommer if he needed anything, I went up to my barracks . . . But they probably used it in the fucking dry run. So, uh, yeah, I mean, if that's kind of the common theme, I mean, it would make sense. Um, I mighta just fucking blanked it outta my mind. Said, 'No, that's not true.'"

"Okay."

"So. Yeah, it's totally possible that that's what happened, and I wouldn't dispute it if that's what was written."

"Okay."

"So."

We stared at each other for a few more seconds as Pickles took advantage of this unexpected license to bear down in earnest on my knee.

————

Overt anger has never come easily to me. I used to watch other children stomp and scream and fail to get what they wanted with the superior detachment of a preteen anthropologist. What use was there in taking things personally and raging at one node in the causal tree? Maturity, it seemed to me, meant trying to find higher reasons, to address problems at the root, to understand. It took me a long time to understand that understanding could be its own kind of cowardice.

For fifteen more minutes I hid behind a pose of innocent curiosity while Alex retreated into the same defensive hardness I had encountered on my mother's balcony so many years before. I was just beginning to resign myself to another failed effort at breaking through when Alex looked up from the section he was reading and laughed in my face.

"You spelled 'maneuver' wrong," he said.

He went back to scanning the page. It was all I could do not to throw my glass of whiskey at his head.

"Hey," I found myself saying instead, and then, when he looked up, "Honestly, dude . . ."

Before even a minute had passed I had stomped through every single safeguard erected by Norm, Amanda, and myself over the years, in all our hours of talking about Alex as if he were a delicate little egg that might shatter at the slightest pressure.

"I trusted you totally," I was saying by the end. "You were family, and I committed everything, my whole career, to telling your story. Which now seems to have been a lie. Like, to my *face*."

Alex stared back at me, stunned. Then came a hardening in his face, what Scott Beech must have meant by "that *switch*," and a blizzard of angry denials.

"I would never look you bald in the eye and say, 'Hey, man, this is . . .' But it's . . . When we had these conversations early on, I mean, it wasn't just . . . I had to admit to *myself* what happened, and I couldn't fucking *do* that. I couldn't *do* that. I *couldn't* do that . . . My dad fucking flying up to Seattle every weekend, and me being like, 'Hey, man, I'm a good kid! I'm a fucking *good kid* . . .' To me, to admit to some of this shit that I've had to . . ."

There was a rising hysteria to his resistance, as if a machine with a misaligned gear deep in its guts were spinning faster and faster, scattering a shrapnel of bolts and fragments. Finally I told him to please for a second just shut up.

"You know what, dude?" I said. "I really don't need to hear this. We've been talking about *your* feelings and *your* experience and what *you've* gone through, almost exclusively, for *years*."

Alex shrank back. The conversation lost none of its rotational energy but began to contract rather than expand, rotating inward toward some unnamable center.

"I get that, man," he said. "It's easy to be selfish, and it's one of the hardest things to be selfless, and say, 'Yeah, I fucked up, this is what I did.' Uh, uh, I'm not admitting that I was solely responsible and a hundred percent on board. Sommer was a total, uh, influence on me, but at the same time, were there points where I should have spoken up, or where I said things that made me look more like a victim than I was? Yeah. Absolutely. But to me, like I said, I, I . . ."

It looked to me as if we were in for another whirl of rationalizations. Instead Alex took a deep breath, let it slowly out, and looked directly into my eyes.

"I can't make excuses," he said. "The fact that I've lost your trust is the worst thing I could hear."

"All I'm looking for—" I began.

"And I apologize," Alex said. "I really do. I fucking apologize."

Something enormous inside me let go. It was as if I were really seeing him for the first time in three years. Alex shook his head.

"I wish you would have told me about this a long time ago," he said. "I will tell you this, man. The thing I'm learning about myself, I'm a good fucking liar."

That was a new word. It hit me right in the chest.

"I do it because I don't want to hurt people. I don't want people to know the truth. I don't want people to get close to me. And I don't want to admit to myself that I fucked up at points. The simple story is, 'Yeah, I gave it to him.' Then you're like, 'Why?' I'm like, 'Well, he told me to.' Then you're like, 'Okay, when? How? Dig deeper into it. Did this, this, and this make sense?' I'm like, 'Well, yeah, but . . .' And the fact that I don't have your trust is brutal to me. I pride myself on being honest with people, on being straight up with people. But this is something that . . . I don't know how to deal with this shit, man. I still don't."

"You *have* to tell the truth about it."

"Yeah, I know," Alex said, wilting. "I know."

"*This* is what's making you alone," I said, realizing it as I spoke. "*This* is what's preventing you from connecting to people. It's killing you, dude."

"I don't want to connect with people on this. I really don't."

"The fact that you're not telling the truth about it is what's keeping it from going away."

"I just don't know how you can be a good person, robbing a bank," Alex said, his voice near to breaking.

"You made a mistake, buddy," I said. "Under intense pressure from someone you trusted and believed in. You were young. You've grown up. Look at all the good you're doing now. You're taking care of a dog, you're managing people at a warehouse, you're taking care of your grandma, your brothers and sisters feel so much closer to you now than they ever felt before. I've been talking to all of them and every single one has told me that as terrible as all this was, in a weird way they're thankful for it because they have a relationship with you now that they never got to have before."

He was crying again, for the third time in my experience.

"I hear that over and over," I said. "From Max, from Carly, from Sam. Everybody sees the good in you. You just have to accept this thing that you did. Under absolutely insane conditions, yes, but you did it, and you have to accept it. Other people will too. The people who care most about you, they already see it and they accept it."

"*I* can't, though. *I* can't."

"Even after all these years?"

"No. I'd never *do* that." His voice dropped to a strange, private whisper, as if he were talking only to himself. "*Never* fucking do that. But I *did* it." His eyes widened, startled at hearing the words from his own mouth. "And I just, I can't . . ."

There was a long pause. Alex smacked the sheaf of paper with his palm, suddenly angry again.

"All right," he said. "So what do you want to know? Just fucking ask me questions. Ask me what you fucking want."

Without thinking about it, I put down my notebook, walked over, and hugged him. He broke down in my arms.

"I really am sorry," he sobbed. "I didn't mean to deceive you. I consider you one of my best friends, and the biggest thing for me is never let down a friend. I just . . . I've lost everything in my life over this. Everything. I'm not happy. I don't want a house. I don't want a fucking job. I just want to be a Ranger. That's all I want to be. I was ready to die at the age of twenty-four. I thought, 'Twenty-four, that's when I'm supposed to die. Over in Afghanistan or Iraq, doing this.' I was fine with it. I loved it. That was all I wanted to do."

I wanted so much for us to be done. But there was another very important thing I had never expressed to Alex: if I had to listen to even one more minute of him mooning about his teenage wet dream of Ranger Battalion, I was going to choke him to death or die trying.

"Which isn't to say," I hastened to add, "you weren't really fucking good at it and didn't go incredibly far in this incredibly challenging and honorable thing. I don't mean to diminish that in any way. I just mean to say that there's a lot else you do that's of value, and what you want to get back to, it doesn't actually exist. It was from a different time in your life."

Alex nodded, calmer now.

"No," he said, "I know. I just—I miss waking up and doing PT. And going to the rifle range, and blowing shit up, and fast-roping, and jumping out of airplanes. I miss all of that. I hate having to sit here with my probation officer and say, 'My roommate's a good guy.' 'Well, he didn't give me his information.' 'Well, I apologize, sir.' I'm trying to make a life, but there isn't any honor in it. I don't go to work and think to myself, 'Man, I earned this beret.'"

———

In the hours to come, as we fought our way together through the tangle of Alex's and Norm's incremental misrepresentations to get back to something like the truth, I suggested a new shorthand for explaining his involvement in the robbery, cobbled together from the truest-sounding things he had said to Amanda after months of pressure: "I didn't think it was real at first, and by the time I started to realize it was, everyone thought I was in, and I didn't have the strength to say no."

"That's hard, man," Alex said the first time I suggested it. "It's hard for me to admit weakness."

"I know it."

"It really is."

"Try it. Try it. I think people will respond to that in ways you can't believe."

"Yeah . . ." Alex said, skeptical. "I mean, it's a hundred percent true. It's just, to me the question has always been why. People ask all these questions, and in order to justify it, you always look for the easiest explanation. One of the biggest things I highlighted during the first forty pages was how everybody's like, 'We thought it was a joke, we didn't think it was real.' It's like, *fuck!* How did it go from being a joke to being real? Being like, 'Yeah, man, let's do it'? Like, the bravado kicks in, and everything like that . . . I don't know . . ."

There was a long silence. I felt a strange glimmer of unease. Wasn't there something I had worried about all those years ago at the *Dr. Phil* taping, something about authority figures forcing Alex to adopt their own interpretations?

"All right, well, fuck," Alex said. He shrugged. "I robbed a bank."

Both of us laughed in shock. He had said those words before, but never like this.

"It is so good to hear you say that."

Seeing my grin, Alex punched the seat of the couch and gave me a tentative smile. "Finally live up to my fucking convictions," he said.

———

The next month was not easy. Norm helped a lot once I sent him the Matrix of Lies. Finally a letter from Alex showed up in my mailbox in Seattle.

Hey guys,

I know this is may seem like a letter written to a large group of people without really addressing anyone specific but I am writing this with every single one of you in mind. This letter represents a conversation that should have happened 8 years ago but is happening because of two people I genuinely respect and hold dear to my heart, Ben and Dad. Ben has been spending the better part of his last seven years telling this fantastic story of his misled manipulated Ranger cousin who unknowingly robbed a bank under the misguidance of his villainous superior. Ben being the fantastic researcher he is started finding holes in this story early on and asked me about them but I shrugged them off with a lie so he took me at my word and continued on. Finally it all came to a head a month or so ago when he finally made me tell the truth. That truth is this. I had full knowledge of the robbery before it happened. I did help plan some of it and I knew what we were doing on the way there and after it happened. I had no reason to do it. I didn't need the money or the thrill. I had a sick feeling in my stomach the whole time and hoped it would turn out to be a joke even though I knew better. Did the training I went through have a role in my participation? I think it did a little bit but nowhere near the amount I have misled you into believing. I knew what we were talking about was stupid and illegal, in my mind I would think, "This is crazy." But I kept it to myself because I didn't want to seem like I was a pussy in front of Sommer I didn't want to show him I was afraid. Admitting I was afraid or didn't want to do something seemed like the ultimate shame when I was in the army. This letter was originally only a few sentences I angrily put together because Ben made me realize the truth about my lies. It has been really hard for me to look at myself and realize the lies I have told. The letter in front of you now is because of a conversation Dad had with me last Friday. He took me to lunch and made a point that hit me hard. I was sick to my stomach when Dad talked to me about how much I had been hurting everyone with all of my bullshit. He gave me the biggest compliment of my life that day with a very hard "but" for me to accept. He told me "When you're the Alex that everyone knows you have the best personality in the room, even better than mine which is hard to do. We haven't seen that Alex for a long time. You've become a bully and all this shit you're telling everyone isn't good for anyone." When he said that it hit me harder than anything I have felt. He was absolutely right. It all came into perspective. I have been letting the 4 months I spent in the army control everything about me. In prison I had an identity that after a while I came to I wouldn't say enjoy but relate to. I cooked burrito bowls on weekends drank pruno on Sundays with a few guys. Learned Mandarin from another inmate named Ning. When I got out I went back to the identity I thought I wanted so bad, the 18-year-old Army Ranger. That's when the lies started. I couldn't admit to myself that I lost everything I worked for because of my choice. I lied about so much that without knowing I started resenting myself. I have been a bully to those closest to me. I have been stand-offish to anyone in the room and always had to be the tough guy always had to have the most badass stories and biggest ambitions. Why? Because I couldn't admit my shame and check my ego. Because I couldn't take the time to realize what Dad has been telling me this whole time. No one cares what you have done they just care about you. The talk with Dad also made me do something I have been avoiding and probably would have for a long time. I had to examine what all of my lies have done to me, and I did. The last year and a half I haven't worked out more than twice a month. I've been drinking way more than I care to admit. If you found me a week where I had been sober for more than three days I was doing pretty good. I would wake up go to work go home sit in bed drink pass out wake up and do it all over again. I've gotten fat, I weigh 195 right now. I'm not writing those truths about myself to ask for pity but to be honest with you and let you know this has truly eaten me away.

I will end by saying this. I did a lot of fun things in the army. I shot a lot of guns jumped out of airplanes fast-roped out of helicopters and blew things up. I never deployed never got shot at and never got to travel the world doing all sorts of crazy things. The last thing I did as an Army Ranger was help plan and execute an armed bank robbery. I am ready to let go of that 18-year-old kids identity and find a new one. Ben I have hurt you more than anyone in this whole process and for that I can never truly ask for your forgiveness but I am sorry. All of you guys helped save my life and I hope to start living it now. I know this is a cliché but as I have been writing this I have literally felt a weight being lifted off my chest. Ben and Dad I want you to know something I went to Jiu Jitsu for the first time in about eight months. I got my ass kicked but when I got in my car and headed home I felt something that I genuinely haven't felt for a long time. Happy. I was sweaty sore and couldn't feel half of my body. I got home took a shower and fell asleep sober. You guys have done more for me than I have ever done for myself and I honestly believe those two conversations have saved my life in every way. Thank you, I love you both so much. You have all been there for me and I need to be there for you. I hope you can someday forgive me for my deceit. Thank you for everything.

Sincerely,

Alex Blum

CHAPTER 28

BIRTH OF A BANK ROBBER

At first he didn't think it was real.

Four figures in sweats and ski masks ran down the alley in ragged formation, empty duffels flapping, two with AK-47s held across their chests and two with dangling pistols. Behind the steering wheel of a pickup truck, the terrified eyes and mouth of a middle-aged woman shrank away down the alley as her truck wove off wildly in reverse, bright red in the afternoon sun.

Alone in the driver's seat of his father's silver Audi, a nineteen-year-old man with short blond hair stared through the windshield. His right hand rested on the stick shift, which he had just moments ago put in reverse. One sandaled foot was jammed against the clutch. The other was frozen in the motion of lifting off the brake toward the gas. The men reached the end of the wooden fence that lined the alley's left edge, rounded the corner, and vanished.

"The robbery was *this big*," Alex said that first night at his house, holding his forefingers a quarter inch away from each other. "It was *this big*. And then . . ." His hands swung wide apart.

———

For the past two weeks, PFC Blum had been working hard to secure his Expert Infantryman Badge before deploying to Iraq.

The first week was all drills. He spent hours breaking down and putting back together an M249 SAW, feeding through a belt with a false round to simulate a jam, calling "Misfire, misfire, misfire!" as he began the procedure to clear it, then doing the same with an M240B, a Mark 19, and a .50-caliber machine gun. A sergeant smoked him over and over for saying "um" when calling in mortar strikes, after which he sequestered himself in his barracks room all evening to beat this tic out of himself by reciting coordinates into his fist.

During the second week Blum said no "ums." He missed no details in sketching an enemy bunker after recon on top of Noble Hill. He gauged distances correctly through his binoculars, changed his night-vision batteries in the dark, handled every misfire correctly, broke down and rebuilt a SAW within two minutes and a pistol within one. He passed his final tests on Thursday afternoon.

An hour later Specialist Sommer stopped by Blum's barracks room to ask him for a ride to the Bank of America branch where he banked.

Sommer was by no means the only superior with whom Blum was friendly. The key to getting ahead as a cherry private at Ranger Battalion was navigating your relationships with the tabs, and much like his father, Blum had a natural flair for moving gracefully among alpha males. Social contact between tabs and privates was officially discouraged—one time on the bus to the land nav course, Blum forgot to call the specialist he was sitting with "Specialist," and a sergeant overheard and screamed at them both—but PFC Blum was the kind of soldier whom superiors tended to like, paying respect where it was due but giving no quarter in cocky banter. He lifted weights regularly with his team leader, Corporal Sager, and several times acted as the designated driver for weekend trips to Tacoma strip clubs, snoozing with his head down on a bar table while tabs tucked dollar bills into G-strings and slammed back shots. This wasn't just a bid for social status and connections that might save his life on deployment; Blum truly felt honored to spend time with older Rangers who impressed him. After four months at battalion he had built an unconscious internal database of his superiors' likes and dislikes. One sergeant liked drinking, chasing women, and golf. Another liked bodybuilding, checking out his profile in reflective surfaces, and brainstorming particularly graphic ways to murder "A-rabs." Specialist Sommer liked watching action movies, playing Mafia-themed video games, and fantasizing about robbing casinos and banks.

By the time Alex followed Elliott through the sliding glass doors of the Bank of America on the afternoon of Thursday, August 3, he knew that this was more than the usual Ranger war-gaming. Sommer had assured him by now that the entire E4 Mafia of other specialists and corporals was on board with his crazy scheme to be weekend vigilantes in Canada, though it seemed clear that no one really expected it to happen. Just before EIB drills had taken over his life two weeks before, Alex had driven Sommer, Palmer, and Byrne to case Chips Casino. But just as Alex had expected, nothing came of all the bullshitting—swarming in with Humvees, landing a helicopter on the roof, showing all these pathetic civilians just how badass Rangers could be—and amid all the EIB prep, he had let it slip from his mind. Now it almost felt as if Sommer were taking him out for one last EIB test.

Inside the Bank of America, PFC Blum took a seat while Specialist Sommer asked a teller for his balance. As they had at so many other facilities, both assessed the tactical problem the space represented, taking mental notes for their subsequent huddle at the nearby Quiznos. When Sommer asked Blum how he would take the bank down, he sketched it out on a napkin: two shooters at the doors, two more to control the interior. It was then that Sommer told him that he wanted Blum to be one of them.

If there was one rule of Ranger banter, it was that you never, ever backed down from a challenge or taunt. The only honorable way out was to escalate it to a point of such obvious absurdity that the tension cracked into laughter.

"Sure, Specialist," Blum said lightly, then tried for a riff based on the Quentin Tarantino movie *Reservoir Dogs*. "Make sure you call yourself Mr. Pink."

Sommer received this with amusement, repeating Steve Buscemi's whining protest: "Why am *I* Mr. Pink? . . . Mr. Pink sounds like Mr. Pussy. How 'bout if I'm Mr. Purple?" Then he said that the robbery would be going down four days from now, on Monday, and that two associates of his would be traveling in from Canada to complete the team.

Blum covered his shock with a fresh burst of riffing—appearing to take this seriously and backing out would only make him look weak if Sommer turned out to have been joking.

"I'm a Maggot," he mock-protested—a member of a gun team rather than a line team. "We don't go in-house."

Sommer said that was fine: Blum could drive instead.

"One of the things that's so crucial to understand," Alex said to me, "is what a force Sommer is as a person. He's such a fast talker, and it seems like he's all over the place, but it would always funnel down to one certain point. You'd be like, 'Yeah, you're full of shit.' And he'd be like, 'Oh, I am? I *might* be.' And you'd be like, 'Is he?' You know what I'm saying?"

———

Friday morning, PFC Blum lined up with the other passing privates in full-battalion formation to hear the battalion commander congratulate them on a job well done. EIB badges were distributed to Captain Fuller, commander of Charlie Company, who passed them to Platoon Sergeant Congdon, who passed them to Sergeant Waterhouse, who went down the line of Maggot Squad to pin them on each soldier.

Alex had ample opportunity in the next three days to tell Specialist Sommer that he didn't want to be involved. He could have refused him that very evening, when he took Sommer and Palmer to a sports supply store to pick up sweatshirts for the team. Instead he rationalized the danger away. Sommer was always making crazy plans. The chances of his actually bringing these shadowy Canadian associates in to rob a bank seemed remote. During their meeting at Englewood Correctional Institute, Alex would tell Amanda Lee that he had considered reporting Sommer to a superior, but the truth is he never really came close. He could very clearly see the image of himself in Platoon Sergeant Congdon's eyes: some idiot cherry taking standard Ranger war-gaming just a little too seriously, maybe even making up incriminating details to save face. Instead Alex endeavored once more to put it out of his mind, cracking wise about Iraq all weekend with his fellow privates and chatting with Anna on the phone, making plans to help her move into the University of Colorado dorm where she would be spending her freshman year.

He had almost managed to forget about it entirely when Sommer dropped by his barracks room again on Sunday night and asked him for a ride to the Greyhound station to pick up his Canadian associates.

"I think that was really the night that it was like, 'Holy fuck, this might actually happen,'" Alex said. "That's when I should have been like, 'Okay, I'm going to get a plane ticket for tonight and fucking go home.'"

Instead he went along with what felt like a strange pageant of criminal playacting. Sommer introduced PFC Blum to the others as the driver for the operation. Alex did not correct him, though he removed himself from their company as soon as possible once they were back at the barracks. In the next eighteen hours, a helpless feeling of irritation grew. He was annoyed at the Canadians for eating Taco Bell food in his backseat and dropping their wrappers on his newly shampooed carpets. He was annoyed at having to lend the specialist his soft armor, then at having to get it back from him the next morning for inspection. He was especially annoyed at the disappearance of his car all afternoon, when all he wanted to do was leave for the airport to catch his flight home to see Anna—he really did tell the friend who was supposed to drive him that he was still "waiting on Specialist Sommer." But for all Alex hoped that the bank robbery would not happen, never once did he muster even a token effort of resistance. What would haunt him later was the way he had worked so hard at every juncture to smooth away his discomfort with a lubricating layer of jokes. On the drive to the bank, the very lunacy of the plan—the fact that the Audi's license plate was uncovered, that the weapons were so obviously military, that Sommer was targeting his own branch—seemed yet another reason to question its seriousness. On some level this all still felt like one more ridiculous tab game. Halfway there, when an armored truck pulled up next to them in traffic, Alex even laughed along when Sommer suggested to the guys in back that they should just hit that instead. Then, when it started to seem as if the specialist might not be joking, it fell to PFC Blum to talk him out of it.

"*I* was the voice of reason there," Alex said. "*I* was the fucked-up voice of reason. Like, 'We got an objective over at the fucking bank. We can't go here and rob these guys and have a shootout in the middle of the street.'"

———

It was immediately obvious to Alex when the team jumped out of the car that he had made a terrible mistake. The fear-stricken face of the woman in the truck, which would come to serve for Amanda and Norm as the emblem of Alex's dormant free will cracking through the mud of his Ranger automatism, was at the time just one nightmarish detail among many: the hot blue sky, the looming blackberry bramble alongside the car, the many bystanders who might already have seen his license plate. Alex backed away down the alley, swung the Audi snug against the curb of South 60th Street, and hyperventilated in silence for what felt like an eternity but was probably no more than thirty seconds. Then he pulled out from the curb, made a U-turn, and turned left on Puget Sound Avenue. Within a block he realized he was driving the wrong way to return to Fort Lewis and made another U-turn. Straight ahead of him, four men in dark sweatshirts entered the crosswalk, caught sight of the Audi, and began jogging toward him up the street.

His first feeling as the men approached was of profound relief: they hadn't actually done it. Barely two minutes had passed since he had dropped them off. Of *course* they hadn't done it.

Half a second later, with the specialist's unmasked face approaching the passenger-side door, relief gave way to dread. PFC Blum had just left a Ranger behind, violating the single most important tenet of the Ranger Creed. Not only that, but a tab—a superior.

The men clambered into the vehicle in a rumble of hilarity and excitement.

"What the hell?" Alex protested, confused.

"Turn left," Sommer said, then commenced whooping and crowing with his coconspirators, celebrating the success of the crime.

———

This may be the point at which Alex became a criminal in more than just name. The fates of the five men in the car, regardless of the paths they had taken to get there, were now inextricably entangled. There was no longer any denying the reality of what PFC Blum had helped bring about, but instead of condemning it, he tried to apologize to Sommer for leaving. Sommer brushed him off.

"You know about us pulling into the cul-de-sac, right?" Alex asked me.

"And a cop went by."

"There were three of them, three cop cars. By the way, it feels very good to be honest with you, just so you know. But yeah, we pulled into that cul-de-sac ready to get into a fucking shootout and I didn't have shit. I was sitting there in board shorts and sandals and these other guys had AKs and pistols and fucking body armor. I mean, fuck."

Sommer still seemed excited by all this, but his demeanor turned on a dime after they dropped off the other three men at a movie theater. Suddenly the specialist seemed to be panicking.

"In front of all the other guys he was like, 'Whoo, we did it! Yeah!' And then as soon as we dropped them all off, he was like, 'What do we do? What do we do? What do *you* think we should do?'"

On one level, this was unnerving. Sommer's past requests for input had all been framed as tests of PFC Blum's expertise, but his old team leader no longer seemed to be in full control. On another level, it was a profound relief. Alex now felt that he and Sommer were of the same mind: stunned and horrified by what had just happened, baffled by how it had come to this. The excitement that Sommer had shown in front of the other guys appeared to have been mere bravado. Alex's own duty seemed clear: to help his friend and mentor through the terrible situation in which they now found themselves, having "Sua Sponte'd it" beyond all belief.

"I was just like, 'Fucking burn it. Get rid of it. Bury everything. Burn it all.' He was like, 'We might have to drive to Canada. We might be in a high-speed chase.' I was like, 'All right, let's fucking do it. Let's drive. I'll go 120 miles an hour. My Audi can handle at least 120.'"

"How were you feeling at that point?" I asked.

"Confused. I think I played off his emotions a lot when he first got in. I was kind of gung-ho for a little bit. But I wasn't elated at all, I wasn't happy at all. From the time before, when it was like, 'Don't let this be real,' it went right back to 'Fuck, please don't let this be real.'"

Sommer opted against PFC Blum's suggestion to burn the money and guns. Instead of going to Canada, though, he had Alex meander through residential streets for nearly an hour and then take them back to base. They passed through the guard station without a hitch. At the barracks, they carried duffel bags full of clothes and shoes right past the CQ desk, and then Sommer had him take a golf bag out to the car, stuff all the guns and money into it, and slide it through Sommer's window. Alex raced upstairs, called a different friend to ask for a ride to the airport, took a minute-long shower, grabbed his hockey bag, and left. Two hours later, having missed his flight, he returned to his barracks room at base, where Sommer and the others brought him his cut of the money. There Sommer informed him that he was as guilty as the rest of them, but it was agreed that, given Alex's inexperience and obvious qualms about the crime, the others would cover for him as best they could. If caught, Alex was instructed to report to the FBI that he hadn't known about the plan in advance, that Sommer had asked him for a ride to the bank and then pulled a gun on him on the way.

Nathan Dunmall's testimony depicts an astonishing openness about the robbery around battalion. Unnamed Rangers wandered in and out with money strewn all over the bed. Scott Byrne too made an appearance. For all his reluctance beforehand about getting involved, he drove the conspirators to the bus station that night for their journey back to Canada, chatting with Sommer on the way about details of the crime and showing off a .45-caliber pistol that he owned. Alex corroborates this festive atmosphere, telling me it gave him the bizarre sense that hitting banks truly was normal Ranger activity. When he himself talked about the robbery with the friend who drove him to the airport, the response wasn't critical. "He wasn't like, 'You have to report this, you have to report this.' He was like, 'Holy shit, that's crazy.' Like—impressed."

Alex accepted $10,000 for his participation. In the next two days, he flashed money in front of Sam and Carly, bantered about his superior military skills with the arresting officers on his way to the Greenwood Village Police Department, and repeated the story of Sommer pulling a gun on him to the FBI, before immediately withdrawing it after being informed that it was ridiculous. There is no question that he is guilty of bank robbery. Though he expressed deep remorse to Amanda from the start and wrote a letter of apology to his parents within days of his arrest, he was already lying in small ways both to them and to himself in order to downplay his involvement, as he would continue to do for months, until Amanda, Jeff, and the government finally wore him down. It is not because he was innocent that he received such a lenient sentence. Like Patty Hearst before him, Alex was a sheltered white kid in a terrible situation whose family had the resources to mount an unusually strong legal defense.

Does it matter that before the crime, Alex's enjoyment of the idea was possible only because he believed it was hypothetical? And that afterward, his tentative displays of pride seem to have been little more than self-justifying bulwarks against the horror of what he had done? Maybe that is how all criminals are made.

CHAPTER 29

THE REST OF US

I was surprised, in the weeks after Alex confessed to me, to find that my sympathy for him increased. PFC Blum was human to me now, a good kid in a bad situation who had simply lacked the moral courage to face the consequences of taking Specialist Sommer's plan seriously and backing out. But it took a long time for me to stop being angry with him for lying. It moved through me less like a storm than like a climate system. How could he have been so false with me for so long? Alex might have thought that evading responsibility would protect him, but in fact it had done the opposite, letting others define his story and leaving him prey to the projection of everyone's worst fears, including my own. It was hard to trust his new commitment to truth. Whenever he and I talked, I was always on edge for him to regress into self-justification and denial, but each time a glimmer of it returned, I heard him catch himself, frustrated at his own tone, before moving on to the next hard revelation.

In March he called to tell me that his probation was officially over.

"Is there some kind of ceremony to mark it?" I asked.

"No," he said, "I just get a letter in the mail that says I was successfully rehabilitated by the United States government."

He told me that there had been one last kerfuffle with his parole officer, a stern, skeptical man who always seemed to think Alex was on the verge of lapsing back to crime.

"Thursday night I get a call from my PO. I was working late. He says, 'Alex, this is Carlos. Something came up. You need to call me immediately.' I call him back. He goes, 'There was an armed bank robbery by where you live and the FBI wants to talk to you about it.' Next Monday the FBI calls me. They're like, 'Yeah, we need you to come in.' So I went in Monday and the same guy who arrested me and interviewed me when it first happened was one of the guys interviewing me for this other bank robbery. John Grusing."

My whole body tensed up. In the years since Alex's arrest, I had heard hours and hours of venom from him toward the FBI agents who had interviewed him.

"Oh man," I said. "Did you talk at all about the first time you saw him?"

"Yeah," Alex said. "He said my case was one of the few that he actually remembers. It was good to see him. We caught up for a while and kind of bullshitted."

I was stunned. "Really? What did he have to say about it?"

"He just said he could tell it was a pretty special circumstance case and that he remembered the whole family. He said he was proud of me for the way my life has gone after getting out."

"What about your long-standing rage toward the FBI?"

"I don't really care anymore," Alex said. "It's not worth it. He even took a picture of my tattoo with my prison number on it. He was like, 'That's an awesome thing, man. That's a cool reminder.'"

It didn't seem likely that anything would come of the investigation of him for this new robbery.

"It happened back in January, so they were getting desperate. It was to the point where they were just like, 'Did you ever *talk* to anyone about robbing a bank?' I was like, 'Here's my time card. This is when I worked. I wasn't there. I didn't talk to anybody about robbing a bank. I don't know anybody who robs banks.' Toward the end, they were just trying to get advice. They were like, 'Well, when you guys talked about robbing a bank, how quick did it happen?' I was like, 'Um . . .' And I told them everything I learned in prison. Like, I told them about how some banks will put cutout trackers in the middle of twenty-dollar bills. This guy in prison who was in for bank robbery in Alaska got away with like $750,000 because he would stuff the money in ice water and it would fry all the trackers. Little shit like that. I think some of it kind of surprised them, so I don't know, maybe it helps them out in the future."

The next time I went through Denver, I was with a new girlfriend. The friend whose rap album I had long ago funded with my grant money happened to be playing a show in town with his new band. I texted Alex to see if he would come along. To my surprise, he showed up at the venue a few hours later. He clearly felt awkward in his cargo shorts, sandals, and broad red shovel of a beard among all the hipsters in the line outside, but after a fortifying head nod with the bouncer and a double Jack Daniel's neat at the bar, he pulled us out to the dance floor.

At first he tried for subdued: shuffling foot to foot, paddling his hands in the air like a bearded penguin. But within minutes he had given up on blending in and was busy compensating for his discomfort by making himself the most conspicuous person in the room, jumping from sandaled foot to sandaled foot on tiptoe as he pumped his fists in the air. He attempted to grab my hand and twirl me. I lurched halfheartedly in place. He gave up and twirled my girlfriend instead. The band segued into a quieter song.

"Are you going to dance with me or not?" he yelled in my direction.

I knew this routine: prodding the respectable guy to loosen up for once. I rolled my eyes.

"This song's too slow," I yelled back. "The next time they play a decent jam, I'll show you how it's done."

I spent the next two minutes regretting my bravado. Then the band struck the opening chord of a song I knew well, jangly and fast, with a hard beat.

After that it's a blur. I remember flashes of light from overhead, my girlfriend bumping against my hip, my cousin's face grinning in surprise and joy, other bodies careening near ours, my friend onstage pulsing his head as he sang like a muscular rooster. He and I had first met during my very unhealthiest year in Seattle. His lyrics were all about escaping the fate of his father, a violent alcoholic who had been in and out of prison all his life. That night's audience did not appear to get it. As the songs got faster and more intense, people drifted one by one to the bar or to the benches outside to smoke. Alex and

I just danced more and more wildly, jumping and yelling along to the words, shaking our heads in laughter at each other's moves. I had never felt more free with him. It was as if we had finally found the language to speak the truth of the last eight years of our friendship. We danced like brothers, like family, like people who shared the same name.

————

A few days later I met our grandmother, Oma, for lunch at her retirement home. A famed beauty and accomplished dancer in her Texas youth, she was still regal in her late eighties, with a cloud of wavy white hair and impeccable taste in jewelry, scarves, and cowboy boots. When I was young, Oma had been the very image of sophisticated charm, a font of dry wit and peach cobblers and an unstoppable force on the tennis court. I had always loved spending time with her. Today, though, I had an ulterior motive. After Alex's confession, I had begun wondering if there was something I had missed about his character—perhaps about the character of all us Blums. Was it merely his friendly, obliging nature that had doomed him, or was something deeper at work? As the wife of the legendary Blum patriarch, Oma seemed the best resource available for understanding the family culture that Opa had striven so hard to create.

"Are you really interested, Ben?" Oma kept asking, incredulous, as she dredged up more details from the depths of her memory.

After lunch she led me to a storage closet down the hall from her room and showed me a crumbling pile of old photograph albums. I brought back as many as I could carry and started going through them on her carpet.

To my surprise, I found the oldest of them the most interesting of all, full of horses, prancing girls, and sun-beaten ranchland—the spiritual originals, it began to seem, from which my own suburban baby photos had been imperfectly copied. The New York side of the family had always loomed largest in my imagination, but the family ethos of assured self-reliance was clearly rooted in Texas. You could tell by the way Oma held her body in even the earliest photos that she knew how to dance. There were glamorous costumed poses in the backyard, a picture of her in the local paper holding a baby bobcat in each arm when she was head yell leader for San Angelo Senior

High School, a photo from the yearbook of Angelo State University, where she had enrolled at age sixteen, labeled "Most Beautiful Girl." Next came a sequence that stopped my heart in my chest: Oma and her dance troupe at the University of Texas in the early 1940s.

The first was of Oma photographed dramatically from below, wearing a cowboy shirt cinched in at the waist of her blue jeans as she stomped one bare foot high in the sky, an expression of utter abandon on her face. Two other individual poses followed, then a shot of all seven women holding hands and leaping into the air in front of the university clock tower, their bare toes pointed down at the receding grass, their faces cast back in the sun. Oma floated in the very center, her dark curls rising around her face. For the era, the image was amazingly modern. A year later the war would come and blast all this away, filling the rest of her college album with cramped portraits in bar booths of GIs in uniform with girls clinging to their elbows, but I felt I could see all the possibilities of Blums yet to come contained in the spring of that joyful body.

When I said goodbye later that afternoon, Oma sent with me a handful of photos of Opa and her getting married and raising their children, as well as something entirely unexpected: a cardboard box containing a ream of typewritten paper that had recently come back to her from its place with my uncle Kurt. I had begun to wonder if Opa's World War II memoir was apocryphal. Suddenly I had it in my hands.

I read the whole thing on the airplane a few days later, hunched in the middle seat with a stack of more than three hundred yellowing sheets on the tray table, which I had to move one by one to my lap. There was no title. "Greetings! etc" it said at the top of the page, the first direct communication I had ever received from my paternal grandfather. The opening scene was of a procession of new recruits undergoing physical screening in a New York City doctor's office on January 4, 1943. I felt a strange thrill when I saw my own name: *O.K. Blum, you're next*. Here, finally, was the blueprint of Blum manhood that Alex and I had been shaped by all our lives.

I read the rest with growing horror. Twenty-six years old when he enlisted, my grandfather was promoted into command of eleven men based solely on his age and appeared desperate from the start to live up to the red-blooded masculinity of his subordinates, none of whom knew he was Jewish. His platoon landed in Normandy six weeks after D-Day, not the one or two days after D-Day that Norm had reported to me, and found themselves assigned to months of mopping-up work far back from the front lines. Sergeant Blum rode with four crew members in an M16 half-track, an awkward-looking truck with tank treads for back wheels and four .50-caliber machine guns mounted in grid formation on a swiveling turret. The M16 had been designed as an antiaircraft weapon, but after struggling against the new breed of German warplanes, it was repurposed for infantry support, a function for which it proved so perfectly suited that it would soon earn the army-wide nickname "Meat Chopper." Opa never once reprimanded his troops for their increasingly disturbing excesses of violence, looking on with a "doubtful grin" as they got in drunken brawls, machine-gunned a crowd of surrendering German soldiers, punched officers from other platoons, robbed a group of teenage captives, and shacked up with German women in occupied villages. Opa gave vivid accounts of sleeping with a total of eleven younger women in the course of the war, several of whom he referred to admiringly as "perfect Aryan specimens." Half-recognizable versions of each of the anecdotes Norm had related to me made their appearance, invariably less flattering and sometimes starring others—it wasn't even Opa himself who had swung those bodies into a pit but French villagers while Opa and a friend drank wine and looked on. Near the end, a rowdy soldier whom Opa had defended on previous occasions shot and killed a teenage girl who resisted his sexual advances, resulting in a court-martial for her murder and Opa's transfer to desk duty in Frankfurt, where he coasted out the remainder of the war before returning home to his first wife in New York, a woman named Marie, whom family lore had conveniently erased. The tone throughout was shockingly jaunty. No casual reader would have guessed that its author was Jewish. In the middle of one of his many graphic sex scenes, Opa cut away from the action for a rare bit of philosophical commentary, delivered with a lecherous wink: *"War is hell."*

After reading the whole thing through, I sat back from my tray table in shocked disgust. I wanted to fling the pile of papers off my lap. What did it mean to have descended from this man? Could this really be the legendary Albert Likes Blum Senior who had inspired such fear and respect in his sons and such eagerness in Alex to enlist?

———

Ten years have passed since the robbery. Slowly and painfully, the conspirators have begun moving on with their lives. Scott Byrne and Richard Olinger were discharged from the Rangers and served short prison sentences. Nathan Dunmall served six and a half years in the United States before receiving a treaty transfer to Canada, where he was paroled to a halfway house within five months. He has since worked as an Amway sales representative and is now the lead estimator and project manager at a construction company. Tigra Robertson and Chad Palmer were the last to be released, in 2015 and early 2016. The only one still in prison is Luke Elliott Sommer. Though his scheduled release date is in 2046, the U.S. Department of Justice has approved his application for transfer to Canada, shocking everyone I have spoken to who is familiar with his case. If the transfer goes through, he will be immediately eligible for parole.

Elliott called to tell me he had proved the twin primes conjecture in the summer of 2015, more than a year after Alex confessed. It's strange how thoroughly this direct lie from his mouth broke my trust in him. Alex's confession had long since removed Elliott's greatest point of leverage over me, preventing me from drawing any more false equivalences between his deceptions and Alex's, but the eager enthusiasm with which he described his fictional JavaScript application made it suddenly obvious to me that there was something profoundly wrong with him, something beyond my ability to fix or even to understand. After Donald Trump announced his candidacy for the presidency, I found myself growing increasingly obsessed with videos of his speeches—the goofy showmanship, the lovable shamelessness, the incredible facility with various entertaining species of untruth. Had Specialist Sommer's crime family sounded as laughable at first as Trump's border wall? It finally began to dawn on me that Sommer might have deliberately kept PFC Blum and others believing that the robbery was a game. I looked back at his text conversations with Tasha, Scott Byrne, and Tigra Robertson and was amazed at the way he had managed to put them at ease with expertly placed lols while extracting everything that he wanted, piece by piece.

A few days later, Alex called to tell me he was quitting his job at the warehouse to pursue his new dream of running his own food truck. I congratulated him, then tried to share my newfound perspective on Sommer. To my surprise, Alex shrugged it off.

"Sommer was a prick," he agreed, "but here's the thing: I should have told him to fuck off. I think at nineteen I just had the hugest ego. I'd just gone through RIP and now I thought I couldn't do wrong. I didn't want to admit I'd fucked up. Dude, I have so much to apologize to you for."

As Alex started into the list, I began to get uncomfortable. It was strange to recall the secret, malignant doubt I had harbored toward him for so long as I got friendlier with Sommer. More and more it seemed to me that my own naïveté and immaturity as a journalist had been equally responsible for the way Alex's story had come to define our lives. I should have questioned harder, pushed back on his bad behavior, been brave enough to confront him. But when I tried to apologize myself, telling Alex I'd had a lot of growing up to do back then, he would hear none of it.

"How do you grow up?" he asked. "How the fuck do you grow up? Did you take a class in college on growing up? Did I take one in prison? This is it. *This* is how you grow up. I think we're better off than the ninety-eight percent of people who never have to go through something like this and learn what growing up means."

I was surprised to find tears in my eyes. The story that had trapped us both for eight years, the story we had come in different ways to think of as ourselves, had finally shattered to pieces around us. We were not the story, though. We were still standing.

A few weeks later, I called Christel to ask how close Elliott was to coming home. Amid all her optimistic chatter about the angles she was working now, it gradually became apparent that his treaty transfer had been held up by the Canadian side. I wasn't sure how I felt about it. With greater clarity on his character, I had begun experiencing a new, more clinical kind of compassion for him. There had been something movingly sincere about his efforts to grapple with his own moral deficits, despite all the pathological lying that surrounded them. His evangelical push seemed to have produced real benefits in the lives of his younger brothers, who had moved past their troubled adolescent years and begun successfully holding down jobs. (Elliott would eventually tell me that he did believe in God, if not precisely the God of his youth, and that he no longer minded my sharing his religious views.) And there was no denying the zeal with which he was pursuing his mathematical education, even if his innate grandiosity occasionally tripped him up. It was hard to wish thirty more years in U.S. federal prison on anyone. Robert Hare's Psychopathy Checklist was in wide use by the Correctional Service of Canada to assess an inmate's risk of reoffending. Perhaps Canada would be able to achieve a clearer view on both the risks Elliott posed and the ways in which he might be able to heal.

———

As the summer ran out, I struggled to reach some kind of peace with my grandfather's memoir. It was so full of that hard male humor at sex and death that I had always accepted as the epitome of Blum manhood, but here it looked like weakness instead of strength, a pressure-release valve for men who were radically estranged from their moral and emotional lives. Were family myths little more than coping mechanisms, insulating sheaths for unbearable truths? What did it do to a man to uphold them his whole life? What did it do to a family to believe them?

In October, Oma turned ninety years old. Cousins, aunts, and uncles flew into Denver from all across the country for a birthday lunch in the banquet hall of a nice Italian restaurant. As waiters filed discreetly in and out to refill our water glasses, I watched more than thirty family members circle round to Oma's place at the central table to pay their respects. She was wearing a fuchsia blazer and a particularly glamorous pair of boots. Her eyes squinted as she broke into embarrassed chuckles at all the attention, hands shifting nervously on the purse in her lap. I took my turn to bend down and give her a hug and a kiss on the cheek.

"Oh, Ben," she said, rolling her eyes with that sardonic self-awareness of hers that all of us adore. "Hello, dear. This is really too much."

A long time before we said hello, I noticed Alex accepting hugs and handshakes from all the uncles and aunts in turn. We knew he was a felon in earnest now, but he had served a prison sentence based on evidence grounded in fact and had paid his restitution in full. As far as the U.S. government was concerned, his debt to society was redeemed. There was something both more worried and more free about his demeanor, a boyish tentativeness that broke out into exuberance when given license. He looked healthier than when I'd seen him last. He spent a long time kneeling by Oma. His gentle manner with her made me think of the Christmas a couple of years after his sentencing when he had showed up for the big family dessert roaring drunk in a shiny new suit, made a beeline for Oma, lurched up so close to her that she had to rock back on her heels, and held out his hand. "Hello, beautiful," he had drawled in his best Texan accent. "May I have this dance?" "Oh Alex," said Oma, laughing and swatting at him. "You are too much."

At the time I had heard a scolding tone in her voice and thought it well deserved. Now, though, having learned more about Opa, and having seen the way Mandi and Christel felt about Elliott, I understood better the obvious pleasure she had felt in the interaction too.

"He was the love of my life," Oma had told me at her retirement home when I asked about Opa. "I loved every minute that we spent together. The only problem was, there weren't enough of them."

Though Opa's chapters on training differed dramatically from Alex's—the atmosphere was collegial, with no smokings or other arbitrary punishments—there were certain undeniable similarities between the protagonists. Each had enlisted in the army with a romantic notion of war, a weakness for self-mythologizing, a genteel anxiety about being man enough, a deficit of moral courage to say no. But their differences were also clear. Alex was kinder, funnier, more eager to please. His relation to his demons was complex, but it was not one of enslavement. Scott Beech, the former line mate who got him his job at the warehouse, had once passed on to me a casual remark Alex made in the months after Kurt's death. "I don't understand why people commit suicide," Alex told him. "I've been given a second chance, and I'm going to live it."

There was a section of Opa's memoir that I kept coming back to. After all the fleeting trysts of the previous pages, he managed in Frankfurt to develop something approximating a relationship with a young German woman named Wilma, whose father suffered recurring traumatic episodes after having spent two days trapped in the rubble from a British bombing. Just before Opa flew back to the United States, he and Wilma sat on a hill above Frankfurt and looked down on the ruins of the city. Then, for four pages of unbroken quotes, Wilma described the night raids.

> First came the fire bombs and in a matter of minutes, the entire city seemed to be ablaze. Then came the heavy explosive bombs. The ground shook and vibrated. A bomb hit the house we were in and the whole building collapsed over our heads. There was no light and people were trapped in the cellar. My mother and father became separated from me. I screamed for them hysterically but had no answer.

After long minutes in the stifling darkness, some men dug them out and they were led to another cellar under a schoolhouse.

> Five blocks away is the zoo and the bombs had broken the elephant and lion cages. The animals crazed by the noise and heat ran into the flames and a screaming death. The bombing increased for about 15 minutes and then as soon as it stopped, more fire bombs began to drop. The schoolhouse caught fire and the heat in the basement became unbearable. Again we ran out of the cellar. We were surrounded by burning buildings, by an entire city in flames. We stood in the street and more fighter planes came and strafed the streets as civilians ran in every direction to escape the hail of bullets. Buildings were falling everywhere. Then came the final part of the raid where the English used their heaviest bombs—I think you call them "blockbusters." These bombs are indescribable. One fell two streets from where I was and when it exploded, we could not breathe. We gasped for breath and turned blue in fact. An old man lying in the street next to me started to writhe in agony and tried to get up but couldn't. He screamed and squirmed and then suddenly lay still. The concussion had killed him. Men and women ran toward some of the buildings and tried to climb the walls! No one knew what he or she was doing. The entire city shook and trembled from the concussions and even above the noise, the human cries of pain, agony and fear could be heard. I saw one man run into a flaming house. He was yelling and laughing, completely mad. He

appeared at a second floor window and he was aflame. He stood there for seconds and then leapt to the ground, a ball of fire.

Here, finally, was the real horror of war, which Opa seemed able to allow himself to experience only by proxy, through the eyes of this sensitive, feeling woman. "She was trembling. She was crying," he observed after Wilma finished her monologue, and then he was flying home in the window seat of a DC-4, looking out over the ruins of Frankfurt and thinking of all the dead who still lay under the rubble.

Law disappears completely when war overruns the soil. Humanity is advanced tremendously, scientifically, but is set back and wounded morally and physically each time war comes. And these moral and physical wounds can never be healed. They will, in years to come, destroy all nations—indeed the world itself.

So ended my grandfather's memoir. He once mailed a copy of it to my father at college, but by then Al Junior was so disenchanted with Al Senior that he never read more than a few pages of it.

"I just wasn't interested at all," Dad recalls. "Looking back, he was probably trying to reach out and open himself up to me in some way. I was so closed off back then. I just wasn't ready for it."

It was my grandfather's last effort to communicate what he had gone through to his family. Al Senior killed himself on May 27, 1981, five months before my birth, the arrival of his first grandchild. It's difficult to say exactly what went into his decision—there were career difficulties, and his health was failing—but when he died, his experiences died with him. I do not think it's wrong to call him a casualty of war.

———

The centerpiece of Oma's birthday party was a slideshow of her life, put together by my mother and my younger brother's wife in part from the photographs I had unearthed from her storage locker. A gasp flew around the room when her Texas dance troupe appeared. Though in many ways Oma had been the backbone of the family for three decades, the legendary deeds of the Blum men had always defined who we were. These were images unlike any we were accustomed to knowing ourselves by.

The slideshow segued to headlines screaming war. There was a picture of the Marine Corps pilot Oma was engaged to, who was shot down in the Pacific theater mere weeks before the war's end. Finally Al Senior appeared, a dashing figure with elegant hands and suspicious eyes. Next came wedding portraits, a house in Scarsdale, babies. After the collapse of Opa's glove company in the late 1960s, I knew, he had become a traveling salesman of women's accessories, spending two weeks on the road for every two he spent at home. Soon he lost that job. The next photographs were from Oma's years supporting the family as a real estate broker in Armonk, where she became an instant star, selling houses to a number of the young hockey players of the New York Rangers while Al Senior stayed at home drinking, smoking, and cooking the occasional meal. Then, after a few shots of the aging couple eating at restaurants near home and in Paris, Opa was simply gone. Oma moved to Colorado at age fifty-five, again sought work as a broker, and helped her children raise their new families. Neither Norm nor my father would admit to a causal link, of course, but it was their mother who had pioneered the family trade that they both went into.

After the slideshow was over, everyone sought a table to sit down for lunch. Alex and I shot each other half-embarrassed looks from across the room. The last time we had seen each other was that night of wild dancing in downtown Denver, but as we gripped hands and then hugged, we slipped easily into our old bantering rhythm. He followed me to a table with my many siblings and stepsiblings.

"Hey," Alex said after the usual pleasantries, "what are you guys getting Oma for her birthday?"

We all exchanged guilty looks. Alex laughed.

"Check this out," he said. He held up his right forearm. There was a fresh-looking splotch of color there above his prison barcode. Everyone leaned in for a closer look. It appeared to be a tattoo of the cartoon characters Calvin and Hobbes, dancing ecstatically atop a background of sheet music. The notes, Alex hastened to point out, formed the letters O M A.

We all glanced around incredulously at each other.

"Has Oma seen that?" I asked.

"Oh, she hates it," Alex said with a grin.

As Dad and Norm gave speeches and my younger brother serenaded Oma with a rendition of "You Are My Sunshine" on acoustic guitar that brought tears out around the room, I thought more about Alex's tattoo. It wasn't as random as it looked: for years now, Alex had been the cousin who checked in on Oma most. Few of the rest of us even lived in Denver anymore. One recent evening, I knew, he had gotten himself all dressed up to escort her to a downtown performance of the Colorado Symphony Orchestra, in whose chorus my mother sang. Now he would have her name on his forearm for the rest of his life. Was this just some kind of a whim? Or did it represent something deeper to him, a commitment to a new and different sense of what it meant to be a Blum?

The afternoon was almost over. Waiters began clearing the tables.

"If I'd known how much fun this would be," Oma reportedly whispered to my mother, "I wouldn't have dreaded it so much."

On the way out, we gathered for a group photograph with Oma in the middle: Norm and Tami looking happy and healthy, Fred and Karen as mellow and friendly as ever, Judy and Terrance both funny and wry, Kurt represented in spirit in the photograph albums on the table in the corner, my parents with their new partners, all the dozens of children and spouses. It was amazing to think that so much love had sprung from one woman. Here we all were: therapists and ad execs, lifeguards and CEOs, stepchildren and second wives and South Korean adoptees, a computer scientist turned writer and an Army Ranger turned bank robber turned food-truck guy. The truth had transformed Alex, but it had also done something to the rest of us. Before, his story had served as fresh support for Al Senior's age-old cynicism toward a world set inevitably against us. Now it had become a lesson in humility, in self-reflection, in holding each other accountable and forgiving each other better. The swords of our grievance had been beaten into plowshares. We too were more ourselves, more fully Blums, more free.

AUTHOR'S NOTE

This is a work of nonfiction: that is to say, an account of true events based on the subjective perspectives of multiple actors complexly implicated in the events, as synthesized by an outside party complexly implicated with the actors. Diligent efforts have been made to represent all this as fairly and accurately as possible.

Most interviews were recorded, but no tape recorder was permitted inside USP McCreary, so the dialogue between Elliott Sommer and myself was reconstructed from notes. Certain interviews conducted across multiple sessions, particularly those with Alex and Norm, have been condensed into one. In a very few cases, I have presented interviews in different order than they were conducted in real life in order to preserve thematic coherence. One introductory monologue from the *Dr. Phil* episode has been transposed into a different section. Certain quotes have been condensed, trimmed, or lightly edited for clarity, particularly Luke Elliott Sommer's speech to Bruce Singer about alleged war crimes, because its forcefulness would have been lost if it were presented at full length. All such choices were made with the intent of filtering out as much noise as possible so the music could be heard, but of course the judgment of what is music and what is noise is at heart a subjective one. I have tried to be true to the spirit of everyone who has been gracious enough to speak to me about their story.

The most difficult choices involved disagreements between interview subjects on factual details. I have allowed some of these contradictions to sit in the text, inviting readers to draw their own conclusions about when and how the truth has been distorted, but in other cases I have relied on those accounts that I judge most credible. I was not always able to verify or disprove certain family anecdotes, but because of their significance to those who related them to me, I decided to include them anyway. They should be interpreted as family lore, a genre closely akin to mythology. Certain characters—Tigra Robertson, Chad Palmer, Scott Byrne, and Bruce Singer most prominently among them—declined to speak with me. I have had to rely on external sources in telling their stories.

The extended excerpts from Alex's prison manuscript about his training, *Breaking Point*, appear here largely intact. However, after Alex confessed to me that he had exaggerated certain details for effect—principally the durations of "smoke sessions"—I decided that the need to avoid misrepresenting army and Ranger training outweighed the need for fidelity to Alex's original text. I have worked with Alex to bring all such details back within the realm of factual accuracy. In addition, the introductory and concluding essays have been lightly condensed to remove repetitions.

The names of four minor characters have been changed: "Don Keegan," "Kathleen," "Amy," and "Marcus Cobb." Any similarity between their fictitious names and the names of persons living or dead is purely coincidental.

In grappling with Alex's story, I have come to believe that although reality itself may lie eternally beyond our comprehension, there is nothing more important to reach for. I do not pretend to know the full truth about the bank robbery that upended the lives of so many of the people I have spoken to, but I have aspired to put more of it in this book than has ever been told before. As Adrienne Rich puts it in her brilliant essay "Women and Honor: Some Notes on Lying," "Truth is not one thing, or even a system. It is an increasing complexity."

ACKNOWLEDGMENTS

I am deeply grateful to all those who have helped bring this book into existence. My transition from science to writing would not have been possible without the open-minded support of my advisers and colleagues, Michael Jordan and David Baker. The Seattle literary world offered enormous incubational energy during this book's formative years, particularly the Richard Hugo House, the Tweeningfulcore writers' collective, the APRIL literary festival, and the late, lamented Pilot Books. Thanks to the New York University Creative Writing Program for critical grounding in the elementals of craft and to the New York Times Foundation for a generous graduate fellowship. Thanks especially to Jonathan Lethem for believing in the book's potential, Zadie Smith for holding me accountable to its best possible incarnation, Darin Strauss for offering helpful suggestions on structure, and Lawrence Weschler for teaching me everything I know about (the fiction of) nonfiction. Thanks to David Mahfouda and the team at Bandwagon for their flexibility and encouragement—no writer could have asked for a better day job.

For providing insight and feedback on countless drafts over the years, I would like to extend special gratitude to James Yeh, Tara Atkinson, and my parents and stepparents, Jude Blum, Ozi Friedrich, Al Blum, and Sari Simchoni. I am enormously grateful to my wife, Leah Vincent, whose editorial contributions in the final year of work were immense and whose emotional support was even greater. Thanks to all others for their generous and discerning comments, particularly Chloe Jones, Kate Lebo, Alex Bush, Brian Christian, Sarah Todes, Yoav Simchoni, and the students of

Jonathan Lethem's spring 2010 workshop at NYU. Thanks to Lee Bob Black for subsidizing the writing at a critical juncture, Kelly Carlin for research support, Kurt Pitzer and Caitlin Rother for their expert journalistic guidance, Matt Gallagher and Arna Hemenway for their insights into army culture, and Robert Engen and Frederic Smoler for their perspectives on the legacy of S.L.A. Marshall. Any missteps in applying their wise counsel are my own. Thanks also to the many fine reporters and writers whose work I have drawn on, including David Baines for his reporting on Rakesh Saxena, James Ross Gardner for his feature on Luke Elliott Sommer for *Seattle Met* magazine, and Jesse Hyde for his superb profile of Clayton Roueche in *Rolling Stone*.

In the course of seven years of work on this project, I held more than two hundred separate interviews with more than forty subjects. Not all were formal, and not all appear in these pages, but each was essential to filling out the deep textures of the story. For their generosity with their time and insights, I would like to thank Bernard Beck, Brandon Beck, Matthias Beck, Scott Beech, Beverly Blum, Carly Blum, Fred Blum, Kurt Blum, Max Blum, Sam Blum, Dave Bowermaster, Judy Brennan, Christel Davidsen, Mike Dion, Anna Dudow, Mike Eadrick, Kim Gordon, Dave Grossman, Bill Hemphill, Todd Karr, Daphne Koller, Stephanie Ness, Laura Pascale, Murray Platt, Dave Preston, Jeff Robinson, Elliott Sommer, Luke Sommer, Mandi Sommer, Reagan Sommer, and Angie Zerr, as well as all those whose contributions were critical but who preferred not to be named. Amanda Lee provided not just critical source material but essential psychological insights and fellowship along the way. Jessiah Stotts's graciousness and strength were an inspiration. Special thanks to the extended Blum family, whose capacity for loving openness astounded me again and again. Special thanks also to Elliott Sommer and the extended Sommer family, who were always gracious and kind to me, even when we didn't see eye to eye.

I am in debt to Tina Bennett, my extraordinary agent, for believing in me from the beginning, and to Bill Thomas for his wisdom, kindness, and vision in helping shape the manuscript into its present form. Finally, my deepest thanks to Alex for accompanying me on what has turned out to be a far harder, longer, and more rewarding journey than either of us could have imagined. May we never stop surprising each other.